EPIC

KALEVALA & FINNISH MYTHS & TALES

ANTHOLOGY OF CLASSIC TALES

Foreword by Tiina Porthan

FLAME TREE PUBLISHING

TALES

This is a FLAME TREE Book

Publisher & Creative Director: Nick Wells
Editorial Director: Catherine Taylor
Project Editor: Jemma North
Special thanks to: Michael Kerrigan

Publisher's Note: Due to the historical nature of the classic text, we're aware that there may be some language used which has the potential to cause offence to the modern reader. However, wishing overall to preserve the integrity of the text, rather than imposing contemporary sensibilities, we have left it unaltered.

FLAME TREE PUBLISHING
6 Melbray Mews, Fulham,
London SW6 3NS, United Kingdom
www.flametreepublishing.com

First published 2026

26 28 30 29 27
1 3 5 7 9 10 8 6 4 2

ISBN: 978-1-83562-779-2
Special ISBN: 978-1-83562-920-8

The cover image is created by Flame Tree Studio based on artwork by Slava Gerj, Gabor Ruszkai. Internal decorations are courtesy Shutterstock.com and the following artists: Net Vector and Karlionau (story headers).

A copy of the CIP data for this book is available from the British Library.

Printed and bound in China

Represented in the EU for product safety and compliance by Authorised Rep Compliance Ltd, Ground Floor, 71 Lower Baggot Street, Dublin, D02 P593, Ireland. Contact at www.arccompliance.com

EPIC

KALEVALA & FINNISH MYTHS & TALES

ANTHOLOGY OF CLASSIC TALES

Foreword by Tiina Porthan

FLAME TREE PUBLISHING

TALES

Contents

Witches, Spirits & Mystical Beings

Animal Stories

Trickery, Enchantment & Magic

The Natural World

Human Stories, Heroes & Morality

Foreword

WHEN I WAS LITTLE, my favourite book was a collection of Finnish folktales. On the edge of my seat, I read about the water creature Vetehinen snatching a girl into his castle, a man having a dead man as his servant, and an evil creature disguising himself as a woman and taking her place as a bride. The horror elements of the stories sent chills down my spine: a pool filled with blood, a dead man sailing in the coffin he had been buried in, and a witch being killed in a sauna. In the *Kalevala*, I was fascinated by the metamorphoses of witch queen Louhi changing herself into a giant eagle and wizard Väinämöinen taking the form of a snake to escape from the underworld. Also the use of magic words to escape dire situations captivated me.

Later, when I dived into other stories and poems of ancient Finnish oral tradition collected into tomes of books, I realized that the whole tradition is permeated with the magic and macabre of the everyday. The otherworld is always present. There is only a thin veil between our world and the magical realm of gods, animals and the dead, and it can be easily lifted. The Finns, living in the land of thousands of lakes, know that if you walk on a sea shore, Vetehinen can grab you anytime and bring you to the deeps, and in the forest, angered gods can throw a blanket over you to hide you from your searchers or send a bear or wolf to attack you. In stories, crossings between worlds are constant: women get married to sea kings, men travel to the underworld to find a bride, and walking into a mountain crevice takes you to a magical land.

While the natural world can be unpredictable, folktales show us things from nature's point of view. A tree mourns why it's being cut down to be used for boats, a fox cries about its children being hunted, and a horse asks why it's being killed even though it has served its masters faithfully. Laments, songs of sadness, reflect the melancholic side of Finns as well as the comforting quality of nature. In all Finnish mythology, animals are people's helpers and allies. In the *Kalevala*, Louhi's daughter asks birds for advice regarding marriage, and the mother of wizard Lemminkäinen gets information about her dead son from a raven, messenger of death.

Instead of being at the mercy of the wrath of gods, the Finns have resorted to a survival mechanism: spells. Magic words were originally known only by a few wizards who had the courage to travel to the underworld to retrieve them from dead ancestors. In the *Kalevala*, Väinämöinen travels to the river of death to the corpse of a dead shaman to retrieve lost words. The shaman wakes up and gives him all his stories. This is the mythical birth of folktales.

Finland has always been known as a land of sorcerers. The *Kalevala* is built on the antagonism between wizards and witches and the battle around a wealth-generating mill, the Sampo. Created to give riches to only a select few, the mill ended up broken on the bottom of the ocean where its fragments turned into the riches of the sea and seeds for agriculture to benefit all humans.

This is how I view the Finnish tradition. From secret words not known by many, the pieces of the magic mill in the form of words, spells and tales spread all over the world to be read and enjoyed by all people even to this day.

Tiina Porthan

Publisher's Note

WE OFFER THIS COLLECTION as a starting point for the general reader in your journey of discovery of ancient Finnish folklore, myths and tales; a topic that remains largely untouched in mainstream media. Despite being from a small part of the world, these stories will reveal imaginative and enchanting characters and otherworlds which will transport readers to the fir tree woodlands and mountains of these tales' homeland. Please note that, aside from the foreword and introduction, the main body of the book is a curated selection of late-nineteenth- and early-twentieth-century texts from noted folklorists, historians, authors and translators. These stories are supported by Elias Lönnrot's epic poem the *Kalevala* translated by John Martin Crawford (1888). More about these scholars and writers can be found at the back of this book.

It should be thus remembered that these texts are of the era during which they were translated, interpreted and written. We must remind the reader that, as tales from mythology and folklore are principally derived from an oral storytelling tradition, their written representation depends on the transcription, translation and interpretation by those who heard them and first put them to paper, and also on whether they are recently re-told versions or more directly sourced from original first-hand accounts. The stories in this book are a mixture, and you can learn more about the sources and authors at the back of the book. Due to the historical nature of such texts, we're aware that there may be some language used which has the potential to cause offence to the modern reader. However, wishing to overall preserve the integrity of the writing, rather than imposing contemporary sensibilities, we have left it largely unaltered.

EPIC

KALEVALA & FINNISH MYTHS & TALES

ANTHOLOGY OF CLASSIC TALES

Foreword by Tiina Porthan

FLAME TREE PUBLISHING

TALES

Kalevala & Finnish Myths & Tales

Introduction

NOTHING IF NOT AMBITIOUS in its scope, Finland's national epic, the *Kalevala,* makes a world of its homeland. Almost literally so: the poem begins with a Creation story centred on what for most us is a small and far-flung land of lakes and woods.

In primeval times, a maiden,
Beauteous Daughter of the Ether,
Passed for ages her existence
In the great expanse of heaven,
O'er the prairies yet enfolded.
Wearisome the maiden growing,
Her existence sad and hopeless,
Thus alone to live for ages
In the infinite expanses
Of the air above the sea-foam,
In the far outstretching spaces,

It is, it seems, to keep her company that she yearns to bring a world into being. Instead she finds she is still alone, swept back and forth by the raging waves of an unending ocean. A prayer to Ukko, god of the heavens, brings down a duck – a seemingly incongruous addition. Yet from her eggs hatch fire and warmth, the sun and moon and their cycling rhythm of day and night. Also, of course, the rocks, the rugged islands and the broad, fair country of the mainland. And the first man, too: Wainamoinen, a hero, a shaman and a singer. Poetry will prove to be the vitalizing force of the *Kalevala's* Finland.

Old and New

Like the English hymnal, the *Kalevala* was 'ancient and modern': as old as Finland, yet as up-to-date as the Romantic sensibility it so appealed to. Romantic writing always did respond to folkloric traditions and the antique paganism with which they appeared to be charged. Superficially, we might say, because the self-consciously wayward modern poet wished to reject the hidebound bourgeois values of the nineteenth century. But that glib dismissal warrants deeper exploration.

Paganism originated with peoples for whom the woods and streams and fields were the whole world; the plants and animals were the most obvious representatives of that world's animating power. The Romantic poets were as drawn to the same things because they represented the idea of a truly authentic and direct relationship with the cosmos unmediated by the institutions and conventions of modern life. Wordsworth claimed to find in the 'Wisdom and Spirit of the Universe' that he could not discover in the conventionally ordered canon of human knowledge.

The things that make the *Kalevala* folkloric are, accordingly, the same things that make it a Romantic poem. The most striking of these is the resonance that we sense with the world of Nature. Celebrated stories may be handed down to us by a 'dear old father' or a 'tender mother', but they may also come from the deep forests and the icy crags. 'There are many other legends,' the Proem says:

Incantations that were taught me,
That I found along the wayside,
Gathered in the fragrant copses,
Blown me from the forest branches,
Culled among the plumes of pine trees,
Scented from the vines and flowers,
Whispered to me as I followed
Flocks in land of honeyed meadows,

As speaker, a semi-fictive bard, Lönnrot isn't just talking about the 'inspiration' poets were conventionally supposed to find in Nature's beauty, peace and quiet. His Proem goes much further, suggesting that he received his composition ready-crafted from the forest. 'Sentences the trees created,' it insists. Then, these verses having been rolled into bundles by some unnamed divinity, they were carried on sledges to his cottage and tied to his garret rafters, hung about his door, laid in his storage-chests... All Lönnrot had to do as poet was 'collect them' and set out his stall.

The Necessity of Naivety

The English Romantic poet John Keats wrote of the need for a poet to have 'negative capability': the capacity to remain in doubt; to accept mystery and strangeness without reaching out for certainty in explanation. The capability is 'negative' not because it's bad, but because it entails our switching off the rationalistic modern compulsion to categorize, to order, to nail down meaning.

'Have you heard the Finnish tale of the girl who sits upon the evening clouds, and weaves a golden shade with silver shuttle? Would you like to...?', So one story ('Castles in the Air') asks us here. The delightful invitation turns out to be a challenge. If we're truly to hear that story, to appreciate its full significance, the tale suggests, a great deal more will be asked of us than simply reading.

Go down to the seashore one evening at sunset, press your right hand against the left side of your breast, and feel if your heart beats warmly and freely, eager for what is beautiful and pure in the world. Look then around you with the eye of a child, and you shall behold wonderful things in the rosy clouds of the sunset.

Granted, the seashore trip may not be practicable, but the receptive reading spirit should not be impossible to attain. It's a choice on our part if, in the storyteller's words, we glance at Nature's beauties 'with an indifferent eye and a cold heart', and so see 'nothing but fleeting clouds and the evening mist, foreboding rain on the morrow.'

All that is beautiful in the world must be beheld with innocent eyes, or it dissolves into vapour, perishes, and becomes naught. This is the canon law of beauty, once for all, I cannot help it.

A World of Humanity

It's all very well for us to be shown the grandeur of creation, the beauty of the world, but sublimity can only take us so far. We are human first and last, and a work of art or literature can only appeal to us if it offers us something on a human scale. An epic of heroics and high adventure, of friendship and feud, of love and war, all rooted in the beauty and remoteness of the Finnish landscape, the *Kalevala* casts a mystic mantle over the most commonly authentic human feelings. In elevating the emotions of real men and women to the status of national destiny; it does for subarctic woods and lakeshores what Virgil's *Aeneid* did for Rome.

If much of the joy of reading folk tales is that of finding the universal in the apparently parochial, there's also the fun of finding the contemporary in some seemingly long lost 'days of yore'. In doing this, however, it highlights the power of much slighter stories to do something of the same, revealing the reason for our love of these traditional tales. The 'Forest Bride' in the story of that name is by all appearances a mouse, tiny, trivial and beneath all notice, but the ultimate prize – a princess, indeed – to the man who, like young Veikko, can see her true worth.

Anthropomorphized Animals

The Mouse Princess is archetypal: the transformation may not be so literal, but just about every animal in a folktale of this sort is a person 'really'. They not only show human characteristics, but also reveal the human foibles (and of course the virtues) of the human characters with whom they interact.

The 'Enchanted Grouse' in another tale hints at being a prince who has suffered a similar transformation. However the fact is never quite confirmed, still less explained – chiefly, of course, because it doesn't matter. The Grouse is instrumental in the story: at the most reductive reading, he is a plot device. But he's also so much more than that, with his initial plight revealing Helli's kindness and loyalty and his magical powers enabling those qualities to be rewarded.

Storytellers from Aesop to Walt Disney have recognized that anthropomorphized animal characters can be engaging. Not only do they add colour and quirkiness: abstracted as they are from human specificity, such characters can more readily be seen as universal types. The animals in 'Mikko the Fox' not only tell us nothing whatsoever about the life of nature: they also offer all sorts of little insights into the vagaries of human life.

Magic and Miracle

This sort of waiving of the rules is, of course, part and parcel of the art of magic. Enchantment is a great facilitator in many of these tales. In the story of 'Knut Fairyflute', the special powers of the pipe that the protagonist finds ends up leading him on a long, meandering and magical journey, as we accompany him through a wildly improbable shaggy-dog story. 'The Little Sister' features a magic cake which rolls along the ground to show Kerttu the way she has to walk. In the story of 'The Sea King's Gift' the magic rhymes that the fisherman's wife remembers hearing as a girl, recounted to her by an old lame man, help to get her and her family out of all sorts of trouble

The Best Policy

But the mundane may often trump the magical in these tales, even as the simplest feelings can be the best, notwithstanding the extravagant powers of enchantment. Courage, heroism, honour, generosity, self-sacrifice: these things matter more than magic in the end. (Indeed a cynic might suggest that they are more extraordinary.)

'The Tale of the True Bride' shows how innocence and honesty win out over a witch's machinations when the wicked Suyettar (who features in the *Kalevala* as Suo'ya-tar, the serpent's mother) uses spells to supplant the fair Ilona in the prince's affections. The good do not by any means always get their happy endings in real life, as we all know, but this story still strikes us as articulating an important truth.

So it is too in the tale of 'The Terrible Olli', in which the protagonist, the youngest of his brothers, and relentlessly put-upon, prevails – despite his ingenuousness – over the grim old Troll. Likewise the Mighty Mikko, who wins a fox's friendship, though his gentle kindness. Despite being a poor woodsman's son with no prospects whatsoever in the world, with the fox's help he rises to high fortunesv– so much so that by story's end he has married a princess and become a lord. The grateful fox who guides him is not simply a representative of Nature, but a gently ironic exemplar of human emotion and a shrewd observer of human character and social life. 'Realistic' the story may not be, but it is nevertheless indisputably 'true' in the sense of resonating with us in our sense of what is right and just.

'The Gifts of the Magician' tells a similar story: a brave young boy rescues a wizard he finds fleeing from a pack of wolves and is repaid by a lifetime's worth of magical rewards. As astonishing as these are, the wonder of this story derives as much from the tricks that it plays upon our received ideas: here the sorcerer is honest and the villain is the king.

A Mischievous Moralism

'The Devil's Bride' is, as its subtitle says, 'The Story of the Boy Who Wouldn't Lose his Temper'. At the most basic level it is a morality tale in which outstanding virtue is rewarded. But it is told with a mischievous wit that removes it as far as is imaginable from the realm of sententiousness. Erkki outwits the Devil by his own devices. Likewise 'the Young Man Who Respected the Dead' in 'The Mysterious Servant': his sense of decorum won't let him look on idly as a group of men belabour the dead body of a merchant who's died in their debt. The servant who suddenly appears to take charge of his affairs and bring him to wealth and happiness is the embodiment of God's favour for his generosity and decency, of course. Again, the story is told with a wry and irreverent humour that redeems it from any hint of pious moralizing.

Alien Attitudes

The way we articulate our sense of rightness does not have to be universal, of course. The collision of different attitudes can be jarring as in 'The Most Beautiful Thing in the Wood', for example, told by the Finnish writer Zachris Topelius. The action takes place, as the title suggests, in a wood. The trees – the fir, the birch, the willow, the lime, the aspen, the mountain ash, even the little juniper bush – argue with each other over which of them should be considered 'the most beautiful thing in the wood'. Each has a claim as all are undoubtedly lovely – especially as they are now, lit up by sunlight on the brightest, sunniest morning of the spring. Eventually, though, they are all upstaged as a little boy and girl from a nearby cottage come walking through the flowers and ferns, pausing to offer up a prayer of thankfulness for the wondrous beauty of their world. The trees hear them and feel 'astonished and reproved'. Sitting high up in the branches of a birch, a bullfinch twitters for them all when he says:

> *Beautiful and glorious is our verdant wood, and all God's nature! But I tell you trees … that of all the pretty and delightful things that God has allowed to grow in this forest, there is nothing more lovely, more innocently pretty, than these two little children, who praise God from the fulness of their hearts, this glorious summer morning.*

There is wit and humour in Topelius's telling of this story. Overall it shines out as strongly as the pious sentimentality perhaps to be expected of a devout Lutheran (1818–95) whose whole adult life would be bound by the 'Victorian' age. The values of the nineteenth century were very different, obviously, from those of today; nor will Topelius's personality necessarily strike a chord with ours. For most of us, however, much as we may enjoy encountering kindred souls in authors, this kind of dissonance can be just as satisfying.

The Teller and the Tale

More important, though, Topelius's highly personalized style serves as a reminder that, however earnestly deadpan the delivery, we are never really simply reading a folktale. No narrative can exist, unmodified, in some 'pure' form. Every tale must be told, and every telling is a reinvention: the story is stamped, however subtly, with its teller's hallmark.

Even the *Kalevala*, despite its undisputed position as its country's 'national epic', may be considered is the property of a people, not of one man.

Mastered by desire impulsive,
By a mighty inward urging,
I am ready now for singing,
Ready to begin the chanting
Of our nation's ancient folk-song
Handed down from by-gone ages.
In my mouth the words are melting,
From my lips the tones are gliding,
From my tongue they wish to hasten;
When my willing teeth are parted,
When my ready mouth is opened,
Songs of ancient wit and wisdom
Hasten from me not unwilling.

Thus begins the prefatory 'Proem' of the poem as it has been bequeathed to us, prompted at once by an 'inward urging' and an external heritage, 'handed down'. The former is immediately recognizable to us as the inspiration of the Romantic poet; the latter echoes the faithful recording of folklore. Both make claims to truth, even if in reality both also expect us to follow Samuel Taylor Coleridge (1772–1834), the great English Romantic, in making a 'willing suspension of disbelief'.

'Poetry,' wrote the great Argentinian writer Jorge Luis Borges (1899–1986) in 1977, 'is not the books in the library.' Rather, he maintained, 'it is the encounter of the reader with the book; the discovery of the book.' A work of literature, for Borges, was no single text but a dialogue between itself and its reader – as indeed, he believed, was our existence as a whole. 'Life itself is a quotation,' he summed up.

For the Story's Sake

Much may be exasperating about the postmodern sensibility that Borges represents, but it takes the complexities and contradictions of the *Kalevala* in its stride. Notionally, this is Finland's 'national epic', but no ancient bard ever declaimed these stories in those exact words, or anything like them. In fact it derives from a compilation of folksongs sung and folktales told in the Karelian dialect. Collected from a number of sources by Elias Lönnrot (1802–84), these were then adapted into standard Finnish and worked into a continuous narrative of verse, published in part in 1835, then in its entirety in 1849. As we find it here, moreover, it's the American translation by John Martin Crawford (1845–1916) published in 1888.

Furthermore, this is a text that the English-speaking reader can hardly help reading through the filter of *The Song of Hiawatha* – even though it was written after Lönnrot's *Kalevala* in 1855, and under its literary influence. Henry Wadsworth Longfellow had read the *Kalevala* (in Finnish, albeit with a little help from Schiefner's German version) and his ambivalently regarded American classic derived its much-parodied metrical form from that work. Since Finnish generally accents the first syllable of any given word, it falls comfortably into trochaic metres. In English, by contrast, these sound at best contrived and at worst (as, some say, in *Hiawatha*) downright comic in their bounciness. Crawford's *Kalevala* is accomplished in avoiding this: rather than repetitive nonsense, we get a sense of the text as cornucopia, an endless spilling-out of folkloric beauty, colour and enchantment.

One advantage of coming to this collection now, rather than a century ago, is our comparative freedom from the anxiety that would have then dogged us then over the 'authenticity' of the work. We no longer expect a poem like this to reveal the 'soul of Finland', as once we might have done. Neither do we dismiss its complex publishing history as somehow diluting or debasing. The least 'literary' of us has been trained by everything from advertising billboards to television shows to appreciate that allusion can be illuminating; derivativeness may possess a dignity all its own. Nor are we troubled – just as well! – by our knowledge that we will never be able to 'hear' these tales in the way that a Karelian villager of the distant past might have done. Yet we do gain an enthralling insight into human nature and to the extraordinary magic and mystery (however we define these things) of Finland.

Kalevala

Introduction

THE NINETEENTH CENTURY SAW A WAVE of nationalism sweeping Europe, from Poland to Italy and from Germany to Greece. Snatched away from Swedish rule by Imperial Russia in 1809, Finland was just the kind of nation that might reasonably have felt the call of freedom. The Czars might have given it the portentous designation of 'Grand Duchy', but it was really just another province of the Empire.

It was, however, doubly disenfranchised: prior to its Russian conquest, Finland had been under Swedish rule since the medieval era. There was no real precedent or paradigm for a 'Finnish nation'. Its Swedish-speaking elite were heirs to centuries of Scandinavian lore and culture. Looking westward, though, they saw nothing to hanker after in the autocratic ways of Charles XIV John; no reason to feel nostalgia for Swedish rule.

The desire for Finland to find itself an identity of its own was still subconscious but becoming irresistible. As yet, though, it was no more than a notion. The country's writers, thinkers and artists had self-consciously to piece together a Finnish identity from the linguistic and cultural bits and pieces they found lying around. Big and compendious and eloquent, Elias Lönnrot's epic brought things to a tipping point, Finland's declaration of imaginative independence.

Kalevala

Proem

Mastered by desire impulsive,
By a mighty inward urging,
I am ready now for singing,
Ready to begin the chanting
Of our nation's ancient folk-song
Handed down from by-gone ages.
In my mouth the words are melting,
From my lips the tones are gliding,
From my tongue they wish to hasten;
When my willing teeth are parted,
When my ready mouth is opened,
Songs of ancient wit and wisdom
Hasten from me not unwilling.

Golden friend, and dearest brother,
Brother dear of mine in childhood,
Come and sing with me the stories,
Come and chant with me the legends,
Legends of the times forgotten,
Since we now are here together,
Come together from our roamings.
Seldom do we come for singing,
Seldom to the one, the other,
O'er this cold and cruel country,
O'er the poor soil of the Northland.
Let us clasp our hands together
That we thus may best remember.
Join we now in merry singing,
Chant we now the oldest folk-lore,
That the dear ones all may hear them,
That the well-inclined may hear them,
Of this rising generation.
These are words in childhood taught me,
Songs preserved from distant ages,
Legends they that once were taken
From the belt of Wainamoinen,
From the forge of Ilmarinen,
From the sword of Kaukomieli,
From the bow of Youkahainen,
From the pastures of the Northland,
From the meads of Kalevala.
These my dear old father sang me
When at work with knife and hatchet
These my tender mother taught me
When she twirled the flying spindle,
When a child upon the matting
By her feet I rolled and tumbled.

Incantations were not wanting
Over Sampo and o'er Louhi,
Sampo growing old in singing,
Louhi ceasing her enchantment.
In the songs died wise Wipunen,
At the games died Lemminkainen.
There are many other legends,
Incantations that were taught me,
That I found along the wayside,
Gathered in the fragrant copses,
Blown me from the forest branches,
Culled among the plumes of pine trees,
Scented from the vines and flowers,
Whispered to me as I followed
Flocks in land of honeyed meadows,
Over hillocks green and golden,
After sable-haired Murikki,
And the many-coloured Kimmo.
Many runes the cold has told me,
Many lays the rain has brought me,
Other songs the winds have sung me;
Many birds from many forests,
Oft have sung me lays in concord
Waves of sea, and ocean billows,
Music from the many waters,
Music from the whole creation,
Oft have been my guide and master.
Sentences the trees created,

Rolled together into bundles,
Moved them to my ancient dwelling,
On the sledges to my cottage,
Tied them to my garret rafters,
Hung them on my dwelling-portals,
Laid them in a chest of boxes,
Boxes lined with shining copper.
Long they lay within my dwelling
Through the chilling winds of winter,
In my dwelling-place for ages.

Shall I bring these songs together
From the cold and frost collect them?
Shall I bring this nest of boxes,
Keepers of these golden legends,
To the table in my cabin,
Underneath the painted rafters,
In this house renowned and ancient?
Shall I now these boxes open,
Boxes filled with wondrous stories?
Shall I now the end unfasten
Of this ball of ancient wisdom,
These ancestral lays unravel?
Let me sing an old-time legend,
That shall echo forth the praises
Of the beer that I have tasted,
Of the sparkling beer of barley.
Bring to me a foaming goblet
Of the barley of my fathers,
Lest my singing grow too weary,
Singing from the water only.
Bring me too a cup of strong-beer,
It will add to our enchantment,
To the pleasure of the evening,
Northland's long and dreary evening,
For the beauty of the day-dawn,
For the pleasure of the morning,
The beginning of the new-day.

Often I have heard them chanting,
Often I have heard them singing,
That the nights come to us singly,
That the Moon beams on us singly,
That the Sun shines on us singly;
Singly also, Wainamoinen,
The renowned and wise enchanter,
Born from everlasting Ether
Of his mother, Ether's daughter.

Rune I: Birth of Wainamoinen

In primeval times, a maiden,
Beauteous Daughter of the Ether,
Passed for ages her existence
In the great expanse of heaven,
O'er the prairies yet enfolded.
Wearisome the maiden growing,
Her existence sad and hopeless,
Thus alone to live for ages
In the infinite expanses
Of the air above the sea-foam,
In the far outstretching spaces,
In a solitude of ether,
She descended to the ocean,
Waves her coach, and waves her pillow.
Thereupon the rising storm-wind
Flying from the East in fierceness,
Whips the ocean into surges,
Strikes the stars with sprays of ocean
Till the waves are white with fervor.
To and fro they toss the maiden,
Storm-encircled, hapless maiden;
With her sport the rolling billows,
With her play the storm-wind forces,
On the blue back of the waters;
On the white-wreathed waves of ocean,
Play the forces of the salt-sea,
With the lone and helpless maiden;
Till at last in full conception,
Union now of force and beauty,
Sink the storm-winds into slumber;
Overburdened now the maiden
Cannot rise above the surface;
Seven hundred years she wandered,
Ages nine of man's existence,
Swam the ocean hither, thither,
Could not rise above the waters,
Conscious only of her travail;
Seven hundred years she laboured
Ere her first-born was delivered.
Thus she swam as water-mother,

Toward the east, and also southward,
Toward the west, and also northward;
Swam the sea in all directions,
Frightened at the strife of storm-winds,
Swam in travail, swam unceasing,
Ere her first-born was delivered.

Then began she gently weeping,
Spake these measures, heavy-hearted:
"Woe is me, my life hard-fated!
Woe is me, in this my travail!
Into what have I now fallen?
Woe is me, that I unhappy,
Left my home in subtle ether,
Came to dwell amid the sea-foam,
To be tossed by rolling billows,
To be rocked by winds and waters,
On the far outstretching waters,
In the salt-sea's vast expanses,
Knowing only pain and trouble!
Better far for me, O Ukko!
Were I maiden in the Ether,
Than within these ocean-spaces,
To become a water-mother!
All this life is cold and dreary,
Painful here is every motion,
As I linger in the waters,
As I wander through the ocean.
Ukko, thou O God, up yonder,
Thou the ruler of the heavens,
Come thou hither, thou art needed,
Come thou hither, I implore thee,
To deliver me from trouble,
To deliver me in travail.
Come I pray thee, hither hasten,
Hasten more that thou art needed,
Haste and help this helpless maiden!"

When she ceased her supplications,
Scarce a moment onward passes,
Ere a beauteous duck descending,
Hastens toward the water-mother,
Comes a-flying hither, thither,
Seeks herself a place for nesting.
Flies she eastward, flies she westward,
Circles northward, circles southward,
Cannot find a grassy hillock,
Not the smallest bit of verdure;
Cannot find a spot protected,
Cannot find a place befitting,
Where to make her nest in safety.
Flying slowly, looking round her,
She descries no place for resting,
Thinking loud and long debating,
And her words are such as follow:
"Build I in the winds my dwelling,
On the floods my place of nesting?
Surely would the winds destroy it,
Far away the waves would wash it."

Then the daughter of the Ether,
Now the hapless water-mother,
Raised her shoulders out of water,
Raised her knees above the ocean,
That the duck might build her dwelling,
Build her nesting-place in safety.
Thereupon the duck in beauty,
Flying slowly, looking round her,
Spies the shoulders of the maiden,
Sees the knees of Ether's daughter,
Now the hapless water-mother,
Thinks them to be grassy hillocks,
On the blue back of the ocean.
Thence she flies and hovers slowly,
Lightly on the knee she settles,
Finds a nesting-place befitting,
Where to lay her eggs in safety.
Here she builds her humble dwelling,
Lays her eggs within, at pleasure,
Six, the golden eggs she lays there,
Then a seventh, an egg of iron;
Sits upon her eggs to hatch them,
Quickly warms them on the knee-cap
Of the hapless water-mother;
Hatches one day, then a second,
Then a third day sits and hatches.
Warmer grows the water round her,
Warmer is her bed in ocean,
While her knee with fire is kindled,
And her shoulders too are burning,
Fire in every vein is coursing.
Quick the maiden moves her shoulders,
Shakes her members in succession,
Shakes the nest from its foundation,

And the eggs fall into ocean,
Dash in pieces on the bottom
Of the deep and boundless waters.
In the sand they do not perish,
Not the pieces in the ocean;
But transformed, in wondrous beauty
All the fragments come together
Forming pieces two in number,
One the upper, one the lower,
Equal to the one, the other.
From one half the egg, the lower,
Grows the nether vault of Terra:
From the upper half remaining,
Grows the upper vault of Heaven;
From the white part come the moonbeams,
From the yellow part the sunshine,
From the motley part the starlight,
From the dark part grows the cloudage;
And the days speed onward swiftly,
Quickly do the years fly over,
From the shining of the new sun
From the lighting of the full moon.

Still the daughter of the Ether,
Swims the sea as water-mother,
With the floods outstretched before her,
And behind her sky and ocean.
Finally about the ninth year,
In the summer of the tenth year,
Lifts her head above the surface,
Lifts her forehead from the waters,
And begins at last her workings,
Now commences her creations,
On the azure water-ridges,
On the mighty waste before her.
Where her hand she turned in water,
There arose a fertile hillock;
Wheresoe'er her foot she rested,
There she made a hole for fishes;
Where she dived beneath the waters,
Fell the many deeps of ocean;
Where upon her side she turned her,
There the level banks have risen;
Where her head was pointed landward,
There appeared wide bays and inlets;
When from shore she swam a distance,
And upon her back she rested,
There the rocks she made and fashioned,
And the hidden reefs created,
Where the ships are wrecked so often,
Where so many lives have perished.

Thus created were the islands,
Rocks were fastened in the ocean,
Pillars of the sky were planted,
Fields and forests were created,
Checkered stones of many colours,
Gleaming in the silver sunlight,
All the rocks stood well established;
But the singer, Wainamoinen,
Had not yet beheld the sunshine,
Had not seen the golden moonlight,
Still remaining undelivered.

Wainamoinen, old and trusty,
Lingering within his dungeon
Thirty summers altogether,
And of winters, also thirty,
Peaceful on the waste of waters,
On the broad sea's yielding bosom,
Well reflected, long considered,
How unborn to live and flourish
In the spaces wrapped in darkness,
In uncomfortable limits,
Where he had not seen the moonlight,
Had not seen the silver sunshine.
Thereupon these words he uttered,
Let himself be heard in this wise:
"Take, O Moon, I pray thee, take me,
Take me, thou, O Sun above me,
Take me, thou, O Bear of heaven,
From this dark and dreary prison,
From these unbefitting portals,
From this narrow place of resting,
From this dark and gloomy dwelling,
Hence to wander from the ocean,
Hence to walk upon the islands,
On the dry land walk and wander,
Like an ancient hero wander,
Walk in open air and breathe it,
Thus to see the moon at evening,
Thus to see the silver sunlight,
Thus to see the Bear in heaven,
That the stars I may consider."

Since the Moon refused to free him,
And the Sun would not deliver,
Nor the Great Bear give assistance,
His existence growing weary,
And his life but an annoyance,
Bursts he then the outer portals
Of his dark and dismal fortress;
With his strong, but unnamed finger,
Opens he the lock resisting;
With the toes upon his left foot,
With the fingers of his right hand,
Creeps he through the yielding portals
To the threshold of his dwelling;
On his knees across the threshold,
Throws himself head foremost, forward
Plunges into deeps of ocean,
Plunges hither, plunges thither,
Turning with his hands the water;
Swims he northward, swims he southward,
Swims he eastward, swims he westward,
Studying his new surroundings.
Thus our hero reached the water,
Rested five years in the ocean,
Six long years, and even seven years,
Till the autumn of the eighth year,
When at last he leaves the waters,
Stops upon a promontory,
On a coast bereft of verdure;
On his knees he leaves the ocean,
On the land he plants his right foot,
On the solid ground his left foot,
Quickly turns his hands about him,
Stands erect to see the sunshine,
Stands to see the golden moonlight,
That he may behold the Great Bear,
That he may the stars consider.
Thus our hero, Wainamoinen,
Thus the wonderful enchanter
Was delivered from his mother,
Ilmatar, the Ether's daughter.

Rune II: Wainamoinen's Sowing

Then arose old Wainamoinen,
With his feet upon the island,
On the island washed by ocean,
Broad expanse devoid of verdure;
There remained he many summers,
There he lived as many winters,
On the island vast and vacant,
Well considered, long reflected,
Who for him should sow the island,
Who for him the seeds should scatter;
Thought at last of Pellerwoinen,
First-born of the plains and prairies,
When a slender boy, called Sampsa,
Who should sow the vacant island,
Who the forest seeds should scatter.
Pellerwoinen, thus consenting,
Sows with diligence the island,
Seeds upon the lands he scatters,
Seeds in every swamp and lowland,
Forest seeds upon the loose earth,
On the firm soil sows the acorns,
Fir trees sows he on the mountains,
Pine trees also on the hill-tops,
Many shrubs in every valley,
Birches sows he in the marshes,
In the loose soil sows the alders,
In the lowlands sows the lindens,
In the moist earth sows the willow,
Mountain-ash in virgin places,
On the banks of streams the hawthorn,
Junipers in hilly regions;
This the work of Pellerwoinen,
Slender Sampsa, in his childhood.
Soon the fertile seeds were sprouting,
Soon the forest trees were growing,
Soon appeared the tops of fir trees,
And the pines were far outspreading;
Birches rose from all the marshes,
In the loose soil grew the alders,
In the mellow soil the lindens;
Junipers were also growing,
Junipers with clustered berries,
Berries on the hawthorn branches.

Now the hero, Wainamoinen,
Stands aloft to look about him,
How the Sampsa-seeds are growing,
How the crop of Pellerwoinen;

Sees the young trees thickly spreading,
Sees the forest rise in beauty;
But the oak-tree has not sprouted,
Tree of heaven is not growing,
Still within the acorn sleeping,
Its own happiness enjoying.
Then he waited three nights longer,
And as many days he waited,
Waited till a week had vanished,
Then again the work examined;
But the oak-tree was not growing,
Had not left her acorn-dwelling.

Wainamoinen, ancient hero,
Spies four maidens in the distance,
Water-brides, he spies a fifth-one,
On the soft and sandy seashore,
In the dewy grass and flowers,
On a point extending seaward,
Near the forests of the island.
Some were mowing, some were raking,
Raking what was mown together,
In a windrow on the meadow.

From the ocean rose a giant,
Mighty Tursas, tall and hardy,
Pressed compactly all the grasses,
That the maidens had been raking,
When a fire within them kindles,
And the flames shot up to heaven,
Till the windrows burned to ashes,
Only ashes now remaining
Of the grasses raked together.
In the ashes of the windrows,
Tender leaves the giant places,
In the leaves he plants an acorn,
From the acorn, quickly sprouting,
Grows the oak-tree, tall and stately,
From the ground enriched by ashes,
Newly raked by water-maidens;
Spread the oak-tree's many branches,
Rounds itself a broad corona,
Raises it above the storm-clouds;
Far it stretches out its branches,
Stops the white-clouds in their courses,
With its branches hides the sunlight,
With its many leaves, the moonbeams,
And the starlight dies in heaven.

Wainamoinen, old and trusty,
Thought awhile, and well considered,
How to kill the mighty oak-tree,
First created for his pleasure,
How to fell the tree majestic,
How to lop its hundred branches.
Sad the lives of man and hero,
Sad the homes of ocean-dwellers,
If the sun shines not upon them,
If the moonlight does not cheer them!
Is there not some mighty hero,
Was there never born a giant,
That can fell the mighty oak-tree,
That can lop its hundred branches?
Wainamoinen, deeply thinking,
Spake these words soliloquizing:
"Kapé, daughter of the Ether,
Ancient mother of my being,
Luonnotar, my nurse and helper,
Loan to me the water-forces,
Great the powers of the waters;
Loan to me the strength of oceans,
To upset this mighty oak-tree,
To uproot this tree of evil,
That again may shine the sunlight,
That the moon once more may glimmer."

Straightway rose a form from ocean,
Rose a hero from the waters,
Nor belonged he to the largest,
Nor belonged he to the smallest,
Long was he as man's forefinger,
Taller than the hand of woman;
On his head a cap of copper,
Boots upon his feet were copper,
Gloves upon his hands were copper,
And its stripes were copper-coloured,
Belt around him made of copper,
Hatchet in his belt was copper;
And the handle of his hatchet
Was as long as hand of woman,
Of a finger's breadth the blade was.
Then the trusty Wainamoinen
Thought awhile and well considered,

And his measures are as follow:
"Art thou, sir, divine or human?
Which of these thou only knowest;
Tell me what thy name and station.
Very like a man thou lookest,
Hast the bearing of a hero,
Though the length of man's first finger,
Scarce as tall as hoof of reindeer."

Then again spake Wainamoinen
To the form from out the ocean:
"Verily I think thee human,
Of the race of pigmy-heroes,
Might as well be dead or dying,
Fit for nothing but to perish."

Answered thus the pigmy-hero,
Spake the small one from the ocean
To the valiant Wainamoinen:
"Truly am I god and hero,
From the tribes that rule the ocean;
Come I here to fell the oak-tree,
Lop its branches with my hatchet."

Wainamoinen, old and trusty,
Answers thus the sea-born hero:
"Never hast thou force sufficient,
Not to thee has strength been given,
To uproot this mighty oak-tree,
To upset this thing of evil,
Nor to lop its hundred branches."

Scarcely had he finished speaking,
Scarcely had he moved his eyelids,
Ere the pigmy full unfolding,
Quick becomes a mighty giant.
With one step he leaves the ocean,
Plants himself, a mighty hero,
On the forest-fields surrounding;
With his head the clouds he pierces,
To his knees his beard extending,
And his locks fall to his ankles;
Far apart appear his eyeballs,
Far apart his feet are stationed,
Farther still his mighty shoulders.
Now begins his axe to sharpen,
Quickly to an edge he whets it,
Using six hard blocks of sandstone,
And of softer whetstones, seven.
Straightway to the oak-tree turning,
Thither stalks the mighty giant,
In his raiment long and roomy,
Flapping in the winds of heaven;
With his second step he totters
On the land of darker colour;
With his third stop firmly planted,
Reaches he the oak-tree's branches,
Strikes the trunk with sharpened hatchet,
With one mighty swing he strikes it,
With a second blow he cuts it;
As his blade descends the third time,
From his axe the sparks fly upward,
From the oak-tree fire outshooting;
Ere the axe descends a fourth time,
Yields the oak with hundred branches,
Shaking earth and heaven in falling.
Eastward far the trunk extending,
Far to westward flew the tree-tops,
To the South the leaves were scattered,
To the North its hundred branches.
Whosoe'er a branch has taken,
Has obtained eternal welfare;
Who secures himself a tree-top,
He has gained the master magic;
Who the foliage has gathered,
Has delight that never ceases.
Of the chips some had been scattered,
Scattered also many splinters,
On the blue back of the ocean,
Of the ocean smooth and mirrored,
Rocked there by the winds and waters,
Like a boat upon the billows;
Storm-winds blew them to the Northland,
Some the ocean currents carried.

Northland's fair and slender maiden,
Washing on the shore a head-dress,
Beating on the rocks her garments,
Rinsing there her silken raiment,
In the waters of Pohyola,
There beheld the chips and splinters,
Carried by the winds and waters.
In a bag the chips she gathered,
Took them to the ancient court-yard,

There to make enchanted arrows,
Arrows for the great magician,
There to shape them into weapons,
Weapons for the skilful archer,
Since the mighty oak has fallen,
Now has lost its hundred branches,
That the North may see the sunshine,
See the gentle gleam of moonlight,
That the clouds may keep
their courses,
May extend the vault of heaven
Over every lake and river,
O'er the banks of every island.

Groves arose in varied beauty,
Beautifully grew the forests,
And again, the vines and flowers.
Birds again sang in the tree-tops,
Noisily the merry thrushes,
And the cuckoos in the birch-trees;
On the mountains grew the berries,
Golden flowers in the meadows,
And the herbs of many colours,
Many kinds of vegetation;
But the barley is not growing.

Wainamoinen, old and trusty,
Goes away and well considers,
By the borders of the waters,
On the ocean's sandy margin,
Finds six seeds of golden barley,
Even seven ripened kernels,
On the shore of upper Northland,
In the sand upon the seashore,
Hides them in his trusty pouches,
Fashioned from the skin of squirrel,
Some were made from skin of marten;
Hastens forth the seeds to scatter,
Quickly sows the barley kernels,
On the brinks of Kalew-waters,
On the Osma-hills and lowlands.

Hark! the titmouse wildly crying,
From the aspen, words as follow:
"Osma's barley will not flourish,
Not the barley of Wainola,
If the soil be not made ready,
If the forest be not levelled,
And the branches burned to ashes."

Wainamoinen, wise and ancient,
Made himself an axe for chopping,
Then began to clear the forest,
Then began the trees to level,
Felled the trees of all descriptions,
Only left the birch-tree standing
For the birds a place of resting,
Where might sing the sweet-voiced cuckoo,
Sacred bird in sacred branches.
Down from heaven came the eagle,
Through the air he came a-flying,
That he might this thing consider;
And he spake the words that follow:
"Wherefore, ancient Wainamoinen,
Hast thou left the slender birch-tree,
Left the birch-tree only standing?"
Wainamoinen thus made answer:
"Therefore is the birch left standing,
That the birds may nest within it,
That the eagle there may rest him,
There may sing the sacred cuckoo."
Spake the eagle, thus replying:
"Good indeed, thy hero-judgement,
That the birch-tree thou hast left us,
Left the sacred birch-tree standing,
As a resting-place for eagles,
And for birds of every feather,
Even I may rest upon it."
Quickly then this bird of heaven,
Kindled fire among the branches;
Soon the flames are fanned by north winds,
And the east-winds lend their forces,
Burn the trees of all descriptions,
Burn them all to dust and ashes,
Only is the birch left standing.

Wainamoinen, wise and ancient,
Brings his magic grains of barley,
Brings he forth his seven seed-grains,
Brings them from his trusty pouches,
Fashioned from the skin of squirrel,
Some were made from skin of marten.
Thence to sow his seeds he hastens,
Hastes the barley-grains to scatter,

Speaks unto himself these measures:
"I the seeds of life am sowing,
Sowing through my open fingers,
From the hand of my Creator,
In this soil enriched with ashes,
In this soil to sprout and flourish.
Ancient mother, thou that livest
Far below the earth and ocean,
Mother of the fields and forests,
Bring the rich soil to producing,
Bring the seed-grains to the sprouting,
That the barley well may flourish.
Never will the earth unaided,
Yield the ripe nutritious barley;
Never will her force be wanting,
If the givers give assistance,
If the givers grace the sowing,
Grace the daughters of creation.
Rise, O earth, from out thy slumber,
From the slumber-land of ages,
Let the barley-grains be sprouting,
Let the blades themselves be starting,
Let the verdant stalks be rising,
Let the ears themselves be growing,
And a hundredfold producing,
From my plowing and my sowing,
From my skilled and honest labour.
Ukko, thou O God, up yonder,
Thou O Father of the heavens,
Thou that livest high in Ether,
Curbest all the clouds of heaven,
Holdest in the air thy counsel,
Holdest in the clouds good counsel,
From the East dispatch a cloudlet,
From the northeast send a rain-cloud,
From the West another send us,
From the northwest, still another,
Quickly from the South a warm-cloud,
That the rain may fall from heaven,
That the clouds may drop their honey,
That the ears may fill and ripen,
That the barley-fields may rustle."

Thereupon benignant Ukko,
Ukko, father of the heavens,
Held his counsel in the cloud-space,
Held good counsel in the Ether;
From the East, he sent a cloudlet,
From the northeast, sent a rain-cloud,
From the West another sent he,
From the northwest, still another,
Quickly from the South a warm-cloud;
Joined in seams the clouds together,
Sewed together all their edges,
Grasped the cloud, and hurled it earthward.
Quick the rain-cloud drops her honey,
Quick the rain-drops fall from heaven,
That the ears may quickly ripen,
That the barley crop may rustle.
Straightway grow the seeds of barley,
From the germ the blade unfolding,
Richly coloured ears arising,
From the rich soil of the fallow,
From the work of Wainamoinen.

Here a few days pass unnoted
And as many nights fly over.
When the seventh day had journeyed,
On the morning of the eighth day,
Wainamoinen, wise and ancient,
Went to view his crop of barley,
How his plowing, how his sowing,
How his labours were resulting;
Found his crop of barley growing,
Found the blades were triple-knotted,
And the ears he found six-sided.

Wainamoinen, old and trusty,
Turned his face, and looked about him,
Lo! there comes a spring-time cuckoo,
Spying out the slender birch-tree,
Rests upon it, sweetly singing:
"Wherefore is the silver birch-tree
Left unharmed of all the forest?"
Spake the ancient Wainamoinen:
"Therefore I have left the birch-tree,
Left the birch-tree only growing,
Home for thee for joyful singing.
Call thou here, O sweet-voiced cuckoo,
Sing thou here from throat of velvet,
Sing thou here with voice of silver,
Sing the cuckoo's golden flute-notes;
Call at morning, call at evening,
Call within the hour of noontide,

For the better growth of forests,
For the ripening of the barley,
For the richness of, the Northland,
For the joy of Kalevala."

Rune III: Wainamoinen and Youkahainen

Wainamoinen, ancient minstrel,
Passed his years in full contentment,
On the meadows of Wainola,
On the plains of Kalevala,
Singing ever wondrous legends,
Songs of ancient wit and wisdom,
Chanting one day, then a second,
Singing in the dusk of evening,
Singing till the dawn of morning,
Now the tales of old-time heroes,
Tales of ages long forgotten,
Now the legends of creation,
Once familiar to the children,
By our children sung no longer,
Sung in part by many heroes,
In these mournful days of evil,
Evil days our race befallen.
Far and wide the story travelled,
Far away men spread the knowledge
Of the chanting of the hero,
Of the song of Wainamoinen;
To the South were heard the echoes,
All of Northland heard the story.

Far away in dismal Northland,
Lived the singer, Youkahainen,
Lapland's young and reckless minstrel.
Once upon a time when feasting,
Dining with his friends and fellows,
Came upon his ears the story,
That there lived a sweeter singer,
On the meadows of Wainola,
On the plains of Kalevala,
Better skilled in chanting legends,
Better skilled than Youkahainen,
Better than the one that taught him.

Straightway then the bard grew angry,
Envy rose within his bosom,
Envy of this Wainamoinen,
Famed to be a sweeter singer;
Hastes he angry to his mother,
To his mother, full of wisdom,

Vows that he will southward hasten,
Hie him southward and betake him
To the dwellings of Wainola,
To the cabins of the Northland,
There as bard to vie in battle,
With the famous Wainamoinen.

"Nay," replies the anxious father,
"Do not go to Kalevala."

"Nay," replies the fearful mother,
"Go not hence to Wainamoinen,
There with him to offer battle;
He will charm thee with his singing
Will bewitch thee in his anger,
He will drive thee back dishonoured,
Sink thee in the fatal snow-drift,
Turn to ice thy pliant fingers,
Turn to ice thy feet and ankles."
These the words of Youkahainen:
"Good the judgement of a father,
Better still, a mother's counsel,
Best of all one's own decision.
I will go and face the minstrel,
Challenge him to sing in contest,
Challenge him as bard to battle,
Sing to him my sweet-toned measures,
Chant to him my oldest legends,
Chant to him my garnered wisdom,
That this best of boasted singers,
That this famous bard of Suomi,
Shall be worsted in the contest,
Shall become a hapless minstrel;
By my songs shall I transform him,
That his feet shall be as flint-stone,
And as oak his nether raiment;
And this famous, best of singers,
Thus bewitched, shall carry ever,
In his heart a stony burden,

On his shoulder bow of marble,
On his hand a flint-stone gauntlet,
On his brow a stony visor."

Then the wizard, Youkahainen,
Heeding not advice paternal,
Heeding not his mother's counsel,
Leads his courser from his stable,
Fire outstreaming from his nostrils,
From his hoofs, the sparks outshooting,
Hitches to his sledge, the fleet-foot,
To his golden sledge, the courser,
Mounts impetuous his snow-sledge,
Leaps upon the hindmost cross-bench,
Strikes his courser with his birch-whip,
With his birch-whip, pearl-enamelled.
Instantly the prancing racer
Springs away upon his journey;
On he, restless, plunges northward,
All day long he onward gallops,
All the next day, onward, onward,
So the third from morn till evening,
Till the third day twilight brings him
To the meadows of Wainola,
To the plains of Kalevala.

As it happened, Wainamoinen,
Wainamoinen, the magician,
Rode that sunset on the highway,
Silently for pleasure driving
Down Wainola's peaceful meadows,
O'er the plains of Kalevala.

Youkahainen, young and fiery,
Urging still his foaming courser,
Dashes down upon the singer,
Does not turn aside in meeting,
Meeting thus in full collision;
Shafts are driven tight together,
Hames and collars wedged and tangled,
Tangled are the reins and traces.
Thus perforce they make a stand-still,
Thus remain and well consider;
Water drips from hame and collar,
Vapors rise from both their horses.
Speaks the minstrel, Wainamoinen:
"Who art thou, and whence? Thou comest
Driving like a stupid stripling,
Careless, dashing down upon me.
Thou hast ruined shafts and traces;
And the collar of my racer
Thou hast shattered into ruin,
And my golden sleigh is broken,
Box and runners dashed to pieces."

Youkahainen then make answer,
Spake at last the words that follow:
"I am youthful Youkahainen,
But make answer first, who thou art,
Whence thou comest, where thou goest,
From what lowly tribe descended?"

Wainamoinen, wise and ancient,
Answered thus the youthful minstrel:
"If thou art but Youkahainen,
Thou shouldst give me all the highway;
I am many years thy senior."

Then the boastful Youkahainen
Spake again to Wainamoinen:
"Young or ancient, little matter,
Little consequence the age is;
He that higher stands in wisdom,
He whose knowledge is the greater,
He that is the sweeter singer,
He alone shall keep the highway,
And the other take the roadside.
Art thou ancient Wainamoinen,
Famous sorcerer and minstrel?
Let us then begin our singing,
Let us sing our ancient legends,
Let us chant our garnered wisdom,
That the one may hear the other,
That the one may judge the other,
In a war of wizard sayings."

Wainamoinen, wise and ancient,
Thus replied in modest accents:
"What I know is very little,
Hardly is it worth the singing,
Neither is my singing wondrous:
All my days I have resided
In the cold and dreary Northland,
In a desert land enchanted,

In my cottage home for ages;
All the songs that I have gathered,
Are the cuckoo's simple measures,
Some of these I may remember;
But since thou perforce demandest,
I accept thy boastful challenge.
Tell me now, my golden youngster,
What thou knowest more than others,
Open now thy store of wisdom."

Thus made answer Youkahainen,
Lapland's young and fiery minstrel:
"Know I many bits of learning,
This I know in perfect clearness:
Every roof must have a chimney,
Every fire-place have a hearth-stone;
Lives of seal are free and merry,
Merry is the life of walrus,
Feeding on incautious salmon,
Daily eating perch and whiting;
Whitings live in quiet shallows,
Salmon love the level bottoms;
Spawns the pike in coldest weather,
And defies the storms of winter.
Slowly perches swim in Autumn,
Wry-backed, hunting deeper water,
Spawn in shallows in the summer,
Bounding on the shore of ocean.
Should this wisdom seem too little,
I can tell thee other matters,
Sing thee other wizard sayings:
All the Northmen plow with reindeer,
Mother-horses plow the Southland,
Inner Lapland plows with oxen;
All the trees on Pisa-mountain,
Know I well in all their grandeur;
On the Horna-rock are fir trees,
Fir trees growing tall and slender;
Slender grow the trees on mountains.
Three, the water-falls in number,
Three in number, inland oceans,
Three in number, lofty mountains,
Shooting to the vault of heaven.
Hallapyora's near to Yaemen,
Katrakoski in Karyala;
Imatra, the falling water,
Tumbles, roaring, into Wuoksi."

Then the ancient Wainamoinen:
"Women's tales and children's wisdom
Do not please a bearded hero,
Hero, old enough for wedlock;
Tell the story of creation,
Tell me of the world's beginning,
Tell me of the creatures in it,
And philosophize a little."

Then the youthful Youkahainen
Thus replied to Wainamoinen:
"Know I well the titmouse-fountains,
Pretty birdling is the titmouse;
And the viper, green, a serpent;
Whitings live in brackish waters;
Perches swim in every river;
Iron rusts, and rusting weakens;
Bitter is the taste of umber;
Boiling water is malicious;
Fire is ever full of danger;
First physician, the Creator;
Remedy the oldest, water;
Magic is the child of sea-foam;
God the first and best adviser;
Waters gush from every mountain;
Fire descended first from heaven;
Iron from the rust was fashioned;
Copper from the rocks created;
Marshes are of lands the oldest;
First of all the trees, the willow;
Fir trees were the first of houses;
Hollowed stones the first of kettles."

Now the ancient Wainamoinen
Thus addresses Youkahainen:
"Canst thou give me now some wisdom,
Is this nonsense all thou knowest?"
Youkahainen thus made answer:
"I can tell thee still a trifle,
Tell thee of the times primeval,
When I plowed the salt-sea's bosom,
When I raked the sea-girt islands,
When I dug the salmon-grottoes,
Hollowed out the deepest caverns,
When I all the lakes created,
When I heaped the mountains round them,
When I piled the rocks about them.

I was present as a hero,
Sixth of wise and ancient heroes,
Seventh of all primeval heroes,
When the heavens were created,
When were formed the ether-spaces,
When the sky was crystal-pillared,
When was arched the beauteous rainbow,
When the Moon was placed in orbit,
When the silver Sun was planted,
When the Bear was firmly stationed,
And with stars the heavens were sprinkled."
Spake the ancient Wainamoinen:
"Thou art surely prince of liars,
Lord of all the host of liars;
Never wert thou in existence,
Surely wert thou never present,
When was plowed the salt-sea's bosom,
When were raked the sea-girt islands,
When were dug the salmon-grottoes,
When were hollowed out the caverns,
When the lakes were all created,
When were heaped the
mountains round them,
When the rocks were piled about them.
Thou wert never seen or heard of
When the earth was first created,
When were made the ether-spaces,
When the air was crystal-pillared,
When the Moon was placed in orbit,
When the silver Sun was planted,
When the Bear was firmly stationed,
When the skies with stars were sprinkled."

Then in anger Youkahainen
Answered ancient Wainamoinen:
"Then, sir, since I fail in wisdom,
With the sword I offer battle;
Come thou, famous bard and minstrel,
Thou the ancient wonder-singer,
Let us try our strength with broadswords,
Let our blades be fully tested."
Spake the ancient Wainamoinen:
"Not thy sword and not thy wisdom,
Not thy prudence, nor thy cunning,
Do I fear a single moment.
Let who may accept thy challenge,
Not with thee, a puny braggart,
Not with one so vain and paltry,
Will I ever measure broadswords."

Then the youthful Youkahainen,
Mouth awry and visage sneering,
Shook his golden locks and answered:
"Whoso fears his blade to measure,
Fears to test his strength at broadswords,
Into wild-boar of the forest,
Swine at heart and swine in visage,
Singing I will thus transform him;
I will hurl such hero-cowards,
This one hither, that one thither,
Stamp him in the mire and bedding,
In the rubbish of the stable."

Angry then grew Wainamoinen,
Wrathful waxed, and fiercely frowning,
Self-composed he broke his silence,
And began his wondrous singing.
Sang he not the tales of childhood,
Children's nonsense, wit of women,
Sang he rather bearded heroes,
That the children never heard of,
That the boys and maidens knew not,
Known but half by bride and bridegroom,
Known in part by many heroes,
In these mournful days of evil,
Evil times our race befallen.
Grandly sang wise Wainamoinen,
Till the copper-bearing mountains,
And the flinty rocks and ledges
Heard his magic tones and trembled;
Mountain cliffs were torn to pieces,
All the ocean heaved and tumbled;
And the distant hills re-echoed.
Lo! the boastful Youkahainen
Is transfixed in silent wonder,
And his sledge with golden trimmings
Floats like brushwood on the billows;
Sings his braces into reed-grass,
Sings his reins to twigs of willow,
And to shrubs his golden cross-bench.
Lo! his birch-whip, pearl-enamelled,
Floats a reed upon the border;
Lo! his steed with golden forehead,
Stands a statue on the waters;

Hames and traces are as fir-boughs,
And his collar, straw and sea-grass.
Still the minstrel sings enchantment,
Sings his sword with golden handle,
Sings it into gleam of lightning,
Hangs it in the sky above him;
Sings his cross-bow, gaily painted,
To a rainbow o'er the ocean;
Sings his quick and feathered arrows
Into hawks and screaming eagles;
Sings his dog with bended muzzle,
Into block of stone beside him;
Sings his cap from off his forehead,
Sings it into wreaths of vapor;
From his hands he sings his gauntlets
Into rushes on the waters;
Sings his vesture, purple-coloured,
Into white clouds in the heavens;
Sings his girdle, set with jewels,
Into twinkling stars around him;
And alas! for Youkahainen,
Sings him into deeps of quick-sand;
Ever deeper, deeper, deeper,
In his torture, sinks the wizard,
To his belt in mud and water.
Now it was that Youkahainen
Comprehended but too clearly
What his folly, what the end was,
Of the journey he had ventured,
Vainly he had undertaken
For the glory of a contest
With the grand, old Wainamoinen.

When at last young Youkahainen,
Pohyola's old and sorry stripling,
Strives his best to move his right foot,
But alas! the foot obeys not;
When he strives to move his left foot,
Lo! he finds it turned to flint-stone.

Thereupon sad Youkahainen,
In the deeps of desperation,
And in earnest supplication,
Thus addresses Wainamoinen:
"O thou wise and worthy minstrel,
Thou the only true magician,
Cease I pray thee thine enchantment,
Only turn away thy magic,
Let me leave this slough of horror,
Loose me from this stony prison,
Free me from this killing torment,
I will pay a golden ransom."
Spake the ancient Wainamoinen:
"What the ransom thou wilt give me
If I cease from mine enchantment,
If I turn away my magic,
Lift thee from thy slough of horror,
Loose thee from thy stony prison,
Free thee from thy killing torment?"
Answered youthful Youkahainen:
"Have at home two magic cross-bows,
Pair of bows of wondrous power,
One so light a child can bend it,
Only strength can bend the other,
Take of these the one that pleases."
Then the ancient Wainamoinen:
"Do not wish thy magic cross-bows,
Have a few of such already,
Thine to me are worse than useless;
I have bows in great abundance,
Bows on every nail and rafter,
Bows that laugh at all the hunters,
Bows that go themselves a-hunting."

Then the ancient Wainamoinen
Sang alas! poor Youkahainen
Deeper into mud and water,
Deeper in the slough of torment.
Youkahainen thus made answer:
"Have at home two magic shallops,
Beautiful the boats and wondrous;
One rides light upon the ocean,
One is made for heavy burdens;
Take of these the one that pleases."
Spake the ancient Wainamoinen:
"Do not wish thy magic shallops,
Have enough of such already;
All my bays are full of shallops,
All my shores are lined with shallops,
Some before the winds are sailors,
Some were built to sail against them."

Still the minstrel of Wainola
Sings again poor Youkahainen

Deeper, deeper into torment,
Into quicksand to his girdle,
Till the Lapland bard in anguish
Speaks again to Wainamoinen:
"Have at home two magic stallions,
One a racer, fleet as lightning,
One was born for heavy burdens;
Take of these the one that pleases."
Spake the ancient Wainamoinen:
"Neither do I wish thy stallions,
Do not need thy hawk-limbed stallions,
Have enough of these already;
Magic stallions swarm my stables,
Eating corn at every manger,
Broad of back to hold the water,
Water on each croup in lakelets."

Still the bard of Kalevala
Sings the hapless Lapland minstrel
Deeper, deeper into torment,
To his shoulders into water.
Spake again young Youkahainen:
"O thou ancient Wainamoinen,
Thou the only true magician,
Cease I pray thee thine enchantment,
Only turn away thy magic,
I will give thee gold abundant,
Countless stores of shining silver;
From the wars my father brought it,
Brought it from the hard-fought battles."
Spake the wise, old Wainamoinen:
"For thy gold I have no longing,
Neither do I wish thy silver,
Have enough of each already;
Gold abundant fills my chambers,
On each nail hang bags of silver,
Gold that glitters in the sunshine,
Silver shining in the moonlight."

Sank the braggart, Youkahainen,
Deeper in his slough of torment,
To his chin in mud and water,
Ever praying, thus beseeching:
"O thou ancient Wainamoinen,
Greatest of the old magicians,
Lift me from this pit of horror,
From this prison-house of torture;
I will give thee all my corn-fields,
Give thee all my corn in garners,
Thus my hapless life to ransom,
Thus to gain eternal freedom."
Wainamoinen thus made answer:
"Take thy corn to other markets,
Give thy garners to the needy;
I have corn in great abundance,
Fields have I in every quarter,
Corn in all my fields is growing;
One's own fields are always richer,
One's own grain is much the sweeter."

Lapland's young and reckless minstrel,
Sorrow-laden, thus enchanted,
Deeper sinks in mud and water,
Fear-enchained and full of anguish,
In the mire, his beard bedrabbled,
Mouth once boastful filled with sea-weed,
In the grass his teeth entangled,
Youkahainen thus beseeches:
"O thou ancient Wainamoinen,
Wisest of the wisdom-singers,
Cease at last thine incantations,
Only turn away thy magic,
And my former life restore me,
Lift me from this stifling torment,
Free mine eyes from sand and water,
I will give thee sister, Aino,
Fairest daughter of my mother,
Bride of thine to be forever,
Bride of thine to do thy pleasure,
Sweep the rooms within thy cottage,
Keep thy dwelling-place in order,
Rinse for thee the golden platters,
Spread thy couch with finest linens,
For thy bed, weave golden covers,
Bake for thee the honey-biscuit."

Wainamoinen, old and truthful,
Finds at last the wished-for ransom,
Lapland's young and fairest daughter,
Sister dear of Youkahainen;
Happy he, that he has won him,
In his age a beauteous maiden,
Bride of his to be forever,
Pride and joy of Kalevala.

Now the happy Wainamoinen,
Sits upon the rock of gladness,
Joyful on the rock of music,
Sings a little, sings and ceases,
Sings again, and sings a third time,
Thus to break the spell of magic,
Thus to lessen the enchantment,
Thus the potent charm to banish.
As the magic spell is broken,
Youkahainen, sad, but wiser,
Drags his feet from out the quicksand,
Lifts his beard from out the water,
From the rocks leads forth his courser,
Brings his sledge back from the rushes,
Calls his whip back from the ocean,
Sets his golden sledge in order,
Throws himself upon the cross-bench,
Snaps his whip and hies him homeward,
Hastens homeward, heavy-hearted,
Sad indeed to meet his mother,
Aino's mother, gray and aged.
Careless thus he hastens homeward,
Nears his home with noise and bustle,
Reckless drives against the pent-house,
Breaks the shafts against the portals,
Breaks his handsome sledge in pieces.

Then his mother, quickly guessing,
Would have chided him for rashness,
But the father interrupted:
"Wherefore dost thou break
thy snow-sledge,
Wherefore dash thy thills in fragments,
Wherefore comest home so strangely,
Why this rude and wild behavior?"

Now alas! poor Youkahainen,
Cap awry upon his forehead,
Falls to weeping, broken-hearted,
Head depressed and mind dejected,
Eyes and lips expressing sadness,
Answers not his anxious father.

Then the mother quickly asked him,
Sought to find his cause for sorrow:
"Tell me, first-born, why thou weepest,
Why thou weepest, heavy-hearted,
Why thy mind is so dejected,
Why thine eyes express such sadness."
Youkahainen then made answer:
"Golden mother, ever faithful,
Cause there is to me sufficient,
Cause enough in what has happened,
Bitter cause for this my sorrow,
Cause for bitter tears and murmurs:
All my days will pass unhappy,
Since, O mother of my being,
I have promised beauteous Aino,
Aino, thy beloved daughter,
Aino, my devoted sister,
To decrepit Wainamoinen,
Bride to be to him forever,
Roof above him, prop beneath him,
Fair companion at his fire-side."

Joyful then arose the mother,
Clapped her hands in glee together,
Thus addressing Youkahainen:
"Weep no more, my son beloved,
Thou hast naught to cause thy weeping,
Hast no reason for thy sorrow,
Often I this hope have cherished;
Many years have I been praying
That this mighty bard and hero,
Wise and valiant Wainamoinen,
Spouse should be to beauteous Aino,
Son-in-law to me, her mother."

But the fair and lovely maiden,
Sister dear of Youkahainen,
Straightway fell to bitter weeping,
On the threshold wept and lingered,
Wept all day and all the night long,
Wept a second, then a third day,
Wept because a bitter sorrow
On her youthful heart had fallen.
Then the gray-haired mother asked her:
"Why this weeping, lovely Aino?
Thou hast found a noble suitor,
Thou wilt rule his spacious dwelling,
At his window sit and rest thee,
Rinse betimes his golden platters,
Walk a queen within his dwelling."
Thus replied the tearful Aino:

"Mother dear, and all-forgiving,
Cause enough for this my sorrow,
Cause enough for bitter weeping:
I must loose my sunny tresses,
Tresses beautiful and golden,
Cannot deck my hair with jewels,
Cannot bind my head with ribbons,
All to be hereafter hidden
Underneath the linen bonnet
That the wife must wear forever;
Weep at morning, weep at evening,
Weep alas! for waning beauty,
Childhood vanished, youth departed,
Silver sunshine, golden moonlight,
Hope and pleasure of my childhood,
Taken from me now forever,
And so soon to be forgotten
At the tool-bench of my brother,
At the window of my sister,
In the cottage of my father."

Spake again the gray-haired mother
To her wailing daughter Aino:
"Cease thy sorrow, foolish maiden,
By thy tears thou art ungrateful,
Reason none for thy repining,
Not the slightest cause for weeping;
Everywhere the silver sunshine
Falls as bright on other households;
Not alone the moonlight glimmers
Through thy father's open windows,
On the work-bench of thy brother;
Flowers bloom in every meadow,
Berries grow on every mountain;
Thou canst go thyself and find them,
All the day long go and find them;
Not alone thy brother's meadows
Grow the beauteous vines
and flowers;
Not alone thy father's mountains
Yield the ripe, nutritious berries;
Flowers bloom in other meadows,
Berries grow on other mountains,
There as here, my lovely Aino."

Rune IV: The Fate of Aino

When the night had passed,
the maiden,
Sister fair of Youkahainen,
Hastened early to the forest,
Birchen shoots for brooms to gather,
Went to gather birchen tassels;
Bound a bundle for her father,
Bound a birch-broom for her mother,
Silken tassels for her sister.
Straightway then she hastened homeward,
By a foot-path left the forest;
As she neared the woodland border,
Lo! the ancient Wainamoinen,
Quickly spying out the maiden,
As she left the birchen woodland,
Trimly dressed in costly raiment,
And the minstrel thus addressed her:
"Aino, beauty of the Northland,
Wear not, lovely maid, for others,
Only wear for me, sweet maiden,
Golden cross upon thy bosom,
Shining pearls upon thy shoulders;
Bind for me thine auburn tresses,
Wear for me thy golden braidlets."
Thus the maiden quickly answered:
"Not for thee and not for others,
Hang I from my neck the crosslet,
Deck my hair with silken ribbons;
Need no more the many trinkets
Brought to me by ship or shallop;
Sooner wear the simplest raiment,
Feed upon the barley bread-crust,
Dwell forever with my mother
In the cabin with my father."

Then she threw the gold cross
from her,
Tore the jewels from her fingers,
Quickly loosed her shining necklace,
Quick untied her silken ribbons,
Cast them all away indignant
Into forest ferns and flowers.
Thereupon the maiden, Aino,
Hastened to her mother's cottage.

At the window sat her father
Whittling on an oaken ax-helve:
"Wherefore weepest, beauteous Aino,
Aino, my beloved daughter?"

"Cause enough for weeping, father,
Good the reasons for my mourning,
This, the reason for my weeping,
This, the cause of all my sorrow:
From my breast I tore the crosslet,
From my belt, the clasp of copper,
From my waist, the belt of silver,
Golden was my pretty crosslet."

Near the door-way sat her brother,
Carving out a birchen ox-bow:
"Why art weeping, lovely Aino,
Aino, my devoted sister?"

"Cause enough for weeping, brother,
Good the reasons for my mourning:
Therefore come I as thou seest,
Rings no longer on my fingers,
On my neck no pretty necklace;
Golden were the rings thou gavest,
And the necklace, pearls and silver!"

On the threshold sat her sister,
Weaving her a golden girdle:
"Why art weeping, beauteous Aino,
Aino, my beloved sister?"

"Cause enough for weeping, sister,
Good the reasons for my sorrow:
Therefore come I as thou seest,
On my head no scarlet fillet,
In my hair no braids of silver,
On mine arms no purple ribbons,
Round my neck no shining necklace,
On my breast no golden crosslet,
In mine ears no golden ear-rings."

Near the door-way of the dairy,
Skimming cream, sat Aino's mother.
"Why art weeping, lovely Aino,
Aino, my devoted daughter?"
Thus the sobbing maiden answered:
"Loving mother, all-forgiving,
Cause enough for this my weeping,
Good the reasons for my sorrow,
Therefore do I weep, dear mother:
I have been within the forest,
Brooms to bind and shoots to gather,
There to pluck some birchen tassels;
Bound a bundle for my father,
Bound a second for my mother,
Bound a third one for my brother,
For my sister silken tassels.
Straightway then I hastened homeward,
By a foot-path left the forest;
As I reached the woodland border
Spake Osmoinen from the cornfield,
Spake the ancient Wainamoinen:
'Wear not, beauteous maid, for others,
Only wear for me, sweet maiden,
On thy breast a golden crosslet,
Shining pearls upon thy shoulders,
Bind for me thine auburn tresses,
Weave for me thy silver braidlets.'
Then I threw the gold-cross from me,
Tore the jewels from my fingers,
Quickly loosed my shining necklace,
Quick untied my silken ribbons,
Cast them all away indignant,
Into forest ferns and flowers.
Then I thus addressed the singer:
'Not for thee and not for others,
Hang I from my neck the crosslet,
Deck my hair with silken ribbons;
Need no more the many trinkets,
Brought to me by ship and shallop;
Sooner wear the simplest raiment,
Feed upon the barley bread-crust,
Dwell forever with my mother
In the cabin with my father.'"

Thus the gray-haired mother answered
Aino, her beloved daughter:
"Weep no more, my lovely maiden,
Waste no more of thy sweet young-life;
One year eat thou my sweet butter,
It will make thee strong and ruddy;
Eat another year fresh bacon,
It will make thee tall and queenly;

Eat a third year only dainties,
It will make thee fair and lovely.
Now make haste to yonder hill-top,
To the store-house on the mountain,
Open there the large compartment,
Thou will find it filled with boxes,
Chests and cases, trunks and boxes;
Open thou the box, the largest,
Lift away the gaudy cover,
Thou will find six golden girdles,
Seven rainbow-tinted dresses,
Woven by the Moon's fair daughters,
Fashioned by the Sun's sweet virgins.
In my young years once I wandered,
As a maiden on the mountains,
In the happy days of childhood,
Hunting berries in the coppice;
There by chance I heard the daughters
Of the Moon as they were weaving;
There I also heard the daughters
Of the Sun as they were spinning
On the red rims of the cloudlets,
O'er the blue edge of the forest,
On the border of the pine-wood,
On a high and distant mountain.
I approached them, drawing nearer,
Stole myself within their hearing,
Then began I to entreat them,
Thus besought them, gently pleading:
'Give thy silver, Moon's fair daughters,
To a poor, but worthy maiden;
Give thy gold, O Sun's sweet virgins,
To this maiden, young and needy.'
Thereupon the Moon's fair daughters
Gave me silver from their coffers;
And the Sun's sweet shining virgins
Gave me gold from their abundance,
Gold to deck my throbbing temples,
For my hair the shining silver.
Then I hastened joyful homeward,
Richly laden with my treasures,
Happy to my mother's cottage;
Wore them one day, then a second,
Then a third day also wore them,
Took the gold then from my temples,
From my hair I took the silver,
Careful laid them in their boxes,
Many seasons have they lain there,
Have not seen them since my childhood.
Deck thy brow with silken ribbon,
Trim with gold thy throbbing temples,
And thy neck with pearly necklace,
Hang the gold-cross on thy bosom,
Robe thyself in pure, white linen
Spun from flax of finest fiber;
Wear withal the richest short-frock,
Fasten it with golden girdle;
On thy feet, put silken stockings,
With the shoes of finest leather;
Deck thy hair with golden braidlets,
Bind it well with threads of silver;
Trim with rings thy fairy fingers,
And thy hands with dainty ruffles;
Come bedecked then to thy chamber,
Thus return to this thy household,
To the greeting of thy kindred,
To the joy of all that know thee,
Flushed thy cheeks as ruddy berries,
Coming as thy father's sunbeam,
Walking beautiful and queenly,
Far more beautiful than moonlight."

Thus she spake to weeping Aino,
Thus the mother to her daughter;
But the maiden, little hearing,
Does not heed her mother's wishes;
Straightway hastens to the court-yard,
There to weep in bitter sorrow,
All alone to weep in anguish.

Waiting long the wailing Aino
Thus at last soliloquizes:
"Unto what can I now liken
Happy homes and joys of fortune?
Like the waters in the river,
Like the waves in yonder lakelet,
Like the crystal waters flowing.
Unto what, the biting sorrow
Of the child of cold misfortune?
Like the spirit of the sea-duck,
Like the icicle in winter,
Water in the well imprisoned.
Often roamed my mind in childhood,
When a maiden free and merry,

Happily through fen and fallow,
Gamboled on the meads with lambkins,
Lingered with the ferns and flowers,
Knowing neither pain nor trouble;
Now my mind is filled with sorrow,
Wanders though the bog and stubble,
Wanders weary through the brambles,
Roams throughout the dismal forest,
Till my life is filled with darkness,
And my spirit white with anguish.
Better had it been for Aino
Had she never seen the sunlight,
Or if born had died an infant,
Had not lived to be a maiden
In these days of sin and sorrow,
Underneath a star so luckless.
Better had it been for Aino,
Had she died upon the eighth day
After seven nights had vanished;
Needed then but little linen,
Needed but a little coffin,
And a grave of smallest measure;
Mother would have mourned a little,
Father too perhaps a trifle,
Sister would have wept the day through,
Brother might have shed a tear-drop,
Thus had ended all the mourning."

Thus poor Aino wept and murmured,
Wept one day, and then a second,
Wept a third from morn till even,
When again her mother asked her:
"Why this weeping, fairest daughter,
Darling daughter, why this grieving?"
Thus the tearful maiden answered:
"Therefore do I weep and sorrow,
Wretched maiden all my life long,
Since poor Aino, thou hast given,
Since thy daughter thou hast promised
To the aged Wainamoinen,
Comfort to his years declining,
Prop to stay him when he totters,
In the storm a roof above him,
In his home a cloak around him;
Better far if thou hadst sent me
Far below the salt-sea surges,
To become the whiting's sister,
And the friend of perch and salmon;
Better far to ride the billows,
Swim the sea-foam as a mermaid,
And the friend of nimble fishes,
Than to be an old man's solace,
Prop to stay him when he totters,
Hand to aid him when he trembles,
Arm to guide him when he falters,
Strength to give him when he weakens;
Better be the whiting's sister
And the friend of perch and salmon,
Than an old man's slave and darling."

Ending thus she left her mother,
Straightway hastened to the mountain,
To the store-house on the summit,
Opened there the box the largest,
From the box six lids she lifted,
Found therein six golden girdles,
Silken dresses seven in number.
Choosing such as pleased her fancy,
She adorned herself as bidden,
Robed herself to look her fairest,
Gold upon her throbbing temples,
In her hair the shining silver,
On her shoulders purple ribbons,
Band of blue around her forehead,
Golden cross, and rings, and jewels,
Fitting ornaments to beauty.

Now she leaves her many treasures,
Leaves the store-house on the mountain,
Filled with gold and silver trinkets,
Wanders over field and meadow,
Over stone-fields waste and barren,
Wanders on through fen and forest,
Through the forest vast and cheerless,
Wanders hither, wanders thither,
Singing careless as she wanders,
This her mournful song and echo:
"Woe is me, my life hard-fated!
Woe to Aino, broken-hearted!
Torture racks my heart and temples,
Yet the sting would not be deeper,
Nor the pain and anguish greater,
If beneath this weight of sorrow,
In my saddened heart's dejection,

I should yield my life forever,
Now unhappy, I should perish!
Lo! the time has come for Aino
From this cruel world to hasten,
To the kingdom of Tuoni,
To the realm of the departed,
To the isle of the hereafter.
Weep no more for me, O Father,
Mother dear, withhold thy censure,
Lovely sister, dry thine eyelids,
Do not mourn me, dearest brother,
When I sink beneath the sea-foam,
Make my home in salmon-grottoes,
Make my bed in crystal waters,
Water-ferns my couch and pillow."

All day long poor Aino wandered,
All the next day, sad and weary,
So the third from morn till evening,
Till the cruel night enwrapped her,
As she reached the sandy margin,
Reached the cold and dismal seashore,
Sat upon the rock of sorrow,
Sat alone in cold and darkness,
Listened only to the music
Of the winds and rolling billows,
Singing all the dirge of Aino.
All that night the weary maiden
Wept and wandered on the border
Through the sand and sea-washed pebbles.

As the day dawns, looking round her,
She beholds three water-maidens,
On a headland jutting seaward,
Water-maidens four in number,
Sitting on the wave-lashed ledges,
Swimming now upon the billows,
Now upon the rocks reposing.
Quick the weeping maiden, Aino,
Hastens there to join the mermaids,
Fairy maidens of the waters.
Weeping Aino, now disrobing,
Lays aside with care her garments,
Hangs her silk robes on the alders,
Drops her gold-cross on the seashore,
On the aspen hangs her ribbons,
On the rocks her silken stockings,
On the grass her shoes of deer-skin,
In the sand her shining necklace,
With her rings and other jewels.
Out at sea a goodly distance,
Stood a rock of rainbow colours,
Glittering in silver sunlight.
Toward it springs the hapless maiden,
Thither swims the lovely Aino,
Up the standing-stone has clambered,
Wishing there to rest a moment,
Rest upon the rock of beauty;
When upon a sudden swaying
To and fro among the billows,
With a crash and roar of waters
Falls the stone of many colours,
Falls upon the very bottom
Of the deep and boundless blue-sea.
With the stone of rainbow colours,
Falls the weeping maiden, Aino,
Clinging to its craggy edges,
Sinking far below the surface,
To the bottom of the blue-sea.
Thus the weeping maiden vanished,
Thus poor Aino sank and perished,
Singing as the stone descended,
Chanting thus as she departed:
"Once to swim I sought the sea-side,
There to sport among the billows;
With the stone of many colours
Sank poor Aino to the bottom
Of the deep and boundless blue-sea,
Like a pretty songbird perished.
Never come a-fishing, father,
To the borders of these waters,
Never during all thy life-time,
As thou lovest daughter Aino.

"Mother dear, I sought the sea-side,
There to sport among the billows;
With the stone of many colours,
Sank poor Aino to the bottom
Of the deep and boundless blue-sea,
Like a pretty songbird perished.
Never mix thy bread, dear mother,
With the blue-sea's foam and waters,
Never during all thy life-time,
As thou lovest daughter Aino.

"Brother dear, I sought the sea-side,
There to sport among the billows;
With the stone of many colours
Sank poor Aino to the bottom
Of the deep and boundless blue-sea,
Like a pretty songbird perished.
Never bring thy prancing war-horse,
Never bring thy royal racer,
Never bring thy steeds to water,
To the borders of the blue-sea,
Never during all thy life-time,
As thou lovest sister Aino.

"Sister dear, I sought the sea-side,
There to sport among the billows;
With the stone of many colours
Sank poor Aino to the bottom
Of the deep and boundless blue-sea,
Like a pretty songbird perished.
Never come to lave thine eyelids
In this rolling wave and sea-foam,
Never during all thy life-time,
As thou lovest sister Aino.
All the waters in the blue-sea
Shall be blood of Aino's body;
All the fish that swim these waters
Shall be Aino's flesh forever;
All the willows on the sea-side
Shall be Aino's ribs hereafter;
All the sea-grass on the margin
Will have grown from Aino's tresses."

Thus at last the maiden vanished,
Thus the lovely Aino perished.
Who will tell the cruel story,
Who will bear the evil tidings
To the cottage of her mother,
Once the home of lovely Aino?
Will the bear repeat the story,
Tell the tidings to her mother?
Nay, the bear must not be herald,
He would slay the herds of cattle.
Who then tell the cruel story,
Who will bear the evil tidings
To the cottage of her father,
Once the home of lovely Aino?
Shall the wolf repeat the story,
Tell the sad news to her father?
Nay, the wolf must not be herald,
He would eat the gentle lambkins.

Who then tell the cruel story,
Who will bear the evil tidings.
To the cottage of her sister?
Will the fox repeat the story
Tell the tidings to her sister?
Nay, the fox must not be herald,
He would eat the ducks and chickens.

Who then tell the cruel story,
Who will bear the evil tidings
To the cottage of her brother,
Once the home of lovely Aino?
Shall the hare repeat the story,
Bear the sad news to her brother?
Yea, the hare shall be the herald,
Tell to all the cruel story.
Thus the harmless hare makes answer:
"I will bear the evil tidings
To the former home of Aino,
Tell the story to her kindred."

Swiftly flew the long-eared herald,
Like the winds he hastened onward,
Galloped swift as flight of eagles;
Neck awry he bounded forward
Till he gained the wished-for cottage,
Once the home of lovely Aino.
Silent was the home, and vacant;
So he hastened to the bath-house,
Found therein a group of maidens,
Working each upon a birch-broom.
Sat the hare upon the threshold,
And the maidens thus addressed him:
"Hie there, Long-legs, or we'll
roast thee,
Hie there, Big-eye, or we'll stew thee,
Roast thee for our lady's breakfast,
Stew thee for our master's dinner,
Make of thee a meal for Aino,
And her brother, Youkahainen!
Better therefore thou shouldst gallop
To thy burrow in the mountains,
Than be roasted for our dinners."

Then the haughty hare made answer,
Chanting thus the fate of Aino:
"Think ye not I journey hither,
To be roasted in the skillet,
To be stewed in yonder kettle;
Let fell Lempo fill thy tables!
I have come with evil tidings,
Come to tell the cruel story
Of the flight and death of Aino,
Sister dear of Youkahainen.
With the stone of many colours
Sank poor Aino to the bottom
Of the deep and boundless waters,
Like a pretty songbird perished;
Hung her ribbons on the aspen,
Left her gold-cross on the seashore,
Silken robes upon the alders,
On the rocks her silken stockings,
On the grass her shoes of deer-skin,
In the sand her shining necklace,
In the sand her rings and jewels;
In the waves, the lovely Aino,
Sleeping on the very bottom
Of the deep and boundless blue-sea,
In the caverns of the salmon,
There to be the whiting's sister
And the friend of nimble fishes."

Sadly weeps the ancient mother
From her blue-eyes bitter tear-drops,
As in sad and wailing measures,
Broken-hearted thus she answers:
"Listen, all ye mothers, listen,
Learn from me a tale of wisdom:
Never urge unwilling daughters
From the dwellings of their fathers,
To the bridegrooms that they love not,
Not as I, inhuman mother,
Drove away my lovely Aino,
Fairest daughter of the Northland."

Sadly weeps the gray-haired mother,
And the tears that fall are bitter,
Flowing down her wrinkled visage,
Till they trickle on her bosom;
Then across her heaving bosom,
Till they reach her garment's border;
Then adown her silken stockings,
Till they touch her shoes of deer-skin;
Then beneath her shoes of deer-skin,
Flowing on and flowing ever,
Part to earth as its possession,
Part to water as its portion.
As the tear-drops fall and mingle,
Form they streamlets three in number,
And their source, the mother's eyelids,
Streamlets formed from pearly tear-drops,
Flowing on like little rivers,
And each streamlet larger growing,
Soon becomes a rushing torrent;
In each rushing, roaring torrent,
There a cataract is foaming,
Foaming in the silver sunlight;
From the cataract's commotion
Rise three pillared rocks in grandeur;
From each rock, upon the summit,
Grow three hillocks clothed in verdure;
From each hillock, speckled birches,
Three in number, struggle skyward;
On the summit of each birch-tree
Sits a golden cuckoo calling,
And the three sing, all in concord:
"Love! O Love!" the first one calleth;
Sings the second, "Suitor! Suitor!"
And the third one calls and echoes,
"Consolation! Consolation!"
He that "Love! O Love!" is calling,
Calls three moons and calls unceasing,
For the love-rejecting maiden
Sleeping in the deep sea-castles.
He that "Suitor! Suitor!" singeth,
Sings six moons and sings unceasing
For the suitor that forever
Sings and sues without a hearing.
He that sadly sings and echoes,
"Consolation! Consolation!"
Sings unceasing all his life long
For the broken-hearted mother
That must mourn and weep forever.

When the lone and wretched mother
Heard the sacred cuckoo singing,
Spake she thus, and sorely weeping:
"When I hear the cuckoo calling,

Then my heart is filled with sorrow;
Tears unlock my heavy eyelids,
Flow adown my furrowed visage,
Tears as large as silver sea pearls;
Older grow my wearied elbows,
Weaker ply my aged fingers,
Wearily, in all its members,
Does my body shake in palsy,
When I hear the cuckoo singing,
Hear the sacred cuckoo calling."

Rune V: Wainamoinen's Lamentation

Far and wide the tidings travelled,
Far away men heard the story
Of the flight and death of Aino,
Sister dear of Youkahainen,
Fairest daughter of creation.

Wainamoinen, brave and truthful,
Straightway fell to bitter weeping,
Wept at morning, wept at evening,
Sleepless, wept the dreary night long,
That his Aino had departed,
That the maiden thus had vanished,
Thus had sunk upon the bottom
Of the blue-sea, deep and boundless.

Filled with grief, the ancient singer,
Wainamoinen of the Northland,
Heavy-hearted, sorely weeping,
Hastened to the restless waters,
This the suitor's prayer and question:
"Tell, Untamo, tell me, dreamer,
Tell me, Indolence, thy visions,
Where the water-gods may linger,
Where may rest Wellamo's maidens?"

Then Untamo thus made answer,
Lazily he told his dreamings:
"Over there, the mermaid-dwellings,
Yonder live Wellamo's maidens,
On the headland robed in verdure,
On the forest-covered island,
In the deep, pellucid waters,
On the purple-coloured seashore;
Yonder is the home of sea-maids,
There the maidens of Wellamo,
Live there in their sea-side chambers,
Rest within their water-caverns,
On the rocks of rainbow colours,
On the juttings of the sea-cliffs."

Straightway hastens Wainamoinen
To a boat-house on the seashore,

Looks with care upon the fish-hooks,
And the lines he well considers;
Lines, and hooks, and poles, and fish-nets,
Places in a boat of copper,
Then begins he swiftly rowing
To the forest-covered island,
To the point enrobed in verdure,
To the purple-coloured headland,
Where the sea-nymphs live and linger.
Hardly does he reach the island
Ere the minstrel starts to angle;
Far away he throws his fish-hook,
Trolls it quickly through the waters,
Turning on a copper swivel
Dangling from a silver fish-line,
Golden is the hook he uses.

Now he tries his silken fish-net,
Angles long, and angles longer,
Angles one day, then a second,
In the morning, in the evening,
Angles at the hour of noontide,
Many days and nights he angles,
Till at last, one sunny morning,
Strikes a fish of magic powers,
Plays like salmon on his fish-line,
Lashing waves across the waters,
Till at length the fish exhausted
Falls a victim to the angler,
Safely landed in the bottom
Of the hero's boat of copper.

Wainamoinen, proudly viewing,
Speaks these words in wonder guessing:
"This the fairest of all sea-fish,
Never have I seen its equal,

Smoother surely than the salmon,
Brighter-spotted than the trout is,
Grayer than the pike of Suomi,
Has less fins than any female,
Not the fins of any male fish,
Not the stripes of sea-born maidens,
Not the belt of any mermaid,
Not the ears of any songbird,
Somewhat like our Northland salmon
From the blue-sea's deepest caverns."

In his belt the ancient hero
Wore a knife insheathed with silver;
From its case he drew the fish-knife,
Thus to carve the fish in pieces,
Dress the nameless fish for roasting,
Make of it a dainty breakfast,
Make of it a meal at noon-day,
Make for him a toothsome supper,
Make the later meal at evening.

Straightway as the fish he touches,
Touches with his knife of silver,
Quick it leaps upon the waters,
Dives beneath the sea's smooth surface,
From the boat with copper bottom,
From the skiff of Wainamoinen.

In the waves at goodly distance,
Quickly from the sea it rises
On the sixth and seventh billows,
Lifts its head above the waters,
Out of reach of fishing-tackle,
Then addresses Wainamoinen,
Chiding thus the ancient hero:
"Wainamoinen, ancient minstrel,
Do not think that I came hither
To be fished for as a salmon,
Only to be chopped in pieces,
Dressed and eaten like a whiting
Make for thee a dainty breakfast,
Make for thee a meal at midday,
Make for thee a toothsome supper,
Make the fourth meal of the Northland."
Spake the ancient Wainamoinen:
"Wherefore didst thou then come hither,
If it be not for my dinner?"

Thus the nameless fish made answer:
"Hither have I come, O minstrel,
In thine arms to rest and linger,
And thyself to love and cherish,
At thy side a life-companion,
And thy wife to be forever;
Deck thy couch with snowy linen,
Smooth thy head upon the pillow,
Sweep thy rooms and make
them cheery,
Keep thy dwelling-place in order,
Build a fire for thee when needed,
Bake for thee the honey-biscuit,
Fill thy cup with barley-water,
Do for thee whatever pleases.

"I am not a scaly sea-fish,
Not a trout of Northland rivers,
Not a whiting from the waters,
Not a salmon of the North-seas,
I, a young and merry maiden,
Friend and sister of the fishes,
Youkahainen's youngest sister,
I, the one that thou dost fish for,
I am Aino whom thou lovest.

"Once thou wert the wise-
tongued hero,
Now the foolish Wainamoinen,
Scant of insight, scant of judgement,
Didst not know enough to keep me,
Cruel-hearted, bloody-handed,
Tried to kill me with thy fish-knife,
So to roast me for thy dinner;
I, a mermaid of Wellamo,
Once the fair and lovely Aino,
Sister dear of Youkahainen."

Spake the ancient Wainamoinen:,
Filled with sorrow, much regretting:
"Since thou'rt Youkahainen's sister,
Beauteous Aino of Pohyola,
Come to me again I pray thee!"

Thus the mermaid wisely answered:
"Nevermore will Aino's spirit
Fly to thee and be ill-treated."

Quickly dived the water-maiden
From the surface of the billow
To the many-coloured pebbles,
To the rainbow-tinted grottoes
Where the mermaids live and linger.

Wainamoinen, not discouraged,
Thought afresh and well reflected,
How to live, and work, and win her;
Drew with care his silken fish-net,
To and fro through foam and billow,
Through the bays and winding channels,
Drew it through the placid waters,
Drew it through the salmon-dwellings,
Through the homes of water-maidens,
Through the waters of Wainola,
Through the blue back of the ocean,
Through the lakes of distant Lapland,
Through the rivers of Youkola,
Through the seas of Kalevala,
Hoping thus to find his Aino.
Many were the fish he landed,
Every form of fish-like creatures,
But he did not catch the sea-maid,
Not Wellamo's water-maiden,
Fairest daughter of the Northland.

Finally the ancient minstrel,
Mind depressed, and heart discouraged,
Spake these words, immersed in sorrow:
"Fool am I, and great my folly,
Having neither wit nor judgement;
Surely once I had some knowledge,
Had some insight into wisdom,
Had at least a bit of instinct;
But my virtues all have left me
In these mournful days of evil,
Vanished with my youth and vigor,
Insight gone, and sense departed,
All my prudence gone to others!
Aino, whom I love and cherish,
All these years have sought to honour,
Aino, now Wellamo's maiden,
Promised friend of mine when needed,
Promised bride of mine forever,
Once I had within my power,
Caught her in Wellamo's grottoes,
Led her to my boat of copper,
With my fish-line made of silver;
But alas! I could not keep her,
Did not know that I had caught her
Till too late to woo and win her;
Let her slip between my fingers
To the home of water-maidens,
To the kingdom of Wellamo."

Wainamoinen then departed,
Empty-handed, heavy-hearted,
Straightway hastened to his country,
To his home in Kalevala,
Spake these words upon his journey:
"What has happened to the cuckoo,
Once the cuckoo bringing gladness,
In the morning, in the evening,
Often bringing joy at noontide?
What has stilled the cuckoo's singing,
What has changed the cuckoo's calling?
Sorrow must have stilled his singing,
And compassion changed his calling,
As I hear him sing no longer,
For my pleasure in the morning,
For my happiness at evening.
Never shall I learn the secret,
How to live and how to prosper,
How upon the earth to rest me,
How upon the seas to wander!
Only were my ancient mother
Living on the face of Northland,
Surely she would well advise me,
What my thought and what my action,
That this cup of grief might pass me,
That this sorrow might escape me,
And this darkened cloud pass over."

In the deep awoke his mother,
From her tomb she spake as follows:
"Only sleeping was thy mother,
Now awakes to give thee answer,
What thy thought and what thine action,
That this cup of grief may pass thee,
That this sorrow may escape thee,
And this darkened cloud pass over.
Hie thee straightway to the Northland,
Visit thou the Suomi daughters;

Thou wilt find them wise and lovely,
Far more beautiful than Aino,
Far more worthy of a husband,
Not such silly chatter-boxes,
As the fickle Lapland maidens.
Take for thee a life-companion,
From the honest homes of Suomi,
One of Northland's honest daughters;
She will charm thee with her sweetness,
Make thee happy through her goodness,
Form perfection, manners easy,
Every step and movement graceful,
Full of wit and good behavior,
Honour to thy home and kindred."

Rune VI: Wainamoinen's Hapless Journey

Wainamoinen, old and truthful,
Now arranges for a journey
To the village of the Northland,
To the land of cruel winters,
To the land of little sunshine,
To the land of worthy women;
Takes his light-foot, royal racer,
Then adjusts the golden bridle,
Lays upon his back the saddle,
Silver-buckled, copper-stirruped,
Seats himself upon his courser,
And begins his journey northward;
Plunges onward, onward, onward,
Galloping along the highway,
In his saddle, gaily fashioned,
On his dappled steed of magic,
Plunging through Wainola's meadows,
O'er the plains of Kalevala.
Fast and far he galloped onward,
Galloped far beyond Wainola,
Bounded o'er the waste of waters,
Till he reached the blue-sea's margin,
Wetting not the hoofs in running.

But the evil Youkahainen
Nursed a grudge within his bosom,
In his heart the worm of envy,
Envy of this Wainamoinen,
Of this wonderful enchanter.
He prepares a cruel cross-bow,
Made of steel and other metals,
Paints the bow in many colours,
Moulds the top-piece out of copper,
Trims his bow with snowy silver,
Gold he uses too in trimming.
Then he hunts for strongest sinews,
Finds them in the stag of Hisi,
Interweaves the flax of Lempo.
Ready is the cruel cross-bow,
String, and shaft, and ends are finished,
Beautiful the bow and mighty,

Surely cost it not a trifle;
On the back a painted courser,
On each end a colt of beauty,
Near the curve a maiden sleeping,
Near the notch a hare is bounding,
Wonderful the bow thus fashioned;
Cuts some arrows for his quiver,
Covers them with finest feathers,
From the oak the shafts he fashions,
Makes the tips of keenest metal.
As the rods and points are finished,
Then he feathers well his arrows
From the plumage of the swallow,
From the wing-quills of the sparrow;
Hardens well his feathered arrows,
And imparts to each new virtues,
Steeps them in the blood of serpents,
In the virus of the adder.

Ready now are all his arrows,
Ready strung, his cruel cross-bow,
Waiting for wise Wainamoinen.
Youkahainen, Lapland's minstrel,
Waits a long time, is not weary,
Hopes to spy the ancient singer;
Spies at day-dawn, spies at evening,
Spies he ceaselessly at noontide,
Lies in wait for the magician,
Waits, and watches, as in envy;
Sits he at the open window,
Stands behind the hedge, and watches;
In the foot-path waits, and listens,

Spies along the balks of meadows;
On his back he hangs his quiver,
In his quiver, feathered arrows
Dipped in virus of the viper,
On his arm the mighty cross-bow,
Waits, and watches, and unwearied,
Listens from the boat-house window,
Lingers at the end of Fog-point,
By the river flowing seaward,
Near the holy stream and whirlpool,
Near the sacred river's fire-fall.

Finally the Lapland minstrel,
Youkahainen of Pohyola,
At the breaking of the day-dawn,
At the early hour of morning,
Fixed his gaze upon the northeast,
Turned his eyes upon the sunrise,
Saw a black cloud on the ocean,
Something blue upon the waters,
And soliloquized as follows:
"Are those clouds on the horizon,
Or perchance the dawn of morning?
Neither clouds on the horizon,
Nor the dawning of the morning;
It is ancient Wainamoinen,
The renowned and wise enchanter,
Riding on his way to Northland;
On his steed, the royal racer,
Magic courser of Wainola."

Quickly now young Youkahainen,
Lapland's vain and evil minstrel,
Filled with envy, grasps his cross-bow,
Makes his bow and arrows ready
For the death of Wainamoinen.

Quick his aged mother asked him,
Spake these words to Youkahainen:
"For whose slaughter is thy cross-bow,
For whose heart thy poisoned arrows?"
Youkahainen thus made answer:
"I have made this mighty cross-bow,
Fashioned bow and poisoned arrows
For the death of Wainamoinen,
Thus to slay the friend of waters;
I must shoot the old magician,
The eternal bard and hero,
Through the heart, and through the liver,
Through the head, and
through the shoulders,
With this bow and feathered arrows
Thus destroy my rival minstrel."

Then the aged mother answered,
Thus reproving, thus forbidding:
"Do not slay good Wainamoinen,
Ancient hero of the Northland,
From a noble tribe descended,
He, my sister's son, my nephew.
If thou slayest Wainamoinen,
Ancient son of Kalevala,
Then alas! all joy will vanish,
Perish all our wondrous singing;
Better on the earth the gladness,
Better here the magic music,
Than within the nether regions,
In the kingdom of Tuoni,
In the realm of the departed,
In the land of the hereafter."

Then the youthful Youkahainen
Thought awhile and well considered,
Ere he made a final answer.

With one hand he raised the cross-bow
But the other seemed to weaken,
As he drew the cruel bow-string.
Finally these words he uttered
As his bosom swelled with envy:
"Let all joy forever vanish,
Let earth's pleasures quickly perish,
Disappear earth's sweetest music,
Happiness depart forever;
Shoot I will this rival minstrel,
Little heeding what the end is."

Quickly now he bends his fire-bow,
On his left knee rests the weapon,
With his right foot firmly planted,
Thus he strings his bow of envy;
Takes three arrows from his quiver,
Choosing well the best among them,
Carefully adjusts the bow-string,

Sets with care the feathered arrow,
To the flaxen string he lays it,
Holds the cross-bow to his shoulder,
Aiming well along the margin,
At the heart of Wainamoinen,
Waiting till he gallops nearer;
In the shadow of a thicket,
Speaks these words while he is waiting
"Be thou, flaxen string, elastic;
Swiftly fly, thou feathered ash-wood,
Swiftly speed, thou deadly missile,
Quick as light, thou poisoned arrow,
To the heart of Wainamoinen.
If my hand too low should hold thee,
May the gods direct thee higher;
If too high mine eye should aim thee,
May the gods direct thee lower."

Steady now he pulls the trigger;
Like the lightning flies the arrow
O'er the head of Wainamoinen;
To the upper sky it darteth,
And the highest clouds it pierces,
Scatters all the flock of
lamb-clouds,
On its rapid journey skyward.

Not discouraged, quick selecting,
Quick adjusting, Youkahainen,
Quickly aiming, shoots a second.
Speeds the arrow swift as lightning;
Much too low he aimed the missile,
Into earth the arrow plunges,
Pierces to the lower regions,
Splits in two the old Sand Mountain.

Nothing daunted, Youkahainen,
Quick adjusting shoots a third one.
Swift as light it speeds its journey,
Strikes the steed of Wainamoinen,
Strikes the light-foot, ocean-swimmer,
Strikes him near his golden girdle,
Through the shoulder of the racer.

Thereupon wise Wainamoinen
Headlong fell upon the waters,
Plunged beneath the rolling billows,
From the saddle of the courser,
From his dappled steed of magic.
Then arose a mighty storm-wind,
Roaring wildly on the waters,
Bore away old Wainamoinen
Far from land upon the billows,
On the high and rolling billows,
On the broad sea's great expanses.

Boasted then young Youkahainen,
Thinking Waino dead and buried,
These the boastful words he uttered:
"Nevermore, old Wainamoinen,
Nevermore in all thy life-time,
While the golden moonlight glistens,
Nevermore wilt fix thy vision
On the meadows of Wainola,
On the plains of Kalevala;
Full six years must swim the ocean,
Tread the waves for seven summers,
Eight years ride the foamy billows,
In the broad expanse of water;
Six long autumns as a fir tree,
Seven winters as a pebble,
Eight long summers as an aspen."

Thereupon the Lapland minstrel
Hastened to his room delighting,
When his mother thus addressed him
"Hast thou slain good Wainamoinen,
Slain the son of Kalevala?"
Youkahainen thus made answer:
"I have slain old Wainamoinen,
Slain the son of Kalevala,
That he now may plow the ocean,
That he now may sweep the waters,
On the billows rock and slumber.
In the salt-sea plunged he headlong,
In the deep sank the magician,
Sidewise turned he to the seashore,
On his back to rock forever,
Thus the boundless sea to travel,
Thus to ride the rolling billows."
This the answer of the mother:
"Woe to earth for this thine action,
Gone forever, joy and singing,
Vanished is the wit of ages!

Thou hast slain good
Wainamoinen,
Slain the ancient wisdom-singer,
Slain the pride of Suwantala,
Slain the hero of Wainola,
Slain the joy of Kalevala."

Rune VII: Wainamoinen's Rescue

Wainamoinen, old and truthful,
Swam through all the deep-sea waters,
Floating like a branch of aspen,
Like a withered twig of willow;
Swam six days in summer weather,
Swam six nights in golden moonlight;
Still before him rose the billows,
And behind him sky and ocean.
Two days more he swam undaunted,
Two long nights he struggled onward.
On the evening of the eighth day,
Wainamoinen grew disheartened,
Felt a very great discomfort,
For his feet had lost their toe-nails,
And his fingers dead and dying.

Wainamoinen, ancient minstrel,
Sad and weary, spake as follows:
"Woe is me, my old life fated!
Woe is me, misfortune's offspring!
Fool was I when fortune favoured,
To forsake my home and kindred,
For a maiden fair and lovely,
Here beneath the starry heavens,
In this cruel waste of waters,
Days and nights to swim and wander,
Here to struggle with the storm-winds,
To be tossed by heaving billows,
In this broad sea's great expanses,
In this ocean vast and boundless.

"Cold my life and sad and dreary,
Painful too for me to linger
Evermore within these waters,
Thus to struggle for existence!
Cannot know how I can prosper,
How to find me food and shelter,
In these cold and lifeless waters,
In these days of dire misfortune.
Build I in the winds my dwelling?
It will find no sure foundation.
Build my home upon the billows?
Surely would the waves destroy it."

Comes a bird from far Pohyola,
From the occident, an eagle,
Is not classed among the largest,
Nor belongs he to the smallest;
One wing touches on the waters,
While the other sweeps the heavens;
O'er the waves he wings his body,
Strikes his beak upon the sea-cliffs,
Flies about, then safely perches,
Looks before him, looks behind him,
There beholds brave Wainamoinen,
On the blue back of the ocean,
And the eagle thus accosts him:
"Wherefore art thou, ancient hero,
Swimming in the deep-sea billows?"
Thus the water-minstrel answered:
"I am ancient Wainamoinen,
Friend and fellow of the waters,
I, the famous wisdom-singer;
Went to woo a Northland maiden,
Maiden from the dismal Darkland,
Quickly galloped on my journey,
Riding on the plain of ocean.
I arrived one morning early,
At the breaking of the day-dawn.
At the bay of Luotola,
Near Youkola's foaming river,
Where the evil Youkahainen
Slew my steed with bow and arrow,
Tried to slay me with his weapons.
On the waters fell I headlong,
Plunged beneath the salt-sea's surface,
From the saddle of the courser,
From my dappled steed of magic.

"Then arose a mighty storm-wind,
From the East and West a whirlwind,
Washed me seaward on the surges,

Seaward, seaward, further, further,
Where for many days I wandered,
Swam and rocked upon the billows,
Where as many nights I struggled,
In the dashing waves and sea-foam,
With the angry winds and waters.

"Woe is me, my life hard-fated!
Cannot solve this heavy problem,
How to live nor how to perish
In this cruel salt-sea water.
Build I in the winds my dwelling?
It will find no sure foundation.
Build my home upon the waters?
Surely will the waves destroy it.
Must I swim the sea forever,
Must I live, or must I perish?
What will happen if I perish,
If I sink below the billows,
Perish here from cold and hunger?"
Thus the bird of Ether answered:
"Be not in the least disheartened,
Place thyself between my shoulders,
On my back be firmly seated,
I will lift thee from the waters,
Bear thee with my pinions upward,
Bear thee wheresoe'er thou willest.
Well do I the day remember
Where thou didst the eagle service,
When thou didst the birds a favour.
Thou didst leave the birch-tree standing,
When were cleared the Osmo-forests,
From the lands of Kalevala,
As a home for weary songbirds,
As a resting-place for eagles."

Then arises Wainamoinen,
Lifts his head above the waters,
Boldly rises from the sea-waves,
Lifts his body from the billows,
Seats himself upon the eagle,
On the eagle's feathered shoulders.
Quick aloft the huge bird bears him,
Bears the ancient Wainamoinen,
Bears him on the path of zephyrs,
Floating on the vernal breezes,
To the distant shore of Northland,
To the dismal Sariola,
Where the eagle leaves his burden,
Flies away to join his fellows.

Wainamoinen, lone and weary,
Straightway fell to bitter weeping,
Wept and moaned in heavy accents,
On the border of the blue-sea,
On a cheerless promontory,
With a hundred wounds tormented,
Made by cruel winds and waters,
With his hair and beard dishevelled
By the surging of the billows.
Three long days he wept disheartened
Wept as many nights in anguish,
Did not know what way to journey,
Could not find a woodland foot-print,
That would point him to the highway,
To his home in Kalevala,
To his much-loved home and kindred.

Northland's young and slender maiden,
With complexion fair and lovely,
With the Sun had laid a wager,
With the Sun and Moon a wager,
Which should rise before the other,
On the morning of the morrow.
And the maiden rose in beauty,
Long before the Sun had risen,
Long before the Moon had wakened,
From their beds beneath the ocean.
Ere the cock had crowed the day-break,
Ere the Sun had broken slumber;
She had sheared six gentle lambkins,
Gathered from them six white fleeces,
Hence to make the rolls for spinning,
Hence to form the threads for weaving,
Hence to make the softest raiment,
Ere the morning dawn had broken,
Ere the sleeping Sun had risen.

When this task the maid had ended,
Then she scrubbed the birchen tables,
Sweeps the ground-floor of the stable,
With a broom of leaves and branches
From the birches of the Northland,
Scrapes the sweepings well together

On a shovel made of copper,
Carries them beyond the stable,
From the doorway to the meadow,
To the meadow's distant border,
Near the surges of the great-sea,
Listens there and looks about her,
Hears a wailing from the waters,
Hears a weeping from the seashore,
Hears a hero-voice lamenting.

Thereupon she hastens homeward,
Hastens to her mother's dwelling,
These the words the maiden utters:
"I have heard a wail from ocean,
Heard a weeping from the sea-coast,
On the shore someone lamenting."

Louhi, hostess of Pohyola,
Ancient, toothless dame of Northland,
Hastens from her door and
court-yard,
Through the meadow to the seashore,
Listens well for sounds of weeping,
For the wail of one in sorrow;
Hears the voice of one in trouble,
Hears a hero-cry of anguish.
Thus the ancient Louhi answers:
"This is not the wail of children,
These are not the tears of women,
In this way weep bearded heroes;
This the hero-cry of anguish."

Quick she pushed her boat to water,
To the floods her goodly vessel,
Straightway rows with lightning swiftness,
To the weeping Wainamoinen;
Gives the hero consolation,
Comfort gives she to the minstrel
Wailing in a grove of willows,
In his piteous condition,
Mid the alder-trees and aspens,
On the border of the salt-sea,
Visage trembling, locks dishevelled,
Ears, and eyes, and lips of sadness.

Louhi, hostess of Pohyola,
Thus addresses Wainamoinen:
"Tell me what has been thy folly,
That thou art in this condition."

Old and truthful Wainamoinen
Lifts aloft his head and answers:
"Well I know that it is folly
That has brought me all this trouble,
Brought me to this land of strangers,
To these regions unbefitting;
Happy was I with my kindred,
In my distant home and country,
There my name was named in honour."

Louhi, hostess of Pohyola,
Thus replied to Wainamoinen:
"I would gain the information,
Should I be allowed to ask thee,
Who thou art of ancient heroes,
Who of all the host of heroes?"
This is Wainamoinen's answer:
"Formerly my name was mentioned,
Often was I heard and honoured,
As a minstrel and magician,
In the long and dreary winters,
Called the Singer of the Northland,
In the valleys of Wainola,
On the plains of Kalevala;
No one thought that such misfortune
Could befall wise Wainamoinen."

Louhi, hostess of Pohyola,
Thus replied in cheering accents:
"Rise, O hero, from discomfort,
From thy bed among the willows;
Enter now upon the new-way,
Come with me to yonder dwelling,
There relate thy strange adventures,
Tell the tale of thy misfortunes."

Now she takes the hapless hero,
Lifts him from his bed of sorrow,
In her boat she safely seats him,
And begins at once her rowing,
Rows with steady hand and mighty
To her home upon the seashore,
To the dwellings of Pohyola.
There she feeds the starving hero,

Rests the ancient Wainamoinen,
Gives him warmth, and food, and shelter,
And the hero soon recovers.
Then the hostess of Pohyola
Questioned thus the ancient singer:
"Wherefore didst thou, Wainamoinen,
Friend and fellow of the waters,
Weep in sad and bitter accents,
On the border of the ocean,
Mid the aspens and the willows?"

This is Wainamoinen's answer:
"Had good reason for my weeping,
Cause enough for all my sorrow;
Long indeed had I been swimming,
Had been buffeting the billows,
In the far outstretching waters.
This the reason for my weeping;
I have lived in toil and torture,
Since I left my home and country,
Left my native land and kindred,
Came to this the land of strangers,
To these unfamiliar portals.
All thy trees have thorns to wound me,
All thy branches, spines to pierce me,
Even birches give me trouble,
And the alders bring discomfort,
My companions, winds and waters,
Only does the Sun seem friendly,
In this cold and cruel country,
Near these unfamiliar portals."

Louhi thereupon made answer:
"Weep no longer, Wainamoinen,
Grieve no more, thou friend of waters,
Good for thee, that thou shouldst linger
At our friendly homes and firesides;
Thou shalt live with us and welcome,
Thou shalt sit at all our tables,
Eat the salmon from our platters,
Eat the sweetest of our bacon,
Eat the whiting from our waters."

Answers thus old Wainamoinen,
Grateful for the invitation:
"Never do I court strange tables,
Though the food be rare and toothsome;
One's own country is the dearest,
One's own table is the sweetest,
One's own home, the most attractive.
Grant, kind Ukko, God above me,
Thou Creator, full of mercy,
Grant that I again may visit
My beloved home and country.
Better dwell in one's own country,
There to drink its healthful waters
From the simple cups of birch-wood,
Than in foreign lands to wander,
There to drink the rarest liquors
From the golden bowls of strangers."

Louhi, hostess of Pohyola,
Thus replied to the magician:
"What reward wilt thou award me,
Should I take thee where thou willest,
To thy native land and kindred,
To thy much-loved home
and fireside,
To the meadows of Wainola,
To the plains of Kalevala?"

These the words of Wainamoinen:
"What would be reward sufficient,
Shouldst thou take me to my people,
To my home and distant country,
To the borders of the Northland,
There to hear the cuckoo singing,
Hear the sacred cuckoo calling?
Shall I give thee golden treasures,
Fill thy cups with finest silver?"

This is Louhi's simple answer:
"O thou ancient Wainamoinen,
Only true and wise magician,
Never will I ask for riches,
Never ask for gold nor silver;
Gold is for the children's flowers,
Silver for the stallion's jewels.
Canst thou forge for me the Sampo,
Hammer me the lid in colours,
From the tips of white-swan feathers
From the milk of greatest virtue,
From a single grain of barley,
From the finest wool of lambkins?

"I will give thee too my daughter,
Will reward thee through the maiden,
Take thee to thy much-loved home-land,
To the borders of Wainola,
There to hear the cuckoo singing,
Hear the sacred cuckoo calling."

Wainamoinen, much regretting,
Gave this answer to her question:
"Cannot forge for thee the Sampo,
Cannot make the lid in colours.
Take me to my distant country,
I will send thee Ilmarinen,
He will forge for thee the Sampo,
Hammer thee the lid in colours,
He may win thy lovely maiden;
Worthy smith is Ilmarinen,
In this art is first and master;
He, the one that forged the heavens.
Forged the air a hollow cover;
Nowhere see we hammer-traces,
Nowhere find a single tongs-mark."

Thus replied the hostess, Louhi:
"Him alone I'll give my daughter,
Promise him my child in marriage,
Who for me will forge the Sampo,
Hammer me the lid in colours,
From the tips of white-swan feathers,
From the milk of greatest virtue,
From a single grain of barley,
From the finest wool of lambkins."

Thereupon the hostess Louhi,
Harnessed quick a dappled courser,
Hitched him to her sledge of birch-wood,
Placed within it Wainamoinen,
Placed the hero on the cross-bench,
Made him ready for his journey;
Then addressed the ancient minstrel,
These the words that Louhi uttered:
"Do not raise thine eyes to heaven,
Look not upward on thy journey,
While thy steed is fresh and frisky,
While the day-star lights thy pathway,
Ere the evening star has risen;
If thine eyes be lifted upward,
While the day-star lights thy pathway,
Dire misfortune will befall thee,
Some sad fate will overtake thee."

Then the ancient Wainamoinen
Fleetly drove upon his journey,
Merrily he hastened homeward,
Hastened homeward, happy-hearted
From the ever-darksome Northland
From the dismal Sariola.

Rune VIII: Maiden of the Rainbow

Pohyola's fair and winsome daughter,
Glory of the land and water,
Sat upon the bow of heaven,
On its highest arch resplendent,
In a gown of richest fabric,
In a gold and silver air-gown,
Weaving webs of golden texture,
Interlacing threads of silver;
Weaving with a golden shuttle,
With a weaving-comb of silver;
Merrily flies the golden shuttle,
From the maiden's nimble fingers,
Briskly swings the lathe in weaving,
Swiftly flies the comb of silver,
From the sky-born maiden's fingers,
Weaving webs of wondrous beauty.

Came the ancient Wainamoinen,
Driving down the highway homeward,
From the ever sunless Northland,
From the dismal Sariola;
Few the furlongs he had driven,
Driven but a little distance,
When he heard the sky-loom buzzing,
As the maiden plied the shuttle.
Quick the thoughtless Wainamoinen
Lifts his eyes aloft in wonder,
Looks upon the vault of heaven,
There beholds the bow of beauty,
On the bow the maiden sitting,

Beauteous Maiden of the Rainbow,
Glory of the earth and ocean,
Weaving there a golden fabric,
Working with the rustling silver.
Wainamoinen, ancient minstrel,
Quickly checks his fleet-foot racer,
Looks upon the charming maiden,
Then addresses her as follows:
"Come, fair maiden, to my snow-sledge,
By my side I wish thee seated."

Thus the Maid of Beauty answers:
"Tell me what thou wishest of me,
Should I join thee in the snow-sledge."
Speaks the ancient Wainamoinen,
Answers thus the Maid of Beauty:
"This the reason for thy coming:
Thou shalt bake me honey-biscuit,
Shalt prepare me barley-water,
Thou shalt fill my foaming beer-cups,
Thou shalt sing beside my table,
Shalt rejoice within my portals,
Walk a queen within my dwelling,
In the Wainola halls and chambers,
In the courts of Kalevala."

Thus the Maid of Beauty answered
From her throne amid the heavens:
"Yesterday at hour of twilight,
Went I to the flowery meadows,
There to rock upon the common,
Where the Sun retires to slumber;
There I heard a songbird singing,
Heard the thrush in simple measures,
Singing sweetly thoughts of maidens,
And the minds of anxious mothers.

"Then I asked the pretty songster,
Asked the thrush this simple question:
'Sing to me, thou pretty songbird,
Sing that I may understand thee,
Sing to me in truthful accents,
How to live in greatest pleasure,
And in happiness the sweetest,
As a maiden with her father,
Or as wife beside her husband.'
"Thus the songbird gave me answer,
Sang the thrush this information:
'Bright and warm are days of summer,
Warmer still is maiden-freedom;
Cold is iron in the winter,
Thus the lives of married women;
Maidens living with their mothers
Are like ripe and ruddy berries;
Married women, far too many,
Are like dogs enchained in kennel,
Rarely do they ask for favours,
Not to wives are favours given.'"

Wainamoinen, old and truthful,
Answers thus the Maid of Beauty:
"Foolish is the thrush thus singing,
Nonsense is the songbird's twitter;
Like to babes are maidens treated,
Wives are queens and highly honoured.
Come, sweet maiden, to my snow-sledge,
I am not despised as hero,
Not the meanest of magicians;
Come with me and I will make thee
Wife and queen in Kalevala."
Thus the Maid of Beauty answered:
"Would consider thee a hero,
Mighty hero, I would call thee,
When a golden hair thou splittest,
Using knives that have no edges;
When thou snarest me a bird's egg
With a snare that I can see not."

Wainamoinen, skilled and ancient,
Split a golden hair exactly,
Using knives that had no edges;
And he snared an egg as nicely
With a snare the maiden saw not.

"Come, sweet maiden, to my snow-sledge,
I have done what thou desirest."
Thus the maiden wisely answered:
"Never enter I thy snow-sledge,
Till thou peelest me the sandstone,
Till thou cuttest me a whip-stick
From the ice, and make no splinters,
Losing not the smallest fragment."
Wainamoinen, true magician,
Nothing daunted, not discouraged,

Deftly peeled the rounded sandstone,
Deftly cut from ice a whip-stick,
Cutting not the finest splinter,
Losing not the smallest fragment.
Then again he called the maiden,
To a seat within his snow-sledge.

But the Maid or Beauty answered,
Answered thus the great magician:
"I will go with that one only
That will make me ship or shallop,
From the splinters of my spindle,
From the fragments of my distaff,
In the waters launch the vessel,
Set the little ship a-floating,
Using not the knee to push it,
Using not the arm to move it,
Using not the hand to touch it,
Using not the foot to turn it,
Using nothing to propel it."

Spake the skilful Wainamoinen,
These the words the hero uttered:
"There is no one in the Northland,
No one under vault of heaven,
Who like me can build a vessel,
From the fragments of the distaff,
From the splinters of the spindle."

Then he took the distaff-fragments,
Took the splinters of the spindle,
Hastened off the boat to fashion,
Hastened to an iron mountain,
There to join the many fragments.
Full of zeal he plies the hammer,
Swings the hammer and the hatchet;
Nothing daunted, builds the vessel,
Works one day and then a second,
Works with steady hand the third day;
On the evening of the third day,
Evil Hisi grasps the hatchet,
Lempo takes the crooked handle,
Turns aside the axe in falling,
Strikes the rocks and breaks to pieces;
From the rocks rebound the fragments,
Pierce the flesh of the magician,
Cut the knee of Wainamoinen.
Lempo guides the sharpened hatchet,
And the veins fell Hisi severs.
Quickly gushes forth a blood-stream,
And the stream is crimson-coloured.

Wainamoinen, old and truthful,
The renowned and wise enchanter,
Thus outspeaks in measured accents:
"O thou keen and cruel hatchet,
O thou axe of sharpened metal,
Thou shouldst cut the trees to fragments,
Cut the pine tree and the willow,
Cut the alder and the birch-tree,
Cut the juniper and aspen,
Shouldst not cut my knee to pieces,
Shouldst not tear my veins asunder."

Then the ancient Wainamoinen
Thus begins his incantations,
Thus begins his magic singing,
Of the origin of evil;
Every word in perfect order,
Makes no effort to remember,
Sings the origin of iron,
That a bolt he well may fashion,
Thus prepare a lock for surety,
For the wounds the axe has given,
That the hatchet has torn open.
But the stream flows like a brooklet,
Rushing like a maddened torrent,
Stains the herbs upon the meadows,
Scarcely is a bit of verdure
That the blood-stream does not cover
As it flows and rushes onward
From the knee of the magician,
From the veins of Wainamoinen.

Now the wise and ancient minstrel
Gathers lichens from the sandstone,
Picks them from the trunks of birches,
Gathers moss within the marshes,
Pulls the grasses from the meadows,
Thus to stop the crimson streamlet,
Thus to close the wounds laid open;
But his work is unsuccessful,
And the crimson stream flows onward.

Wainamoinen, ancient minstrel,
Feeling pain and fearing languor,
Falls to weeping, heavy-hearted;
Quickly now his steed he hitches,
Hitches to the sledge of birch-wood,
Climbs with pain upon the cross-bench,
Strikes his steed in quick succession,
Snaps his whip above the racer,
And the steed flies onward swiftly;
Like the winds he sweeps the highway,
Till he nears a Northland village,
Where the way is triple-parted.

Wainamoinen, old and truthful,
Takes the lowest of the highways,
Quickly nears a spacious cottage,
Quickly asks before the doorway:
"Is there any one here dwelling,
That can know the pain I suffer,
That can heal this wound of hatchet.
That can check this crimson streamlet?"

Sat a boy within a corner,
On a bench beside a baby,
And he answered thus the hero:
"There is no one in this dwelling
That can know the pain thou feelest,
That can heal the wounds of hatchet,
That can check the crimson streamlet;
Someone lives in yonder cottage,
That perchance can do thee service."

Wainamoinen, ancient minstrel,
Whips his courser to a gallop,
Dashes on along the highway;
Only drives a little distance,
On the middle of the highways,
To a cabin on the road-side,
Asks one standing on the threshold,
Questions all through open windows,
These the words the hero uses:
"Is there no one in this cabin,
That can know the pain I suffer,
That can heal this wound of hatchet,
That can check this crimson streamlet?"

On the floor a witch was lying,
Near the fire-place lay the beldame,
Thus she spake to Wainamoinen,
Through her rattling teeth she answered:
"There is no one in this cabin
That can know the pain thou feelest,
That can heal the wounds of hatchets,
That can check the crimson streamlet;
Someone lives in yonder cottage,
That perchance can do thee service."

Wainamoinen, nothing daunted,
Whips his racer to a gallop,
Dashes on along the highway;
Only drives a little distance,
On the upper of the highways,
Gallops to a humble cottage,
Asks one standing near the penthouse,
Sitting on the penthouse-doorsill:
"Is there no one in this cottage,
That can know the pain I suffer,
That can heal this wound of hatchet,
That can check this crimson streamlet?"

Near the fireplace sat an old man,
On the hearthstone sat the gray-beard,
Thus he answered Wainamoinen:
"Greater things have been accomplished,
Much more wondrous things effected,
Through but three words of the master;
Through the telling of the causes,
Streams and oceans have been tempered,
River cataracts been lessened,
Bays been made of promontories,
Islands raised from deep sea-bottoms."

Rune IX: Origin of Iron

Wainamoinen, thus encouraged,
Quickly rises in his snow-sledge,
Asking no one for assistance,
Straightway hastens to the cottage,
Takes a seat within the dwelling.
Come two maids with silver pitchers,

Bringing also golden goblets;
Dip they up a very little,
But the very smallest measure
Of the blood of the magician,
From the wounds of Wainamoinen.

From the fire-place calls the old man,
Thus the gray-beard asks
the minstrel:
"Tell me who thou art of heroes,
Who of all the great magicians?
Lo! thy blood fills seven sea-boats,
Eight of largest birchen vessels,
Flowing from some hero's veinlets,
From the wounds of some magician.
Other matters I would ask thee;
Sing the cause of this thy trouble,
Sing to me the source of metals,
Sing the origin of iron,
How at first it was created."

Then the ancient Wainamoinen
Made this answer to the gray-beard:
"Know I well the source of metals,
Know the origin of iron;
I can tell how steel is fashioned.
Of the mothers air is oldest,
Water is the oldest brother,
And the fire is second brother,
And the youngest brother, iron;
Ukko is the first creator.
Ukko, maker of the heavens,
Cut apart the air and water,
Ere was born the metal, iron.
Ukko, maker of the heavens,
Firmly rubbed his hands together,
Firmly pressed them on his knee-cap,
Then arose three lovely maidens,
Three most beautiful of daughters;
These were mothers of the iron,
And of steel of bright-blue colour.
Tremblingly they walked the heavens,
Walked the clouds with silver linings,
With their bosoms overflowing
With the milk of future iron,
Flowing on and flowing ever,
From the bright rims of the cloudlets
To the earth, the valleys filling,
To the slumber-calling waters.

"Ukko's eldest daughter sprinkled
Black milk over river channels
And the second daughter sprinkled
White milk over hills and mountains,
While the youngest daughter sprinkled
Red milk over seas and oceans.
Where the black milk had been sprinkled,
Grew the dark and ductile iron;
Where the white milk had been sprinkled,
Grew the iron, lighter-coloured;
Where the red milk had been sprinkled,
Grew the red and brittle iron.

"After Time had gone a distance,
Iron hastened Fire to visit,
His beloved elder brother,
Thus to know his brother better.
Straightway Fire began his roarings,
Laboured to consume his brother,
His beloved younger brother.
Straightway Iron sees his danger,
Saves himself by fleetly fleeing,
From the fiery flame's advances,
Fleeing hither, fleeing thither,
Fleeing still and taking shelter
In the swamps and in the valleys,
In the springs that loudly bubble,
By the rivers winding seaward,
On the broad backs of the marshes,
Where the swans their nests have builded,
Where the wild geese hatch their goslings.

"Thus is iron in the swamp-lands,
Stretching by the water-courses,
Hidden well for many ages,
Hidden in the birchen forests,
But he could not hide forever
From the searchings of his brother;
Here and there the fire has caught him,
Caught and brought him to his furnace,
That the spears, and swords, and axes,
Might be forged and duly hammered.
In the swamps ran blackened waters,
From the heath the bears came ambling,

And the wolves ran through the marshes.
Iron then made his appearance,
Where the feet of wolves had trodden,
Where the paws of bears had trampled.

"Then the blacksmith, Ilmarinen,
Came to earth to work the metal;
He was born upon the Coal-mount,
Skilled and nurtured in the coal-fields;
In one hand, a copper hammer,
In the other, tongs of iron;
In the night was born the blacksmith,
In the morn he built his smithy,
Sought with care a favoured hillock,
Where the winds might fill his bellows;
Found a hillock in the swamp-lands,
Where the iron hid abundant;
There he built his smelting furnace,
There he laid his leathern bellows,
Hastened where the wolves had travelled,
Followed where the bears had trampled,
Found the iron's young formations,
In the wolf-tracks of the marshes,
In the foot-prints of the gray-bear.

"Then the blacksmith, Ilmarinen,
Thus addressed the sleeping iron:
'Thou most useful of the metals,
Thou art sleeping in the marshes,
Thou art hid in low conditions,
Where the wolf treads in the swamp-lands,
Where the bear sleeps in the thickets.
Hast thou thought and well considered,
What would be thy future station,
Should I place thee in the furnace,
Thus to make thee free and useful?'

"Then was Iron sorely frightened,
Much distressed and filled with horror,
When of Fire he heard the mention,
Mention of his fell destroyer.

"Then again speaks Ilmarinen,
Thus the smith addresses Iron:
'Be not frightened, useful metal,
Surely Fire will not consume thee,
Will not burn his youngest brother,
Will not harm his nearest kindred.
Come thou to my room and furnace,
Where the fire is freely burning,
Thou wilt live, and grow, and prosper,
Wilt become the swords of heroes,
Buckles for the belts of women.'

"Ere arose the star of evening,
Iron ore had left the marshes,
From the water-beds had risen,
Had been carried to the furnace,
In the fire the smith had laid it,
Laid it in his smelting furnace.
Ilmarinen starts the bellows,
Gives three motions of the handle,
And the iron flows in streamlets
From the forge of the magician,
Soon becomes like baker's leaven,
Soft as dough for bread of barley.
Then out-screamed the metal, Iron:
'Wondrous blacksmith, Ilmarinen,
Take, O take me from thy furnace,
From this fire and cruel torture.'

"Ilmarinen thus made answer:
'I will take thee from my furnace,
Thou art but a little frightened,
Thou shalt be a mighty power,
Thou shalt slay the best of heroes,
Thou shalt wound thy dearest brother.'

"Straightway Iron made this promise,
Vowed and swore in strongest accents,
By the furnace, by the anvil,
By the tongs, and by the hammer,
These the words he vowed
and uttered:
'Many trees that I shall injure,
Shall devour the hearts of mountains,
Shall not slay my nearest kindred,
Shall not kill the best of heroes,
Shall not wound my dearest brother;
Better live in civil freedom,
Happier would be my life-time,
Should I serve my fellow-beings,
Serve as tools for their convenience,
Than as implements of warfare,

Slay my friends and nearest kindred,
Wound the children of my mother.'

"Now the master, Ilmarinen,
The renowned and skilful blacksmith,
From the fire removes the iron,
Places it upon the anvil,
Hammers well until it softens,
Hammers many fine utensils,
Hammers spears, and swords, and axes,
Hammers knives, and forks, and hatchets,
Hammers tools of all descriptions.

"Many things the blacksmith needed,
Many things he could not fashion,
Could not make the tongue of iron,
Could not hammer steel from iron,
Could not make the iron harden.
Well considered Ilmarinen,
Deeply thought and long reflected.
Then he gathered birchen ashes,
Steeped the ashes in the water,
Made a lye to harden iron,
Thus to form the steel most needful.
With his tongue he tests the mixture,
Weighs it long and well considers,
And the blacksmith speaks as follows:
'All this labour is for nothing,
Will not fashion steel from iron,
Will not make the soft ore harden.'

"Now a bee flies from the meadow,
Blue-wing coming from the flowers,
Flies about, then safely settles
Near the furnace of the smithy.

"Thus the smith the bee addresses,
These the words of Ilmarinen:
'Little bee, thou tiny birdling,
Bring me honey on thy winglets,
On thy tongue, I pray thee,
bring me
Sweetness from the fragrant meadows,
From the little cups of flowers,
From the tips of seven petals,
That we thus may aid the water
To produce the steel from iron.'

"Evil Hisi's bird, the hornet,
Heard these words of Ilmarinen,
Looking from the cottage gable,
Flying to the bark of birch-trees,
While the iron bars were heating,
While the steel was being tempered;
Swiftly flew the stinging hornet,
Scattered all the Hisi horrors,
Brought the blessing of the serpent,
Brought the venom of the adder,
Brought the poison of the spider,
Brought the stings of all the insects,
Mixed them with the ore and water,
While the steel was being tempered.

"Ilmarinen, skilful blacksmith,
First of all the iron-workers,
Thought the bee had surely brought him
Honey from the fragrant meadows,
From the little cups of flowers,
From the tips of seven petals,
And he spake the words that follow:
'Welcome, welcome, is thy coming,
Honeyed sweetness from the flowers
Thou hast brought to aid the water,
Thus to form the steel from iron!'

"Ilmarinen, ancient blacksmith,
Dipped the iron into water,
Water mixed with many poisons,
Thought it but the wild bee's honey;
Thus he formed the steel from iron.
When he plunged it into water,
Water mixed with many poisons,
When he placed it in the furnace,
Angry grew the hardened iron,
Broke the vow that he had taken,
Ate his words like dogs and devils,
Mercilessly cut his brother,
Madly raged against his kindred,
Caused the blood to flow in streamlets
From the wounds of man and hero.
This, the origin of iron,
And of steel of light blue colour."

From the hearth arose the gray-beard,
Shook his heavy locks and answered:

"Now I know the source of iron,
Whence the steel and whence its evils;
Curses on thee, cruel iron,
Curses on the steel thou givest,
Curses on thee, tongue of evil,
Cursed be thy life forever!
Once thou wert of little value,
Having neither form nor beauty,
Neither strength nor great importance,
When in form of milk thou rested,
When for ages thou wert hidden
In the breasts of God's three daughters,
Hidden in their heaving bosoms,
On the borders of the cloudlets,
In the blue vault of the heavens.

"Thou wert once of little value,
Having neither form nor beauty,
Neither strength nor great importance,
When like water thou wert resting
On the broad back of the marshes,
On the steep declines of mountains,
When thou wert but formless matter,
Only dust of rusty colour.

"Surely thou wert void of greatness,
Having neither strength nor beauty,
When the moose was trampling
on thee,
When the roebuck trod upon thee,
When the tracks of wolves were in thee,
And the bear-paws scratched thy body.
Surely thou hadst little value
When the skilful Ilmarinen,
First of all the iron-workers,
Brought thee from the
blackened swamp-lands,
Took thee to his ancient smithy,
Placed thee in his fiery furnace.
Truly thou hadst little vigor,
Little strength, and little danger,
When thou in the fire wert hissing,
Rolling forth like seething water,
From the furnace of the smithy,
When thou gavest oath the strongest,
By the furnace, by the anvil,
By the tongs, and by the hammer,
By the dwelling of the blacksmith,
By the fire within the furnace.

"Now forsooth thou hast grown mighty,
Thou canst rage in wildest fury;
Thou hast broken all thy pledges,
All thy solemn vows hast broken,
Like the dogs thou shamest honour,
Shamest both thyself and kindred,
Tainted all with breath of evil.
Tell who drove thee to this mischief,
Tell who taught thee all thy malice,
Tell who gavest thee thine evil!
Did thy father, or thy mother,
Did the eldest of thy brothers,
Did the youngest of thy sisters,
Did the worst of all thy kindred
Give to thee thine evil nature?
Not thy father, nor thy mother,
Not the eldest of thy brothers,
Not the youngest of thy sisters,
Not the worst of all thy kindred,
But thyself hast done this mischief,
Thou the cause of all our trouble.
Come and view thine evil doings,
And amend this flood of damage,
Ere I tell thy gray-haired mother,
Ere I tell thine aged father.
Great indeed a mother's anguish,
Great indeed a father's sorrow,
When a son does something evil,
When a child runs wild and lawless.

"Crimson streamlet, cease thy flowing
From the wounds of Wainamoinen;
Blood of ages, stop thy coursing
From the veins of the magician;
Stand like heaven's crystal pillars,
Stand like columns in the ocean,
Stand like birch-trees in the forest,
Like the tall reeds in the marshes,
Like the high-rocks on the sea-coast,
Stand by power of mighty magic!

"Should perforce thy will impel thee,
Flow thou on thine endless circuit,
Through the veins of Wainamoinen,

Through the bones, and through the muscles,
Through the lungs, and heart, and liver,
Of the mighty sage and singer;
Better be the food of heroes,
Than to waste thy strength and virtue,
On the meadows and the woodlands,
And be lost in dust and ashes.
Flow forever in thy circle;
Thou must cease this crimson out-flow;
Stain no more the grass and flowers,
Stain no more these golden hill-tops,
Pride and beauty of our heroes.
In the veins of the magician,
In the heart of Wainamoinen,
Is thy rightful home and storehouse.
Thither now withdraw thy forces,
Thither hasten, swiftly flowing;
Flow no more as crimson currents,
Fill no longer crimson lakelets,
Must not rush like brooks in spring-tide,
Nor meander like the rivers.

"Cease thy flow, by word of magic,
Cease as did the falls of Tyrya,
As the rivers of Tuoni,
When the sky withheld her rain-drops,
When the sea gave up her waters,
In the famine of the seasons,
In the years of fire and torture.
If thou heedest not this order,
I shall offer other measures,
Know I well of other forces;
I shall call the Hisi irons,
In them I shall boil and roast thee,
Thus to check thy crimson flowing,
Thus to save the wounded hero.

"If these means be inefficient,
Should these measures prove unworthy,
I shall call omniscient Ukko,
Mightiest of the creators,
Stronger than all ancient heroes,
Wiser than the world-magicians;
He will check the crimson out-flow,
He will heal this wound of hatchet.

"Ukko, God of love and mercy,
God and Master of the heavens,
Come thou hither, thou art needed,
Come thou quickly I beseech thee,
Lend thy hand to aid thy children,
Touch this wound with healing fingers,
Stop this hero's streaming life-blood,
Bind this wound with tender leaflets,
Mingle with them healing flowers,
Thus to check this crimson current,
Thus to save this great magician,
Save the life of Wainamoinen."

Thus at last the blood-stream ended,
As the magic words were spoken.
Then the gray-beard, much rejoicing,
Sent his young son to the smithy,
There to make a healing balsam,
From the herbs of tender fibre,
From the healing plants and flowers,
From the stalks secreting honey,
From the roots, and leaves, and blossoms.

On the way he meets an oak-tree,
And the oak the son addresses:
"Hast thou honey in thy branches,
Does thy sap run full of sweetness?"
Thus the oak-tree wisely answers:
"Yea, but last night dripped the honey
Down upon my spreading branches,
And the clouds their fragrance sifted,
Sifted honey on my leaflets,
From their home within the heavens."

Then the son takes oak-wood splinters,
Takes the youngest oak-tree branches,
Gathers many healing grasses,
Gathers many herbs and flowers,
Rarest herbs that grow in Northland,
Places them within the furnace
In a kettle made of copper;
Lets them steep and boil together,
Bits of bark chipped from the oak-tree,
Many herbs of healing virtues;
Steeps them one day, then a second,
Three long days of summer weather,
Days and nights in quick succession;

Then he tries his magic balsam,
Looks to see if it is ready,
If his remedy is finished;
But the balsam is unworthy.

Then he added other grasses,
Herbs of every healing virtue,
That were brought from distant nations,
Many hundred leagues from Northland,
Gathered by the wisest minstrels,
Thither brought by nine enchanters.
Three days more he steeped the balsam,
Three nights more the fire he tended,
Nine the days and nights he watched it,
Then again he tried the ointment,
Viewed it carefully and tested,
Found at last that it was ready,
Found the magic balm was finished.

Near by stood a branching birch-tree,
On the border of the meadow,
Wickedly it had been broken,
Broken down by evil Hisi;
Quick he takes his balm of healing,
And anoints the broken branches,
Rubs the balsam in the fractures,
Thus addresses then the birch-tree:
"With this balsam I anoint thee,
With this salve thy wounds I cover,
Cover well thine injured places;
Now the birch-tree shall recover,
Grow more beautiful than ever."

True, the birch-tree soon recovered,
Grew more beautiful than ever,
Grew more uniform its branches,
And its bole more strong and stately.
Thus it was he tried the balsam,
Thus the magic salve he tested,
Touched with it the splintered sandstone,
Touched the broken blocks of granite,
Touched the fissures in the mountains,
And the broken parts united,
All the fragments grew together.

Then the young boy quick returning
With the balsam he had finished,
To the gray-beard gave the ointment,
And the boy these measures uttered:
"Here I bring the balm of healing,
Wonderful the salve I bring thee;
It will join the broken granite,
Make the fragments grow together,
Heal the fissures in the mountains,
And restore the injured birch-tree."

With his tongue the old man tested,
Tested thus the magic balsam,
Found the remedy effective,
Found the balm had magic virtues;
Then anointed he the minstrel,
Touched the wounds of Wainamoinen,
Touched them with his magic balsam,
With the balm of many virtues;
Speaking words of ancient wisdom,
These the words the gray-beard uttered:
"Do not walk in thine own virtue,
Do not work in thine own power,
Walk in strength of thy Creator;
Do not speak in thine own wisdom,
Speak with tongue of mighty Ukko.
In my mouth, if there be sweetness,
It has come from my Creator;
If my hands are filled with beauty,
All the beauty comes from Ukko."

When the wounds had been anointed,
When the magic salve had
touched them,
Straightway ancient Wainamoinen
Suffered fearful pain and anguish,
Sank upon the floor in torment,
Turning one way, then another,
Sought for rest and found it nowhere,
Till his pain the gray-beard banished,
Banished by the aid of magic,
Drove away his killing torment
To the court of all our trouble,
To the highest hill of torture,
To the distant rocks and ledges,
To the evil-bearing mountains,
To the realm of wicked Hisi.
Then he took some silken fabric,
Quick he tore the silk asunder,

Making equal strips for wrapping,
Tied the ends with silken ribbons,
Making thus a healing bandage;
Then he wrapped with skilful fingers
Wainamoinen's knee and ankle,
Wrapped the wounds of the magician,
And this prayer the gray-
beard uttered
"Ukko's fabric is the bandage,
Ukko's science is the surgeon,
These have served the wounded hero,
Wrapped the wounds of the magician.
Look upon us, God of mercy,
Come and guard us, kind Creator,
And protect us from all evil!
Guide our feet lest they may stumble,
Guard our lives from every danger,
From the wicked wilds of Hisi."

Wainamoinen, old and truthful,
Felt the mighty aid of magic,
Felt the help of gracious Ukko,
Straightway stronger grew in body,
Straightway were the wounds united,
Quick the fearful pain departed.
Strong and hardy grew the hero,
Straightway walked in perfect freedom,
Turned his knee in all directions,
Knowing neither pain nor trouble.

Then the ancient Wainamoinen
Raised his eyes to high Jumala,
Looked with gratitude to heaven,
Looked on high, in joy and gladness,
Then addressed omniscient Ukko,
This the prayer the minstrel uttered:
"O be praised, thou God of mercy,
Let me praise thee, my Creator,
Since thou gavest me assistance,
And vouchsafed me thy protection,
Healed my wounds and stilled mine anguish,
Banished all my pain and trouble,
Caused by Iron and by Hisi.
O, ye people of Wainola,
People of this generation,
And the folk of future ages,
Fashion not in emulation,
River boat, nor ocean shallop,
Boasting of its fine appearance;
God alone can work completion,
Give to cause its perfect ending,
Never hand of man can find it,
Never can the hero give it,
Ukko is the only Master."

Rune X: Ilmarinen Forges the Sampo

Wainamoinen, the magician,
Takes his steed of copper colour,
Hitches quick his fleet-foot courser,
Puts his racer to the snow-sledge,
Straightway springs upon the cross-seat,
Snaps his whip adorned with jewels.
Like the winds the steed flies onward,
Like a lightning flash, the racer
Makes the snow-sledge creak and rattle,
Makes the highway quickly vanish,
Dashes on through fen and forest,
Over hills and through the valleys,
Over marshes, over mountains,
Over fertile plains and meadows;
Journeys one day, then a second,
So a third from morn till evening,
Till the third day evening brings him
To the endless bridge of Osmo,
To the Osmo-fields and pastures,
To the plains of Kalevala;
When the hero spake as follows:
"May the wolves devour
the dreamer,
Eat the Laplander for dinner,
May disease destroy the braggart,
Him who said that I should never
See again my much-loved
home-land,
Nevermore behold my kindred,
Never during all my life-time,
Never while the sunshine brightens,
Never while the moonlight glimmers
On the meadows of Wainola,
On the plains of Kalevala."

Then began old Wainamoinen,
Ancient bard and famous singer,
To renew his incantations;
Sang aloft a wondrous pine tree,
Till it pierced the clouds in growing
With its golden top and branches,
Till it touched the very heavens,
Spread its branches in the ether,
In the ever-shining sunlight.
Now he sings again enchanting,
Sings the Moon to shine forever
In the fir tree's emerald branches;
In its top he sings the Great Bear.
Then he quickly journeys homeward,
Hastens to his golden portals,
Head awry and visage wrinkled,
Crooked cap upon his forehead,
Since as ransom he had promised
Ilmarinen, magic artist,
Thus to save his life from torture
On the distant fields of Northland,
In the dismal Sariola.

When his stallion he had halted
On the Osmo-field and meadow,
Quickly rising in his snow-sledge,
The magician heard one knocking,
Breaking coal within the smithy,
Beating with a heavy hammer.
Wainamoinen, famous minstrel,
Entering the smithy straightway,
Found the blacksmith, Ilmarinen,
Knocking with his copper hammer.
Ilmarinen spake as follows:
"Welcome, brother Wainamoinen,
Old and worthy Wainamoinen!
Why so long hast thou been absent,
Where hast thou so long been hiding?"

Wainamoinen then made answer,
These the words of the magician:
"Long indeed have I been living,
Many dreary days have wandered,
Many cheerless nights have lingered,
Floating on the cruel ocean,
Weeping in the fens and woodlands
Of the never-pleasant Northland,
In the dismal Sariola;
With the Laplanders I've wandered,
With the people filled with witchcraft."

Promptly answers Ilmarinen,
These the words the blacksmith uses:
"O thou ancient Wainamoinen,
Famous and eternal singer,
Tell me of thy journey northward,
Of thy wanderings in Lapland,
Of thy dismal journey homeward."
Spake the minstrel, Wainamoinen:
"I have much to tell thee, brother,
Listen to my wondrous story:
In the Northland lives a virgin,
In a village there, a maiden,
That will not accept a lover,
That a hero's hand refuses,
That a wizard's heart disdaineth;
All of Northland sings her praises,
Sings her worth and magic beauty,
Fairest maiden of Pohyola,
Daughter of the earth and ocean.
From her temples beams the moonlight,
From her breast, the gleam of sunshine,
From her forehead shines the rainbow,
On her neck, the seven starlets,
And the Great Bear from her shoulder.

"Ilmarinen, worthy brother,
Thou the only skilful blacksmith,
Go and see her wondrous beauty,
See her gold and silver garments,
See her robed in finest raiment,
See her sitting on the rainbow,
Walking on the clouds of purple.
Forge for her the magic Sampo,
Forge the lid in many colours,
Thy reward shall be the virgin,
Thou shalt win this bride of beauty;
Go and bring the lovely maiden
To thy home in Kalevala."
Spake the brother, Ilmarinen:
"O thou cunning Wainamoinen,
Thou hast promised me already
To the ever-darksome Northland,
Thy devoted head to ransom,

Thus to rescue thee from trouble.
I shall never visit Northland,
Shall not go to see thy maiden,
Do not love the Bride of Beauty;
Never while the moonlight glimmers,
Shall I go to dreary Pohya,
To the plains of Sariola,
Where the people eat each other,
Sink their heroes in the ocean,
Not for all the maids of Lapland."
Spake the brother, Wainamoinen:
"I can tell thee greater wonders,
Listen to my wondrous story:
I have seen the fir tree blossom,
Seen its flowers with emerald branches,
On the Osmo-fields and woodlands;
In its top, there shines the moonlight,
And the Bear lives in its branches."
Ilmarinen thus made answer:
"I cannot believe thy story,
Cannot trust thy tale of wonder,
Till I see the blooming fir tree,
With its many emerald branches,
With its Bear and golden moonlight."
This is Wainamoinen's answer:
"Wilt thou not believe my story?
Come with me and I will show thee
If my lips speak fact or fiction."

Quick they journey to discover,
Haste to view the wondrous
fir tree;
Wainamoinen leads the journey,
Ilmarinen closely follows.
As they near the Osmo-borders,
Ilmarinen hastens forward
That he may behold the wonder,
Spies the Bear within the fir-top,
Sitting on its emerald branches,
Spies the gleam of golden moonlight.

Spake the ancient Wainamoinen:,
These the words the singer uttered:
"Climb this tree, dear Ilmarinen,
And bring down the golden moonbeams,
Bring the Moon and Bear down with thee
From the fir tree's lofty branches."
Ilmarinen, full consenting,
Straightway climbed the golden fir tree,
High upon the bow of heaven,
Thence to bring the golden moonbeams,
Thence to bring the Bear of heaven,
From the fir tree's topmost branches.

Thereupon the blooming fir tree
Spake these words to Ilmarinen:
"O thou senseless, thoughtless hero,
Thou hast neither wit nor instinct;
Thou dost climb my golden branches,
Like a thing of little judgement,
Thus to get my pictured moonbeams,
Take away my silver starlight,
Steal my Bear and blooming branches."

Quick as thought old Wainamoinen
Sang again in magic accents,
Sang a storm-wind in the heavens,
Sang the wild winds into fury,
And the singer spake as follows:
"Take, O storm-wind, take the forgeman,
Carry him within thy vessel,
Quickly hence, and land the hero
On the ever-darksome Northland,
On the dismal Sariola."

Now the storm-wind quickly darkens,
Quickly piles the air together,
Makes of air a sailing vessel,
Takes the blacksmith, Ilmarinen,
Fleetly from the fir tree branches,
Toward the never-pleasant Northland,
Toward the dismal Sariola.
Through the air sailed Ilmarinen,
Fast and far the hero travelled,
Sweeping onward, sailing northward,
Riding in the track of storm-winds,
O'er the Moon, beneath the sunshine,
On the broad back of the
Great Bear,
Till he neared Pohyola's woodlands,
Neared the homes of Sariola,
And alighted undiscovered,
Was not noticed by the hunters,
Was not scented by the watch-dogs.

Louhi, hostess of Pohyola,
Ancient, toothless dame of Northland,
Standing in the open court-yard,
Thus addresses Ilmarinen,
As she spies the hero-stranger:
"Who art thou of ancient heroes,
Who of all the host of heroes,
Coming here upon the storm-wind,
O'er the sledge-path of the ether,
Scented not by Pohya's watch-dogs?"
This is Ilmarinen's answer:
"I have surely not come hither
To be barked at by the watch-dogs,
At these unfamiliar portals,
At the gates of Sariola."

Thereupon the Northland hostess
Asks again the hero-stranger:
"Hast thou ever been acquainted
With the blacksmith of Wainola,
With the hero, Ilmarinen,
With the skilful smith and artist?
Long I've waited for his coming,
Long this one has been expected,
On the borders of the Northland,
Here to forge for me the Sampo."
Spake the hero, Ilmarinen:
"Well indeed am I acquainted
With the blacksmith, Ilmarinen,
I myself am Ilmarinen,
I, the skilful smith and artist."

Louhi, hostess of the Northland,
Toothless dame of Sariola,
Straightway rushes to her dwelling,
These the words that Louhi utters:
"Come, thou youngest of my daughters,
Come, thou fairest of my maidens,
Dress thyself in finest raiment,
Deck thy hair with rarest jewels,
Pearls upon thy swelling bosom,
On thy neck, a golden necklace,
Bind thy head with silken ribbons,
Make thy cheeks look fresh and ruddy,
And thy visage fair and winsome,
Since the artist, Ilmarinen,
Hither comes from Kalevala,
Here to forge for us the Sampo,
Hammer us the lid in colours."

Now the daughter of the Northland,
Honoured by the land and water,
Straightway takes her choicest raiment,
Takes her dresses rich in beauty,
Finest of her silken wardrobe,
Now adjusts her silken fillet,
On her brow a band of copper,
Round her waist a golden girdle,
Round her neck a pearly necklace,
Shining gold upon her bosom,
In her hair the threads of silver.
From her dressing-room she hastens,
To the hall she hastes and listens,
Full of beauty, full of joyance,
Ears erect and eyes bright-beaming,
Ruddy cheeks and charming visage,
Waiting for the hero-stranger.

Louhi, hostess of Pohyola,
Leads the hero, Ilmarinen,
To her dwelling-rooms in Northland,
To her home in Sariola,
Seats him at her well-filled table,
Gives to him the finest viands,
Gives him every needed comfort,
Then addresses him as follows:
"O thou blacksmith, Ilmarinen,
Master of the forge and smithy,
Canst thou forge for me the Sampo,
Hammer me the lid in colours,
From the tips of white-swan feathers,
From the milk of greatest virtue,
From a single grain of barley,
From the finest wool of lambkins?
Thou shalt have my fairest daughter,
Recompense for this thy service."
These the words of Ilmarinen:
"I will forge for thee the Sampo,
Hammer thee the lid in colours,
From the tips of white-swan feathers,
From the milk of greatest virtue,
From a single grain of barley,
From the finest wool of lambkins,
Since I forged the arch of heaven,

Forged the air a concave cover,
Ere the earth had a beginning."

Thereupon the magic blacksmith
Went to forge the wondrous Sampo,
Went to find a blacksmith's workshop,
Went to find the tools to work with;
But he found no place for forging,
Found no smithy, found no bellows,
Found no chimney, found no anvil,
Found no tongs, and found no hammer.

Then the artist, Ilmarinen.
Spake these words, soliloquizing:
"Only women grow discouraged,
Only knaves leave work unfinished,
Not the devils, nor the heroes,
Nor the Gods of greater knowledge."

Then the blacksmith, Ilmarinen,
Sought a place to build a smithy,
Sought a place to plant a bellows,
On the borders of the Northland,
On the Pohya-hills and meadows;
Searched one day, and then a second;
Ere the evening of the third day,
Came a rock within his vision,
Came a stone with rainbow-colours.
There the blacksmith, Ilmarinen,
Set at work to build his smithy,
Built a fire and raised a chimney;
On the next day laid his bellows,
On the third day built his furnace,
And began to forge the Sampo.

The eternal magic artist,
Ancient blacksmith, Ilmarinen,
First of all the iron-workers,
Mixed together certain metals,
Put the mixture in the caldron,
Laid it deep within the furnace,
Called the hirelings to the forging.
Skilfully they work the bellows,
Tend the fire and add the fuel,
Three most lovely days of summer,
Three short nights of bright midsummer,
Till the rocks begin to blossom,
In the foot-prints of the workmen,
From the magic heat and furnace.

On the first day, Ilmarinen
Downward bent and well examined,
On the bottom of his furnace,
Thus to see what might be forming
From the magic fire and metals.
From the fire arose a cross-bow,
With the brightness of the moonbeams,
Golden bow with tips of silver;
On the shaft was shining copper,
And the bow was strong and wondrous,
But alas! it was ill-natured,
Asking for a hero daily,
Two the heads it asked on feast-days.

Ilmarinen, skilful artist,
Was not pleased with this creation,
Broke the bow in many pieces,
Threw them back within the furnace,
Kept the workmen at the bellows,
Tried to forge the magic Sampo.

On the second day, the blacksmith
Downward bent and well examined,
On the bottom of the furnace;
From the fire, a skiff of metals,
Came a boat of purple colour,
All the ribs were coloured golden,
And the oars were forged from copper;
Thus the skiff was full of beauty,
But alas! a thing of evil;
Forth it rushes into trouble,
Hastens into every quarrel,
Hastes without a provocation
Into every evil combat.

Ilmarinen, metal artist,
Is not pleased with this creation,
Breaks the skiff in many fragments,
Throws them back within the furnace,
Keeps the workmen at the bellows,
Thus to forge the magic Sampo.

On the third day, Ilmarinen,
First of all the metal-workers,

Downward bent and well examined,
On the bottom of the furnace;
There he saw a heifer rising,
Golden were the horns of Kimmo,
On her head the Bear of heaven,
On her brow a disc of sunshine,
Beautiful the cow of magic;
But alas! she is ill-tempered,
Rushes headlong through the forest,
Rushes through the swamps and meadows,
Wasting all her milk in running.

Ilmarinen, the magician,
Is not pleased with this creation,
Cuts the magic cow in pieces,
Throws them in the fiery furnace,
Sets the workmen at the bellows,
Thus to forge the magic Sampo.

On the fourth day, Ilmarinen
Downward bent and well examined,
To the bottom of the furnace;
There beheld a plow in beauty
Rising from the fire of metals,
Golden was the point and plowshare,
And the beam was forged from copper,
And the handles, molten silver,
Beautiful the plow and wondrous;
But alas! it is ill-mannered,
Plows up fields of corn and barley,
Furrows through the richest meadows.

Ilmarinen, metal artist,
Is not pleased with this creation,
Quickly breaks the plow in pieces,
Throws them back within the furnace,
Lets the winds attend the bellows,
Lets the storm-winds fire the metals.
Fiercely vie the winds of heaven,
East-wind rushing, West-wind roaring,
South-wind crying, North-wind howling,
Blow one day and then a second,
Blow the third from morn till even,
When the fire leaps through
the windows,
Through the door the sparks fly upward,
Clouds of smoke arise to heaven;
With the clouds the black smoke mingles,
As the storm-winds ply the bellows.

On the third night Ilmarinen,
Bending low to view his metals,
On the bottom of the furnace,
Sees the magic Sampo rising,
Sees the lid in many colours.
Quick the artist of Wainola
Forges with the tongs and anvil,
Knocking with a heavy hammer,
Forges skilfully the Sampo;
On one side the flour is grinding,
On another salt is making,
On a third is money forging,
And the lid is many-coloured.
Well the Sampo grinds when finished,
To and fro the lid in rocking,
Grinds one measure at the day-break,
Grinds a measure fit for eating,
Grinds a second for the market,
Grinds a third one for the store-house.

Joyfully the dame of Northland,
Louhi, hostess of Pohyola,
Takes away the magic Sampo,
To the hills of Sariola,
To the copper-bearing mountains,
Puts nine locks upon the wonder,
Makes three strong roots creep around it;
In the earth they grow nine fathoms,
One large root beneath the mountain,
One beneath the sandy sea-bed,
One beneath the mountain-dwelling.

Modestly pleads Ilmarinen
For the maiden's willing answer,
These the words of the magician:
"Wilt thou come with me, fair maiden,
Be my wife and queen forever?
I have forged for thee the Sampo,
Forged the lid in many colours."

Northland's fair and lovely daughter
Answers thus the metal-worker:
"Who will in the coming spring-time,
Who will in the second summer,

Guide the cuckoo's song and echo?
Who will listen to his calling,
Who will sing with him in autumn,
Should I go to distant regions,
Should this cheery maiden vanish
From the fields of Sariola,
From Pohyola's fens and forests,
Where the cuckoo sings and echoes?
Should I leave my father's dwelling,
Should my mother's berry vanish,
Should these mountains lose their cherry,
Then the cuckoo too would vanish,
All the birds would leave the forest,
Leave the summit of the mountain,
Leave my native fields and woodlands,
Never shall I, in my life-time,
Say farewell to maiden freedom,
Nor to summer cares and labours,
Lest the harvest be ungarnered,
Lest the berries be ungathered,
Lest the songbirds leave the forest,
Lest the mermaids leave the waters,
Lest I sing with them no longer."

Ilmarinen, the magician,
The eternal metal-forger,
Cap awry and head dejected,
Disappointed, heavy-hearted,
Empty-handed, well considers,
How to reach his distant country,
Reach his much-loved home and kinded,
Gain the meadows of Wainola,
From the never-pleasant Northland,
From the darksome Sariola.
Louhi thus addressed the suitor:
"O thou blacksmith, Ilmarinen,
Why art thou so heavy-hearted,
Why thy visage so dejected?
Hast thou in thy mind to journey
From the vales and hills of Pohya,
To the meadows of Wainola,
To thy home in Kalevala?"
This is Ilmarinen's answer:
"Thitherward my mind is tending,
To my home-land let me journey,
With my kindred let me linger,
Be at rest in mine own country."

Straightway Louhi, dame of Northland,
Gave the hero every comfort,
Gave him food and rarest viands,
Placed him in a boat of copper,
In a copper-banded vessel,
Called the winds to his assistance,
Made the North-wind guide him homeward.
Thus the skilful Ilmarinen
Travels toward his native country,
On the blue back of the waters,
Travels one day, then a second,
Till the third day evening brings him
To Wainola's peaceful meadows,
To his home in Kalevala.

Straightway ancient Wainamoinen
Thus addresses Ilmarinen:
"O my brother, metal artist,
Thou eternal wonder-worker,
Didst thou forge the magic Sampo,
Forge the lid in many colours?"

Spake the brother, Ilmarinen,
These the words the master uttered:
"Yea, I forged the magic Sampo,
Forged the lid in many colours;
To and fro the lid in rocking
Grinds one measure at the day-dawn,
Grinds a measure fit for eating,
Grinds a second for the market,
Grinds a third one for the store-house.
Louhi has the wondrous Sampo,
I have not the Bride of Beauty."

Rune XI: Lemminkainen's Lament

This the time to sing of Ahti,
Son of Lempo, Kaukomieli,
Also known as Lemminkainen.
Ahti was the king of islands,
Grew amid the island-dwellings,
At the site of his dear mother,

On the borders of the ocean,
On the points of promontories.
Ahti fed upon the salmon,
Fed upon the ocean whiting,
Thus became a mighty hero,
In his veins the blood of ages,
Head erect and form commanding,
Growth of mind and body perfect;
But alas! he had his failings,
Bad indeed his heart and morals,
Roaming in unworthy places,
Staying days and nights in sequence
At the homes of merry maidens,
At the dances of the virgins,
With the maids of braided tresses.

Up in Sahri lived a maiden,
Lived the fair and winsome Kulli,
Lovely as a summer-flower,
From a kingly house descended,
Grew to perfect form and beauty,
Living in her father's cottage,
Home of many ancient heroes;
Beautiful was she and queenly,
Praised throughout the whole of Ehstland;
From afar men came to woo her,
To the birthplace of the virgin,
To the household of her mother.

For his son the day-star wooes her,
But she will not go to Sun-land,
Will not shine beside the day-star,
In his haste to bring the summer.
For her son, the bright Moon wooes her,
But she will not go to Moon-land,
By the bright Moon will not glimmer,
Will not run through boundless ether.

For his son the Night-star wooes her,
But she will not go to Star-land,
Will not twinkle in the starlight,
Through the dreary nights in winter.

Lovers come from distant Ehstland,
Others come from far-off Ingern,
But they cannot win the maiden,
This the answer that she gives them

"Vainly are your praises lavished
Vainly is your silver offered,
Wealth and praise are no temptation;
Never shall I go to Ehstland,
Never shall I go a-rowing
On the waters of the Ingern,
Shall not cross the Sahri-waters,
Never eat the fish of Ehstland,
Never taste the Ehstland viands.
Ingerland shall never see me,
Will not row upon her rivers,
Will not step within her borders;
Hunger there, and fell starvation,
Wood is absent, fuel wanting,
Neither water, wheat, nor barley,
Even rye is not abundant."

Lemminkainen of the islands,
Warlike hero, Kaukomieli,
Undertakes to win the maiden,
Woo and win the Sahri-flower,
Win a bride so highly honoured,
Win the maid with golden tresses,
Win the Sahri maid of beauty;
But his mother gives him warning:
"Nay," replies his gray-haired mother,
"Do not woo, my son beloved,
Maiden of a higher station;
She will never make thee happy
With her lineage of Sahri."

Spake the hero, Lemminkainen,
These the words of Kaukomieli:
"Should I come from lowly station,
Though my tribe is not the highest,
I shall woo to please my fancy,
Woo the maiden fair and lovely,
Choose a wife for worth
and beauty."
This the anxious mother's answer:
"Lemminkainen, son beloved,
Listen to advice maternal:
Do not go to distant Sahri,
To her tribe of many branches;
All the maidens there will
taunt thee,
All the women will deride thee."

Lemminkainen, little hearing,
Answers thus his mother's pleading:
"I will still the sneers of women,
Silence all the taunts of maidens,
I will crush their haughty bosoms,
Smite the hands and cheeks of infants;
Surely this will check their insults,
Fitting ending to derision!"
This the answer of the mother:
"Woe is me, my son beloved!
Woe is me, my life hard-fated!
Shouldst thou taunt the Sahri daughters,
Or insult the maids of virtue,
Shouldst thou laugh them to derision,
There will rise a great contention,
Fierce the battle that will follow.
All the hosts of Sahri-suitors,
Armed in thousands will attack thee,
And will slay thee for thy folly."

Nothing listing, Lemminkainen,
Heeding not his mother's warning,
Led his war-horse from the stables,
Quickly hitched the fiery charger,
Fleetly drove upon his journey,
To the distant Sahri-village,
There to woo the Sahri-flower,
There to win the Bride of Beauty.

All the aged Sahri-women,
All the young and lovely maidens
Laughed to scorn the coming stranger
Driving careless through the alleys,
Wildly driving through the court-yard,
Now upsetting in the gate-way,
Breaking shaft, and hame, and runner.

Then the fearless Lemminkainen,
Mouth awry and visage wrinkled,
Shook his sable locks and answered:
"Never in my recollection
Have I heard or seen such treatment,
Never have I been derided,
Never suffered sneers of women,
Never suffered scorn of virgins,
Not in my immortal life-time.
Is there any place befitting
On the Sahri-plains and pastures,
Where to join in songs and dances?
Is there here a hall for pleasure,
Where the Sahri-maidens linger,
Merry maids with braided tresses?"

Thereupon the Sahri-maidens
Answered from their promontory:
"Room enough is there in Sahri,
Room upon the Sahri-pastures,
Room for pleasure-halls and dances;
Sing and dance upon our meadows,
Be a shepherd on the mountains,
Shepherd-boys have room for dancing;
Indolent the Sahri-children,
But the colts are fat and frisky."

Little caring, Lemminkainen
Entered service there as shepherd,
In the daytime on the pastures,
In the evening, making merry
At the games of lively maidens,
At the dances with the virgins,
With the maids with braided tresses.
Thus it was that Lemminkainen,
Thus the shepherd, Kaukomieli,
Quickly hushed the women's laughter,
Quickly quenched the taunts of maidens,
Quickly silenced their derision.
All the dames and Sahri-daughters
Soon were feasting Lemminkainen,
At his side they danced and lingered.
Only was there one among them,
One among the Sahri-virgins,
Harbored neither love nor wooers,
Favoured neither gods nor heroes,
This the lovely maid Kyllikki,
This the Sahri's fairest flower.
Lemminkainen, full of pleasure,
Handsome hero, Kaukomieli,
Rowed a hundred boats in pieces,
Pulled a thousand oars to fragments,
While he wooed the Maid of Beauty,
Tried to win the fair Kyllikki.

Finally the lovely maiden,
Fairest daughter of the Northland,

Thus addresses Lemminkainen:
"Why dost linger here, thou weak one,
Why dost murmur on these borders,
Why come wooing at my fireside,
Wooing me in belt of copper?
Have no time to waste upon thee,
Rather give this stone its polish,
Rather would I turn the pestle
In the heavy sandstone mortar;
Rather sit beside my mother
In the dwellings of my father.
Never shall I heed thy wooing,
Neither wights nor whisks I care for,
Sooner have a slender husband
Since I have a slender body;
Wish to have him fine of figure,
Since perchance I am well-shapen;
Wish to have him tall and stately,
Since my form perchance is queenly;
Never waste thy time in wooing
Sahri's maid and favoured flower."

Time had gone but little distance,
Scarcely had a month passed over,
When upon a merry evening,
Where the maidens meet for dancing,
In the glen beyond the meadow,
On a level patch of verdure,
Came too soon the maid Kyllikki,
Sahri's pride, the Maid of Beauty;
Quickly followed Lemminkainen,
With his stallion proudly prancing,
Fleetest racer of the Northland,
Fleetly drives beyond the meadow,
Where the maidens meet for dancing,
Snatches quick the maid Kyllikki,
On the settle seats the maiden,
Quickly draws the leathern cover,
And adjusts the brichen cross-bar,
Whips his courser to a gallop.
With a rush, and roar, and rattle,
Speeds he homeward like the
storm-wind,
Speaks these words to those that listen:
"Never, never, anxious maidens,
Must ye give the information,
That I carried off Kyllikki
To my distant home and kindred.
If ye do not heed this order,
Ye shall badly fare as maidens;
I shall sing to war your suitors,
Sing them under spear and broadsword,
That for months, and years, and ages,
Never ye will see their faces,
Never hear their merry voices,
Never will they tread these uplands,
Never will they join these dances,
Never will they drive these highways

Sad the wailing of Kyllikki,
Sad the weeping flower of Sahri!
Listen to her tearful pleading:
"Give, O give me back my freedom,
Free me from the throes of thralldom,
Let this maiden wander homeward,
By some foot-path let me wander
To my father who is grieving,
To my mother who is weeping;
Let me go or I will curse thee!
If thou wilt not give me freedom,
Wilt not let me wander homeward,
Where my loved ones wait my coming,
I have seven stalwart brothers,
Seven sons of father's brother,
Seven sons of mother's sister,
Who pursue the tracks of red-deer,
Hunt the hare upon the heather;
They will follow thee and slay thee,
Thus I'll gain my wished-for freedom."

Lemminkainen, little heeding,
Would not grant the maiden's wishes,
Would not heed her plea for mercy.

Spake again the waiting virgin,
Pride and beauty of the Northland:
"Joyful was I with my kindred,
Joyful born and softly nurtured;
Merrily I spent my childhood,
Happy I, in virgin-freedom,
In the dwelling of my father,
By the bedside of my mother,
With my lineage in Sahri;
But alas! all joy has vanished,

All my happiness departed,
All my maiden beauty waneth
Since I met thine evil spirit,
Shameless hero of dishonour,
Cruel fighter of the islands,
Merciless in civil combat."

Spake the hero, Lemminkainen,
These the words of Kaukomieli:
"Dearest maiden, fair Kyllikki,
My sweet strawberry of Pohya,
Still thine anguish, cease thy weeping,
Be thou free from care and sorrow,
Never shall I do thee evil,
Never will my hands maltreat thee,
Never will mine arms abuse thee,
Never will my tongue revile thee,
Never will my heart deceive thee.

"Tell me why thou hast this anguish,
Why thou hast this bitter sorrow,
Why this sighing and lamenting,
Tell me why this wail of sadness?
Banish all thy cares and sorrows,
Dry thy tears and still thine anguish,
I have cattle, food, and shelter,
I have home, and friends, and kindred,
Kine upon the plains and uplands,
In the marshes berries plenty,
Strawberries upon the mountains;
I have kine that need no milking,
Handsome kine that need no feeding,
Beautiful if not well-tended;
Need not tie them up at evening,
Need not free them in the morning,
Need not hunt them, need not feed them,
Need not give them salt nor water.

"Thinkest thou my race is lowly,
Dost thou think me born ignoble,
Does my lineage agrieve thee?
Was not born in lofty station,
From a tribe of noble heroes,
From a worthy race descended;
But I have a sword of fervor,
And a spear yet filled with courage,
Surely these are well descended,
These were born from hero-races,
Sharpened by the mighty Hisi,
By the gods were forged and burnished;
Therefore will I give thee greatness,
Greatness of my race and nation,
With my broadsword filled with fervor,
With my spear still filled with courage."

Anxiously the sighing maiden
Thus addresses Lemminkainen:
"O thou Ahti, son of Lempo,
Wilt thou take this trusting virgin,
As thy faithful life-companion,
Take me under thy protection,
Be to me a faithful husband,
Swear to me an oath of honour,
That thou wilt not go to battle,
When for gold thou hast a longing,
When thou wishest gold and silver?"
This is Lemminkainen's answer:
"I will swear an oath of honour,
That I'll never go to battle,
When for gold I feel a longing,
When I wish for gold and silver.
Swear thou also on thine honour,
Thou wilt go not to the village,
When desire for dance impels thee,
Wilt not visit village-dances."

Thus the two made oath together,
Registered their vows in heaven,
Vowed before omniscient Ukko,
Ne'er to go to war vowed Ahti,
Never to the dance, Kyllikki.

Lemminkainen, full of joyance,
Snapped his whip above his courser,
Whipped his racer to a gallop,
And these words the hero uttered:
"Fare ye well, ye Sahri-meadows,
Roots of firs, and stumps of birch-trees.
That I wandered through in summer,
That I travelled o'er in winter,
Where ofttimes in rainy seasons,
At the evening hour I lingered,
When I sought to win the virgin,
Sought to win the Maid of Beauty,

Fairest of the Sahri-flowers.
Fare ye well, ye Sahri-woodlands,
Seas and oceans, lakes and rivers,
Vales and mountains, isles and inlets,
Once the home of fair Kyllikki!"

Quick the racer galloped homeward,
Galloped on along the highway,
Toward the meadows of Wainola,
To the plains of Kalevala.

As they neared the Ahti-dwellings,
Thus Kyllikki spake in sorrow:
"Cold and drear is thy cottage,
Seeming like a place deserted;
Who may own this dismal cabin,
Who the one so little honoured?"

Spake the hero, Lemminkainen,
These the words that Ahti uttered:
"Do not grieve about my cottage,
Have no care about my chambers;
I shall build thee other dwellings,
I shall fashion them much better,
Beams, and posts, and sills, and rafters,
Fashioned from the sacred birch-wood."

Now they reach the home of Ahti,
Lemminkainen's home and birthplace,
Enter they his mother's cottage;
There they meet his aged mother,
These the words the mother uses:
"Long indeed hast thou been absent,
Long in foreign lands hast wandered,
Long in Sahri thou hast lingered!"
This is Lemminkainen's answer:
"All the host of Sahri-women,
All the chaste and lovely maidens,
All the maids with braided tresses,
Well have paid for their derision,
For their scorn and for their laughter,
That they basely heaped upon me.
I have brought the best among them
In my sledge to this thy cottage;
Well I wrapped her in my fur-robes,
Kept her warm enwrapped in bear-skin,
Brought her to my mother's dwelling,
As my faithful life-companion;
Thus I paid the scornful maidens,
Paid them well for their derision.

"Cherished mother of my being,
I have found the long-sought jewel,
I have won the Maid of Beauty.
Spread our couch with finest linen,
For our heads the softest pillows,
On our table rarest viands,
So that I may dwell in pleasure
With my spouse, the bride of honour,
With the pride of distant Sahri."
This the answer of the mother:
"Be thou praised, O gracious Ukko,
Loudly praised, O thou Creator,
Since thou givest me a daughter,
Ahti's bride, my second daughter,
Who can stir the fire at evening,
Who can weave me finest fabrics,
Who can twirl the useful spindle,
Who can rinse my silken ribbons,
Who can full the richest garments.

"Son beloved, praise thy Maker,
For the winning of this virgin,
Pride and joy of distant Sahri!
Kind indeed is thy Creator,
Wise the ever-knowing Ukko!
Pure the snow upon the mountains,
Purer still thy Bride of Beauty;
White the foam upon the ocean,
Whiter still her virgin-spirit;
Graceful on the lakes, the
white-swan,
Still more graceful, thy companion;
Beautiful the stars in heaven,
Still more beautiful, Kyllikki.
Larger make our humble cottage,
Wider build the doors and windows,
Fashion thou the ceilings higher,
Decorate the walls in beauty,
Now that thou a bride hast taken
From a tribe of higher station,
Purest maiden of creation,
From the meadow-lands of Sahri,
From the upper shores of Northland."

Rune XII: Kyllikki's Broken Vow

Lemminkainen, artful husband,
Reckless hero, Kaukomieli,
Constantly beside his young wife,
Passed his life in sweet contentment,
And the years rolled swiftly onward;
Ahti thought not of the battles,
Nor Kyllikki of the dances.
Once upon a time it happened
That the hero, Lemminkainen,
Went upon the lake a-fishing,
Was not home at early evening,
As the cruel night descended;
To the village went Kyllikki,
To the dance of merry maidens.

Who will tell the evil story,
Who will bear the information
To the husband, Lemminkainen?
Ahti's sister tells the story,
And the sister's name, Ainikki.

Soon she spreads the cruel tidings,
Straightway gives the information,
Of Kyllikki's perjured honour,
These the words Ainikki utters:
"Ahti, my beloved brother,
To the village went Kyllikki,
To the hall of many strangers,
To the plays and village dances,
With the young men and the maidens,
With the maids of braided tresses,
To the halls of joy and pleasure."

Lemminkainen, much dejected,
Broken-hearted, flushed with anger,
Spake these words in measured accents:
"Mother dear, my gray-haired mother,
Wilt thou straightway wash my linen
In the blood of poison-serpents,
In the black blood of the adder?
I must hasten to the combat,
To the camp-fires of the Northland,
To the battle-fields of Lapland;
To the village went Kyllikki,
To the play of merry maidens,
To the games and village dances,
With the maids of braided tresses."
Straightway speaks the wife, Kyllikki:
"My beloved husband, Ahti,
Do not go to war, I pray thee.
In the evening I lay sleeping,
Slumbering I saw in dream-land
Fire upshooting from the chimney,
Flames arising, mounting skyward,
From the windows of this dwelling,
From the summits of these rafters,
Piercing through our upper chambers,
Roaring like the fall of waters,
Leaping from the floor and ceiling,
Darting from the halls and doorways."

But the doubting Lemminkainen
Makes this answer to Kyllikki:
"I discredit dreams of women,
Have no faith in vows of maidens!
Faithful mother of my being,
Hither bring my mail of copper;
Strong desire is stirring in me
For the cup of deadly combat,
For the mead of martial conquest."
This the pleading mother's answer:
"Lemminkainen, son beloved,
Do not go to war I pray thee;
We have foaming beer abundant,
In our vessels beer of barley,
Held in casks by oaken spigots;
Drink this beer of peace and pleasure,
Let us drink of it together."
Spake the hero, Lemminkainen:
"I shall taste no more the viands,
In the home of false Kyllikki;
Rather would I drink the water
From the painted tips of birch-oars;
Sweeter far to me the water,
Than the beverage of dishonour,
At my mother's home and fireside!

"Hither bring my martial doublet,
Bring me now the sword of battle,
Bring my father's sword of honour;

I must go to upper Northland,
To the battle-fields of Lapland,
There to win me gold and silver."
This the anxious mother's answer:
"My beloved Kaukomieli,
We have gold in great abundance,
Gold and silver in the store-room;
Recently upon the uplands,
In the early hours of morning,
Toiled the workmen in the corn-fields,
Plowed the meadows filled with serpents,
When the plowshare raised the cover
From a chest of gold and silver,
Countless was the gold uncovered,
Hid beneath the grassy meadow;
This the treasure I have brought thee,
Take the countless gold in welcome."
Spake the hero, Lemminkainen:
"Do not wish thy household silver,
From the wars I'll earn my silver;
Gold and silver from the combat
Are to me of greater value
Than the wealth thou hast discovered.
Bring me now my heavy armor,
Bring me too my spear and broadsword;
To the Northland I must hasten,
To the bloody wars of Lapland,
Thither does my pride impel me,
Thitherward my heart is turning.

"I have heard a tale of Lapland,
Some believe the wondrous story,
That a maid in Pimentola
Lives that does not care for suitors,
Does not care for bearded heroes."
This the aged mother's answer:
"Warlike Ahti, son beloved,
In thy home thou hast Kyllikki,
Fairest wife of all the islands;
Strange to see two wives abiding
In the home of but one husband."
Spake the hero, Lemminkainen:
"To the village runs Kyllikki;
Let her run to village dances,
Let her sleep in other dwellings,
With the village youth find pleasure,
With the maids of braided tresses."
Seeks the mother to detain him,
Thus the anxious mother answers:
"Do not go, my son beloved,
Ignorant of Pohya-witchcraft,
To the distant homes of Northland
Till thou hast the art of magic,
Till thou hast some little wisdom;
Do not go to fields of battle,
To the fires of Northland's children,
To the slaughter-fields of Lapland,
Till of magic thou art master.
There the Lapland maids will charm thee,
Turyalanders will bewitch thee,
Sing thy visage into charcoal,
Head and shoulders to the furnace,
Into ashes sing thy fore-arm,
Into fire direct thy footsteps."
Spake the warlike Lemminkainen:
"Wizards often have bewitched me,
And the fascinating serpents;
Lapland wizards, three in number,
On an eve in time of summer,
Sitting on a rock at twilight,
Not a garment to protect them,
Once bewitched me with their magic;
This much they have taken from me,
This the sum of all my losses:
What the hatchet gains from flint-stone,
What the auger bores from granite,
What the heel chips from the iceberg,
And what death purloins from tomb-stones.

"Horribly the wizards threatened,
Tried to sink me with their magic,
In the water of the marshes,
In the mud and treacherous quicksand,
To my chin in mire and water;
But I too was born a hero,
Born a hero and magician,
Was not troubled by their magic.

"Straightway I began my singing,
Sang the archers with their arrows,
Sang the spearmen with their weapons,
Sang the swordsmen with their poniards,
Sang the singers with their singing,

The enchanters with their magic,
To the rapids of the rivers,
To the highest fall of waters,
To the all-devouring whirlpool,
To the deepest depths of ocean,
Where the wizards still are sleeping,
Sleeping till the grass shoots upward
Through the beards and wrinkled faces,
Through the locks of the enchanters,
As they sleep beneath the billows."
Still entreats the anxious mother,
Still beseeches Lemminkainen,
Trying to restrain the hero,
While Kyllikki begs forgiveness;
This the language of the mother:
"Do not go, my son beloved,
To the villages of Northland,
Nor to Lapland's frigid borders;
Dire misfortune will befall thee,
Star of evil settle o'er thee,
Lemminkainen's end, destruction.

"Couldst thou speak in tongues a hundred,
I could not believe thee able,
Through the magic of thy singing,
To enchant the sons of Lapland
To the bottom of the ocean;
Dost not know the Tury-language,
Canst but speak the tongue of Suomi,
Canst not win by witless magic."

Lemminkainen, reckless hero,
Also known as Kaukomieli,
Stood beside his mother, combing
Out his sable locks and musing,
Brushing down his beard, debating,
Steadfast still in his decision,
Quickly hurls his brush in anger,
Hurls it to the wall opposing,
Gives his mother final answer,
These the words that Ahti uses:
"Dire misfortune will befall me,
Some sad fate will overtake me,
Evil come to Lemminkainen,
When the blood flows from that hair-brush,
When blood oozes from those bristles."
Thus the warlike Lemminkainen
Goes to never-pleasant Lapland,
Heeding not his mother's warning,
Heeding not her prohibition.

Thus the hero, Kaukomieli,
Quick equips himself for warfare,
On his head a copper helmet,
On his shoulders caps of copper,
On his body iron armor,
Steel, the belt around his body;
As he girds himself for battle,
Ahti thus soliloquizing:
"Strong the hero in his armor,
Strong indeed in copper helmet,
Powerful in mail of iron,
Stronger far than any hero
On the dismal shores of Lapland,
Need not fear their wise enchanters,
Need not fear their strongest foemen,
Need not fear a war with wizards."

Grasped he then the sword of battle,
Firmly grasped the heavy broadsword
That Tuoni had been grinding,
That the gods had brightly burnished,
Thrust it in the leathern scabbard,
Tied the scabbard to his armor.

How do heroes guard from danger,
Where protect themselves from evil?
Heroes guard their homes and firesides,
Guard their doors, and roofs, and windows,
Guard the posts that hold the torch-lights,
Guard the highways to the court-yard,
Guard the ends of all the gate-ways.
Heroes guard themselves from women,
Carefully from merry maidens;
If in this their strength be wanting,
Easy fall the heroes, victims
To the snares of the enchanters.
Furthermore are heroes watchful
Of the tribes of warlike giants,
Where the highway doubly branches,
On the borders of the blue-rock,
On the marshes filled with evil,
Near the mighty fall of waters,
Near the circling of the whirlpool,

Near the fiery springs and rapids.
Spake the stout-heart, Lemminkainen:
"Rise ye heroes of the broadsword,
Ye, the earth's eternal heroes,
From the deeps, ye sickle-bearers,
From the brooks, ye crossbow-shooters,
Come, thou forest, with thine archers,
Come, ye thickets, with your armies,
Mountain spirits, with your powers,
Come, fell Hisi, with thy horrors,
Water-mother, with thy dangers,
Come, Wellamo, with thy mermaids,
Come, ye maidens from the valleys,
Come, ye nymphs from winding rivers,
Be protection to this hero,
Be his day-and-night companions,
Body-guard to Lemminkainen,
Thus to blunt the spears of wizards,
Thus to dull their pointed arrows,
That the spears of the enchanters,
That the arrows of the archers,
That the weapons of the foemen,
May not harm this bearded hero.

"Should this force be insufficient,
I can call on other powers,
I can call the gods above me,
Call the great god of the heavens,
Him who gives the clouds their courses,
Him who rules through boundless ether,
Who directs the march of storm-winds.

"Ukko, thou O God above me,
Thou the father of creation,
Thou that speakest through the thunder,
Thou whose weapon is the lightning,
Thou whose voice is borne by ether,
Grant me now thy mighty fire-sword,
Give me here thy burning arrows,
Lightning arrows for my quiver,
Thus protect me from all danger,
Guard me from the wiles of witches,
Guide my feet from every evil,
Help me conquer the enchanters,
Help me drive them from the Northland;
Those that stand in front of battle,
Those that fill the ranks behind me,
Those around me, those above me,
Those beneath me, help me banish,
With their knives, and swords,
and cross-bows,
With their spears of keenest temper,
With their tongues of evil magic;
Help me drive these Lapland wizards
To the deepest depths of ocean,
There to wrestle with Wellamo."

Then the reckless Lemminkainen
Whistled loudly for his stallion,
Called the racer from the hurdles,
Called his brown steed from the pasture,
Threw the harness on the courser,
Hitched the fleet-foot to the snow-sledge,
Leaped upon the highest cross-bench,
Cracked his whip above the racer,
And the steed flies onward swiftly,
Bounds the sleigh upon its journey,
And the golden plain re-echoes;
Travels one day, then a second,
Travels all the next day northward,
Till the third day evening brings him
To a sorry Northland village,
On the dismal shores of Lapland.

Here the hero, Lemminkainen,
Drove along the lowest highway,
Through the streets along the border,
To a court-yard in the hamlet,
Asked one standing in the doorway:
"Is there one within this dwelling,
That can loose my stallion's breastplate,
That can lift his heavy collar,
That these shafts can rightly lower?"

On the floor a babe was playing,
And the young child gave this answer:
"There is no one in this dwelling
That can loose thy stallion's breastplate,
That can lift his heavy collar,
That the shafts can rightly lower."

Lemminkainen, not discouraged,
Whips his racer to a gallop,
Rushes forward through the village,

On the middle of the highways,
To the court-yard in the centre,
Asks one standing in the threshold,
Leaning on the penthouse door-posts:
"Is there any one here dwelling
That can slip my stallion's bridle,
That can loose his leathern breast-straps,
That can tend my royal racer?"

From the fire-place spake a wizard,
From her bench the witch made answer:
"Thou canst find one in this dwelling,
That can slip thy courser's bridle,
That can loose his heavy breastplate,
That can tend thy royal racer.
There are here a thousand heroes
That can make thee hasten homeward,
That can give thee fleet-foot stallions,
That can chase thee to thy country,
Reckless rascal and magician,
To thy home and fellow minstrels,
To the uplands of thy father,
To the cabins of thy mother,
To the work-bench of thy brother,
To the dairy of thy sister,
Ere the evening star has risen,
Ere the sun retires to slumber."

Lemminkainen, little fearing,
Gives this answer to the wizard:
"I should slay thee for thy pertness,
That thy clatter might be silenced."

Then he whipped his fiery charger,
And the steed flew onward swiftly,
On the upper of the highways,
To the court-yard on the summit.

When the reckless Lemminkainen
Had approached the upper court-yard,
Uttered he the words that follow:
"O thou Hisi, stuff this watch-dog,
Lempo, stuff his throat and nostrils,
Close the mouth of this wild barker,
Bridle well the vicious canine,
That the watcher may be silent
While the hero passes by him."

Then he stepped within the court-room,
With his whip he struck the flooring,
From the floor arose a vapor,
In the fog appeared a pigmy,
Who unhitched the royal racer,
From his back removed the harness,
Gave the weary steed attention.
Then the hero, Lemminkainen,
Carefully advanced and listened.
No one saw the strange magician,
No one heard his cautious footsteps;
Heard he songs within the dwelling,
Through the moss-stuffed chinks heard voices,
Through the walls he heard them singing,
Through the doors the peals of laughter.

Then he spied within the court-rooms,
Lurking slyly in the hall-ways,
Found the court-rooms filled with singers,
By the walls were players seated,
Near the doors the wise men hovered,
Skilful ones upon the benches,
Near the fires the wicked wizards;
All were singing songs of Lapland,
Singing songs of evil Hisi.

Now the minstrel, Lemminkainen,
Changes both his form and stature,
Passes through the inner door-ways,
Enters he the spacious court-hall,
And these words the hero utters:
"Fine the singing quickly ending,
Good the song that quickly ceases;
Better far to keep thy wisdom
Than to sing it on the house-tops."

Comes the hostess of Pohyola,
Fleetly rushing through the door-way,
To the centre of the court-room,
And addresses thus the stranger:
"Formerly a dog lay watching,
Was a cur of iron-colour,
Fond of flesh, a bone-devourer,
Loved to lick the blood of strangers.
Who then art thou of the heroes,
Who of all the host of heroes,
That thou art within my court-rooms,

That thou comest to my dwelling,
Was not seen without my portals,
Was not scented by my watch-dogs?"
Spake the reckless Lemminkainen:
"Do not think that I come hither
Having neither wit nor wisdom,
Having neither art nor power,
Wanting in ancestral knowledge,
Lacking prudence of the fathers,
That thy watch-dogs may devour me.

"My devoted mother washed me,
When a frail and tender baby,
Three times in the nights of summer,
Nine times in the nights of autumn,
That upon my journeys northward
I might sing the ancient wisdom,
Thus protect myself from danger;
When at home I sing as wisely
As the minstrels of thy hamlet."

Then the singer, Lemminkainen,
Ancient hero, Kaukomieli,
Quick began his incantations,
Straightway sang the songs of witchcraft,
From his fur-robe darts the lightning,
Flames outshooting from his eye-balls,
From the magic of his singing,
From his wonderful enchantment.
Sang the very best of singers
To the very worst of minstrels,
Filled their mouths with dust
and ashes,
Piled the rocks upon their shoulders,
Stilled the best of Lapland witches,
Stilled the sorcerers and wizards.
Then he banished all their heroes,
Banished all their proudest minstrels,
This one hither, that one thither,
To the lowlands poor in verdure,
To the unproductive uplands,
To the oceans wanting whiting,
To the waterfalls of Rutya,
To the whirlpool hot and flaming,
To the waters decked with sea-foam,
Into fires and boiling waters,
Into everlasting torment.

Then the hero, Lemminkainen,
Sang the foemen with their broadswords,
Sang the heroes with their weapons,
Sang the eldest, sang the youngest,
Sang the middle-aged, enchanted;
Only one he left his senses,
He a poor, defenseless shepherd,
Old and sightless, halt
and wretched,
And the old man's name was Nasshut.
Spake the miserable shepherd:
"Thou hast old and young enchanted,
Thou hast banished all our heroes,
Why hast spared this wretched shepherd?"
This is Lemminkainen's answer:
"Therefore have I not bewitched thee:
Thou art old, and blind,
and wretched
Feeble-minded thou, and harmless,
Loathsome now without my magic.
Thou didst, in thy better life-time,
When a shepherd filled with malice,
Ruin all thy mother's berries,
Make thy sister, too unworthy,
Ruin all thy brother's cattle,
Drive to death thy father's stallions,
Through the marshes, o'er the meadows,
Through the lowlands, o'er the mountains,
Heeding not thy mother's counsel."

Thereupon the wretched Nasshut,
Angry grew and swore for vengeance,
Straightway limping through the
door-way,
Hobbled on beyond the court-yard,
O'er the meadow-lands and pastures,
To the river of the deathland,
To the holy stream and whirlpool,
To the kingdom of Tuoni,
To the islands of Manala;
Waited there for Kaukomieli,
Listened long for Lemminkainen,
Thinking he must pass this river
On his journey to his country,
On the highway to the islands,
From the upper shores of Pohya,
From the dreary Sariola.

Rune XIII: Lemminkainen's Second Wooing

Spake the ancient Lemminkainen
To the hostess of Pohyola:
"Give to me thy lovely daughter,
Bring me now thy winsome maiden,
Bring the best of Lapland virgins,
Fairest virgin of the Northland."
Louhi, hostess of Pohyola,
Answered thus the wild magician:
"I shall never give my daughter,
Never give my fairest maiden,
Not the best one, nor the worst one,
Not the largest, nor the smallest;
Thou hast now one wife-companion,
Thou has taken hence one hostess,
Carried off the fair Kyllikki."

This is Lemminkainen's answer:
"To my home I took Kyllikki,
To my cottage on the island,
To my entry-gates and kindred;
Now I wish a better hostess,
Straightway bring thy fairest daughter,
Worthiest of all thy virgins,
Fairest maid with sable tresses."
Spake the hostess of Pohyola:
"Never will I give my daughter
To a hero false and worthless,
To a minstrel vain and evil;
Therefore, pray thou for my maiden,
Therefore, woo the sweet-faced flower,
When thou bringest me the wild-moose
From the Hisi fields and forests."

Then the artful Lemminkainen
Deftly whittled out his javelins,
Quickly made his leathern bow-string,
And prepared his bow and arrows,
And soliloquized as follows:
"Now my javelins are made ready,
All my arrows too are ready,
And my oaken cross-bow bended,
But my snow-shoes are not builded,
Who will make me worthy snow-shoes?"
Lemminkainen, grave and thoughtful,
Long reflected, well considered,
Where the snow-shoes could be fashioned,
Who the artist that could make them;
Hastened to the Kauppi-smithy,
To the smithy of Lylikki,
Thus addressed the snow-shoe artist:
"O thou skilful Woyalander,
Kauppi, ablest smith of Lapland,
Make me quick two worthy snow-shoes,
Smooth them well and make them hardy,
That in Tapio the wild-moose,
Roaming through the Hisi-forests,
I may catch and bring to Louhi,
As a dowry for her daughter."

Then Lylikki thus made answer,
Kauppi gave this prompt decision:
"Lemminkainen, reckless minstrel,
Thou wilt hunt in vain the wild-moose,
Thou wilt catch but pain and torture,
In the Hisi fens and forests."

Little heeding, Lemminkainen
Spake these measures to Lylikki:
"Make for me the worthy snow-shoes,
Quickly work and make them ready;
Go I will and catch the blue-moose
Where in Tapio it browses,
In the Hisi woods and snow-fields."

Then Lylikki, snow-shoe-maker,
Ancient Kauppi, master artist,
Whittled in the fall his show-shoes,
Smoothed them in the winter evenings,
One day working on the runners,
All the next day making stick-rings,
Till at last the shoes were finished,
And the workmanship was perfect.
Then he fastened well the shoe-straps,
Smooth as adder's skin the woodwork,
Soft as fox-fur were the stick-rings;
Oiled he well his wondrous snow-shoes
With the tallow of the reindeer;
When he thus soliloquizes,

These the accents of Lylikki:
"Is there any youth in Lapland,
Any in this generation,
That can travel in these snow-shoes,
That can move the lower sections?"

Spake the reckless Lemminkainen,
Full of hope, and life, and vigor:
"Surely there is one in Lapland.
In this rising generation,
That can travel in these snow-shoes,
That the right and left can manage."

To his back he tied the quiver,
Placed the bow upon his shoulder,
With both hands he grasped his snow-cane,
Speaking meanwhile words as follow:
"There is nothing in the woodlands,
Nothing in the world of Ukko,
Nothing underneath the heavens,
In the uplands, in the lowlands,
Nothing in the snow-fields running,
Not a fleet deer of the forest,
That could not be overtaken
With the snow-shoes of Lylikki,
With the strides of Lemminkainen."

Wicked Hisi heard these measures,
Juutas listened to their echoes;
Straightway Hisi called the wild-moose,
Juutas fashioned soon a reindeer,
And the head was made of punk-wood,
Horns of naked willow branches,
Feet were furnished by the rushes,
And the legs, by reeds aquatic,
Veins were made of withered grasses,
Eyes, from daisies of the meadows,
Ears were formed of water-flowers,
And the skin of tawny fir-bark,
Out of sappy wood, the muscles,
Fair and fleet, the magic reindeer.

Juutas thus instructs the wild-moose,
These the words of wicked Hisi:
"Flee away, thou moose of Juutas,
Flee away, thou Hisi-reindeer,
Like the winds, thou rapid courser,
To the snow-homes of the ranger,
To the ridges of the mountains,
To the snow-capped hills of Lapland,
That thy hunter may be worn out,
Thy pursuer be tormented,
Lemminkainen be exhausted."

Thereupon the Hisi-reindeer,
Juutas-moose with branching antlers,
Fleetly ran through fen and forest,
Over Lapland's hills and valleys,
Through the open fields and court-yards,
Through the penthouse doors and gate-ways,
Turning over tubs of water,
Threw the kettles from the fire-pole,
And upset the dishes cooking.
Then arose a fearful uproar,
In the court-yards of Pohyola,
Lapland-dogs began their barking,
Lapland-children cried in terror,
Lapland-women roared with laughter,
And the Lapland-heroes shouted.

Fleetly followed Lemminkainen,
Followed fast, and followed faster,
Hastened on behind the wild-moose,
Over swamps and through
the woodlands,
Over snow-fields vast and pathless,
Over high uprising mountains,
Fire out-shooting from his runners,
Smoke arising from his snow-cane:
Could not hear the wild-moose bounding,
Could not sight the flying fleet-foot;
Glided on through field and forest,
Glided over lakes and rivers,
Over lands beyond the smooth-sea,
Through the desert plains of Hisi,
Glided o'er the plains of Kalma,
Through the kingdom of Tuoni,
To the end of Kalma's empire,
Where the jaws of Death stand open,
Where the head of Kalma lowers,
Ready to devour the stranger,
To devour wild Lemminkainen;
But Tuoni cannot reach him,
Kalma cannot overtake him.

Distant woods are yet untravelled,
Far away a woodland corner
Stands unsearched by Kaukomieli,
In the North's extensive borders,
In the realm of dreary Lapland.
Now the hero, on his snow-shoes,
Hastens to the distant woodlands,
There to hunt the moose of Piru.
As he nears the woodland corner,
There he hears a frightful uproar,
From the Northland's distant borders,
From the dreary fields of Lapland,
Hears the dogs as they are barking,
Hears the children loudly screaming,
Hears the laughter of the women,
Hears the shouting of the heroes.
Thereupon wild Lemminkainen
Hastens forward on his snow-shoes,
To the place where dogs are barking,
To the distant woods of Lapland.

When the reckless Kaukomieli
Had approached this Hisi corner,
Straightway he began to question:
"Why this laughter of the women,
Why the screaming of the children,
Why the shouting of the heroes,
Why this barking of the watch-dogs?"
This reply was promptly given:
"This the reason for this uproar,
Women laughing, children screaming,
Heroes shouting, watch-dogs barking:
Hisi's moose came running hither,
Hither came the Piru-Reindeer,
Hither came with hoofs of silver,
Through the open fields and court-yards,
Through the penthouse doors and gate-ways,
Turning over tubs of water,
Threw the kettles from the fire-pole,
And upset the dishes cooking."

Then the hero, Lemminkainen,
Straightway summoned all his courage,
Pushed ahead his mighty snow-shoes,
Swift as adders in the stubble,
Levelled bushes in the marshes,
Like the swift and fiery serpents,
Spake these words of magic import,
Keeping balance with his snow-staff:
"Come thou might of Lapland heroes,
Bring to me the moose of Juutas;
Come thou strength of Lapland-women,
And prepare the boiling caldron;
Come, thou might of Lapland children,
Bring together fire and fuel;
Come, thou strength of Lapland-kettles,
Help to boil the Hisi wild-moose."

Then with mighty force and courage,
Lemminkainen hastened onward,
Striking backward, shooting forward;
With a long sweep of his snow-shoe,
Disappeared from view the hero;
With the second, shooting further,
Was the hunter out of hearing;
With the third the hero glided
On the shoulders of the wild-moose;
Took a pole of stoutest oak-wood,
Took some bark-strings from the willow,
Wherewithal to bind the moose-deer,
Bind him to his oaken hurdle.
To the moose he spake as follows:
"Here remain, thou moose of Juutas
Skip about, my bounding courser,
In my hurdle jump and frolic,
Captive from the fields of Piru,
From the Hisi glens and mountains."

Then he stroked the captured wild-moose,
Patted him upon his forehead,
Spake again in measured accents:
"I would like awhile to linger,
I would love to rest a moment
In the cottage of my maiden,
With my virgin, young and lovely."

Then the Hisi-moose grew angry,
Stamped his feet and shook his antlers,
Spake these words to Lemminkainen:
"Surely Lempo soon will got thee,
Shouldst thou sit beside the maiden,
Shouldst thou linger by the virgin."

Now the wild-moose stamps and rushes,
Tears in two the bands of willow,
Breaks the oak-wood pole in pieces,
And upturns the hunter's hurdle,
Quickly leaping from his captor,
Bounds away with strength of freedom,
Over hills and over lowlands,
Over swamps and over snow-fields,
Over mountains clothed in heather,
That the eye may not behold him,
Nor the hero's ear detect him.

Thereupon the mighty hunter
Angry grows, and much disheartened,
Starts again the moose to capture,
Gliding off behind the courser.
With his might he plunges forward;
At the instep breaks his snow-shoe,
Breaks the runners into fragments,
On the mountings breaks his javelins,
In the centre breaks his snow-staff,
And the moose bounds on before him,
Through the Hisi-woods and snow-fields,
Out of reach of Lemminkainen.

Then the reckless Kaukomieli
Looked with bended head, ill-humored,
One by one upon the fragments,
Speaking words of ancient wisdom:
"Northland hunters, never, never,
Go defiant to thy forests,
In the Hisi vales and mountains,
There to hunt the moose of Juutas,
Like this senseless, reckless hero;
I have wrecked my magic snow-shoes,
Ruined too my useful snow-staff,
And my javelins I have broken,
While the wild-moose runs in safety
Through the Hisi fields and forests."

Rune XIV: Death of Lemminkainen

Lemminkainen, much disheartened,
Deeply thought and long considered,
What to do, what course to follow,
Whether best to leave the wild-moose
In the fastnesses of Hisi,
And return to Kalevala,
Or a third time hunt the ranger,
Hoping thus to bring him captive,
Thus return at last a victor
To the forest home of Louhi,
To the joy of all her daughters,
To the wood-nymph's happy fireside.

Taking courage Lemminkainen
Spake these words in supplication:
"Ukko, thou O God above me,
Thou Creator of the heavens,
Put my snow-shoes well in order,
And endow them both with swiftness,
That I rapidly may journey
Over marshes, over snow-fields,
Over lowlands, over highlands,
Through the realms of wicked Hisi,
Through the distant plains of Lapland,
Through the paths of Lempo's wild-moose,
To the forest hills of Juutas.
To the snow-fields shall I journey,
Leave the heroes to the woodlands,
On the way to Tapiola,
Into Tapio's wild dwellings.

"Greeting bring I to the mountains,
Greeting to the vales and uplands,
Greet ye, heights with forests covered,
Greet ye, ever-verdant fir trees,
Greet ye, groves of whitened aspen,
Greetings bring to those that greet you,
Fields, and streams, and woods of Lapland.
Bring me favour, mountain-woodlands,
Lapland-deserts, show me kindness,
Mighty Tapio, be gracious,
Let me wander through thy forests,
Let me glide along thy rivers,
Let this hunter search thy snow-fields,
Where the wild-moose herds in numbers
Where the bounding reindeer lingers.

"O Nyrikki, mountain hero,
Son of Tapio of forests,
Hero with the scarlet head-gear,
Notches make along the pathway,
Landmarks upward to the mountains,
That this hunter may not wander,
May not fall, and falling perish
In the snow-fields of thy kingdom,
Hunting for the moose of Hisi,
Dowry for the pride of Northland.

"Mistress of the woods, Mielikki,
Forest-mother, formed in beauty,
Let thy gold flow out abundant,
Let thy silver onward wander,
For the hero that is seeking
For the wild-moose of thy kingdom;
Bring me here thy keys of silver,
From the golden girdle round thee;
Open Tapio's rich chambers,
And unlock the forest fortress,
While I here await the booty,
While I hunt the moose of Lempo.

"Should this service be too menial
Give the order to thy servants,
Send at once thy servant-maidens,
And command it to thy people.
Thou wilt never seem a hostess,
If thou hast not in thy service,
Maidens ready by the hundreds,
Thousands that await thy bidding,
Who thy herds may watch and nurture,
Tend the game of thy dominions.

"Tall and slender forest-virgin,
Tapio's beloved daughter,
Blow thou now thy honey flute-notes,
Play upon thy forest-whistle,
For the hearing of thy mistress,
For thy charming woodland-mistress,
Make her hear thy sweet-toned playing,
That she may arise from slumber.
Should thy mistress not awaken
At the calling of thy flute-notes,
Play again, and play unceasing,
Make the golden tongue re-echo."

Wild and daring Lemminkainen
Steadfast prays upon his journey,
Calling on the gods for succor,
Hastens off through fields and moorlands,
Passes on through cruel brush-wood,
To the colliery of Hisi,
To the burning fields of Lempo;
Glided one day, then a second,
Glided all the next day onward,
Till he came to Big-stone mountain,
Climbed upon its rocky summit,
Turned his glances to the northwest,
Toward the Northland moors and marshes;
There appeared the Tapio-mansion.
All the doors were golden-coloured,
Shining in the gleam of sunlight
Through the thickets on the mountains,
Through the distant fields of Northland.

Lemminkainen, much encouraged,
Hastens onward from his station
Through the lowlands, o'er the uplands,
Over snow-fields vast and vacant,
Under snow-robed firs and aspens,
Hastens forward, happy-hearted,
Quickly reaches Tapio's court-yards,
Halts without at Tapio's windows,
Slyly looks into her mansion,
Spies within some kindly women,
Forest-dames outstretched before him,
All are clad in scanty raiment,
Dressed in soiled and ragged linens.
Spake the stranger Lemminkainen:
"Wherefore sit ye, forest-mothers,
In your old and simple garments,
In your soiled and ragged linen?
Ye, forsooth! are too untidy,
Too unsightly your appearance
In your tattered gowns apparelled.
When I lived within the forest,
There were then three mountain castles,
One of horn and one of ivory,
And the third of wood constructed;
In their walls were golden windows,
Six the windows in each castle,
Through these windows I discovered
All the host of Tapio's mansion,

Saw its fair and stately hostess;
Saw great Tapio's lovely daughter,
Saw Tellervo in her beauty,
With her train of charming maidens;
All were dressed in golden raiment,
Rustled all in gold and silver.
Then the forest's queenly hostess,
Still the hostess of these woodlands,
On her arms wore golden bracelets,
Golden rings upon her fingers,
In her hair were sparkling jewels,
On her head were golden fillets,
In her ears were golden ear-rings,
On her neck a pearly necklace,
And her braidlets, silver-tinselled.

"Lovely hostess of the forest,
Metsola's enchanting mistress,
Fling aside thine ugly straw-shoes,
Cast away the shoes of birch-bark,
Doff thy soiled and ragged linen,
Doff thy gown of shabby fabric,
Don the bright and festive raiment,
Don the gown of merry-making,
While I stay within thy borders,
While I seek my forest-booty,
Hunt the moose of evil Hisi.
Here my visit will be irksome,
Here thy guest will be ill-humored,
Waiting in thy fields and woodlands,
Hunting here the moose of Lempo,
Finding not the Hisi-ranger,
Shouldst thou give me no enjoyment,
Should I find no joy, nor respite.
Long the eve that gives no pleasure,
Long the day that brings no guerdon!

"Sable-bearded god of forests,
In thy hat and coat of ermine,
Robe thy trees in finest fibers,
Deck thy groves in richest fabrics,
Give the fir trees shining silver,
Deck with gold the slender balsams,
Give the spruces copper belting,
And the pine trees silver girdles,
Give the birches golden flowers,
Deck their stems with silver fret-work,
This their garb in former ages,
When the days and nights were brighter,
When the fir trees shone like sunlight,
And the birches like the moonbeams;
Honey breathed throughout the forest,
Settled in the glens and highlands
Spices in the meadow-borders,
Oil out-pouring from the lowlands.

"Forest daughter, lovely virgin,
Golden maiden, fair Tulikki,
Second of the Tapio-daughters,
Drive the game within these borders,
To these far-extending snow-fields.
Should the reindeer be too sluggish,
Should the moose-deer move too slowly
Cut a birch-rod from the thicket,
Whip them hither in their beauty,
Drive the wild-moose to my hurdle,
Hither drive the long-sought booty
To the hunter who is watching,
Waiting in the Hisi-forests.

"When the game has started hither,
Keep them in the proper highway,
Hold thy magic hands before them,
Guard them well on either road-side,
That the elk may not escape thee,
May not dart adown some by-path.
Should, perchance, the moose-deer wander
Through some by-way of the forest,
Take him by the ears and antlers,
Hither lead the pride of Lempo.

"If the path be filled with brush-wood
Cast the brush-wood to the road-side;
If the branches cross his pathway,
Break the branches into fragments;
Should a fence of fir or alder
Cross the way that leads him hither,
Make an opening within it,
Open nine obstructing fences;
If the way be crossed by streamlets,
If the path be stopped by rivers,
Make a bridge of silken fabric,
Weaving webs of scarlet colour,
Drive the deer-herd gently over,

Lead them gently o'er the waters,
O'er the rivers of thy forests,
O'er the streams of thy dominions.

"Thou, the host of Tapio's mansion,
Gracious host of Tapiola,
Sable-bearded god of woodlands,
Golden lord of Northland forests,
Thou, O Tapio's worthy hostess,
Queen of snowy woods, Mimerkki,
Ancient dame in sky-blue vesture,
Fenland-queen in scarlet ribbons,
Come I to exchange my silver,
To exchange my gold and silver;
Gold I have, as old as moonlight,
Silver of the age of sunshine,
In the first of years was gathered,
In the heat and pain of battle;
It will rust within my pouches,
Soon will wear away and perish,
If it be not used in trading."

Long the hunter, Lemminkainen,
Glided through the fen and forest,
Sang his songs throughout the woodlands,
Through three mountain glens he sang them,
Sang the forest hostess friendly,
Sang he, also, Tapio friendly,
Friendly, all the forest virgins,
All of Metsola's fair daughters.

Now they start the herds of Lempo,
Start the wild-moose from his shelter,
In the realms of evil Hisi,
Tapio's highest mountain-region;
Now they drive the ranger homeward,
To the open courts of Piru,
To the hero that is waiting,
Hunting for the moose of Juutas.

When the herd had reached the castle,
Lemminkainen threw his lasso
O'er the antlers of the blue-moose,
Settled on the neck and shoulders
Of the mighty moose of Hisi.
Then the hunter, Kaukomieli,
Stroked his captive's neck in safety,
For the moose was well-imprisoned.

Thereupon gay Lemminkainen
Filled with joyance spake as follows:
"Pride of forests, queen of woodlands,
Metsola's enchanted hostess,
Lovely forest dame, Mielikki,
Mother-donor of the mountains,
Take the gold that I have promised,
Come and take away the silver;
Spread thy kerchief well before me,
Spread out here thy silken neck-wrap,
Underneath the golden treasure,
Underneath the shining silver,
That to earth it may not settle,
Scattered on the snows of winter."

Then the hero went a victor
To the dwellings of Pohyola,
And addressed these words to Louhi:
"I have caught the moose of Hisi,
In the Metsola-dominions,
Give, O hostess, give thy daughter,
Give to me thy fairest virgin,
Bride of mine to be hereafter."

Louhi, hostess of the Northland,
Gave this answer to the suitor:
"I will give to thee my daughter,
For thy wife my fairest maiden,
When for me thou'lt put a bridle
On the flaming horse of Hisi,
Rapid messenger of Lempo,
On the Hisi-plains and pastures."

Nothing daunted, Lemminkainen
Hastened forward to accomplish
Louhi's second test of heroes,
On the cultivated lowlands,
On the sacred fields and forests.
Everywhere he sought the racer,
Sought the fire-expiring stallion,
Fire out-shooting from his nostrils.
Lemminkainen, fearless hunter,
Bearing in his belt his bridle,
On his shoulders, reins and halter,

Sought one day, and then a second,
Finally, upon the third day,
Went he to the Hisi-mountain,
Climbed, and struggled to the summit;
To the east he turned his glances,
Cast his eyes upon the sunrise,
There beheld the flaming courser,
On the heath among the fir trees.
Lempo's fire-expiring stallion
Fire and mingled smoke out-shooting
From his mouth, and eyes, and nostrils.

Spake the daring Lemminkainen,
This the hero's supplication:
"Ukko, thou O God above me,
Thou that rulest all the storm-clouds,
Open thou the vault of heaven,
Open windows through the ether,
Let the icy rain come falling,
Let the heavy hailstones shower
On the flaming horse of Hisi,
On the fire-expiring stallion."

Ukko, the benign Creator,
Heard the prayer of Lemminkainen,
Broke apart the dome of heaven,
Rent the heights of heaven asunder,
Sent the iron-hail in showers,
Smaller than the heads of horses,
Larger than the heads of heroes,
On the flaming steed of Lempo,
On the fire-expiring stallion,
On the terror of the Northland.

Lemminkainen, drawing nearer,
Looked with care upon the courser,
Then he spake the words that follow:
"Wonder-steed of mighty Hisi,
Flaming horse of Lempo's mountain,
Bring thy mouth of gold, assenting,
Gently place thy head of silver
In this bright and golden halter,
In this silver-mounted bridle.
I shall never harshly treat thee,
Never make thee fly too fleetly,
On the way to Sariola,
On the tracks of long duration,
To the hostess of Pohyola,
To her magic courts and stables,
Will not lash thee on thy journey;
I shall lead thee gently forward,
Drive thee with the reins of kindness,
Cover thee with silken blankets."

Then the fire-haired steed of Juutas,
Flaming horse of mighty Hisi,
Put his head of shining silver,
In the bright and golden head-stall,
In the silver-mounted bridle.
Thus the hero, Lemminkainen,
Easy bridles Lempo's stallion,
Flaming horse of evil Piru;
Lays the bits within his fire-mouth,
On his silver head, the halter,
Mounts the fire-expiring courser,
Brandishes his whip of willow,
Hastens forward on his journey,
Bounding o'er the hills and mountains,
Dashing through the valleys northward,
O'er the snow-capped hills of Lapland,
To the courts of Sariola.

Then the hero, quick dismounting,
Stepped within the court of Louhi,
Thus addressed the Northland hostess:
"I have bridled Lempo's fire-horse,
I have caught the Hisi-racer,
Caught the fire-expiring stallion,
In the Piru plains and pastures,
Ridden him within thy borders;
I have caught the moose of Lempo,
I have done what thou demandest;
Give, I pray thee, now thy daughter,
Give to me thy fairest maiden,
Bride of mine to be forever."

Louhi, hostess of Pohyola,
Made this answer to the suitor:
"I will only give my daughter,
Give to thee my fairest virgin,
Bride of thine to be forever,
When for me the swan thou killest
In the river of Tuoni,
Swimming in the black death-river,

In the sacred stream and whirlpool;
Thou canst try one cross-bow only,
But one arrow from thy quiver."

Then the reckless Lemminkainen,
Handsome hero, Kaukomieli,
Braved the third test of the hero,
Started out to hunt the wild-swan,
Hunt the long-necked, graceful swimmer,
In Tuoni's coal-black river,
In Manala's lower regions.
Quick the daring hunter journeyed,
Hastened off with fearless footsteps,
To the river of Tuoni,
To the sacred stream and whirlpool,
With his bow upon his shoulder,
With his quiver and one arrow.

Nasshut, blind and crippled shepherd,
Wretched shepherd of Pohyola,
Stood beside the deathland river,
Near the sacred stream and whirlpool,
Guarding Tuonela's waters,
Waiting there for Lemminkainen,
Listening there for Kaukomieli,
Waiting long the hero's coming.
Finally he hears the footsteps
Of the hero on his journey,
Hears the tread of Lemminkainen,
As he journeys nearer, nearer,
To the river of Tuoni,
To the cataract of deathland,
To the sacred stream and whirlpool.
Quick the wretched shepherd, Nasshut,
From the death-stream sends a serpent,
Like an arrow from a cross-bow,
To the heart of Lemminkainen,
Through the vitals of the hero.

Lemminkainen, little conscious,
Hardly knew that he was injured,
Spake these measures as he perished:
"Ah! unworthy is my conduct,
Ah! unwisely have I acted,
That I did not heed my mother,
Did not take her goodly counsel,
Did not learn her words of magic.
Oh! for three words with my mother,
How to live, and how to suffer,
In this time of dire misfortune,
How to bear the stings of serpents,
Tortures of the reed of waters,
From the stream of Tuonela!

"Ancient mother who hast borne me,
Who hast trained me from my childhood,
Learn, I pray thee, where I linger,
Where alas! thy son is lying,
Where thy reckless hero suffers.
Come, I pray thee, faithful mother,
Come thou quickly, thou art needed,
Come deliver me from torture,
From the death-jaws of Tuoni,
From the sacred stream and whirlpool."

Northland's old and wretched shepherd,
Nasshut, the despised protector
Of the flocks of Sariola,
Throws the dying Lemminkainen,
Throws the hero of the islands,
Into Tuonela's river,
To the blackest stream of deathland,
To the worst of fatal whirlpools.
Lemminkainen, wild and daring,
Helpless falls upon the waters,
Floating down the coal-black current,
Through the cataract and rapids
To the tombs of Tuonela.

There the blood-stained son of deathland,
There Tuoni's son and hero,
Cuts in pieces Lemminkainen,
Chops him with his mighty hatchet,
Till the sharpened axe strikes flint-sparks
From the rocks within his chamber,
Chops the hero into fragments,
Into five unequal portions,
Throws each portion to Tuoni,
In Manala's lowest kingdom,
Speaks these words when he has ended:
"Swim thou there, wild Lemminkainen,
Flow thou onward in this river,
Hunt forever in these waters,
With thy cross-bow and thine arrow,

Shoot the swan within this empire,
Shoot our water-birds in welcome!"

Thus the hero, Lemminkainen,
Thus the handsome Kaukomieli,
The untiring suitor, dieth
In the river of Tuoni,
In the death-realm of Manala.

Rune XV: Lemminkainen's Restoration

Lemminkainen's aged mother
Anxious roams about the islands,
Anxious wonders in her chambers,
What the fate of Lemminkainen,
Why her son so long has tarried;
Thinks that something ill has happened
To her hero in Pohyola.
Sad, indeed, the mother's anguish,
As in vain she waits his coming,
As in vain she asks the question,
Where her daring son is roaming,
Whether to the fir tree mountain,
Whether to the distant heath-land,
Or upon the broad sea's ridges,
On the floods and rolling waters,
To the war's contending armies,
To the heat and din of battle,
Steeped in blood of valiant heroes,
Evidence of fatal warfare.

Daily does the wife Kyllikki
Look about her vacant chamber,
In the home of Lemminkainen,
At the court of Kaukomieli;
Looks at evening, looks at morning,
Looks, perchance, upon his hair-brush,
Sees alas! the blood-drops oozing,
Oozing from the golden bristles,
And the blood-drops, scarlet-coloured.

Then the beauteous wife, Kyllikki,
Spake these words in deeps of anguish:
"Dead or wounded is my husband,
Or at best is filled with trouble,
Lost perhaps in Northland forests,
In some glen unknown to heroes,
Since alas! the blood is flowing
From the brush of Lemminkainen,
Red drops oozing from the bristles."
Thereupon the anxious mother
Looks upon the bleeding hair-brush
And begins this wail of anguish:
"Woe is me, my life hard-fated,
Woe is me, all joy departed!
For alas! my son and hero,
Valiant hero of the islands,
Son of trouble and misfortune!
Some sad fate has overtaken
My ill-fated Lemminkainen!
Blood is flowing from his hair-brush,
Oozing from its golden bristles,
And the drops are scarlet-coloured."

Quick her garment's hem she clutches,
On her arm she throws her long-robes,
Fleetly flies upon her journey;
With her might she hastens northward,
Mountains tremble from her footsteps,
Valleys rise and heights are lowered,
Highlands soon become as lowlands,
All the hills and valleys levelled.
Soon she gains the Northland village,
Quickly asks about her hero,
These the words the mother utters:
"O thou hostess of Pohyola,
Where hast thou my Lemminkainen?
Tell me of my son and hero!"

Louhi, hostess of the Northland,
Gives this answer to the mother:
"Nothing know I of thy hero,
Of the hero of the islands;
Where thy son may be I know not,
Cannot lend the information;
Once I gave thy son a courser,
Hitched the racer to his snow-sledge,
This the last of Lemminkainen;
May perchance be drowned in Wuhne,
Frozen in the icy ocean,
Fallen prey to wolves in hunger,

In a bear's den may have perished."
Lemminkainen's mother answers:
"Thou art only speaking falsehoods,
Northland wolves cannot devour us,
Nor the bears kill Kaukomieli;
He can slay the wolves of Pohya
With the fingers of his left hand;
Bears of Northland he would silence
With the magic of his singing.
"Hostess of Pohyola, tell me
Whither thou hast sent my hero;
I shall burst thy many garners,
Shall destroy the magic Sampo,
If thou dost not tell me truly
Where to find my Lemminkainen."
Spake the hostess of Pohyola:
"I have well thy hero treated,
Well my court has entertained him,
Gave him of my rarest viands,
Fed him at my well-filled tables,
Placed him in a boat of copper,
Thus to float adown the current,
This the last of Lemminkainen;
Cannot tell where he has wandered,
Whether in the foam of waters,
Whether in the boiling torrent,
Whether in the drowning whirlpool."

Lemminkainen's mother answers:
"Thou again art speaking falsely;
Tell me now the truth I pray thee,
Make an end of thy deception,
Where is now my Lemminkainen,
Whither hast thou sent my hero,
Young and daring son of Kalew?
If a third time thou deceivest,
I will send thee plagues, unnumbered,
I will send thee fell destruction,
Certain death will overtake thee."
Spake the hostess of Pohyola:
"This the third time that I answer,
This the truth that I shall tell thee:
I have sent the Kalew-hero
To the Hisi-fields and forests,
There to hunt the moose of Lempo;
Sent him then to catch the fire-horse,
Catch the fire-expiring stallion,
On the distant plains of Juutas,
In the realm of cruel Hisi.
Then I sent him to the Death-stream,
In the kingdom of Tuoni,
With his bow and but one arrow,
There to shoot the swan as dowry
For my best and fairest daughter;
Have not heard about thy hero
Since he left for Tuonela;
May in misery have fallen,
May have perished in Manala;
Has not come to ask my daughter,
Has not come to woo the maiden,
Since he left to hunt the death-swan."

Now the mother seeks her lost one,
For her son she weeps and trembles,
Like the wolf she bounds through fenlands,
Like the bear, through forest thickets,
Like the wild-boar, through the marshes,
Like the hare, along the sea-coast,
To the sea-point, like the hedgehog,
Like the wild-duck swims the waters,
Casts the rubbish from her pathway,
Tramples down opposing brush-wood,
Stops at nothing in her journey;
Seeks a long time for her hero,
Seeks, and seeks, and does not find him.

Now she asks the trees the question,
And the forest gives this answer:
"We have care enough already,
Cannot think about thy matters;
Cruel fates have we to battle,
Pitiful our own misfortunes!
We are felled and chopped in pieces,
Cut in blocks for hero-fancy,
We are burned to death as fuel,
No one cares how much we suffer."

Now again the mother wanders,
Seeks again her long-lost hero,
Seeks, and seeks, and does not find him.
Paths arise and come to meet her,
And she questions thus the pathways:
"Paths of hope that God has fashioned,
Have ye seen my Lemminkainen,

Has my son and golden hero
Travelled through thy many kingdoms?"
Sad, the many pathways answer:
"We ourselves have cares sufficient,
Cannot watch thy son and hero,
Wretched are the lives of pathways,
Deep indeed our own misfortunes;
We are trodden by the red-deer,
By the wolves, and bears, and roebucks,
Driven o'er by heavy cart-wheels,
By the feet of dogs are trodden,
Trodden under foot of heroes,
Foot-paths for contending armies."

Seeks again the frantic mother,
Seeks her long-lost son and hero,
Seeks, and seeks, and does not find him;
Finds the Moon within her orbit,
Asks the Moon in pleading measures:
"Golden Moon, whom God has stationed
In the heavens, the Sun's companion,
Hast thou seen my Kaukomieli,
Hast thou seen my silver apple,
Anywhere in thy dominions?"
Thus the golden Moon makes answer:
"I have trouble all-sufficient,
Cannot watch thy daring hero;
Long the journey I must travel,
Sad the fate to me befallen,
Pitiful mine own misfortunes,
All alone the nights to wander,
Shine alone without a respite,
In the winter ever watching,
In the summer sink and perish."

Still the mother seeks, and wanders,
Seeks, and does not find her hero;
Sees the Sun in the horizon,
And the mother thus entreats him:
"Silver Sun, whom God has fashioned,
Thou that giveth warmth and comfort,
Hast thou lately seen my hero,
Hast thou seen my Lemminkainen,
Wandering in thy dominions?"
Thus the Sun in kindness answers:
"Surely has thy hero perished,
To ingratitude a victim;
Lemminkainen died and vanished
In Tuoni's fatal river,
In the waters of Manala,
In the sacred stream and whirlpool,
In the cataract and rapids,
Sank within the drowning current
To the realm of Tuonela,
To Manala's lower regions."

Lemminkainen's mother weeping,
Wailing in the deeps of anguish,
Mourns the fate of Kaukomieli,
Hastens to the Northland smithy,
To the forge of Ilmarinen,
These the words the mother utters:
"Ilmarinen, metal-artist,
Thou that long ago wert forging,
Forging earth a concave cover,
Yesterday wert forging wonders,
Forge thou now, immortal blacksmith,
Forge a rake with shaft of copper,
Forge the teeth of strongest metal,
Teeth in length a hundred fathoms,
And five hundred long the handle."

Ilmarinen does as bidden,
Makes the rake in full perfection.

Lemminkainen's anxious mother
Takes the magic rake and hastens
To the river of Tuoni,
Praying to the Sun as follows:
"Thou, O Sun, by God created,
Thou that shinest on thy Maker,
Shine for me in heat of magic,
Give me warmth, and strength, and courage,
Shine a third time full of power,
Lull to sleep the wicked people,
Still the people of Manala,
Quiet all Tuoni's empire."

Thereupon the Sun of Ukko,
Dearest child of the Creator,
Flying through the groves of Northland,
Sitting on a curving birch-tree,
Shines a little while in ardor,
Shines again in greater fervor,

Shines a third time full of power,
Lulls to sleep the wicked people
In the Manala home and kingdom,
Still the heroes with their broadswords,
Makes the lancers halt and totter,
Stills the stoutest of the spearmen,
Quiets Tuoni's ghastly empire.
Now the Sun retires in magic,
Hovers here and there a moment
Over Tuoni's hapless sleepers,
Hastens upward to his station,
To his Jumala home and kingdom.

Lemminkainen's faithful mother
Takes the rake of magic metals,
Rakes the Tuoni river bottoms,
Rakes the cataract and whirlpool,
Rakes the swift and boiling current
Of the sacred stream of deathland,
In the Manala home and kingdom.
Searching for her long-lost hero,
Rakes a long time, finding nothing;
Now she wades the river deeper,
To her belt in mud and water,
Deeper, deeper, rakes the death-stream,
Rakes the river's deepest caverns,
Raking up and down the current,
Till at last she finds his tunic,
Heavy-hearted, finds his jacket;
Rakes again and rakes unceasing,
Finds the hero's shoes and stockings,
Sorely troubled, finds these relics;
Now she wades the river deeper,
Rakes the Manala shoals and shallows,
Rakes the deeps at every angle;
As she draws the rake the third time
From the Tuoni shores and waters,
In the rake she finds the body
Of her long-lost Lemminkainen,
In the metal teeth entangled,
In the rake with copper handle.

Thus the reckless Lemminkainen,
Thus the son of Kalevala,
Was recovered from the bottom
Of the Manala lake and river.
There were wanting many fragments,
Half the head, a hand, a fore-arm,
Many other smaller portions,
Life, above all else, was missing.
Then the mother, well reflecting,
Spake these words in bitter weeping:
"From these fragments, with my magic,
I will bring to life my hero."

Hearing this, the raven answered,
Spake these measures to the mother:
"There is not in these a hero,
Thou canst not revive these fragments;
Eels have fed upon his body,
On his eyes have fed the whiting;
Cast the dead upon the waters,
On the streams of Tuonela,
Let him there become a walrus,
Or a seal, or whale, or porpoise."

Lemminkainen's mother does not
Cast the dead upon the waters,
On the streams of Tuonela;
She again with hope and courage,
Rakes the river lengthwise, crosswise,
Through the Manala pools and caverns,
Rakes up half the head, a fore-arm,
Finds a hand and half the back-bone,
Many other smaller portions;
Shapes her son from all the fragments,
Shapes anew her Lemminkainen,
Flesh to flesh with skill she places,
Gives the bones their proper stations,
Binds one member to the other,
Joins the ends of severed vessels,
Counts the threads of all the venules,
Knits the parts in apposition;
Then this prayer the mother offers:

"Suonetar, thou slender virgin,
Goddess of the veins of heroes,
Skilful spinner of the vessels,
With thy slender, silver spindle,
With thy spinning-wheel of copper,
Set in frame of molten silver,
Come thou hither, thou art needed;
Bring the instruments for mending,
Firmly knit the veins together,

At the end join well the venules,
In the wounds that still are open,
In the members that are injured.

"Should this aid be inefficient,
There is living in the ether,
In a boat enriched with silver,
In a copper boat, a maiden,
That can bring to thee assistance.
Come, O maiden, from the ether,
Virgin from the belt of heaven,
Row throughout these veins, O maiden,
Row through all these lifeless members,
Through the channels of the long-bones,
Row through every form of tissue.
Set the vessels in their places,
Lay the heart in right position,
Make the pulses beat together,
Join the smallest of the veinlets,
And unite with skill the sinews.
Take thou now a slender needle,
Silken thread within its eyelet,
Ply the silver needle gently,
Sew with care the wounds together.

"Should this aid be inefficient,
Thou, O God, that knowest all things,
Come and give us thine assistance,
Harness thou thy fleetest racer,
Call to aid thy strongest courser,
In thy scarlet sledge come swiftly,
Drive through all the bones and channels,
Drive throughout these lifeless tissues,
Drive thy courser through each vessel,
Bind the flesh and bones securely,
In the joints put finest silver,
Purest gold in all the fissures.

"Where the skin is broken open,
Where the veins are torn asunder,
Mend these injuries with magic;
Where the blood has left the body,
There make new blood flow abundant;
Where the bones are rudely broken,
Set the parts in full perfection;
Where the flesh is bruised and loosened,
Touch the wounds with magic balsam,
Do not leave a part imperfect;
Bone, and vein, and nerve, and sinew,
Heart, and brain, and gland, and vessel,
Heal as Thou alone canst heal them."

These the means the mother uses,
Thus she joins the lifeless members,
Thus she heals the death-like tissues,
Thus restores her son and hero
To his former life and likeness;
All his veins are knit together,
All their ends are firmly fastened,
All the parts in apposition,
Life returns, but speech is wanting,
Deaf and dumb, and blind, and senseless.
Now the mother speaks as follows:
"Where may I procure the balsam,
Where the drops of magic honey,
To anoint my son and hero,
Thus to heal my Lemminkainen,
That again his mouth may open,
May again begin his singing,
Speak again in words of wonder,
Sing again his incantations?

"Tiny bee, thou honey-birdling,
Lord of all the forest flowers,
Fly away and gather honey,
Bring to me the forest-sweetness,
Found in Metsola's rich gardens,
And in Tapio's fragrant meadows,
From the petals of the flowers,
From the blooming herbs and grasses,
Thus to heal my hero's anguish,
Thus to heal his wounds of evil."

Thereupon the honey-birdling
Flies away on wings of swiftness,
Into Metsola's rich gardens,
Into Tapio's flowery meadows,
Gathers sweetness from the meadows,
With the tongue distills the honey
From the cups of seven flowers,
From the bloom of countless grasses;
Quick from Metsola returning,
Flying, humming, darting onward,
With his winglets honey-laden,

With the store of sweetest odors,
To the mother brings the balsam.
Lemminkainen's anxious mother
Takes the balm of magic virtues,
And anoints the injured hero,
Heals his wounds and stills his anguish;
But the balm is inefficient,
For her son is deaf and speechless.

Then again out-speaks the mother:
"Little bee, my honey-birdling,
Fly away in one direction,
Fly across the seven oceans,
In the eighth, a magic island,
Where the honey is enchanted,
To the distant Turi-castles,
To the chambers of Palwoinen;
There the honey is effective,
There, the wonder-working balsam,
This may heal the wounded hero;
Bring me of this magic ointment,
That I may anoint his eyelids,
May restore his injured senses."

Thereupon the honey-birdling
Flies away o'er seven oceans,
To the old enchanted island;
Flies one day, and then a second,
On the verdure does not settle,
Does not rest upon the flowers;
Flies a third day, fleetly onward,
Till a third day evening brings him
To the island in the ocean,
To the meadows rich in honey,
To the cataract and fire-flow,
To the sacred stream and whirlpool.

There the honey was preparing,
There the magic balm distilling
In the tiny earthen vessels,
In the burnished copper kettles,
Smaller than a maiden's thimble,
Smaller than the tips of fingers.
Faithfully the busy insect
Gathers the enchanted honey
From the magic Turi-cuplets
In the chambers of Palwoinen.

Time had gone but little distance,
Ere the bee came loudly humming,
Flying fleetly, honey-laden;
In his arms were seven vessels,
Seven, the vessels on each shoulder;
All were filled with honey-balsam,
With the balm of magic virtues.

Lemminkainen's tireless mother
Quick anoints her speechless hero,
With the magic Turi-balsam,
With the balm of seven virtues;
Nine the times that she anoints him
With the honey of Palwoinen,
With the wonder-working balsam;
But the balm is inefficient,
For the hero still is speechless.
Then again out-speaks the mother:
"Honey-bee, thou ether birdling,
Fly a third time on thy journey,
Fly away to high Jumala,
Fly thou to the seventh heaven,
Honey there thou'lt find abundant,
Balsam of the highest virtue,
Only used by the Creator,
Only made from the breath of Ukko.
God anoints his faithful children,
With the honey of his wisdom,
When they feel the pangs of sorrow,
When they meet the powers of evil.
Dip thy winglets in this honey,
Steep thy plumage in His sweetness,
Hither bring the all-sufficient
Balsam of the great Creator;
This will still my hero's anguish,
This will heal his wounded tissues,
This restore his long-lost vision,
Make the Northland hills re-echo
With the magic of his singing,
With his wonderful enchantment."
Thus the honey-bee made answer:
"I can never fly to heaven,
To the seventh of the heavens,
To the distant home of Ukko,
With these wings of little virtue."
Lemminkainen's mother answered:
"Thou canst surely fly to heaven,

To the seventh of the heavens,
O'er the Moon, beneath the sunshine,
Through the dim and distant starlight.
On the first day, flying upward,
Thou wilt near the Moon in heaven,
Fan the brow of Kootamoinen;
On the second thou canst rest thee
On the shoulders of Otava;
On the third day, flying higher,
Rest upon the seven starlets,
On the heads of Hetewanè;
Short the journey that is left thee,
Inconsiderable the distance
To the home of mighty Ukko,
To the dwellings of the blessed."

Thereupon the bee arising,
From the earth flies swiftly upward,
Hastens on with graceful motion,
By his tiny wings borne heavenward,
In the paths of golden moonbeams,
Touches on the Moon's bright borders,
Fans the brow of Kootamoinen,
Rests upon Otava's shoulders,
Hastens to the seven starlets,
To the heads of Hetewanè,
Flies to the Creator's castle,
To the home of generous Ukko,
Finds the remedy preparing,
Finds the balm of life distilling,
In the silver-tinted caldrons,
In the purest golden kettles;
On one side, heart-easing honey,
On a second, balm of joyance,
On the third, life-giving balsam.
Here the magic bee, selecting,
Culls the sweet, life-giving balsam,
Gathers too, heart-easing honey,
Heavy-laden hastens homeward.

Time had travelled little distance,
Ere the busy bee came humming
To the anxious mother waiting,
In his arms a hundred cuplets,
And a thousand other vessels,
Filled with honey, filled with balsam,
Filled with the balm of the Creator.
Lemminkainen's mother quickly
Takes them on her tongue and tests them,
Finds a balsam all-sufficient.
Then the mother spake as follows:
"I have found the long-sought balsam,
Found the remedy of Ukko,
Wherewith God anoints his people,
Gives them life, and faith, and wisdom,
Heals their wounds and stills their anguish,
Makes them strong against temptation,
Guards them from the evil-doers."

Now the mother well anointing,
Heals her son, the magic singer,
Eyes, and ears, and tongue, and temples,
Breaks, and cuts, and seams, anointing,
Touching well the life-blood centres,
Speaks these words of magic import
To the sleeping Lemminkainen:
"Wake, arise from out thy slumber,
From the worst of low conditions,
From thy state of dire misfortune!"

Quickly wakes the son and hero,
Rises from the depths of slumber,
Speaks again in magic accents,
These the first words of the singer:
"Long, indeed, have I been sleeping,
Long unconscious of existence,
But my sleep was full of sweetness,
Sweet the sleep in Tuonela,
Knowing neither joy nor sorrow!"
This the answer of his mother:
"Longer still thou wouldst have slumbered,
Were it not for me, thy mother;
Tell me now, my son beloved,
Tell me that I well may hear thee,
Who enticed thee to Manala,
To the river of Tuoni,
To the fatal stream and whirlpool?"

Then the hero, Lemminkainen,
Gave this answer to his mother:
"Nasshut, the decrepit shepherd
Of the flocks of Sariola,
Blind, and halt, and poor, and wretched,
And to whom I did a favour;

From the slumber-land of envy
Nasshut sent me to Manala,
To the river of Tuoni;
Sent a serpent from the waters,
Sent an adder from the death-stream,
Through the heart of Lemminkainen;
Did not recognize the serpent,
Could not speak the serpent-language,
Did not know the sting of adders."
Spake again the ancient mother:
"O thou son of little insight,
Senseless hero, fool-magician,
Thou didst boast betimes thy magic
To enchant the wise enchanters,
On the dismal shores of Lapland,
Thou didst think to banish heroes,
From the borders of Pohyola;
Didst not know the sting of serpents,
Didst not know the reed of waters,
Nor the magic word-protector!
Learn the origin of serpents,
Whence the poison of the adder.

"In the floods was born the serpent,
From the marrow of the gray-duck,
From the brain of ocean-swallows;
Suoyatar had made saliva,
Cast it on the waves of ocean,
Currents drove it outward, onward,
Softly shone the sun upon it,
By the winds 'twas gently cradled,
Gently nursed by winds and waters,
By the waves was driven shoreward,
Landed by the surging billows.
Thus the serpent, thing of evil,
Filling all the world with trouble,
Was created in the waters
Born from Suoyatar, its maker."

Then the mother of the hero
Rocked her son to rest and comfort,
Rocked him to his former being,
To his former life and spirit,
Into greater magic powers;
Wiser, handsomer than ever
Grew the hero of the islands;
But his heart was full of trouble,
And his mother, ever watchful,
Asked the cause of his dejection.
This is Lemminkainen's answer:
"This the cause of all my sorrow;
Far away my heart is roaming,
All my thoughts forever wander
To the Northland's blooming virgins,
To the maids of braided tresses.
Northland's ugly hostess, Louhi,
Will not give to me her daughter,
Fairest maiden of Pohyola,
Till I kill the swan of Mana,
With my bow and but one arrow,
In the river of Tuoni."
Lemminkainen's mother answers,
In the sacred stream and whirlpool.
"Let the swan swim on in safety,
Give the water-bird his freedom,
In the river of Manala,
In the whirlpool of Tuoni;
Leave the maiden in the Northland,
With her charms and fading beauty;
With thy fond and faithful mother,
Go at once to Kalevala,
To thy native fields and fallows.
Praise thy fortune, all sufficient,
Praise, above all else, thy Maker.
Ukko gave thee aid when needed,
Thou wert saved by thy Creator,
From thy long and hopeless slumber,
In the waters of Tuoni,
In the chambers of Manala.
I unaided could not save thee,
Could not give the least assistance;
God alone, omniscient Ukko,
First and last of the creators,
Can revive the dead and dying,
Can protect his worthy people
From the waters of Manala,
From the fatal stream
and whirlpool,
In the kingdom of Tuoni."

Lemminkainen, filled with wisdom,
With his fond and faithful mother,
Hastened straightway on his journey
To his distant home and kindred,

To the Wainola fields and meadows,
To the plains of Kalevala.

Here I leave my Kaukomieli,
Leave my hero Lemminkainen,
Long I leave him from my singing,
Turn my song to other heroes,
Send it forth on other pathways,
Sing some other golden legend.

Rune XVI: Wainamoinen's Boat Building

Wainamoinen, ancient minstrel,
The eternal wisdom-singer,
For his boat was working lumber,
Working long upon his vessel,
On a fog-point jutting seaward,
On an island, forest-covered;
But the lumber failed the master,
Beams were wanting for his vessel,
Beams and scantling, ribs and flooring.
Who will find for him the lumber,
Who procure the timber needed
For the boat of Wainamoinen,
For the bottom of his vessel?

Pellerwoinen of the prairies,
Sampsa, slender-grown and ancient,
He will seek the needful timber,
He procure the beams of oak-wood
For the boat of Wainamoinen,
For the bottom of his vessel.

Quick he starts upon his journey
To the eastern fields and forests,
Hunts throughout the Northland mountain
To a second mountain wanders,
To a third he hastens, searching,
Golden axe upon his shoulder,
In his hand a copper hatchet.
Comes an aspen-tree to meet him
Of the height of seven fathoms.
Sampsa takes his axe of copper,
Starts to fell the stately aspen,
But the aspen quickly halting,
Speaks these words to Pellerwoinen:
"Tell me, hero, what thou wishest,
What the service thou art needing?"
Sampsa Pellerwoinen answers:
"This indeed, the needed service
That I ask of thee, O aspen:
Need thy lumber for a vessel,
For the boat of Wainamoinen,
Wisest of the wisdom-singers."

Quick and wisely speaks the aspen,
Thus its hundred branches answer:
"All the boats that have been fashioned
From my wood have proved but failures;
Such a vessel floats a distance,
Then it sinks upon the bottom
Of the waters it should travel.
All my trunk is filled with hollows,
Three times in the summer seasons
Worms devour my stem and branches,
Feed upon my heart and tissues."

Pellerwoinen leaves the aspen,
Hunts again through all the forest,
Wanders through the woods
of Northland,
Where a pine tree comes to meet him,
Of the height of fourteen fathoms.

With his axe he chops the pine tree,
Strikes it with his axe of copper,
As he asks the pine this question:
"Will thy trunk give worthy timber
For the boat of Wainamoinen,
Wisest of the wisdom-singers?"
Loudly does the pine tree answer:
"All the ships that have been fashioned
From my body are unworthy;
I am full of imperfections,
Cannot give thee needed timber
Wherewithal to build thy vessel;
Ravens live within my branches,
Build their nests and hatch
their younglings,
Three times in my trunk in summer."

Sampsa leaves the lofty pine tree,
Wanders onward, onward, onward,
To the woods of gladsome summer,
Where an oak-tree comes to meet him,
In circumference, three fathoms,
And the oak he thus addresses:
"Ancient oak-tree, will thy body
Furnish wood to build a vessel,
Build a boat for Wainamoinen,
Master-boat for the magician,
Wisest of the wisdom-singers?"
Thus the oak replies to Sampsa:
"I for thee will gladly furnish
Wood to build the hero's vessel;
I am tall, and sound, and hardy,
Have no flaws within my body;
Three times in the months of summer,
In the warmest of the seasons,
Does the sun dwell in my tree-top,
On my trunk the moonlight glimmers,
In my branches sings the cuckoo,
In my top her nestlings slumber."

Now the ancient Pellerwoinen
Takes the hatchet from his shoulder,
Takes his axe with copper handle,
Chops the body of the oak-tree;
Well he knows the art of chopping.
Soon he fells the tree majestic,
Fells the mighty forest-monarch,
With his magic axe and power.
From the stems he lops the branches,
Splits the trunk in many pieces,
Fashions lumber for the bottom,
Countless boards, and ribs, and braces,
For the singer's magic vessel,
For the boat of the magician.

Wainamoinen, old and skilful,
The eternal wonder-worker,
Builds his vessel with enchantment,
Builds his boat by art of magic,
From the timber of the oak-tree,
From its posts, and planks, and flooring.
Sings a song, and joins the frame-work;
Sings a second, sets the siding;
Sings a third time, sets the row-locks;
Fashions oars, and ribs, and rudder,
Joins the sides and ribs together.
When the ribs were firmly fastened,
When the sides were tightly jointed,
Then alas! three words were wanting,
Lost the words of master-magic,
How to fasten in the ledges,
How the stern should be completed,
How complete the boat's forecastle.
Then the ancient Wainamoinen,
Wise and wonderful enchanter,
Heavy-hearted spake as follows:
"Woe is me, my life hard-fated!
Never will this magic vessel
Pass in safety o'er the water,
Never ride the rough sea-billows."

Then he thought and long considered,
Where to find these words of magic,
Find the lost-words of the Master:
"From the brains of countless swallows,
From the heads of swans in dying,
From the plumage of the gray-duck?"

For these words the hero searches,
Kills of swans a goodly number,
Kills a flock of fattened gray-duck,
Kills of swallows countless numbers,
Cannot find the words of magic,
Not the lost-words of the Master.
Wainamoinen, wisdom-singer,
Still reflected and debated:
"I perchance may find the lost-words
On the tongue of summer-reindeer,
In the mouth of the white squirrel."

Now again he hunts the lost-words,
Hastes to find the magic sayings,
Kills a countless host of reindeer,
Kills a rafterful of squirrels,
Finds of words a goodly number,
But they are of little value,
Cannot find the magic lost-word.
Long he thought and well considered:
"I can find of words a hundred
In the dwellings of Tuoni,
In the Manala fields and castles."

Wainamoinen quickly journeys
To the kingdom of Tuoni,
There to find the ancient wisdom,
There to learn the secret doctrine;
Hastens on through fen and forest,
Over meads and over marshes,
Through the ever-rising woodlands,
Journeys one week through the brambles,
And a second through the hazels,
Through the junipers the third week,
When appear Tuoni's islands,
And the Manala fields and castles.

Wainamoinen, brave and ancient,
Calls aloud in tones of thunder,
To the Tuonela deeps and dungeons,
And to Manala's magic castle:
"Bring a boat, Tuoni's daughter,
Bring a ferry-boat, O maiden,
That may bear me o'er this channel,
O'er this black and fatal river."

Quick the daughter of Tuoni,
Magic maid of little stature,
Tiny virgin of Manala,
Tiny washer of the linen,
Tiny cleaner of the dresses,
At the river of Tuoni,
In Manala's ancient castles,
Speaks these words to Wainamoinen,
Gives this answer to his calling:
"Straightway will I bring the row-boat,
When the reasons thou hast given
Why thou comest to Manala
In a hale and active body."

Wainamoinen, old and artful,
Gives this answer to the maiden:
"I was brought here by Tuoni,
Mana raised me from the coffin."
Speaks the maiden of Manala:
"This a tale of wretched liars;
Had Tuoni brought thee hither,
Mana raised thee from the coffin,
Then Tuoni would be with thee,
Manalainen too would lead thee,
With Tuoni's hat upon thee,
On thy hands, the gloves of Mana;
Tell the truth now, Wainamoinen,
What has brought thee to Manala?"

Wainamoinen, artful hero,
Gives this answer, still finessing:
"Iron brought me to Manala,
To the kingdom of Tuoni."
Speaks the virgin of the deathland,
Mana's wise and tiny daughter:
"Well I know that this is falsehood,
Had the iron brought thee hither,
Brought thee to Tuoni's kingdom,
Blood would trickle from thy vesture,
And the blood-drops, scarlet-coloured.
Speak the truth now, Wainamoinen,
This the third time that I ask thee."

Wainamoinen, little heeding,
Still finesses to the daughter:
"Water brought me to Manala,
To the kingdom of Tuoni."
This the tiny maiden's answer:
"Well I know thou speakest falsely;
If the waters of Manala,
If the cataract and whirlpool,
Or the waves had brought thee hither,
From thy robes the drops would trickle,
Water drip from all thy raiment.
Tell the truth and I will serve thee,
What has brought thee to Manala?"

Then the stubborn Wainamoinen
Told this falsehood to the maiden:
"Fire has brought me to Manala,
To the kingdom of Tuoni."
Spake again Tuoni's daughter:
"Well I know the voice of falsehood.
If the fire had brought thee hither,
Brought thee to Tuoni's empire,
Singed would be thy locks and eyebrows,
And thy beard be crisped and tangled.
O, thou foolish Wainamoinen,
If I row thee o'er the ferry,
Thou must speak the truth in answer,
This the last time I will ask thee;
Make an end of thy deception.

What has brought thee to Manala,
Still unharmed by pain or sickness,
Still untouched by Death's dark angels?"
Spake the ancient Wainamoinen:
"At the first I spake, not truly,
Now I give thee rightful answer:
I a boat with ancient wisdom,
Fashioned with my powers of magic,
Sang one day and then a second,
Sang the third day until evening,
When I broke the magic main-spring,
Broke my magic sledge in pieces,
Of my song the fleetest runners;
Then I come to Mana's kingdom,
Came to borrow here a hatchet,
Thus to mend my sledge of magic,
Thus to join the parts together.
Send the boat now quickly over,
Send me, quick, Tuoni's row-boat,
Help me cross this fatal river,
Cross the channel of Manala."

Spake the daughter of Tuoni,
Mana's maiden thus replying:
"Thou art sure a stupid fellow,
Foresight wanting, judgement lacking,
Having neither wit nor wisdom,
Coming here without a reason,
Coming to Tuoni's empire;
Better far if thou shouldst journey
To thy distant home and kindred;
Many they that visit Mana,
Few return from Mana's kingdom."

Spake the good old Wainamoinen:
"Women old retreat from danger,
Not a man of any courage,
Not the weakest of the heroes.
Bring thy boat, Tuoni's daughter,
Tiny maiden of Manala,
Come and row me o'er the ferry."

Mana's daughter does as bidden,
Brings her boat to Wainamoinen,
Quickly rows him through the channel,
O'er the black and fatal river,
To the kingdom of Manala,
Speaks these words to the magician:
"Woe to thee! O Wainamoinen!
Wonderful indeed, thy magic,
Since thou comest to Manala,
Comest neither dead nor dying."

Tuonetar, the deathland hostess,
Ancient hostess of Tuoni,
Brings him pitchers filled with
strong beer,
Fills her massive golden goblets,
Speaks these measures to the stranger:
"Drink, thou ancient Wainamoinen,
Drink the beer of king Tuoni!"

Wainamoinen, wise and cautious,
Carefully inspects the liquor,
Looks a long time in the pitchers,
Sees the spawning of the black-frogs,
Sees the young of poison-serpents,
Lizards, worms, and writhing adders,
Thus addresses Tuonetar:
"Have not come with this intention,
Have not come to drink thy poisons,
Drink the beer of Tuonela;
Those that drink Tuoni's liquors,
Those that sip the cups of Mana,
Court the Devil and destruction,
End their lives in want and ruin."
Tuonetar makes this answer:
"Ancient minstrel, Wainamoinen,
Tell me what has brought thee hither,
Brought thee to the realm of Mana,
To the courts of Tuonela,
Ere Tuoni sent his angels
To thy home in Kalevala,
There to cut thy magic life-thread."
Spake the singer, Wainamoinen:
"I was building me a vessel,
At my craft was working, singing,
Needed three words of the Master,
How to fasten in the ledges,
How the stern should be completed,
How complete the boat's forecastle.
This the reason of my coming
To the empire of Tuoni,
To the castles of Manala:

Came to learn these magic sayings,
Learn the lost-words of the Master."
Spake the hostess, Tuonetar:
"Mana never gives these sayings,
Canst not learn them from Tuoni,
Not the lost-words of the Master;
Thou shalt never leave this kingdom,
Never in thy magic life-time,
Never go to Kalevala,
To Wainola's peaceful meadows.
To thy distant home and country."

Quick the hostess, Tuonetar,
Waves her magic wand of slumber
O'er the head of Wainamoinen,
Puts to rest the wisdom-hero,
Lays him on the couch of Mana,
In the robes of living heroes,
Deep the sleep that settles o'er him.
In Manala lived a woman,
In the kingdom of Tuoni,
Evil witch and toothless wizard,
Spinner of the threads of iron,
Moulder of the bands of copper,
Weaver of a hundred fish-nets,
Of a thousand nets of copper,
Spinning in the days of summer,
Weaving in the winter evenings,
Seated on a rock in water.

In the kingdom of Tuoni
Lived a man, a wicked wizard,
Three the fingers of the hero,
Spinner he of iron meshes,
Maker too of nets of copper,
Countless were his nets of metal,
Moulded on a rock in water,
Through the many days of summer.

Mana's son with crooked fingers,
Iron-pointed, copper fingers,
Pulls of nets, at least a thousand,
Through the river of Tuoni,
Sets them lengthwise, sets them crosswise,
In the fatal, darksome river,
That the sleeping Wainamoinen,
Friend and brother of the waters,
May not leave the isle of Mana,
Never in the course of ages,
Never leave the deathland castles,
Never while the moonlight glimmers
On the empire of Tuoni.

Wainamoinen, wise and wary,
Rising from his couch of slumber,
Speaks these words as he is waking:
"Is there not some mischief brewing,
Am I not at last in danger,
In the chambers of Tuoni,
In the Manala home and household?"

Quick he changes his complexion,
Changes too his form and feature,
Slips into another body;
Like a serpent in a circle,
Rolls black-dyed upon the waters;
Like a snake among the willows,
Crawls he like a worm of magic,
Like an adder through the grasses,
Through the coal-black stream of deathland,
Through a thousand nets of copper
Interlaced with threads of iron,
From the kingdom of Tuoni,
From the castles of Manala.

Mana's son, the wicked wizard,
With his iron-pointed fingers,
In the early morning hastens
To his thousand nets of copper,
Set within the Tuoni river,
Finds therein a countless number
Of the death-stream fish and serpents;
Does not find old Wainamoinen,
Wainamoinen, wise and wary,
Friend and fellow of the waters.

When the wonder-working hero
Had escaped from Tuonela,
Spake he thus in supplication:
"Gratitude to thee, O Ukko,
Do I bring for thy protection!
Never suffer other heroes,
Of thy heroes not the wisest,

To transgress the laws of nature;
Never let another singer,
While he lives within the body,
Cross the river of Tuoni,
As thou lovest thy creations.
Many heroes cross the channel,
Cross the fatal stream of Mana,
Few return to tell the story,
Few return from Tuonela,
From Manala's courts and castles."
Wainamoinen calls his people,
On the plains of Kalevala,
Speaks these words of ancient wisdom,
To the young men, to the maidens,
To the rising generation:
"Every child of Northland, listen:
If thou wishest joy eternal,
Never disobey thy parents,
Never evil treat the guiltless,
Never wrong the feeble-minded,
Never harm thy weakest fellow,
Never stain thy lips with falsehood,
Never cheat thy trusting neighbor,
Never injure thy companion,
Lest thou surely payest penance
In the kingdom of Tuoni,
In the prison of Manala;
There, the home of all the wicked,
There the couch of the unworthy,
There the chambers of the guilty.
Underneath Manala's fire-rock
Are their ever-flaming couches,
For their pillows hissing serpents,
Vipers green their writhing covers,
For their drink the blood of adders,
For their food the pangs of hunger,
Pain and agony their solace;
If thou wishest joy eternal,
Shun the kingdom of Tuoni!"

Rune XVII: Wainamoinen Finds the Lost Word

Wainamoinen, old and truthful,
Did not learn the words of magic
In Tuoni's gloomy regions,
In the kingdom of Manala.
Thereupon he long debated,
Well considered, long reflected,
Where to find the magic sayings;
When a shepherd came to meet him,
Speaking thus to Wainamoinen:
"Thou canst find of words a hundred,
Find a thousand wisdom-sayings,
In the mouth of wise Wipunen,
In the body of the hero;
To the spot I know the foot-path,
To his tomb the magic highway,
Trodden by a host of heroes;
Long the distance thou must travel,
On the sharpened points of needles;
Then a long way thou must journey
On the edges of the broadswords;
Thirdly thou must travel farther
On the edges of the hatchets."
Wainamoinen, old and trustful,
Well considered all these journeys,
Travelled to the forge and smithy,
Thus addressed the metal-worker:
"Ilmarinen, worthy blacksmith,
Make a shoe for me of iron,
Forge me gloves of burnished copper,
Mould a staff of strongest metal,
Lay the steel upon the inside,
Forge within the might of magic;
I am going on a journey
To procure the magic sayings,
Find the lost-words of the Master,
From the mouth of the magician,
From the tongue of wise Wipunen."
Spake the artist, Ilmarinen:
"Long ago died wise Wipunen,
Disappeared these many ages,
Lays no more his snares of copper,
Sets no longer traps of iron,
Cannot learn from him the wisdom,
Cannot find in him the lost-words."

Wainamoinen, old and hopeful,
Little heeding, not discouraged,
In his metal shoes and armor,
Hastens forward on his journey,
Runs the first day fleetly onward,
On the sharpened points of needles;
Wearily he strides the second,
On the edges of the broadswords
Swings himself the third day forward,
On the edges of the hatchets.

Wise Wipunen, wisdom-singer,
Ancient bard, and great magician,
With his magic songs lay yonder,
Stretched beside him, lay his sayings,
On his shoulder grew the aspen,
On each temple grew the birch-tree,
On his mighty chin the alder,
From his beard grew willow-bushes,
From his mouth the dark green fir tree,
And the oak-tree from his forehead.

Wainamoinen, coming closer,
Draws his sword, lays bare his hatchet
From his magic leathern scabbard,
Fells the aspen from his shoulder,
Fells the birch-tree from his temples,
From his chin he fells the alder,
From his beard, the branching willows,
From his mouth the dark-green fir tree,
Fells the oak-tree from his forehead.

Now he thrusts his staff of iron
Through the mouth of wise Wipunen,
Pries his mighty jaws asunder,
Speaks these words of master-magic:
"Rise, thou master of magicians,
From the sleep of Tuonela,
From thine everlasting slumber!"

Wise Wipunen, ancient singer,
Quickly wakens from his sleeping,
Keenly feels the pangs of torture,
From the cruel staff of iron;
Bites with mighty force the metal,
Bites in twain the softer iron,
Cannot bite the steel asunder,
Opens wide his mouth in anguish.
Wainamoinen of Wainola,
In his iron-shoes and armor,
Careless walking, headlong stumbles
In the spacious mouth and fauces
Of the magic bard, Wipunen.
Wise Wipunen, full of song-charms,
Opens wide his mouth and swallows
Wainamoinen and his magic,
Shoes, and staff, and iron armor.
Then outspeaks the wise Wipunen:
"Many things before I've eaten,
Dined on goat, and sheep, and reindeer,
Bear, and ox, and wolf, and wild-boar,
Never in my recollection,
Have I tasted sweeter morsels!"
Spake the ancient Wainamoinen:
"Now I see the evil symbols,
See misfortune hanging o'er me,
In the darksome Hisi-hurdles,
In the catacombs of Kalma."

Wainamoinen long considered
How to live and how to prosper,
How to conquer this condition.
In his belt he wore a poniard,
With a handle hewn from birch-wood,
From the handle builds a vessel,
Builds a boat through magic science;
In this vessel rows he swiftly
Through the entrails of the hero,
Rows through every gland and vessel
Of the wisest of magicians.
Old Wipunen, master-singer,
Barely feels the hero's presence,
Gives no heed to Wainamoinen.
Then the artist of Wainola
Straightway sets himself to forging,
Sets at work to hammer metals;
Makes a smithy from his armor,
Of his sleeves he makes the bellows,
Makes the air-valve from his fur-coat,
From his stockings, makes the muzzle,
Uses knees instead of anvil,
Makes a hammer of his fore-arm;
Like the storm-wind roars the bellows,
Like the thunder rings the anvil;

Forges one day, then a second,
Forges till the third day closes,
In the body of Wipunen,
In the sorcerer's abdomen.

Old Wipunen, full of magic,
Speaks these words in wonder, guessing:
"Who art thou of ancient heroes,
Who of all the host of heroes?
Many heroes I have eaten,
And of men a countless number,
Have not eaten such as thou art;
Smoke arises from my nostrils,
From my mouth the fire is streaming,
In my throat are iron-clinkers.

"Go, thou monster, hence to wander,
Flee this place, thou plague of Northland,
Ere I go to seek thy mother,
Tell the ancient dame thy mischief;
She shall bear thine evil conduct,
Great the burden she shall carry;
Great a mother's pain and anguish,
When her child runs wild and lawless;
Cannot comprehend the meaning,
Nor this mystery unravel,
Why thou camest here, O monster,
Camest here to give me torture.
Art thou Hisi sent from heaven,
Some calamity from Ukko?
Art, perchance, some new creation,
Ordered here to do me evil?
If thou art some evil genius,
Some calamity from Ukko,
Sent to me by my Creator,
Then am I resigned to suffer;
God does not forsake the worthy,
Does not ruin those that trust him,
Never are the good forsaken.
If by man thou wert created,
If some hero sent thee hither,
I shall learn thy race of evil,
Shall destroy thy wicked tribe-folk.

"Thence arose the violation,
Thence arose the first destruction,
Thence came all the evil-doings:
From the neighborhood of wizards,
From the homes of the magicians,
From the caves of vicious spirits,
From the haunts of fortune-tellers,
From the cabins of the witches,
From the castles of Tuoni,
From the bottom of Manala,
From the ground with envy swollen,
From Ingratitude's dominions,
From the rocky shoals and quicksands,
From the marshes filled with danger,
From the cataract's commotion,
From the bear-caves in the mountains,
From the wolves within the thickets,
From the roarings of the pine tree,
From the burrows of the fox-dog,
From the woodlands of the reindeer,
From the caves and Hisi-hurdles,
From the battles of the giants,
From uncultivated pastures,
From the billows of the oceans,
From the streams of boiling waters,
From the waterfalls of Rutya,
From the limits of the storm-clouds,
From the pathways of the thunders,
From the flashings of the lightnings,
From the distant plains of Pohya,
From the fatal stream and whirlpool,
From the birthplace of Tuoni.

"Art thou coming from these places?
Hast thou, evil, hastened hither,
To the heart of sinless hero,
To devour my guiltless body,
To destroy this wisdom-singer?
Get thee hence, thou dog of Lempo,
Leave, thou monster from Manala,
Flee from mine immortal body,
Leave my liver, thing of evil,
In my body cease thy forging,
Cease this torture of my vitals,
Let me rest in peace and slumber.

"Should I want in means efficient,
Should I lack the magic power
To outroot thine evil genius,
I shall call a better hero,

Call upon a higher power,
To remove this dire misfortune,
To annihilate this monster.
I shall call the will of woman,
From the fields, the old-time heroes,
Mounted heroes from the sand-hills,
Thus to rescue me from danger,
From these pains and ceaseless tortures.

"If this force prove inefficient,
Should not drive thee from my body,
Come, thou forest, with thy heroes,
Come, ye junipers and pine trees,
With your messengers of power,
Come, ye mountains, with
your wood-nymphs,
Come, ye lakes, with all your mermaids,
Come, ye hundred ocean-spearmen,
Come, torment this son of Hisi,
Come and kill this evil monster.

"If this call is inefficient,
Does not drive thee from my vitals,
Rise, thou ancient water-mother,
With thy blue-cap from the ocean,
From the seas, the lakes, the rivers,
Bring protection to thy hero,
Comfort bring and full assistance,
That I guiltless may not suffer,
May not perish prematurely.

"Shouldst thou brave this invocation,
Kapè, daughter of Creation,
Come, thou beauteous, golden maiden,
Oldest of the race of women,
Come and witness my misfortunes,
Come and turn away this evil,
Come, remove this biting torment,
Take away this plague of Piru.

"If this call be disregarded,
If thou wilt not leave me guiltless,
Ukko, on the arch of heaven,
In the thunder-cloud dominions,
Come thou quickly, thou art needed,
Come, protect thy tortured hero,
Drive away this magic demon,
Banish ever his enchantment,
With his sword and flaming furnace,
With his fire-enkindling bellows.

"Go, thou demon, hence to wander,
Flee, thou plague of Northland heroes;
Never come again for shelter,
Nevermore build thou thy dwelling
In the body of Wipunen;
Take at once thy habitation
To the regions of thy kindred,
To thy distant fields and firesides;
When thy journey thou hast ended,
Gained the borders of thy country,
Gained the meads of thy Creator,
Give a signal of thy coming,
Rumble like the peals of thunder,
Glisten like the gleam of lightning,
Knock upon the outer portals,
Enter through the open windows,
Glide about the many chambers,
Seize the host and seize the hostess,
Knock their evil heads together,
Wring their necks and hurl their bodies
To the black-dogs of the forest.

"Should this prove of little value,
Hover like the bird of battle,
O'er the dwellings of the master,
Scare the horses from the mangers,
From the troughs affright the cattle,
Twist their tails, and horns, and forelocks,
Hurl their carcasses to Lempo.

"If some scourge the winds have sent me,
Sent me on the air of spring-tide,
Brought me by the frosts of winter,
Quickly journey whence thou camest,
On the air-path of the heavens,
Perching not upon some aspen,
Resting not upon the birch-tree;
Fly away to copper mountains,
That the copper-winds may nurse thee,
Waves of ether, thy protection.

"Didst those come from high Jumala,
From the hems of ragged snow-clouds,

Quick ascend beyond the cloud-space,
Quickly journey whence thou camest,
To the snow-clouds, crystal-sprinkled,
To the twinkling stars of heaven;
There thy fire may burn forever,
There may flash thy forked lightnings,
In the Sun's undying furnace.

"Wert thou sent here by the
spring-floods,
Driven here by river-torrents?
Quickly journey whence thou camest,
Quickly hasten to the waters,
To the borders of the rivers,
To the ancient water-mountain,
That the floods again may rock thee,
And thy water-mother nurse thee.

"Didst thou come from Kalma's kingdom,
From the castles of the deathland?
Haste thou back to thine own country,
To the Kalma-halls and castles,
To the fields with envy swollen,
Where contending armies perish.

"Art thou from the Hisi-woodlands,
From ravines in Lempo's forest,
From the thickets of the pine-wood,
From the dwellings of the fir-glen?
Quick retrace thine evil footsteps
To the dwellings of thy master,
To the thickets of thy kindred;
There thou mayest dwell at pleasure,
Till thy house decays about thee,
Till thy walls shall mould and crumble.

"Evil genius, thee I banish,
Got thee hence, thou horrid monster,
To the caverns of the white-bear,
To the deep abysm of serpents,
To the vales, and swamps,
and fenlands,
To the ever-silent waters,
To the hot-springs of the mountains,
To the dead-seas of the Northland,
To the lifeless lakes and rivers,
To the sacred stream and whirlpool.

"Shouldst thou find no place of resting,
I will banish thee still farther,
To the Northland's distant borders,
To the broad expanse of Lapland,
To the ever-lifeless deserts,
To the unproductive prairies,
Sunless, moonless, starless, lifeless,
In the dark abyss of Northland;
This for thee, a place befitting,
Pitch thy tents and feast forever
On the dead plains of Pohyola.

"Shouldst thou find no means of living,
I will banish thee still farther,
To the cataract of Rutya,
To the fire-emitting whirlpool,
Where the firs are ever falling,
To the windfalls of the forest;
Swim hereafter in the waters
Of the fire-emitting whirlpool,
Whirl thou ever in the current
Of the cataract's commotion,
In its foam and boiling waters.

"Should this place be unbefitting,
I will drive thee farther onward,
To Tuoni's coal-black river,
To the endless stream of Mana,
Where thou shalt forever linger;
Thou canst never leave Manala,
Should I not thy head deliver,
Should I never pay thy ransom;
Thou canst never safely journey
Through nine brother-rams abutting,
Through nine brother-bulls opposing,
Through nine brother-stallions thwarting,
Thou canst not re-cross Death-river
Thickly set with iron netting,
Interlaced with threads of copper.

"Shouldst thou ask for steeds for saddle,
Shouldst thou need a fleet-foot courser,
I will give thee worthy racers,
I will give thee saddle-horses;
Evil Hisi has a charger,
Crimson mane, and tail, and foretop,
Fire emitting from his nostrils,

As he prances through his pastures;
Hoofs are made of strongest iron,
Legs are made of steel and copper,
Quickly scales the highest mountains,
Darts like lightning through the valleys,
When a skilful master rides him.

"Should this steed be insufficient,
I will give thee Lempo's snow-shoes,
Give thee Hisi's shoes of elm-wood,
Give to thee the staff of Piru,
That with these thou mayest journey
Into Hisi's courts and castles,
To the woods and fields of Juutas;
If the rocks should rise before thee,
Dash the flinty rocks in pieces,
Hurl the fragments to the heavens;
If the branches cross thy pathway,
Make them turn aside in greeting;
If some mighty hero hail thee,
Hurl him headlong to the woodlands.

"Hasten hence, thou thing of evil,
Heinous monster, leave my body,
Ere the breaking of the morning
Ere the Sun awakes from slumber,
Ere the sinning of the cuckoo;
Haste away, thou plague
of Northland,
Haste along the track of moonbeams,
Wander hence, forever wander,
To the darksome fields of Pohya.

"If at once thou dost not leave me,
I will send the eagle's talons,
Send to thee the beaks of vultures,
To devour thine evil body,
Hurl thy skeleton to Hisi.
Much more quickly cruel Lempo
Left my vitals when commanded,
When I called the aid of Ukko,
Called the help of my Creator.
Flee, thou motherless offendant,
Flee, thou fiend of Sariola,
Flee, thou hound without a master,
Ere the morning Sun arises,
Ere the Moon withdraws to slumber!"

Wainamoinen, ancient hero,
Speaks at last to old Wipunen:
"Satisfied am I to linger
In these old and spacious caverns,
Pleasant here my home and dwelling;
For my meat I have thy tissues,
Have thy heart, and spleen, and liver,
For my drink the blood of ages,
Goodly home for Wainamoinen.

"I shall set my forge and bellows
Deeper, deeper in thy vitals;
I shall swing my heavy hammer,
Swing it with a greater power
On thy heart, and lungs, and liver;
I shall never, never leave thee
Till I learn thine incantations,
Learn thy many wisdom-sayings,
Learn the lost-words of the Master;
Never must these words be hidden,
Earth must never lose this wisdom,
Though the wisdom-singers perish."

Old Wipunen, wise magician,
Ancient prophet, filled with power,
Opens full his store of knowledge,
Lifts the covers from his cases,
Filled with old-time incantations,
Filled with songs of times primeval,
Filled with ancient wit and wisdom;
Sings the very oldest folk-songs,
Sings the origin of witchcraft,
Sings of Earth and its beginning,
Sings the first of all creations,
Sings the source of good and evil,
Sung alas! by youth no longer,
Only sung in part by heroes
In these days of sin and sorrow.
Evil days our land befallen.
Sings the orders of enchantment.
How, upon the will of Ukko,
By command of the Creator,
How the air was first divided,
How the water came from ether,
How the earth arose from water,
How from earth came vegetation,
Fish, and fowl, and man, and hero.

Sings again the wise Wipunen,
How the Moon was first created,
How the Sun was set in heaven,
Whence the colours of the rainbow,
Whence the ether's crystal pillars,
How the skies with stars were sprinkled.

Then again sings wise Wipunen,
Sings in miracles of concord,
Sings in magic tones of wisdom,
Never was there heard such singing;
Songs he sings in countless numbers,
Swift his notes as tongues of serpents,
All the distant hills re-echo;
Sings one day, and then a second,
Sings a third from dawn till evening,
Sings from evening till the morning;
Listen all the stars of heaven,
And the Moon stands still and listens
Fall the waves upon the deep-sea,
In the bay the tides cease rising,
Stop the rivers in their courses,
Stops the waterfall of Rutya,
Even Jordan ceases flowing,
And the Wuoksen stops and listens.

When the ancient Wainamoinen
Well had learned the magic sayings,
Learned the ancient songs and legends,
Learned the words of ancient wisdom,
Learned the lost-words of the Master,
Well had learned the secret doctrine,
He prepared to leave the body
Of the wisdom-bard, Wipunen,
Leave the bosom of the master,
Leave the wonderful enchanter.
Spake the hero, Wainamoinen:
"O, thou Antero Wipunen,
Open wide thy mouth and fauces,
I have found the magic lost-words,
I will leave thee now forever,
Leave thee and thy wondrous singing,
Will return to Kalevala,
To Wainola's fields and firesides."
Thus Wipunen spake in answer:
"Many are the things I've eaten,
Eaten bear, and elk, and reindeer,
Eaten ox, and wolf, and wild-boar,
Eaten man, and eaten hero,
Never, never have I eaten
Such a thing as Wainamoinen;
Thou hast found what thou desirest,
Found the three words of the Master;
Go in peace, and ne'er returning,
Take my blessing on thy going."

Thereupon the bard Wipunen
Opens wide his mouth, and wider;
And the good, old Wainamoinen
Straightway leaves the wise enchanter,
Leaves Wipunen's great abdomen;
From the mouth he glides and journeys
O'er the hills and vales of Northland,
Swift as red-deer of the forest,
Swift as yellow-breasted marten,
To the firesides of Wainola,
To the plains of Kalevala.

Straightway hastes he to the smithy
Of his brother, Ilmarinen,
Thus the iron-artist greets him:
"Hast thou found the long-lost wisdom,
Hast thou heard the secret doctrine,
Hast thou learned the master magic,
How to fasten in the ledges,
How the stern should be completed,
How complete the ship's forecastle?"
Wainamoinen thus made answer:
"I have learned of words a hundred,
Learned a thousand incantations,
Hidden deep for many ages,
Learned the words of ancient wisdom,
Found the keys of secret doctrine,
Found the lost-words of the Master."

Wainamoinen, magic-builder,
Straightway journeys to his vessel,
To the spot of magic labour,
Quickly fastens in the ledges,
Firmly binds the stern together
And completes the boat's forecastle.
Thus the ancient Wainamoinen
Built the boat with magic only,
And with magic launched his vessel,

Using not the hand to touch it,
Using not the foot to move it,
Using not the knee to turn it,
Using nothing to propel it.
Thus the third task was completed,
For the hostess of Pohyola,
Dowry for the Maid
of Beauty
Sitting on the arch of heaven,
On the bow of many colours.

Rune XVIII: The Rival Suitors

Wainamoinen, old and truthful,
Long considered, long debated,
How to woo and win the daughter
Of the hostess of Pohyola,
How to lead the Bride of Beauty,
Fairy maiden of the rainbow,
To the meadows of Wainola,
From the dismal Sariola.

Now he decks his magic vessel,
Paints the boat in blue and scarlet,
Trims in gold the ship's forecastle,
Decks the prow in molten silver;
Sings his magic ship down gliding,
On the cylinders of fir tree;
Now erects the masts of pine-wood,
On each mast the sails of linen,
Sails of blue, and white, and scarlet,
Woven into finest fabric.

Wainamoinen, the magician,
Steps aboard his wondrous vessel,
Steers the bark across the waters,
On the blue back of the broad sea,
Speaks these words in sailing northward,
Sailing to the dark Pohyola:
"Come aboard my ship, O Ukko,
Come with me, thou God of mercy,
To protect thine ancient hero,
To support thy trusting servant,
On the breasts of raging billows,
On the far out-stretching waters.

"Rock, O winds, this wondrous vessel,
Causing not a single ripple;
Rolling waves, bear ye me northward,
That the oar may not be needed
In my journey to Pohyola,
O'er this mighty waste of waters."

Ilmarinen's beauteous sister,
Fair and goodly maid, Annikki,
Of the Night and Dawn, the daughter,
Who awakes each morning early,
Rises long before the daylight,
Stood one morning on the seashore,
Washing in the foam her dresses,
Rinsing out her silken ribbons,
On the bridge of scarlet colour,
On the border of the highway,
On a headland jutting seaward,
On the forest-covered island.
Here Annikki, looking round her,
Looking through the fog and ether,
Looking through the clouds
of heaven,
Gazing far out on the blue-sea,
Sees the morning sun arising,
Glimmering along the billows,
Looks with eyes of distant vision
Toward the sunrise on the waters,
Toward the winding streams
of Suomi,
Where the Wina-waves were flowing.

There she sees, on the horizon,
Something darkle in the sunlight,
Something blue upon the billows,
Speaks these words in wonder guessing:
"What is this upon the surges,
What this blue upon the waters,
What this darkling in the sunlight?
'Tis perhaps a flock of wild-geese,
Or perchance the blue-duck flying;
Then upon thy wings arising,
Fly away to highest heaven.

"Art thou then a shoal of sea-trout,
Or perchance a school of salmon?

Dive then to the deep sea-bottom,
In the waters swim and frolic.

"Art thou then a cliff of granite,
Or perchance a mighty oak-tree,
Floating on the rough sea-billows?
May the floods then wash and beat thee,
Break thee to a thousand fragments."

Wainamoinen, sailing northward,
Steers his wondrous ship of magic
Toward the headland jutting seaward,
Toward the island forest-covered.

Now Annikki, goodly maiden,
Sees it is the magic vessel
Of a wonderful enchanter,
Of a mighty bard and hero,
And she asks this simple question:
"Art thou then my father's vessel,
Or my brother's ship of magic?
Haste away then to thy harbor,
To thy refuge in Wainola.
Hast thou come a goodly distance?
Sail then farther on thy journey,
Point thy prow to other waters."

It was not her father's vessel,
Not a sail-boat from the distance,
'Twas the ship of Wainamoinen,
Bark of the eternal singer;
Sails within a hailing distance,
Swims still nearer o'er the waters,
Brings one word and takes another,
Brings a third of magic import.

Speaks the goodly maid, Annikki,
Of the Night and Dawn, the daughter,
To the sailor of the vessel:
"Whither sailest, Wainamoinen,
Whither bound, thou friend of waters,
Pride and joy of Kalevala?"

From the vessel Wainamoinen
Gives this answer to the maiden:
"I have come to catch some sea-trout,
Catch the young and toothsome whiting,
Hiding in these reeds and rushes."
This the answer of Annikki:

"Do not speak to me in falsehood,
Know I well the times of fishing;
Long ago my honoured father
Was a fisherman in Northland,
Came to catch the trout and whiting,
Fished within these seas and rivers.
Very well do I remember
How the fisherman disposes,
How he rigs his fishing vessel,
Lines, and gaffs, and poles, and fish-nets;
Hast not come a-fishing hither.
Whither goest, Wainamoinen,
Whither sailest, friend of waters?"
Spake the ancient Wainamoinen:
"I have come to catch some wild-geese,
Catch the hissing birds of Suomi,
In these far-extending borders,
In the Sachsensund dominions."
Good Annikki gives this answer:
"Know I well a truthful speaker,
Easily detect a falsehood;
Formerly my aged father
Often came a-hunting hither,
Came to hunt the hissing wild-geese,
Hunt the red-bill of these waters.
Very well do I remember
How the hunter rigs his vessel,
Bows, and arrows, knives, and quiver,
Dogs enchained within the vessel,
Pointers hunting on the seashore,
Setters seeking in the marshes;
Tell the truth now Wainamoinen,
Whither is thy vessel sailing?"
Spake the hero of the Northland:
"To the wars my ship is sailing,
To the bloody fields of battle,
Where the streams run scarlet-coloured,
Where the paths are paved with bodies."
These the words of fair Annikki:
"Know I well the paths to battle;
Formerly my aged father
Often sounded war's alarum,
Often led the hosts to conquest;
In each ship a hundred rowers,

And in arms a thousand heroes,
On the prow a thousand cross-bows,
Swords, and spears, and battle-axes;
Know I well the ship of battle.
Speak no longer fruitless falsehoods,
Whither sailest, Wainamoinen,
Whither steerest, friend of waters?"
These the words of Wainamoinen:
"Come, O maiden, to my vessel,
In my magic ship be seated,
Then I'll give thee truthful answer."

Thus Annikki, silver-tinselled,
Answers ancient Wainamoinen:
"With the winds I'll fill thy vessel,
To thy bark I'll send the storm-winds
And capsize thy ship of magic,
Break in pieces its forecastle,
If the truth thou dost not tell me,
If thou dost not cease thy falsehoods,
If thou dost not tell me truly
Whither sails thy magic vessel."
These the words of Wainamoinen:
"Now I make thee truthful answer,
Though at first I spake deception:
I am sailing to the Northland
To the dismal Sariola,
Where the ogres live and flourish,
Where they drown the worthy heroes,
There to woo the Maid of Beauty
Sitting on the bow of heaven,
Woo and win the fairy virgin,
Bring her to my home and kindred,
To the firesides of Wainola."

Then Annikki, graceful maiden,
Of the Night and Dawn, the daughter,
As she heard the rightful answer,
Knew the truth was fully spoken,
Straightway left her coats unbeaten,
Left unwashed her linen garments,
Left unrinsed her silks and ribbons
On the highway by the seashore,
On the bridge of scarlet colour;
On her arm she threw her long-robes,
Hastened off with speed of roebuck
To the shops of Ilmarinen,
To the iron-forger's furnace,
To the blacksmith's home and smithy,
Here she found the hero-artist,
Forging out a bench of iron,
And adorning it with silver.
Soot lay thick upon his forehead,
Soot and coal upon his shoulders.

On the threshold speaks Annikki,
These the words his sister uses:
"Ilmarinen, dearest brother,
Thou eternal artist-forger,
Forge me now a loom of silver,
Golden rings to grace my fingers,
Forge me gold and silver ear-rings,
Six or seven golden girdles,
Golden crosslets for my bosom,
For my head forge golden trinkets,
And I'll tell a tale surprising,
Tell a story that concerns thee
Truthfully I'll tell the story."

Then the blacksmith Ilmarinen
Spake and these the words he uttered:
"If thou'lt tell the tale sincerely,
I will forge the loom of silver,
Golden rings to grace thy fingers,
Forge thee gold and silver ear-rings,
Six or seven golden girdles,
Golden crosslets for thy bosom,
For thy head forge golden trinkets;
But if thou shouldst tell me falsely,
I shall break thy beauteous jewels,
Break thine ornaments in pieces,
Hurl them to the fire and furnace,
Never forge thee other trinkets."
This the answer of Annikki:
"Ancient blacksmith, Ilmarinen,
Dost thou ever think to marry
Her already thine affianced,
Beauteous Maiden of the Rainbow,
Fairest virgin of the Northland,
Chosen bride of Sariola?
Shouldst thou wish the Maid of Beauty,
Thou must forge, and forge unceasing,
Hammering the days and nights through;
Forge the summer hoofs for horses,

Forge them iron hoofs for winter,
In the long nights forge the snow-sledge,
Gaily trim it in the daytime,
Haste thou then upon thy journey
To thy wooing in the Northland,
To the dismal Sariola;
Thither journeys one more clever,
Sails another now before thee,
There to woo thy bride affianced,
Thence to lead thy chosen virgin,
Woo and win the Maid of Beauty;
Three long years thou hast been wooing.
Wainamoinen now is sailing
On the blue back of the waters,
Sitting at his helm of copper;
On the prow are golden carvings,
Beautiful his boat of magic,
Sailing fleetly o'er the billows,
To the never-pleasant Northland,
To the dismal Sariola."

Ilmarinen stood in wonder,
Stood a statue at the story;
Silent grief had settled o'er him,
Settled o'er the iron-artist;
From one hand the tongs descended,
From the other fell the hammer,
As the blacksmith made this answer:
"Good Annikki, worthy sister,
I shall forge the loom of silver,
Golden rings to grace thy fingers,
Forge thee gold and silver ear-rings,
Six or seven golden girdles,
Golden crosslets for thy bosom;
Go and heat for me the bath-room,
Fill with heat the honey-chambers,
Lay the faggots on the fire-place,
Lay the smaller woods around them,
Pour some water through the ashes,
Make a soap of magic virtue,
Thus to cleanse my blackened visage,
Thus to cleanse the blacksmith's body,
Thus remove the soot and ashes."

Then Annikki, kindly sister,
Quickly warmed her brother's bath-room,
Warmed it with the knots of fir trees,
That the thunder-winds had broken;
Gathered pebbles from the fire-stream,
Threw them in the heating waters;
Broke the tassels from the birch-trees,
Steeped the foliage in honey,
Made a lye from milk and ashes,
Made of these a strong decoction,
Mixed it with the fat and marrow
Of the reindeer of the mountains,
Made a soap of magic virtue,
Thus to cleanse the iron-artist,
Thus to beautify the suitor,
Thus to make the hero worthy.

Ilmarinen, ancient blacksmith,
The eternal metal-worker,
Forged the wishes of his sister,
Ornaments for fair Annikki,
Rings, and bracelets, pins and ear-drops,
Forged for her six golden girdles,
Forged a weaving loom of silver,
While the maid prepared the bath-room,
Set his toilet-room in order.

To the maid he gave the trinkets,
Gave the loom of molten silver,
And the sister thus made answer:
"I have heated well thy bath-room,
Have thy toilet-things in order,
Everything as thou desirest;
Go prepare thyself for wooing,
Lave thy head to flaxen whiteness,
Make thy cheeks look fresh and ruddy,
Lave thyself in Love's aroma,
That thy wooing prove successful."

Ilmarinen, magic artist,
Quick repairing to his bath-room,
Bathed his head to flaxen whiteness,
Made his cheeks look fresh and ruddy,
Laved his eyes until they sparkled
Like the moonlight on the waters;
Wondrous were his form and features,
And his cheeks like ruddy berries.
These the words of Ilmarinen:
"Fair Annikki, lovely sister,
Bring me now my silken raiment,

Bring my best and richest vesture,
Bring me now my softest linen,
That my wooing prove successful."

Straightway did the helpful sister
Bring the finest of his raiment,
Bring the softest of his linen,
Raiment fashioned by his mother;
Brought to him his silken stockings,
Brought him shoes of marten-leather,
Brought a vest of sky-blue colour,
Brought him scarlet-coloured trousers,
Brought a coat with scarlet trimming,
Brought a red shawl trimmed in ermine
Fourfold wrapped about his body;
Brought a fur-coat made of seal-skin,
Fastened with a thousand bottons,
And adorned with countless jewels;
Brought for him his magic girdle,
Fastened well with golden buckles,
That his artist-mother fashioned;
Brought him gloves with golden wristlets,
That the Laplanders had woven
For a head of many ringlets;
Brought the finest cap in Northland,
That his ancient father purchased
When he first began his wooing.

Ilmarinen, blacksmith-artist,
Clad himself to look his finest,
When he thus addressed a servant:
"Hitch for me a fleet-foot racer,
Hitch him to my willing snow-sledge,
For I start upon a journey
To the distant shores of Pohya,
To the dismal Sariola."
Spake the servant thus in answer:
"Thou hast seven fleet-foot racers,
Munching grain within their mangers,
Which of these shall I make ready?"
Spake the blacksmith, Ilmarinen:
"Take the fleetest of my coursers,
Put the gray steed in the harness,
Hitch him to my sledge of magic;
Place six cuckoos on the break-board,
Seven bluebirds on the cross-bars,
Thus to charm the Northland maidens,
Thus to make them look and listen,
As the cuckoos call and echo.
Bring me too my largest bear-skin,
Fold it warm about the cross-bench;
Bring me then my marten fur-robes,
As a cover and protection."

Straightway then the trusty servant
Of the blacksmith, Ilmarinen,
Put the gray steed in the harness,
Hitched the racer to the snow-sledge,
Placed six cuckoos on the break-board,
Seven bluebirds on the cross-bars,
On the front to sing and twitter;
Then he brought the largest bear-skin,
Folded it upon the cross-bench;
Brought the finest robes of marten,
Warm protection for the master.

Ilmarinen, forger-artist,
The eternal metal-worker,
Earnestly entreated Ukko:
"Send thy snow-flakes, Ukko, father,
Let them gently fall from heaven,
Let them cover all the heather,
Let them hide the berry-bushes,
That my sledge may glide in freedom
O'er the hills to Sariola!"

Ukko sent the snow from heaven,
Gently dropped the crystal snow-flakes,
Lending thus his kind assistance
To the hero, Ilmarinen,
On his journey to the Northland.

Reins in hand, the ancient artist
Seats him in his metal snow-sledge,
And beseeches thus his Master:
"Good luck to my reins and traces,
Good luck to my shafts and runners!
God protect my magic snow-sledge,
Be my safeguard on my journey
To the dismal Sariola!"

Now the ancient Ilmarinen
Draws the reins upon the racer,
Snaps his whip above the courser,

To the gray steed gives this order,
And the charger plunges northward:
"Haste away, my flaxen stallion,
Haste thee onward, noble white-face,
To the never-pleasant Pohya,
To the dreary Sariola!"

Fast and faster flies the fleet-foot,
On the curving snow-capped sea-coast,
On the borders of the lowlands,
O'er the alder-hills and mountains.
Merrily the steed flies onward,
Bluebirds singing, cuckoos calling,
On the seashore looking northward,
Through the sand and falling snow-flakes
Blinding winds, and snow, and sea-foam,
Cloud the hero, Ilmarinen,
As he glides upon his journey,
Looking seaward for the vessel
Of the ancient Wainamoinen;
Travels one day, then a second,
Travels all the next day northward,
Till the third day Ilmarinen
Overtakes old Wainamoinen,
Hails him in his magic vessel,
And addresses thus the minstrel:
"O thou ancient Wainamoinen,
Let us woo in peace the maiden,
Fairest daughter of the Northland,
Sitting on the bow of heaven,
Let each labour long to win her,
Let her wed the one she chooses,
Him selecting, let her follow."
Wainamoinen thus makes answer:
"I agree to thy proposal,
Let us woo in peace the maiden,
Not by force, nor faithless measures,
Shall we woo the Maid of Beauty,
Let her follow him she chooses;
Let the unsuccessful suitor
Harbor neither wrath nor envy
For the hero that she follows."

Thus agreeing, on they journey,
Each according to his pleasure;
Fleetly does the steed fly onward,
Quickly flies the magic vessel,
Sailing on the broad sea northward;
Ilmarinen's fleet-foot racer
Makes the hills of Northland tremble,
As he gallops on his journey
To the dismal Sariola.

Wainamoinen calls the south winds,
And they fly to his assistance;
Swiftly sails his ship of beauty,
Swiftly plows the rough sea-billows
In her pathway to Pohyola.

Time had gone but little distance,
Scarce a moment had passed over,
Ere the dogs began their barking,
In the mansions of the Northland,
In the courts of Sariola,
Watch-dogs of the court of Louhi;
Never had they growled so fiercely,
Never had they barked so loudly,
Never with their tails had beaten
Northland into such an uproar.
Spake the master of Pohyola:
"Go and learn, my worthy daughter,
Why the watch-dogs have been barking,
Why the black-dog signals danger."
Quickly does the daughter answer:
"I am occupied, dear father,
I have work of more importance,
I must tend my flock of lambkins,
I must turn the nether millstone,
Grind to flour the grains of barley,
Run the grindings through the sifter,
Only have I time for grinding."

Lowly growls the faithful watch-dog,
Seldom does he growl so strangely.
Spake the master of Pohyola:
"Go and learn, my trusted consort,
Why the Northland dogs are barking,
Why the black-dog signals danger."
Thus his aged wife makes answer:
"Have no time, nor inclination,
I must feed my hungry household,
Must prepare a worthy dinner,
I must bake the toothsome biscuit,
Knead the dough till it is ready,

Only have I strength for kneading."
Spake the master of Pohyola:
"Dames are always in a hurry,
Maidens too are ever busy,
Whether warming at the oven,
Or asleep upon their couches;
Go my son, and learn the danger,
Why the black-dog growls displeasure."
Quickly does the son give answer:
"Have no time, nor inclination,
Am in haste to grind my hatchet;
I must chop this log to cordwood,
For the fire must cut the faggots,
I must split the wood in fragments,
Large the pile and small the fire-wood,
Only have I strength for chopping."

Still the watch-dog growls in anger,
Growl the whelps within the mansion,
Growl the dogs chained in the kennel,
Growls the black-dog on the hill-top,
Setting Northland in an uproar.
Spake the master of Pohyola:
"Never, never does my black-dog
Growl like this without a reason;
Never does he bark for nothing,
Does not growl at angry billows,
Nor the sighing of the pine trees."

Then the master of Pohyola
Went himself to learn the reason
For the barking of the watch-dogs;
Strode he through the spacious court-yard,
Through the open fields beyond it,
To the summit of the uplands.
Looking toward his black-dog barking,
He beholds the muzzle pointed
To a distant, stormy hill-top,
To a mound with alders covered;
There he learned the rightful reason,
Why his dogs had barked so loudly,
Why had growled the wool-tail bearer,
Why his whelps had signalled danger.
At full sail, he saw a vessel,
And the ship was scarlet-coloured,
Entering the bay of Lempo;
Saw a sledge of magic colours,
Gliding up the curving seashore,
O'er the snow-fields of Pohyola.

Then the master of the Northland
Hastened straightway to his dwelling,
Hastened forward to his court-room,
These the accents of the master:
"Often strangers journey hither,
On the blue back of the ocean,
Sailing in a scarlet vessel,
Rocking in the bay of Lempo;
Often strangers come in sledges
To the honey-lands of Louhi."

Spake the hostess of Pohyola:
"How shall we obtain a token
Why these strangers journey hither?
My beloved, faithful daughter,
Lay a branch upon the fire-place,
Let it burn with fire of magic;
If it trickle drops of scarlet,
War and bloodshed do they bring us;
If it trickle drops of water,
Peace and plenty bring the strangers."

Northland's fair and slender maiden,
Beautiful and modest daughter,
Lays a sorb-branch on the fire-place,
Lights it with the fire of magic;
Does not trickle drops of scarlet,
Trickles neither blood, nor water,
From the wand come drops of honey.

From the corner spake Suowakko,
This the language of the wizard:
"If the wand is dripping honey,
Then the strangers that are coming
Are but worthy friends and suitors."

Then the hostess of the Northland,
With the daughter of the hostess,
Straightway left their work, and hastened
From their dwelling to the court-yard;
Looked about in all directions,
Turned their eyes upon the waters,
Saw a magic-coloured vessel
Rocking slowly in the harbor,

Having sailed the bay of Lempo,
Triple sails, and masts, and rigging,
Sable was the nether portion,
And the upper, scarlet-coloured,
At the helm an ancient hero
Leaning on his oars of copper;
Saw a fleet-foot racer running,
Saw a red sledge lightly follow,
Saw the magic sledge emblazoned,
Guided toward the courts of Louhi;
Saw and heard six golden cuckoos
Sitting on the break-board, calling,
Seven bluebirds richly coloured
Singing from the yoke and cross-bar;
In the sledge a magic hero,
Young, and strong, and proud, and handsome,
Holding reins upon the courser.
Spake the hostess of Pohyola:
"Dearest daughter, winsome maiden,
Dost thou wish a noble suitor?
Should these heroes come to woo thee,
Wouldst thou leave thy home and country,
Be the bride of him that pleases,
Be his faithful life-companion?

"He that comes upon the waters,
Sailing in a magic vessel,
Having sailed the bay of Lempo,
Is the good, old Wainamoinen;
In his ship are countless treasures,
Richest presents from Wainola.

"He that rides here in his snow-sledge
In his sledge of magic beauty,
With the cuckoos and the bluebirds,
Is the blacksmith, Ilmarinen,
Cometh hither empty-handed,
Only brings some wisdom-sayings.
When they come within the dwelling,
Bring a bowl of honeyed viands,
Bring a pitcher with two handles,
Give to him that thou wouldst follow;
Give it to old Wainamoinen,
Him that brings thee countless treasures,
Costly presents in his vessel,
Priceless gems from Kalevala."
Spake the Northland's lovely daughter,
This the language of the maiden:
"Good, indeed, advice maternal,
But I will not wed for riches,
Wed no man for countless treasures;
For his worth I'll choose a husband,
For his youth and fine appearance,
For his noble form and features;
In the olden times the maidens
Were not sold by anxious mothers
To the suitors that they loved not.
I shall choose without his treasures
Ilmarinen for his wisdom,
For his worth and good behavior,
Him that forged the wondrous Sampo,
Hammered thee the lid in colours."
Spake the hostess of Pohyola:
"Senseless daughter, child of folly,
Thus to choose the ancient blacksmith,
From whose brow drips perspiration,
Evermore to rinse his linen,
Lave his hands, and eyes, and forehead,
Keep his ancient house in order;
Little use his wit and wisdom
When compared with gold and silver."
This the answer of the daughter:
"I will never, never, never,
Wed the ancient Wainamoinen
With his gold and priceless jewels;
Never will I be a helpmate
To a hero in his dotage,
Little thanks my compensation."

Wainamoinen, safely landing
In advance of Ilmarinen,
Pulls his gaily-covered vessel
From the waves upon the sea-beach,
On the cylinders of birch-wood,
On the rollers copper-banded,
Straightway hastens to the guest-room
Of the hostess of Pohyola,
Of the master of the Northland,
Speaks these words upon the threshold
To the famous Maid of Beauty:
"Come with me, thou lovely virgin,
Be my bride and life-companion,
Share with me my joys and sorrows,
Be my honoured wife hereafter!"

This the answer of the maiden:
"Hast thou built for me the vessel,
Built for me the ship of magic
From the fragments of the distaff,
From the splinters of the spindle?"
Wainamoinen thus replying:
"I have built the promised vessel,
Built the wondrous ship for sailing,
Firmly joined the parts by magic;
It will weather roughest billows,
Will outlive the winds and waters,
Swiftly glide upon the blue back
Of the deep and boundless ocean;
It will ride the waves in beauty,
Like an airy bubble rising,
Like a cork on lake and river,
Through the angry seas of Northland,
Through Pohyola's peaceful waters."

Northland's fair and slender daughter
Gives this answer to her suitor:
"Will not wed a sea-born hero,
Do not care to rock the billows,
Cannot live with such a husband;
Storms would bring us pain and trouble,
Winds would rack our hearts and temples;
Therefore thee I cannot follow,
Cannot keep thy home in order,
Cannot be thy life-companion,
Cannot wed old Wainamoinen."

Rune XIX: Ilmarinen's Wooing

Ilmarinen, hero-blacksmith,
The eternal metal-worker,
Hastens forward to the court-room
Of the hostess of Pohyola,
Of the master of the Northland,
Hastens through the open portals
Into Louhi's home and presence.
Servants come with silver pitchers,
Filled with Northland's richest brewing;
Honey-drink is brought and offered
To the blacksmith of Wainola,
Ilmarinen thus replying:
"I shall not in all my life-time
Taste the drink that thou hast brought me,
Till I see the Maid of Beauty,
Fairy Maiden of the Rainbow;
I will drink with her in gladness,
For whose hand I journey hither."
Spake the hostess of Pohyola:
"Trouble does the one selected
Give to him that wooes and watches;
Not yet are her feet in sandals,
Thine affianced is not ready.
Only canst thou woo my daughter,
Only canst thou win the maiden,
When thou hast by aid of magic
Plowed the serpent-field of Hisi,
Plowed the field of hissing vipers,
Touching neither beam nor handles.
Once this field was plowed by Piru,
Lempo furrowed it with horses,
With a plowshare made of copper,
With a beam of flaming iron;
Never since has any hero
Brought this field to cultivation."

Ilmarinen of Wainola
Straightway hastens to the chamber
Of the Maiden of the Rainbow,
Speaks these words in hesitation:
"Thou of Night and Dawn the daughter,
Tell me, dost thou not remember
When for thee I forged the Sampo,
Hammered thee the lid in colours?
Thou didst swear by oath the strongest,
By the forge and by the anvil,
By the tongs and by the hammer,
In the ears of the Almighty,
And before omniscient Ukko,
Thou wouldst follow me hereafter,
Be my bride, my life-companion,
Be my honoured wife forever.
Now thy mother is exacting,
Will not give to me her daughter,
Till by means of magic only,
I have plowed the field
of serpents,
Plowed the hissing soil of Hisi."

The affianced Bride of Beauty
Gives this answer to the suitor:
"O, thou blacksmith, Ilmarinen,
The eternal wonder-forger,
Forge thyself a golden plowshare,
Forge the beam of shining silver,
And of copper forge the handles;
Then with ease, by aid of magic,
Thou canst plow the field of serpents,
Plow the hissing soil of Hisi."
Ilmarinen, welcome suitor,
Straightway builds a forge
and smithy,
Places gold within the furnace,
In the forge he lays the silver,
Forges then a golden plowshare,
Forges, too, a beam of silver,
Forges handles out of copper,
Forges boots and gloves of iron,
Forges him a mail of metal,
For his limbs a safe protection,
Safe protection for his body.
Then a horse of fire selecting,
Harnesses the flaming stallion,
Goes to plow the field of serpents,
Plow the viper-lands of Hisi.
In the field were countless vipers,
Serpents there of every species,
Crawling, writhing, hissing, stinging,
Harmless all against the hero,
Thus he stills the snakes of Lempo:
"Vipers, ye by God created,
Neither best nor worst of creatures,
Ye whose wisdom comes from Ukko,
And whose venom comes from Hisi,
Ukko is your greater Master,
By His will your heads are lifted;
Get ye hence before my plowing,
Writhe ye through the grass
and stubble,
Crawl ye to the nearest thicket,
Keep your heads beneath the heather,
Hunt your holes to Mana's kingdom
If your poison-heads be lifted,
Then will mighty Ukko smite them
With his iron-pointed arrows,
With the lightning of his anger."
Thus the blacksmith, Ilmarinen,
Safely plows the field of serpents,
Lifts the vipers in his plowing,
Buries them beneath the furrow,
Harmless all against his magic.
When the task had been completed,
Ilmarinen, quick returning,
Thus addressed Pohyola's hostess:
"I have plowed the field of Hisi,
Plowed the field of hissing serpents,
Stilled and banished all the vipers;
Give me, ancient dame, thy daughter,
Fairest maiden of the Northland."
Spake the hostess of Pohyola:
"Shall not grant to thee
my daughter,
Shall not give my lovely virgin,
Till Tuoni's bear is muzzled,
Till Manala's wolf is conquered,
In the forests of the deathland,
In the boundaries of Mana.
Hundreds have been sent to hunt him,
No one yet has been successful,
All have perished in Manala."

Thereupon young Ilmarinen
To the maiden's chamber hastens,
Thus addresses his affianced:
"Still another test demanded,
I must go to Tuonela,
Bridle there the bear of Mana,
Bring him from the deathland forests,
From Tuoni's grove and empire!"
This advice the maiden gives him:
"O thou artist, Ilmarinen,
The eternal metal-worker,
Forge of steel a magic bridle,
On a rock beneath the water,
In the foaming triple currents;
Make the straps of steel
and copper,
Bridle then the bear of Mana,
Lead him from Tuoni's forests."

Then the blacksmith, Ilmarinen,
Forged of steel a magic bridle,
On a rock beneath the water,

In the foam of triple currents;
Made the straps of steel and copper,
Straightway went the bear to muzzle,
In the forests of the deathland,
Spake these words in supplication:
"Terhenetar, ether-maiden,
Daughter of the fog and snow-flake,
Sift the fog and let it settle
O'er the hills and lowland thickets,
Where the wild-bear feeds and lingers,
That he may not see my coming,
May not hear my stealthy footsteps!"

Terhenetar hears his praying,
Makes the fog and snow-flake settle
On the coverts of the wild-beasts;
Thus the bear he safely bridles,
Fetters him in chains of magic,
In the forests of Tuoni,
In the blue groves of Manala.

When this task had been completed,
Ilmarinen, quick returning,
Thus addressed the ancient Louhi:
"Give me, worthy dame, thy daughter,
Give me now my bride affianced,
I have brought the bear of Mana
From Tuoni's fields and forests."

Spake the hostess of Pohyola
To the blacksmith, Ilmarinen:
"I will only give my daughter,
Give to thee the Maid of Beauty,
When the monster-pike thou catchest
In the river of Tuoni,
In Manala's fatal waters,
Using neither hooks, nor fish-nets,
Neither boat, nor fishing-tackle;
Hundreds have been sent to catch him,
No one yet has been successful,
All have perished in Manala."

Much disheartened, Ilmarinen
Hastened to the maiden's chamber,
Thus addressed the rainbow-maiden:
"Now a third test is demanded,
Much more difficult than ever;
I must catch the pike of Mana,
In the river of Tuoni,
And without my fishing-tackle,
Hard the third test of the hero!"
This advice the maiden gives him:
"O thou hero, Ilmarinen,
Never, never be discouraged:
In thy furnace, forge an eagle,
From the fire of ancient magic;
He will catch the pike of Mana,
Catch the monster-fish in safety,
From the death-stream of Tuoni,
From Manala's fatal waters."
Then the suitor, Ilmarinen,
The eternal artist-forgeman,
In the furnace forged an eagle
From the fire of ancient wisdom;
For this giant bird of magic
Forged he talons out of iron,
And his beak of steel and copper;
Seats himself upon the eagle,
On his back between the wing-bones,
Thus addresses he his creature,
Gives the bird of fire this order:
"Mighty eagle, bird of beauty,
Fly thou whither I direct thee,
To Tuoni's coal-black river,
To the blue deeps of the Death-stream,
Seize the mighty fish of Mana,
Catch for me this water-monster."

Swiftly flies the magic eagle,
Giant-bird of worth and wonder,
To the river of Tuoni,
There to catch the pike of Mana;
One wing brushes on the waters,
While the other sweeps the heavens;
In the ocean dips his talons,
Whets his beak on mountain-ledges.

Safely landing, Ilmarinen,
The immortal artist-forger,
Hunts the monster of the Death-stream,
While the eagle hunts and fishes
In the waters of Manala.
From the river rose a monster,
Grasped the blacksmith, Ilmarinen,

Tried to drag him to his sea-cave;
Quick the eagle pounced upon him,
With his metal-beak he seized him,
Wrenched his head, and rent his body,
Hurled him back upon the bottom
Of the deep and fatal river,
Freed his master, Ilmarinen.

Then arose the pike of Mana,
Came the water-dog in silence,
Of the pikes was not the largest,
Nor belonged he to the smallest;
Tongue the length of double hatchets,
Teeth as long as fen-rake handles,
Mouth as broad as triple streamlets,
Back as wide as seven sea-boats,
Tried to snap the magic blacksmith,
Tried to swallow Ilmarinen.
Swiftly swoops the mighty eagle,
Of the birds was not the largest,
Nor belonged he to the smallest;
Beak a hundred fathoms measured,
Mouth as wide as seven streamlets,
Tongue as long as seven javelins,
Like five crooked scythes his talons;
Swoops upon the pike of Mana.
Quick the giant fish endangered,
Darts and flounders in the river,
Dragging down the mighty eagle,
Lashing up the very bottom
To the surface of the river;
When the mighty bird uprising
Leaves the wounded pike in water,
Soars aloft on worsted pinions
To his home in upper ether;
Soars awhile, and sails, and circles,
Circles o'er the reddened waters,
Swoops again on lightning-pinions,
Strikes with mighty force his talons
Into the shoulder of his victim;
Strikes the second of his talons
On the flinty mountain-ledges,
On the rocks with iron hardened;
From the cliffs rebound his talons,
Slip the flinty rocks o'erhanging,
And the monster-pike resisting
Dives again beneath the surface
To the bottom of the river,
From the talons of the eagle;
Deep, the wounds upon the body
Of the monster of Tuoni.
Still a third time soars the eagle,
Soars, and sails, and quickly circles,
Swoops again upon the monster,
Fire out-shooting from his pinions,
Both his eyeballs flashing lightning;
With his beak of steel and copper
Grasps again the pike of Mana;
Firmly planted are his talons
In the rocks and in his victim,
Drags the monster from the river,
Lifts the pike above the waters,
From Tuoni's coal-black river,
From the blue back of Manala.

Thus the third time does the eagle
Bring success from former failures;
Thus at last the eagle catches
Mana's pike, the worst of fishes,
Swiftest swimmer of the waters,
From the river of Tuoni;
None could see Manala's river,
For the myriad of fish-scales;
Hardly could one see through ether,
For the feathers of the eagle,
Relicts of the mighty contest.

Then the bird of copper talons
Took the pike, with scales of silver,
To the pine tree's topmost branches,
To the fir tree plumed with needles,
Tore the monster-fish in pieces,
Ate the body of his victim,
Left the head for Ilmarinen.
Spake the blacksmith to the eagle:
"O thou bird of evil nature,
What thy thought and what thy motive?
Thou hast eaten what I needed,
Evidence of my successes;
Thoughtless eagle, witless instinct,
Thus to mar the spoils of conquest!"

But the bird of metal talons
Hastened onward, soaring upward,

Rising higher into ether,
Rising, flying, soaring, sailing,
To the borders of the long-clouds,
Made the vault of ether tremble,
Split apart the dome of heaven,
Broke the coloured bow of Ukko,
Tore the Moon-horns from
their sockets,
Disappeared beyond the Sun-land,
To the home of the triumphant.

Then the blacksmith, Ilmarinen,
Took the pike-head to the hostess
Of the ever-dismal Northland,
Thus addressed the ancient Louhi:
"Let this head forever serve thee
As a guest-bench for thy dwelling,
Evidence of hero-triumphs;
I have caught the pike of Mana,
I have done as thou demandest,
Three my victories in deathland,
Three the tests of magic heroes;
Wilt thou give me now thy daughter,
Give to me the Maid of Beauty?"
Spake the hostess of Pohyola:
"Badly is the test accomplished,
Thou has torn the pike in pieces,
From his neck the head is severed,
Of his body thou hast eaten,
Brought to me this worthless relic!"
These the words of Ilmarinen:
"When the victory is greatest,
Do we suffer greatest losses!
From the river of Tuoni,
From the kingdom of Manala,
I have brought to thee this trophy,
Thus the third task is completed.
Tell me is the maiden ready,
Wilt thou give the bride affianced?"
Spake the hostess of Pohyola:
"I will give to thee my daughter,
Will prepare my snow-white virgin,
For the suitor, Ilmarinen;
Thou hast won the Maid of Beauty,
Bride is she of thine hereafter,
Fit companion of thy fireside,
Help and joy of all thy lifetime."

On the floor a child was sitting,
And the babe this tale related.
"There appeared within this dwelling,
Came a bird within the castle,
From the East came flying hither,
From the East, a monstrous eagle,
One wing touched the vault of heaven,
While the other swept the ocean;
With his tail upon the waters,
Reached his beak beyond the cloudlets,
Looked about, and eager watching,
Flew around, and sailing, soaring,
Flew away to hero-castle,
Knocked three times with beak of copper
On the castle-roof of iron;
But the eagle could not enter.

"Then the eagle, looking round him,
Flew again, and sailed, and circled,
Flew then to the mothers' castle,
Loudly rapped with heavy knocking
On the mothers' roof of copper;
But the eagle could not enter.

"Then the eagle, looking round him,
Flew a third time, sailing, soaring,
Flew then to the virgins' castle,
Knocked again with beak of copper,
On the virgins' roof of linen,
Easy for him there to enter;
Flew upon the castle-chimney,
Quick descending to the chamber,
Pulled the clapboards from the studding,
Tore the linen from the rafters,
Perched upon the chamber-window,
Near the walls of many colours,
On the cross-bars gaily-feathered,
Looked upon the curly-headed,
Looked upon their golden ringlets,
Looked upon the snow-white virgins,
On the purest of the maidens,
On the fairest of the daughters,
On the maid with pearly necklace,
On the maiden wreathed in flowers;
Perched awhile, and looked, admiring,
Swooped upon the Maid of Beauty,
On the purest of the virgins,

On the whitest, on the fairest,
On the stateliest and grandest,
Swooped upon the rainbow-daughter
Of the dismal Sariola;
Grasped her in his mighty talons,
Bore away the Maid of Beauty,
Maid of fairest form and feature,
Maid adorned with pearly necklace,
Decked in feathers iridescent,
Fragrant flowers upon her bosom,
Scarlet band around her forehead,
Golden rings upon her fingers,
Fairest maiden of the Northland."
Spake the hostess of Pohyola,
When the babe his tale had ended:
"Tell me how, my child beloved,
Thou hast learned about the maiden,
Hast obtained the information,
How her flaxen ringlets nestled,
How the maiden's silver glistened,
How the virgin's gold was lauded.
Shone the silver Sun upon thee,
Did the moonbeams bring this knowledge?"
From the floor the child made answer:
"Thus I gained the information,
Moles of good-luck led me hither,
To the home of the distinguished,
To the guest-room of the maiden,
Good-name bore her worthy father,
He that sailed the magic vessel;
Better-name enjoyed the mother,
She that baked the bread of barley,
She that kneaded wheaten biscuits,
Fed her many guests in Northland.

"Thus the information reached me,
Thus the distant stranger heard it,
Heard the virgin had arisen:
Once I walked within the court-yard,
Stepping near the virgin's chamber,
At an early hour of morning,
Ere the Sun had broken slumber;
Whirling rose the soot in cloudlets,
Blackened wreaths of smoke came rising
From the chamber of the maiden,
From thy daughter's lofty chimney;
There the maid was busy grinding,
Moved the handles of the millstone
Making voices like the cuckoo,
Like the ducks the side-holes sounded,
And the sifter like the goldfinch,
Like the sea-pearls sang the grindstones.

"Then a second time I wandered
To the border of the meadow;
In the forest was the maiden
Rocking on a fragrant hillock,
Dyeing red in iron vessels,
And in copper kettles, yellow.

"Then a third time did I wander
To the lovely maiden's window;
There I saw thy daughter weaving,
Heard the flying of her shuttle,
Heard the beating of her loom-lathe,
Heard the rattling of her treddles,
Heard the whirring of her yarn-reel."
Spake the hostess of Pohyola:
"Now alas! beloved daughter,
I have often taught this lesson:
'Do not sing among the pine trees,
Do not call adown the valleys,
Do not hang thy head in walking,
Do not bare thine arms, nor shoulders,
Keep the secrets of thy bosom,
Hide thy beauty and thy power.'

"This I told thee in the autumn,
Taught thee in the summer season,
Sang thee in the budding spring-time,
Sang thee when the snows were falling:
'Let us build a place for hiding,
Let us build the smallest windows,
Where may weave my fairest daughter,
Where my maid may ply her shuttle,
Where my joy may work unnoticed
By the heroes of the Northland,
By the suitors of Wainola.'"

From the floor the child made answer,
Fourteen days the young child numbered:
"Easy 'tis to hide a war-horse
In the Northland fields and stables;
Hard indeed to hide a maiden,

Having lovely form and features!
Build of stone a distant castle
In the middle of the ocean,
Keep within thy lovely maiden,
Train thou there thy winsome daughter,
Not long hidden canst thou keep her.
Maidens will not grow and flourish,
Kept apart from men and heroes,
Will not live without their suitors,
Will not thrive without their wooers;
Thou canst never hide a maiden,
Neither on the land nor water."

Now the ancient Wainamoinen,
Head down-bent and heavy-hearted,
Wanders to his native country,
To Wainola's peaceful meadows,
To the plains of Kalevala,
Chanting as he journeys homeward:
"I have passed the age for wooing,
Woe is me, rejected suitor,
Woe is me, a witless minstrel,
That I did not woo and marry,
When my face was young and winsome,
When my hand was warm and welcome!
Youth dethrones my age and station,
Wealth is nothing, wisdom worthless,
When a hero goes a-wooing
With a poor but younger brother.
Fatal error that a hero
Does not wed in early manhood,
In his youth does not be master
Of a worthy wife and household."

Thus the ancient Wainamoinen
Sends the edict to his people:
"Old men must not go a-wooing,
Must not swim the sea of anger,
Must not row upon a wager,
Must not run a race for glory,
With the younger sons of Northland."

Rune XX: The Brewing of Beer

Now we sing the wondrous legends,
Songs of wedding-feasts and dances,
Sing the melodies of wedlock,
Sing the songs of old tradition;
Sing of Ilmarinen's marriage
To the Maiden of the Rainbow,
Fairest daughter of the Northland,
Sing the drinking-songs of Pohya.

Long prepared they for the wedding
In Pohyola's halls and chambers,
In the courts of Sariola;
Many things that Louhi ordered,
Great indeed the preparations
For the marriage of the daughter,
For the feasting of the heroes,
For the drinking of the strangers,
For the feeding of the poor-folk,
For the people's entertainment.

Grew an ox in far Karjala,
Not the largest, nor the smallest,
Was the ox that grew in Suomi;
But his size was all-sufficient,
For his tail was sweeping Jamen,
And his head was over Kemi,
Horns in length a hundred fathoms,
Longer than the horns his mouth was;
Seven days it took a weasel
To encircle neck and shoulders;
One whole day a swallow journeyed
From one horn-tip to the other,
Did not stop between for resting.
Thirty days the squirrel travelled
From the tail to reach the shoulders,
But he could not gain the horn-tip
Till the Moon had long passed over.

This young ox of huge dimensions,
This great calf of distant Suomi,
Was conducted from Karjala
To the meadows of Pohyola;
At each horn a hundred heroes,
At his head and neck a thousand.
When the mighty ox was lassoed,
Led away to Northland pastures,

Peacefully the monster journeyed
By the bays of Sariola,
Ate the pasture on the borders;
To the clouds arose his shoulders,
And his horns to highest heaven.
Not in all of Sariola
Could a butcher be discovered
That could kill the ox for Louhi,
None of all the sons of Northland,
In her hosts of giant people,
In her rising generation,
In the hosts of those grown older.

Came a hero from a distance,
Wirokannas from Karelen,
And these words the gray-beard uttered:
"Wait, O wait, thou ox of Suomi,
Till I bring my ancient war-club;
Then I'll smite thee on thy forehead,
Break thy skull, thou willing victim!
Nevermore wilt thou in summer
Browse the woods of Sariola,
Bare our pastures, fields, and forests;
Thou, O ox, wilt feed no longer
Through the length and
breadth of Northland,
On the borders of this ocean!"

When the ancient Wirokannas
Started out the ox to slaughter,
When Palwoinen swung his war-club,
Quick the victim turned his forehead,
Flashed his flaming eyes upon him;
To the fir tree leaped the hero,
In the thicket hid Palwoinen,
Hid the gray-haired Wirokannas.

Everywhere they seek a butcher,
One to kill the ox of Suomi,
In the country of Karelen,
And among the Suomi-giants,
In the quiet fields of Ehstland,
On the battle-fields of Sweden,
Mid the mountaineers of Lapland,
In the magic fens of Turya;
Seek him in Tuoni's empire,
In the death-courts of Manala.
Long the search, and unsuccessful,
On the blue back of the ocean,
On the far-outstretching pastures.

There arose from out the sea-waves,
Rose a hero from the waters,
On the white-capped, roaring breakers,
From the water's broad expanses;
Nor belonged he to the largest,
Nor belonged he to the smallest;
Made his bed within a sea-shell,
Stood erect beneath a flour-sieve,
Hero old, with hands of iron,
And his face was copper-coloured;
Quick the hero full unfolded,
Like the full corn from the kernel.
On his head a hat of flint-stone,
On his feet were sandstone-sandals,
In his hand a golden cleaver,
And the blade was copper-handled.
Thus at last they found a butcher,
Found the magic ox a slayer.
Nothing has been found so mighty
That it has not found a master.

As the sea-god saw his booty,
Quickly rushed he on his victim,
Hurled him to his knees before him,
Quickly felled the calf of Suomi,
Felled the young ox of Karelen.
Bountifully meat was furnished;
Filled at least a thousand hogsheads
Of his blood were seven boatfuls,
And a thousand weight of suet,
For the banquet of Pohyola,
For the marriage-feast of Northland.

In Pohyola was a guest-room,
Ample was the hall of Louhi,
Was in length a hundred furlongs,
And in breadth was nearly fifty;
When upon the roof a rooster
Crowed at break of early morning,
No one on the earth could hear him;
When the dog barked at
one entrance,
None could hear him at the other.

Louhi, hostess of Pohyola,
Hastens to the hall and court-room,
In the centre speaks as follows:
"Whence indeed will come the liquor,
Who will brew me beer from barley,
Who will make the mead abundant,
For the people of the Northland,
Coming to my daughter's marriage,
To her drinking-feast and nuptials?
Cannot comprehend the malting,
Never have I learned the secret,
Nor the origin of brewing."
Spake an old man from his corner:
"Beer arises from the barley,
Comes from barley, hops, and water,
And the fire gives no assistance.
Hop-vine was the son of Remu,
Small the seed in earth was planted,
Cultivated in the loose soil,
Scattered like the evil serpents
On the brink of Kalew-waters,
On the Osmo-fields and borders.
There the young plant grew and flourished,
There arose the climbing hop-vine,
Clinging to the rocks and alders.

"Man of good-luck sowed the barley
On the Osmo hills and lowlands,
And the barley grew and flourished,
Grew and spread in rich abundance,
Fed upon the air and water,
On the Osmo plains and highlands,
On the fields of Kalew-heroes.

"Time had travelled little distance,
Ere the hops in trees were humming,
Barley in the fields was singing,
And from Kalew's well the water,
This the language of the trio:
'Let us join our triple forces,
Join to each the other's powers;
Sad alone to live and struggle,
Little use in working singly,
Better we should toil together.'

"Osmotar, the beer-preparer,
Brewer of the drink refreshing,
Takes the golden grains of barley,
Taking six of barley-kernels,
Taking seven tips of hop-fruit,
Filling seven cups with water,
On the fire she sets the caldron,
Boils the barley, hops, and water,
Lets them steep, and seethe, and bubble
Brewing thus the beer delicious,
In the hottest days of summer,
On the foggy promontory,
On the island forest-covered;
Poured it into birch-wood barrels,
Into hogsheads made of oak-wood.

"Thus did Osmotar of Kalew
Brew together hops and barley,
Could not generate the ferment.
Thinking long and long debating,
Thus she spake in troubled accents:
'What will bring the effervescence,
Who will add the needed factor,
That the beer may foam and sparkle,
May ferment and be delightful?'

"Kalevatar, magic maiden,
Grace and beauty in her fingers,
Swiftly moving, lightly stepping,
In her trimly-buckled sandals,
Steps upon the birch-wood bottom,
Turns one way, and then another,
In the centre of the caldron;
Finds within a splinter lying,
From the bottom lifts the fragment,
Turns it in her fingers, musing:
'What may come of this I know not,
In the hands of magic maidens,
In the virgin hands of Kapo,
Snowy virgin of the Northland!'

"Kalevatar took the splinter
To the magic virgin, Kapo,
Who by unknown force and insight,
Rubbed her hands and knees together,
And produced a snow-white squirrel;
Thus instructed she her creature,
Gave the squirrel these directions:
'Snow-white squirrel, mountain-jewel,

Flower of the field and forest,
Haste thee whither I would send thee,
Into Metsola's wide limits,
Into Tapio's seat of wisdom;
Hasten through the heavy tree-tops,
Wisely through the thickest branches,
That the eagle may not seize thee,
Thus escape the bird of heaven.
Bring me ripe cones from the fir tree,
From the pine tree bring me seedlings,
Bring them to the hands of Kapo,
For the beer of Osmo's daughter.'

"Quickly hastened forth the squirrel,
Quickly sped the nimble broad-tail,
Swiftly hopping on its journey
From one thicket to another,
From the birch-tree to the aspen,
From the pine tree to the willow,
From the sorb-tree to the alder,
Jumping here and there with method,
Crossed the eagle-woods in safety,
Into Metsola's wide limits,
Into Tapio's seat of wisdom;
There perceived three magic pine trees,
There perceived three smaller fir trees,
Quickly climbed the dark-green branches,
Was not captured by the eagle,
Was not mangled in his talons;
Broke the young cones from the fir tree,
Cut the shoots of pine tree branches,
Hid the cones within his pouches,
Wrapped them in his fur-grown mittens,
Brought them to the hands of Kapo,
To the magic virgin's fingers.
Kapo took the cones selected,
Laid them in the beer for ferment,
But it brought no effervescence,
And the beer was cold and lifeless.

"Osmotar, the beer-preparer,
Kapo, brewer of the liquor,
Deeply thought and long considered:
'What will bring the effervescence,
Who will lend me aid efficient,
That the beer may foam and sparkle,
May ferment and be refreshing?'

"Kalevatar, sparkling maiden,
Grace and beauty in her fingers,
Softly moving, lightly stepping,
In her trimly-buckled sandals,
Steps again upon the bottom,
Turns one way and then another,
In the centre of the caldron,
Sees a chip upon the bottom,
Takes it from its place of resting,
Looks upon the chip and muses:
'What may come of this I know not,
In the hands of mystic maidens,
In the hands of magic Kapo,
In the virgin's snow-white fingers.'

"Kalevatar took the birch-chip
To the magic maiden, Kapo,
Gave it to the white-faced maiden.
Kapo, by the aid of magic,
Rubbed her hands and knees together,
And produced a magic marten,
And the marten, golden-breasted;
Thus instructed she her creature,
Gave the marten these directions:
'Thou, my golden-breasted marten,
Thou my son of golden colour,
Haste thou whither I may send thee,
To the bear-dens of the mountain,
To the grottoes of the growler,
Gather yeast upon thy fingers,
Gather foam from lips of anger,
From the lips of bears in battle,
Bring it to the hands of Kapo,
To the hands of Osmo's daughter.'

"Then the marten golden-breasted,
Full consenting, hastened onward,
Quickly bounding on his journey,
Lightly leaping through the distance
Leaping o'er the widest rivers,
Leaping over rocky fissures,
To the bear-dens of the mountain,
To the grottoes of the growler,
Where the wild-bears fight each other,
Where they pass a dread existence,
Iron rocks, their softest pillows,
In the fastnesses of mountains;

From their lips the foam was dripping,
From their tongues the froth of anger;
This the marten deftly gathered,
Brought it to the maiden, Kapo,
Laid it in her dainty fingers.

"Osmotar, the beer-preparer,
Brewer of the beer of barley,
Used the beer-foam as a ferment;
But it brought no effervescence,
Did not make the liquor sparkle.

"Osmotar, the beer-preparer,
Thought again, and long debated:
'Who or what will bring the ferment,
That my beer may not be lifeless?'

"Kalevatar, magic maiden,
Grace and beauty in her fingers,
Softly moving, lightly stepping,
In her trimly-buckled sandals,
Steps again upon the bottom,
Turns one way and then another,
In the centre of the caldron,
Sees a pod upon the bottom,
Lifts it in her snow-white fingers,
Turns it o'er and o'er, and muses:
'What may come of this I know not,
In the hands of magic maidens,
In the hands of mystic Kapo,
In the snowy virgin's fingers?'

"Kalevatar, sparkling maiden,
Gave the pod to magic Kapo;
Kapo, by the aid of magic,
Rubbed the pod upon her knee-cap,
And a honey-bee came flying
From the pod within her fingers,
Kapo thus addressed her birdling:
'Little bee with honeyed winglets,
King of all the fragrant flowers,
Fly thou whither I direct thee,
To the islands in the ocean,
To the water-cliffs and grottoes,
Where asleep a maid has fallen,
Girdled with a belt of copper;
By her side are honey-grasses,
By her lips are fragrant flowers,
Herbs and flowers honey-laden;
Gather there the sweetened juices,
Gather honey on thy winglets,
From the calyces of flowers,
From the tips of seven petals,
Bring it to the hands of Kapo,
To the hands of Osmo's daughter.'

"Then the bee, the swift-winged birdling,
Flew away with lightning-swiftness
On his journey to the islands,
O'er the high waves of the ocean;
Journeyed one day, then a second,
Journeyed all the next day onward,
Till the third day evening brought him
To the islands in the ocean,
To the water-cliffs and grottoes;
Found the maiden sweetly sleeping,
In her silver-tinselled raiment,
Girdled with a belt of copper,
In a nameless meadow, sleeping,
In the honey-fields of magic;
By her side were honeyed grasses,
By her lips were fragrant flowers,
Silver stalks with golden petals;
Dipped its winglets in the honey,
Dipped its fingers in the juices
Of the sweetest of the flowers,
Brought the honey back to Kapo,
To the mystic maiden's fingers.

"Osmotar, the beer-preparer,
Placed the honey in the liquor;
Kapo mixed the beer and honey,
And the wedding-beer fermented;
Rose the live beer upward, upward,
From the bottom of the vessels,
Upward in the tubs of birch-wood,
Foaming higher, higher, higher,
Till it touched the oaken handles,
Overflowing all the caldrons;
To the ground it foamed and sparkled,
Sank away in sand and gravel.

"Time had gone but little distance,
Scarce a moment had passed over,

Ere the heroes came in numbers
To the foaming beer of Northland,
Rushed to drink the sparkling liquor.
Ere all others Lemminkainen
Drank, and grew intoxicated
On the beer of Osmo's daughter,
On the honey-drink of Kalew.

"Osmotar, the beer-preparer,
Kapo, brewer of the barley,
Spake these words in saddened accents:
'Woe is me, my life hard-fated,
Badly have I brewed the liquor,
Have not brewed the beer in wisdom,
Will not live within its vessels,
Overflows and fills Pohyola!'

"From a tree-top sings the redbreast,
From the aspen calls the robin:
'Do not grieve, thy beer is worthy,
Put it into oaken vessels,
Into strong and willing barrels
Firmly bound with hoops of copper.'

"Thus was brewed the beer of Northland,
At the hands of Osmo's daughter;
This the origin of brewing
Beer from Kalew-hops and barley;
Great indeed the reputation
Of the ancient beer of Kalew,
Said to make the feeble hardy,
Famed to dry the tears of women,
Famed to cheer the broken-hearted,
Make the aged young and supple,
Make the timid brave and mighty,
Make the brave men ever braver,
Fill the heart with joy and gladness,
Fill the mind with wisdom-sayings,
Fill the tongue with ancient legends,
Only makes the fool more foolish."

When the hostess of Pohyola
Heard how beer was first fermented,
Heard the origin of brewing,
Straightway did she fill with water
Many oaken tubs and barrels;
Filled but half the largest vessels,
Mixed the barley with the water,
Added also hops abundant;
Well she mixed the triple forces
In her tubs of oak and birch-wood,
Heated stones for months succeeding,
Thus to boil the magic mixture,
Steeped it through the days of summer,
Burned the wood of many forests,
Emptied all the springs of Pohya;
Daily did the forests lesson,
And the wells gave up their waters,
Thus to aid the hostess, Louhi,
In the brewing of the liquors,
From the water, hops, and barley,
And from honey of the islands,
For the wedding-feast of Northland,
For Pohyola's great carousal
And rejoicings at the marriage
Of the Maiden of the Rainbow
To the blacksmith, Ilmarinen,
Metal-worker of Wainola.

Smoke is seen upon the island,
Fire, upon the promontory,
Black smoke rising to the heavens
From the fire upon the island;
Fills with clouds the half of Pohya,
Fills Karelen's many hamlets;
All the people look and wonder,
This the chorus of the women:
"Whence are rising all these smoke-clouds,
Why this dreadful fire in Northland?
Is not like the smoke of camp-fires,
Is too large for fires of shepherds!"

Lemminkainen's ancient mother
Journeyed in the early morning
For some water to the fountain,
Saw the smoke arise to heaven,
In the region of Pohyola,
These the words the mother uttered:
"'Tis the smoke of battle-heroes,
From the heat of warring armies!"

Even Ahti, island-hero,
Ancient wizard, Lemminkainen,
Also known as Kaukomieli,

Looked upon the scene in wonder,
Thought awhile and spake as follows:
"I would like to see this nearer,
Learn the cause of all this trouble,
Whence this smoke and great confusion,
Whether smoke from heat of battle,
Or the bonfires of the shepherds."

Kaukomieli gazed and pondered,
Studied long the rising smoke-clouds;
Came not from the heat of battle,
Came not from the shepherd bonfires;
Heard they were the fires of Louhi
Brewing beer in Sariola,
On Pohyola's promontory;
Long and oft looked Lemminkainen,
Strained in eagerness his vision,
Stared, and peered, and
thought, and wondered,
Looked abashed and envy-swollen,
Spake these words upon his island:
"O beloved, second mother,
Northland's well-intentioned hostess,
Brew thy beer of honey-flavor,
Make thy liquors foam and sparkle,
For thy many friends invited,
Brew it well for Lemminkainen,
For his marriage in Pohyola
With the Maiden of the Rainbow."

Finally the beer was ready,
Beverage of noble heroes,
Stored away in casks and barrels,
There to rest awhile in silence,
In the cellars of the Northland,
In the copper-banded vessels,
In the magic oaken hogsheads,
Plugs and faucets made of copper.
Then the hostess of Pohyola
Skilfully prepared the dishes,
Laid them all with careful fingers
In the boiling-pans and kettles,
Ordered countless loaves of barley,
Ordered many liquid dishes,
All the delicacies of Northland,
For the feasting of her people,
For their richest entertainment,
For the nuptial songs and dances,
At the marriage of her daughter
With the blacksmith, Ilmarinen.

When the loaves were baked and ready,
When the dishes all were seasoned,
Time had gone but little distance,
Scarce a moment had passed over,
Ere the beer, in casks imprisoned,
Loudly rapped, and sang, and murmured:
"Come, ye heroes, come and take me,
Come and let me cheer your spirits,
Make you sing the songs of wisdom,
That with honour ye may praise me,
Sing the songs of beer immortal!"

Straightway Louhi sought a minstrel,
Magic bard and artist-singer,
That the beer might well be lauded,
Might be praised in song and honour.
First as bard they brought a salmon,
Also brought a pike from ocean,
But the salmon had no talent,
And the pike had little wisdom;
Teeth of pike and gills of salmon
Were not made for singing legends.

Then again they sought a singer,
Magic minstrel, beer-enchanter,
Thus to praise the drink of heroes,
Sing the songs of joy and gladness;
And a boy was brought for singing;
But the boy had little knowledge,
Could not praise the beer in honour;
Children's tongues are filled with questions,
Children cannot speak in wisdom,
Cannot sing the ancient legends.

Stronger grew the beer imprisoned
In the copper-banded vessels,
Locked behind the copper faucets,
Boiled, and foamed, and sang,
and murmured:
"If ye do not bring a singer,
That will sing my worth immortal,
That will sing my praise deserving,
I will burst these bands of copper,

Burst the heads of all these barrels;
Will not serve the best of heroes
Till he sings my many virtues."

Louhi, hostess of Pohyola,
Called a trusted maiden-servant,
Sent her to invite the people
To the marriage of her daughter,
These the words that Louhi uttered:
"O my trusted, truthful maiden,
Servant-maid to me belonging,
Call together all my people,
Call the heroes to my banquet,
Ask the rich, and ask the needy,
Ask the blind and deaf, and crippled,
Ask the young, and ask the aged;
Go thou to the hills, and hedges,
To the highways, and the by-ways,
Urge them to my daughter's wedding;
Bring the blind, and sorely troubled,
In my boats upon the waters,
In my sledges bring the halting,
With the old, and sick, and needy;
Ask the whole of Sariola,
Ask the people of Karelen,
Ask the ancient Wainamoinen,
Famous bard and wisdom-singer;
But I give command explicit
Not to ask wild Lemminkainen,
Not the island-dweller, Ahti!"
This the question of the servant:
"Why not ask wild Lemminkainen,
Ancient islander and minstrel?"

Louhi gave this simple answer:
"Good the reasons that I give thee
Why the wizard, Lemminkainen,
Must not have an invitation
To my daughter's feast and marriage:
Ahti courts the heat of battle,
Lemminkainen fosters trouble,
Skilful fighter of the virtues;
Evil thinking, acting evil,
He would bring but pain and sorrow,
He would jest and jeer at maidens
In their trimly buckled raiment,
Cannot ask the evil-minded!"
Thus again the servant questions:
"Tell me how to know this Ahti,
Also known as Lemminkainen,
That I may not ask him hither;
Do not know the isle of Ahti,
Nor the home of Kaukomieli!"
Spake the hostess of Pohyola:
"Easy 'tis to know the wizard,
Easy find the Ahti-dwelling:
Ahti lives on yonder island,
On that point dwells Lemminkainen,
In his mansion near the water,
Far at sea his home and dwelling."

Thereupon the trusted maiden
Spread the wedding-invitations
To the people of Pohyola,
To the tribes of Kalevala;
Asked the friendless, asked the homeless
Asked the labourers and shepherds,
Asked the fishermen and hunters,
Asked the deaf, the dumb, the crippled,
Asked the young, and asked the aged,
Asked the rich, and asked the needy;
Did not give an invitation
To the reckless Lemminkainen,
Island-dweller of the ocean.

Rune XXI: Ilmarinen's Wedding Feast

Louhi, hostess of the Northland,
Ancient dame of Sariola,
While at work within her dwelling,
Heard the whips crack on the fenlands,
Heard the rattle of the sledges;
To the northward turned her glances,
Turned her vision to the sunlight,
And her thoughts ran on as follow:
"Who are these in bright apparel,
On the banks of Pohya-waters,
Are they friends or hostile armies?"

Then the hostess of the Northland
Looked again and well considered,

Drew much nearer to examine,
Found they were not hostile armies,
Found that they were friends and suitors.
In the midst was Ilmarinen,
Son-in-law to ancient Louhi.

When the hostess of Pohyola
Saw the son-in-law approaching,
She addressed the words that follow:
"I had thought the winds were raging,
That the piles of wood were falling,
Thought the pebbles in commotion,
Or perchance the ocean roaring;
Then I hastened nearer, nearer,
Drew still nearer and examined,
Found the winds were not in battle,
Found the piles of wood unshaken,
Found the ocean was not roaring,
Nor the pebbles in commotion;
Found my son-in-law was coming
With his heroes and attendants,
Heroes counted by the hundreds.

"Should you ask of me the question,
How I recognized the bridegroom
Mid the hosts of men and heroes,
I should answer, I should tell you:
'As the hazel-bush in copses,
As the oak-tree in the forest,
As the Moon among the planets;
Drives the groom a coal-black courser,
Running like the famished black-dog,
Flying like the hungry raven,
Graceful as the lark at morning,
Golden cuckoos, six in number,
Twitter on the birchen cross-bow;
There are seven bluebirds singing
On the racer's hame and collar.'"

Noises hear they in the court-yard,
On the highway hear the sledges,
To the court comes Ilmarinen,
With his body-guard of heroes;
In the midst the chosen suitor,
Not too far in front of others,
Not too far behind his fellows.
Spake the hostess of Pohyola:

"Hie ye hither, men and heroes,
Haste, ye watchers, to the stables,
There unhitch the suitor's stallion,
Lower well the racer's breast-plate,
There undo the straps and buckles,
Loosen well the shafts and traces,
And conduct the suitor hither,
Give my son-in-law good welcome!"

Ilmarinen turned his racer
Into Louhi's yard and stables,
And descended from his snow-sledge.
Spake the hostess of Pohyola:
"Come, thou servant of my bidding,
Best of all my trusted servants,
Take at once the bridegroom's courser
From the shafts adorned with silver,
From the curving arch of willow,
Lift the harness trimmed in copper,
Tie the white-face to the manger,
Treat the suitor's steed with kindness,
Lead him carefully to shelter
By his soft and shining bridle,
By his halter tipped with silver;
Let him roll among the sand-hills,
On the bottoms soft and even,
On the borders of the snow-banks,
In the fields of milky colour.

"Lead the hero's steed to water,
Lead him to the Pohya-fountains,
Where the living streams are flowing,
Sweet as milk of human kindness,
From the roots of silvery birches,
Underneath the shade of aspens.

"Feed the courser of the suitor,
With the sweetest corn and barley,
On the summer-wheat and clover,
In the caldron steeped in sweetness;
Feed him at the golden manger,
In the boxes lined with copper,
At my manger richly furnished,
In the warmest of the stables;
Tie him with a silk-like halter,
To the golden rings and staples,
To the hooks of purest silver,

Set in beams of birch and oak-wood;
Feed him on the hay the sweetest,
Feed him on the corn nutritious,
Give the best my barns can furnish.

"Curry well the suitor's courser
With the curry-comb of fish-bone,
Brush his hair with silken brushes,
Put his mane and tail in order,
Cover well with flannel blankets,
Blankets wrought in gold and silver,
Buckles forged from shining copper.

"Come, ye small lads of the village,
Lead the suitor to my chambers,
With your auburn locks uncovered,
From your hands remove your mittens,
See if ye can lead the hero
Through the door without his stooping,
Lifting not the upper cross-bar,
Lowering not the oaken threshold,
Moving not the birchen casings,
Great the hero who must enter.

"Ilmarinen is too stately,
Cannot enter through the portals,
Not the son-in-law and bridegroom,
Till the portals have been heightened;
Taller by a head the suitor
Than the door-ways of the mansion."

Quick the servants of Pohyola
Tore away the upper cross-bar,
That his cap might not be lifted;
Made the oaken threshold lower
That the hero might not stumble;
Made the birch-wood portals wider,
Opened full the door of welcome,
Easy entrance for the suitor.

Speaks the hostess of the Northland
As the bridegroom freely passes
Through the doorway of her dwelling:
"Thanks are due to thee, O Ukko,
That my son-in-law has entered!
Let me now my halls examine;
Make the bridal chambers ready,
Finest linen on my tables,
Softest furs upon my benches,
Birchen flooring scrubbed to whiteness,
All my rooms in perfect order."

Then the hostess of Pohyola
Visited her spacious dwelling,
Did not recognize her chambers;
Every room had been remodeled,
Changed by force of mighty magic;
All the halls were newly burnished,
Hedge-hog bones were used for ceilings,
Bones of reindeer for foundations,
Bones of wolverine for door-sills,
For the cross-bars bones of roebuck,
Apple-wood were all the rafters,
Alder-wood, the window-casings,
Scales of trout adorned the windows,
And the fires were set in flowers.
All the seats were made of silver,
All the floors of copper-tiling,
Gold-adorned were all the tables,
On the floor were silken mattings,
Every fire-place set in copper,
Every hearth-stone cut from marble,
On each shelf were coloured sea-shells,
Kalew's tree was their protection.

To the court-room came the hero,
Chosen suitor from Wainola,
These the words of Ilmarinen:
"Send, O Ukko, health and pleasure
To this ancient home and dwelling,
To this mansion richly fashioned!"
Spake the hostess of Pohyola:
"Let thy coming be auspicious
To these halls of thee unworthy,
To the home of thine affianced,
To this dwelling lowly fashioned,
Mid the lindens and the aspens.

"Come, ye maidens that should serve me,
Come, ye fellows from the village,
Bring me fire upon the birch-bark,
Light the fagots of the fir tree,
That I may behold the bridegroom,
Chosen suitor of my daughter,

Fairy Maiden of the Rainbow,
See the colour of his eyeballs,
Whether they are blue or sable,
See if they are warm and faithful."

Quick the young lads from the village
Brought the fire upon the birch-bark,
Brought it on the tips of pine-wood;
And the fire and smoke commingled
Roll and roar about the hero,
Blackening the suitor's visage,
And the hostess speaks as follows:
"Bring the fire upon a taper,
On the waxen tapers bring it!"

Then the maidens did as bidden,
Quickly brought the lighted tapers,
Made the suitor's eyeballs glisten,
Made his cheeks look fresh and ruddy;
Made his eyes of sable colour
Sparkle like the foam of waters,
Like the reed-grass on the margin,
Coloured as the ocean jewels,
Iridescent as the rainbow.

"Come, ye fellows of the hamlets,
Lead my son-in-law and hero
To the highest seat at table,
To the seat of greatest honour,
With his back upon the blue-wall,
Looking on my bounteous tables,
Facing all the guests of Northland."

Then the hostess of Pohyola
Served her guests in great abundance,
Richest drinks and rarest viands,
First of all she served the bridegroom;
On his platters, honeyed biscuit,
And the sweetest river salmon,
Seasoned butter, roasted bacon,
All the dainties of Pohyola.
Then the helpers served the others,
Filled the plates of all invited
With the varied food of Northland.
Spake the hostess of Pohyola:
"Come, ye maidens from the village,
Hither bring the beer in pitchers,
In the urns with double handles,
To the many guests in-gathered,
Ere all others, serve the bridegroom."

Thereupon the merry maidens
Brought the beer in silver pitchers
From the copper-banded vessels,
For the wedding-guests assembled;
And the beer, fermenting, sparkled
On the beard of Ilmarinen,
On the beards of many heroes.

When the guests had all partaken
Of the wondrous beer of barley,
Spake the beer in merry accents
Through the tongues of the magicians,
Through the tongue of many
a hero,
Through the tongue of Wainamoinen,
Famed to be the sweetest singer
Of the Northland bards and minstrels,
These the words of the enchanter:
"O thou beer of honeyed flavor,
Let us not imbibe in silence,
Let some hero sing thy praises,
Sing thy worth in golden measures;
Let the hostess start the singing,
Let the bridegroom sound thy virtues!
Have our songs thus quickly vanished,
Have our joyful tongues grown silent?
Evil then has been the brewing,
Then the beer must be unworthy,
That it does not cheer the singer,
Does not move the merry minstrel,
That the golden guests are joyless,
And the cuckoo is not singing.
Never will these benches echo
Till the bench-guests chant
thy virtues;
Nor the floor resound thy praises
Till the floor-guests sing in concord;
Nor the windows join the chorus
Till the window-guests have spoken;
All the tables will keep silence
Till the heroes toast thy virtues;
Little singing from the chimney
Till the chimney-guests have chanted."

On the floor a child was sitting,
Thus the little boy made answer:
"I am small and young in singing,
Have perchance but little wisdom;
Be that as it may, my seniors,
Since the elder minstrels sing not,
Nor the heroes chant their legends,
Nor the hostess lead the singing,
I will sing my simple stories,
Sing my little store of knowledge,
To the pleasure of the evening,
To the joy of the invited."

Near the fire reclined an old man,
And the gray-beard thus made answer:
"Not the time for children's singing,
Children's wisdom is too ready,
Children's songs are filled with trifles,
Filled with shrewd and vain deceptions,
Maiden-songs are full of follies;
Leave the songs and incantations
To the ancient wizard-singers;
Leave the tales of times primeval
To the minstrel of Wainola,
To the hero of the Northland,
To the ancient Wainamoinen."
Thereupon Osmoinen answered:
"Are there not some sweeter singers
In this honoured congregation,
That will clasp their hands together,
Sing the ancient songs unbroken,
Thus begin the incantations,
Make these ancient halls re-echo
For the pleasure of the evening,
For the joy of the in-gathered?"
From the hearth-stone spake, the gray-beard
"Not a singer of Pohyola,
Not a minstrel, nor magician,
That was better skilled in chanting
Legends of the days departed,
Than was I when I was singing,
In my years of vain ambition;
Then I chanted tales of heroes,
On the blue back of the waters,
Sang the ballads of my people,
In the vales and on the mountains,
Through the verdant fields and forests;
Sweet my voice and skilled my singing,
All my songs were highly lauded,
Rippled like the quiet rivers,
Easy-flowing like the waters,
Easy-gliding as the snow-shoes,
Like the ship upon the ocean.

"Woe is me, my days are ended,
Would not recognize my singing,
All its sweetness gone to others,
Flows no more like rippling waters,
Makes no more the hills re-echo!
Now my songs are full of discord,
Like the rake upon the stubble,
Like the sledge upon the gravel,
Like the boat upon the seashore!"

Then the ancient Wainamoinen
Spake these words in magic measures:
"Since no other bard appeareth
That will clasp my hand in singing,
I will sing some simple legends,
Sing my garnered store of wisdom,
Make these magic halls re-echo
With my tales of ancient story,
Since a bard I was created,
Born an orator and singer;
Do not ask the ways of others,
Follow not the paths of strangers."

Wainamoinen, famous minstrel,
Song's eternal, wise supporter,
Then began the songs of pleasure,
Made the halls resound with joyance,
Filled the rooms with wondrous singing;
Sang the ancient bard-magician
All the oldest wisdom-sayings,
Did not fail in voice nor legends,
All the wisest thoughts remembered.

Thus the ancient Wainamoinen
Sang the joy of all assembled,
To the pleasure of the evening,
To the merriment of maidens,
To the happiness of heroes;
All the guests were stilled in wonder

At the magic of his singing,
At the songs of the magician.

Spake again wise Wainamoinen,
When his wonder-tales had ended:
"I have little worth or power,
Am a bard of little value,
Little consequence my singing,
Mine abilities as nothing,
If but Ukko, my Creator,
Should intone his wisdom-sayings,
Sing the source of good and evil,
Sing the origin of matter,
Sing the legends of omniscience,
Sing his songs in full perfection.
God could sing the floods to honey,
Sing the sands to ruddy berries,
Sing the pebbles into barley,
Sing to beer the running waters,
Sing to salt the rocks of ocean,
Into corn-fields sing the forests,
Into gold the forest-fruitage,
Sing to bread the hills and mountains,
Sing to eggs the rounded sandstones;
He could touch the springs of magic,
He could turn the keys of nature,
And produce within thy pastures,
Hurdles filled with sheep and reindeer,
Stables filled with fleet-foot stallions,
Kine in every field and fallow;
Sing a fur-robe for the bridegroom,
For the bride a coat of ermine,
For the hostess, shoes of silver,
For the hero, mail of copper.

"Grant O Ukko, my Creator,
God of love, and truth, and justice,
Grant thy blessing on our feasting,
Bless this company assembled,
For the good of Sariola,
For the happiness of Northland!
May this bread and beer bring joyance,
May they come in rich abundance,
May they carry full contentment
To the people of Pohyola,
To the cabin and the mansion;
May the hours we spend in singing,
In the morning, in the evening,
Fill our hearts with joy and gladness!
Hear us in our supplications,
Grant to us thy needed blessings,
Send enjoyment, health, and comfort,
To the people here assembled,
To the host and to the hostess,
To the bride and to the bridegroom,
To the sons upon the waters,
To the daughters at their weavings,
To the hunters on the mountains,
To the shepherds in the fenlands,
That our lives may end in honour,
That we may recall with pleasure
Ilmarinen's magic marriage
To the Maiden of the Rainbow,
Snow-white virgin of the Northland."

Rune XXII: The Bride's Farewell

When the marriage was completed,
When the many guests had feasted,
At the wedding of the Northland,
At the Dismal-land carousal,
Spake the hostess of Pohyola
To the blacksmith, Ilmarinen:
"Wherefore, bridegroom, dost thou linger,
Why art waiting, Northland hero?
Sittest for the father's pleasure,
For affection of the mother,
For the splendor of the maidens,
For the beauty of the daughter?
Noble son-in-law and brother,
Wait thou longer, having waited
Long already for the virgin,
Thine affianced is not ready,
Not prepared, thy life-companion,
Only are her tresses braided.

"Chosen bridegroom, pride of Pohya,
Wait thou longer, having waited
Long already for the virgin,
Thy beloved is preparing,
Only is one hand made ready.

"Famous artist, Ilmarinen,
Wait still longer, having waited
Long already for the virgin,
Thy beloved is not ready,
Only is one foot in fur-shoes,"
Spake again the ancient Louhi:
"Chosen suitor of my daughter,
Thou hast thrice in kindness waited,
Wait no longer for the virgin,
Thy beloved now is ready,
Well prepared thy life-companion,
Fairy Maiden of the Rainbow.

"Beauteous daughter, join thy suitor,
Follow him, thy chosen husband,
Very near is the uniting,
Near indeed thy separation.
At thy hand the honoured bridegroom,
Near the door he waits to lead thee,
Guide thee to his home and kindred;
At the gate his steed is waiting,
Restless champs his silver bridle,
And the sledge awaits thy presence.

"Thou wert anxious for a suitor,
Ready to accept his offer,
Wert in haste to take his jewels,
Place his rings upon thy fingers;
Now, fair daughter, keep thy promise;
To his sledge, with happy footsteps,
Hie in haste to join the bridegroom,
Gaily journey to the village
With thy chosen life-companion,
With thy suitor, Ilmarinen.
Little hast thou looked about thee,
Hast not raised thine eyes above thee,
Beauteous maiden of the Northland.
Hast thou made a rueful bargain,
Full of wailing thine engagement,
And thy marriage full of sorrow,
That thy father's ancient cottage
Thou art leaving now forever,
Leaving also friends and kindred,
For the blacksmith, Ilmarinen?

"O how beautiful thy childhood,
In thy father's dwelling-places,
Nurtured like a tender flower,
Like the strawberry in spring-time;
Soft thy couch and sweet thy slumber,
Warm thy fires and rich thy table;
From the fields came corn in plenty,
From the highlands, milk and berries,
Wheat and barley in abundance,
Fish, and fowl, and hare, and bacon,
From thy father's fields and forests.

"Never wert thou, child, in sorrow,
Never hadst thou grief nor trouble,
All thy cares were left to fir trees,
All thy worry to the copses,
All thy weeping to the willows,
All thy sighing to the lindens,
All thy thinking to the aspens
And the birches on the mountains,
Light and airy as the leaflet,
As a butterfly in summer,
Ruddy as a mountain-berry,
Beautiful as vernal flowers.

"Now thou leavest home and kindred,
Wanderest to other firesides,
Goest to another mother,
Other sisters, other brothers,
Goest to a second father,
To the servant-folk of strangers,
From thy native hills and lowlands.
There and here the homes will differ,
Happier thy mother's hearth-stone;
Other horns will there be sounded,
Other portals there swing open,
Other hinges there be creaking;
There the doors thou canst not enter
Like the daughters of Wainola,
Canst not tend the fires and ovens
As will please the minds of strangers.

"Didst thou think, my fairest maiden,
Thou couldst wed and on the morrow
Couldst return, if thou shouldst wish it,
To thy father's court and dwelling?
Not for one, nor two, nor three days,
Wilt thou leave thy mother's chambers,
Leave thy sisters and thy brothers,

Leave thy father's hills and lowlands.
Long the time the wife must wander,
Many months and years must wander,
Work, and struggle, all her life long,
Even though the mother liveth.
Great, indeed, must be the changes
When thou comest back to Pohya,
Changed, thy friends and nearest kindred,
Changed, thy father's ancient dwellings,
Changed, the valleys and the mountains,
Other birds will sing thy praises!"

When the mother thus had spoken,
Then the daughter spake, departing:
"In my early days of childhood
Often I intoned these measures:
'Art a virgin, yet no virgin,
Guided by an aged mother,
In a brother's fields and forests,
In the mansion of a father!
Only wilt become a virgin,
Only when thou hast a suitor,
Only when thou wedst a hero,
One foot on the father's threshold,
And the other for the snow-sledge
That will speed thee and thy husband
To his native vales and highlands!'

"I have wished thus many summers,
Sang it often in my childhood,
Hoped for this as for the flowers,
Welcome as the birds of spring-time.
Thus fulfilled are all my wishes,
Very near is my departure,
One foot on my father's threshold,
And the other for the journey
With my husband to his people;
Cannot understand the reason
That has changed my former feelings,
Cannot leave thee now with gladness,
Cannot go with great rejoicing
From my dear, old home and kindred,
Where as maiden I have lingered,
From the courts where I was nurtured,
From my father's hand and guidance,
From my faithful mother's counsel.
Now I go, a maid of sorrow,
Heavy-hearted to the bridegroom,
Like the bride of Night in winter,
Like the ice upon the rivers.

"Such is not the mind of others,
Other brides of Northland heroes;
Others do not leave unhappy,
Have no tears, nor cares, nor sorrows,
I alas! must weep and murmur,
Carry to my grave great sadness,
Heart as dark as Death's black river.

"Such the feelings of the happy,
Such the minds of merry maidens:
Like the early dawn of spring-time,
Like the rising Sun in summer;
No such radiance awaits me,
With my young heart filled with terror;
Happiness is not my portion,
Like the flat-shore of the ocean,
Like the dark rift of the storm-cloud,
Like the cheerless nights of winter!
Dreary is the day in autumn,
Dreary too the autumn evening,
Still more dreary is my future!"

An industrious old maiden,
Ever guarding home and kindred,
Spake these words of doubtful comfort:
"Dost thou, beauteous bride, remember,
Canst thou not recall my counsels?
These the words that I have taught thee:
'Look not joyfully for suitors,
Never heed the tongues of wooers,
Look not in the eyes of charmers,
At their feet let fall thy vision.
He that hath a mouth for sweetness,
He that hath an eye for beauty,
Offers little that will comfort;
Lempo sits upon his forehead,
In his mouth dwells dire Tuoni.'

"Thus, fair bride, did I advise thee,
Thus advised my sister's daughter:
Should there come the best of suitors,
Noblest wooers, proudest lovers,
Give to all these wisdom-sayings,

Let thine answer be as follows:
'Never will I think it wisdom,
Never will it be my pleasure,
To become a second daughter,
Linger with my husband's mother;
Never shall I leave my father,
Never wander forth to bondage,
At the bidding of a bridegroom:
Never shall I be a servant,
Wife and slave to any hero,
Never will I be submissive
To the orders of a husband.'

"Fairest bride, thou didst not heed me,
Gav'st no thought to my advices,
Didst not listen to my counsel;
Wittingly thy feet have wandered
Into boiling tar and water,
Hastened to thy suitor's snow-sledge,
To the bear-dens of thy husband,
On his sledge to be ill-treated,
Carried to his native country,
To the bondage of his people,
There, a subject to his mother.
Thou hast left thy mother's dwelling,
To the schooling of the master;
Hard indeed the master's teachings,
Little else than constant torture;
Ready for thee are his bridles,
Ready for thy hands the shackles,
Were not forged for any other;
Soon, indeed, thou'lt feel the hardness,
Feel the weight of thy misfortune,
Feel thy second father's censure,
And his wife's inhuman treatment,
Hear the cold words of thy brother,
Quail before thy haughty sister.

"Listen, bride, to what I tell thee:
In thy home thou wert a jewel,
Wert thy father's pride and pleasure,
'Moonlight,' did thy father call thee,
And thy mother called thee 'Sunshine,'
'Sea-foam' did thy brother call thee,
And thy sister called thee 'Flower.'
When thou leavest home and kindred
Goest to a second mother,
Often she will give thee censure,
Never treat thee as her daughter,
Rarely will she give thee counsel,
Never will she sound thy praises.
'Brush-wood,' will the father call thee,
'Sledge of Rags,' thy husband's mother,
'Flight of Stairs,' thy stranger brother,
'Scare-crow,' will the sister call thee,
Sister of thy blacksmith-husband;
Then wilt think of my good counsels,
Then wilt wish in tears and murmurs,
That as steam thou hadst ascended,
That as smoke thy soul had risen,
That as sparks thy life had vanished.
As a bird thou canst not wander
From thy nest to circle homeward,
Canst not fall and die like leaflets,
As the sparks thou canst not perish,
Like the smoke thou canst not vanish.

"Youthful bride, and darling sister,
Thou hast bartered all thy friendships,
Hast exchanged thy loving father,
Thou hast left thy faithful mother
For the mother of thy husband;
Hast exchanged thy loving brother,
Hast renounced thy gentle sister,
For the kindred of thy suitor;
Hast exchanged thy snow-white covers
For the rocky couch of sorrow;
Hast exchanged these crystal waters
For the waters of Wainola;
Hast renounced these sandy seashores
For the muddy banks of Kalew;
Northland glens thou hast forsaken
For thy husband's barren meadows;
Thou hast left thy berry-mountains
For the stubble-fields and deserts.

"Thou, O maiden, hast been thinking
Thou wouldst happy be in wedlock;
Neither work, nor care, nor sorrow,
From this night would be thy portion,
With thy husband for protection.
Not to sleep art thou conducted,
Not to happiness, nor joyance,
Wakefulness, thy night-companion,

And thy day-attendant, trouble;
Often thou wilt drink of sorrow,
Often long for vanished pleasures.

"When at home thou hadst no head-gear,
Thou hadst also little sadness;
When thy couch was not of linen,
No unhappiness came nigh thee;
Head-gear brings but pain and sorrow,
Linen breeds bad dispositions,
Linen brings but deeps of anguish,
And the flax untimely mourning.

"Happy in her home, the maiden,
Happy at her father's fireside,
Like the master in his mansion,
Happy with her bows and arrows.
'Tis not thus with married women;
Brides of heroes may be likened
To the prisoners of Moskva,
Held in bondage by their masters.

"As a wife, must weep and labour,
Carry trouble on both shoulders;
When the next hour passes over,
Thou must tend the fire and oven,
Must prepare thy husband's dinner,
Must direct thy master's servants.
When thine evening meal is ready,
Thou must search for hidden wisdom
In the brain of perch and salmon,
In the mouths of ocean whiting,
Gather wisdom from the cuckoo,
Canst not learn it from thy mother,
Mother dear of seven daughters;
Cannot find among her treasures
Where were born the human instincts,
Where were born the minds of heroes,
Whence arose the maiden's beauty,
Whence the beauty of her tresses,
Why all life revives in spring-time.

"Weep, O weep, my pretty young bride.
When thou weepest, weep sincerely,
Weep great rivers from thine eyelids,
Floods of tears in field and fallow,
Lakelets in thy father's dwelling;
Weep thy rooms to overflowing,
Shed thy tears in great abundance,
Lest thou weepest on returning
To thy native hills and valleys,
When thou visitest thy father
In the smoke of waning glory,
On his arm a withered tassel.

"Weep, O weep, my lovely maiden,
When thou weepest, weep in earnest,
Weep great rivers from thine eyelids;
If thou dost not weep sincerely,
Thou wilt weep on thy returning
To thy Northland home and kindred,
When thou visitest thy mother
Old and breathless near the hurdles,
In her arms a barley-bundle.

"Weep, O weep, sweet bride of beauty,
When thou weepest, weep profusely;
If thou dost not weep in earnest,
Thou wilt weep on thy returning
To thy native vales and highlands,
When thou visitest thy brother
Lying wounded by the way-side,
In his hand but empty honours.

"Weep, O weep, my sister's daughter,
Weep great rivers from thine eyelids;
If thou dost not weep sufficient,
Thou wilt weep on thy returning
To the scenes of happy childhood,
When thou visitest thy sister
Lying, prostrate in the meadow,
In her hand a birch-wood mallet."

When the ancient maid had ended,
Then the young bride sighed in anguish,
Straightway fell to bitter weeping,
Spake these words in deeps of sorrow:
"O, ye sisters, my beloved,
Ye companions of my childhood,
Playmates of my early summers,
Listen to your sister's counsel:
Cannot comprehend the reason,
Why my mind is so dejected,
Why this weariness and sadness,

This untold and unseen torture,
Cannot understand the meaning
Of this mighty weight of sorrow!
Differently I had thought it,
I had hoped for greater pleasures,
I had hoped to sing as cuckoos,
On the hill-tops call and echo,
When I had attained this station,
Reached at last the goal expectant;
But I am not like the cuckoo,
Singing, merry on the hill-tops;
I am like the songless blue-duck,
As she swims upon the waters,
Swims upon the cold, cold ocean,
Icicles upon her pinions.

"Ancient father, gray-haired mother,
Whither do ye wish to lead me,
Whither take this bride, thy daughter,
That this sorrow may pass over,
Where this heavy heart may lighten,
Where this grief may turn to gladness?
Better it had been, O mother,
Hadst thou nursed a block of birch-wood,
Hadst thou clothed the coloured sandstone,
Rather than this hapless maiden,
For the fulness of these sorrows,
For this keen and killing trouble.

"Many sympathizers tell me:
'Foolish bride, thou art ungrateful,
Do not grieve, thou child of sorrow,
Thou hast little cause for weeping.'

"O, deceive me not, my people,
Do not argue with me falsely,
For alas! I have more troubles
Than the waterfalls have pebbles,
Than the Ingerland has willows,
Than the Suomi-hills have berries;
Never could the Pohya plow-horse
Pull this mighty weight of sorrow,
Shaking not his birchen cross-bar,
Breaking not his heavy collar;
Never could the Northland reindeer
Heavy shod and stoutly harnessed,
Draw this load of care and trouble."

By the stove a babe was playing,
And the young child spake as follows:
"Why, O fair bride, art thou weeping,
Why these tears of pain and sadness?
Leave thy troubles to the elk-herds,
And thy grief to sable fillies,
Let the steeds of iron bridles
Bear the burden of thine anguish,
Horses have much larger foreheads,
Larger shoulders, stronger sinews,
And their necks are made for labour,
Stronger are their bones and muscles,
Let them bear thy heavy burdens.
There is little good in weeping,
Useless are thy tears of sorrow;
Art not led to swamps and lowlands,
Nor to banks of little rivers;
Thou art led to fields of flowers,
Led to fruitful trees and forests,
Led away from beer of Pohya
To the sweeter mead of Kalew.
At thy shoulder waits thy husband,
On thy right side, Ilmarinen,
Constant friend and life-protector,
He will guard thee from all evil;
Husband ready, steed in waiting,
Gold-and-silver-mounted harness,
Hazel-birds that sing and flutter
On the courser's yoke and cross-bar;
Thrushes also sing and twitter
Merrily on hame and collar,
Seven bluebirds, seven cuckoos,
Sing thy wedding-march in concord.

"Be no longer full of sorrow,
Dry thy tears, thou bride of beauty,
Thou hast found a noble husband,
Better wilt thou fare than ever,
By the side of Ilmarinen,
Artist husband, metal-master,
Bread-provider of thy table,
On the arm of the fish-catcher,
On the breast of the elk-hunter,
By the side of the bear-killer.
Thou hast won the best of suitors,
Hast obtained a mighty hero;

Never idle is his cross-bow,
On the nails his quivers hang not,
Neither are his dogs in kennel,
Active agents is his hunting.
Thrice within the budding spring-time
In the early hours of morning
He arises from his fare-couch,
From his slumber in the brush-wood,
Thrice within the sowing season,
On his eyes the deer has fallen,
And the branches brushed his vesture,
And his locks been combed by fir-boughs.
Hasten homeward with thy husband,
Where thy hero's friends await thee,
Where his forests sing thy welcome.

"Ilmarinen there possesses
All the birds that fly in mid-air,
All the beasts that haunt the woodlands,
All that feed upon the mountains,
All that graze on hill and valley,
Sheep and cattle by the thousands;
Sweet the grass upon his meadows,
Sweet the barley in his uplands,
In the lowlands corn abundant,
Wheat upon the elm-wood fallows,
Near the streamlets rye is waving,
Waving grain on many acres,
On his mountains gold and silver,
Rich his mines of shining copper,
Highlands filled with magic metals,
Chests of jewels in his store-house,
All the wealth of Kalevala."

Rune XXIII: Osmotar, the Bride Adviser

Now the bride must be instructed,
Who will teach the Maid of Beauty,
Who instruct the Rainbow-daughter?
Osmotar, the wisdom-maiden,
Kalew's fair and lovely virgin,
Osmotar will give instructions
To the bride of Ilmarinen,
To the orphaned bride of Pohya,
Teach her how to live in pleasure,
How to live and reign in glory,
Win her second mother's praises,
Joyful in her husband's dwelling.

Osmotar in modest accents
Thus the anxious bride addresses:
"Maid of Beauty, lovely sister,
Tender plant of Louhi's gardens,
Hear thou what thy sister teaches,
Listen to her sage instructions:
Go thou hence, my much beloved,
Wander far away, my flower,
Travel on enwrapped in colours,
Glide away in silks and ribbons,
From this house renowned and ancient,
From thy father's halls and court-yards
Haste thee to thy husband's village,
Hasten to his mother's household;
Strange, the rooms in other dwellings,
Strange, the modes in other hamlets.

"Full of thought must be thy going,
And thy work be well considered,
Quite unlike thy home in Northland,
On the meadows of thy father,
On the highlands of thy brother,
Singing through thy mother's fenlands,
Culling daisies with thy sister.

"When thou goest from thy father
Thou canst take whatever pleases,
Only three things leave behind thee:
Leave thy day-dreams to thy sister,
Leave thou kindness for thy mother,
To thy brother leave thy labours,
Take all else that thou desirest.
Throw away thine incantations,
Cast thy sighing to the pine trees,
And thy maidenhood to zephyrs,
Thy rejoicings to the couches,
Cast thy trinkets to the children,
And thy leisure to the gray-beards,
Cast all pleasures to thy playmates,
Let them take them to the woodlands,
Bury them beneath the mountain.

*"Thou must hence acquire new habits,
Must forget thy former customs,
Mother-love must be forsaken,
Thou must love thy husband's mother,
Lower must thy head be bended,
Kind words only must thou utter.*

*"Thou must hence acquire new habits,
Must forget thy former customs,
Father-love must be forsaken,
Thou must love thy husband's father,
Lower must thy head be bended,
Kind words only must thou utter.
"Thou must hence acquire new habits,
Must forget thy former customs,
Brother-love must be forsaken,
Thou must love thy husband's brother,
Lower must thy head be bended,
Kind words only must thou utter.*

*"Thou must hence acquire new habits
Must forget thy former customs,
Sister-love must be forsaken,
Thou must love thy husband's sister,
Lower must thy head be bended,
Kind words only must thou utter.*

*"Never in the course of ages,
Never while the moonlight glimmers,
Wickedly approach thy household,
Nor unworthily, thy servants,
Nor thy courts with indiscretion;
Let thy dwellings sing good manners,
And thy walls re-echo virtue.
After mind the hero searches,
And the best of men seek honour,
Seek for honesty and wisdom;
If thy home should be immoral,
If thine inmates fail in virtue,
Then thy gray-beards would be black-dogs
In sheep's clothing at thy firesides;
All thy women would be witches,
Wicked witches in thy chambers,
And thy brothers be as serpents
Crawling through thy husband's mansion;
All thy sisters would be famous
For their evil thoughts and conduct.*

*"Equal honours must be given
To thy husband's friends and kindred;
Lower must thy head be bended,
Than within thy mother's dwelling,
Than within thy father's guest-room,
When thou didst thy kindred honour.
Ever strive to give good counsel,
Wear a countenance of sunshine,
Bear a head upon thy shoulders
Filled with wise and ancient sayings;
Open bright thine eyes at morning
To behold the silver sunrise,
Sharpen well thine ears at evening,
Thus to hear the rooster crowing;
When he makes his second calling,
Straightway thou must rise from slumber,
Let the aged sleep in quiet;
Should the rooster fail to call thee,
Let the moonbeams touch thine eyelids,
Let the Great Bear be thy keeper;
Often go thou and consult them,
Call upon the Moon for counsel,
Ask the Bear for ancient wisdom,
From the stars divine thy future;
When the Great Bear faces southward,
When his tail is pointing northward,
This is time to break with slumber,
Seek for fire within the ashes,
Place a spark upon the tinder,
Blow the fire through all the fuel.
If no spark is in the ashes,
Then go wake thy hero-husband,
Speak these words to him on waking:
'Give me fire, O my beloved,
Give a single spark, my husband,
Strike a little fire from flintstone,
Let it fall upon my tinder.'*

*"From the spark, O Bride of Beauty,
Light thy fires, and heat thine ovens,
In the holder, place the torch-light,
Find thy pathway to the stables,
There to fill the empty mangers;
If thy husband's cows be lowing,
If thy brother's steeds be neighing,
Then the cows await thy coming,
And the steeds for thee are calling,*

Hasten, stooping through the hurdles,
Hasten through the yards and stables,
Feed thy husband's cows with pleasure,
Feed with care the gentle lambkins,
Give the cows the best of clover,
Hay, and barley, to the horses,
Feed the calves of lowing mothers,
Feed the fowl that fly to meet thee.

"Never rest upon the haymow,
Never sleep within the hurdles,
When the kine are fed and tended,
When the flocks have all been watered;
Hasten thence, my pretty matron,
Like the snow-flakes to thy dwelling,
There a crying babe awaits thee,
Weeping in his couch neglected,
Cannot speak and tell his troubles,
Speechless babe, and weeping infant,
Cannot say that he is hungry,
Whether pain or cold distresses,
Greets with joy his mother's footsteps.
Afterward repair in silence
To thy husband's rooms and presence,
Early visit thou his chambers,
In thy hand a golden pitcher,
On thine arm a broom of birch-wood,
In thy teeth a lighted taper,
And thyself the fourth in order.
Sweep thou then thy hero's dwelling,
Dust his benches and his tables,
Wash the flooring well with water.

"If the baby of thy sister
Play alone within his corner,
Show the little child attention,
Bathe his eyes and smoothe his ringlets,
Give the infant needed comforts;
Shouldst thou have no bread of barley,
In his hand adjust some trinket.

"Lastly, when the week has ended,
Give thy house a thorough cleansing,
Benches, tables, walls, and ceilings;
What of dust is on the windows,
Sweep away with broom of birch-twigs,
All thy rooms must first be sprinkled,
That the dust may not be scattered,
May not fill the halls and chambers.
Sweep the dust from every crevice,
Leave thou not a single atom;
Also sweep the chimney-corners,
Do not then forget the rafters,
Lest thy home should seem untidy,
Lest thy dwelling seem neglected.

"Hear, O maiden, what I tell thee,
Learn the tenor of my teaching:
Never dress in scanty raiment,
Let thy robes be plain and comely,
Ever wear the whitest linen,
On thy feet wear tidy fur-shoes,
For the glory of thy husband,
For the honour of thy hero.
Tend thou well the sacred sorb-tree,
Guard the mountain-ashes planted
In the court-yard, widely branching;
Beautiful the mountain-ashes,
Beautiful their leaves and flowers,
Still more beautiful the berries.
Thus the exiled one demonstrates
That she lives to please her husband,
Tries to make her hero happy.

"Like the mouse, have ears for hearing,
Like the hare, have feet for running,
Bend thy neck and turn thy visage
Like the juniper and aspen,
Thus to watch with care thy goings,
Thus to guard thy feet from stumbling,
That thou mayest walk in safety.

"When thy brother comes from plowing,
And thy father from his garners,
And thy husband from the woodlands,
From his chopping, thy beloved,
Give to each a water-basin,
Give to each a linen-towel,
Speak to each some pleasant greeting.

"When thy second mother hastens
To thy husband's home and kindred,
In her hand a corn-meal measure,
Haste thou to the court to meet her,

Happy-hearted, bow before her,
Take the measure from her fingers,
Happy, bear it to thy husband.

"If thou shouldst not see distinctly
What demands thy next attention,
Ask at once thy hero's mother:
'Second mother, my beloved,
Name the task to be accomplished
By thy willing second daughter,
Tell me how to best perform it.'

"This should be the mother's answer:
'This the manner of thy workings,
Thus thy daily work accomplish:
Stamp with diligence and courage,
Grind with will and great endurance,
Set the millstones well in order,
Fill the barley-pans with water,
Knead with strength the dough for baking,
Place the fagots on the fire-place,
That thy ovens may be heated,
Bake in love the honey-biscuit,
Bake the larger loaves of barley,
Rinse to cleanliness thy platters,
Polish well thy drinking-vessels.

"If thou hearest from the mother,
From the mother of thy husband,
That the cask for meal is empty,
Take the barley from the garners,
Hasten to the rooms for grinding.
When thou grindest in the chambers,
Do not sing in glee and joyance,
Turn the grinding-stones in silence,
To the mill give up thy singing,
Let the side-holes furnish music;
Do not sigh as if unhappy,
Do not groan as if in trouble,
Lest the father think thee weary,
Lest thy husband's mother fancy
That thy groans mean discontentment,
That thy sighing means displeasure.
Quickly sift the flour thou grindest,
Take it to the casks in buckets,
Bake thy hero's bread with pleasure,
Knead the dough with care and patience,
That thy biscuits may be worthy,
That the dough be light and airy.

"Shouldst thou see a bucket empty,
Take the bucket on thy shoulder,
On thine arm a silver-dipper,
Hasten off to fill with water
From the crystal river flowing;
Gracefully thy bucket carry,
Bear it firmly by the handles,
Hasten houseward like the zephyrs,
Hasten like the air of autumn;
Do not tarry near the streamlet,
At the waters do not linger,
That the father may not fancy,
Nor the ancient dame imagine,
That thou hast beheld thine image,
Hast admired thy form and features,
Hast admired thy grace and beauty
In the mirror of the fountain,
In the crystal streamlet's eddies.

"Shouldst thou journey to the woodlands,
There to gather aspen-fagots,
Do not go with noise and bustle,
Gather all thy sticks in silence,
Gather quietly the birch-wood,
That the father may not fancy,
And the mother not imagine,
That thy calling came from anger,
And thy noise from discontentment.

"If thou goest to the store-house
To obtain the flour of barley,
Do not tarry on thy journey,
On the threshold do not linger,
That the father may not fancy,
And the mother not imagine,
That the meal thou hast divided
With the women of the village.

"If thou goest to the river,
There to wash thy birchen platters,
There to cleanse thy pans and buckets,
Lest thy work be done in neatness,
Rinse the sides, and rinse the handles,
Rinse thy pitchers to perfection,

Spoons, and forks, and knives,
and goblets,
Rinse with care thy cooking-vessels,
Closely watch the food-utensils,
That the dogs may not deface them,
That the kittens may not mar them,
That the eagles may not steal them,
That the children may not break them;
Many children in the village,
Many little heads and fingers,
That will need thy careful watching,
Lest they steal the things of value.

"When thou goest to thy bathing,
Have the brushes ready lying
In the bath-room clean and smokeless;
Do not, linger in the water,
At thy bathing do not tarry,
That the father may not fancy,
And the mother not imagine,
Thou art sleeping on the benches,
Rolling in the laps of comfort.

"From thy bath, when thou returnest,
To his bathing tempt the father,
Speak to him the words that follow:
'Father of my hero-husband,
Clean are all the bath-room benches,
Everything in perfect order;
Go and bathe for thine enjoyment,
Pour the water all-sufficient,
I will lend thee needed service.'

"When the time has come for spinning,
When the hours arrive for weaving,
Do not ask the help of others,
Look not in the stream for knowledge,
For advice ask not the servants,
Nor the spindle from the sisters,
Nor the weaving-comb from strangers.
Thou thyself must do the spinning,
With thine own hand ply the shuttle,
Loosely wind the skeins of wool-yarn,
Tightly wind the balls of flax-thread,
Wind them deftly in the shuttle;
Fit the warp upon the rollers,
Beat the woof and warp together,
Swiftly ply the weaver's shuttle,
Weave good cloth for all thy vestments,
Weave of woolen, webs for dresses
From the finest wool of lambkins,
One thread only in thy weaving.

"Hear thou what I now advise thee:
Brew thy beer from early barley,
From the barley's new-grown kernels,
Brew it with the magic virtues,
Malt it with the sweets of honey,
Do not stir it with the birch-rod,
Stir it with thy skilful fingers;
When thou goest to the garners,
Do not let the seed bring evil,
Keep the dogs outside the brew-house,
Have no fear of wolves in hunger,
Nor the wild-beasts of the mountains,
When thou goest to thy brewing,
Shouldst thou wander forth at midnight.

"Should some stranger come to
see thee,
Do not worry for his comfort;
Ever does the worthy household
Have provisions for the stranger,
Bits of meat, and bread, and biscuit,
Ample for the dinner-table;
Seat the stranger in thy dwelling,
Speak with him in friendly accents,
Entertain the guest with kindness,
While his dinner is preparing.
When the stranger leaves thy threshold,
When his farewell has been spoken,
Lead him only to the portals,
Do not step without the doorway,
That thy husband may not fancy,
And the mother not imagine,
Thou hast interest in strangers.

"Shouldst thou ever make a journey
To the centre of the village,
There to gain some needed object,
While thou speakest in the hamlet,
Let thy words be full of wisdom,
That thou shamest not thy kindred,
Nor disgrace thy husband's household.

"Village-maidens oft will ask thee,
Mothers of the hamlet question:
'Does thy husband's mother
greet thee
As in childhood thou wert greeted,
In thy happy home in Pohya?'
Do not answer in negation,
Say that she has always given
Thee the best of her provisions,
Given thee the kindest greetings,
Though it be but once a season.

"Listen well to what I tell thee:
As thou goest from thy father
To thy husband's distant dwelling,
Thou must not forget thy mother,
Her that gave thee life and beauty,
Her that nurtured thee in childhood,
Many sleepless nights she nursed thee;
Often were her wants neglected,
Numberless the times she rocked thee;
Tender, true, and ever faithful,
Is the mother to her daughter.
She that can forget her mother,
Can neglect the one that nursed her,
Should not visit Mana's castle,
In the kingdom of Tuoni;
In Manala she would suffer,
Suffer frightful retribution,
Should her mother be forgotten;
Should her dear one be neglected,
Mana's daughters will torment her,
And Tuoni's sons revile her,
They will ask her much as follows:
'How couldst thou forget thy mother,
How neglect the one that nursed thee?
Great the pain thy mother suffered,
Great the trouble that thou gavest
When thy loving mother brought thee
Into life for good or evil,
When she gave thee earth-existence,
When she nursed thee but an infant,
When she fed thee in thy childhood,
When she taught thee what
thou knowest,
Mana's punishments upon thee,
Since thy mother is forgotten!'"

On the floor a witch was sitting,
Near the fire a beggar-woman,
One that knew the ways of people,
These the words the woman uttered:
"Thus the crow calls in the winter:
'Would that I could be a singer,
And my voice be full of sweetness,
But, alas! my songs are worthless,
Cannot charm the weakest creature;
I must live without the singing,
Leave the songs to the musicians,
Those that live in golden houses,
In the homes of the beloved;
Homeless therefore I must wander,
Like a beggar in the corn-fields,
And with none to do me honour.'

"Hear now, sister, what I tell thee,
Enter thou thy husband's dwelling,
Follow not his mind, nor fancies,
As my husband's mind I followed;
As a flower was I when budding,
Sprouting like a rose in spring-time,
Growing like a slender maiden,
Like the honey-gem of glory,
Like the playmates of my childhood,
Like the goslings of my father,
Like the blue-ducks of my mother,
Like my brother's water-younglings,
Like the bullfinch of my sister;
Grew I like the heather-flower,
Like the berry of the meadow,
Played upon the sandy seashore,
Rocked upon the fragrant upland,
Sang all day adown the valley,
Thrilled with song the hill
and mountain,
Filled with mirth the glen and forest,
Lived and frolicked in the woodlands.

"Into traps are foxes driven
By the cruel pangs of hunger,
Into traps, the cunning ermine;
Thus are maidens wooed and wedded,
In their hunger for a husband.
Thus created is the virgin,
Thus intended is the daughter,

Subject to her hero-husband,
Subject also to his mother.

"Then to other fields I hastened,
Like a berry from the border,
Like a cranberry for roasting,
Like a strawberry for dinner;
All the elm-trees seemed to wound me,
All the aspens tried to cut me,
All the willows tried to seize me,
All the forest tried to slay me.
Thus I journeyed to my husband,
Thus I travelled to his dwelling,
Was conducted to his mother.
Then there were, as was reported,
Six compartments built of pine-wood,
Twelve the number of the chambers,
And the mansion filled with garrets,
Studding all the forest border,
Every by-way filled with flowers;
Streamlets bordered fields of barley,
Filled with wheat and corn, the islands,
Grain in plenty in the garners,
Rye unthrashed in great abundance,
Countless sums of gold and silver,
Other treasures without number.
When my journey I had ended,
When my hand at last was given,
Six supports were in his cabin,
Seven poles as rails for fencing.
Filled with anger were the bushes,
All the glens disfavour showing,
All the walks were lined with trouble,
Evil-tempered were the forests,
Hundred words of evil import,
Hundred others of unkindness.
Did not let this bring me sorrow,
Long I sought to merit praises,
Long I hoped to find some favour,
Strove most earnestly for kindness;
When they led me to the cottage,
There I tried some chips to gather,
Knocked my head against the portals
Of my husband's lowly dwelling.

"At the door were eyes of strangers,
Sable eyes at the partition,
Green with envy in his cabin,
Evil heroes in the back-ground,
From each mouth the fire was streaming,
From each tongue the sparks out-flying,
Flying from my second father,
From his eyeballs of unkindness.
Did not let this bring me trouble,
Tried to live in peace and pleasure,
In the homestead of my husband;
In humility I suffered,
Skipped about with feet of rabbit,
Flew along with steps of ermine,
Late I laid my head to slumber,
Early rose as if a servant,
Could not win a touch of kindness,
Could not merit love nor honour,
Though I had dislodged the mountains,
Though the rocks had I torn open.

"Then I turned the heavy millstone,
Ground the flour with care and trouble,
Ground the barley-grains in patience,
That the mother might be nourished,
That her fury-throat might swallow
What might please her taste and fancy,
From her gold-enamelled platters,
From the corner of her table.

"As for me, the hapless daughter,
All my flour was from the siftings
On the table near the oven,
Ate I from the birchen ladle;
Oftentimes I brought the mosses
Gathered in the lowland meadows,
Baked them into loaves for eating;
Brought the water from the river,
Thirsty, sipped it from the dipper,
Ate of fish the worst in Northland,
Only smelts, and worthless swimmers,
Rocking in my boat of birch-bark;
Never ate I fish or biscuit
From my second mother's fingers.

"Blades I gathered in the summers,
Twisted barley-stalks in winter,
Like the labourers of heroes,
Like the servants sold in bondage.

In the thresh-house of my husband,
Evermore to me was given
Flail the heaviest and longest,
And to me the longest lever,
On the shore the strongest beater,
And the largest rake in haying;
No one thought my burden heavy,
No one thought that I could suffer,
Though the best of heroes faltered,
And the strongest women weakened.

"Thus did I, a youthful housewife,
At the right time, all my duties,
Drenched myself in perspiration,
Hoped for better times to follow;
But I only rose to labour,
Knowing neither rest nor pleasure.
I was blamed by all the household,
With ungrateful tongues derided,
Now about my awkward manners,
Now about my reputation,
Censuring my name and station.
Words unkind were heaped upon me,
Fell like hail on me unhappy,
Like the frightful flash of lightning,
Like the heavy hail of spring-time.
I did not despair entirely,
Would have lived to labour longer
Underneath the tongue of malice,
But the old-one spoiled my temper,
Roused my deepest ire and hatred;
Then my husband grew a wild-bear,
Grew a savage wolf of Hisi.

"Only then I turned to weeping,
And reflected in my chamber,
Thought of all my former pleasures
Of the happy days of childhood,
Of my father's joyful firesides,
Of my mother's peaceful cottage,
Then began I thus to murmur:
'Well thou knowest, ancient mother,
How to make thy sweet bud blossom,
How to train thy tender shootlet;
Did not know where to ingraft it,
Placed, alas! the little scion
In the very worst of places,
On an unproductive hillock,
In the hardest limb of cherry,
Where it could not grow and flourish,
There to waste its life, in weeping,
Hapless in her lasting sorrow.
Worthier had been my conduct,
In the regions that are better,
In the court-yards that are wider,
In compartments that are larger,
Living with a loving husband,
Living with a stronger hero.
Shoe of birch-bark was my suitor,
Shoe of Laplanders, my husband;
Had the body of a raven,
Voice and visage like the jackdaw,
Mouth and claws were from the black-wolf,
The remainder from the wild-bear.
Had I known that mine affianced
Was a fount of pain and evil,
To the hill-side I had wandered,
Been a pine tree on the highway,
Been a linden on the border,
Like the black-earth made my visage,
Grown a beard of ugly bristles,
Head of loam and eyes of lightning,
For my ears the knots of birches,
For my limbs the trunks of aspens.'

"This the manner of my singing
In the hearing of my husband,
Thus I sang my cares and murmurs
Thus my hero near the portals
Heard the wail of my displeasure,
Then he hastened to my chamber;
Straightway knew I by his footsteps,
Well concluded he was angry,
Knew it by his steps implanted;
All the winds were still in slumber,
Yet his sable locks stood endwise,
Fluttered round his head in fury,
While his horrid mouth stood open;
To and fro his eyes were rolling,
In one hand a branch of willow,
In the other, club of alder;
Struck at me with might of malice,
Aimed the cudgel at my forehead.

"When the evening had descended,
When my husband thought of slumber
Took he in his hand a whip-stalk,
With a whip-lash made of deer-skin,
Was not made for any other,
Only made for me unhappy.

"When at last I begged for mercy,
When I sought a place for resting,
By his side I courted slumber,
Merciless, my husband seized me,
Struck me with his arm of envy,
Beat me with the whip of torture,
Deer-skin-lash and stalk of birch-wood.
From his couch I leaped impulsive,
In the coldest night of winter,
But the husband fleetly followed,
Caught me at the outer portals,
Grasped me by my streaming tresses,
Tore my ringlets from my forehead,
Cast in curls upon the night-winds
To the freezing winds of winter.
What the aid that I could ask for,
Who could free me from my torment?
Made I shoes of magic metals,
Made the straps of steel and copper,
Waited long without the dwelling,
Long I listened at the portals,
Hoping he would end his ravings,
Hoping he would sink to slumber,
But he did not seek for resting,
Did not wish to still his fury.
Finally the cold benumbed me;
As an outcast from his cabin,
I was forced to walk and wander,
When I, freezing, well reflected,
This the substance of my thinking:
'I will not endure this torture,
Will not bear this thing forever,
Will not bear this cruel treatment,
Such contempt I will not suffer
In the wicked tribe of Hisi,
In this nest of evil Piru.'

"Then I said, 'Farewell forever!'
To my husband's home and kindred,
To my much-loved home and husband;
Started forth upon a journey
To my father's distant hamlet,
Over swamps and over snow-fields,
Wandered over towering mountains,
Over hills and through the valleys,
To my brother's welcome meadows,
To my sister's home and birthplace.

"There were rustling withered pine trees,
Finely-feathered firs were fading,
Countless ravens there were cawing,
All the jackdaws harshly singing,
This the chorus of the ravens:
'Thou hast here a home no longer,
This is not the happy homestead
Of thy merry days of childhood.'

"Heeding not this woodland chorus,
Straight I journeyed to the dwelling
Of my childhood's friend and brother,
Where the portals spake in concord,
And the hills and valleys answered,
This their saddened song and echo:
'Wherefore dost thou journey hither,
Comest thou for joy or sorrow,
To thy father's old dominions?
Here unhappiness awaits thee,
Long departed is thy father,
Dead and gone to visit Ukko,
Dead and gone thy faithful mother,
And thy brother is a stranger,
While his wife is chill and heartless!'

"Heeding not these many warnings,
Straightway to my brother's cottage
Were my weary feet directed,
Laid my hand upon the door-latch
Of my brother's dismal cottage,
But the latch was cold and lifeless.
When I wandered to the chamber,
When I waited at the doorway,
There I saw the heartless hostess,
But she did not give me greeting,
Did not give her hand in welcome;
Proud, alas! was I unhappy,
Did not make the first advances,
Did not offer her my friendship,

And my hand I did not proffer;
Laid my hand upon the oven,
All its former warmth departed!
On the coal I laid my fingers,
All the latent heat had left it.
On the rest-bench lay my brother,
Lay outstretched before the fire-place,
Heaps of soot upon his shoulders,
Heaps of ashes on his forehead.
Thus the brother asked the stranger,
Questioned thus his guest politely:
'Tell me what thy name and station,
Whence thou comest o'er the waters!'
"This the answer that I gave him:
'Hast thou then forgot thy sister,
Does my brother not remember,
Not recall his mother's daughter?
We are children of one mother,
Of one bird were we the fledgelings,
In one nest were hatched and nurtured.'"

"Then the brother fell to weeping,
From his eyes great tear-drops flowing,
To his wife the brother whispered,
Whispered thus unto the housewife:
'Bring thou beer to give my sister,
Quench her thirst and cheer her spirits.'

"Full of envy, brought the sister
Only water filled with evil,
Water for the infant's eyelids,
Soap and water from the bath-room.

"To his wife the brother whispered,
Whispered thus unto the housewife:
'Bring thou salmon for my sister,
For my sister so long absent,
Thus to still her pangs of hunger.'

"Thereupon the wife obeying,
Brought, in envy, only cabbage
That the children had been eating,
And the house-dogs had been licking,
Leavings of the black-dog's breakfast.

"Then I left my brother's dwelling,
Hastened to the ancient homestead,
To my mother's home deserted;
Onward, onward did I wander,
Hastened onward by the cold-sea,
Dragged my body on in anguish,
To the cottage-doors of strangers,
To the unfamiliar portals,
For the care of the neglected,
For the needy of the village,
For the children poor and orphaned.

"There are many wicked people,
Many slanderers of women,
Many women evil-minded,
That malign their sex through envy.
Many they with lips of evil,
That belie the best of maidens,
Prove the innocent are guilty
Of the worst of misdemeanors,
Speak aloud in tones unceasing,
Speak, alas! with wicked motives,
Spread the follies of their neighbors
Through the tongues of self-pollution.
Very few, indeed, the people
That will feed the poor and hungry,
That will bid the stranger welcome;
Very few to treat her kindly,
Innocent, and lone, and needy,
Few to offer her a shelter
From the chilling storms of winter,
When her skirts with ice are stiffened,
Coats of ice her only raiment!

"Never in my days of childhood,
Never in my maiden life-time,
Never would believe the story,
Though a hundred tongues had told it,
Though a thousand voices sang it,
That such evil things could happen,
That such misery could follow,
Such misfortune could befall one
Who has tried to do her duty,
Who has tried to live uprightly,
Tried to make her people happy."

Thus the young bride was instructed,
Beauteous Maiden of the Rainbow,
Thus by Osmotar, the teacher.

Rune XXIV: The Bride's Farewell

Osmotar, the bride-instructor,
Gives the wedding-guests this counsel,
Speaks these measures to the bridegroom:
"Ilmarinen, artist-brother,
Best of all my hero-brothers,
Of my mother's sons the dearest,
Gentlest, truest, bravest, grandest,
Listen well to what I tell thee
Of the Maiden of the Rainbow,
Of thy beauteous life-companion:
Bridegroom, praise thy fate hereafter,
Praise forever thy good fortune;
If thou praisest, praise sincerely,
Good the maiden thou hast wedded,
Good the bride that Ukko gives thee,
Graciously has God bestowed her.
Sound her praises to thy father,
Praise her virtues to thy mother,
Let thy heart rejoice in secret,
That thou hast the Bride of Beauty,
Lovely Maiden of the Rainbow!

"Brilliant near thee stands
the maiden,
At thy shoulder thy companion,
Happy under thy protection,
Beautiful as golden moonlight,
Beautiful upon thy bosom,
Strong to do thy kindly bidding,
Labour with thee as thou wishest,
Rake the hay upon thy meadows,
Keep thy home in full perfection,
Spin for thee the finest linen,
Weave for thee the richest fabrics,
Make for thee the softest raiment,
Make thy weaver's loom as merry
As the cuckoo of the forest;
Make the shuttle glide in beauty
Like the ermine of the woodlands;
Make the spindle twirl as deftly
As the squirrel spins the acorn;
Village-maidens will not slumber
While thy young bride's loom
is humming,
While she plies the graceful shuttle.

"Bridegroom of the Bride of Beauty,
Noblest of the Northland heroes,
Forge thyself a scythe for mowing,
Furnish it with oaken handle,
Carve it in thine ancient smithy,
Hammer it upon thine anvil,
Have it ready for the summer,
For the merry days of sunshine;
Take thy bride then to the lowlands,
Mow the grass upon thy meadows,
Rake the hay when it is ready,
Make the reeds and grasses rustle,
Toss the fragrant heads of clover,
Make thy hay in Kalevala
When the silver sun is shining.

"When the time has come
for weaving,
To the loom attract the weaver,
Give to her the spools and shuttles,
Let the willing loom be worthy,
Beautiful the frame and settle;
Give to her what may be needed,
That the weaver's song may echo,
That the lathe may swing and rattle,
May be heard within the village,
That the aged may remark it,
And the village-maidens question:
'Who is she that now is weaving,
What new power now plies the shuttle?'
"Make this answer to the question:
'It is my beloved weaving,
My young bride that plies the shuttle.'

"Shall the weaver's weft be loosened,
Shall the young bride's loom
be tightened?
Do not let the weft be loosened,
Nor the weaver's loom be tightened;
Such the weaving of the daughters
Of the Moon beyond the cloudlets;
Such the spinning of the maidens
Of the Sun in high Jumala,
Of the daughters of the Great Bear,
Of the daughters of the Evening.

"Bridegroom, thou beloved hero,
Brave descendant of thy fathers,
When thou goest on a journey,
When thou drivest on the highway,
Driving with the Rainbow-daughter,
Fairest bride of Sariola,
Do not lead her as a titmouse,
As a cuckoo of the forest,
Into unfrequented places,
Into copses of the borders,
Into brier-fields and brambles,
Into unproductive marshes;
Let her wander not, nor stumble
On opposing rocks and rubbish.
Never in her father's dwelling,
Never in her mother's court-yard,
Has she fallen into ditches,
Stumbled hard against the fences,
Run through brier-fields, nor brambles,
Fallen over rocks, nor rubbish.

"Magic bridegroom of Wainola,
Wise descendant of the heroes,
Never let thy young wife suffer,
Never let her be neglected,
Never let her sit in darkness,
Never leave her unattended.
Never in her father's mansion,
In the chambers of her mother,
Has she sat alone in darkness,
Has she suffered for attention;
Sat she by the crystal window,
Sat and rocked, in peace and plenty,
Evenings for her father's pleasure,
Mornings for her mother's sunshine.
Never mayest thou, O bridegroom,
Lead the Maiden of the Rainbow
To the mortar filled with sea-grass,
There to grind the bark for cooking,
There to bake her bread from stubble,
There to knead her dough from tan-bark
Never in her father's dwelling,
Never in her mother's mansion,
Was she taken to the mortar,
There to bake her bread from sea-grass.
Thou shouldst lead the Bride of Beauty
To the garner's rich abundance,
There to draw the till of barley,
Grind the flour and knead for baking,
There to brew the beer for drinking,
Wheaten flour for honey-biscuits.

"Hero-bridegroom of Wainola,
Never cause thy Bride of Beauty
To regret her day of marriage;
Never make her shed a tear-drop,
Never fill her cup with sorrow.
Should there ever come an evening
When thy wife shall feel unhappy,
Put the harness on thy racer,
Hitch the fleet-foot to the snow-sledge,
Take her to her father's dwelling,
To the household of her mother;
Never in thy hero-lifetime,
Never while the moonbeams glimmer,
Give thy fair spouse evil treatment,
Never treat her as thy servant;
Do not bar her from the cellar,
Do not lock thy best provisions;
Never in her father's mansion,
Never by her faithful mother
Was she treated as a hireling.

"Honoured bridegroom of the Northland,
Proud descendant of the fathers,
If thou treatest well thy young wife,
Worthily wilt thou be treated;
When thou goest to her homestead,
When thou visitest her father,
Thou shalt meet a cordial welcome.

"Censure not the Bride of Beauty,
Never grieve thy Rainbow-maiden,
Never say in tones reproachful,
She was born in lowly station,
That her father was unworthy;
Honoured are thy bride's relations,
From an old-time tribe, her kindred;
When of corn they sowed a measure,
Each one's portion was a kernel;
When they sowed a cask of flax-seed,
Each received a thread of linen.
Never, never, magic husband,
Treat thy beauty-bride unkindly,

Teach her not with lash of servants,
Strike her not with thongs of leather;
Never has she wept in anguish
From the birch-whip of her mother.
Stand before her like a rampart,
Be to her a strong protection,
Do not let thy mother chide her,
Let thy father not upbraid her,
Never let thy guests offend her;
Should thy servants bring annoyance,
They may need the master's censure;
Do not harm the Bride of Beauty,
Never injure her thou lovest;
Three long years hast thou been wooing,
Hoping every month to win her.

"Counsel with the bride of heaven,
To thy young wife give instruction,
Kindly teach thy bride in secret,
In the long and dreary evenings,
When thou sittest at the fireside;
Teach one year, in words of kindness,
Teach with eyes of love a second,
In the third year teach with firmness.
If she should not heed thy teaching,
Should not hear thy kindly counsel
After three long years of effort,
Cut a reed upon the lowlands,
Cut a nettle from the border,
Teach thy wife with harder measures.
In the fourth year, if she heed not,
Threaten her with sterner treatment,
With the stalks of rougher edges,
Use not yet the thongs of leather,
Do not touch her with the birch-whip.
If she does not heed this warning,
Should she pay thee no attention,
Cut a rod upon the mountains,
Or a willow in the valleys,
Hide it underneath thy mantle,
That the stranger may not see it,
Show it to thy wife in secret,
Shame her thus to do her duty,
Strike not yet, though disobeying.
Should she disregard this warning,
Still refuse to heed thy wishes,
Then instruct her with the willow,
Use the birch-rod from the mountains
In the closet of thy dwelling,
In the attic of thy mansion;
Strike, her not upon the common,
Do not conquer her in public,
Lest the villagers should see thee,
Lest the neighbors hear her weeping,
And the forests learn thy troubles.
Touch thy wife upon the shoulders,
Let her stiffened back be softened.
Do not touch her on the forehead,
Nor upon the ears, nor visage;
If a ridge be on her forehead,
Or a blue mark on her eyelids,
Then her mother would perceive it,
And her father would take notice,
All the village-workmen see it,
And the village-women ask her
'Hast thou been in heat of battle,
Hast thou struggled in a conflict,
Or perchance the wolves have torn thee,
Or the forest-bears embraced thee,
Or the black-wolf be thy husband,
And the bear be thy protector?'"

By the fire-place lay a gray-beard,
On the hearth-stone lay a beggar,
And the old man spake as follows:
"Never, never, hero-husband,
Follow thou thy young wife's wishes,
Follow not her inclinations,
As, alas! I did, regretful;
Bought my bride the bread of barley,
Veal, and beer, and best of butter,
Fish and fowl of all descriptions,
Beer I bought, home-brewed and sparkling,
Wheat from all the distant nations,
All the dainties of the Northland;
All of this was unavailing,
Gave my wife no satisfaction,
Often came she to my chamber,
Tore my sable locks in frenzy,
With a visage fierce and frightful,
With her eyeballs flashing anger,
Scolding on and scolding ever,
Ever speaking words of evil,
Using epithets the vilest,

Thought me but a block for chopping.
Then I sought for other measures,
Used on her my last resources,
Cut a birch-whip in the forest,
And she spake in tones endearing;
Cut a juniper or willow,
And she called me 'hero-darling';
When with lash my wife I threatened,
Hung she on my neck with kisses."

Thus the bridegroom was instructed,
Thus the last advices given.

Then the Maiden of the Rainbow,
Beauteous bride of Ilmarinen,
Sighing heavily and moaning,
Fell to weeping, heavy-hearted,
Spake these words from depths of sorrow:
"Near, indeed, the separation,
Near, alas! the time for parting,
Near the time for my departure;
O the anguish of the parting,
O the pain of separation,
From these walls renowned and ancient,
From this village of the Northland,
From these scenes of peace and plenty,
Where my faithful mother taught me,
Where my father gave instruction
To me in my happy childhood,
When my years were few and tender!
As a child I did not fancy,
Never thought of separation
From the confines of this cottage,
From these dear old hills and mountains,
But, alas! I now must journey,
Since I now cannot escape it;
Empty is the bowl of parting,
All the farewell-beer is taken,
And my husband's sledge is waiting,
With the break-board looking southward,
Looking from my father's dwelling.

"How shall I give compensation,
How repay, on my departure,
All the kindness of my mother,
All the counsel of my father,
All the friendship of my brother,
All my sister's warm affection?
Gratitude to thee, dear father,
For my former-life and blessings,
For the comforts of thy table,
For the pleasures of my childhood!
Gratitude to thee, dear mother,
For thy tender care and guidance,
For my birth and for my culture,
Nurtured by thy purest life-blood!
Gratitude to thee, dear brother,
Gratitude to thee, sweet sister,
To the servants of my childhood,
To my many friends and playmates!

"Never, never, aged father,
Never, thou, beloved mother,
Never, ye, my kindred spirits,
Never harbor care, nor sorrow,
Never fall to bitter weeping,
Since thy child has gone to others,
To the distant home of strangers,
To the meadows of Wainola,
From her father's fields and firesides.
Shines the Sun of the Creator,
Shines the golden Moon of Ukko,
Glitter all the stars of heaven,
In the firmament of ether,
Full as bright on other homesteads;
Not upon my father's uplands,
Not upon my home in childhood,
Shines the Star of Joyance only.

"Now the time has come for parting
From my father's golden firesides,
From my brother's welcome hearth-stone,
From the chambers of my sister,
From my mother's happy dwelling;
Now I leave the swamps and lowlands,
Leave the grassy vales and mountains,
Leave the crystal lakes and rivers,
Leave the shores and sandy shallows,
Leave the white-capped surging billows,
Where the maidens swim and linger,
Where the mermaids sing and frolic;
Leave the swamps to those that wander,
Leave the corn-fields to the plowman,
Leave the forests to the weary,

Leave the heather to the rover,
Leave the copses to the stranger,
Leave the alleys to the beggar,
Leave the court-yards to the rambler,
Leave the portals to the servant,
Leave the matting to the sweeper,
Leave the highways to the roebuck,
Leave the woodland-glens to lynxes,
Leave the lowlands to the wild-geese,
And the birch-tree to the cuckoo.
Now I leave these friends of childhood,
Journey southward with my husband,
To the arms of Night and Winter,
O'er the ice-grown seas of Northland.
"Should I once again, returning,
Pay a visit to my tribe-folk,
Mother would not hear me calling,
Father would not see me weeping,
Calling at my mother's grave-stone,
Weeping o'er my buried father,
On their graves the fragrant flowers,
Junipers and mournful willows,
Verdure from my mother's tresses,
From the gray-beard of my father.

"Should I visit Sariola,
Visit once again these borders,
No one here would bid me welcome.
Nothing in these hills would greet me,
Save perchance a few things only,
By the fence a clump of osiers,
And a land-mark at the corner,
Which in early youth I planted,
When a child of little stature.

"Mother's kine perhaps will know me,
Which so often I have watered,
Which I oft have fed and tended,
Lowing now at my departure,
In the pasture cold and cheerless;
Sure my mother's kine will welcome
Northland's daughter home returning.
Father's steeds may not forget me,
Steeds that I have often ridden,
When a maiden free and happy,
Neighing now for me departing,
In the pasture of my brother,
In the stable of my father;
Sure my father's steeds will know me,
Bid Pohyola's daughter welcome.
Brother's faithful dogs may know me,
That I oft have fed and petted,
Dogs that I have taught to frolic,
That now mourn for me departing,
In their kennels in the court-yard,
In their kennels cold and cheerless;
Sure my brother's dogs will welcome
Pohya's daughter home returning.
But the people will not know me,
When I come these scenes to visit,
Though the fords remain as ever,
Though unchanged remain the rivers,
Though untouched the flaxen fish-nets
On the shores await my coming.

"Fare thou well, my dear old homestead,
Fare ye well, my native bowers;
It would give me joy unceasing
Could I linger here forever.
Now farewell, ye halls and portals,
Leading to my father's mansion;
It would give me joy unceasing
Could I linger here forever.
Fare ye well, familiar gardens
Filled with trees and fragrant flowers;
It would give me joy unceasing,
Could I linger here forever.
Send to all my farewell greetings,
To the fields, and groves, and berries;
Greet the meadows with their daisies,
Greet the borders with their fences,
Greet the lakelets with their islands,
Greet the streams with trout disporting,
Greet the hills with stately pine trees,
And the valleys with their birches.
Fare ye well, ye streams and lakelets,
Fertile fields, and shores of ocean,
All ye aspens on the mountains,
All ye lindens of the valleys,
All ye beautiful stone-lindens,
All ye shade-trees by the cottage,
All ye junipers and willows,
All ye shrubs with berries laden,
Waving grass and fields of barley,

Arms of elms, and oaks, and alders,
Fare ye well, dear scenes of childhood,
Happiness of days departed!"

Ending thus, Pohyola's daughter
Left her native fields and fallows,
Left the darksome Sariola,
With her husband, Ilmarinen,
Famous son of Kalevala.

But the youth remained for singing,
This the chorus of the children:
"Hither came a bird of evil,
Flew in fleetness from the forest,
Came to steal away our virgin,
Came to win the Maid of Beauty;
Took away our fairest flower,
Took our mermaid from the waters,
Won her with his youth and beauty,
With his keys of ancient wisdom.
Who will lead us to the sea-beach,
Who conduct us to the rivers?
Now the buckets will be idle,
On the hooks will rest the fish-poles,
Now unswept will lie the matting,
And unswept the halls of birch-wood,
Copper goblets be unburnished,
Dark the handles of the pitchers,
Fare thou well, dear Rainbow Maiden."

Ilmarinen, happy bridegroom,
Hastened homeward with the daughter
Of the hostess of Pohyola,
With the beauty of the Northland;
Fleetly flew the hero's snow-sledge,
Loudly creaked, and roared, and rattled
Down the banks of Northland waters,
By the side of Honey-inlet,
On the back of Sandy Mountain.
Stones went rolling from the highway,
Like the winds the sledge flew onward,
On the yoke rang hoops of iron,
Loud the spotted wood resounded,
Loudly creaked the bands of willow,
All the birchen cross-bars trembled,
And the copper-bells rang music,
In the racing of the fleet-foot,
In the courser's gallop homeward;
Journeyed one day, then a second,
Journeyed still the third day onward,
In one hand the reins of magic,
While the other grasped the maiden,
One foot resting on the cross-bar,
And the other in the fur-robes.
Merrily the steed flew homeward,
Quickly did the highways shorten,
Till at last upon the third day,
As the sun was fast declining,
There appeared the blacksmith's furnace,
Nearer, Ilmarinen's dwelling,
Smoke arising high in ether,
Clouds of smoke to lofty heaven,
From the village of Wainola,
From the suitor's forge and smithy,
From the chimneys of the hero,
From the home of the successful.

Rune XXV: Wainamoinen's Wedding Songs

At the home of Ilmarinen
Long had they been watching, waiting,
For the coming of the blacksmith,
With his bride from Sariola.
Weary were the eyes of watchers,
Waiting from the father's portals,
Looking from the mother's windows;
Weary were the young knees standing
At the gates of the magician;
Weary grew the feet of children,
Tramping to the walls and watching;
Worn and torn, the shoes of heroes,
Running on the shore to meet him.

Now at last upon a morning
Of a lovely day in winter,
Heard they from the woods the rumble
Of a snow-sledge swiftly bounding.
Lakko, hostess of Wainola,
She the lovely Kalew-daughter,
Spake these words in great excitement:
"'Tis the sledge of the magician,

Comes at last the metal-worker
From the dismal Sariola,
By his side the Bride of Beauty!
Welcome, welcome, to this hamlet,
Welcome to thy mother's hearth-stone,
To the dwelling of thy father,
By thine ancestors erected!"

Straightway came great Ilmarinen
To his cottage drove the blacksmith,
To the fireside of his father,
To his mother's ancient dwelling.
Hazel-birds were sweetly singing
On the newly-bended collar;
Sweetly called the sacred cuckoos
From the summit of the break-board;
Merry, jumped the graceful squirrel
On the oaken shafts and cross-bar.

Lakko, Kalew's fairest hostess,
Beauteous daughter of Wainola,
Spake these words of hearty welcome:
"For the new moon hopes the village,
For the Sun, the happy maidens,
For the boat, the swelling water;
I have not the moon expected,
For the sun have not been waiting,
I have waited for my hero,
Waited for the Bride of Beauty;
Watched at morning, watched at evening,
Did not know but some misfortune,
Some sad fate had overtaken
Bride and bridegroom on their journey;
Thought the maiden growing weary,
Weary of my son's attentions,
Since he faithfully had promised
To return to Kalevala,
Ere his foot-prints had departed
From the snow-fields of his father.
Every morn I looked and listened,
Constantly I thought and wondered
When his sledge would rumble homeward,
When it would return triumphant
To his home, renowned and ancient.
Had a blind and beggared straw-horse
Hobbled to these shores awaiting,
With a sledge of but two pieces,
Well the steed would have been lauded,
Had it brought my son beloved,
Had it brought the Bride of Beauty.
Thus I waited long, impatient,
Looking out from morn till even,
Watching with my head extended,
With my tresses streaming southward,
With my eyelids widely opened,
Waiting for my son's returning
To this modest home of heroes,
To this narrow place of resting.
Finally am I rewarded,
For the sledge has come triumphant,
Bringing home my son and hero,
By his side the Rainbow maiden,
Red her cheeks, her visage winsome,
Pride and joy of Sariola.

"Wizard-bridegroom of Wainola,
Take thy courser to the stable,
Lead him to the well-filled manger,
To the best of grain and clover;
Give to us thy friendly greetings,
Greetings send to all thy people.
When thy greetings thou hast ended,
Then relate what has befallen
To our hero in his absence.
Hast thou gone without adventure
To the dark fields of Pohyola,
Searching for the Maid of Beauty?
Didst thou scale the hostile ramparts,
Didst thou take the virgin's mansion,
Passing o'er her mother's threshold,
Visiting the halls of Louhi?

"But I know without the asking,
See the answer to my question:
Comest from the North a victor,
On thy journey well contented;
Thou hast brought the Northland daughter,
Thou hast razed the hostile portals,
Thou hast stormed the forts of Louhi,
Stormed the mighty walls opposing,
On thy journey to Pohyola,
To the village of the father.
In thy care the bride is sitting,
In thine arms, the Rainbow-maiden,

At thy side, the pride of Northland,
Mated to the highly-gifted.
Who has told the cruel story,
Who the worst of news has scattered,
That thy suit was unsuccessful,
That in vain thy steed had journeyed?
Not in vain has been thy wooing,
Not in vain thy steed has travelled
To the dismal homes of Lapland;
He has journeyed heavy laden,
Shaken mane, and tail, and forelock,
Dripping foam from lips and nostrils,
Through the bringing of the maiden,
With the burden of the husband.
"Come, thou beauty, from the snow-sledge,
Come, descend thou from the cross-bench,
Do not linger for assistance,
Do not tarry to be carried;
If too young the one that lifts thee,
If too proud the one in waiting,
Rise thou, graceful, like a young bird,
Hither glide along the pathway,
On the tan-bark scarlet-coloured,
That the herds of kine have evened,
That the gentle lambs have trodden,
Smoothened by the tails of horses.
Haste thou here with gentle footsteps,
Through the pathway smooth and tidy,
On the tiles of even surface,
On thy second father's court-yard,
To thy second mother's dwelling,
To thy brother's place of resting,
To thy sister's silent chambers.
Place thy foot within these portals,
Step across this waiting threshold,
Enter thou these halls of joyance,
Underneath these painted rafters,
Underneath this roof of ages.
During all the winter evenings,
Through the summer gone forever,
Sang the tiling made of ivory,
Wishing thou wouldst walk upon it;
Often sang the golden ceiling,
Hoping thou wouldst walk beneath it,
And the windows often whistled,
Asking thee to sit beside them;
Even on this merry morning,
Even on the recent evening,
Sat the aged at their windows,
On the seashore ran the children,
Near the walls the maidens waited,
Ran the boys upon the highway,
There to watch the young bride's coming,
Coming with her hero-husband.

"Hail, ye courtiers of Wainola,
With the heroes of the fathers,
Hail to thee, Wainola's hamlet,
Hail, ye halls with heroes peopled,
Hail, ye rooms with all your inmates,
Hail to thee, sweet golden moonlight,
Hail to thee, benignant Ukko,
Hail companions of the bridegroom!
Never has there been in Northland
Such a wedding-train of honour,
Never such a bride of beauty.

"Bridegroom, thou beloved hero,
Now untie the scarlet ribbons,
And remove the silken muffler,
Let us see the honey-maiden,
See the Daughter of the Rainbow.
Seven years hast thou been wooing,
Hast thou brought the maid affianced,
Hast thou sought a sweeter cuckoo,
Sought one fairer than the moonlight,
Sought a mermaid from the ocean?
But I know without the asking,
See the answer to my question:
Thou hast brought the sweet-voiced cuckoo,
Thou hast found the swan of beauty,
Plucked the sweetest flower of Northland,
Culled the fairest of the jewels,
Gathered Pohya's sweetest berry!"

Sat a babe upon the matting,
And the young child spake as follows:
"Brother, what is this thou bringest,
Aspen-log or trunk of willow,
Slender as the mountain-linden?
Bridegroom, well dost thou remember,
Thou hast hoped it all thy life-time,
Hoped to bring the Maid of Beauty,
Thou a thousand times hast said it,

Better far than any other,
Not one like the croaking raven,
Nor the magpie from the border,
Nor the scarecrow from the corn-fields,
Nor the vulture from the desert.
What has this one done of credit,
In the summer that has ended?
Where the gloves that she has knitted,
Where the mittens she has woven?
Thou hast brought her empty-handed,
Not a gift she brings thy father;
In thy chests the mice are nesting,
Long-tails feeding on thy vestments,
And thy bride cannot repair them."

Lakko, hostess of Wainola,
She the faithful Kalew-daughter,
Hears the young child's speech in wonder,
Speaks these words of disapproval:
"Silly prattler, cease thy talking,
Thou hast spoken in dishonour;
Let all others be astonished,
Heap thy malice on thy kindred,
Must not harm the Bride of Beauty,
Rainbow-daughter of the Northland.
False indeed is this thy prattle,
All thy words are full of evil,
Fallen from thy tongue of mischief,
From the lips of one unworthy.
Excellent the hero's young bride,
Best of all in Sariola,
Like the strawberry in summer,
Like the daisy from the meadow,
Like the cuckoo from the forest,
Like the bluebird from the aspen,
Like the redbreast from the heather,
Like the martin from the linden;
Never couldst thou find in Ehstland
Such a virgin as this daughter,
Such a graceful beauteous maiden,
With such dignity of carriage,
With such arms of pearly whiteness,
With a neck so fair and lovely.
Neither is she empty-handed,
She has brought us furs abundant,
Brought us many silken garments,
Richest weavings of Pohyola.
Many beauteous things the maiden,
With the spindle has accomplished,
Spun and woven with her fingers;
Dresses of the finest texture
She in winter has upfolded,
Bleached them in the days of spring-time,
Dried them at the hour of noon-day,
For our couches finest linen,
For our heads the softest pillows,
For our comfort woollen blankets,
For our necks the silken ribbons."
To the bride speaks gracious Lakko:
"Goodly wife, thou Maid of Beauty,
Highly wert thou praised as daughter,
In thy father's distant country;
Here thou shalt be praised forever
By the kindred of thy husband;
Thou shalt never suffer sorrow,
Never give thy heart to grieving;
In the swamps thou wert not nurtured,
Wert not fed beside the brooklets;
Thou wert born 'neath stars auspicious,
Nurtured from the richest garners,
Thou wert taken to the brewing
Of the sweetest beer in Northland.

"Beauteous bride from Sariola,
Shouldst thou see me bringing hither
Casks of corn, or wheat, or barley,
Bringing rye in great abundance,
They belong to this thy household;
Good the plowing of thy husband,
Good his sowing and his reaping.

"Bride of Beauty from the Northland,
Thou wilt learn this home to manage,
Learn to labour with thy kindred;
Good the home for thee to dwell in,
Good enough for bride and daughter.
At thy hand will rest the milk-pail,
And the churn awaits thine order;
It is well here for the maiden,
Happy will the young bride labour,
Easy are the resting-benches;
Here the host is like thy father,
Like thy mother is the hostess,
All the sons are like thy brothers,

Like thy sisters are the daughters.

"Shouldst thou ever have a longing
For the whiting of the ocean,
For thy father's Northland salmon,
For thy brother's hazel-chickens,
Ask them only of thy husband,
Let thy hero-husband bring them.
There is not in all of Northland,
Not a creature of the forest,
Not a bird beneath the ether,
Not a fish within the waters,
Not the largest, nor the smallest,
That thy husband cannot capture.
It is well here for the maiden,
Here the bride may live in freedom,
Need not turn the heavy millstone,
Need not move the iron pestle;
Here the wheat is ground by water,
For the rye, the swifter current,
While the billows wash the vessels
And the surging waters rinse them.
Thou hast here a lovely village,
Finest spot in all of Northland,
In the lowlands sweet the verdure,
In the uplands, fields of beauty,
With the lake-shore near the hamlet,
Near thy home the running water,
Where the goslings swim and frolic,
Water-birds disport in numbers."

Thereupon the bride and bridegroom
Were refreshed with richest viands,
Given food and drink abundant,
Fed on choicest bits of reindeer,
On the sweetest loaves of barley,
On the best of wheaten biscuits,
On the richest beer of Northland.
Many things were on the table,
Many dainties of Wainola,
In the bowls of scarlet colour,
In the platters deftly painted,
Many cakes with honey sweetened,
To each guest was butter given,
Many bits of trout and whiting,
Larger salmon carved in slices,
With the knives of molten silver,
Rimmed with gold the silver handles,
Beer of barley ceaseless flowing,
Honey-drink that was not purchased,
In the cellar flows profusely,
Beer for all, the tongues to quicken,
Mead and beer the minds to freshen.
Who is there to lead the singing,
Lead the songs of Kalevala?

Wainamoinen, old and truthful,
The eternal, wise enchanter,
Quick begins his incantations,
Straightway sings the songs that follow.
"Golden brethren, dearest kindred,
Ye, my loved ones, wise and worthy
Ye companions, highly-gifted,
Listen to my simple sayings:
Rarely stand the geese together,
Sisters do not mate each other,
Not together stand the brothers,
Nor the children of one mother,
In the countries of the Northland.

"Shall we now begin the singing,
Sing the songs of old tradition?
Singers can but sing their wisdom,
And the cuckoo call the spring-time,
And the goddess of the heavens
Only dyes the earth in beauty;
So the goddesses of weaving
Can but weave from dawn till twilight,
Ever sing the youth of Lapland
In their straw-shoes full of gladness,
When the coarse-meat of the roebuck,
Or of blue-moose they have eaten.
Wherefore should I not be singing,
And the children not be chanting
Of the biscuits of Wainola,
Of the bread of Kalew-waters?
Even sing the lads of Lapland
In their straw-shoes filled with joyance,
Drinking but a cup of water,
Eating but the bitter tan-bark.
Wherefore should I not be singing,
And the children not be chanting
Of the beer of Kalevala,
Brewed from barley in perfection,

Dressed in quaint and homely costume,
As they sit beside their hearth-stones.
Wherefore should I not be singing,
And the children too be chanting
Underneath these painted rafters,
In these halls renowned and ancient?
This the place for men to linger,
This the court-room for the maidens,
Near the foaming beer of barley,
Honey-brewed in great abundance,
Very near, the salmon-waters,
Near, the nets for trout and whiting,
Here where food is never wanting,
Where the beer is ever brewing.
Here Wainola's sons assemble,
Here Wainola's daughters gather,
Here they never eat in trouble,
Here they live without regretting,
In the life-time of the landlord,
While the hostess lives and prospers.

"Who shall first be sung and lauded?
Shall it be the bride or bridegroom?
Let us praise the bridegroom's father,
Let the hero-host be chanted,
Him whose home is in the forest,
Him who built upon the mountains,
Him who brought the trunks of lindens,
With their tops and slender branches,
Brought them to the best of places,
Joined them skilfully together,
For the mansion of the nation,
For this famous hero-dwelling,
Walls procured upon the lowlands,
Rafters from the pine and fir tree,
From the woodlands beams of oak-wood,
From the berry-plains the studding,
Bark was furnished by the aspen,
And the mosses from the fenlands.
Trimly builded is this mansion,
In a haven warmly sheltered;
Here a hundred men have laboured,
On the roof have stood a thousand,
As this spacious house was building,
As this roof was tightly jointed.
Here the ancient mansion-builder,
When these rafters were erected,
Lost in storms his locks of sable,
Scattered by the winds of heaven.
Often has the hero-landlord
On the rocks his gloves forgotten,
Left his hat upon the willows,
Lost his mittens in the marshes;
Oftentimes the mansion-builder,
In the early hours of morning,
Ere his workmen had awakened,
Unperceived by all the village,
Has arisen from his slumber,
Left his cabin in the snow-fields,
Combed his locks among the branches,
Bathed his eyes in dews of morning.

"Thus obtained the pleasant landlord
Friends to fill his spacious dwelling,
Fill his benches with magicians,
Fill his windows with enchanters,
Fill his halls with wizard-singers,
Fill his floors with ancient speakers,
Fill his ancient court with strangers,
Fill his hurdles with the needy;
Thus the Kalew-host is lauded.

"Now I praise the genial hostess,
Who prepares the toothsome dinner,
Fills with plenty all her tables,
Bakes the honeyed loaves of barley,
Kneads the dough with magic fingers,
With her arms of strength and beauty,
Bakes her bread in copper ovens,
Feeds her guests and bids them welcome,
Feeds them on the toothsome bacon,
On the trout, and pike, and whiting,
On the rarest fish in ocean,
On the dainties of Wainola.

"Often has the faithful hostess
Risen from her couch in silence,
Ere the crowing of the watcher,
To prepare the wedding-banquet,
Make her tables look attractive,
Brew the honey-beer of wedlock.
Excellently has the housewife,
Has the hostess filled with wisdom,
Brewed the beer from hops and barley,

From the corn of Kalevala,
From the wheat-malt honey-seasoned,
Stirred the beer with graceful fingers,
At the oven in the penthouse,
In the chamber swept and polished.
Neither did the prudent hostess,
Beautiful, and full of wisdom,
Let the barley sprout too freely,
Lest the beer should taste of black-earth,
Be too bitter in the brewing;
Often went she to the garners,
Went alone at hour of midnight,
Was not frightened by the black-wolf,
Did not fear the beasts of woodlands.
"Now the hostess I have lauded,
Let me praise the favoured suitor,
Now the honoured hero-bridegroom,
Best of all the village-masters.
Clothed in purple is the hero,
Raiment brought from distant nations,
Tightly fitting to his body;
Snugly sets his coat of ermine,
To the floor it hangs in beauty,
Trailing from his neck and shoulders,
Little of his vest appearing,
Peeping through his outer raiment,
Woven by the Moon's fair daughters,
And his vestment silver-tinselled.
Dressed in neatness is the suitor,
Round his waist a belt of copper,
Hammered by the Sun's sweet maidens,
Ere the early fires were lighted,
Ere the fire had been discovered.
Dressed in richness is the bridegroom,
On his feet are silken stockings,
Silken ribbons on his ankles,
Gold and silver interwoven.
Dressed in beauty is the bridegroom,
On his feet are shoes of deer-skin,
Like the swans upon the water,
Like the blue-duck on the sea-waves,
Like the thrush among the willows,
Like the water-birds of Northland.
Well adorned the hero-suitor,
With his locks of golden colour,
With his gold-beard finely braided,
Hero-hat upon his forehead,
Piercing through the forest branches,
Reaching to the clouds of heaven,
Bought with countless gold and silver,
Priceless is the suitor's head-gear.

"Now the bridegroom has been lauded,
I will praise the young bride's playmate,
Day-companion in her childhood,
In the maiden's magic mansion.
Whence was brought the merry maiden,
From the village of Tanikka?
Thence was never brought the playmate,
Playmate of the bride in childhood.
Has she come from distant nations,
From the waters of the Dwina,
O'er the ocean far-outstretching?
Not from Dwina came the maiden,
Did not sail across the waters;
Grew as berry in the mountains,
As a strawberry of sweetness,
On the fields the child of beauty,
In the glens the golden flower.
Thence has come the young bride's playmate,
Thence arose her fair companion.
Tiny are her feet and fingers,
Small her lips of scarlet colour,
Like the maiden's loom of Suomi;
Eyes that shine in kindly beauty
Like the twinkling stars of heaven;
Beam the playmate's throbbing temples
Like the moonlight on the waters.
Trinkets has the bride's companion,
On her neck a golden necklace,
In her tresses, silken ribbons,
On her arms are golden bracelets,
Golden rings upon her fingers,
Pearls are set in golden ear-rings;
Loops of gold upon her temples,
And with pearls her brow is studded.
Northland thought the Moon was shining
When her jeweled ear-rings glistened;
Thought the Sun had left his station
When her girdle shone in beauty;
Thought a ship was homeward sailing
When her coloured head-gear fluttered.
Thus is praised the bride's companion,
Playmate of the Rainbow-maiden.

"Now I praise the friends assembled,
All appear in graceful manners;
If the old are wise and silent,
All the youth are free and merry,
All the guests are fair and worthy.
Never was there in Wainola,
Never will there be in Northland,
Such a company assembled;
All the children speak in joyance,
All the aged move sedately;
Dressed in white are all the maidens,
Like the hoar-frost of the morning,
Like the welcome dawn of
spring-time,
Like the rising of the daylight.
Silver then was more abundant,
Gold among the guests in plenty,
On the hills were money-pockets,
Money-bags along the valleys,
For the friends that were invited,
For the guests in joy assembled.
All the friends have now been lauded,
Each has gained his mead of honour."

Wainamoinen, old and truthful,
Song-deliverer of Northland,
Swung himself upon the fur-bench
Of his magic sledge of copper,
Straightway hastened to his hamlet,
Singing as he journeyed onward,
Singing charms and incantations,
Singing one day, then a second,
All the third day chanting legends.
On the rocks the runners rattled,
Hung the sledge upon a birch-stump,
Broke it into many pieces,
With the magic of his singing;
Double were the runners bended,
All the parts were torn asunder,
And his magic sledge was ruined.

Then the good, old Wainamoinen
Spake these words in meditation:
"Is there one among this number,
In this rising generation,
Or perchance among the aged,
In the passing generation,
That will go to Mana's kingdom,
To the empire of Tuoni,
There to get the magic auger
From the master of Manala,
That I may repair my snow-sledge,
Or a second sledge may fashion?"

What the younger people answered
Was the answer of the aged:
"Not among the youth of Northland,
Nor among the aged heroes,
Is there one of ample courage,
That has bravery sufficient,
To attempt the reckless journey
To the kingdom of Tuoni,
To Manala's fields and castles,
Thence to bring Tuoni's auger,
Wherewithal to mend thy snow-sledge,
Build anew thy sledge of magic."

Thereupon old Wainamoinen,
The eternal wisdom-singer,
Went again to Mana's empire,
To the kingdom of Tuoni,
Crossed the sable stream of
deathland,
To the castles of Manala,
Found the auger of Tuoni,
Brought the instrument in safety.
Straightway sings old Wainamoinen,
Sings to life a purple forest,
In the forest, slender birches,
And beside them, mighty oak-trees,
Shapes them into shafts and runners,
Moulds them by his will and power,
Makes anew his sledge of magic.

On his steed he lays the harness,
Binds him to his sledge securely,
Seats himself upon the cross-bench,
And the racer gallops homeward,
To the manger filled and waiting,
To the stable of his master;
Brings the ancient Wainamoinen,
Famous bard and wise enchanter,
To the threshold of his dwelling,
To his home in Kalevala.

Rune XXVI: Origin of the Serpent

Ahti, living on the island,
Near the Kauko-point and harbor,
Plowed his fields for rye and barley,
Furrowed his extensive pastures,
Heard with quickened ears an uproar,
Heard the village in commotion,
Heard a noise along the seashore,
Heard the foot-steps on the ice-plain,
Heard the rattle of the sledges;
Quick his mind divined the reason,
Knew it was Pohyola's wedding,
Wedding of the Rainbow-virgin.
Quick he stopped in disappointment,
Shook his sable locks in envy,
Turned his hero-head in anger,
While the scarlet blood ceased flowing
Through his pallid face and temples;
Ceased his plowing and his sowing,
On the field he left the furrows;
On his steed he lightly mounted,
Straightway galloped
fleetly homeward
To his well-beloved mother,
To his mother old and golden,
Gave his mother these directions,
These the words of Lemminkainen:
"My beloved, faithful mother,
Quickly bring me beer and viands,
Bring me food for I am hungry,
Food and drink for me abundant,
Have my bath-room quickly heated,
Quickly set the room in order,
That I may refresh my body,
Dress myself in hero-raiment."

Lemminkainen's aged mother
Brings her hero food in plenty,
Beer and viands for the hungry,
For her thirsting son and hero;
Quick she heats the ancient bath-room,
Quickly sets his bath in order.

Then the reckless Lemminkainen
Ate his meat with beer inspiring,
Hastened to his bath awaiting;
Only was the bullfinch bathing,
With the many-coloured bunting;
Quick the hero laved his temples,
Laved himself to flaxen whiteness,
Quick returning to his mother,
Spake in haste the words that follow:
"My beloved, helpful mother,
Go at once to yonder mountain,
To the store-house on the hill-top,
Bring my vest of finest texture,
Bring my hero-coat of purple,
Bring my suit of magic colours,
Thus to make me look attractive,
Thus to robe myself in beauty."

First the ancient mother asked him,
Asked her son this simple question:
"Whither dost thou go, my hero?
Dost thou go to hunt the roebuck,
Chase the lynx upon the mountains,
Shoot the squirrel in the woodlands?"

Spake the reckless Lemminkainen,
Also known as Kaukomieli:
"Worthy mother of my being,
Go I not to hunt the roebuck,
Chase the lynx upon the mountains,
Shoot the squirrel on the tree-tops;
I am going to Pohyola,
To the feasting of her people.
Bring at once my purple vestments,
Straightway bring my nuptial outfit,
Let me don it for the marriage
Of the maiden of the Northland."

But the ancient dame dissented,
And the wife forebade the husband;
Two of all the best of heroes,
Three of nature's fairest daughters,
Strongly urged wild Lemminkainen
Not to go to Sariola,
To Pohyola's great carousal,
To the marriage-feast of Northland,
"Since thou hast not been invited,
Since they do not wish thy presence."

Spake the reckless Lemminkainen.
These the words of Kaukomieli:
"Where the wicked are invited,
There the good are always welcome,
Herein lies my invitation;
I am constantly reminded
By this sword of sharpened edges,
By this magic blade and scabbard,
That Pohyola needs my presence."

Lemminkainen's aged mother
Sought again to stay her hero:
"Do not go, my son beloved,
To the feasting in Pohyola;
Full of horrors are the highways,
On the road are many wonders,
Three times Death appears to frighten,
Thrice destruction hovers over!"

Spake the reckless Lemminkainen,
These the words of Kaukomieli:
"Death is seen by aged people,
Everywhere they see perdition,
Death can never frighten heroes,
Heroes do not fear the spectre;
Be that as it may, dear mother,
Tell that I may understand thee,
Name the first of all destructions,
Name the first and last destroyers!"
Lemminkainen's mother answered:
"I will tell thee, son and hero,
Not because I wish to speak it,
But because the truth is worthy;
I will name the chief destruction,
Name the first of the destroyers.
When thou hast a distance journeyed,
Only one day hast thou travelled,
Comes a stream along the highway,
Stream of fire of wondrous beauty,
In the stream a mighty fire-spout,
In the spout a rock uprising,
On the rock a fiery hillock,
On the top a flaming eagle,
And his crooked beak he sharpens,
Sharpens too his bloody talons,
For the coming of the stranger,
For the people that approach him."

Spake the reckless Lemminkainen,
Handsome hero, Kaukomieli:
"Women die beneath the eagle,
Such is not the death of heroes;
Know I well a magic lotion,
That will heal the wounds of eagles;
Make myself a steed of alders,
That will walk as my companion,
That will stride ahead majestic;
As a duck I'll drive behind him,
Drive him o'er the fatal waters,
Underneath the flaming eagle,
With his bloody beak and talons.
Worthy mother of my being,
Name the second of destroyers."
Lemminkainen's mother answered:
"This the second of destroyers:
When thou hast a distance wandered,
Only two days hast thou travelled,
Comes a pit of fire to meet thee,
In the centre of the highway,
Eastward far the pit extending,
Stretches endless to the westward,
Filled with burning coals and pebbles,
Glowing with the heat of ages;
Hundreds has this monster swallowed,
In his jaws have thousands perished,
Hundreds with their trusty broadswords,
Thousands on their fiery chargers."

Spake the reckless Lemminkainen,
Handsome hero, Kaukomieli:
"Never will the hero perish
In the jaws of such a monster;
Know I well the means of safety,
Know a remedy efficient:
I will make of snow a master,
On the snow-clad fields, a hero,
Drive the snow-man on before me,
Drive him through the flaming vortex,
Drive him through the fiery furnace,
With my magic broom of copper;
I will follow in his shadow,
Follow close the magic image,
Thus escape the frightful monster,
With my golden locks uninjured,
With my flowing beard untangled.

Ancient mother of my being,
Name the last of the destructions,
Name the third of the destroyers."
Lemminkainen's mother answered:
"This the third of fatal dangers:
Hast thou gone a greater distance,
Hast thou travelled one day longer,
To the portals of Pohyola,
To the narrowest of gate-ways,
There a wolf will rise to meet thee,
There the black-bear sneak upon thee;
In Pohyola's darksome portals,
Hundreds in their jaws have perished,
Have devoured a thousand heroes;
Wherefore will they not destroy thee,
Since thy form is unprotected?"

Spake the reckless Lemminkainen,
Handsome hero, Kaukomieli:
"Let them eat the gentle lambkins,
Feed upon their tender tissues,
They cannot devour this hero;
I am girded with my buckler,
Girded with my belt of copper,
Armlets wear I of the master,
From the wolf and bear protected,
Will not hasten to Untamo.
I can meet the wolf of Lempo,
For the bear I have a balsam,
For his mouth I conjure bridles,
For the wolf, forge chains of iron;
I will smite them as the willow,
Chop them into little fragments,
Thus I'll gain the open court-yard,
Thus triumphant end my journey."
Lemminkainen's mother answered:
"Then thy journey is not ended,
Greater dangers still await thee,
Great the wonders yet before thee,
Horrors three within thy pathway;
Three great dangers of the hero
Still await thy reckless footsteps,
These the worst of all thy dangers:
When thou hast still farther wandered,
Thou wilt reach the Court of Pohya,
Where the walls are forged from iron,
And from steel the outer bulwark;
Rises from the earth to heaven,
Back again to earth returning;
Double spears are used for railings,
On each spear are serpents winding,
On each rail are stinging adders;
Lizards too adorn the bulwarks,
Play their long tails in the sunlight,
Hissing lizards, venomed serpents,
Jump and writhe upon the rampart,
Turn their horrid heads to meet thee;
On the greensward lie the monsters,
On the ground the things of evil,
With their pliant tongues of venom,
Hissing, striking, crawling, writhing;
One more horrid than the others,
Lies before the fatal gate-way,
Longer than the longest rafters,
Larger than the largest portals;
Hisses with the tongue of anger,
Lifts his head in awful menace,
Raises it to strike none other
Than the hero of the islands."

Spake the warlike Lemminkainen,
Handsome hero, Kaukomieli:
"By such things the children perish,
Such is not the death of heroes;
Know I well the fire to manage,
I can quench the flames of passion,
I can meet the prowling wild-beasts,
Can appease the wrath of serpents,
I can heal the sting of adders,
I have plowed the serpent-pastures,
Plowed the adder-fields of Northland;
While my hands were unprotected,
Held the serpents in my fingers,
Drove the adders to Manala,
On my hands the blood of serpents,
On my feet the fat of adders.
Never will thy hero stumble
On the serpents of the Northland;
With my heel I'll crush the monsters,
Stamp the horrid things to atoms;
I will banish them from Pohya,
Drive them to Manala's kingdom,
Step within Pohyola's mansion,
Walk the halls of Sariola!"

Lemminkainen's mother answered:
"Do not go, my son beloved,
To the firesides of Pohyola,
Through the Northland fields and fallows;
There are warriors with broadswords,
Heroes clad in mail of copper,
Are on beer intoxicated,
By the beer are much embittered;
They will charm thee, hapless creature,
On the tips of swords of magic;
Greater heroes have been conjured,
Stronger ones have been outwitted."
Spake the reckless Lemminkainen:
"Formerly thy son resided
In the hamlets of Pohyola;
Laplanders cannot enchant me,
Nor the Turyalanders harm me;
I the Laplander will conjure,
Charm him with my magic powers,
Sing his shoulders wide asunder,
In his chin I'll sing a fissure,
Sing his collar-bone to pieces,
Sing his breast to thousand fragments."
Lemminkainen's mother answered:
"Foolish son, ungrateful wizard,
Boasting of thy former visit,
Boasting of thy fatal journey!
Once in Northland thou wert living,
In the homesteads of Pohyola;
There thou tried to swim the whirlpool,
Tasted there the dog-tongue waters,
Floated down the fatal current,
Sank beneath its angry billows;
Thou hast seen Tuoni's river,
Thou hast measured Mana's waters,
There today thou wouldst be sleeping,
Had it not been for thy mother!
What I tell thee well remember,
Shouldst thou gain Pohyola's chambers,
Filled with stakes thou'lt find the court-yard,
These to hold the heads of heroes;
There thy head will rest forever,
Shouldst thou go to Sariola."
Spake the warlike Lemminkainen:
"Fools indeed may heed thy counsel,
Cowards too may give attention;
Those of seven conquest-summers
Cannot heed such weak advising.
Bring to me my battle-armor,
Bring my magic mail of copper,
Bring me too my father's broadsword,
Keep the old man's blade from rusting;
Long it has been cold and idle,
Long has lain in secret places,
Long and constantly been weeping,
Long been asking for a bearer."

Then he took his mail of copper,
Took his ancient battle-armor,
Took his father's sword of magic,
Tried its point against the oak-wood,
Tried its edge upon the sorb-tree;
In his hand the blade was bended,
Like the limber boughs of willow,
Like the juniper in summer.
Spake the hero, Lemminkainen:
"There is none in Pohya's hamlets,
In the courts of Sariola,
That with me can measure broadswords,
That can meet this blade ancestral."

From the nail he took a cross-bow,
Took the strongest from the rafters,
Spake these words in meditation:
"I shall recognize as worthy,
Recognize that one a hero
That can bend this mighty cross-bow,
That can break its magic sinews,
In the hamlets of Pohyola."

Lemminkainen, filled with courage,
Girds himself in suit of battle,
Dons his mighty mail of copper,
To his servant speaks as follows:
"Trusty slave, and whom I purchased,
Whom I bought with gold and silver,
Quick prepare my fiery charger,
Harness well my steed of battle;
I am going to the feasting,
To the banquet-fields of Lempo."

Quick obeys the faithful servant,
Hitches well the noble war-horse,
Quick prepares the fire-red stallion,

Speaks these words when all is ready:
"I have done what thou hast bidden,
Ready harnessed is the charger,
Waiting to obey his master."

Comes the hour of the departing
Of the hero, Lemminkainen,
Right hand ready, left unwilling,
All his anxious fingers pain him,
Till at last in full obedience,
All his members give permission;
Starts the hero on his journey,
While the mother gives him counsel,
At the threshold of the dwelling,
At the highway of the court-yard:
"Child of courage, my beloved,
Son of strength, my wisdom-hero,
If thou goest to the feasting,
Shouldst thou reach the great carousal,
Drink thou only a half a cupful,
Drink the goblet to the middle,
Always give the half remaining,
Give the worse half to another,
To another more unworthy;
In the lower half are serpents,
Worms, and frogs, and hissing lizards,
Feeding on the slimy bottom."

Furthermore she tells her hero,
Gives her son these sage directions,
On the border of the court-yard,
At the portals farthest distant:
"If thou goest to the banquet,
Shouldst thou reach the great carousal,
Occupy but half the settle,
Take but half a stride in walking,
Give the second half to others,
To another less deserving;
Only thus thou'lt be a hero,
Thus become a son immortal;
In the guest-rooms look courageous,
Bravely move about the chambers,
In the gatherings of heroes,
With the hosts of magic valor."

Thereupon wild Lemminkainen
Quickly leaped upon the cross-bench
Of his battle-sledge of wonder,
Raised his pearl-enamelled birch-rod,
Snapped his whip above his charger,
And the steed flew onward fleetly,
Galloped on his distant journey.

He had travelled little distance,
When a flight of hazel-chickens
Quick arose before his coming,
Flew before the foaming racer.
There were left some feathers lying,
Feathers of the hazel-chickens,
Lying in the hero's pathway.
These the reckless Lemminkainen
Gathered for their magic virtues,
Put them in his pouch of leather,
Did not know what things might happen
On his journey to Pohyola;
All things have some little value,
In a strait all things are useful.

Then he drove a little distance,
Galloped farther on the highway,
When his courser neighed in danger,
And the fleet-foot ceased his running.
Then the stout-heart, Lemminkainen,
Handsome hero, Kaukomieli,
Rose upon his seat in wonder,
Craned his neck and looked about him.
Found it as his mother told him,
Found a stream of fire opposing;
Ran the fire-stream like a river,
Ran across the hero's pathway.
In the river was a fire-fall,
In the cataract a fire-rock,
On the rock a fiery hillock,
On its summit perched an eagle,
From his throat the fire was streaming
To the crater far below him,
Fire out-shooting from his feathers,
Glowing with a fiery splendor;
Long he looked upon the hero,
Long he gazed on Lemminkainen,
Then the eagle thus addressed him:
"Whither art thou driving, Ahti,
Whither going, Lemminkainen?"
Kaukomieli spake in answer:

"To the feastings of Pohyola,
To the drinking-halls of Louhi,
To the banquet of her people;
Move aside and let me journey,
Move a little from my pathway,
Let this wanderer pass by thee,
I am warlike Lemminkainen."

This the answer of the eagle,
Screaming from his throat of splendor:
"Though thou art wild Lemminkainen,
I shall let thee wander onward,
Through my fire-throat let thee journey,
Through these flames shall be thy passage
To the banquet-halls of Louhi,
To Pohyola's great carousal!"

Little heeding, Kaukomieli
Thinks himself in little trouble,
Thrusts his fingers in his pockets,
Searches in his pouch of leather,
Quickly takes the magic feathers,
Feathers from the hazel-chickens,
Rubs them into finest powder,
Rubs them with his magic fingers,
Whence a flight of birds arises,
Hazel-chickens from the feathers,
Large the bevy of the young birds.
Quick the wizard, Lemminkainen,
Drives them to the eagle's fire-mouth,
Thus to satisfy his hunger,
Thus to quench the fire out-streaming.
Thus escapes the reckless hero,
Thus escapes the first of dangers,
Passes thus the first destroyer,
On his journey to Pohyola.

With his whip he strikes his courser,
With his birch-whip, pearl-enamelled;
Straightway speeds the fiery charger,
Noiselessly upon his journey,
Gallops fast and gallops faster,
Till the flying steed in terror
Neighs again and ceases running.
Lemminkainen, quickly rising,
Cranes his neck and looks about him,
Sees his mother's words were truthful,
Sees her augury well-taken.
Lo! before him yawned a fire-gulf,
Stretching crosswise through his pathway;
Far to east the gulf extending,
To the west an endless distance,
Filled with stones and burning pebbles,
Running streams of burning matter.

Little heeding, Lemminkainen
Cries aloud in prayer to Ukko:
"Ukko, thou O God above me,
Dear Creator, omnipresent,
From the northwest send a storm-cloud,
From the east, dispatch a second,
From the south send forth a third one;
Let them gather from the southwest,
Sew their edges well together,
Fill thou well the interspaces,
Send a snow-fall high as heaven,
Let it fall from upper ether,
Fall upon the flaming fire-pit,
On the cataract and whirlpool!"

Mighty Ukko, the Creator,
Ukko, father omnipresent,
Dwelling in the courts of heaven,
Sent a storm-cloud from the northwest,
From the east he sent a second,
From the south despatched a third one,
Let them gather from the southwest,
Sewed their edges well together,
Filled their many interspaces,
Sent a snow-fall high as heaven,
From the giddy heights of ether,
Sent it seething to the fire-pit,
On the streams of burning matter;
From the snow-fall in the fire-pond,
Grows a lake with rolling billows.
Quick the hero, Lemminkainen,
Conjures there of ice a passage
From one border to the other,
Thus escapes his second danger,
Thus his second trouble passes.

Then the reckless Lemminkainen
Raised his pearl-enamelled birch-rod,
Snapped his whip above his racer,

And the steed flew onward swiftly,
Galloped on his distant journey
O'er the highway to Pohyola;
Galloped fast and galloped faster,
Galloped on a greater distance,
When the stallion loudly neighing,
Stopped and trembled on the highway.
Then the lively Lemminkainen
Raised himself upon the cross-bench,
Looked to see what else had happened;
Lo! a wolf stands at the portals,
In the passage-way a black-bear,
At the high-gate of Pohyola,
At the ending of the journey.

Thereupon young Lemminkainen,
Handsome hero, Kaukomieli,
Thrusts his fingers in his pockets,
Seeks his magic pouch of leather,
Pulls therefrom a lock of ewe-wool,
Rubs it firmly in his fingers,
In his hands it falls to powder;
Breathes the breath of life upon it,
When a flock of sheep arises,
Goats and sheep of sable colour;
On the flock the black-wolf pounces,
And the wild-bear aids the slaughter,
While the reckless Lemminkainen
Rushes by them on his journey;
Gallops on a little distance,
To the court of Sariola,
Finds the fence of molten iron,
And of steel the rods and pickets,
In the earth a hundred fathoms,
To the azure sky, a thousand,
Double-pointed spears projecting;
On each spear were serpents twisted,
Adders coiled in countless numbers,
Lizards mingled with the serpents,
Tails entangled pointing earthward,
While their heads were skyward whirling,
Writhing, hissing mass of evil.

Then the stout-heart, Kaukomieli,
Deeply thought and long considered:
"It is as my mother told me,
This the wall that she predicted,
Stretching from the earth to heaven;
Downward deep are serpents creeping,
Deeper still the rails extending;
High as highest flight of eagles,
Higher still the wall shoots upward."

But the hero, Lemminkainen,
Little cares, nor feels disheartened,
Draws his broadsword from its scabbard,
Draws his mighty blade ancestral,
Hews the wall with might of magic,
Breaks the palisade in pieces,
Hews to atoms seven pickets,
Chops the serpent-wall to fragments;
Through the breach he quickly passes
To the portals of Pohyola.

In the way, a serpent lying,
Lying crosswise in the entry,
Longer than the longest rafters,
Larger than the posts of oak-wood;
Hundred-eyed, the heinous serpent,
And a thousand tongues, the monster,
Eyes as large as sifting vessels,
Tongues as long as shafts of javelins,
Teeth as large as hatchet-handles,
Back as broad as skiffs of ocean.
Lemminkainen does not venture
Straightway through this host opposing,
Through the hundred heads of adders,
Through the thousand tongues of serpents.
Spake the magic Lemminkainen:
"Venomed viper, thing of evil,
Ancient adder of Tuoni,
Thou that crawlest in the stubble,
Through the flower-roots of Lempo,
Who has sent thee from thy kingdom,
Sent thee from thine evil coverts,
Sent thee hither, crawling, writhing,
In the pathway I would travel?
Who bestowed thy mouth of venom,
Who insisted, who commanded,
Thou shouldst raise thy head toward heaven,
Who thy tail has given action?
Was this given by the father,
Did the mother give this power,
Or the eldest of the brothers,

Or the youngest of the sisters,
Or some other of thy kindred?

"Close thy mouth, thou thing of evil,
Hide thy pliant tongue of venom,
In a circle wrap thy body,
Coil thou like a shield in silence,
Give to me one-half the pathway,
Let this wanderer pass by thee,
Or remove thyself entirely;
Get thee hence to yonder heather,
Quick retreat to bog and stubble,
Hide thyself in reeds and rushes,
In the brambles of the lowlands.
Like a ball of flax enfolding,
Like a sphere of aspen-branches,
With thy head and tail together,
Roll thyself to yonder mountain;
In the heather is thy dwelling,
Underneath the sod thy caverns.
Shouldst thou raise thy head in anger,
Mighty Ukko will destroy it,
Pierce it with his steel-tipped arrows,
With his death-balls made of iron!"

Hardly had the hero ended,
When the monster, little heeding,
Hissing with his tongue in anger,
Plying like the forked lightning,
Pounces with his mouth of venom
At the head of Lemminkainen;
But the hero, quick recalling,
Speaks the master-words of knowledge,
Words that came from distant ages,
Words his ancestors had taught him,
Words his mother learned in childhood,
These the words of Lemminkainen:
"Since thou wilt not heed mine order,
Since thou wilt not leave the highway,
Puffed with pride of thine own greatness,
Thou shall burst in triple pieces.
Leave thy station for the borders,
I will hunt thine ancient mother,
Sing thine origin of evil,
How arose thy head of horror;
Suoyatar, thine ancient mother,
Thing of evil, thy creator!

"Suoyatar once let her spittle
Fall upon the waves of ocean;
This was rocked by winds and waters,
Shaken by the ocean-currents,
Six years rocked upon the billows,
Rocked in water seven summers,
On the blue back of the ocean,
On the billows high as heaven;
Lengthwise did the billows draw it,
And the sunshine gave it softness,
To the shore the billows washed it,
On the coast the waters left it.

"Then appeared Creation's daughters,
Three the daughters thus appearing,
On the roaring shore of ocean,
There beheld the spittle lying,
And the daughters spake as follows:
'What would happen from this spittle,
Should the breath of the Creator
Fall upon the writhing matter,
Breathe the breath of life upon it,
Give the thing the sense of vision?'

"The Creator heard these measures,
Spake himself the words that follow:
'Evil only comes from evil,
This is the expectoration
Of fell Suoyatar, its mother;
Therefore would the thing be evil,
Should I breathe a soul within it,
Should I give it sense of vision.'

"Hisi heard this conversation,
Ever ready with his mischief,
Made himself to be creator,
Breathed a soul into the spittle,
To fell Suoyatar's fierce anger.
Thus arose the poison-monster,
Thus was born the evil serpent,
This the origin of evil.

"Whence the life that gave her action?
From the carbon-pile of Hisi.
Whence then was her heart created?
From the heart-throbs of her mother.
Whence arose her brain of evil?

From the foam of rolling waters.
Whence was consciousness awakened?
From the waterfall's commotion.
Whence arose her head of venom?
From the seed-germs of the ivy.
Whence then came her eyes of fury?
From the flaxen seeds of Lempo.
Whence the evil ears for hearing?
From the foliage of Hisi.
Whence then was her mouth created?
This from Suoyatar's foam-currents.
Whence arose thy tongue of anger?
From the spear of Keitolainen.
Whence arose thy fangs of poison?
From the teeth of Mana's daughter.
Whence then was thy back created?
From the carbon-posts of Piru.
How then was thy tail created?
From the brain of the hobgoblin.
Whence arose thy writhing entrails?
From the death-belt of Tuoni.

"This thine origin, O Serpent,
This thy charm of evil import,
Vilest thing of God's creation,
Writhing, hissing thing of evil,
With the colour of Tuoni,
With the shade of earth and heaven,
With the darkness of the storm-cloud.
Get thee hence, thou loathsome monster,
Clear the pathway of this hero.
I am mighty Lemminkainen,
On my journey to Pohyola,
To the feastings and carousals,
In the halls of darksome Northland."

Thereupon the snake uncoiling,
Hundred-eyed and heinous monster,
Crawled away to other portals,
That the hero, Kaukomieli,
Might proceed upon his errand,
To the dismal Sariola,
To the feastings and carousals
In the banquet-halls of Pohya.

Rune XXVII: The Unwelcome Guest

I have brought young Kaukomieli,
Brought the Islander and hero,
Also known as Lemminkainen,
Through the jaws of death and ruin,
Through the darkling deeps of Kalma,
To the homesteads of Pohyola,
To the dismal courts of Louhi;
Now must I relate his doings,
Must relate to all my hearers,
How the merry Lemminkainen,
Handsome hero, Kaukomieli,
Wandered through Pohyola's chambers,
Through the halls of Sariola,
How the hero went unbidden
To the feasting and carousal,
Uninvited to the banquet.

Lemminkainen full of courage,
Full of life, and strength, and magic,
Stepped across the ancient threshold,
To the centre of the court-room,
And the floors of linwood trembled,
Walls and ceilings creaked and murmured.

Spake the reckless Lemminkainen,
These the words that Ahti uttered:
"Be ye greeted on my coming,
Ye that greet, be likewise greeted!
Listen, all ye hosts of Pohya;
Is there food about this homestead,
Barley for my hungry courser,
Beer to give a thirsty stranger?"

Sat the host of Sariola
At the east end of the table,
Gave this answer to the questions:
"Surely is there in this homestead,
For thy steed an open stable,
Never will this host refuse thee,
Shouldst thou act a part becoming,
Worthy, coming to these portals,
Waiting near the birchen rafters,
In the spaces by the kettles,
By the triple hooks of iron."

Then the reckless Lemminkainen
Shook his sable locks and answered:
"Lempo may perchance come hither,
Let him fill this lowly station,
Let him stand between the kettles,
That with soot he may be blackened.
Never has my ancient father,
Never has the dear old hero,
Stood upon a spot unworthy,
At the portals near the rafters;
For his steed the best of stables,
Food and shelter gladly furnished,
And a room for his attendants,
Corners furnished for his mittens,
Hooks provided for his snow-shoes,
Halls in waiting for his helmet.
Wherefore then should I not find here
What my father found before me?"

To the centre walked the hero,
Walked around the dining table,
Sat upon a bench and waited,
On a bench of polished fir-wood,
And the kettle creaked beneath him.
Spake the reckless Lemminkainen:
"As a guest am I unwelcome,
Since the waiters bring no viands,
Bring no dishes to the stranger?"

Ilpotar, the Northland hostess,
Then addressed the words that follow:
"Lemminkainen, thou art evil,
Thou art here, but not invited,
Thou hast not the look of kindness,
Thou wilt give me throbbing temples,
Thou art bringing pain and sorrow.
All our beer is in the barley,
All the malt is in the kernel,
All our grain is still ungarnered,
And our dinner has been eaten;
Yesterday thou shouldst have been here,
Come again some future season."

Whereupon wild Lemminkainen
Pulled his mouth awry in anger,
Shook his coal-black locks and answered:
"All the tables here are empty,
And the feasting-time is over;
All the beer has left the goblets,
Empty too are all the pitchers,
Empty are the larger vessels.
O thou hostess of Pohyola,
Toothless dame of dismal Northland,
Badly managed is thy wedding,
And thy feast is ill-conducted,
Like the dogs hast thou invited;
Thou hast baked the honey-biscuit,
Wheaten loaves of greatest virtue,
Brewed thy beer from hops and barley,
Sent abroad thine invitations,
Six the hamlets thou hast honoured,
Nine the villages invited
By thy merry wedding-callers.
Thou hast asked the poor and lowly,
Asked the hosts of common people,
Asked the blind, and deaf, and crippled,
Asked a multitude of beggars,
Toilers by the day, and hirelings;
Asked the men of evil habits,
Asked the maids with braided tresses,
I alone was not invited.
How could such a slight be given,
Since I sent thee kegs of barley?
Others sent thee grain in cupfuls,
Brought it sparingly in dippers,
While I sent thee fullest measure,
Sent the half of all my garners,
Of the richest of my harvest,
Of the grain that I had gathered.
Even now young Lemminkainen,
Though a guest of name and station,
Has no beer, no food, no welcome,
Naught for him art thou preparing,
Nothing cooking in thy kettles,
Nothing brewing in thy cellars
For the hero of the Islands,
At the closing of his journey."

Ilpotar, the ancient hostess,
Gave this order to her servants:
"Come, my pretty maiden-waiter,
Servant-girl to me belonging,
Lay some salmon to the broiling,
Bring some beer to give the stranger!"

Small of stature was the maiden,
Washer of the banquet-platters,
Rinser of the dinner-ladles,
Polisher of spoons of silver,
And she laid some food in kettles,
Only bones and heads of whiting,
Turnip-stalks and withered cabbage,
Crusts of bread and bits of biscuit.
Then she brought some beer in pitchers,
Brought of common drink the vilest,
That the stranger, Lemminkainen,
Might have drink, and meat in welcome,
Thus to still his thirst and hunger.
Then the maiden spake as follows:
"Thou art sure a mighty hero,
Here to drink the beer of Pohya,
Here to empty all our vessels!"

Then the minstrel, Lemminkainen,
Closely handled all the pitchers,
Looking to the very bottoms;
There beheld he writhing serpents,
In the centre adders swimming,
On the borders worms and lizards.
Then the hero, Lemminkainen,
Filled with anger, spake as follows:
"Get ye hence, ye things of evil,
Get ye hence to Tuonela,
With the bearer of these pitchers,
With the maid that brought ye hither,
Ere the evening Moon has risen,
Ere the day-star seeks the ocean!
O thou wretched beer of barley,
Thou hast met with great dishonour,
Into disrepute hast fallen,
But I'll drink thee, notwithstanding,
And the rubbish cast far from me."

Then the hero to his pockets
Thrust his first and unnamed finger,
Searching in his pouch of leather;
Quick withdraws a hook for fishing,
Drops it to the pitcher's bottom,
Through the worthless beer of barley;
On his fish-hook hang the serpents,
Catches many hissing adders,
Catches frogs in magic numbers,
Catches blackened worms in thousands,
Casts them to the floor before him,
Quickly draws his heavy broadsword,
And decapitates the serpents.

Now he drinks the beer remaining,
When the wizard speaks as follows:
"As a guest am I unwelcome,
Since no beer to me is given
That is worthy of a hero;
Neither has a ram been butchered,
Nor a fattened calf been slaughtered,
Worthy food for Lemminkainen."

Then the landlord of Pohyola
Answered thus the Island-minstrel:
"Wherefore hast thou journeyed hither,
Who has asked thee for thy presence?"
Spake in answer Lemminkainen:
"Happy is the guest invited,
Happier when not expected;
Listen, son of Pohylander,
Host of Sariola, listen:
Give me beer for ready payment,
Give me worthy drink for money!"

Then the landlord of Pohyola,
In bad humor, full of anger,
Conjured in the earth a lakelet,
At the feet of Kaukomieli,
Thus addressed the Island-hero:
"Quench thy thirst from yonder lakelet,
There, the beer that thou deservest!"

Little heeding, Lemminkainen
To this insolence made answer:
"I am neither bear nor roebuck,
That should drink this filthy water,
Drink the water of this lakelet."

Ahti then began to conjure,
Conjured he a bull before him,
Bull with horns of gold and silver,
And the bull drank from the lakelet,
Drank he from the pool in pleasure.
Then the landlord of Pohyola
There a savage wolf created,

Set him on the floor before him
To destroy the bull of magic.
Lemminkainen, full of courage,
Conjured up a snow-white rabbit,
Set him on the floor before him
To attract the wolf's attention.
Then the landlord of Pohyola
Conjured there a dog of Lempo,
Set him on the floor before him
To destroy the magic rabbit.
Lemminkainen, full of mischief,
Conjured on the roof a squirrel,
That by jumping on the rafters
He might catch the dog's attention.
But the master of the Northland
Conjured there a golden marten,
And he drove the magic squirrel
From his seat upon the rafters.
Lemminkainen, full of mischief,
Made a fox of scarlet colour,
And it ate the golden marten.
Then the master of Pohyola
Conjured there a hen to flutter
Near the fox of scarlet colour.
Lemminkainen, full of mischief,
Thereupon a hawk created,
That with beak and crooked talons
He might tear the hen to pieces.

Spake the landlord of Pohyola,
These the words the tall man uttered:
"Never will this feast be bettered
Till the guests are less in number;
I must do my work as landlord,
Get thee hence, thou evil stranger,
Cease thy conjurings of evil,
Leave this banquet of my people,
Haste away, thou wicked wizard,
To thine Island-home and people!"
Spake the reckless Lemminkainen:
"Thus no hero will be driven,
Not a son of any courage
Will be frightened by thy presence,
Will be driven from thy banquet."

Then the landlord of Pohyola
Snatched his broadsword from the rafters,
Drew it rashly from the scabbard,
Thus addressing Lemminkainen:
"Ahti, Islander of evil,
Thou the handsome Kaukomieli,
Let us measure then our broadswords,
Let our skill be fully tested;
Surely is my broadsword better
Than the blade within thy scabbard."
Spake the hero, Lemminkainen:
"That my blade is good and trusty,
Has been proved on heads of heroes,
Has on many bones been tested;
Be that as it may, my fellow,
Since thine order is commanding,
Let our swords be fully tested,
Let us see whose blade is better.
Long ago my hero-father
Tested well this sword in battle,
Never failing in a conflict.
Should his son be found less worthy?"

Then he grasped his mighty broadsword,
Drew the fire-blade from the scabbard
Hanging from his belt of copper.
Standing on their hilts their broadswords,
Carefully their blades were measured,
Found the sword of Northland's master
Longer than the sword of Ahti
By the half-link of a finger.
Spake the reckless Lemminkainen.
"Since thou hast the longer broadsword,
Thou shalt make the first advances,
I am ready for thy weapon."

Thereupon Pohyola's landlord
With the wondrous strength of anger,
Tried in vain to slay the hero,
Strike the crown of Lemminkainen;
Chipped the splinters from the rafters,
Cut the ceiling into fragments,
Could not touch the Island-hero.

Thereupon brave Kaukomieli,
Thus addressed Pohyola's master:
"Have the rafters thee offended?
What the crimes they have committed,
Since thou hewest them in pieces?

Listen now, thou host of Northland,
Reckless landlord of Pohyola,
Little room there is for swordsmen
In these chambers filled with women;
We shall stain these painted rafters,
Stain with blood these floors and ceilings;
Let us go without the mansion,
In the field is room for combat,
On the plain is space sufficient;
Blood looks fairer in the court-yard,
Better in the open spaces,
Let it dye the snow-fields scarlet."

To the yard the heroes hasten,
There they find a monstrous ox-skin,
Spread it on the field of battle;
On the ox-skin stand the swordsmen.
Spake the hero, Lemminkainen:
"Listen well, thou host of Northland,
Though thy broadsword is the longer,
Though thy blade is full of horror,
Thou shalt have the first advantage;
Use with skill thy boasted broadsword
Ere the final bout is given,
Ere thy head be chopped in pieces;
Strike with skill, or thou wilt perish,
Strike, and do thy best for Northland."

Thereupon Pohyola's landlord
Raised on high his blade of battle,
Struck a heavy blow in anger,
Struck a second, then a third time,
But he could not touch his rival,
Could not draw a single blood-drop
From the veins of Lemminkainen,
Skillful Islander and hero.
Spake the handsome Kaukomieli:
"Let me try my skill at fencing,
Let me swing my father's broadsword,
Let my honoured blade be tested!"
But the landlord of Pohyola,
Does not heed the words of Ahti,
Strikes in fury, strikes unceasing,
Ever aiming, ever missing.
When the skillful Lemminkainen
Swings his mighty blade of magic,
Fire disports along his weapon,
Flashes from his sword of honour,
Glistens from the hero's broadsword,
Balls of fire disporting, dancing,
On the blade of mighty Ahti,
Overflow upon the shoulders
Of the landlord of Pohyola.
Spake the hero, Lemminkainen:
"O thou son of Sariola,
See! indeed thy neck is glowing
Like the dawning of the morning,
Like the rising Sun in ocean!"

Quickly turned Pohyola's landlord,
Thoughtless host of darksome Northland,
To behold the fiery splendor
Playing on his neck and shoulders.
Quick as lightning, Lemminkainen,
With his father's blade of battle,
With a single blow of broadsword,
With united skill and power,
Lopped the head of Pohya's master;
As one cleaves the stalks of turnips,
As the ear falls from the corn-stalk,
As one strikes the fins from salmon,
Thus the head rolled from the shoulders
Of the landlord of Pohyola,
Like a ball it rolled and circled.

In the yard were pickets standing,
Hundreds were the sharpened pillars,
And a head on every picket,
Only one was left un-headed.
Quick the victor, Lemminkainen,
Took the head of Pohya's landlord,
Spiked it on the empty picket.

Then the Islander, rejoicing,
Handsome hero, Kaukomieli,
Quick returning to the chambers,
Gave this order to the hostess:
"Evil maiden, bring me water,
Wherewithal to cleanse my fingers
From the blood of Northland's master,
Wicked host of Sariola."

Ilpotar, the Northland hostess,
Fired with anger, threatened vengeance,

Conjured men with heavy broadswords,
Heroes clad in copper-armor,
Hundred warriors with their javelins,
And a thousand bearing cross-bows,
To destroy the Island-hero,
For the death of Lemminkainen.

Kaukomieli soon discovered
That the time had come for leaving,
That his presence was unwelcome
At the feasting of Pohyola,
At the banquet of her people.

Rune XXVIII: The Mother's Counsel

Ahti, hero of the Islands,
Wild magician, Lemminkainen,
Also known as Kaukomieli,
Hastened from the great carousal,
From the banquet-halls of Louhi,
From the ever-darksome Northland,
From the dismal Sariola.
Stormful strode he from the mansion,
Hastened like the smoke of battle,
From the court-yard of Pohyola,
Left his crimes and misdemeanors
In the halls of ancient Louhi.
Then he looked in all directions,
Seeking for his tethered courser,
Anxious looked in field and stable,
But he did not find his racer;
Found a black thing in the fallow,
Proved to be a clump of willows.
Who will well advise the hero,
Who will give him wise directions,
Guide the wizard out of trouble,
Give his hero-locks protection,
Keep his magic head from danger
From the warriors of Northland?

Noise is heard within the village,
And a din from other homesteads,
From the battle-hosts of Louhi,
Streaming from the doors and window,
Of the homesteads of Pohyola.

Thereupon young Lemminkainen,
Handsome Islander and hero,
Changing both his form and features,
Clad himself in other raiment,
Changing to another body,
Quick became a mighty eagle,
Soared aloft on wings of magic,
Tried to fly to highest heaven,
But the moonlight burned his temples,
And the sunshine singed his feathers.

Then entreating, Lemminkainen,
Island-hero, turned to Ukko,
This the prayer that Ahti uttered:
"Ukko, God of love and mercy,
Thou the Wisdom of the heavens,
Wise Director of the lightning,
Thou the Author of the thunder,
Thou the Guide of all the cloudlets,
Give to me thy cloak of vapor,
Throw a silver cloud around me,
That I may in its protection
Hasten to my native country,
To my mother's Island-dwelling,
Fly to her that waits my coming,
With a mother's grave forebodings."

Farther, farther, Lemminkainen
Flew and soared on eagle-pinions,
Looked about him, backwards, forwards,
Spied a gray-hawk soaring near him,
In his eyes the fire of splendor,
Like the eyes of Pohyalanders,
Like the eyes of Pohya's spearmen,
And the gray-hawk thus addressed him:
"Ho! there! hero, Lemminkainen,
Art thou thinking of our combat
With the hero-heads of Northland?"

Thus the Islander made answer,
These the words of Kaukomieli:
"O thou gray-hawk, bird of beauty,
Fly direct to Sariola,
Fly as fast as wings can bear thee;
When thou hast arrived in safety,

On the plains of darksome Northland,
Tell the archers and the spearmen,
They will never catch the eagle,
In his journey from Pohyola,
To his Island-home and fortress."

Then the Ahti-eagle hastened
Straightway to his mother's cottage,
In his face the look of trouble,
In his heart the pangs of sorrow.
Ahti's mother ran to meet him,
When she spied him in the pathway,
Walking toward her island-dwelling;
These the words the mother uttered:
"Of my sons thou art the bravest,
Art the strongest of my children;
Wherefore then comes thine annoyance,
On returning from Pohyola?
Wert thou worsted at the banquet,
At the feast and great carousal?
At thy cups, if thou wert injured,
Thou shalt here have better treatment,
Thou shalt have the cup thy father
Brought me from the hero-castle."
Spake the reckless Lemminkainen:
"Worthy mother, thou that nursed me,
If I had been maimed at drinking,
I the landlord would have worsted,
Would have slain a thousand heroes,
Would have taught them useful lessons."
Lemminkainen's mother answered:
"Wherefore then art thou indignant,
Didst thou meet disgrace and insult,
Did they rob thee of thy courser?
Buy thou then a better courser
With the riches of thy mother,
With thy father's horded treasures."
Spake the hero, Lemminkainen:
"Faithful mother of my being,
If my steed had been insulted,
If for him my heart was injured,
I the landlord would have punished,
Would have punished all the horsemen,
All of Pohya's strongest riders."
Lemminkainen's mother answered:
"Tell me then thy dire misfortune,
What has happened to my hero,
On his journey to Pohyola?
Have the Northland maidens scorned thee,
Have the women ridiculed thee?
If the maidens scorned thy presence,
If the women gave derision,
There are others thou canst laugh at,
Thou canst scorn a thousand women."
Said the reckless Lemminkainen:
"Honoured mother, fond and faithful,
If the Northland dames had scorned me
Or the maidens laughed derision,
I the maidens would have punished,
Would have scorned a thousand women."
Lemminkainen's mother answered:
"Wherefore then are thou indignant,
Thus annoyed, and heavy-hearted,
On returning from Pohyola?
Was thy feasting out of season,
Was the banquet-beer unworthy,
Were thy dreams of evil import
When asleep in darksome Northland?"
This is Lemminkainen's answer:
"Aged women may remember
What they dream on beds of trouble;
I have seen some wondrous visions,
Since I left my Island-cottage.
My beloved, helpful mother,
Fill my bag with good provisions,
Flour and salt in great abundance,
Farther must thy hero wander,
He must leave his home behind him,
Leave his pleasant Island-dwelling,
Journey from this home of ages;
Men are sharpening their broadswords,
Sharpening their spears and lances,
For the death of Lemminkainen."

Then again the mother questioned,
Hurriedly she asked the reason:
"Why the men their swords were whetting,
Why their spears are being sharpened."

Spake the reckless Lemminkainen,
Handsome hero, Kaukomieli:
"Therefore do they whet their broadswords,
Therefore sharpen they their lances:
It is for thy son's destruction,

At his heart are aimed their lances.
In the court-yard of Pohyola,
There arose a great contention,
Fierce the battle waged against me;
But I slew the Northland hero,
Killed the host of Sariola;
Quick to arms rose Louhi's people,
All the spears and swords of Northland
Were directed at thy hero;
All of Pohya turned against me,
Turned against a single foeman."
This the answer of the mother:
"I had told thee this beforehand,
I had warned thee of this danger,
And forbidden thee to journey
To the hostile fields of Northland.
Here my hero could have lingered,
Passed his life in full contentment,
Lived forever with his mother,
With his mother for protection,
In the court-yard with his kindred;
Here no war would have arisen,
No contention would have followed.
Whither wilt thou go, my hero,
Whither will my loved one hasten,
To escape thy fierce pursuers,
To escape from thy misdoings,
From thy sins to hide in safety,
From thy crimes and misdemeanors,
That thy head be not endangered,
That thy body be not mangled,
That thy locks be not outrooted?"
Spake the reckless Lemminkainen:
"Know I not a spot befitting,
Do not know a place of safety,
Where to hide from my pursuers,
That will give me sure protection
From the crimes by me committed.
Helpful mother of my being,
Where to flee wilt thou advise me?"
This the answer of the mother:
"I do not know where I can send thee;
Be a pine tree on the mountain,
Or a juniper in lowlands?
Then misfortune may befall thee;
Often is the mountain pine tree
Cut in splints for candle-lighters;
And the juniper is often
Peeled for fence-posts for the pastures.
Go a birch-tree to the valleys,
Or an elm-tree to the glenwood?
Even then may trouble find thee,
Misery may overtake thee;
Often is the lowland birch-tree
Cut to pieces in the ware-house;
Often is the elm-wood forest
Cleared away for other plantings.
Be a berry on the highlands,
Cranberry upon the heather,
Strawberry upon the mountains,
Blackberry along the fences?
Even there will trouble find thee,
There misfortune overtake thee,
For the berry-maids would pluck thee,
Silver-tinselled girls would get thee.
Be a pike then in the ocean,
Or a troutlet in the rivers?
Then would trouble overtake thee,
Would become thy life-companion;
Then the fisherman would catch thee,
Catch thee in his net of flax-thread,
Catch thee with his cruel fish-hook.
Be a wolf then in the forest,
Or a black-bear in the thickets?
Even then would trouble find thee,
And disaster cross thy pathway;
Sable hunters of the Northland
Have their spears and cross-bows ready
To destroy the wolf and black-bear."
Spake the reckless Lemminkainen:
"Know I well the worst of places,
Know where Death will surely follow,
Where misfortune's eye would find me;
Since thou gavest me existence,
Gavest nourishment in childhood,
Whither shall I flee for safety,
Whither hide from death and danger?
In my view is fell destruction,
Dire misfortune hovers o'er me;
On the morrow come the spearmen,
Countless warriors from Pohya,
Ahti's head their satisfaction."
This the answer of the mother:
"I can name a goodly refuge,

Name a land of small dimensions,
Name a distant ocean-island,
Where my son may live in safety.
Thither archers never wander,
There thy head cannot be severed;
But an oath as strong as heaven,
Thou must swear before thy mother;
Thou wilt not for sixty summers
Join in war or deadly combat,
Even though thou wishest silver,
Wishest gold and silver treasures."
Spake the grateful Lemminkainen:
"I will swear an oath of honour,
That I'll not in sixty summers
Draw my sword in the arena,
Test the warrior in battle;
I have wounds upon my shoulders,
On my breast two scars of broadsword,
Of my former battles, relics,
Relics of my last encounters,
On the battle-fields of Northland,
In the wars with men and heroes."
Lemminkainen's mother answered:
"Go thou, take thy father's vessel,
Go and hide thyself in safety,
Travel far across nine oceans;
In the tenth, sail to the centre,
To the island, forest-covered,
To the cliffs above the waters,
Where thy father went before thee,
Where he hid from his pursuers,
In the times of summer conquests,
In the darksome days of battle;
Good the isle for thee to dwell in,
Goodly place to live and linger;
Hide one year, and then a second,
In the third return in safety
To thy mother's island dwelling,
To thy father's ancient mansion,
To my hero's place of resting."

Rune XXIX: The Isle of Refuge

Lemminkainen, full of joyance,
Handsome hero, Kaukomieli,
Took provisions in abundance,
Fish and butter, bread and bacon,
Hastened to the Isle of Refuge,
Sailed away across the oceans,
Spake these measures on departing:
"Fare thee well, mine Island-dwelling,
I must sail to other borders,
To an island more protective,
Till the second summer passes;
Let the serpents keep the island,
Lynxes rest within the glen-wood,
Let the blue-moose roam the mountains,
Let the wild-geese eat the barley.
Fare thee well, my helpful mother!
When the warriors of the Northland,
From the dismal Sariola,
Come with swords, and spears,
and cross-bows,
Asking for my head in vengeance,
Say that I have long departed,
Left my mother's Island-dwelling,
When the barley had been garnered."

Then he launched his boat of copper,
Threw the vessel to the waters,
From the iron-banded rollers,
From the cylinders of oak-wood,
On the masts the sails he hoisted,
Spread the magic sails of linen,
In the stern the hero settled
And prepared to sail his vessel,
One hand resting on the rudder.

Then the sailor spake as follows,
These the words of Lemminkainen:
"Blow, ye winds, and drive me onward,
Blow ye steady, winds of heaven,
Toward the island in the ocean,
That my bark may fly in safety
To my father's place of refuge,
To the far and nameless island!"

Soon the winds arose as bidden,
Rocked the vessel o'er the billows,
O'er the blue back of the waters,
O'er the vast expanse of ocean;

Blew two months and blew unceasing,
Blew a third month toward the island,
Toward his father's Isle of Refuge.

Sat some maidens on the seaside,
On the sandy beach of ocean,
Turned about in all directions,
Looking out upon the billows;
One was waiting for her brother,
And a second for her father,
And a third one, anxious, waited
For the coming of her suitor;
There they spied young Lemminkainen,
There perceived the hero's vessel
Sailing o'er the bounding billows;
It was like a hanging cloudlet,
Hanging twixt the earth and heaven.

Thus the island-maidens wondered,
Thus they spake to one another:
"What this stranger on the ocean,
What is this upon the waters?
Art thou one of our sea-vessels?
Wert thou builded on this island?
Sail thou straightway to the harbor,
To the island-point of landing
That thy tribe may be discovered."

Onward did the waves propel it,
Rocked his vessel o'er the billows,
Drove it to the magic island,
Safely landed Lemminkainen
On the sandy shore and harbor.

Spake he thus when he had landed,
These the words that Ahti uttered:
"Is there room upon this island,
Is there space within this harbor,
Where my bark may lie at anchor,
Where the sun may dry my vessel?"

This the answer of the virgins,
Dwellers on the Isle of Refuge:
"There is room within this harbor,
On this island, space abundant,
Where thy bark may lie at anchor,
Where the sun may dry thy vessel;
Lying ready are the rollers,
Cylinders adorned with copper;
If thou hadst a hundred vessels,
Shouldst thou come with boats a thousand,
We would give them room in welcome."

Thereupon wild Lemminkainen
Rolled his vessel in the harbor,
On the cylinders of copper,
Spake these words when he had ended:
"Is there room upon this island,
Or a spot within these forests,
Where a hero may be hidden
From the coming din of battle,
From the play of spears and arrows?"
Thus replied the Island-maidens:
"There are places on this island,
On these plains a spot befitting,
Where to hide thyself in safety,
Hero-son of little valor.
Here are many, many castles,
Many courts upon this island;
Though there come a thousand heroes,
Though a thousand spearmen follow,
Thou canst hide thyself in safety."
Spake the hero, Lemminkainen:
"Is there room upon this island,
Where the birch-tree grows abundant,
Where this son may fell the forest,
And may cultivate the fallow?"
Answered thus the Island-maidens:
"There is not a spot befitting,
Not a place upon the island,
Where to rest thy wearied members,
Not the smallest patch of birch-wood,
Thou canst bring to cultivation.
All our fields have been divided,
All these woods have been apportioned,
Fields and forests have their owners."

Lemminkainen asked this question,
These the words of Kaukomieli:
"Is there room upon this island,
Worthy spot in field or forest,
Where to sing my songs of magic,
Chant my gathered store of wisdom,
Sing mine ancient songs and legends?"

Answered thus the Island-maidens:
"There is room upon this island,
Worthy place in these dominions,
Thou canst sing thy garnered wisdom,
Thou canst chant thine ancient legends,
Legends of the times primeval,
In the forest, in the castle,
On the island-plains and pastures."
Then began the reckless minstrel
To intone his wizard-sayings;
Sang the alders to the waysides,
Sang the oaks upon the mountains,
On the oak-trees sang he branches,
On each branch he sang an acorn,
On the acorns, golden rollers,
On each roller, sang a cuckoo;
Then began the cuckoos, calling,
Gold from every throat came streaming,
Copper fell from every feather,
And each wing emitted silver,
Filled the isle with precious metals.
Sang again young Lemminkainen,
Conjured on, and sang, and chanted,
Sang to precious stones the sea-sands,
Sang the stones to pearls resplendent,
Robed the groves in iridescence,
Sang the island full of flowers,
Many-coloured as the rainbow.
Sang again the magic minstrel,
In the court a well he conjured,
On the well a golden cover,
On the lid a silver dipper,
That the boys might drink the water,
That the maids might lave their eyelids.
On the plains he conjured lakelets,
Sang the duck upon the waters,
Golden-cheeked and silver-headed,
Sang the feet from shining copper;
And the Island-maidens wondered,
Stood entranced at Ahti's wisdom,
At the songs of Lemminkainen,
At the hero's magic power.

Spake the singer, Lemminkainen,
Handsome hero, Kaukomieli:
"I would sing a wondrous legend,
Sing in miracles of sweetness,
If within some hall or chamber,
I were seated at the table.
If I sing not in the castle,
In some spot by walls surrounded,
Then I sing my songs to zephyrs,
Fling them to the fields and forests."
Answered thus the Island-maidens:
"On this isle are castle-chambers,
Halls for use of magic singers,
Courts complete for chanting legends,
Where thy singing will be welcome,
Where thy songs will not be scattered
To the forests of the island,
Nor thy wisdom lost in ether."

Straightway Lemminkainen journeyed
With the maidens to the castle;
There he sang and conjured pitchers
On the borders of the tables,
Sang and conjured golden goblets
Foaming with the beer of barley;
Sang he many well-filled vessels,
Bowls of honey-drink abundant,
Sweetest butter, toothsome biscuit,
Bacon, fish, and veal, and venison,
All the dainties of the Northland,
Wherewithal to still his hunger.
But the proud-heart, Lemminkainen,
Was not ready for the banquet,
Did not yet begin his feasting,
Waited for a knife of silver,
For a knife of golden handle;
Quick he sang the precious metals,
Sang a blade from purest silver,
To the blade a golden handle,
Straightway then began his feasting,
Quenched his thirst and stilled his hunger,
Charmed the maidens on the island.

Then the minstrel, Lemminkainen,
Roamed throughout the island-hamlets,
To the joy of all the virgins,
All the maids of braided tresses;
Wheresoe'er he turned his footsteps,
There appeared a maid to greet him;
When his hand was kindly offered,
There his hand was kindly taken;

When he wandered out at evening,
Even in the darksome places,
There the maidens bade him welcome;
There was not an island-village
Where there were not seven castles,
In each castle seven daughters,
And the daughters stood in waiting,
Gave the hero joyful greetings,
Only one of all the maidens
Whom he did not greet with pleasure.

Thus the merry Lemminkainen
Spent three summers in the ocean,
Spent a merry time in refuge,
In the hamlets on the island,
To the pleasure of the maidens,
To the joy of all the daughters;
Only one was left neglected,
She a poor and graceless spinster,
On the isle's remotest border,
In the smallest of the hamlets.

Then he thought about his journey
O'er the ocean to his mother,
To the cottage of his father.
There appeared the slighted spinster,
To the Northland son departing,
Spake these words to Lemminkainen:
"O, thou handsome Kaukomieli,
Wisdom-bard, and magic singer,
Since this maiden thou hast slighted,
May the winds destroy thy vessel,
Dash thy bark to countless fragments
On the ocean-rocks and ledges!"

Lemminkainen's thoughts were homeward,
Did not heed the maiden's murmurs,
Did not rise before the dawning
Of the morning on the island,
To the pleasure of the maiden
Of the much-neglected hamlet.
Finally at close of evening,
He resolved to leave the island,
He resolved to waken early,
Long before the dawn of morning;
Long before the time appointed,
He arose that he might wander
Through the hamlets of the island,
Bid adieu to all the maidens,
On the morn of his departure.
As he wandered hither, thither,
Walking through the village pathways
To the last of all the hamlets;
Saw he none of all the castles,
Where three dwellings were not standing;
Saw he none of all the dwellings
Where three heroes were not watching;
Saw he none of all the heroes,
Who was not engaged in grinding
Swords, and spears, and battle-axes,
For the death of Lemminkainen.
And these words the hero uttered:
"Now alas! the Sun arises
From his couch within the ocean,
On the frailest of the heroes,
On the saddest child of Northland;
On my neck the cloak of Lempo
Might protect me from all evil,
Though a hundred foes assail me,
Though a thousand archers follow."

Then he left the maids ungreeted,
Left his longing for the daughters
Of the nameless Isle of Refuge,
With his farewell-words unspoken,
Hastened toward the island-harbor,
Toward his magic bark at anchor;
But he found it burned to ashes,
Sweet revenge had fired his vessel,
Lighted by the slighted spinster.
Then he saw the dawn of evil,
Saw misfortune hanging over,
Saw destruction round about him.
Straightway he began rebuilding
Him a magic sailing-vessel,
New and wondrous, full of beauty;
But the hero needed timber,
Boards, and planks, and beams, and braces,
Found the smallest bit of lumber,
Found of boards but seven fragments,
Of a spool he found three pieces,
Found six pieces of the distaff;
With these fragments builds his vessel,
Builds a ship of magic virtue,

Builds the bark with secret knowledge,
Through the will of the magician;
Strikes one blow, and builds the first part,
Strikes a second, builds the centre,
Strikes a third with wondrous power,
And the vessel is completed.

Thereupon the ship he launches,
Sings the vessel to the ocean,
And these words the hero utters:
"Like a bubble swim these waters,
Like a flower ride the billows;
Loan me of thy magic feathers,
Three, O eagle, four, O raven,
For protection to my vessel,
Lest it flounder in the ocean!"

Now the sailor, Lemminkainen,
Seats himself upon the bottom
Of the vessel he has builded,
Hastens on his journey homeward,
Head depressed and evil-humored,
Cap awry upon his forehead,
Mind dejected, heavy-hearted,
That he could not dwell forever
In the castles of the daughters
Of the nameless Isle of Refuge.

Spake the minstrel, Lemminkainen,
Handsome hero, Kaukomieli:
"Leave I must this merry island,
Leave her many joys and pleasures,
Leave her maids with braided tresses,
Leave her dances and her daughters,
To the joys of other heroes;
But I take this comfort with me:
All the maidens on the island,
Save the spinster who was slighted,
Will bemoan my loss for ages,
Will regret my quick departure;
They will miss me at the dances,
In the halls of mirth and joyance,
In the homes of merry maidens,
On my father's Isle of Refuge."

Wept the maidens on the island,
Long lamenting, loudly calling
To the hero sailing homeward:
"Whither goest, Lemminkainen,
Why depart, thou best of heroes?
Dost thou leave from inattention,
Is there here a dearth of maidens,
Have our greetings been unworthy?"

Sang the magic Lemminkainen
To the maids as he was sailing,
This in answer to their calling:
"Leaving not for want of pleasure,
Do not go from dearth of women
Beautiful the island-maidens,
Countless as the sands their virtues.
This the reason of my going,
I am longing for my home-land,
Longing for my mother's cabins,
For the strawberries of Northland,
For the raspberries of Kalew,
For the maidens of my childhood,
For the children of my mother."

Then the merry Lemminkainen
Bade farewell to all the island;
Winds arose and drove his vessel
On the blue back of the ocean,
O'er the far-extending waters,
Toward the island of his mother.
On the shore were grouped
the daughters
Of the magic Isle of Refuge,
On the rocks sat the forsaken,
Weeping stood the island-maidens,
Golden daughters, loud-lamenting.
Weep the maidens of the island
While the sail-yards greet their vision,
While the copper-beltings glisten;
Do not weep to lose the sail-yards,
Nor to lose the copper-beltings;
Weep they for the loss of Ahti,
For the fleeing Kaukomieli
Guiding the departing vessel.
Also weeps young Lemminkainen,
Sorely weeps, and loud-lamenting,
Weeps while he can see the island,
While the island hill-tops glisten;
Does not mourn the island-mountains,

Weeps he only for the maidens,
Left upon the Isle of Refuge.

Thereupon sailed Kaukomieli
On the blue back of the ocean;
Sailed one day, and then a second,
But, alas! upon the third day,
There arose a mighty storm-wind,
And the sky was black with fury.
Blew the black winds from the northwest,
From the southeast came the whirlwind,
Tore away the ship's forecastle,
Tore away the vessel's rudder,
Dashed the wooden hull to pieces.
Thereupon wild Lemminkainen
Headlong fell upon the waters;
With his head he did the steering,
With his hands and feet, the rowing;
Swam whole days and nights unceasing,
Swam with hope and strength united,
Till at last appeared a cloudlet,
Growing cloudlet to the westward,
Changing to a promontory,
Into land within the ocean.

Swiftly to the shore swam Ahti,
Hastened to a magic castle,
Found therein a hostess baking,
And her daughters kneading barley,
And these words the hero uttered:
"O, thou hostess, filled with kindness,
Couldst thou know my pangs of hunger,
Couldst thou guess my name and station,
Thou wouldst hasten to the storehouse,
Bring me beer and foaming liquor,
Bring the best of thy provisions,
Bring me fish, and veal, and bacon,
Butter, bread, and honeyed biscuits,
Set for me a wholesome dinner,
Wherewithal to still my hunger,
Quench the thirst of Lemminkainen.
Days and nights have I been swimming,
Buffeting the waves of ocean,
Seemed as if the wind protected,
And the billows gave me shelter."

Then the hostess, filled with kindness,
Hastened to the mountain storehouse,
Cut some butter, veal, and bacon,
Bread, and fish, and honeyed biscuit,
Brought the best of her provisions,
Brought the mead and beer of barley,
Set for him a toothsome dinner,
Wherewithal to still his hunger,
Quench the thirst of Lemminkainen.

When the hero's feast had ended,
Straightway was a magic vessel
Given by the kindly hostess
To the weary Kaukomieli,
Bark of beauty, new and hardy,
Wherewithal to aid the stranger
In his journey to his home-land,
To the cottage of his mother.

Quickly sailed wild Lemminkainen
On the blue back of the ocean;
Sailed he days and nights unceasing,
Till at last he reached the borders
Of his own loved home and country;
There beheld he scenes familiar,
Saw the islands, capes, and rivers,
Saw his former shipping-stations,
Saw he many ancient landmarks,
Saw the mountains with their fir trees,
Saw the pine trees on the hill-tops,
Saw the willows in the lowlands;
Did not see his father's cottage,
Nor the dwellings of his mother.
Where a mansion once had risen,
There the alder-trees were growing,
Shrubs were growing on the homestead,
Junipers within the court-yard.
Spake the reckless Lemminkainen:
"In this glen I played and wandered,
On these stones I rocked for ages,
On this lawn I rolled and tumbled,
Frolicked on these woodland-borders,
When a child of little stature.
Where then is my mother's dwelling,
Where the castles of my father?
Fire, I fear, has found the hamlet,
And the winds dispersed the ashes."

Then he fell to bitter weeping,
Wept one day and then a second,
Wept the third day without ceasing;
Did not mourn the ancient homestead,
Nor the dwellings of his father;
Wept he for his darling mother,
Wept he for the dear departed,
For the loved ones of the island.

Then he saw the bird of heaven,
Saw an eagle flying near him,
And he asked the bird this question:
"Mighty eagle, bird majestic,
Grant to me the information,
Where my mother may have wandered,
Whither I may go and find her!"

But the eagle knew but little,
Only knew that Ahti's people
Long ago together perished;
And the raven also answered
That his people had been scattered
By the swords, and spears, and arrows,
Of his enemies from Pohya.
Spake the hero, Lemminkainen:
"Faithful mother, dear departed,
Thou who nursed me in my childhood,
Art thou dead and turned to ashes,
Didst thou perish for my follies,
O'er thy head are willows weeping,
Junipers above thy body,
Alders watching o'er thy slumbers?
This my punishment for evil,
This the recompense of folly!
Fool was I, a son unworthy,
That I measured swords in Northland
With the landlord of Pohyola.
To my tribe came fell destruction,
And the death of my dear mother,
Through my crimes and misdemeanors."

Then the minstrel looked about him,
Anxious, looked in all directions,
And beheld some gentle foot-prints,
Saw a pathway lightly trodden
Where the heather had been beaten.
Quick as thought the path he followed,
Through the meadows, through the brambles,
O'er the hills, and through the valleys,
To a forest, vast and cheerless;
Travelled far and travelled farther,
Still a greater distance travelled,
To a dense and hidden glenwood,
In the middle of the island;
Found therein a sheltered cabin,
Found a small and darksome dwelling
Built between the rocky ledges,
In the midst of triple pine trees;
And within he spied his mother,
Found his gray-haired mother weeping.

Lemminkainen loud rejoices,
Cries in tones of joyful greetings,
These the words that Ahti utters:
"Faithful mother, well-beloved,
Thou that gavest me existence,
Happy I, that thou art living,
That thou hast not yet departed
To the kingdom of Tuoni,
To the islands of the blessed,
I had thought that thou hadst perished,
Hadst been murdered by my foemen,
Hadst been slain with bows and arrows.
Heavy are mine eyes from weeping,
And my cheeks are white with sorrow,
Since I thought my mother slaughtered
For the sins I had committed!"
Lemminkainen's mother answered:
"Long, indeed, hast thou been absent,
Long, my son, hast thou been living
In thy father's Isle of Refuge,
Roaming on the secret island,
Living at the doors of strangers,
Living in a nameless country,
Refuge from the Northland foemen."
Spake the hero, Lemminkainen:
"Charming is that spot for living,
Beautiful the magic island,
Rainbow-coloured was the forest,
Blue the glimmer of the meadows,
Silvered were the pine tree branches,
Golden were the heather-blossoms;
All the woodlands dripped with honey,
Eggs in every rock and crevice,

Honey flowed from birch and sorb-tree,
Milk in streams from fir and aspen,
Beer-foam dripping from the willows,
Charming there to live and linger,
All their edibles delicious.
This their only source of trouble:
Great the fear for all the maidens,
All the heroes filled with envy,
Feared the coming of the stranger;
Thought that all the island-maidens,
Thought that all the wives and daughters,
All the good, and all the evil,
Gave thy son too much attention;
Thought the stranger, Lemminkainen,
Saw the Island-maids too often;
Yet the virgins I avoided,
Shunned the good and shunned the evil,
Shunned the host of charming daughters,
As the black-wolf shuns the sheep-fold,
As the hawk neglects the chickens."

Rune XXX: The Frost-fiend

Lemminkainen, reckless minstrel,
Handsome hero, Kaukomieli,
Hastens as the dawn is breaking,
At the dawning of the morning,
To the resting-place of vessels,
To the harbor of the island,
Finds the vessels sorely weeping,
Hears the wailing of the rigging,
And the ships intone this chorus:
"Must we wretched lie forever
In the harbor of this island,
Here to dry and fall in pieces?
Ahti wars no more in Northland,
Wars no more for sixty summers,
Even should he thirst for silver,
Should he wish the gold of battle."

Lemminkainen struck his vessels
With his gloves adorned with copper,
And addressed the ships as follows:
"Mourn no more, my ships of fir-wood,
Strong and hardy is your rigging,
To the wars ye soon may hasten,
Hasten to the seas of battle;
Warriors may swarm your cabins
Ere tomorrow's morn has risen."

Then the reckless Lemminkainen
Hastened to his aged mother,
Spake to her the words that follow:
"Weep no longer, faithful mother,
Do not sorrow for thy hero,
Should he leave for scenes of battle,
For the hostile fields of Pohya;
Sweet revenge has fired my spirit,
And my soul is well determined,
To avenge the shameful insult
That the warriors of Northland
Gave to thee, defenseless woman."

To restrain him seeks his mother,
Warns her son again of danger:
"Do not go, my son beloved,
To the wars in Sariola;
There the jaws of Death await thee,
Fell destruction lies before thee!"

Lemminkainen, little heeding,
Still determined, speaks as follows:
"Where may I secure a swordsman,
Worthy of my race of heroes,
To assist me in the combat?
Often I have heard of Tiera,
Heard of Kura of the islands,
This one I will take to help me,
Magic hero of the broadsword;
He will aid me in the combat,
Will protect me from destruction."

Then he wandered to the islands,
On the way to Tiera's hamlet,
These the words that Ahti utters
As he nears the ancient dwellings:
"Dearest friend, my noble Tiera,
My beloved hero-brother,
Dost thou other times remember,
When we fought and bled together,
On the battle-fields of Northland?

There was not an island-village
Where there were not seven mansions,
In each mansion seven heroes,
And not one of all these foemen
Whom we did not slay with broadswords,
Victims of our skill and valor."

Near the window sat the father
Whittling out a javelin-handle;
Near the threshold sat the mother
Skimming cream and making butter;
Near the portal stood the brother
Working on a sledge of birch-wood;
Near the bridge-pass were the sisters
Washing out their varied garments.

Spake the father from the window,
From the threshold spake the mother,
From the portals spake the brother,
And the sisters from the bridge-pass:
"Tiera has no time for combat,
And his broadsword cannot battle;
Tiera is but late a bridegroom,
Still unveiled his bride awaits him."

Near the hearth was Tiera lying,
Lying by the fire was Kura,
Hastily one foot was shoeing,
While the other lay in waiting.
From the hook he takes his girdle,
Buckles it around his body,
Takes a javelin from its resting,
Not the largest, nor the smallest,
Buckles on his mighty scabbard,
Dons his heavy mail of copper;
On each javelin pranced a charger,
Wolves were howling from his helmet,
On the rings the bears were growling.
Tiera poised his mighty javelin,
Launched the spear upon its errand;
Hurled the shaft across the pasture,
To the border of the forest,
O'er the clay-fields of Pohyola,
O'er the green and fragrant meadows,
Through the distant hills of Northland.
Then great Tiera touched his javelin
To the mighty spear of Ahti,
Pledged his aid to Lemminkainen,
As his combatant and comrade.
Thereupon wild Kaukomieli
Pushed his boat upon the waters;
Like the serpent through the heather,
Like the creeping of the adder,
Sails the boat away to Pohya,
O'er the seas of Sariola.
Quick the wicked hostess, Louhi,
Sends the black-frost of the heavens
To the waters of Pohyola,
O'er the far-extending sea-plains,
Gave the black-frost these directions:
"Much-loved Frost, my son and hero,
Whom thy mother has instructed,
Hasten whither I may send thee,
Go wherever I command thee,
Freeze the vessel of this hero,
Lemminkainen's bark of magic,
On the broad back of the ocean,
On the far-extending waters;
Freeze the wizard in his vessel,
Freeze to ice the wicked Ahti,
That he never more may wander,
Never waken while thou livest,
Or at least till I shall free him,
Wake him from his icy slumber!"

Frost, the son of wicked parents,
Hero-son of evil manners,
Hastens off to freeze the ocean,
Goes to fasten down the flood-gates,
Goes to still the ocean-currents.
As he hastens on his journey,
Takes the leaves from all the forest,
Strips the meadows of their verdure,
Robs the flowers of their colours.
When his journey he had ended,
Gained the border of the ocean,
Gained the seashore curved and endless,
On the first night of his visit,
Freezes he the lakes and rivers,
Freezes too the shore of ocean,
Freezes not the ocean-billows,
Does not check the ocean-currents.
On the sea a finch is resting,
Bird of song upon the waters,

But his feet are not yet frozen,
Neither is his head endangered.
When the second night Frost lingered,
He began to grow important,
He became a fierce intruder,
Fearless grew in his invasions,
Freezes everything before him;
Sends the fiercest cold of Northland,
Turns to ice the boundless waters.
Ever thicker, thicker, thicker,
Grew the ice on sea and ocean,
Ever deeper, deeper, deeper,
Fell the snow on field and forest,
Froze the hero's ship of beauty,
Cold and lifeless bark of Ahti;
Sought to freeze wild Lemminkainen,
Freeze him lifeless as his vessel,
Asked the minstrel for his life-blood,
For his ears, and feet, and fingers.

Then the hero, Lemminkainen,
Angry grew and filled with magic,
Hurled the black-frost to the fire-god,
Threw him to the fiery furnace,
Held him in his forge of iron,
Then addressed the frost as follows:
"Frost, thou evil son of Northland,
Dire and only son of Winter,
Let my members not be stiffened,
Neither ears, nor feet, nor fingers,
Neither let my head be frozen.
Thou hast other things to feed on,
Many other heads to stiffen;
Leave in peace the flesh of heroes,
Let this minstrel pass in safety,
Freeze the swamps, and lakes, and rivers,
Fens and forests, hills and valleys;
Let the cold stones grow still colder,
Freeze the willows in the waters,
Let the aspens freeze and suffer,
Let the bark peel from the birch-trees,
Let the pines burst on the mountains,
Let this hero pass in safety,
Do not let his locks be stiffened.

"If all these prove insufficient,
Feed on other worthy matters;
Let the hot stones freeze asunder,
Let the flaming rocks be frozen,
Freeze the fiery blocks of iron,
Freeze to ice the iron mountains;
Stiffen well the mighty Wuoksi,
Let Imatra freeze to silence;
Freeze the sacred stream and whirlpool,
Let their boiling billows stiffen,
Or thine origin I'll sing thee,
Tell thy lineage of evil.
Well I know thine evil nature,
Know thine origin and power,
Whence thou camest, where thou goest,
Know thine ancestry of evil.
Thou wert born upon the aspen,
Wert conceived upon the willows,
Near the borders of Pohyola,
In the courts of dismal Northland;
Sin-begotten was thy father,
And thy mother was Dishonour.

"While in infancy who fed thee
While thy mother could not nurse thee?
Surely thou wert fed by adders,
Nursed by foul and slimy serpents;
north winds rocked thee into slumber,
Cradled thee in roughest weather,
In the worst of willow-marshes,
In the springs forever flowing,
Evil-born and evil-nurtured,
Grew to be an evil genius,
Evil was thy mind and spirit,
And the infant still was nameless,
Till the name of Frost was given
To the progeny of evil.

"Then the young lad lived in hedges,
Dwelt among the weeds and willows,
Lived in springs in days of summer,
On the borders of the marshes,
Tore the lindens in the winter,
Stormed among the glens and forests,
Raged among the sacred birch-trees,
Rattled in the alder-branches,
Froze the trees, the shoots, the grasses,
Evened all the plains and prairies,
Ate the leaves within the woodlands,

Made the stalks drop down their blossoms,
Peeled the bark on weeds and willows.

"Thou hast grown to large proportions,
Hast become too tall and mighty;
Dost thou labour to benumb me,
Dost thou wish mine ears and fingers,
Of my feet wouldst thou deprive me?
Do not strive to freeze this hero,
In his anguish and misfortune;
In my stockings I shall kindle
Fire to drive thee from my presence,
In my shoes lay flaming fagots,
Coals of fire in every garment,
Heated sandstones in my rigging;
Thus will hold thee at a distance.
Then thine evil form I'll banish
To the farthest Northland borders;
When thy journey is completed,
When thy home is reached in safety,
Freeze the caldrons in the castle,
Freeze the coal upon the hearthstone,
In the dough, the hands of women,
On its mother's lap, the infant,
Freeze the colt beside its mother.

"If thou shouldst not heed this order,
I shall banish thee still farther,
To the carbon-piles of Hisi,
To the chimney-hearth of Lempo,
Hurl thee to his fiery furnace,
Lay thee on the iron anvil,
That thy body may be hammered
With the sledges of the blacksmith,
May be pounded into atoms,
Twixt the anvil and the hammer.

"If thou shouldst not heed this order,
Shouldst not leave me to my freedom,
Know I still another kingdom,
Know another spot of resting;
I shall drive thee to the summer,
Lead thy tongue to warmer climates,
There a prisoner to suffer,
Never to obtain thy freedom
Till thy spirit I deliver,
Till I go myself and free thee."

Wicked Frost, the son of Winter,
Saw the magic bird of evil
Hovering above his spirit,
Straightway prayed for Ahti's mercy,
These the words the Frost-fiend uttered:
"Let us now agree together,
Neither one to harm the other,
Never in the course of ages,
Never while the moonlight glimmers
On the snow-capped hills of Northland.
If thou hearest that I bring thee
Cold to freeze thy feet and fingers,
Hurl me to the fiery furnace,
Hammer me upon the anvil
Of the blacksmith, Ilmarinen;
Lead my tongue to warmer climates,
Banish me to lands of summer,
There a prisoner to suffer,
Nevermore to gain my freedom."

Thereupon wild Lemminkainen
Left his vessel in the ocean,
Frozen in the ice of Northland,
Left his warlike boat forever,
Started on his cheerless journey
To the borders of Pohyola,
And the mighty Tiera followed
In the tracks of his companion.
On the ice they journeyed northward
Briskly walked upon the ice-plain,
Walked one day, and then a second,
Till the closing of the third day,
When the Hunger-land approached them,
When appeared Starvation-island.

Here the hardy Lemminkainen
Hastened forward to the castle,
This the hero's prayer and question:
"Is there food within this castle,
Fish or fowl within its larders,
To refresh us on our journey,
Mighty heroes, cold and weary?

When the hero, Lemminkainen,
Found no food within the castle,
Neither fish, nor fowl, nor bacon,
Thus he cursed it and departed:

"May the fire destroy these chambers,
May the waters flood this dwelling,
Wash it to the seas of Mana!"

Then they hastened onward, onward,
Hastened on through field and forest,
Over by-ways long untrodden,
Over unknown paths and snow-fields;
Here the hardy Lemminkainen,
Reckless hero, Kaukomieli,
Pulled the soft wool from the ledges,
Gathered lichens from the tree-trunks,
Wove them into magic stockings,
Wove them into shoes and mittens,
On the settles of the hoar-frost,
In the stinging cold of Northland.

Then he sought to find some pathway,
That would guide their wayward footsteps,
And the hero spake as follows:
"O thou Tiera, friend beloved,
Shall we reach our destination,
Wandering for days together,
Through these Northland fields and forests?"
Kura thus replies to Ahti:
"We, alas! have come for vengeance,
Come for blood and retribution,
To the battle-fields of Northland,
To the dismal Sariola,
Here to leave our souls and bodies,
Here to starve, and freeze, and perish,
In the dreariest of places,
In this sun-forsaken country!
Never shall we gain the knowledge,
Never learn it, never tell it,
Which the pathway that can guide us
To the forest-beds to suffer,
To the Pohya-plains to perish,
In the home-land of the ravens,
Fitting food for crows and eagles.
Often do the Northland vultures
Hither come to feed their fledgelings;
Hither bring the birds of heaven
Bits of flesh and blood of heroes;
Often do the beaks of ravens
Tear the flesh of kindred corpses,
Often do the eagle's talons
Carry bones and trembling vitals,
Such as ours, to feed their nestlings,
In their rocky homes and ledges.

"Oh! my mother can but wonder,
Never can divine the answer,
Where her reckless son is roaming,
Where her hero's blood is flowing,
Whether in the swamps and lowlands,
Whether in the heat of battle,
Or upon the waves of the ocean,
Or upon the hop-field mountains,
Or along some forest by-way.
Nothing can her mind discover
Of the frailest of her heroes,
Only think that he has perished.
Thus the hoary-headed mother
Weeps and murmurs in her chambers:
'Where is now my son beloved,
In the kingdom of Manala?
Sow thy crops, thou dread Tuoni,
Harrow well the fields of Kalma!
Now the bow receives its respite
From the fingers of my Tiera;
Bow and arrow now are useless,
Now the merry birds can fatten
In the fields, and fens, and forests;
Bears may live in dens of freedom,
On the fields may sport the elk-herds.'"
Spake the reckless Lemminkainen:
"Thus it is, mine aged mother,
Thou that gavest me existence!
Thou hast reared thy broods of chickens,
Hatched and reared thy flights
of white-swans,
All of them the winds have scattered,
Or the evil Lempo frightened;
One flew hither, and one thither,
And a third one, lost forever!
Think thou of our former pleasures,
Of our better days together,
When I wandered like the flowers,
Like the berry in the meadows.
Many saw my form majestic,
Many thought me well-proportioned.
Now is not as then with Ahti,
Into evil days have fallen,

Since I see but storms and darkness!
Then my eyes beheld but sunshine,
Then we did not weep and murmur,
Did not fill our hearts with sorrow,
When the maids in joy were singing,
When the virgins twined their tresses;
Then the women joined in joyance,
Whether brides were happy-wedded,
Whether bridegrooms choose discreetly,
Whether they were wise or unwise.

"But we must not grow disheartened,
Let the Island-maidens cheer us;
Here we are not yet enchanted,
Not bewitched by magic singing,
On the paths not left to perish,
Sink and perish on our journey.
Full of youth we should not suffer,
Strong, we should not die unworthy,
Whom the wizards have enchanted,
Have bewitched with songs of magic;
Sorcerers may charm and conquer,
Bury them within their dungeons,
Hide them spell-bound in their cabins.
Let the wizards charm each other,
And bewitch their magic offspring,
Bring their tribes to fell destruction.
Never did my gray-haired father
Bow submission to a wizard,
Offer worship to magicians.
These the words my father uttered,
These the thoughts his son advances:

'Guard us, thou O great Creator,
Shield us, thou O God of mercy,
With thine arms of grace protect us,
Help us with thy strength and wisdom,
Guide the minds of all thy heroes,
Keep aright the thoughts of women,
Keep the old from speaking evil,
Keep the young from sin and folly,
Be to us a help forever,
Be our Guardian and our Father,
That our children may not wander
From the ways of their Creator,
From the path that God has given!'"

Then the hero Lemminkainen,
Made from cares the fleetest racers,
Sable racers from his sorrows,
Reins he made from days of evil,
From his sacred pains made saddles.
To the saddle, quickly springing,
Galloped he away from trouble,
To his dear and aged mother;
And his comrade, faithful Tiera,
Galloped to his Island-dwelling.

Now departs wild Lemminkainen,
Brave and reckless Kaukomieli,
From these ancient songs and legends;
Only guides his faithful Kura
To his waiting bride and kindred,
While these lays and incantations
Shall be turned to other heroes.

Rune XXXI: Kullerwoinen, Son of Evil

In the ancient times a mother
Hatched and raised some
swans and chickens,
Placed the chickens in the brushwood,
Placed her swans upon the river;
Came an eagle, hawk, and falcon,
Scattered all her swans and chickens,
One was carried to Karyala,
And a second into Ehstland,
Left a third at home in Pohya.
And the one to Ehstland taken
Soon became a thriving merchant;
He that journeyed to Karyala
Flourished and was called Kalervo;
He that hid away in Pohya
Took the name of Untamoinen,
Flourished to his father's sorrow,
To the heart-pain of his mother.

Untamoinen sets his fish-nets
In the waters of Kalervo;
Kullerwoinen sees the fish-nets,
Takes the fish home in his basket.
Then Untamo, evil-minded,

Angry grew and sighed for vengeance,
Clutched his fingers for the combat,
Bared his mighty arms for battle,
For the stealing of his salmon,
For the robbing of his fish-nets.
Long they battled, fierce the struggle,
Neither one could prove the victor;
Should one beat the other fiercely,
He himself was fiercely beaten.

Then arose a second trouble;
On the second and the third days,
Kalerwoinen sowed some barley
Near the barns of Untamoinen;
Untamoinen's sheep in hunger
Ate the crop of Kullerwoinen;
Kullerwoinen's dog in malice
Tore Untamo's sheep in pieces;
Then Untamo sorely threatened
To annihilate the people
Of his brother, Kalerwoinen,
To exterminate his tribe-folk,
To destroy the young and aged,
To out-root his race and kingdom;
Conjures men with broadswords girded,
For the war he fashions heroes,
Fashions youth with spears adjusted,
Bearing axes on their shoulders;
Conjures thus a mighty army,
Hastens to begin a battle,
Bring a war upon his brother.

Kalerwoinen's wife in beauty
Sat beside her chamber-window,
Looking out along the highway,
Spake these words in wonder guessing:
"Do I see some smoke arising,
Or perchance a heavy storm-cloud,
Near the border of the forest,
Near the ending of the prairie?"

It was not some smoke arising,
Nor indeed a heavy storm-cloud,
It was Untamoinen's soldiers
Marching to the place of battle.
Warriors of Untamoinen
Came equipped with spears and arrows,
Killed the people of Kalervo,
Slew his tribe and all his kindred,
Burned to ashes many dwellings,
Levelled many courts and cabins,
Only left Kalervo's daughter,
With her unborn child, survivors
Of the slaughter of Untamo;
And she led the hostile army
To her father's halls and mansion,
Swept the rooms and made them cheery,
Gave the heroes home-attentions.

Time had gone but little distance,
Ere a boy was born in magic
Of the virgin, Untamala,
Of a mother, trouble-laden,
Him the mother named Kullervo,
"Pearl of Combat," said Untamo.
Then they laid the child of wonder,
Fatherless, the magic infant,
In the cradle of attention,
To be rocked, and fed, and guarded;
But he rocked himself at pleasure,
Rocked until his locks stood endwise;
Rocked one day, and then a second,
Rocked the third from morn till noontide;
But before the third day ended,
Kicks the boy with might of magic,
Forwards, backwards, upwards, downwards,
Kicks in miracles of power,
Bursts with might his swaddling garments;
Creeping from beneath his blankets,
Knocks his cradle into fragments,
Tears to tatters all his raiment,
Seemed that he would grow a hero,
And his mother, Untamala,
Thought that he, when full of stature,
When he found his strength and reason,
Would become a great magician,
First among a thousand heroes.

When three months the boy had thriven,
He began to speak as follows:
"When my form is full of stature,
When these arms grow strong and hardy,
Then will I avenge the murder
Of Kalervo and his people!"

Untamoinen hears the saying,
Speaks these words to those about him:
"To my tribe he brings destruction,
In him grows a new Kalervo!"

Then the heroes well considered,
And the women gave their counsel,
How to kill the magic infant,
That their tribe may live in safety.
It appeared the boy would prosper;
Finally, they all consenting,
He was placed within a basket,
And with willows firmly fastened,
Taken to the reeds and rushes,
Lowered to the deepest waters,
In his basket there to perish.

When three nights had circled over,
Messengers of Untamoinen
Went to see if he had perished
In his basket in the waters;
But the prodigy was living,
Had not perished in the rushes;
He had left his willow-basket,
Sat in triumph on a billow,
In his hand a rod of copper,
On the rod a golden fish-line,
Fishing for the silver whiting,
Measuring the deeps beneath him;
In the sea was little water,
Scarcely would it fill three measures.

Untamoinen then reflected,
This the language of the wizard:
"Whither shall we take this wonder,
Lay this prodigy of evil,
That destruction may o'ertake him,
Where the boy will sink and perish?"

Then his messengers he ordered
To collect dried poles of brushwood,
Birch-trees with their hundred branches,
Pine trees full of pitch and resin,
Ordered that a pyre be builded,
That the boy might be cremated,
That Kullervo thus might perish.
High they piled the arid branches,
Dried limbs from the sacred birch-tree,
Branches from a hundred fir trees,
Knots and branches full of resin;
Filled with bark a thousand sledges,
Seasoned oak, a hundred measures;
Piled the brushwood to the tree-tops,
Set the boy upon the summit,
Set on fire the pile of brushwood,
Burned one day, and then a second,
Burned the third from morn till evening.

When Untamo sent his heralds
To inspect the pyre and wizard,
There to learn if young Kullervo
Had been burned to dust and ashes,
There they saw the young boy sitting
On a pyramid of embers,
In his hand a rod of copper,
Raking coals of fire about him,
To increase their heat and power;
Not a hair was burned nor injured,
Not a ringlet singed nor shrivelled.

Then Untamo, evil-humored,
Thus addressed his trusted heralds:
"Whither shall the boy be taken,
To what place this thing of evil,
That destruction may o'ertake him.
That the boy may sink and perish?"

Then they hung him to an oak-tree,
Crucified him in the branches,
That the wizard there might perish.

When three days and nights had ended,
Untamoinen spake as follows:
"It is time to send my heralds
To inspect the mighty oak-tree,
There to learn if young Kullervo
Lives or dies among the branches."

Thereupon he sent his servants,
And the heralds brought this message:
"Young Kullervo has not perished,
Has not died among the branches
Of the oak-tree where we hung him.
In the oak he maketh pictures

With a wand between his fingers;
Pictures hang from all the branches,
Carved and painted by Kullervo;
And the heroes, thick as acorns,
With their swords and spears adjusted,
Fill the branches of the oak-tree,
Every leaf becomes a soldier."

Who can help the grave Untamo
Kill the boy that threatens evil
To Untamo's tribe and country,
Since he will not die by water,
Nor by fire, nor crucifixion?
Finally it was decided
That his body was immortal,
Could not suffer death nor torture.

In despair grave Untamoinen
Thus addressed the boy, Kullervo:
"Wilt thou live a life becoming,
Always do my people honour,
Should I keep thee in my dwelling?
Shouldst thou render servant's duty,
Then thou wilt receive thy wages,
Reaping whatsoe'er thou sowest;
Thou canst wear the golden girdle,
Or endure the tongue of censure."

When the boy had grown a little,
Had increased in strength and stature,
He was given occupation,
He was made to tend an infant,
Made to rock the infant's cradle.
These the words of Untamoinen:
"Often look upon the young child,
Feed him well and guard from danger,
Wash his linen in the river,
Give the infant good attention."

Young Kullervo, wicked wizard,
Nurses one day then a second;
On the morning of the third day,
Gives the infant cruel treatment,
Blinds its eyes and breaks its fingers;
And when evening shadows gather,
Kills the young child while it slumbers,
Throws its body to the waters,
Breaks and burns the infant's cradle.
Untamoinen thus reflected:
"Never will this fell Kullervo
Be a worthy nurse for children,
Cannot rock a babe in safety;
Do not know how I can use him,
What employment I can give him!"

Then he told the young magician
He must fell the standing forest,
And Kullervo gave this answer:
"Only will I be a hero,
When I wield the magic hatchet;
I am young, and fair, and mighty,
Far more beautiful than others,
Have the skill of six magicians."

Thereupon he sought the blacksmith,
This the order of Kullervo:
"Listen, O thou metal-artist,
Forge for me an axe of copper,
Forge the mighty axe of heroes,
Wherewith I may fell the forest,
Fell the birch, and oak, and aspen."

This behest the blacksmith honours,
Forges him an axe of copper,
Wonderful the blade he forges.
Kullerwoinen grinds his hatchet,
Grinds his blade from morn
till evening,
And the next day makes the handle;
Then he hastens to the forest,
To the upward-sloping mountain,
To the tallest of the birches,
To the mightiest of oak-trees;
There he swings his axe of copper,
Swings his blade with might
of magic,
Cuts with sharpened edge the aspen,
With one blow he fells the oak-tree,
With a second blow, the linden;
Many trees have quickly fallen,
By the hatchet of Kullervo.
Then the wizard spake as follows:
"This the proper work of Lempo,
Let dire Hisi fell the forest!"

In the birch he sank his hatchet,
Made an uproar in the woodlands,
Called aloud in tones of thunder,
Whistled to the distant mountains,
Till they echoed to his calling,
When Kullervo spake as follows:
"May the forest, in the circle
Where my voice rings, fall and perish,
In the earth be lost forever!
May no tree remain unlevelled,
May no saplings grow in spring-time,
Never while the moonlight glimmers,
Where Kullervo's voice has echoed,
Where the forest hears my calling;
Where the ground with seed is planted,
And the grain shall sprout and flourish,
May it never come to ripeness,
May the ears of corn be blasted!"

When the strong man, Untamoinen,
Went to look at early evening,
How Kullervo was progressing,
In his labours in the forest;
Little was the work accomplished,
Was not worthy of a hero;
Untamoinen thus reflected:
"Young Kullervo is not fitted
For the work of clearing forests,
Wastes the best of all the timber,
To my lands he brings destruction;
I shall set him making fences."

Then the youth began the building
Of a fence for Untamoinen;
Took the trunks of stately fir trees,
Trimmed them with his blade for fence-posts,
Cut the tallest in the woodlands,
For the railing of his fences;
Made the smaller poles and cross-bars
From the longest of the lindens;
Made the fence without a pass-way,
Made no wicket in his fences,
And Kullervo spake these measures:
"He that does not rise as eagles,
Does not sail on wings through ether,
Cannot cross Kullervo's pickets,
Nor the fences he has builded."

Untamoinen left his mansion
To inspect the young boy's labours,
View the fences of Kullervo;
Saw the fence without a pass-way,
Not a wicket in his fences;
From the earth the
fence extended
To the highest clouds of heaven.
These the words of Untamoinen:
"For this work he is not fitted,
Useless is the fence thus builded;
Is so high that none can cross it,
And there is no passage through it:
He shall thresh the rye and barley."

Young Kullervo, quick preparing,
Made an oaken flail for threshing,
Threshed the rye to finest powder,
Threshed the barley into atoms,
And the straw to worthless fragments.

Untamoinen went at evening,
Went to see Kullervo's threshing,
View the work of Kullerwoinen;
Found the rye was ground to powder,
Grains of barley crushed to atoms,
And the straw to worthless rubbish.

Untamoinen then grew angry,
Spake these words in bitter accents:
"Kullerwoinen as a workman
Is a miserable failure;
Whatsoever work he touches
Is but ruined by his witchcraft;
I shall carry him to Ehstland,
In Karyala I shall sell him
To the blacksmith, Ilmarinen,
There to swing the heavy hammer."

Untamoinen sells Kullervo,
Trades him off in far Karyala,
To the blacksmith, Ilmarinen,
To the master of the metals,
This the sum received in payment:
Seven worn and worthless sickles,
Three old caldrons worse
than useless,

Three old scythes, and hoes, and axes,
Recompense, indeed, sufficient
For a boy that will not labour
For the good of his employer.

Rune XXXII: Kullervo as a Shepherd

Kullerwoinen, wizard-servant
Of the blacksmith, Ilmarinen,
Purchased slave from Untamoinen,
Magic son with sky-blue stockings,
With a head of golden ringlets,
In his shoes of marten-leather,
Waiting little, asked the blacksmith,
Asked the host for work at morning,
In the evening asked the hostess,
These the words of Kullerwoinen:
"Give me work at early morning,
In the evening, occupation,
Labour worthy of thy servant."

Then the wife of Ilmarinen,
Once the Maiden of the Rainbow,
Thinking long, and long debating,
How to give the youth employment,
How the purchased slave could labour;
Finally a shepherd made him,
Made him keeper of her pastures;
But the over-scornful hostess,
Baked a biscuit for the herdsman,
Baked a loaf of wondrous thickness,
Baked the lower-half of oat-meal,
And the upper-half of barley,
Baked a flint-stone in the centre,
Poured around it liquid butter,
Then she gave it to the shepherd,
Food to still the herdsman's hunger;
Thus she gave the youth instructions:
"Do not eat the bread in hunger,
Till the herd is in the woodlands!"

Then the wife of Ilmarinen
Sent her cattle to the pasture,
Thus addressing Kullerwoinen:
"Drive the cows to yonder bowers,
To the birch-trees and the aspens,
That they there may feed and fatten,
Fill themselves with milk and butter,
In the open forest-pastures,
On the distant hills and mountains,
In the glens among the birch-trees,
In the lowlands with the aspens,
In the golden pine tree forests,
In the thickets silver-laden.

"Guard them, thou O kind Creator,
Shield them, omnipresent Ukko,
Shelter them from every danger,
And protect them from all evil,
That they may not want, nor wander
From the paths of peace and plenty.
As at home thou didst protect them
In the shelters and the hurdles,
Guard them now beneath the heavens,
Shelter them in woodland pastures,
That the herds may live and prosper
To the joy of Northland's hostess,
And against the will of Lempo.

"If my herdsman prove unworthy,
If the shepherd-maids seem evil,
Let the pastures be their shepherds,
Let the alders guard the cattle,
Make the birch-tree their protector,
Let the willow drive them homeward,
Ere the hostess go to seek them,
Ere the milkmaids wait and worry.
Should the birch-tree not protect them,
Nor the aspen lend assistance,
Nor the linden be their keeper,
Nor the willow drive them homeward,
Wilt thou give them better herdsmen,
Let Creation's beauteous daughters
Be their kindly shepherdesses.
Thou hast many lovely maidens,
Many hundreds that obey thee,
In the Ether's spacious circles,
Beauteous daughters of creation.

"Summer-daughter, magic maiden,
Southern mother of the woodlands,

Pine tree daughter, Kateyatar,
Pihlayatar, of the aspen,
Alder-maiden, Tapio's daughter,
Daughter of the glen, Millikki,
And the mountain-maid, Tellervo,
Of my herds be ye protectors,
Keep them from the evil-minded,
Keep them safe in days of summer,
In the times of fragrant flowers,
While the tender leaves are whispering,
While the Earth is verdure-laden.

"Summer-daughter, charming maiden,
Southern mother of the woodlands,
Spread abroad thy robes of safety,
Spread thine apron o'er the forest,
Let it cover all my cattle,
And protect the unprotected,
That no evil winds may harm them,
May not suffer from the storm-clouds.
Guard my flocks from every danger,
Keep them from the hands of wild-beasts,
From the swamps with sinking pathways,
From the springs that bubble trouble,
From the swiftly running waters,
From the bottom of the whirlpool,
That they may not find misfortune,
May not wander to destruction,
In the marshes sink and perish,
Though against God's best intentions,
Though against the will of Ukko.

"From a distance bring a bugle,
Bring a shepherd's horn from heaven,
Bring the honey-flute of Ukko,
Play the music of creation,
Blow the pipes of the magician,
Play the flowers on the highlands,
Charm the hills, and dales, and mountains,
Charm the borders of the forest,
Fill the forest-trees with honey,
Fill with spice the fountain-borders.

"For my herds give food and shelter,
Feed them all on honeyed pastures,
Give them drink at honeyed fountains
Feed them on thy golden grasses,
On the leaves of silver saplings,
From the springs of life and beauty,
From the crystal-waters flowing,
From the waterfalls of Rutya,
From the uplands green and golden,
From the glens enriched in silver.
Dig thou also golden fountains
On the four sides of the willow,
That the cows may drink in sweetness,
And their udders swell with honey,
That their milk may flow in streamlets;
Let the milk be caught in vessels,
Let the cow's gift be not wasted,
Be not given to Manala.

"Many are the sons of evil,
That to Mana take their milkings,
Give their milk to evil-doers,
Waste it in Tuoni's empire;
Few there are, and they the worthy,
That can get the milk from Mana;
Never did my ancient mother
Ask for counsel in the village,
Never in the courts for wisdom;
She obtained her milk from Mana,
Took the sour-milk from the dealers,
Sweet-milk from the greater distance,
From the kingdom of Manala,
From Tuoni's fields and pastures;
Brought it in the dusk of evening,
Through the by-ways in the darkness,
That the wicked should not know it,
That it should not find destruction.

"This the language of my mother,
And these words I also echo:
'Whither does the cow's gift wander,
Whither has the milk departed?
Has it gone to feed the strangers,
Banished to the distant village,
Gone to feed the hamlet-lover,
Or perchance to feed the forest,
Disappeared within the woodlands,
Scattered o'er the hills and mountains,
Mingled with the lakes and rivers?
It shall never go to Mana,
Never go to feed the stranger,

Never to the village-lover;
Neither shall it feed the forest,
Nor be lost upon the mountains,
Neither sprinkled in the woodlands,
Nor be mingled with the waters;
It is needed for our tables,
Worthy food for all our children.'

"Summer-daughter, maid of beauty,
Southern daughter of Creation,
Give Suotikki tender fodder,
To Watikki, give pure water,
To Hermikki milk abundant,
Fresh provisions to Tuorikki,
From Mairikki let the milk flow,
Fresh milk from my cows in plenty,
Coming from the tips of grasses,
From the tender herbs and leaflets,
From the meadows rich in honey,
From the mother of the forest,
From the meadows sweetly dripping,
From the berry-laden branches,
From the heath of flower-maidens,
From the verdure-maiden bowers,
From the clouds of milk-providers,
From the virgin of the heavens,
That the milk may flow abundant
From the cows that I have given
To the keeping of Kullervo.

"Rise thou virgin of the valley,
From the springs arise in beauty,
Rise thou maiden of the fountain,
Beautiful, arise in ether,
Take the waters from the cloudlets,
And my roaming herds besprinkle,
That my cows may drink and flourish,
May be ready for the coming
Of the shepherdess of evening.

"O Millikki, forest-hostess,
Mother of the herds at pasture,
Send the tallest of thy servants,
Send the best of thine assistants,
That my herds may well be guarded,
Through the pleasant days of summer,
Given us by our Creator.

"Beauteous virgin of the woodlands,
Tapio's most charming daughter,
Fair Tellervo, forest-maiden,
Softly clad in silken raiment,
Beautiful in golden ringlets,
Do thou give my herds protection,
In the Metsola dominions,
On the hills of Tapiola;
Shield them with thy hands of beauty,
Stroke them gently with thy fingers,
Give to them a golden lustre,
Make them shine like fins of salmon,
Grow them robes as soft as ermine.

"When the evening star brings darkness,
When appears the hour of twilight,
Send my lowing cattle homeward,
Milk within their vessels coursing,
Water on their backs in lakelets.
When the Sun has set in ocean,
When the evening-bird is singing,
Thus address my herds of cattle:

"Ye that carry horns, now hasten
To the sheds of Ilmarinen;
Ye enriched in milk go homeward,
To the hostess now in waiting,
Home, the better place for sleeping,
Forest-beds are full of danger;
When the evening comes in darkness,
Straightway journey to the milkmaids
Building fires to light the pathway
On the turf enriched in honey,
In the pastures berry-laden!

"Thou, O Tapio's son, Nyrikki,
Forest-son, enrobed in purple,
Cut the fir trees on the mountains,
Cut the pines with cones of beauty,
Lay them o'er the streams for bridges,
Cover well the sloughs of quicksand,
In the swamps and in the lowlands,
That my herd may pass in safety,
On their long and dismal journey,
To the clouds of smoke may hasten,
Where the milkmaids wait their coming.
If the cows heed not this order,

Do not hasten home at evening,
Then, O service-berry maiden,
Cut a birch-rod from the glenwood,
From the juniper, a whip-stick,
Near to Tapio's spacious mansion,
Standing on the ash-tree mountain,
Drive my wayward, lowing cattle,
Into Metsola's wide milk-yards,
When the evening-star is rising.

"Thou, O Otso, forest-apple,
Woodland bear, with honeyed fingers,
Let us make a lasting treaty,
Make a vow for future ages,
That thou wilt not kill my cattle,
Wilt not eat my milk-providers;
That I will not send my hunters
To destroy thee and thy kindred,
Never in the days of summer,
The Creator's warmest season.

"Dost thou hear the tones of cow-bells,
Hear the calling of the bugles,
Hide thyself within the meadow,
Sink upon the turf in slumber,
Bury both thine ears in clover,
Crouch within some alder-thicket
Climb between the mossy ledges,
Visit thou some rocky cavern,
Flee away to other mountains,
Till thou canst not hear the cow-bells,
Nor the calling of the herdsmen.

"Listen, Otso of the woodlands,
Sacred bear with honeyed fingers,
To approach the herd of cattle
Thou thyself art not forbidden,
But thy tongue, and teeth, and fingers,
Must not touch my herd in summer,
Must not harm my harmless creatures.
Go around the scented meadows,
Amble through the milky pastures,
From the tones of bells and shepherds.
Should the herd be on the mountain,
Go thou quickly to the marshes;
Should my cattle browse the lowlands,
Sleep thou then within the thicket;
Should they feed upon the uplands,
Thou must hasten to the valley;
Should the herd graze at the bottom,
Thou must feed upon the summit.

"Wander like the golden cuckoo,
Like the dove of silver brightness,
Like a little fish in ocean;
Hide thy claws within thy hair-foot,
Shut thy wicked teeth in darkness,
That my herd may not be frightened,
May not think themselves in danger.
Leave my cows in peace and plenty,
Let them journey home in order,
Through the vales and mountain by-ways,
Over plains and through the forest,
Harming not my harmless creatures.

"Call to mind our former pledges,
At the river of Tuoni,
Near the waterfall and whirlpool,
In the ears of our Creator.
Thrice to Otso was it granted,
In the circuit of the summer,
To approach the land of cow-bells,
Where the herdsmen's voices echo;
But to thee it was not granted,
Otso never had permission
To attempt a wicked action,
To begin a work of evil.
Should the blinding thing of malice
Come upon thee in thy roamings,
Should thy bloody teeth feel hunger,
Throw thy malice to the mountains,
And thy hunger to the pine trees,
Sink thy teeth within the aspens,
In the dead limbs of the birches,
Prune the dry stalks from the willows.
Should thy hunger still impel thee,
Go thou to the berry-mountain,
Eat the fungus of the forest,
Feed thy hunger on the ant-hills,
Eat the red roots of the bear-tree,
Metsola's rich cakes of honey,
Not the grass my herd would feed on.
Or if Metsola's rich honey
Should ferment before the eating,

On the hills of golden colour,
On the mountains filled with silver,
There is other food for hunger,
Other drink for thirsting Otso,
Everlasting will the food be,
And the drink be never wanting.

"Let us now agree in honour,
And conclude a lasting treaty
That our lives may end in pleasure,
May be merry in the summer,
Both enjoy the woods in common,
Though our food must be distinctive.
Shouldst thou still desire to fight me,
Let our contests be in winter,
Let our wars be on the snow-fields.
Swamps will thaw in days of summer,
Warm, the water in the rivers.
Therefore shouldst thou break this treaty,
Shouldst thou come where golden cattle
Roam these woodland hills and valleys,
We will slay thee with our cross-bows;
Should our arrow-men be absent,
We have here some archer-women,
And among them is the hostess,
That can use the fatal weapon,
That can bring thee to destruction,
Thus will end the days of trouble
That thou bringest to our people,
And against the will of Ukko.

"Ukko, ruler in the heavens,
Lend an ear to my entreaty,
Metamorphose all my cattle,
Through the mighty force of magic,
Into stumps and stones convert them,
If the enemy should wander,
Near my herd in days of summer.

"If I had been born an Otso,
I would never stride and amble
At the feet of aged women;
Elsewhere there are hills and valleys,
Farther on are honey-pastures,
Where the lazy bear may wander,
Where the indolent may linger;
Sneak away to yonder mountain,
That thy tender flesh may lessen,
In the blue-glen's deep recesses,
In the bear-dens of the forest.
Thou canst move through fields of acorns,
Through the sand and ocean-pebbles,
There for thee is tracked a pathway,
Through the woodlands on the sea-coast,
To the Northland's farthest limits,
To the dismal plains of Lapland,
There 'tis well for thee to lumber,
There to live will be a pleasure.
Shoeless there to walk in summer,
Stockingless in days of autumn,
On the blue back of the mountain,
Through the swamps and fertile lowlands.

"If thou canst not journey thither,
Canst not find the Lapland-highway,
Hasten on a little distance,
In the bear-path leading northward.
To the grove of Tuonela,
To the honey-plains of Kalma,
Swamps there are in which to wander,
Heaths in which to roam at pleasure,
There are Kiryos, there are Karyos,
And of beasts a countless number,
With their fetters strong as iron,
Fattening within the forest.
Be ye gracious, groves and mountains,
Full of grace, ye darksome thickets,
Peace and plenty to my cattle,
Through the pleasant days of summer,
The Creator's warmest season.

"Knippana, O King of forests,
Thou the gray-beard of the woodlands,
Watch thy dogs in fen and fallow,
Lay a sponge within one nostril,
And an acorn in the other,
That they may not scent my cattle;
Tie their eyes with silken fillets,
That they may not see my herdlings,
May not see my cattle grazing.

"Should all this seem inefficient,
Drive away thy barking children,
Let them run to other forests,

Let them hunt in other marshes,
From these verdant strips of meadow,
From these far outstretching borders,
Hide thy dogs within thy caverns,
Firmly tie thy yelping children,
Tie them with thy golden fetters,
With thy chains adorned with silver,
That they may not do me damage,
May not do a deed of mischief.

"Should all this prove inefficient,
Thou, O Ukko, King of heaven,
Wise director, full of mercy,
Hear the golden words I utter,
Hear a voice that breathes affection,
From the alder make a muzzle,
For each dog within the kennel;
Should the alder prove too feeble,
Cast a band of purest copper;
Should the copper prove
a failure,
Forge a band of ductile iron;
Should the iron snap asunder,
In each nose a small-ring fasten,
Made of molten gold and silver,
Chain thy dogs in forest-caverns,
That my herd may not be injured."

Then the wife of Ilmarinen,
Life-companion of the blacksmith,
Opened all her yards and stables,
Led her herd across the meadow,
Placed them in the herdman's keeping,
In the care of Kullerwoinen.

Rune XXXIII: Kullervo and the Cheat-cake

Thereupon the lad, Kullervo,
Laid his luncheon in his basket,
Drove the herd to mountain-pastures,
O'er the hills and through the marshes,
To their grazings in the woodlands,
Speaking as he careless wandered:
"Of the youth am I the poorest,
Hapless lad and full of trouble,
Evil luck to me befallen!
I, alas! must idly wander
O'er the hills and through the valleys,
As a watch-dog for the cattle!"

Then he sat upon the greensward,
In a sunny spot selected,
Singing, chanting words as follow:
"Shine, O shine, thou Sun of heaven,
Cast thy rays, thou fire of Ukko,
On the herdsman of the blacksmith,
On the head of Kullerwoinen,
On this poor and luckless shepherd,
Not in Ilmarinen's smithy,
Nor the dwellings of his people;
Good the table of the hostess,
Cuts the best of wheaten biscuit,
Honey-cakes she cuts in slices,
Spreading each with golden butter;
Only dry bread has the herdsman,
Eats with pain the oaten bread-crusts,
Filled with chaff his arid biscuit,
Feeds upon the worst of straw-bread,
Pine tree bark, the bread he
feeds on,
Sipping water from the birch-bark,
Drinking from the tips of grasses!
Go, O Sun, and go, O barley,
Haste away, thou light of Ukko,
Hide within the mountain pine trees,
Go, O wheat, to yonder thickets,
To the trees of purple berries,
To the junipers and alders,
Safely lead the herdsman homeward
To the biscuit golden-buttered,
To the honeyed cakes and viands!"

While the shepherd lad was singing
Kullerwoinen's song and echo,
Ilmarinen's wife was feasting
On the sweetest bread of Northland,
On the toothsome cakes of barley,
On the richest of provisions;
Only laid aside some cabbage,
For the herdsman, Kullerwoinen;
Set apart some wasted fragments,

Leavings of the dogs at dinner,
For the shepherd, home returning.

From the woods a bird came flying,
Sang this song to Kullerwoinen:
"'Tis the time for forest-dinners,
For the fatherless companion
Of the herds to eat his viands,
Eat the good things from his basket!"

Kullerwoinen heard the songster,
Looked upon the Sun's long shadow,
Straightway spake the words that follow:
"True, the singing of the songbird,
It is time indeed for feasting,
Time to eat my basket-dinner."

Thereupon young Kullerwoinen
Called his herd to rest in safety,
Sat upon a grassy hillock,
Took his basket from his shoulders,
Took therefrom the arid oat-loaf,
Turned it over in his fingers,
Carefully the loaf inspected,
Spake these words of ancient wisdom:
"Many loaves are fine to look on,
On the outside seem delicious,
On the inside, chaff and tan-bark!"

Then the shepherd, Kullerwoinen,
Drew his knife to cut his oat-loaf,
Cut the hard and arid biscuit;
Cuts against a stone imprisoned,
Well imbedded in the centre,
Breaks his ancient knife in pieces;
When the shepherd youth, Kullervo,
Saw his magic knife had broken,
Weeping sore, he spake as follows:
"This, the blade that I hold sacred,
This the one thing that I honour,
Relic of my mother's people!
On the stone within this oat-loaf,
On this cheat-cake of the hostess,
I my precious knife have broken.
How shall I repay this insult,
How avenge this woman's malice,
What the wages for deception?"

From a tree the raven answered:
"O thou little silver buckle,
Only son of old Kalervo,
Why art thou in evil humor,
Wherefore sad in thy demeanor?
Take a young shoot from the thicket,
Take a birch-rod from the valley,
Drive thy herd across the lowlands,
Through the quicksands of the marshes;
To the wolves let one half wander,
To the bear-dens, lead the other;
Sing the forest wolves together,
Sing the bears down from the mountains,
Call the wolves thy little children,
And the bears thy standard-bearers;
Drive them like a cow-herd homeward,
Drive them home like spotted cattle,
Drive them to thy master's milk-yards;
Thus thou wilt repay the hostess
For her malice and derision."

Thereupon the wizard answered,
These the words of Kullerwoinen:
"Wait, yea wait, thou bride of Hisi!
Do I mourn my mother's relic,
Mourn the keep-sake thou hast broken?
Thou thyself shalt mourn as sorely
When thy cows come home at evening!"

From the tree he cuts a birch-wand,
From the juniper a whip-stick,
Drives the herd across the lowlands,
Through the quicksands of the marshes,
To the wolves lets one half wander,
To the bear-dens leads the other;
Calls the wolves his little children,
Calls the bears his standard-bearers,
Changes all his herd of cattle
Into wolves and bears by magic.

In the west the Sun is shining,
Telling that the night is coming.
Quick the wizard, Kullerwoinen,
Wanders o'er the pine tree mountain,
Hastens through the forest homeward,
Drives the wolves and bears before him
Toward the milk-yards of the hostess;

To the herd he speaks as follows,
As they journey on together:
"Tear and kill the wicked hostess,
Tear her guilty flesh in pieces,
When she comes to view her cattle,
When she stoops to do her milking!"

Then the wizard, Kullerwoinen,
From an ox-bone makes a bugle,
Makes it from Tuonikki's cow-horn,
Makes a flute from Kiryo's shin-bone,
Plays a song upon his bugle,
Plays upon his flute of magic,
Thrice upon the home-land hill-tops,
Six times near the coming gate-ways.

Ilmarinen's wife and hostess
Long had waited for the coming
Of her herd with Kullerwoinen,
Waited for the milk at evening,
Waited for the new-made butter,
Heard the footsteps in the cow-path,
On the heath she heard the bustle,
Spake these joyous words of welcome:
"Be thou praised, O gracious Ukko,
That my herd is home returning!
But I hear a bugle sounding,
'Tis the playing of my herdsman,
Playing on a magic cow-horn,
Bursting all our ears with music!"

Kullerwoinen, drawing nearer,
To the hostess spake as follows:
"Found the bugle in the woodlands,
And the flute among the rushes;
All thy herd are in the passage,
All thy cows within the hurdles,
This the time to build the camp-fire,
This the time to do the milking!"

Ilmarinen's wife, the hostess,
Thus addressed an aged servant:
"Go, thou old one, to the milking,
Have the care of all my cattle,
Do not ask for mine assistance,
Since I have to knead the biscuit."
Kullerwoinen spake as follows:
"Always does the worthy hostess,
Ever does the wisdom-mother
Go herself and do the milking,
Tend the cows within the hurdles!"

Then the wife of Ilmarinen
Built a field-fire in the passage,
Went to milk her cows awaiting,
Looked upon her herd in wonder,
Spake these happy words of greeting:
"Beautiful, my herd of cattle,
Glistening like the skins of lynxes,
Hair as soft as fur of ermine,
Peaceful waiting for the milk-pail!"

On the milk-stool sits the hostess,
Milks one moment, then a second,
Then a third time milks and ceases;
When the bloody wolves disguising,
Quick attack the hostess milking,
And the bears lend their assistance,
Tear and mutilate her body
With their teeth and sharpened fingers.
Kullerwoinen, cruel wizard,
Thus repaid the wicked hostess,
Thus repaid her evil treatment.

Quick the wife of Ilmarinen
Cried aloud in bitter anguish,
Thus addressed the youth, Kullervo:
"Evil son, thou bloody herdsman,
Thou hast brought me wolves in malice,
Driven bears within my hurdles!"
These the words of Kullerwoinen:
"Have I evil done as shepherd,
Worse the conduct of the hostess;
Baked a stone inside my oat-cake,
On the inside, rock and tan-bark,
On the stone my knife, was broken,
Treasure of my mother's household,
Broken virtue of my people!"
Ilmarinen's wife made answer:
"Noble herdsman, Kullerwoinen,
Change, I pray thee, thine opinion,
Take away thine incantations,
From the bears and wolves release me,
Save me from this spell of torture;

I will give thee better raiment,
Give the best of milk and butter,
Set for thee the sweetest table;
Thou shalt live with me in welcome,
Need not labour for thy keeping.
If thou dost not free me quickly,
Dost not break this spell of magic,
I shall sink into the deathland,
Shall return to Tuonela."
This is Kullerwoinen's answer:
"It is best that thou shouldst perish,
Let destruction overtake thee,
There is ample room in Mana,
Room for all the dead in Kalma,
There the worthiest must slumber,
There must rest the good and evil."
Ilmarinen's wife made answer:
"Ukko, thou O God in heaven,
Span the strongest of thy cross-bows,
Test the weapon by thy wisdom,
Lay an arrow forged from copper,
On the cross-bow of thy forging;
Rightly aim thy flaming arrow,
With thy magic hurl the missile,
Shoot this wizard through the vitals,
Pierce the heart of Kullerwoinen
With the lightning of the heavens,
With thine arrows tipped with copper."
Kullerwoinen prays as follows:
"Ukko, God of truth and justice.
Do not slay thy magic servant,
Slay the wife of Ilmarinen,
Kill in her the worst of women,
In these hurdles let her perish,
Lest she wander hence in freedom,
To perform some other mischief,
Do some greater deed of malice!"

Quick as lightning fell the hostess,
Quick the wife of Ilmarinen
Fell and perished in the hurdles,
On the ground before her cottage;
Thus the death of Northland's hostess,
Cherished wife of Ilmarinen,
Once the Maiden of the Rainbow,
Wooed and watched for
many summers,
Pride and joy of Kalevala!

Rune XXXIV: Kullervo Finds His Tribe Folk

Kullerwoinen, young magician,
In his beauteous, golden ringlets,
In his magic shoes of deer-skin,
Left the home of Ilmarinen
Wandered forth upon his journey,
Ere the blacksmith heard the tidings
Of the cruel death and torture
Of his wife and joy-companion,
Lest a bloody fight should follow.

Kullerwoinen left the smithy,
Blowing on his magic bugle,
Joyful left the lands of Ilma,
Blowing blithely on the heather,
Made the distant hills re-echo,
Made the swamps and mountains tremble,
Made the heather-blossoms answer
To the music of his cow-horn,
In its wild reverberations,
To the magic of his playing.
Songs were heard within the smithy,
And the blacksmith stopped and listened,
Hastened to the door and window,
Hastened to the open court-yard,
If perchance he might discover
What was playing on the heather,
What was sounding through the forest.
Quick he learned the cruel story,
Learned the cause of the rejoicing,
Saw the hostess dead before him,
Knew his beauteous wife had perished,
Saw the lifeless form extended,
In the court-yard of his dwelling.
Thereupon the metal-artist
Fell to bitter tears and wailings,
Wept through all the dreary
night-time,
Deep the grief that settled o'er him,
Black as night his darkened future,
Could not stay his tears of sorrow.

Kullerwoinen hastened onward,
Straying, roaming, hither, thither,
Wandered on through field and forest,
O'er the Hisi-plains and woodlands.
When the darkness settled o'er him,
When the bird of night was flitting,
Sat the fatherless at evening,
The forsaken sat and rested
On a hillock of the forest.
Thus he murmured, heavy-hearted:
"Why was I, alas! created,
Why was I so ill-begotten,
Since for months and years I wander,
Lost among the ether-spaces?
Others have their homes to dwell in,
Others hasten to their firesides
As the evening gathers round them:
But my home is in the forest,
And my bed upon the heather,
And my bath-room is the rain-cloud.

"Never didst thou, God of mercy,
Never in the course of ages,
Give an infant birth unwisely;
Wherefore then was I created,
Fatherless to roam in ether,
Motherless and lone to wander?
Thou, O Ukko, art my father,
Thou hast given me form and feature;
As the sea-gull on the ocean,
As the duck upon the waters,
Shines the Sun upon the swallow,
Shines as bright upon the sparrow,
Gives the joy-birds song and gladness,
Does not shine on me unhappy;
Nevermore will shine the sunlight,
Never will the moonlight glimmer
On this hapless son and orphan;
Do not know my hero-father,
Cannot tell who was my mother;
On the shore, perhaps the gray-duck
Left me in the sand to perish.
Young was I and small of stature,
When my mother left me orphaned;
Dead, my father and my mother,
Dead, my honoured tribe of heroes;
Shoes they left me that are icy,
Stockings filled with frosts of ages,
Let me on the freezing ice-plains
Fall to perish in the rushes;
From the giddy heights of mountains
Let me tumble to destruction.

"O, thou wise and good Creator,
Why my birth and what my service?
I shall never fall and perish
On the ice-plains, in the marshes,
Never be a bridge in swamp-land,
Not while I have arms of virtue
That can serve my honoured kindred!"

Then Kullervo thought to journey
To the village of Untamo,
To avenge his father's murder,
To avenge his mother's tortures,
And the troubles of his tribe-folk.
These the words of Kullerwoinen:
"Wait, yea wait, thou Untamoinen,
Thou destroyer of my people;
When I meet thee in the combat,
I will slay thee and thy kindred,
I will burn thy homes to ashes!"

Came a woman on the highway,
Dressed in blue, the aged mother,
To Kullervo spake as follows:
"Whither goest, Kullerwoinen,
Whither hastes the wayward hero?"
Kullerwoinen gave this answer:
"I have thought that I would journey
To the far-off land of strangers,
To the village of Untamo,
To avenge my father's murder,
To avenge my mother's tortures,
And the troubles of my tribe-folk."
Thus the gray-haired woman answered:
"Surely thou dost rest in error,
For thy tribe has never perished,
And thy mother still is living
With thy father in the Northland,
Living with the old Kalervo."

"O, thou ancient dame beloved,
Worthy mother of the woodlands,

Tell me where my father liveth,
Where my loving mother lingers!"

"Yonder lives thine aged father,
And thy loving mother with him,
On the farthest shore of Northland,
On the long-point of the fish-lake!"

"Tell me, O thou woodland-mother,
How to journey to my people,
How to find mine honoured tribe-folk."

"Easy is the way for strangers:
Thou must journey through the forest,
Hasten to the river-border,
Travel one day, then a second,
And the third from morn till even,
To the northwest, thou must journey.
If a mountain comes to meet thee,
Go around the nearing mountain,
Westward hold thy weary journey,
Till thou comest to a river,
On thy right hand flowing eastward;
Travel to the river border,
Where three water-falls will greet thee;
When thou comest to a headland,
On the point thou'lt see a cottage
Where the fishermen assemble;
In this cottage is thy father,
With thy mother and her daughters,
Beautiful thy maiden sisters."

Kullerwoinen, the magician,
Hastens northward on his journey,
Walks one day, and then a second,
Walks the third from morn till evening;
To the northwest walks Kullervo,
Till a mountain comes to meet him,
Walks around the nearing mountain;
Westward, westward, holds his journey,
Till he sees a river coming;
Hastens to the river border,
Walks along the streams and rapids
Till three waterfalls accost him;
Travels till he meets a headland,
On the point he spies a cottage,
Where the fishermen assemble.
Quick he journeys to the cabin,
Quick he passes through the portals
Of the cottage on the headland,
Where he finds his long-lost kindred;
No one knows the youth, Kullervo,
No one knows whence comes the stranger,
Where his home, nor where he goeth.
These the words of young Kullervo:
"Dost thou know me not, my mother,
Dost thou know me not, my father?
I am hapless Kullerwoinen,
Whom the heroes of Untamo
Carried to their distant country,
When my height was but a hand-breadth."
Quick the hopeful mother answers:
"O my worthy son, beloved,
O my precious silver-buckle,
Hast thou with thy mind of magic,
Wandered through the fields of Northland
Searching for thy home and kindred?
As one dead I long have mourned thee,
Had supposed thee in Manala.
Once I had two sons and heroes,
Had two good and beauteous daughters,
Two of these have long been absent,
Elder son and elder daughter;
For the wars my son departed,
While my daughter strayed and perished;
If my son is home returning,
Yet my daughter still is absent."
Kullerwoinen asked his mother:
"Whither did my sister wander,
What direction did she journey?"
This the answer of the mother:
"This the story of thy sister:
Went for berries to the woodlands,
To the mountains went my daughter,
Where the lovely maiden vanished,
Where my pretty berry perished,
Died some death beyond my knowledge,
Nameless is the death she suffered.
Who is mourning for the daughter?
No one mourns her as her mother,
Walks and wanders, mourns and searches,
For her fairest child and daughter;
Therefore did the mother wander,
Searching for thy lovely sister,

Like the bear she roamed the forest,
Ran the glenways like the adder,
Searched one day and then a second,
Searched the third from morn till even,
Till she reached the mountain-summit,
There she called and called her daughter,
Till the distant mountains answered,
Called to her who had departed:
'Where art thou, my lovely maiden,
Come my daughter to thy mother!'

"Thus I called, and sought thy sister,
This the answer of the mountains,
Thus the hills and valleys echoed:
'Call no more, thou weeping mother,
Weep no more for the departed;
Nevermore in all thy lifetime,
Never in the course of ages,
Will she join again her kindred,
At her brother's landing-places,
In her father's humble dwelling.'"

Rune XXXV: Kullervo's Evil Deeds

Kullerwoinen, youthful wizard,
In his blue and scarlet stockings,
Henceforth lingered with his parents;
But he could not change his nature,
Could not gain a higher wisdom,
Could not win a better judgement;
As a child he was ill-nurtured,
Early rocked in stupid cradles,
By a nurse of many follies,
By a minister of evil.

To his work went Kullerwoinen,
Strove to make his labours worthy;
First, Kullervo went a-fishing,
Set his fishing-nets in ocean;
With his hands upon the row-locks,
Kullerwoinen spake as follows:
"Shall I pull with all my forces,
Pull with strength of youthful heroes,
Or with weakness of the aged?"

From the stern arose a gray-beard,
And he answered thus Kullervo:
"Pull with all thy youthful vigor;
Shouldst thou row with magic power,
Thou couldst not destroy this vessel,
Couldst not row this boat to fragments."

Thereupon the youth, Kullervo,
Rowed with all his youthful vigor,
With the mighty force of magic,
Rowed the bindings from the vessel,
Ribs of juniper he shattered,
Rowed the aspen-oars to pieces.

When the aged sire, Kalervo,
Saw the work of Kullerwoinen,
He addressed his son as follows:
"Dost not understand the rowing;
Thou hast burst the bands asunder,
Bands of juniper and willow,
Rowed my aspen-boat to pieces;
To the fish-nets drive the salmon,
This, perchance, will suit thee better."

Thereupon the son, Kullervo,
Hastened to his work as bidden,
Drove the salmon to the fish-nets,
Spake in innocence as follows:
"Shall I with my youthful vigor
Scare the salmon to the fish-nets,
Or with little magic vigor
Shall I drive them to their capture?"
Spake the master of the fish-nets:
"That would be but work of women,
Shouldst thou use but little power
In the frighting of the salmon!"

Kullerwoinen does as bidden,
Scares the salmon with the forces
Of his mighty arms and shoulders,
With the strength of youth and magic,
Stirs the water thick with black-earth,
Beats the scare-net into pieces,
Into pulp he beats the salmon.

When the aged sire, Kalervo,
Saw the work of Kullerwoinen,

To his son these words he uttered:
"Dost not understand this labour,
For this work thou art not suited,
Canst not scare the perch and salmon
To the fish-nets of thy father;
Thou hast ruined all my fish-nets,
Torn my scare-net into tatters,
Beaten into pulp the whiting,
Torn my net-props into fragments,
Beaten into bits my wedges.
Leave the fishing to another;
See if thou canst pay the tribute,
Pay my yearly contribution;
See if thou canst better travel,
On the way show better judgement!"

Thereupon the son, Kullervo,
Hapless youth in purple vestments,
In his magic shoes of deer-skin,
In his locks of golden colour,
Sallied forth to pay the taxes,
Pay the tribute for his people.
When the youth had paid the tribute,
Paid the yearly contribution,
He returned to join the snow-sledge,
Took his place upon the cross-bench,
Snapped his whip above the courser,
And began his journey homeward;
Rattled on along the highway,
Measured as he galloped onward
Wainamoinen's hills and valleys,
And his fields in cultivation.

Came a golden maid to meet him,
On her snow-shoes came a virgin,
O'er the hills of Wainamoinen,
O'er his cultivated lowlands.

Quick the wizard-son, Kullervo,
Checked the motion of his racer,
Thus addressed the charming maiden:
"Come, sweet maiden, to my snow-sledge,
In my fur-robes rest and linger!"
As she ran, the maiden answered:
"Let the Death-maid sit beside thee,
Rest and linger in thy fur-robes!"

Thereupon the youth, Kullervo,
Snapped his whip above the courser;
Fleet as wind he gallops homeward,
Dashes down along the highway;
With the roar of falling waters,
Gallops onward, onward, onward,
O'er the broad-back of the ocean,
O'er the icy plains of Lapland.

Comes a winsome maid to meet him,
Golden-haired, and wearing snow-shoes,
On the far outstretching ice-plains;
Quick the wizard checks his racer,
Charmingly accosts the maiden,
Chanting carefully these measures:
"Come, thou beauty, to my snow-sledge,
Hither come, and rest, and linger!"
Tauntingly the maiden answered:
"Take Tuoni to thy snow-sledge,
At thy side let Manalainen
Sit with thee, and rest, and linger!"

Quick the wizard, Kullerwoinen,
Struck his fiery, prancing racer,
With the birch-whip of his father.
Like the lightning flew the fleet-foot,
Galloped on the highway homeward;
O'er the hills the snow-sledge bounded,
And the coming mountains trembled.
Kullerwoinen, wild magician,
Measures, on his journey homeward,
Northland's far-extending borders,
And the fertile plains of Pohya.
Comes a beauteous maid to meet him,
With a tin-pin on her bosom,
On the heather of Pohyola,
O'er the Pohya-hills and moorlands.

Quick the wizard son, Kullervo,
Holds the bridle of his courser,
Charmingly intones these measures:
"Come, fair maiden, to my snow-sledge,
In these fur-robes rest, and linger;
Eat with me the golden apples,
Eat the hazel-nut in joyance,
Drink with me the beer delicious,
Eat the dainties that I give thee."

This the answer of the maiden
With the tin-pin on her bosom:
"I have scorn to give thy snow-sledge,
Scorn for thee, thou wicked wizard;
Cold is it beneath thy fur-robes,
And thy sledge is chill and cheerless."

Thereupon the youth, Kullervo,
Wicked wizard of the Northland,
Drew the maiden to his snow-sledge,
Drew her to a seat beside him,
Quickly in his furs enwrapped her;
And the tin-adorned made answer,
These the accents of the maiden:
"Loose me from thy magic power,
Let me leave at once thy presence,
Lest I speak in wicked accents,
Lest I say the prayer of evil;
Free me now as I command thee,
Or I'll tear thy sledge to pieces,
Throw these fur-robes to the north winds."

Straightway wicked Kullerwoinen,
Evil wizard and magician,
Opens all his treasure-boxes,
Shows the maiden gold and silver,
Shows her silken wraps of beauty,
Silken hose with golden borders,
Golden belts with silver buckles,
Jewelry that dims the vision,
Blunts the conscience of the virgin.
Silver leads one to destruction,
Gold entices from uprightness.
Kullerwoinen, wicked wizard,
Flatters lovingly the maiden,
One hand on the reins of leather,
One upon the maiden's shoulder;
Thus they journey through the evening,
Pass the night in merry-making.

When the day-star led the morning,
When the second day was dawning,
Then the maid addressed Kullervo,
Questioned thus the wicked wizard:
"Of what tribe art thou descended,
Of what race thy hero-father?
Tell thy lineage and kindred."

This, Kullervo's truthful answer:
"Am not from a mighty nation,
Not the greatest, nor the smallest,
But my lineage is worthy:
Am Kalervo's son of folly,
Am a child of contradictions,
Hapless son of cold misfortune.
Tell me of thy race of heroes,
Tell thine origin and kindred."
This the answer of the maiden:
"Came not from a race primeval,
Not the largest, nor the smallest,
But my lineage is worthy;
Am Kalervo's wretched daughter,
Am his long-lost child of error,
Am a maid of contradictions,
Hapless daughter of misfortune.

"When a child I lived in plenty
In the dwellings of my mother;
To the woods I went for berries,
Went for raspberries to uplands,
Gathered strawberries on mountains,
Gathered one day then a second;
But, alas! upon the third day,
Could not find the pathway homeward,
Forestward the highways led me,
All the footpaths, to the woodlands.
Long I sat in bitter weeping,
Wept one day and then a second,
Wept the third from morn till even.
Then I climbed a lofty mountain,
There I called in wailing accents,
And the woodlands gave this answer,
Thus the distant hills re-echoed:
'Call no longer, foolish virgin,
All thy calls and tears are useless;
There is none to give thee answer,
Far away, thy home and people.'

"On the third and on the fourth days,
On the fifth, and sixth, and seventh,
Constantly I sought to perish;
But in vain were all my efforts,
Could not die upon the mountains.
If this wretched maid had perished,
In the summer of the third year,

She had fed earth's vegetation,
She had blossomed as a flower,
Knowing neither pain nor sorrow."
Scarcely had the maiden spoken,
When she bounded from the snow-sledge,
Rushed upon the rolling river,
To the cataract's commotion,
To the fiery stream and whirlpool.
Thus Kullervo's lovely sister
Hastened to her own destruction,
To her death by fire and water,
Found her peace in Tuonela,
In the sacred stream of Mana.

Then the wicked Kullerwoinen
Fell to weeping, sorely troubled,
Wailed, and wept, and heavy-hearted,
Spake these words in bitter sorrow:
"Woe is me, my life hard-fated!
I have slain my virgin-sister,
Shamed the daughter of my mother;
Woe to thee, my ancient father!
Woe to thee, my gray-haired mother!
Wherefore was I born and nurtured,
Why this hapless child's existence?
Better fate to Kullerwoinen,
Had he never seen the daylight,
Or, if born, had never thriven
In these mournful days of evil!
Death has failed to do his duty,
Sickness sinned in passing by me,
Should have slain me in the cradle,
When the seventh day had ended!"

Thereupon he slips the collar
Of his prancing royal racer,
Mounts the silver-headed fleet-foot,
Gallops like the lightning homeward;
Gallops only for a moment,
When he halts his foaming courser
At the cabin of his father.
In the court-yard stood the mother,
Thus the wicked son addressed her:
"Faithful mother, fond and tender,
Hadst thou slain me when an infant,
Smoked my life out in the chamber,
In a winding-sheet hadst thrown me
To the cataract and whirlpool,
In the fire hadst set my cradle,
After seven nights had ended,
Worthy would have been thy service.
Had the village-maidens asked thee:
'Where is now the little cradle,
Wherefore is the bath-room empty?'
This had been a worthy answer:
'I have burned the wizard's cradle,
Cast the infant to the fire-dogs;
In the bath-room corn is sprouting,
From the barley malt is brewing.'"

Thereupon the aged mother
Asks her wizard-son these questions:
"What has happened to my hero,
What new fate has overcome thee?
Comest thou as from Tuoni,
From the castles of Manala?"
This, Kullervo's frank confession:
"Infamous the tale I bring thee,
My confession is dishonour:
On the way I met a maiden,
Met thy long-lost, wayward daughter,
Did not recognize my sister,
Fatal was the sin committed!
When the taxes had been settled,
When the tribute had been gathered,
Came a matchless maid to meet me,
Whom I witless led to sorrow,
This my mother's long-lost daughter.
When she saw in me her brother,
Quick she bounded from the snow-sledge,
Hastened to the roaring waters,
To the cataract's commotion,
To the fiery stream and whirlpool,
Hastened to her full destruction.

"Now, alas! must I determine,
Now must find a spot befitting,
Where thy sinful son may perish;
Tell me, all-forgiving mother,
Where to end my life of trouble;
Let me stop the black-wolf's howling,
Let me satisfy the hunger
Of the vicious bear of Northland;
Let the shark or hungry sea-dog

Be my dwelling-place hereafter!"
This the answer of the mother:
"Do not go to stop the howling
Of the hungry wolf of Northland;
Do not haste to still the black-bear
Growling in his forest-cavern;
Let not shark, nor vicious sea-dog
Be thy dwelling-place hereafter.
Spacious are the rooms of Suomi,
Limitless the Sawa-borders,
Large enough to hide transgression,
Man's misdeeds to hide for ages,
With his sins and evil actions.
Six long years man's sins lie hidden
In the border-land of Kalma,
Even nine for magic heroes,
Till the years bring consolation,
Till they quiet all his mourning."
Kullerwoinen, wicked wizard,
Answers thus his grieving mother:
"Shall not haste to hide
from sorrow,
Shall not flee from my misconduct;
To the jaws of death I hasten,
To the open courts of Kalma,
To the hunting-grounds of Pohya,
To the battle-fields of heroes.
Untamoinen still is living,
Unmolested roams the wicked,
Unavenged my father's grievance,
Unavenged my mother's tortures,
Unavenged the wrongs I suffer!"

Rune XXXVI: Kullerwoinen's Victory and Death

Kullerwoinen, wicked wizard,
In his purple-coloured stockings,
Now prepares himself for battle;
Grinds a long time on his broadsword,
Sharpens well his trusty weapon,
And his mother speaks as follows:
"Do not go, my son beloved,
Go not to the wars, my hero,
Struggle not with hostile spearsmen.
Whoso goes to war for nothing,
Undertakes a fearful combat,
Undertakes a fatal issue;
Those that war without a reason
Will be slaughtered for their folly,
Easy prey to bows and arrows.
Go thou with a goat to battle,
Shouldst thou go to fight
the roebuck,
'Tis the goat that will be vanquished,
And the roebuck will be slaughtered;
With a frog thou'lt journey homeward,
Victor, with but little honour!"
These the words of Kullerwoinen:
"Shall not journey through the marshes,
Shall not sink upon the heather,
On the home-land of the raven,
Where the eagles scream at day-break.
When I yield my life forever,
Bravely will I fall in battle,
Fall upon the field of glory,
Beautiful to die in armor,
And the clang and clash of armies,
Beautiful the strife for conquest!
Thus Kullervo soon will hasten
To the kingdom of Tuoni,
To the realm of the departed,
Undeformed by wasting sickness."
This the answer of the mother:
"If thou diest in the conflict,
Who will stay to guard thy father,
Who will give thy sire protection?"
These the words of Kullerwoinen:
"Let him die upon the court-yard,
Sleeping out his life of sorrow!"

"Who then will protect thy mother,
Be her shield in times of danger?"

"Let her die within the stable,
Or the cabin where she lingers!"

"Who then will defend thy brother,
Give him aid in times of trouble?"

"Let him die within the forest,
Sleep his life away unheeded!"

"Who will comfort then thy sister,
Who will aid her in affliction?"

"Let her sink beneath the waters,
Perish in the crystal fountain,
Where the brook flows on in beauty,
Like a silver serpent winding
Through the valley to the ocean!"

Thereupon the wild Kullervo
Hastens from his home to battle,
To his father speaks, departing:
"Fare thou well, my aged father!
Wilt thou weep for me, thy hero,
When thou hearest I have perished,
Fallen from thy tribe forever,
Perished on the field of glory?"
Thus the father speaks in answer:
"I shall never mourn the downfall
Of my evil son, Kullervo;
Shall not weep when thou hast perished;
Shall beget a second hero
That will do me better service,
That will think and act in wisdom."
Kullerwoinen gives this answer:
"Neither shall I mourn thy downfall,
Shall not weep when thou hast perished;
I shall make a second father,
Make the head from loam and sandstone,
Make the eyes from swamp-land berries,
Make the beard from withered sea-grass,
Make the feet from roots of willow,
Make the form from birch-wood fungus."

Thereupon the youth, Kullervo,
To his brother speaks as follows:
"Fare thou well, beloved brother!
Wilt thou weep for me departed,
Shouldst thou hear that I have perished,
Fallen on the field of battle?"
This the answer of the brother:
"I shall never mourn the downfall
Of my brother, Kullerwoinen,
Shall not weep when thou hast perished;
I shall find a second brother,
Find one worthier and wiser!"
This is Kullerwoinen's answer:
"Neither shall I mourn thy downfall,
Shall not weep when thou hast perished;
I shall form a second brother,
Make the head from dust and ashes,
Make the eyes from pearls of ocean,
Make the beard from withered verdure,
Make the form from pulp of birch-wood."
To his sister speaks Kullervo:
"Fare thou well, beloved sister!
Surely thou wilt mourn my downfall,
Weep for me when I have perished,
When thou hearest I have fallen
In the heat and din of battle,
Fallen from thy race forever!"
But the sister makes this answer:
"Never shall I mourn thy downfall,
Shall not weep when thou hast perished;
I shall seek a second brother,
Seek a brother, purer, better,
One that will not shame his sister!"
Kullerwoinen thus makes answer:
"Neither shall I mourn thee fallen,
Shall not weep when thou hast perished;
I shall form a second sister,
Make the head from whitened marble,
Make the eyes from golden moonbeams,
Make the tresses from the rainbow,
Make the ears from ocean-flowers,
And her form from gold and silver.

"Fare thou well, beloved mother,
Mother, beautiful and faithful!
Wilt thou weep when I have perished,
Fallen on the field of glory,
Fallen from thy race forever?"
Thus the mother speaks in answer:
"Canst not fathom love maternal,
Canst not smother her affection;
Bitterly I'll mourn thy downfall,
I would weep if thou shouldst perish,
Shouldst thou leave my race forever;
I would weep in court or cabin,
Sprinkle all these fields with tear-drops,
Weep great rivers to the ocean,
Weep to melt the snows of Northland,
Make the hillocks green with weeping,
Weep at morning, weep at evening,

Weep three years in bitter sorrow
O'er the death of Kullerwoinen!"

Thereupon the wicked wizard
Went rejoicing to the combat;
In delight to war he hastened
O'er the fields, and fens, and fallows,
Shouting loudly on the heather,
Singing o'er the hills and mountains,
Rushing through the glens and forests,
Blowing war upon his bugle.

Time had gone but little distance,
When a messenger appearing,
Spake these words to Kullerwoinen:
"Lo! thine aged sire has perished,
Fallen from thy race forever;
Hasten home and do him honour,
Lay him in the lap of Kalma."
Kullerwoinen made this answer:
"Has my aged father perished,
There is home a sable stallion
That will take him to his slumber,
Lay him in the lap of Kalma."

Then Kullervo journeyed onward,
Calling war upon his bugle,
Till a messenger appearing,
Brought this word to Kullerwoinen:
"Lo! thy brother too has perished,
Dead he lies within the forest,
Manalainen's trumpet called him;
Home return and do him honour,
Lay him in the lap of Kalma."
Kullerwoinen thus replying:
"Has my hero-brother perished,
There is home a sable stallion
That will take him to his slumber,
Lay him in the lap of Kalma."

Young Kullervo journeyed onward
Over vale and over mountain,
Playing on his reed of battle,
Till a messenger appearing
Brought the warrior these tidings:
"Lo! thy sister too has perished,
Perished in the crystal fountain,
Where the waters flow in beauty,
Like a silver serpent winding
Through the valley to the ocean;
Home return and do her honour,
Lay her in the lap of Kalma."
These the words of Kullerwoinen:
"Has my beauteous sister perished,
Fallen from my race forever,
There is home a sable filly
That will take her to her resting,
Lay her in the lap of Kalma."

Still Kullervo journeyed onward,
Through the fens he went rejoicing,
Sounding war upon his bugle,
Till a messenger appearing
Brought to him these words of sorrow:
"Lo! thy mother too has perished,
Died in anguish, broken-hearted;
Home return and do her honour,
Lay her in the lap of Kalma."
These the measures of Kullervo:
"Woe is me, my life hard-fated,
That my mother too has perished,
She that nursed me in my cradle,
Made my couch a golden cover,
Twirled for me the spool and spindle!
Lo! Kullervo was not present
When his mother's life departed;
May have died upon the mountains,
Perished there from cold and hunger.
Lave the dead form of my mother
In the crystal waters flowing;
Wrap her in the robes of ermine,
Tie her hands with silken ribbon,
Take her to the grave of ages,
Lay her in the lap of Kalma.
Bury her with songs of mourning,
Let the singers chant my sorrow;
Cannot leave the fields of battle
While Untamo goes unpunished,
Fell destroyer of my people."

Kullerwoinen journeyed onward,
Still rejoicing, to the combat,
Sang these songs in supplication:
"Ukko, mightiest of rulers,

Loan to me thy sword of battle,
Grant to me thy matchless weapon,
And against a thousand armies
I will war and ever conquer."
Ukko gave the youth his broadsword,
Gave his blade of magic powers
To the wizard, Kullerwoinen.
Thus equipped, the mighty hero
Slew the people of Untamo,
Burned their villages to ashes;
Only left the stones and ovens,
And the chimneys of their hamlets.

Then the conqueror, Kullervo,
Turned his footsteps to his home-land,
To the cabin of his father,
To his ancient fields and forests.
Empty did he find the cabin,
And the forests were deserted;
No one came to give him greeting,
None to give the hand of welcome;
Laid his fingers on the oven,
But he found it cold and lifeless;
Then he knew to satisfaction
That his mother lived no longer;
Laid his hand upon the fire-place,
Cold and lifeless were the
hearth-stones;
Then he knew to satisfaction
That his sister too had perished;
Then he sought the landing-places,
Found no boats upon the rollers;
Then he knew to satisfaction
That his brother too had perished;
Then he looked upon the fish-nets,
And he found them torn and tangled;
And he knew to satisfaction
That his father too had perished.

Bitterly he wept and murmured,
Wept one day, and then a second,
On the third day spake as follows:
"Faithful mother, fond and tender,
Why hast left me here to sorrow
In this wilderness of trouble?
But thou dost not hear my calling,
Though I sing in magic accents,
Though my tear-drops speak lamenting,
Though my heart bemoans thine absence."

From her grave awakes the mother,
To Kullervo speaks these measures:
"Thou has still the dog remaining,
He will lead thee to the forest;
Follow thou the faithful watcher,
Let him lead thee to the woodlands,
To the farthest woodland border,
To the caverns of the wood-nymphs;
There the forest maidens linger,
They will give thee food and shelter,
Give my hero joyful greetings."

Kullerwoinen, with his watch-dog,
Hastens onward through the forest,
Journeys on through fields and fallows;
Journeys but a little distance,
Till he comes upon the summit
Where he met his long-lost sister;
Finds the turf itself is weeping,
Finds the glen-wood filled with sorrow,
Finds the heather shedding tear-drops,
Weeping are the meadow-flowers,
O'er the ruin of his sister.

Kullerwoinen, wicked wizard,
Grasps the handle of his broadsword,
Asks the blade this simple question:
"Tell me, O my blade of honour,
Dost thou wish to drink my life-blood,
Drink the blood of Kullerwoinen?"

Thus his trusty sword makes answer,
Well divining his intentions:
"Why should I not drink thy life-blood,
Blood of guilty Kullerwoinen,
Since I feast upon the worthy,
Drink the life-blood of the righteous?"

Thereupon the youth, Kullervo,
Wicked wizard of the Northland,
Lifts the mighty sword of Ukko,
Bids adieu to earth and heaven;
Firmly thrusts the hilt in heather,
To his heart he points the weapon,

Throws his weight upon his broadsword,
Pouring out his wicked life-blood,
Ere he journeys to Manala.
Thus the wizard finds destruction,
This the end of Kullerwoinen,
Born in sin, and nursed in folly.

Wainamoinen, ancient minstrel,
As he hears the joyful tidings,
Learns the death of fell Kullervo,
Speaks these words of ancient wisdom:
"O, ye many unborn nations,
Never evil nurse your children,
Never give them out to strangers,
Never trust them to the foolish!
If the child is not well nurtured,
Is not rocked and led uprightly,
Though he grow to years of manhood,
Bear a strong and shapely body,
He will never know discretion,
Never eat the bread of honour,
Never drink the cup of wisdom."

Rune XXXVII: Ilmarinen's Bride of Gold

Ilmarinen, metal-worker,
Wept one day, and then a second,
Wept the third from morn till evening,
O'er the death of his companion,
Once the Maiden of the Rainbow;
Did not swing his heavy hammer,
Did not touch its copper handle,
Made no sound within his smithy,
Made no blow upon his anvil,
Till three months had circled over;
Then the blacksmith spake as follows:
"Woe is me, unhappy hero!
Do not know how I can prosper;
Long the days, and cold, and dreary,
Longer still the nights, and colder;
I am weary in the evening,
In the morning still am weary,
Have no longing for the morning,
And the evening is unwelcome;
Have no pleasure in the future,
All my pleasures gone forever,
With my faithful life-companion
Slaughtered by the hand of witchcraft!
Often will my heart-strings quiver
When I rest within my chamber,
When I wake at dreamy midnight,
Half-unconscious, vainly searching
For my noble wife departed."

Wifeless lived the mourning blacksmith,
Altered in his form and features;
Wept one month and then another,
Wept three months in full succession.
Then the magic metal-worker
Gathered gold from deeps
of ocean,
Gathered silver from the mountains,
Gathered many heaps of birch-wood.
Filled with fagots thirty sledges,
Burned the birch-wood into ashes;
Put the ashes in the furnace,
Laid the gold upon the embers,
Lengthwise laid a piece of silver
Of the size of lambs in autumn,
Or the fleet-foot hare in winter;
Places servants at the bellows,
Thus to melt the magic metals.
Eagerly the servants labour,
Gloveless, hatless, do the workmen
Fan the flames within the furnace.

Ilmarinen, magic blacksmith,
Works unceasing at his forging,
Thus to mould a golden image,
Mould a bride from gold and silver;
But the workmen fail their master,
Faithless stand they at the bellows.
Wow the artist, Ilmarinen,
Fans the flame with force
of magic,
Blows one day, and then a second,
Blows the third from morn till even;
Then he looks within the furnace,
Looks around the oven-border,
Hoping there to see an image
Rising from the molten metals.

Comes a lambkin from the furnace,
Rising from the fire of magic,
Wearing hair of gold and copper,
Laced with many threads of silver;
All rejoice but Ilmarinen
At the beauty of the image.
This the language of
the blacksmith:
"May the wolf admire thy graces;
I desire a bride of beauty
Born from molten gold
and silver!"

Ilmarinen, the magician,
To the furnace threw the lambkin;
Added gold in great abundance,
And increased the mass of silver,
Added other magic metals,
Set the workmen at the bellows;
Zealously the servants labour,
Gloveless, hatless, do
the workmen
Fan the flames within the furnace.

Ilmarinen, wizard-forgeman,
Works unceasing with his metals,
Moulding well a golden image,
Wife of molten gold and silver;
But the workmen fail their master,
Faithless do they ply the bellows.

Now the artist, Ilmarinen,
Fans the flames by force of magic;
Blows one day, and then a second,
Blows a third from morn till evening,
When he looks within the furnace,
Looks around the oven-border,
Hoping there to see an image
Rising from the molten metals.
From the flames a colt arises,
Golden-maned and silver-headed,
Hoofs are formed of shining copper.
All rejoice but Ilmarinen
At the wonderful creation;
This the language of
the blacksmith:
"Let the bears admire thy graces;
I desire a bride of beauty
Born of many magic metals."
Thereupon the wonder-forger
Drives the colt back to the furnace,
Adds a greater mass of silver,
And of gold the rightful measure,
Sets the workmen at the bellows.
Eagerly the servants labour,
Gloveless, hatless, do
the workmen
Fan the flames within the furnace.

Ilmarinen, the magician,
Works unceasing at his witchcraft,
Moulding well a golden maiden,
Bride of molten gold and silver;
But the workmen fail their master,
Faithlessly they ply the bellows.

Now the blacksmith, Ilmarinen,
Fans the flames with magic powers,
Blows one day, and then a second,
Blows a third from morn till even;
Then he looks within his furnace,
Looks around the oven-border,
Trusting there to see a maiden
Coming from the molten metals.
From the fire a virgin rises,
Golden-haired and silver-headed,
Beautiful in form and feature.
All are filled with awe
and wonder,
But the artist and magician.
Ilmarinen, metal-worker,
Forges nights and days unceasing,
On the bride of his creation;
Feet he forges for the maiden,
Hands and arms, of gold and silver;
But her feet are not for walking,
Neither can her arms embrace him.
Ears he forges for the virgin,
But her ears are not for hearing;
Forges her a mouth of beauty,
Eyes he forges bright and sparkling;
But the magic mouth is speechless,
And the eyes are not for seeing.
Spake the artist, Ilmarinen:

"This, indeed, a priceless maiden,
Could she only speak in wisdom,
Could she breathe the breath
of Ukko!"
Thereupon he lays the virgin
On his silken couch of slumber,
On his downy place of resting.
Ilmarinen heats his bath-room,
Makes it ready for his service,
Binds together silken brushes,
Brings three cans of crystal water,
Wherewithal to lave the image,
Lave the golden maid of beauty.
When this task had been completed,
Ilmarinen, hoping, trusting,
Laid his golden bride to slumber,
On his downy couch of resting;
Ordered many silken wrappings,
Ordered bear-skins, three
in number,
Ordered seven lambs-wool blankets,
Thus to keep him warm in slumber,
Sleeping by the golden image
He had forged from magic metals.
Warm the side of Ilmarinen
That was wrapped in furs
and blankets;
Chill the parts beside the maiden,
By his bride of gold and silver;
One side warm, the
other lifeless,
Turning into ice from coldness.
Spake the artist, Ilmarinen:
"Not for me was born this virgin
From the magic molten metals;
I shall take her to Wainola,
Give her to old Wainamoinen,
As a bride and life-companion,
Comfort to him in his dotage."

Ilmarinen, much disheartened,
Takes the virgin to Wainola,
To the plains of Kalevala,
To his brother speaks as follows:
"O, thou ancient Wainamoinen,
Look with favour on this image;
Make the maiden fair and lovely,
Beautiful in form and feature,
Suited to thy years declining!"

Wainamoinen, old and truthful,
Looked in wonder on the virgin,
On the golden bride of beauty,
Spake these words to Ilmarinen:
"Wherefore dost thou bring this maiden,
Wherefore bring to Wainamoinen
Bride of molten gold and silver?"
Spake in answer Ilmarinen:
"Wherefore should I bring this image,
But for purposes the noblest?
I have brought her as companion
To thy life in years declining,
As a joy and consolation,
When thy days are full of trouble!"
Spake the good, old Wainamoinen:
"Magic brother, wonder-forger,
Throw the virgin to the furnace,
To the flames, thy golden image,
Forge from her a thousand trinkets.
Take the image into Ehstland,
Take her to the plains of Pohya,
That for her the mighty powers
May engage in deadly contest,
Worthy trophy for the victor;
Not for me this bride of wonder,
Neither for my worthy people.
I shall never wed an image
Born from many magic metals,
Never wed a silver maiden,
Never wed a golden virgin."
Then the hero of the waters
Called together all his people,
Spake these words of
ancient wisdom:
"Every child of Northland, listen,
Whether poor, or fortune-favoured:
Never bow before an image
Born of molten gold and silver;
Never while the sunlight brightens,
Never while the moonlight glimmers,
Choose a maiden of the metals,
Choose a bride from gold created;
Cold the lips of golden maiden,
Silver breathes the breath of sorrow."

Rune XXXVIII: Ilmarinen's Fruitless Wooing

Ilmarinen, the magician,
The eternal metal-artist,
Lays aside the golden image,
Beauteous maid of magic metals;
Throws the harness on his courser,
Binds him to his sledge of
birch-wood,
Seats himself upon the cross-bench,
Snaps the whip above the racer,
Thinking once again to journey
To the mansions of Pohyola,
There to woo a bride in honour,
Second daughter of the Northland.

On he journeyed, restless, northward,
Journeyed one day, then a second,
So the third from morn till evening,
When he reached a Northland-village
On the plains of Sariola.

Louhi, hostess of Pohyola,
Standing in the open court-yard,
Spied the hero, Ilmarinen,
Thus addressed the metal-worker:
"Tell me how my child is living,
How the Bride of Beauty prospers,
As a daughter to thy mother."

Then the blacksmith, Ilmarinen,
Head bent down and brow dejected,
Thus addressed the Northland hostess:
"O, thou dame of Sariola,
Do not ask me of thy daughter,
Since, alas! in Tuonela
Sleeps the Maiden of the Rainbow,
Sleeps in death the Bride of Beauty,
Underneath the fragrant heather,
In the kingdom of Manala.
Come I for a second daughter,
For the fairest of thy virgins.
Beauteous hostess of Pohyola,
Give to me thy youngest maiden,
For my former wife's compartments,
For the chambers of
her sister."

Louhi, hostess of the Northland,
Spake these words to Ilmarinen:
"Foolish was the Northland-hostess,
When she gave her fairest virgin,
In the bloom of youth and beauty
To the blacksmith of Wainola,
Only to be led to Mana,
Like a lambkin to the slaughter!
I shall never give my daughter,
Shall not give my youngest maiden
Bride of thine to be hereafter,
Life-companion at thy fireside.
Sooner would I give the fair one
To the cataract and whirlpool,
To the river of Manala,
To the waters of Tuoni!"

Then the blacksmith, Ilmarinen,
Drew away his head, disdainful,
Shook his sable locks in anger,
Entered to the inner court-room,
Where the maiden sat in waiting,
Spake these measures to the daughter:
"Come with me, thou bright-eyed maiden,
To the cottage where thy sister
Lived and lingered in contentment,
Baked for me the toothsome biscuit,
Brewed for me the beer of barley,
Kept my dwelling-place in order."

On the floor a babe was lying,
Thus he sang to Ilmarinen:
"Uninvited, leave this mansion,
Go, thou stranger, from this dwelling;
Once before thou camest hither,
Only bringing pain and trouble,
Filling all our hearts with sorrow.
Fairest daughter of my mother,
Do not give this suitor welcome,
Look not on his eyes with pleasure,
Nor admire his form and features.
In his mouth are only wolf-teeth,
Cunning fox-claws in his mittens,
In his shoes art only bear-claws,
In his belt a hungry dagger;

Weapons these of blood and murder,
Only worn by the unworthy."

Then the daughter spake as follows
To the blacksmith, Ilmarinen:
"Follow thee this maid will never,
Never heed unworthy suitors;
Thou hast slain the Bride of Beauty,
Once the Maiden of the Rainbow,
Thou wouldst also slay her sister.
I deserve a better suitor,
Wish a truer, nobler husband,
Wish to ride in richer sledges,
Have a better home-protection;
Never will I sweep the cottage
And the coal-place of a blacksmith."

Then the hero, Ilmarinen,
The eternal metal-artist,
Turned his head away, disdainful,
Shook his sable locks in anger,
Quickly seized the trembling maiden,
Held her in his grasp of iron,
Hastened from the court of Louhi,
To his sledge upon the highway.
In his sleigh he seats the virgin,
Snugly wraps her in his fur-robes,
Snaps his whip above the racer,
Gallops on the high-road homeward;
With one hand the reins he tightens,
With the other holds the maiden.
Speaks the virgin-daughter, weeping:
"We have reached the lowland-berries,
Here the herbs of water-borders;
Leave me here to sink and perish
As a child of cold misfortune.
Wicked Ilmarinen, listen!
If thou dost not quickly free me,
I will break thy sledge to pieces,
Throw thy fur-robes to the north winds."
Ilmarinen makes this answer:
"When the blacksmith builds his snow-sledge,
All the parts are hooped with iron;
Therefore will the beauteous maiden
Never beat my sledge to fragments."

Then the silver-tinselled daughter
Wept and wailed in bitter accents,
Wrung her hands in desperation,
Spake again to Ilmarinen:
"If thou dost not quickly free me,
I shall change to ocean-salmon,
Be a whiting of the waters."

"Thou wilt never thus escape me,
As a pike I'll fleetly follow."

Then the maiden of Pohyola
Wept and wailed in bitter accents,
Wrung her hands in desperation,
Spake again to Ilmarinen;
"If thou dost not quickly free me,
I shall hasten to the forest,
Mid the rocks become an ermine!"

"Thou wilt never thus escape me,
As a serpent I will follow."

Then the beauty of the Northland,
Wailed and wept in bitter accents,
Wrung her hands in desperation,
Spake once more to Ilmarinen:
"Surely, if thou dost not free me,
As a lark I'll fly the ether,
Hide myself within the storm-clouds."

"Neither wilt thou thus escape me,
As an eagle I will follow."

They had gone but little distance,
When the courser shied and halted,
Frighted at some passing object;
And the maiden looked in wonder,
In the snow beheld some foot-prints,
Spake these words to Ilmarinen:
"Who has run across our highway?"

"'Tis the timid hare", he answered.
Thereupon the stolen maiden
Sobbed, and moaned, in deeps of sorrow,
Heavy-hearted, spake these measures:
"Woe is me, ill-fated virgin!
Happier far my life hereafter,

If the hare I could but follow
To his burrow in the woodlands!
Crook-leg's fur to me is finer
Than the robes of Ilmarinen."

Ilmarinen, the magician,
Tossed his head in full resentment,
Galloped on the highway homeward;
Travelled but a little distance,
When again his courser halted,
Frighted at some passing stranger.
Quick the maiden looked and wondered,
In the snow beheld some foot-prints,
Spake these measures to the blacksmith:
"Who has crossed our snowy pathway?"

"'Tis a fox", replied the minstrel.
Thereupon the beauteous virgin
Moaned again in depths of anguish,
Sang these accents, heavy-hearted:
"Woe is me, ill-fated maiden!
Happier far my life hereafter,
With the cunning fox to wander,
Than with this ill-mannered suitor;
Reynard's fur to me is finer
Than the robes of Ilmarinen."

Thereupon the metal-worker
Shut his lips in sore displeasure,
Hastened on the highway homeward;
Travelled but a little distance,
When again his courser halted.

Quick the maiden looked in wonder,
In the snow beheld some foot-prints,
Spake these words to the magician:
"Who again has crossed our pathway?"

"'Tis the wolf", said Ilmarinen.
Thereupon the fated daughter
Fell again to bitter weeping,
And intoned these words of sorrow:
"Woe is me, a hapless maiden!
Happier far my life hereafter,
Brighter far would be my future,
If these tracks I could but follow;
On the wolf the hair is finer
Than the furs of Ilmarinen,
Faithless suitor of the Northland."

Then the minstrel of Wainola
Closed his lips again in anger,
Shook his sable locks, resentful,
Snapped the whip above the racer,
And the steed flew onward swiftly,
O'er the way to Kalevala,
To the village of the blacksmith.

Sad and weary from his journey,
Ilmarinen, home-returning,
Fell upon his couch in slumber,
And the maiden laughed derision.

In the morning, slowly waking,
Head confused, and locks dishevelled,
Spake the wizard, words as follow:
"Shall I set myself to singing
Magic songs and incantations?
Shall I now enchant this maiden
To a black-wolf on the mountains,
To a salmon of the ocean?
Shall not send her to the woodlands,
All the forest would be frighted;
Shall not send her to the waters,
All the fish would flee in terror;
This my sword shall drink her life-blood,
End her reign of scorn and hatred."

Quick the sword feels his intention,
Quick divines his evil purpose,
Speaks these words to Ilmarinen:
"Was not born to drink the life-blood
Of a maiden pure and lovely,
Of a fair but helpless virgin."

Thereupon the magic minstrel,
Filled with rage, began his singing;
Sang the very rocks asunder,
Till the distant hills re-echoed;
Sang the maiden to a sea-gull,
Croaking from the ocean-ledges,
Calling from the ocean-islands,
Screeching on the sandy sea-coast,
Flying to the winds opposing.

When his conjuring had ended,
Ilmarinen joined his snow-sledge,
Whipped his steed upon a gallop,
Hastened to his ancient smithy,
To his home in Kalevala.

Wainamoinen, old and truthful,
Comes to meet him on the highway,
Speaks these words to the magician:
"Ilmarinen, worthy brother,
Wherefore comest heavy-hearted
From the dismal Sariola?
Does Pohyola live and prosper?"
Spake the minstrel, Ilmarinen:
"Why should not Pohyola prosper?
There the Sampo grinds unceasing,
Noisy rocks the lid in colours;
Grinds one day the flour for eating,
Grinds the second flour for selling,
Grinds the third day flour for keeping;
Thus it is Pohyola prospers.
While the Sampo is in Northland,
There is plowing, there is sowing,
There is growth of every virtue,
There is welfare never-ending."
Spake the ancient Wainamoinen:
"Ilmarinen, artist-brother,
Where then is the Northland-daughter,
Far renowned and beauteous maiden,
For whose hand thou hast
been absent?"
These the words of Ilmarinen:
"I have changed the hateful virgin
To a sea-gull on the ocean;
Now she calls above the waters,
Screeches from the ocean-islands;
On the rocks she calls and murmurs,
Vainly calling for a suitor."

Rune XXXIX: Wainamoinen's Sailing

Wainamoinen, old and faithful,
Spake these words to Ilmarinen:
"O thou wonder-working brother,
Let us go to Sariola,
There to gain the magic Sampo,
There to see the lid in colours."
Ilmarinen gave this answer:
"Hard indeed to seize the Sampo,
Neither can the lid be captured
From the never-pleasant Northland,
From the dismal Sariola.
Louhi took away the Sampo,
Carried off the lid in colours
To the stone-mount of Pohyola;
Hid it in the copper mountain,
Where nine locks secure the treasure.
Many young roots sprout around it,
Grow nine fathoms deep in sand-earth,
One great root beneath the mountain,
In the cataract a second,
And a third beneath the castle
Built upon the mount of ages."
Spake the ancient Wainamoinen:
"Brother mine, and wonder-worker,
Let us go to Sariola,
That we may secure the Sampo;
Let us build a goodly vessel,
Bring the Sampo to Wainola,
Bring away the lid in colours,
From the stone-berg of Pohyola,
From the copper-bearing mountain.
Where the miracle lies anchored."
Ilmarinen thus made answer:
"By the land the way is safer,
Lempo travels on the ocean,
Ghastly Death upon his shoulder;
On the sea the waves will drift us,
And the storm-winds wreck our vessel;
Then our hands must do the rowing,
And our feet must steer us homeward."
Spake the ancient Wainamoinen:
"Safe indeed by land to journey,
But the way is rough and trying,
Long the road and full of turnings;
Lovely is the ship on ocean,
Beautiful to ride the billows,
Journey easy o'er the waters,
Sailing in a trusty vessel;
Should the West-wind cross our pathway,
Will the South-wind drive us northward.

Be that as it may, my brother,
Since thou dost not love the water,
By the land then let us journey.
Forge me now the sword of battle,
Forge for me the mighty fire-sword,
That I may destroy the wild-beasts,
Frighten all the Northland people,
As we journey for the Sampo
To the cold and dismal village,
To the never-pleasant Northland,
To the dismal Sariola."

Then the blacksmith, Ilmarinen,
The eternal forger-artist,
Laid the metals in the furnace,
In the fire laid steel and iron,
In the hot-coals, gold and silver,
Rightful measure of the metals;
Set the workmen at the furnace,
Lustily they plied the bellows.
Like the wax the iron melted,
Like the dough the hard steel softened,
Like the water ran the silver,
And the liquid gold flowed after.

Then the minstrel, Ilmarinen,
The eternal wonder-forger,
Looks within his magic furnace,
On the border of his oven,
There beholds the fire-sword forming,
Sees the blade with golden handle;
Takes the weapon from the furnace,
Lays it on his heavy anvil
For the falling of the hammer;
Forges well the blade of magic,
Well the heavy sword he tempers,
Ornaments the hero-weapon
With the finest gold and silver.

Wainamoinen, the magician,
Comes to view the blade of conquest,
Lifts admiringly the fire-sword,
Then these words the hero utters:
"Does the weapon match the soldier,
Does the handle suit the bearer?
Yea, the blade and hilt are moulded
To the wishes of the minstrel."
On the sword-point gleams the moonlight,
On the blade the sun is shining,
On the hilt the bright stars twinkle,
On the edge a horse is neighing,
On the handle plays a kitten,
On the sheath a dog is barking.

Wainamoinen wields his fire-sword,
Tests it on the iron-mountain,
And these words the hero utters:
"With this broadsword I could quickly
Cleave in twain the mount of Pohya,
Cut the flinty rocks asunder."
Spake the blacksmith, Ilmarinen:
"Wherewith shall I guard from danger,
How protect myself from evil,
From the ills by land and water?
Shall I wear an iron armor,
Belt of steel around my body?
Stronger is a man in armor,
Safer in a mail of copper."

Now the time has come to journey
To the never-pleasant Northland;
Wainamoinen, ancient minstrel,
And his brother, Ilmarinen,
Hasten to the field and forest,
Searching for their fiery coursers,
In each shining belt a bridle,
With a harness on their shoulders.
In the woods they find a race;
In the glen a steed of battle,
Ready for his master's service.
Wainamoinen, old and trusty,
And the blacksmith, Ilmarinen,
Throw the harness on the courser,
Hitch him to the sledge of conquest,
Hasten on their journey northward;
Drive along the broad sea's margin
Till they hear someone lamenting,
On the strand hear something wailing
Near the landing-place of vessels.

Wainamoinen, ancient minstrel,
Speaks these words in wonder, guessing:
"This must be some maiden weeping,
Some fair daughter thus lamenting;

Let us journey somewhat nearer,
To discover whence this wailing."

Drew they nearer, nearer, nearer,
Hoping thus to find a maiden
Weeping on the sandy seashore.
It was not a maiden weeping,
But a vessel, sad, and lonely,
Waiting on the shore and wailing.
Spake the ancient Wainamoinen:
"Why art weeping, goodly vessel,
What the cause of thy lamenting?
Art thou mourning for thy row-locks,
Is thy rigging ill-adjusted?
Dost thou weep since thou art anchored
On the shore in times of trouble?"
Thus the war-ship spake in answer:
"To the waters would this vessel
Haste upon the well-tarred rollers,
As a happy maiden journeys
To the cottage of her husband.
I, alas! a goodly vessel,
Weep because I lie at anchor,
Weep and wail because no hero
Sets me free upon the waters,
Free to ride the rolling billows.
It was said when I was fashioned,
Often sung when I was building,
That this bark should be for battle,
Should become a mighty war-ship,
Carry in my hull great treasures,
Priceless goods across the ocean.
Never have I sailed to conquest,
Never have I carried booty;
Other vessels not as worthy
To the wars are ever sailing,
Sailing to the songs of battle.
Three times in the summer season
Come they home with treasures laden,
In their hulls bring gold and silver;
I, alas! a worthy vessel,
Many months have lain at anchor,
I, a war-ship well constructed,
Am decaying in the harbor,
Never having sailed to conquest;
Worms are gnawing at my vitals,
In my hull their dwelling-places,
And ill-omened birds of heaven
Build their nests within my rigging;
Frogs and lizards of the forest
Play about my oars and rudder;
Three times better for this vessel
Were he but a valley birch-tree,
Or an aspen on the heather,
With the squirrels in his branches,
And the dogs beneath them barking!"

Wainamoinen, old and faithful,
Thus addressed the ship at anchor:
"Weep no more, thou goodly vessel,
Man-of-war, no longer murmur;
Thou shalt sail to Sariola,
Sing the war-songs of the Northland,
Sail with us to deadly combat.
Wert thou built by the Creator,
Thou canst sail the roughest waters,
Sidewise journey o'er the ocean;
Dost not need the hand to touch thee,
Dost not need the foot to turn thee,
Needing nothing to propel thee."
Thus the weeping boat made answer:
"Cannot sail without assistance,
Neither can my brother-vessels
Sail unaided o'er the waters,
Sail across the waves undriven."
Spake the ancient Wainamoinen:
"Should I lead thee to the broad sea,
Wilt thou journey north unaided,
Sail without the help of rowers,
Sail without the aid of south winds,
Sail without the helm to guide thee?"
Thus the wailing ship replying:
"Cannot sail without assistance,
Neither can my brother-vessels
Sail without the aid of rowers,
Sail without the help of south winds,
Nor without the helm to guide them."
These the words of Wainamoinen:
"Wilt thou run with aid of oarsmen
When the south winds give assistance,
Guided by a skillful pilot?"
This the answer of the war-ship:
"Quickly can I course these waters,
When my oars are manned by rowers,

When my sails are filled with south winds,
All my goodly brother-vessels
Sail the ocean with assistance,
When the master holds the rudder."

Then the ancient Wainamoinen
Left the racer on the sea-side,
Tied him to the sacred birch-tree,
Hung the harness on a willow,
Rolled the vessel to the waters,
Sang the ship upon the broad sea,
Asked the boat this simple question:
"O thou vessel, well appearing
From the mighty oak constructed,
Art thou strong to carry treasures
As in view thou art commanding?"
Thus the goodly ship made answer:
"Strong am I to carry treasures,
In my hull a golden cargo;
I can bear a hundred oarsmen,
And of warriors a thousand."

Wainamoinen, the magician,
Then began his wondrous singing.
On one side the magic vessel,
Sang he youth with golden virtues,
Bearded youth with strength of heroes,
Sang them into mail of copper.
On the other side the vessel,
Sang he silver-tinselled maidens,
Girded them with belts of copper,
Golden rings upon their fingers.
Sings again the great magician,
Fills the magic ship with heroes,
Ancient heroes, brave and mighty;
Sings them into narrow limits,
Since the young men came before them.

At the helm himself he seated,
Near the last beam of the vessel,
Steered his goodly boat in joyance,
Thus addressed the willing war-ship:
"Glide upon the trackless waters,
Sail away, my ship of magic,
Sail across the waves before thee,
Speed thou like a dancing bubble,
Like a flower upon the billows!"

Then the ancient Wainamoinen
Set the young men to the rowing,
Let the maidens sit in waiting.
Eagerly the youthful heroes
Bend the oars and try the row-locks,
But the distance is not lessened.
Then the minstrel, Wainamoinen,
Set the maidens to the rowing,
Let the young men rest in waiting.
Eagerly the merry maidens
Bend the aspen-oars in rowing,
But the distance is not lessened.
Then the master, Wainamoinen,
Set the old men to the rowing,
Let the youth remain in waiting.
Lustily the aged heroes
Bend and try the oars of aspen,
But the distance is not lessened.

Then the blacksmith, Ilmarinen,
Grasped the oars with master-magic,
And the boat leaped o'er the surges,
Swiftly sped across the billows;
Far and wide the oars resounded,
Quickly was the distance lessened.
With a rush and roar of waters
Ilmarinen sped his vessel,
Benches, ribs, and row-locks creaking,
Oars of aspen far resounding;
Flap the sails like wings of moor-cocks,
And the prow dips like a white-swan;
In the rear it croaks like ravens,
Loud the oars and rigging rattle.

Straightway ancient Wainamoinen,
Sitting by the bending rudder,
Turns his magic vessel landward,
To a jutting promontory,
Where appears a Northland-village.
On the point stands Lemminkainen,
Kaukomieli, black magician,
Ahti, wizard of Wainola,
Wishing for the fish of Pohya,
Weeping for his fated dwelling,
For his perilous adventures,
Hard at work upon a vessel,

On the sail-yards of a fish-boat,
Near the hunger-point and island,
Near the village-home deserted.
Good the ears of the magician,
Good the wizard's eyes for seeing;
Casts his vision to the southeast,
Turns his eyes upon the sunset,
Sees afar a wondrous rainbow,
Farther on, a cloudlet hanging;
But the bow was a deception,
And the cloudlet a delusion;
'Tis a vessel swiftly sailing,
'Tis a war-ship flying northward,
O'er the blue back of the broad sea,
On the far-extending waters,
At the helm the master standing,
At the oars a mighty hero.
Spake the reckless Lemminkainen:
"Do not know this wondrous vessel,
Not this well-constructed war-ship,
Coming from the distant Suomi,
Rowing for the hostile Pohya."

Thereupon wild Lemminkainen
Called aloud in tones of thunder
O'er the waters to the vessel;
Made the distant hills re-echo
With the music of his calling:
"Whence this vessel on the waters,
Whose the war-ship sailing hither?"

Spake the master of the vessel
To the reckless Lemminkainen:
"Who art thou from fen or forest,
Senseless wizard from the woodlands,
That thou dost not know this vessel,
Magic war-ship of Wainola?
Dost not know him at the rudder,
Nor the hero at the row-locks?"
Spake the wizard, Lemminkainen:
"Well I know the helm-director,
And I recognize the rower;
Wainamoinen, old and trusty,
At the helm directs the vessel;
Ilmarinen does the rowing.
Whither is the vessel sailing,
Whither wandering, my heroes?"
Spake the ancient Wainamoinen:
"We are sailing to the Northland,
There to gain the magic Sampo,
There to get the lid in colours,
From the stone-berg of Pohyola,
From the copper-bearing mountain."
Spake the evil Lemminkainen:
"O, thou good, old Wainamoinen,
Take me with thee to Pohyola,
Make me third of magic heroes,
Since thou goest for the Sampo,
Goest for the lid in colours;
I shall prove a valiant soldier,
When thy wisdom calls for fighting;
I am skilled in arts of warfare!"

Wainamoinen, ancient minstrel,
Gave assent to Ahti's wishes;
Thereupon wild Lemminkainen
Hastened to Wainola's war-ship,
Bringing floats of aspen-timber,
To the ships of Wainamoinen.

Thus the hero of the Northland
Speaks to reckless Lemminkainen:
"There is aspen on my vessel,
Aspen-floats in great abundance,
And the boat is heavy-laden.
Wherefore dost thou bring the aspen
To the vessel of Wainola?"
Lemminkainen gave this answer:
"Not through caution sinks a vessel,
Nor a hay-stack by its proppings;
Seas abound in hidden dangers,
Heavy storms arise and threaten
Fell destruction to the sailor
That would brave the angry billows."
Spake the good, old Wainamoinen:
"Therefore is this warlike vessel
Built of trusty steel and copper,
Trimmed and bound in toughest iron,
That the winds may not destroy it,
May not harm my ship of magic."

Rune XL: Birth of the Harp

Wainamoinen, ancient minstrel,
Onward steered his goodly vessel,
From the isle of Lemminkainen,
From the borders of the village;
Steered his war-ship through the waters,
Sang it o'er the ocean-billows,
Joyful steered it to Pohyola.

On the banks were maidens standing,
And the daughters spake these measures:
"List the music on the waters!
What this wonderful rejoicing,
What this singing on the billows?
Far more beautiful this singing,
This rejoicing on the waters,
Than our ears have heard in Northland."

Wainamoinen, the magician,
Steered his wonder-vessel onward,
Steered one day along the seashore,
Steered the next through shallow waters,
Steered the third day through the rivers.

Then the reckless Lemminkainen
Suddenly some words remembered,
He had heard along the fire-stream
Near the cataract and whirlpool,
And these words the hero uttered:
"Cease, O cataract, thy roaring,
Cease, O waterfall, thy foaming!
Maidens of the foam and current,
Sitting on the rocks in water,
On the stone-blocks in the river,
Take the foam and white-capped billows
In your arms and still their anger,
That our ships may pass in safety!
Aged dame beneath the eddy,
Thou that livest in the sea-foam,
Swimming, rise above the waters,
Lift thy head above the whirlpool,
Gather well the foam and billows
In thine arms and still their fury,
That our ship may pass in safety!
Ye, O rocks beneath the current,
Underneath the angry waters,
Lower well your heads of danger,
Sink below our magic vessel,
That our ship may pass in safety!

"Should this prayer prove inefficient,
Kimmo, hero son of Kammo,
Bore an outlet with thine auger,
Cut a channel for this vessel
Through the rocks beneath the waters,
That our ship may pass in safety!
Should all this prove unavailing,
Hostess of the running water,
Change to moss these rocky ledges,
Change this vessel to an air-bag,
That between these rocks and billows
It may float, and pass in safety!

"Virgin of the sacred whirlpool,
Thou whose home is in the river,
Spin from flax of strongest fiber,
Spin a thread of crimson colour,
Draw it gently through the water,
That the thread our ship may follow,
And our vessel pass in safety!
Goddess of the helm, thou daughter
Of the ocean-winds and sea-foam,
Take thy helm endowed with mercy,
Guide our vessel through these dangers,
Hasten through these floods enchanted,
Passing by the house of envy,
By the gates of the enchanters,
That our ship may pass in safety!

"Should this prayer prove inefficient,
Ukko, Ruler of creation,
Guide our vessel with thy fire-sword,
Guide it with thy blade of lightning,
Through the dangers of these rapids,
Through the cataract and whirlpool,
That our ship may pass in safety!"

Thereupon old Wainamoinen
Steered his boat through winds and waters,
Through the rocky chinks and channels,
Through the surges wildly tossing;

And the vessel passed in safety
Through the dangers of the current,
Through the sacred stream and whirlpool.
As it gains the open waters,
Gains at length the broad-lake's bosom,
Suddenly its motion ceases,
On some object firmly anchored.
Thereupon young Ilmarinen,
With the aid of Lemminkainen,
Plunges in the lake the rudder,
Struggles with the aid of magic;
But he cannot move the vessel,
Cannot free it from its moorings.

Wainamoinen, old and truthful,
Thus addresses his companion:
"O thou hero, Lemminkainen,
Stoop and look beneath this war-ship,
See on what this boat is anchored,
See on what our craft is hanging,
In this broad expanse of water,
In the broad-lake's deepest soundings,
If upon some rock or tree-snag,
Or upon some other hindrance."

Thereupon wild Lemminkainen
Looked beneath the magic vessel,
Peering through the crystal waters,
Spake and these the words he uttered:
"Does not rest upon a sand-bar,
Nor upon a rock, nor tree-snag,
But upon the back and shoulders
Of the mighty pike of Northland,
On the fin-bones of the monster."

Wainamoinen, old and trusty,
Spake these words to Lemminkainen:
"Many things we find in water,
Rocks, and trees, and fish, and sea-duck;
Are we on the pike's broad shoulders,
On the fin-bones of the monster,
Pierce the waters with thy broadsword,
Cut the monster into pieces."

Thereupon wild Lemminkainen,
Reckless wizard, filled with courage,
Pulls his broadsword from his girdle,
From its sheath, the bone-divider,
Strikes with might of magic hero,
Headlong falls into the water;
And the blacksmith, Ilmarinen,
Lifts the wizard from the river,
Speaks these words to dripping Ahti:
"Accidents will come to mortals,
Accidents will come to heroes,
By the hundreds, by the thousands,
Even to the gods above us!"

Then the blacksmith, Ilmarinen,
Drew his broadsword from his girdle,
From its sheath his blade of honour,
Tried to slay the pike of Northland
With the weapon of his forging;
But he broke his sword in pieces,
Did not harm the water-monster.

Wainamoinen, old and trusty,
Thus addresses his companions:
"Poor apologies for heroes!
When occasion calls for victors,
When we need some great magician,
Need a hero filled with valor,
Then the arm that comes is feeble,
And the mind insane or witless,
Strength and reason gone to others!"

Straightway ancient Wainamoinen,
Miracle of strength and wisdom,
Draws his fire-sword from his girdle,
Wields the mighty blade of magic,
Strikes the waters as the lightning,
Strikes the pike beneath the vessel,
And impales the mighty monster;
Raises him above the surface,
In the air the pike he circles,
Cuts the monster into pieces;
To the water falls the pike-tail,
To the ship the head and body;
Easily the ship moves onward.

Wainamoinen, old and faithful,
To the shore directs his vessel,
On the strand the boat he anchors,
Looks in every nook and corner

For the fragments of the monster;
Gathers well the parts together,
Speaks these words to those about him:
"Let the oldest of the heroes
Slice for me the pike of Northland,
Slice the fish to fitting morsels."

Answered all the men and heroes,
And the maidens spake, assenting:
"Worthier the catcher's fingers,
Wainamoinen's hands are sacred!"

Thereupon the wise magician
Drew a fish-knife from his girdle,
Sliced the pike to fitting morsels,
Spake again to those about him:
"Let the youngest of the maidens
Cook for me the pike of Northland,
Set for me a goodly dinner!"

All the maidens quick responded,
All the virgins vied in cooking;
Neither could outdo the other,
Thus the pike was rendered toothsome.
Feasted all the old magicians,
Feasted all the younger heroes,
Feasted all the men and maidens;
On the rocks were left the fish-bones,
Only relics of their feasting.

Wainamoinen, ancient minstrel,
Looked upon the pile of fragments,
On the fish-bones looked and pondered,
Spake these words in meditation:
"Wondrous things might be constructed
From the relics of this monster,
Were they in the blacksmith's furnace,
In the hands of the magician,
In the hands of Ilmarinen."
Spake the blacksmith of Wainola:
"Nothing fine can be constructed
From the bones and teeth of fishes
By the skillful forger-artist,
By the hands of the magician."
These the words of Wainamoinen:
"Something wondrous might be builded
From these jaws, and teeth, and fish-bones;
Might a magic harp be fashioned,
Could an artist be discovered
That could shape them to my wishes."

But he found no fish-bone artist
That could shape the harp of joyance
From the relics of their feasting,
From the jaw-bones of the monster,
To the will of the magician.
Thereupon wise Wainamoinen
Set himself at work designing;
Quick became a fish-bone artist,
Made a harp of wondrous beauty,
Lasting joy and pride of Suomi.
Whence the harp's enchanting arches?
From the jaw-bones of the monster.
Whence the necessary harp-pins?
From the pike-teeth firmly fastened.
Whence the sweetly singing harp-strings?
From the tail of Lempo's stallion.
Thus was born the harp of magic
From the mighty pike of Northland,
From the relics from the feasting
Of the heroes of Wainola.
All the young men came to view it,
All the aged with their children,
Mothers with their beauteous daughters,
Maidens with their golden tresses;
All the people on the islands
Came to view the harp of joyance,
Pride and beauty of the Northland.

Wainamoinen, ancient minstrel,
Let the aged try the harp-strings,
Gave it to the young magicians,
To the dames and to their daughters,
To the maidens, silver-tinselled,
To the singers of Wainola.
When the young men touched
the harp-strings,
Then arose the notes of discord;
When the aged played upon it,
Dissonance their only music.
Spake the wizard, Lemminkainen:
"O ye witless, worthless children,
O ye senseless, useless maidens,
O ye wisdom-lacking heroes,

Cannot play this harp of magic,
Cannot touch the notes of concord!
Give to me this thing of beauty,
Hither bring the harp of fish-bones,
Let me try my skillful fingers."
Lemminkainen touched the harp-strings,
Carefully the strings adjusted,
Turned the harp in all directions,
Fingered all the strings in sequence,
Played the instrument of wonder,
But it did not speak in concord,
Did not sing the notes of joyance.
Spake the ancient Wainamoinen:
"There is none among these maidens,
None among these youthful heroes,
None among the old magicians
That can play the harp of magic,
Touch the notes of joy and pleasure.
Let us take the harp to Pohya,
There to find a skillful player
That can touch the strings in concord."

Then they sailed to Sariola,
To Pohyola took the wonder,
There to find the harp a master.
All the heroes of Pohyola,
All the boys and all the maidens,
Ancient dames, and bearded minstrels,
Vainly touched the harp of beauty.

Louhi, hostess of the Northland,
Took the harp-strings in her fingers;
All the youth of Sariola,
Youth of every tribe and station,
Vainly touched the harp of fish-bone;
Could not find the notes of joyance,
Dissonance their only pleasure;
Shrieked the harp-strings like the whirlwinds,
All the tones wore harsh and frightful.

In a corner slept a blind man,
Lay a gray-beard on the oven,
Rousing from his couch of slumber,
Murmured thus within his corner:
"Cease at once this wretched playing,
Make an end of all this discord;
It benumbs mine ears for hearing,
Racks my brain, despoils my senses,
Robs me of the sweets of sleeping.
If the harp of Suomi's people
True delight cannot engender,
Cannot bring the notes of pleasure,
Cannot sing to sleep the aged,
Cast the thing upon the waters,
Sink it in the deeps of ocean,
Take it back to Kalevala,
To the home of him that made it,
To the hands of its creator."

Thereupon the harp made answer,
To the blind man sang these measures:
"Shall not fall upon the waters,
Shall not sink within the ocean;
I will play for my creator,
Sing in melody and concord
In the fingers of my master."

Carefully the harp was carried
To the artist that had made it,
To the hands of its creator,
To the feet of Wainamoinen.

Rune XLI: Wainamoinen's Harp Songs

Wainamoinen, ancient minstrel,
The eternal wisdom-singer,
Laves his hands to snowy whiteness,
Sits upon the rock of joyance,
On the stone of song he settles,
On the mount of silver clearness,
On the summit, golden coloured;
Takes the harp by him created,
In his hands the harp of fish-bone,
With his knee the arch supporting,
Takes the harp-strings in his fingers,
Speaks these words to those assembled:
"Hither come, ye Northland people,
Come and listen to my playing,
To the harp's entrancing measures,
To my songs of joy and gladness."

Then the singer of Wainola
Took the harp of his creation,
Quick adjusting, sweetly tuning,
Deftly plied his skillful fingers
To the strings that he had fashioned.
Now was gladness rolled on gladness,
And the harmony of pleasure
Echoed from the hills and mountains:
Added singing to his playing,
Out of joy did joy come welling,
Now resounded marvelous music,
All of Northland stopped and listened.
Every creature in the forest,
All the beasts that haunt the woodlands,
On their nimble feet came bounding,
Came to listen to his playing,
Came to hear his songs of joyance.
Leaped the squirrels from the branches,
Merrily from birch to aspen;
Climbed the ermines on the fences,
O'er the plains the elk-deer bounded,
And the lynxes purred with pleasure;
Wolves awoke in far-off swamp-lands,
Bounded o'er the marsh and heather,
And the bear his den deserted,
Left his lair within the pine-wood,
Settled by a fence to listen,
Leaned against the listening gate-posts,
But the gate-posts yield beneath him;
Now he climbs the fir tree branches
That he may enjoy and wonder,
Climbs and listens to the music
Of the harp of Wainamoinen.

Tapiola's wisest senior,
Metsola's most noble landlord,
And of Tapio, the people,
Young and aged, men and maidens,
Flew like red-deer up the mountains
There to listen to the playing,
To the harp of Wainamoinen.
Tapiola's wisest mistress,
Hostess of the glen and forest,
Robed herself in blue and scarlet,
Bound her limbs with silken ribbons,
Sat upon the woodland summit,
On the branches of a birch-tree,
There to listen to the playing,
To the high-born hero's harping,
To the songs of Wainamoinen.

All the birds that fly in mid-air
Fell like snow-flakes from the heavens,
Flew to hear the minstrel's playing,
Hear the harp of Wainamoinen.
Eagles in their lofty eyrie
Heard the songs of the enchanter;
Swift they left their unfledged young ones,
Flew and perched around the minstrel.
From the heights the hawks descended,
From the clouds down swooped the falcon,
Ducks arose from inland waters,
Swans came gliding from the marshes;
Tiny finches, green and golden,
Flew in flocks that darkened sunlight,
Came in myriads to listen,
Perched upon the head and shoulders
Of the charming Wainamoinen,
Sweetly singing to the playing
Of the ancient bard and minstrel.
And the daughters of the welkin,
Nature's well-beloved daughters,
Listened all in rapt attention;
Some were seated on the rainbow,
Some upon the crimson cloudlets,
Some upon the dome of heaven.

In their hands the Moon's fair daughters
Held their weaving-combs of silver;
In their hands the Sun's sweet maidens
Grasped the handles of their distaffs,
Weaving with their golden shuttles,
Spinning from their silver spindles,
On the red rims of the cloudlets,
On the bow of many colours.
As they hear the minstrel playing,
Hear the harp of Wainamoinen,
Quick they drop their combs of silver,
Drop the spindles from their fingers,
And the golden threads are broken,
Broken are the threads of silver.

All the fish in Suomi-waters
Heard the songs of the magician,

Came on flying fins to listen
To the harp of Wainamoinen.
Came the trout with graceful motions,
Water-dogs with awkward movements,
From the water-cliffs the salmon,
From the sea-caves came the whiting,
From the deeper caves the bill-fish;
Came the pike from beds of sea-fern,
Little fish with eyes of scarlet,
Leaning on the reeds and rushes,
With their heads above the surface;
Came to hear the harp of joyance,
Hear the songs of the enchanter.
Ahto, king of all the waters,
Ancient king with beard of sea-grass,
Raised his head above the billows,
In a boat of water-lilies,
Glided to the coast in silence,
Listened to the wondrous singing,
To the harp of Wainamoinen.
These the words the sea-king uttered:
"Never have I heard such playing,
Never heard such strains of music,
Never since the sea was fashioned,
As the songs of this enchanter,
This sweet singer, Wainamoinen."

Satko's daughters from the blue-deep,
Sisters of the wave-washed ledges,
On the coloured strands were sitting,
Smoothing out their sea-green tresses
With the combs of molten silver,
With their silver-handled brushes,
Brushes forged with golden bristles.
When they hear the magic playing,
Hear the harp of Wainamoinen,
Fall their brushes on the billows,
Fall their combs with silver handles
To the bottom of the waters,
Unadorned their heads remaining,
And uncombed their sea-green tresses.

Came the hostess of the waters,
Ancient hostess robed in flowers,
Rising from her deep sea-castle,
Swimming to the shore in wonder,
Listened to the minstrel's playing,
To the harp of Wainamoinen.
As the magic tones re-echoed,
As the singer's song out-circled,
Sank the hostess into slumber,
On the rocks of many colours,
On her watery couch of joyance,
Deep the sleep that settled o'er her.

Wainamoinen, ancient minstrel,
Played one day and then a second,
Played the third from morn till even.
There was neither man nor hero,
Neither ancient dame, nor maiden,
Not in Metsola a daughter,
Whom he did not touch to weeping;
Wept the young, and wept the aged,
Wept the mothers, wept the daughters
Wept the warriors and heroes
At the music of his playing,
At the songs of the magician.

Wainamoinen's tears came flowing,
Welling from the master's eyelids,
Pearly tear-drops coursing downward,
Larger than the whortle-berries,
Finer than the pearls of ocean,
Smoother than the eggs of moor-hens,
Brighter than the eyes of swallows.
From his eyes the tear-drops started,
Flowed adown his furrowed visage,
Falling from his beard in streamlets,
Trickled on his heaving bosom,
Streaming o'er his golden girdle,
Coursing to his garment's border,
Then beneath his shoes of ermine,
Flowing on, and flowing ever,
Part to earth for her possession,
Part to water for her portion.
As the tear-drops fall and mingle,
Form they streamlets from the eyelids
Of the minstrel, Wainamoinen,
To the blue-mere's sandy margin,
To the deeps of crystal waters,
Lost among the reeds and rushes.
Spake at last the ancient minstrel:
"Is there one in all this concourse,
One in all this vast assembly

That can gather up my tear-drops
From the deep, pellucid waters?"

Thus the younger heroes answered,
Answered thus the bearded seniors:
"There is none in all this concourse,
None in all this vast assembly,
That can gather up thy tear-drops
From the deep, pellucid waters."
Spake again wise Wainamoinen:
"He that gathers up my tear-drops
From the deeps of crystal waters
Shall receive a beauteous plumage."
Came a raven, flying, croaking,
And the minstrel thus addressed him:
"Bring, O raven, bring my tear-drops
From the crystal lake's abysses;
I will give thee beauteous plumage,
Recompense for golden service."
But the raven failed his master.

Came a duck upon the waters,
And the hero thus addressed him:
"Bring, O water-bird, my tear-drops;
Often thou dost dive the deep-sea,
Sink thy bill upon the bottom
Of the waters thou dost travel;
Dive again my tears to gather,
I will give thee beauteous plumage,
Recompense for golden service."
Thereupon the duck departed,
Hither, thither, swam, and circled,
Dived beneath the foam and billow,
Gathered Wainamoinen's tear-drops
From the blue-sea's pebbly bottom,
From the deep, pellucid waters;
Brought them to the great magician,
Beautifully formed and coloured,
Glistening in the silver sunshine,
Glimmering in the golden moonlight,
Many-coloured as the rainbow,
Fitting ornaments for heroes,
Jewels for the maids of beauty.
This the origin of sea-pearls,
And the blue-duck's beauteous plumage.

Rune XLII: Capture of the Sampo

Wainamoinen, old and truthful,
With the blacksmith, Ilmarinen,
With the reckless son of Lempo,
Handsome hero, Kaukomieli,
On the sea's smooth plain departed,
On the far-extending waters,
To the village, cold and dreary,
To the never-pleasant Northland,
Where the heroes fall and perish.
Ilmarinen led the rowers
On one side the magic war-ship,
And the reckless Lemminkainen
Led the rowers on the other.
Wainamoinen, old and trusty,
Laid his hand upon the rudder,
Steered his vessel o'er the waters,
Through the foam and angry billows
To Pohyola's place of landing,
To the cylinders of copper,
Where the war-ships lie at anchor.
When they had arrived at Pohya,
When their journey they had ended,
On the land they rolled their vessel,
On the copper-banded rollers,
Straightway journeyed to the village,
Hastened to the halls and hamlets
Of the dismal Sariola.

Louhi, hostess of the Northland,
Thus addressed the stranger-heroes:
"Magic heroes of Wainola,
What the tidings ye are bringing
To the people of my village?"

Wainamoinen, ancient minstrel,
Gave this answer to the hostess:
"All the hosts of Kalevala
Are inquiring for the Sampo,
Asking for the lid in colours;
Hither have these heroes journeyed
To divide the priceless treasure."

Thus the hostess spake in answer:
"No one would divide a partridge,
Nor a squirrel, with three heroes;
Wonderful the magic Sampo,
Plenty does it bring to Northland;
And the coloured lid re-echoes
From the copper-bearing mountains,
From the stone-berg of Pohyola,
To the joy of its possessors."

Wainamoinen, ancient minstrel,
Thus addressed the ancient Louhi:
"If thou wilt not share the Sampo,
Give to us an equal portion,
We will take it to Wainola,
With its lid of many colours,
Take by force the hope of Pohya."

Thereupon the Northland hostess
Angry grew and sighed for vengeance;
Called her people into council,
Called the hosts of Sariola,
Heroes with their trusted broadswords,
To destroy old Wainamoinen
With his people of the Northland.

Wainamoinen, wise and ancient,
Hastened to his harp of fish-bone,
And began his magic playing;
All of Pohya stopped and listened,
Every warrior was silenced
By the notes of the magician;
Peaceful-minded grew the soldiers,
All the maidens danced with pleasure,
While the heroes fell to weeping,
And the young men looked in wonder.

Wainamoinen plays unceasing,
Plays the maidens into slumber,
Plays to sleep the young and aged,
All of Northland sleeps and listens.
Wise and wondrous Wainamoinen,
The eternal bard and singer,
Searches in his pouch of leather,
Draws therefrom his slumber-arrows,
Locks the eyelids of the sleepers,
Of the heroes of Pohyola,
Sings and charms to deeper slumber
All the warriors of the Northland.
Then the heroes of Wainola
Hasten to obtain the Sampo,
To procure the lid in colours
From the copper-bearing mountains.
From behind nine locks of copper,
In the stone-berg of Pohyola.

Wainamoinen, ancient minstrel,
Then began his wondrous singing,
Sang in gentle tones of magic,
At the entrance to the mountain,
At the border of the stronghold;
Trembled all the rocky portals,
And the iron-banded pillars
Fell and crumbled at his singing.

Ilmarinen, magic blacksmith,
Well anointed all the hinges,
All the bars and locks anointed,
And the bolts flew back by magic,
All the gates unlocked in silence,
Opened for the great magician.
Spake the minstrel Wainamoinen:
"O thou daring Lemminkainen,
Friend of mine in times of trouble,
Enter thou within the mountain,
Bring away the wondrous Sampo,
Bring away the lid in colours!"

Quick the reckless Lemminkainen,
Handsome hero, Kaukomieli,
Ever ready for a venture,
Hastens to the mountain-caverns,
There to find the famous Sampo,
There to get the lid in colours;
Strides along with conscious footsteps,
Thus himself he vainly praises:
"Great am I and full of glory,
Wonder-hero, son of Ukko,
I will bring away the Sampo,
Turn about the lid in colours,
Turn it on its magic hinges!"

Lemminkainen finds the wonder,
Finds the Sampo in the mountain,

Labours long with strength heroic,
Tugs with might and main to turn it;
Motionless remains the treasure,
Deeper sinks the lid in colours,
For the roots have grown about it,
Grown nine fathoms deep in sand-earth.

Lived a mighty ox in Northland,
Powerful in bone and sinew,
Beautiful in form and colour,
Horns the length of seven fathoms,
Mouth and eyes of wondrous beauty.

Lemminkainen, reckless hero,
Harnesses the ox in pasture,
Takes the master-plow of Pohya,
Plows the roots about the Sampo,
Plows around the lid in colours,
And the sacred Sampo loosens,
Falls the coloured lid in silence.
Straightway ancient Wainamoinen
Brings the blacksmith, Ilmarinen,
Brings the daring Lemminkainen,
Lastly brings the magic Sampo,
From the stone-berg of Pohyola,
From the copper-bearing mountain,
Hides it in his waiting vessel,
In the war-ship of Wainola.

Wainamoinen called his people,
Called his crew of men and maidens,
Called together all his heroes,
Rolled his vessel to the water,
Into billowy deeps and dangers.
Spake the blacksmith, Ilmarinen:
"Whither shall we take the Sampo,
Whither take the lid in colours,
From the stone-berg of Pohyola,
From this evil spot of Northland?"

Wainamoinen, wise and faithful,
Gave this answer to the question:
"Thither shall we take the Sampo,
Thither take the lid in colours,
To the fog-point on the waters,
To the island forest-covered;
There the treasure may be hidden,
May remain in peace for ages,
Free from trouble, free from danger,
Where the sword will not molest it."

Then the minstrel, Wainamoinen,
Joyful, left the Pohya borders,
Homeward sailed, and happy-hearted,
Spake these measures on departing:
"Turn, O man-of-war, from Pohya,
Turn thy back upon the strangers,
Turn thou to my distant country!
Rock, O winds, my magic vessel,
Homeward drive my ship, O billows,
Lend the rowers your assistance,
Give the oarsmen easy labour,
On this vast expanse of waters!
Give me of thine oars, O Ahto,
Lend thine aid, O King of sea-waves,
Guide as with thy helm in safety,
Lay thy hand upon the rudder,
And direct our war-ship homeward;
Let the hooks of metal rattle
O'er the surging of the billows,
On the white-capped waves' commotion."

Then the master, Wainamoinen,
Guided home his willing vessel;
And the blacksmith, Ilmarinen,
With the lively Lemminkainen,
Led the mighty host of rowers,
And the war-ship glided homeward
O'er the sea's unruffled surface,
O'er the mighty waste of waters.
Spake the reckless Lemminkainen:
"Once before I rode these billows,
There were viands for the heroes,
There was singing for the maidens;
But today I hear no singing,
Hear no songs upon the vessel,
Hear no music on the waters."

Wainamoinen, wise and ancient,
Answered thus wild Lemminkainen:
"Let none sing upon the blue-sea,
On the waters, no rejoicing;
Singing would prolong our journey,
Songs disturb the host of rowers;

Soon will die the silver sunlight,
Darkness soon will overtake us,
On this evil waste of waters,
On this blue-sea, smooth and level."
These the words of Lemminkainen:
"Time will fly on equal pinions
Whether we have songs or silence;
Soon will disappear the daylight,
And the night as quickly follow,
Whether we be sad or joyous."

Wainamoinen, the magician,
O'er the blue backs of the billows,
Steered one day, and then a second,
Steered the third from morn till even,
When the wizard, Lemminkainen,
Once again addressed the master:
"Why wilt thou, O famous minstrel,
Sing no longer for thy people,
Since the Sampo thou hast captured,
Captured too the lid in colours?"
These the words of Wainamoinen:
"'Tis not well to sing too early!
Time enough for songs of joyance
When we see our home-land mansions,
When our journeyings have ended!"
Spake the reckless Lemminkainen:
"At the helm, if I were sitting,
I would sing at morn and evening,
Though my voice has little sweetness;
Since thy songs are not forthcoming
Listen to my wondrous singing!"

Thereupon wild Lemminkainen,
Handsome hero, Kaukomieli,
Raised his voice above the waters,
O'er the sea his song resounded;
But his measures were discordant,
And his notes were harsh
and frightful.
Sang the wizard, Lemminkainen,
Screeched the reckless Kaukomieli,
Till the mighty war-ship trembled;
Far and wide was heard his singing,
Heard his songs upon the waters,
Heard within the seventh village,
Heard beyond the seven oceans.

Sat a crane within the rushes,
On a hillock clothed in verdure,
And the crane his toes was counting;
Suddenly he heard the singing
Of the wizard, Lemminkainen;
And the bird was justly frightened
At the songs of the magician.
Then with horrid voice, and screeching,
Flew the crane across the broad sea
To the lakes of Sariola,
O'er Pohyola's hills and hamlets,
Screeching, screaming, over Northland,
Till the people of the darkness
Were awakened from their slumbers.
Louhi hastens to her hurdles,
Hastens to her droves of cattle,
Hastens also to her garners,
Counts her herds, inspects her store-house;
Undisturbed she finds her treasures.

Quick she journeys to the entrance
To the copper-bearing mountain,
Speaks these words as she approaches:
"Woe is me, my life hard-fated,
Woe to Louhi, broken-hearted!
Here the tracks of the destroyers,
All my locks and bolts are broken
By the hands of cruel strangers!
Broken are my iron hinges,
Open stand the mountain-portals
Leading to the Northland-treasure.
Has Pohyola lost her Sampo?"

Then she hastened to the chambers
Where the Sampo had been grinding;
But she found the chambers empty,
Lid and Sampo gone to others,
From the stone-berg of Pohyola,
From behind nine locks of copper,
In the copper-bearing mountain.

Louhi, hostess of the Northland,
Angry grew and cried for vengeance;
As she found her fame departing,
Found her strength fast disappearing,
Thus addressed the sea-fog virgin:
"Daughter of the morning-vapors,

Sift thy fogs from distant cloud-land,
Sift the thick air from the heavens,
Sift thy vapors from the ether,
On the blue back of the broad sea,
On the far extending waters,
That the ancient Wainamoinen,
Friend of ocean-wave and billow,
May not baffle his pursuers!

"Should this prayer prove unavailing,
Iku-Turso, son of Old-age,
Raise thy head above the billows,
And destroy Wainola's heroes,
Sink them to thy deep sea-castles,
There devour them at thy pleasure;
Bring thou back the golden Sampo
To the people of Pohyola!

"Should these words be ineffective,
Ukko, mightiest of rulers,
Golden king beyond the welkin,
Sitting on a throne of silver,
Fill thy skies with heavy storm-clouds,
Call thy fleetest winds about thee,
Send them o'er the seven broad seas,
There to find the fleeing vessel,
That the ancient Wainamoinen
May not baffle his pursuers!"

Quick the virgin of the vapors
Breathed a fog upon the waters,
Made it settle on the war-ship
Of the heroes of the Northland,
Held the minstrel, Wainamoinen,
Anchored in the fog and darkness;
Bound him one day, then a second,
Then a third till dawn of morning,
In the middle of the blue-sea,
Whence he could not flee in safety
From the wrath of his pursuers.

When the third night had departed,
Resting in the sea, and helpless,
Wainamoinen spake as follows:
"Not a man of strength and courage,
Not the weakest of the heroes,
Who upon the sea will suffer,
Sink and perish in the vapors,
Perish in the fog and darkness!"

With his sword he smote the billows,
From his magic blade flowed honey;
Quick the vapor breaks, and rises,
Leaves the waters clear for rowing;
Far extend the sky and waters,
Large the ring of the horizon,
And the troubled sea enlarges.

Time had journeyed little distance,
Scarce a moment had passed over,
When they heard a mighty roaring,
Heard a roaring and a rushing
Near the border of the vessel,
Where the foam was shooting skyward
O'er the boat of Wainamoinen.
Straightway youthful Ilmarinen
Sank in gravest apprehension,
From his cheeks the blood departed;
Pulled his cap down o'er his forehead,
Shook and trembled with emotion.

Wainamoinen, ancient minstrel,
Casts his eyes upon the waters
Near the broad rim of his war-ship;
There perceives an ocean-wonder
With his head above the sea-foam.

Wainamoinen, brave and mighty,
Seizes quick the water-monster,
Lifts him by his ears and questions:
"Iku-Turso, son of Old-age,
Why art rising from the blue-sea?
Wherefore dost thou leave thy castle,
Show thyself to mighty heroes,
To the heroes of Wainola?"

Iku-Turso, son of Old-age,
Ocean monster, manifested
Neither pleasure, nor displeasure,
Was not in the least affrighted,
Did not give the hero answer.

Whereupon the ancient minstrel,
Asked the second time the monster,

Urgently inquired a third time:
"Iku-Turso, son of Old-age,
Why art rising from the waters,
Wherefore dost thou leave the blue-sea?"
Iku-Turso gave this answer:
"For this cause I left my castle
Underneath the rolling billows:
Came I here with the intention
To destroy the Kalew-heroes,
And return the magic Sampo
To the people of Pohyola.
If thou wilt restore my freedom,
Spare my life from pain and sorrow,
I will quick retrace my journey,
Nevermore to show my visage
To the people of Wainola,
Never while the moonlight glimmers
On the hills of Kalevala!"

Then the singer, Wainamoinen,
Freed the monster, Iku-Turso,
Sent him to his deep sea-castles,
Spake these words to him departing:
"Iku-Turso, son of Old-age,
Nevermore arise from ocean,
Nevermore let Northland-heroes
See thy face above the waters!"

Nevermore has Iku-Turso
Risen to the ocean-level;
Never since have Northland sailors
Seen the head of this sea-monster.

Wainamoinen, old and truthful,
Onward rowed his goodly vessel,
Journeyed but a little distance,
Scarce a moment had passed over,
When the King of all creators,
Mighty Ukko of the heavens,
Made the winds blow full of power,
Made the storms arise in fury,
Made them rage upon the waters.
From the west the winds came roaring,
From the northeast came in anger,
Winds came howling from the southwest,
Came the winds from all directions,
In their fury, rolling, roaring,
Tearing branches from the lindens,
Hurling needles from the pine trees,
Blowing flowers from the heather,
Grasses blowing from the meadow,
Tearing up the very bottom
Of the deep and boundless blue-sea.
Roared the winds and lashed the waters
Till the waves were white with fury;
Tossed the war-ship high in ether,
Tossed away the harp of fish-bone,
Magic harp of Wainamoinen,
To the joy of King Wellamo,
To the pleasure of his people,
To the happiness of Ahto,
Ahto, rising from his caverns,
On the floods beheld his people
Carry off the harp of magic
To their home below the billows.

Wainamoinen, ancient minstrel,
Heavy-hearted, spake these measures:
"I have lost what I created,
I have lost the harp of joyance;
Now my strength has gone to others,
All my pleasure too departed,
All my hope and comfort vanished!
Nevermore the harp of fish-bone
Will enchant the hosts of Suomi!"

Then the blacksmith, Ilmarinen,
Sorrow-laden, spake as follows:
"Woe is me, my life hard-fated!
Would that I had never journeyed
On these waters filled with dangers,
On the rolling waste before me,
In this war-ship false and feeble.
Winds and storms have I encountered,
Wretched days of toil and trouble,
I have witnessed in the Northland;
Never have I met such dangers
On the land, nor on the ocean,
Never in my hero life-time!"

Then the ancient Wainamoinen
Spake and these the words he uttered:
"Weep no more, my goodly comrades,
In my bark let no one murmur;

Weeping cannot mend disaster,
Tears can never still misfortune,
Mourning cannot save from evil.

"Sea, command thy warring forces,
Bid thy children cease their fury!
Ahto, still thy surging billows!
Sink, Wellamo, to thy slumber,
That our boat may move in safety.
Rise, ye storm-winds, to your kingdoms,
Lift your heads above the waters,
To the regions of your kindred,
To your people and dominions,
Cut the trees within the forest,
Bend the lindens of the valley,
Let our vessel sail in safety!"

Then the reckless Lemminkainen,
Handsome wizard, Kaukomieli,
Spake these words in supplication:
"Come, O eagle, Turyalander,
Bring three feathers from thy pinions,
Three, O raven, three, O eagle,
To protect this bark from evil!"

All the heroes of Wainola
Call their forces to the rescue,
And repair the sinking vessel.
By the aid of master-magic,
Wainamoinen saved his war-ship,
Saved his people from destruction,
Well repaired his ship to battle
With the roughest seas of Northland;
Steers his mighty boat in safety
Through the perils of the whirlpool,
Through the watery deeps and dangers.

Rune XLIII: The Sampo Lost in the Sea

Louhi, hostess of Pohyola,
Called her many tribes together,
Gave the archers bows and arrows,
Gave her brave men spears
and broadswords;
Fitted out her mightiest war-ship,
In the vessel placed her army,
With their swords a hundred heroes,
With their bows a thousand archers;
Quick erected masts and sail-yards,
On the masts her sails of linen
Hanging like the clouds of heaven,
Like the white-clouds in the ether;
Sailed across the seas of Pohya,
To re-take the wondrous Sampo
From the heroes of Wainola.

Wainamoinen, old and faithful,
Sailed across the deep, blue waters,
Spake these words to Lemminkainen:
"O thou daring son of Lempo,
Best of all my friends and heroes,
Mount the highest of the topmasts,
Look before you into ether,
Look behind you at the heavens,
Well examine the horizon,
Whether clear or filled with trouble."

Climbed the daring Lemminkainen,
Ever ready for a venture,
To the highest of the mastheads;
Looked he eastward, also westward,
Looked he northward, also southward,
Then addressed wise Wainamoinen:
"Clear the sky appears before me,
But behind a dark horizon;
In the north a cloud is rising,
And a longer cloud at northwest."
Wainamoinen thus made answer:
"Art thou speaking truth or fiction?
I am fearful that the war-ships
Of Pohyola are pursuing;
Look again with keener vision."

Thereupon wild Lemminkainen
Looked again and spake as follows:
"In the distance seems a forest,
In the south appears an island,
Aspen-groves with falcons laden,
Alders laden with the wood-grouse."
Spake the ancient Wainamoinen:
"Surely thou art speaking falsehood;

'Tis no forest in the distance,
Neither aspen, birch, nor alders,
Laden with the grouse, or falcon;
I am fearful that Pohyola
Follows with her magic armies;
Look again with keener vision."

Then the daring Lemminkainen
Looked the third time from the topmast,
Spake and these the words he uttered:
"From the north a boat pursues us,
Driven by a hundred rowers,
Carrying a thousand heroes!"

Knew at last old Wainamoinen,
Knew the truth of his inquiry,
Thus addressed his fleeing people:
"Row, O blacksmith, Ilmarinen,
Row, O mighty Lemminkainen,
Row, all ye my noble oarsmen,
That our boat may skim the waters,
May escape from our pursuers!"

Rowed the blacksmith, Ilmarinen,
Rowed the mighty Lemminkainen,
With them rowed the other heroes;
Heavily groaned the helm of birch-wood,
Loudly rattled all the row-locks;
All the vessel shook and trembled,
Like a cataract it thundered
As it plowed the waste of waters,
Tossing sea-foam to the heavens.
Strongly rowed Wainola's forces,
Strongly were their arms united;
But the distance did not widen
Twixt the boat and their pursuers.

Quick the hero, Wainamoinen,
Saw misfortune hanging over,
Saw destruction in the distance;
Heavy-hearted, long reflecting,
Trouble-laden, spake as follows:
"Only is there one salvation,
Know one miracle for safety!"

Then he grasped his box of tinder,
From the box he took a flint-stone,
Of the tinder took some fragments,
Cast the fragments on the waters,
Spake these words of master-magic.
"Let from these arise a mountain
From the bottom of the deep-sea,
Let a rock arise in water,
That the war-ship of Pohyola,
With her thousand men and heroes,
May be wrecked upon the summit,
By the aid of surging billows."

Instantly a reef arises,
In the sea springs up a mountain,
Eastward, westward, through the waters.
Came the war-ship of the Northland,
Through the floods the boat came steering,
Sailed against the mountain-ledges,
Fastened on the rocks in water,
Wrecked upon the Mount of Magic.
In the deep-sea fell the topmasts,
Fell the sails upon the billows,
Carried by the winds and waters
O'er the waves of toil and trouble.

Louhi, hostess of Pohyola,
Tries to free her sinking vessel,
Tries to rescue from destruction;
But she cannot raise the war-ship,
Firmly fixed upon the mountain;
Shattered are the ribs and rudder,
Ruined is the ship of Pohya.

Then the hostess of the Northland,
Much disheartened, spake as follows:
"Where the force, in earth or heaven,
That will help a soul in trouble?"

Quick she changes form and feature,
Makes herself another body;
Takes five sharpened scythes of iron,
Also takes five goodly sickles,
Shapes them into eagle-talons;
Takes the body of the vessel,
Makes the frame-work of an eagle;
Takes the vessel's ribs and flooring,
Makes them into wings and breastplate;
For the tail she shapes the rudder;

In the wings she plants a thousand
Seniors with their bows and arrows;
Sets a thousand magic heroes
In the body, armed with broadswords;
In the tail a hundred archers,
With their deadly spears and cross-bows,
Thus the bird is hero-feathered.
Quick she spreads her mighty pinions,
Rises as a monster-eagle,
Flies on high, and soars, and circles;
With one wing she sweeps the heavens,
While the other sweeps the waters.
Spake the hero's ocean-mother:
"O thou ancient Wainamoinen,
Turn thy vision to the northeast,
Cast thine eyes upon the sunrise,
Look behind thy fleeing vessel,
See the eagle of misfortune!"

Wainamoinen turned as bidden,
Turned his vision to the northeast,
Cast his eyes upon the sunrise,
There beheld the Northland-hostess,
Wicked witch of Sariola,
Flying as a monster-eagle,
Swooping on his mighty war-ship;
Flies and perches on the topmast,
On the sail-yards firmly settles;
Nearly overturns the vessel
Of the heroes of Wainola,
Underneath the weight of envy.

Then the hero, Ilmarinen,
Turned to Ukko as his refuge,
Thus entreated his Creator:
"Ukko, thou O God in heaven,
Thou Creator full of mercy,
Guard us from impending danger,
That thy children may not perish,
May not meet with fell destruction.
Hither bring thy magic fire-cloak,
That thy people, thus protected,
May resist Pohyola's forces,
Well may fight against the hostess
Of the dismal Sariola,
May not fall before her weapons,
May not in the deep-sea perish!"

Then the ancient Wainamoinen
Thus addressed the ancient Louhi:
"O thou hostess of Pohyola,
Wilt thou now divide the Sampo,
On the fog-point in the water,
On the island forest-covered?"
Thus the Northland hostess answered:
"I will not divide the Sampo,
Not with thee, thou evil wizard,
Not with wicked Wainamoinen!"

Quick the mighty eagle, Louhi,
Swoops upon the lid in colours,
Grasps the Sampo in her talons;
But the daring Lemminkainen
Straightway draws his blade of battle,
Draws his broadsword from his girdle,
Cleaves the talons of the eagle,
One toe only is uninjured,
Speaks these magic words of conquest:
"Down, ye spears, and down, ye broadswords,
Down, ye thousand witless heroes,
Down, ye feathered hosts of Louhi!"

Spake the hostess of Pohyola,
Calling, screeching, from the sail-yards:
"O thou faithless Lemminkainen,
Wicked wizard, Kaukomieli,
To deceive thy trusting mother!
Thou didst give to her thy promise,
Not to go to war for ages,
Not to war for sixty summers,
Though desire for gold impels thee,
Though thou wishest gold and silver!

Wainamoinen, ancient hero,
The eternal wisdom-singer,
Thinking he had met destruction,
Snatched the rudder from the waters,
With it smote the monster-eagle,
Smote the eagle's iron talons,
Smote her countless feathered heroes.
From her breast her hosts descended,
Spearmen fell upon the billows,
From the wings descend a thousand,

From the tail, a hundred archers.
Swoops again the bird of Pohya
To the bottom of the vessel,
Like the hawk from birch or aspen,
Like the falcon from the linden;
Grasps the Sampo with one talon,
Drags the treasure to the waters,
Drops the magic lid in colours
From the red rim of the war-ship
To the bottom of the deep-sea,
Where the Sampo breaks in pieces,
Scatters through the Alue-waters,
In the mighty deeps for ages,
To increase the ocean's treasures,
Treasures for the hosts of Ahto.
Nevermore will there be wanting
Richness for the Ahto-nation,
Never while the moonlight brightens
On the waters of the Northland.

Many fragments of the Sampo
Floated on the purple waters,
On the waters deep and boundless,
Rocked by winds and waves of Suomi,
Carried by the rolling billows
To the sea-sides of Wainola.

Wainamoinen, ancient minstrel,
Saw the fragments of the treasure
Floating on the billows landward,
Fragments of the lid in colours,
Much rejoicing, spake as follows:
"Thence will come the sprouting seed-grain,
The beginning of good fortune,
The unending of resources,
From the plowing and the sowing,
From the glimmer of the moonlight,
From the splendor of the sunshine,
On the fertile plains of Suomi,
On the meads of Kalevala."

Louhi, hostess of Pohyola,
Thus addressed old Wainamoinen:
"Know I other mighty measures,
Know I means that are efficient,
And against thy golden moonlight,
And the splendor of thy sunshine,
And thy plowing, and thy reaping;
In the rocks I'll sink the moonbeams,
Hide the sun within the mountain,
Let the frost destroy thy sowings,
Freeze the crops on all thy corn-fields;
Iron-hail I'll send from heaven,
On the richness of thine acres,
On the barley of thy planting;
I will drive the bear from forests,
Send thee Otso from the thickets,
That he may destroy thy cattle,
May annihilate thy sheep-folds,
May destroy thy steeds at pasture.
I will send thee nine diseases,
Each more fatal than the other,
That will sicken all thy people,
Make thy children sink and perish,
Nevermore to visit Northland,
Never while the moonlight glimmers
On the plains of Kalevala!"
Thus the ancient bard made answer:
"Not a Laplander can banish
Wainamoinen and his people;
Never can a Turyalander
Drive my tribes from Kalevala;
God alone has power to banish,
God controls the fate of nations,
Never trusts the arms of evil,
Never gives His strength to others.
As I trust in my Creator,
Call upon benignant Ukko,
He will guard my crops from danger,
Drive the Frost-fiend from my
corn-fields,
Drive great Otso to his caverns.

"Wicked Louhi of Pohyola,
Thou canst banish evil-doers,
In the rocks canst hide the wicked,
In thy mountains lock the guilty;
Thou canst never hide the moonlight,
Never hide the silver sunshine,
In the caverns of thy kingdom.
Freeze the crops of thine own planting,
Freeze the barley of thy sowing,
Send thine iron-hail from heaven
To destroy the Lapland corn-fields,

To annihilate thy people,
To destroy the hosts of Pohya;
Send great Otso from the heather,
Send the sharp-tooth from the forest,
To the fields of Sariola,
On the herds and flocks of Louhi!"

Thus the wicked hostess answered:
"All my power has departed,
All my strength has gone to others,
All my hope is in the deep-sea;
In the waters lies my Sampo!"

Then the hostess of Pohyola
Home departed, weeping, wailing,
To the land of cold and darkness;
Only took some worthless fragments
Of the Sampo to her people;
Carried she the lid to Pohya,
In the blue-sea left the handle;
Hence the poverty of Northland,
And the famines of Pohyola.

Wainamoinen, ancient minstrel,
Hastened to the broad sea's margin,
Stepped upon the shore in joyance;
Found there fragments of the Sampo,
Fragments of the lid in colours,
On the borders of the waters,
On the curving sands and sea-sides;
Gathered well the Sampo-relics
From the waters near the fog-point,
On the island forest-covered.

Spake the ancient Wainamoinen:,
Spake these words in supplication:
"Grant, O Ukko, our Creator,
Grant to us, thy needful children,
Peace, and happiness, and plenty,
That our lives may be successful,
That our days may end in honour,
On the vales and hills of Suomi,
On the prairies of Wainola,
In the homes of Kalevala!
"Ukko, wise and good Creator,
Ukko, God of love and mercy,
Shelter and protect thy people
From the evil-minded heroes,
From the wiles of wicked women,
That our country's plagues may leave us,
That thy faithful tribes may prosper.
Be our friend and strong protector,
Be the helper of thy children,
In the night a roof above them,
In the day a shield around them,
That the sunshine may not vanish,
That the moonlight may not lessen,
That the killing frosts may leave them,
And destructive hail pass over.
Build a metal wall around us,
From the valleys to the heavens;
Build of stone a mighty fortress
On the borders of Wainola,
Where thy people live and labour,
As their dwelling-place forever,
Sure protection to thy people,
Where the wicked may not enter,
Nor the thieves break through and pilfer,
Never while the moonlight glistens,
And the Sun brings golden blessings
To the plains of Kalevala."

Rune XLIV: Birth of the Second Harp

Wainamoinen, ancient minstrel,
Long reflecting, sang these measures:
"It is now the time befitting
To awaken joy and gladness,
Time for me to touch the harp-strings,
Time to sing the songs primeval,
In these spacious halls and mansions,
In these homes of Kalevala;
But, alas! my harp lies hidden,
Sunk upon the deep-sea's bottom,
To the salmon's hiding-places,
To the dwellings of the whiting,
To the people of Wellamo,
Where the Northland-pike assemble.

Nevermore will I regain it,
Ahto never will return it,
Joy and music gone forever!

"O thou blacksmith, Ilmarinen,
Forge for me a rake of iron,
Thickly set the teeth of copper,
Many fathoms long the handle;
Make a rake to search the waters,
Search the broad sea to the bottom,
Rake the weeds and reeds together,
Rake them to the curving seashore,
That I may regain my treasure,
May regain my harp of fish-bone
From the whiting's place of resting,
From the caverns of the salmon,
From the castles of Wellamo."

Thereupon young Ilmarinen,
The eternal metal-worker,
Forges well a rake of iron,
Teeth in length a hundred fathoms,
And a thousand long the handle,
Thickly sets the teeth of copper.
Straightway ancient Wainamoinen
Takes the rake of magic metals,
Travels but a little distance,
To the cylinders of oak-wood,
To the copper-banded rollers,
Where he finds two ships awaiting,
One was new, the other ancient.

Wainamoinen, old and faithful,
Thus addressed the new-made vessel:
"Go, thou boat of master-magic,
Hasten to the willing waters,
Speed away upon the blue-sea,
And without the hand to move thee;
Let my will impel thee seaward."
Quick the boat rolled to the billows
On the cylinders of oak-wood,
Quick descended to the waters,
Willingly obeyed his master.

Wainamoinen, the magician,
Then began to rake the sea-beds,
Raked up all the water-flowers,
Bits of broken reeds and rushes,
Deep-sea shells and coloured pebbles,
Did not find his harp of fish-bone,
Lost forever to Wainola!

Thereupon the ancient minstrel
Left the waters, homeward hastened,
Cap pulled down upon his forehead,
Sang this song with sorrow laden:
"Nevermore shall I awaken
With my harp-strings, joy and gladness!
Nevermore will Wainamoinen
Charm the people of the Northland
With the harp of his creation!
Nevermore my songs will echo
O'er the hills of Kalevala!"

Thereupon the ancient singer
Went lamenting through the forest,
Wandered through the sighing pine-woods,
Heard the wailing of a birch-tree,
Heard a juniper complaining;
Drawing nearer, waits and listens,
Thus the birch-tree he addresses:
"Wherefore, brother, art thou weeping,
Merry birch enrobed in silver,
Silver-leaved and silver-tasselled?
Art thou shedding tears of sorrow,
Since thou art not led to battle,
Not enforced to war with wizards?"
Wisely does the birch make answer:
"This the language of the many,
Others speak as thou, unjustly,
That I only live in pleasure,
That my silver leaves and tassels
Only whisper my rejoicings;
That I have no cares, no sorrows,
That I have no hours unhappy,
Knowing neither pain nor trouble.
I am weeping for my smallness,
Am lamenting for my weakness,
Have no sympathy, no pity,
Stand here motionless for ages,
Stand alone in fen and forest,
In these woodlands vast and joyless.
Others hope for coming summers,
For the beauties of the spring-time;

I, alas! a helpless birch-tree,
Dread the changing of the seasons,
I must give my bark to others,
Lose my leaves and silken tassels.
Often come the Suomi children,
Peel my bark and drink my life-blood:
Wicked shepherds in the summer,
Come and steal my belt of silver,
Of my bark make berry-baskets,
Dishes make, and cups for drinking.
Oftentimes the Northland maidens
Cut my tender limbs for birch-brooms,
Bind my twigs and silver tassels
Into brooms to sweep their cabins;
Often have the Northland heroes
Chopped me into chips for burning;
Three times in the summer season,
In the pleasant days of spring-time,
Foresters have ground their axes
On my silver trunk and branches,
Robbed me of my life for ages;
This my spring-time joy and pleasure,
This my happiness in summer,
And my winter days no better!
When I think of former troubles,
Sorrow settles on my visage,
And my face grows white with anguish;
Often do the winds of winter
And the hoar-frost bring me sadness,
Blast my tender leaves and tassels,
Bear my foliage to others,
Rob me of my silver raiment,
Leave me naked on the mountain,
Lone, and helpless, and disheartened!"
Spake the good, old Wainamoinen:
"Weep no longer, sacred birch-tree,
Mourn no more, my friend and brother,
Thou shalt have a better fortune;
I will turn thy grief to joyance,
Make thee laugh and sing with gladness."

Then the ancient Wainamoinen
Made a harp from sacred birch-wood,
Fashioned in the days of summer,
Beautiful the harp of magic,
By the master's hand created
On the fog-point in the Big-Sea,
On the island forest-covered,
Fashioned from the birch the archings,
And the frame-work from the aspen.
These the words of the magician:
"All the archings are completed,
And the frame is fitly finished;
Whence the hooks and pins for tuning,
That the harp may sing in concord?"

Near the way-side grew an oak-tree,
Skyward grew with equal branches,
On each twig an acorn growing,
Golden balls upon each acorn,
On each ball a singing cuckoo.
As each cuckoo's call resounded,
Five the notes of song that issued
From the songster's throat of joyance;
From each throat came liquid music,
Gold and silver for the master,
Flowing to the hills and hillocks,
To the silvery vales and mountains;
Thence he took the merry harp-pins,
That the harp might play in concord.
Spake again wise Wainamoinen:
"I the pins have well completed,
Still the harp is yet unfinished;
Now I need five strings for playing,
Where shall I procure the
harp-strings?"
Then the ancient bard and minstrel
Journeyed through the fen and forest.
On a hillock sat a maiden,
Sat a virgin of the valley;
And the maiden was not weeping,
Joyful was the sylvan daughter,
Singing with the woodland songsters,
That the eventide might hasten,
In the hope that her beloved
Would the sooner sit beside her.

Wainamoinen, old and trusted,
Hastened, tripping to the virgin,
Asked her for her golden ringlets,
These the words of the magician:
"Give me, maiden, of thy tresses,
Give to me thy golden ringlets;
I will weave them into harp-strings,

To the joy of Wainamoinen,
To the pleasure of his people."

Thereupon the forest-maiden
Gave the singer of her tresses,
Gave him of her golden ringlets,
And of these he made the harp-strings.
Sources of eternal pleasure
To the people of Wainola.

Thus the sacred harp is finished,
And the minstrel, Wainamoinen,
Sits upon the rock of joyance,
Takes the harp within his fingers,
Turns the arch up, looking skyward;
With his knee the arch supporting,
Sets the strings in tuneful order,
Runs his fingers o'er the harp-strings,
And the notes of pleasure follow.
Straightway ancient Wainamoinen,
The eternal wisdom-singer,
Plays upon his harp of birch-wood.
Far away is heard the music,
Wide the harp of joy re-echoes;
Mountains dance and valleys listen,
Flinty rocks are torn asunder,
Stones are hurled upon the waters,
Pebbles swim upon the Big-Sea,
Pines and lindens laugh with pleasure,
Alders skip about the heather,
And the aspen sways in concord.

All the daughters of Wainola
Straightway leave their shining needles,
Hasten forward like the current,
Speed along like rapid rivers,
That they may enjoy and wonder.
Laugh the younger men and maidens,
Happy-hearted are the matrons
Flying swift to hear the playing,
To enjoy the common pleasure,
Hear the harp of Wainamoinen.
Aged men and bearded seniors,
Gray-haired mothers with their daughters
Stop in wonderment and listen.
Creeps the babe in full enjoyment
As he hears the magic singing,
Hears the harp of Wainamoinen.
All of Northland stops in wonder,
Speaks in unison these measures:
"Never have we heard such playing,
Never heard such strains of music,
Never since the earth was fashioned,
As the songs of this magician,
This sweet singer, Wainamoinen!"

Far and wide the sweet tones echo,
Ring throughout the seven hamlets,
O'er the seven islands echo;
Every creature of the Northland
Hastens forth to look and listen,
Listen to the songs of gladness,
To the harp of Wainamoinen.
All the beasts that haunt the woodlands
Fall upon their knees and wonder
At the playing of the minstrel,
At his miracles of concord.
All the songsters of the forests
Perch upon the trembling branches,
Singing to the wondrous playing
Of the harp of Wainamoinen.
All the dwellers of the waters
Leave their beds, and caves, and grottoes,
Swim against the shore and listen
To the playing of the minstrel,
To the harp of Wainamoinen.
All the little things in nature,
Rise from earth, and fall from ether,
Come and listen to the music,
To the notes of the enchanter,
To the songs of the magician,
To the harp of Wainamoinen.

Plays the singer of the Northland,
Plays in miracles of sweetness,
Plays one day, and then a second,
Plays the third from morn till even;
Plays within the halls and cabins,
In the dwellings of his people,
Till the floors and ceilings echo,
Till resound the roofs of pine-wood,
Till the windows speak and tremble,
Till the portals echo joyance,
And the hearth-stones sing in pleasure.

As he journeys through the forest,
As he wanders through the woodlands,
Pine and sorb-tree bid him welcome,
Birch and willow bend obeisance,
Beech and aspen bow submission;
And the linden waves her branches
To the measure of his playing,
To the notes of the magician.
As the minstrel plays and wanders,
Sings upon the mead and heather,
Glen and hill his songs re-echo,
Ferns and flowers laugh
in pleasure,
And the shrubs attune their voices
To the music of the harp-strings,
To the songs of Wainamoinen.

Rune XLV: Birth of the Nine Diseases

Louhi, hostess of the Northland,
Heard the word in Sariola,
Heard the news with ears of envy,
That Wainola lives and prospers,
That Osmoinen's wealth increases,
Through the ruins of the Sampo,
Ruins of the lid in colours.
Thereupon her wrath she kindled,
Well considered, long reflected,
How she might prepare destruction
For the people of Wainola,
For the tribes of Kalevala.

With this prayer she turns to Ukko,
Thus entreats the god of thunder:
"Ukko, thou who art in heaven,
Help me slay Wainola's people
With thine iron-hail of justice,
With thine arrows tipped with lightning,
Or from sickness let them perish,
Let them die the death deserving;
Let the men die in the forest,
And the women in the hurdles!"

The blind daughter of Tuoni,
Old and wicked witch, Lowyatar,
Worst of all the deathland women,
Ugliest of Mana's children,
Source of all the host of evils,
All the ills and plagues of Northland,
Black in heart, and soul, and visage,
Evil genius of Lappala,
Made her couch along the wayside,
On the fields of sin and sorrow;
Turned her back upon the east-wind,
To the source of stormy weather,
To the chilling winds of morning.

When the winds arose at evening,
Heavy-laden grew Lowyatar,
Through the east-wind's impregnation,
On the sand-plains, vast and barren.
Long she bore her weight of trouble,
Many morns she suffered anguish,
Till at last she leaves the desert,
Makes her couch within the forest,
On a rock upon the mountain;
Labours long to leave her burden
By the mountain-springs and fountains,
By the crystal waters flowing,
By the sacred stream and whirlpool,
By the cataract and fire-stream;
But her burden does not lighten.
Blind Lowyatar, old and ugly,
Knew not where to look for succor,
How to lose her weight of sorrow,
Where to lay her evil children.

Spake the Highest from the heavens,
These the words of mighty Ukko:
"Is a triangle in Swamp-field,
Near the border of the ocean,
In the never-pleasant Northland,
In the dismal Sariola;
Thither go and lay thy burden,
In Pohyola leave thine offspring;
There the Laplanders await thee,
There will bid thy children welcome."

Thereupon the blind Lowyatar,
Blackest daughter of Tuoni,
Mana's old and ugly maiden,

Hastened on her journey northward,
To the chambers of Pohyola,
To the ancient halls of Louhi,
There to lay her heavy burdens,
There to leave her evil offspring.

Louhi, hostess of the Northland,
Old and toothless witch of Pohya,
Takes Lowyatar to her mansion;
Silently she leads the stranger
To the bath-rooms of her chamber,
Pours the foaming beer of barley,
Lubricates the bolts and hinges,
That their movements may be secret,
Speaks these measures to Lowyatar:
"Faithful daughter of Creation,
Thou most beautiful of women,
First and last of ancient mothers,
Hasten on thy feet to ocean,
To the ocean's centre hasten,
Take the sea-foam from the waters,
Take the honey of the mermaids,
And anoint thy sacred members,
That thy labours may be lightened.

"Should all this be unavailing,
Ukko, thou who art in heaven,
Hasten hither, thou art needed,
Come thou to thy child in trouble,
Help the helpless and afflicted.
Take thy golden-coloured sceptre,
Charm away opposing forces,
Strike the pillars of the stronghold,
Open all resisting portals,
That the great and small may wander
From their ancient hiding-places,
Through the courts and halls of freedom."

Finally the blind Lowyatar,
Wicked witch of Tuonela,
Was delivered of her burden,
Laid her offspring in the cradle,
Underneath the golden covers.
Thus at last were born nine children,
In an evening of the summer,
From Lowyatar, blind and ancient,
Ugly daughter of Tuoni.

Faithfully the virgin-mother
Guards her children in affection,
As an artist loves and nurses
What his skillful hands have fashioned.

Thus Lowyatar named her offspring,
Colic, Pleurisy, and Fever,
Ulcer, Plague, and dread Consumption,
Gout, Sterility, and Cancer.
And the worst of these nine children
Blind Lowyatar quickly banished,
Drove away as an enchanter,
To bewitch the lowland people,
To engender strife and envy.

Louhi, hostess of Pohyola,
Banished all the other children
To the fog-point in the ocean,
To the island forest-covered;
Banished all the fatal creatures,
Gave these wicked sons of evil
To the people of Wainola,
To the youth of Kalevala,
For the Kalew-tribe's destruction.
Quick Wainola's maidens sicken,
Young and aged, men and heroes,
With the worst of all diseases,
With diseases new and nameless;
Sick and dying is Wainola.

Thereupon old Wainamoinen,
Wise and wonderful enchanter,
Hastens to his people's rescue,
Hastens to a war with Mana,
To a conflict with Tuoni,
To destroy the evil children
Of the evil maid, Lowyatar.
Wainamoinen heats the bath-rooms,
Heats the blocks of healing-sandstone
With the magic wood of Northland,
Gathered by the sacred river;
Water brings in covered buckets
From the cataract and whirlpool;
Brooms he brings enwrapped with ermine,
Well the bath the healer cleanses,
Softens well the brooms of birch-wood;
Then a honey-heat he wakens,

Fills the rooms with healing vapors,
From the virtue of the pebbles
Glowing in the heat of magic,
Thus he speaks in supplication:
"Come, O Ukko, to my rescue,
God of mercy, lend thy presence,
Give these vapor-baths new virtues,
Grant to them the powers of healing,
And restore my dying people;
Drive away these fell diseases,
Banish them to the unworthy,
Let the holy sparks enkindle,
Keep this heat in healing limits,
That it may not harm thy children,
May not injure the afflicted.
When I pour the sacred waters
On the heated blocks of sandstone,
May the water turn to honey
Laden with the balm of healing.
Let the stream of magic virtues
Ceaseless flow to all my children,
From this bath enrolled in sea-moss,
That the guiltless may not suffer,
That my tribe-folk may not perish,
Till the Master gives permission,
Until Ukko sends his minions,
Sends diseases of his choosing,
To destroy my trusting people.
Let the hostess of Pohyola,
Wicked witch that sent these troubles,
Suffer from a gnawing conscience,
Suffer for her evil doings.
Should the Master of Wainola
Lose his magic skill and weaken,
Should he prove of little service
To deliver from misfortune,
To deliver from these evils,
Then may Ukko be our healer,
Be our strength and wise Physician.

"Omnipresent God of mercy,
Thou who livest in the heavens,
Hasten hither, thou art needed,
Hasten to thine ailing children,
To observe their cruel tortures,
To dispel these fell diseases,
Drive destruction from our borders.
Bring with thee thy mighty fire-sword,
Bring to me thy blade of lightning,
That I may subdue these evils,
That these monsters I may banish,
Send these pains, and ills, and tortures,
To the empire of Tuoni,
To the kingdom of the east-winds,
To the islands of the wicked,
To the caverns of the demons,
To the rocks within the mountains,
To the hidden beds of iron,
That the rocks may fall and sicken,
And the beds of iron perish.
Rocks and metals do not murmur
At the hands of the invader.

"Torture-daughter of Tuoni,
Sitting on the mount of anguish,
At the junction of three rivers,
Turning rocks of pain and torture,
Turn away these fell diseases
Through the virtues of the blue-stone;
Lead them to the water-channels,
Sink them in the deeps of ocean,
Where the winds can never find them,
Where the sunlight never enters.

"Should this prayer prove unavailing,
O, Health-virgin, maid of beauty
Come and heal my dying people,
Still their agonies and anguish,
Give them consciousness and comfort,
Give them healthful rest and slumber;
These diseases take and banish,
Take them in thy copper vessel,
To thy caves within the mountains,
To the summit of the Pain-rock,
Hurl them to thy boiling caldrons.
In the mountain is a touch-stone,
Lucky-stone of ancient story,
With a hole bored through the centre,
Through this pour these pains and tortures,
Wretched feelings, thoughts of evil,
Human ailments, days unlucky,
Tribulations, and misfortunes,
That they may not rise at evening,
May not see the light of morning."

Ending thus, old Wainamoinen,
The eternal, wise enchanter,
Rubbed his sufferers with balsams,
Rubbed the tissues, red and painful,
With the balm of healing flowers,
Balsams made of herbs enchanted,
Sprinkled all with healing vapors,
Spake these words in supplication.
"Ukko, thou who art in heaven,
God of justice, and of mercy,
Send us from the east a rain-cloud,
Send a dark cloud from
the northwest,
From the north let fall a third one,
Send us mingled rain and honey,
Balsam from the great Physician,
To remove this plague of Northland.
What I know of healing measures,
Only comes from my Creator;
Lend me, therefore, of thy wisdom,
That I may relieve my people,
Save them from the fell destroyer.
If my hands should fall in virtue.
Let the hands of Ukko follow,
God alone can save from trouble.
Come to us with thine enchantment,
Speak the magic words of healing,
That my people may not perish;
Give to all alleviation
From their sicknesses and sorrows;
In the morning, in the evening,
Let their wasting ailments vanish;
Drive the Death-child from Wainola,
Nevermore to visit Northland,
Never in the course of ages,
Never while the moonlight glimmers
O'er the lakes of Kalevala."

Wainamoinen, the enchanter,
The eternal wisdom-singer,
Thus expelled the nine diseases,
Evil children of Lowyatar,
Healed the tribes of Kalevala,
Saved his people from destruction.

RUNE XLVI: Otso the Honey Eater

Came the tidings to Pohyola,
To the village of the Northland,
That Wainola had recovered
From her troubles and misfortunes,
From her sicknesses and sorrows.

Louhi, hostess of the Northland,
Toothless dame of Sariola,
Envy-laden, spake these measures:
"Know I other means of trouble,
I have many more resources;
I will drive the bear before me,
From the heather and the mountain,
Drive him from the fen and forest,
Drive great Otso from the glen-wood
On the cattle of Wainola,
On the flocks of Kalevala."

Thereupon the Northland hostess
Drove the hungry bear of Pohya
From his cavern to the meadows,
To Wainola's plains and pastures.

Wainamoinen, ancient minstrel,
To his brother spake as follows:
"O thou blacksmith, Ilmarinen,
Forge a spear from magic metals,
Forge a lancet triple-pointed,
Forge the handle out of copper,
That I may destroy great Otso,
Slay the mighty bear of Northland,
That he may not eat my horses,
Nor destroy my herds of cattle,
Nor the flocks upon my pastures."

Thereupon the skillful blacksmith
Forged a spear from magic metals,
Forged a lancet triple-pointed,
Not the longest, nor the shortest,
Forged the spear in wondrous beauty.
On one side a bear was sitting,
Sat a wolf upon the other,
On the blade an elk lay sleeping,
On the shaft a colt was running,
Near the hilt a roebuck bounding.

Snows had fallen from the heavens,
Made the flocks as white as ermine
Or the hare, in days of winter,
And the minstrel sang these measures:
"My desire impels me onward
To the Metsola-dominions,
To the homes of forest-maidens,
To the courts of the white virgins;
I will hasten to the forest,
Labour with the woodland-forces.

"Ruler of the Tapio-forests,
Make of me a conquering hero,
Help me clear these boundless woodlands.
O Mielikki, forest-hostess,
Tapio's wife, thou fair Tellervo,
Call thy dogs and well enchain them,
Set in readiness thy hunters,
Let them wait within their kennels.

"Otso, thou O Forest-apple,
Bear of honey-paws and fur-robes,
Learn that Wainamoinen follows,
That the singer comes to meet thee;
Hide thy claws within thy mittens,
Let thy teeth remain in darkness,
That they may not harm the minstrel,
May be powerless in battle.
Mighty Otso, much beloved,
Honey-eater of the mountains,
Settle on the rocks in slumber,
On the turf and in thy caverns;
Let the aspen wave above thee,
Let the merry birch-tree rustle
O'er thy head for thy protection.
Rest in peace, thou much-loved Otso,
Turn about within thy thickets,
Like the partridge at her brooding,
In the spring-time like the wild-goose."

When the ancient Wainamoinen
Heard his dog bark in the forest,
Heard his hunter's call and echo,
He addressed the words that follow:
"Thought it was the cuckoo calling,
Thought the pretty bird was singing;
It was not the sacred cuckoo,
Not the liquid notes of songsters,
'Twas my dog that called and murmured,
'Twas the echo of my hunter
At the cavern-doors of Otso,
On the border of the woodlands."

Wainamoinen, old and trusty,
Finds the mighty bear in waiting,
Lifts in joy the golden covers,
Well inspects his shining fur-robes;
Lifts his honey-paws in wonder,
Then addresses his Creator:
"Be thou praised, O mighty Ukko,
As thou givest me great Otso,
Givest me the Forest-apple,
Thanks be paid to thee unending."
To the bear he spake these measures:
"Otso, thou my well beloved,
Honey-eater of the woodlands,
Let not anger swell thy bosom;
I have not the force to slay thee,
Willingly thy life thou givest
As a sacrifice to Northland.
Thou hast from the tree descended,
Glided from the aspen branches,
Slippery the trunks in autumn,
In the fog-days, smooth the branches.
Golden friend of fen and forest,
In thy fur-robes rich and beauteous,
Pride of woodlands, famous Light-foot,
Leave thy cold and cheerless dwelling,
Leave thy home within the alders,
Leave thy couch among the willows,
Hasten in thy purple stockings,
Hasten from thy walks restricted,
Come among the haunts of heroes,
Join thy friends in Kalevala.
We shall never treat thee evil,
Thou shalt dwell in peace and plenty,
Thou shalt feed on milk and honey,
Honey is the food of strangers.
Haste away from this thy covert,
From the couch of the unworthy,
To a couch beneath the rafters
Of Wainola's ancient dwellings.
Haste thee onward o'er the snow-plain,
As a leaflet in the autumn;

Skip beneath these birchen branches,
As a squirrel in the summer,
As a cuckoo in the spring-time."

Wainamoinen, the magician,
The eternal wisdom-singer,
O'er the snow-fields hastened homeward,
Singing o'er the hills and mountains,
With his guest, the ancient Otso,
With his friend, the famous Light-foot,
With the Honey-paw of Northland.

Far away was heard the singing,
Heard the playing of the hunter,
Heard the songs of Wainamoinen;
All the people heard and wondered,
Men and maidens, young and aged,
From their cabins spake as follows:
"Hear the echoes from the woodlands,
Hear the bugle from the forest,
Hear the flute-notes of the songsters,
Hear the pipes of forest-maidens!"

Wainamoinen, old and trusty,
Soon appears within the court-yard.
Rush the people from their cabins,
And the heroes ask these questions:
"Has a mine of gold been opened,
Hast thou found a vein of silver,
Precious jewels in thy pathway?
Does the forest yield her treasures,
Give to thee the Honey-eater?
Does the hostess of the woodlands,
Give to thee the lynx and adder,
Since thou comest home rejoicing,
Playing, singing, on thy snow-shoes?"

Wainamoinen, ancient minstrel,
Gave this answer to his people:
"For his songs I caught the adder,
Caught the serpent for his wisdom;
Therefore do I come rejoicing,
Singing, playing, on my snow-shoes.
Not the mountain lynx, nor serpent,
Comes, however, to our dwellings;
The Illustrious is coming,
Pride and beauty of the forest,
'Tis the Master comes among us,
Covered with his friendly fur-robe.
Welcome, Otso, welcome, Light-foot,
Welcome, Loved-one from the glenwood!
If the mountain guest is welcome,
Open wide the gates of entry;
If the bear is thought unworthy,
Bar the doors against the stranger."
This the answer of the tribe-folk:
"We salute thee, mighty Otso,
Honey-paw, we bid thee welcome,
Welcome to our courts and cabins,
Welcome, Light-foot, to our tables
Decorated for thy coming!
We have wished for thee for ages,
Waiting since the days of childhood,
For the notes of Tapio's bugle,
For the singing of the wood-nymphs,
For the coming of dear Otso,
For the forest gold and silver,
Waiting for the year of plenty,
Longing for it as for summer,
As the shoe waits for the snow-fields,
As the sledge for beaten highways,
As the maiden for her suitor,
And the wife her husband's coming;
Sat at evening by the windows,
At the gates have sat at morning,
Sat for ages at the portals,
Near the granaries in winter,
Till the snow-fields warmed and vanished,
Till the sails unfurled in joyance,
Till the earth grew green and blossomed,
Thinking all the while as follows:
'Where is our beloved Otso,
Why delays our forest-treasure?
Has he gone to distant Ehstland,
To the upper glens of Suomi?'"
Spake the ancient Wainamoinen:
"Whither shall I lead the stranger,
Whither take the golden Light-foot?
Shall I lead him to the garner,
To the house of straw conduct him?"
This the answer of his tribe-folk:
"To the dining-hall lead Otso,
Greatest hero of the Northland.
Famous Light-foot, Forest-apple,

Pride and glory of the woodlands,
Have no fear before these maidens,
Fear not curly-headed virgins,
Clad in silver-tinselled raiment;
Maidens hasten to their chambers
When dear Otso joins their number,
When the hero comes among them."
This the prayer of Wainamoinen:
"Grant, O Ukko, peace and plenty
Underneath these painted rafters,
In this ornamented dwelling;
Thanks be paid to gracious Ukko!"
Spake again the ancient minstrel:
"Whither shall we lead dear Otso,
Whither take the fur-clad stranger?"
This the answer of his people:
"Hither let the fur-robed Light-foot
Be saluted on his coming;
Let the Honey-paw be welcomed
To the hearth-stone of the penthouse,
Welcomed to the boiling caldrons,
That we may admire his fur-robe,
May behold his cloak with joyance.
Have no care, thou much-loved Otso,
Let not anger swell thy bosom
As thy coat we view with pleasure;
We thy fur shall never injure,
Shall not make it into garments
To protect unworthy people."

Thereupon wise Wainamoinen
Pulled the sacred robe from Otso,
Spread it in the open court-yard,
Cut the members into fragments,
Laid them in the heating caldrons,
In the copper-bottomed vessels.
O'er the fire the crane was hanging,
On the crane were hooks of copper,
On the hooks the broiling vessels
Filled with bear-steak for the feasting,
Seasoned with the salt of Dwina,
From the Saxon-land imported,
From the distant Dwina-waters,
From the salt-sea brought in shallops.

Ready is the feast of Otso;
From the fire are swung the kettles
On the crane of polished iron;
In the centres of the tables
Is the bear displayed in dishes,
Golden dishes, decorated;
Of the fir tree and the linden
Were the tables newly fashioned;
Drinking cups were forged from copper,
Knives of gold and spoons of silver;
Filled the vessels to their borders
With the choicest bits of Light-foot,
Fragments of the Forest-apple.
Spake the ancient Wainamoinen:
"Ancient one with bosom golden,
Potent voice in Tapio's council,
Metsola's most lovely hostess,
Hostess of the glen and forest,
Hero-son of Tapiola,
Stalwart youth in cap of scarlet,
Tapio's most beauteous virgin,
Fair Tellervo of the woodlands,
Metsola with all her people,
Come, and welcome, to the feasting,
To the marriage-feast of Otso!
All sufficient, the provisions,
Food to eat and drink abundant,
Plenty for the hosts assembled,
Plenty more to give the village."
This the question of the people:
"Tell us of the birth of Otso!
Was he born within a manger,
Was he nurtured in the bath-room
Was his origin ignoble?"
This is Wainamoinen's answer:
"Otso was not born a beggar,
Was not born among the rushes,
Was not cradled in a manger;
Honey-paw was born in ether,
In the regions of the Moon-land,
On the shoulders of Otava,
With the daughters of creation.

"Through the ether walked a maiden,
On the red rims of the cloudlets,
On the border of the heavens,
In her stockings purple-tinted,
In her golden-coloured sandals.
In her hand she held a wool-box,

With a hair-box on her shoulder;
Threw the wool upon the ocean,
And the hair upon the rivers;
These are rocked by winds and waters,
Water-currents bear them onward,
Bear them to the sandy seashore,
Land them near the woods of honey,
On an island forest-covered.

"Fair Mielikki, woodland hostess,
Tapio's most cunning daughter,
Took the fragments from the sea-side,
Took the white wool from the waters,
Sewed the hair and wool together,
Laid the bundle in her basket,
Basket made from bark of birch-wood,
Bound with cords the magic bundle;
With the chains of gold she bound it
To the pine tree's topmost branches.
There she rocked the thing of magic,
Rocked to life the tender baby,
Mid the blossoms of the pine tree,
On the fir-top set with needles;
Thus the young bear well was nurtured,
Thus was sacred Otso cradled
On the honey-tree of Northland,
In the middle of the forest.

"Sacred Otso grew and flourished,
Quickly grew with graceful movements,
Short of feet, with crooked ankles,
Wide of mouth and broad of forehead,
Short his nose, his fur-robe velvet;
But his claws were not well fashioned,
Neither were his teeth implanted.
Fair Mielikki, forest hostess,
Spake these words in meditation:
'Claws I should be pleased to give him,
And with teeth endow the wonder,
Would he not abuse the favour.'

"Swore the bear a promise sacred,
On his knees before Mielikki,
Hostess of the glen and forest,
And before omniscient Ukko,
First and last of all creators,
That he would not harm the worthy,
Never do a deed of evil.
Then Mielikki, woodland hostess,
Wisest maid of Tapiola,
Sought for teeth and claws to give him,
From the stoutest mountain-ashes,
From the juniper and oak tree,
From the dry knots of the alder.
Teeth and claws of these were worthless,
Would not render goodly service.

"Grew a fir tree on the mountain,
Grew a stately pine in Northland,
And the fir had silver branches,
Bearing golden cones abundant;
These the sylvan maiden gathered,
Teeth and claws of these she fashioned
In the jaws and feet of Otso,
Set them for the best of uses.
Then she freed her new-made creature,
Let the Light-foot walk and wander,
Let him lumber through the marshes,
Let him amble through the forest,
Roll upon the plains and pastures;
Taught him how to walk a hero,
How to move with graceful motion,
How to live in ease and pleasure,
How to rest in full contentment,
In the moors and in the marshes,
On the borders of the woodlands;
How unshod to walk in summer,
Stockingless to run in autumn;
How to rest and sleep in winter
In the clumps of alder-bushes
Underneath the sheltering fir tree,
Underneath the pine's protection,
Wrapped securely in his fur-robes,
With the juniper and willow.
This the origin of Otso,
Honey-eater of the Northlands,
Whence the sacred booty cometh."
Thus again the people questioned:
"Why became the woods so gracious,
Why so generous and friendly?
Why is Tapio so humored,
That he gave his dearest treasure,
Gave to thee his Forest-apple,
Honey-eater of his kingdom?

Was he startled with thine arrows,
Frightened with the spear and broadsword?"

Wainamoinen, the magician,
Gave this answer to the question:
"Filled with kindness was the forest,
Glen and woodland full of greetings,
Tapio showing greatest favour.
Fair Mielikki, forest hostess,
Metsola's bewitching daughter,
Beauteous woodland maid, Tellervo,
Gladly led me on my journey,
Smoothed my pathway through
the glen-wood.
Marked the trees upon the mountains,
Pointing me to Otso's caverns,
To the Great Bear's golden island.

"When my journeyings had ended,
When the bear had been discovered,
Had no need to launch my javelins,
Did not need to aim the arrow;
Otso tumbled in his vaulting,
Lost his balance in his cradle,
In the fir tree where he slumbered;
Tore his breast upon the branches,
Freely gave his life to others.

"Mighty Otso, my beloved,
Thou my golden friend and hero,
Take thy fur-cap from thy forehead,
Lay aside thy teeth forever,
Hide thy fingers in the darkness,
Close thy mouth and still thine anger,
While thy sacred skull is breaking.

"Now I take the eyes of Otso,
Lest he lose the sense of seeing,
Lest their former powers shall weaken;
Though I take not all his members,
Not alone must these be taken.

"Now I take the ears of Otso,
Lest he lose the sense of hearing,
Lest their former powers shall weaken;
Though I take not all his members,
Not alone must these be taken.

"Now I take the nose of Otso,
Lest he lose the sense of smelling,
Lest its former powers shall weaken;
Though I take not all his members,
Not alone must this be taken.

"Now I take the tongue of Otso,
Lest he lose the sense of tasting,
Lest its former powers shall weaken;
Though I take not all his members,
Not alone must this be taken.

"Now I take the brain of Otso,
Lest he lose the means of thinking,
Lest his consciousness should fail him,
Lest his former instincts weaken;
Though I take not all his members,
Not alone must this be taken.

"I will reckon him a hero,
That will count the teeth of Light-foot,
That will loosen Otso's fingers
From their settings firmly fastened."

None he finds with strength sufficient
To perform the task demanded.
Therefore ancient Wainamoinen
Counts the teeth of sacred Otso;
Loosens all the claws of Light-foot,
With his fingers strong as copper,
Slips them from their firm foundations,
Speaking to the bear these measures:
"Otso, thou my Honey-eater,
Thou my Fur-ball of the woodlands,
Onward, onward, must thou journey
From thy low and lonely dwelling,
To the court-rooms of the village.
Go, my treasure, through the pathway
Near the herds of swine and cattle,
To the hill-tops forest covered,
To the high and rising mountains,
To the spruce-trees filled with needles,
To the branches of the pine tree;
There remain, my Forest-apple,
Linger there in lasting slumber,
Where the silver bells are ringing,
To the pleasure of the shepherd."

Thus beginning, and thus ending,
Wainamoinen, old and truthful,
Hastened from his emptied tables,
And the children thus addressed him:
"Whither hast thou led thy booty,
Where hast left thy Forest-apple,
Sacred Otso of the woodlands?
Hast thou left him on the iceberg,
Buried him upon the snow-field?
Hast thou sunk him in the quicksand,
Laid him low beneath the heather?"
Wainamoinen spake in answer:
"Have not left him on the iceberg,
Have not buried him in snow-fields;
There the dogs would soon devour him,
Birds of prey would feast upon him;
Have not hidden him in Swamp-land,
Have not buried him in heather;
There the worms would live upon him,
Insects feed upon his body.
Thither I have taken Otso,
To the summit of the Gold-hill,
To the copper-bearing mountain,
Laid him in his silken cradle
In the summit of a pine tree,
Where the winds and sacred branches
Rock him to his lasting slumber,
To the pleasure of the hunter,
To the joy of man and hero.
To the east his lips are pointing,
While his eyes are northward looking;
But dear Otso looks not upward,
For the fierceness of the storm-winds
Would destroy his sense of vision."

Wainamoinen, ancient minstrel,
Touched again his harp of joyance,
Sang again his songs enchanting,
To the pleasure of the evening,
To the joy of morn arising.
Spake the singer of Wainola:
"Light for me a torch of pine-wood,
For the darkness is appearing,
That my playing may be joyous
And my wisdom-songs find welcome."
Then the ancient sage and singer,
Wise and worthy Wainamoinen,
Sweetly sang, and played, and chanted,
Through the long and dreary evening,
Ending thus his incantation:
"Grant, O Ukko, my Creator,
That the people of Wainola
May enjoy another banquet
In the company of Light-foot;
Grant that we may long remember
Kalevala's feast with Otso!

"Grant, O Ukko, my Creator,
That the signs may guide our footsteps,
That the notches in the pine tree
May direct my faithful people
To the bear-dens of the woodlands;
That great Tapio's sacred bugle
May resound through glen and forest;
That the wood-nymph's call may echo,
May be heard in field and hamlet,
To the joy of all that listen!
Let great Tapio's horn for ages
Ring throughout the fen and forest,
Through the hills and dales of Northland
O'er the meadows and the mountains,
To awaken song and gladness
In the forests of Wainola,
On the snowy plains of Suomi,
On the meads of Kalevala,
For the coming generations."

Rune XLVII: Louhi Steals Sun, Moon and Fire

Wainamoinen, ancient minstrel,
Touched again his magic harp-strings,
Sang in miracles of concord,
Filled the north with joy and gladness.
Melodies arose to heaven,
Songs arose to Luna's chambers,
Echoed through the Sun's bright windows
And the Moon has left her station,
Drops and settles in the birch-tree;
And the Sun comes from his castle,
Settles in the fir tree branches,
Comes to share the common pleasure,

Comes to listen to the singing,
To the harp of Wainamoinen.

Louhi, hostess of Pohyola,
Northland's old and toothless wizard,
Makes the Sun and Moon her captives;
In her arms she takes fair Luna
From her cradle in the birch-tree,
Calls the Sun down from his station,
From the fir tree's bending branches,
Carries them to upper Northland,
To the darksome Sariola;
Hides the Moon, no more to glimmer,
In a rock of many colours;
Hides the Sun, to shine no longer,
In the iron-banded mountain;
Thereupon these words she utters:
"Moon of gold and Sun of silver,
Hide your faces in the caverns
Of Pohyola's dismal mountain;
Shine no more to gladden Northland,
Till I come to give ye freedom,
Drawn by coursers nine in number,
Sable coursers of one mother!"

When the golden Moon had vanished,
And the silver Sun had hidden
In the iron-banded caverns,
Louhi stole the fire from Northland,
From the regions of Wainola,
Left the mansions cold and cheerless,
And the cabins full of darkness.
Night was king and reigned unbroken,
Darkness ruled in Kalevala,
Darkness in the home of Ukko.
Hard to live without the moonlight,
Harder still without the sunshine;
Ukko's life is dark and dismal,
When the Sun and Moon desert him.

Ukko, first of all creators,
Lived in wonder at the darkness;
Long reflected, well considered,
Why this miracle in heaven,
What this accident in nature
To the Moon upon her journey;
Why the Sun no more is shining,
Why has disappeared the moonlight.
Then great Ukko walked the heavens,
To the border of the cloudlets,
In his purple-coloured vestments,
In his silver-tinselled sandals,
Seeking for the golden moonlight,
Looking for the silver sunshine.
Lightning Ukko struck in darkness
From the edges of his fire-sword;
Shot the flames in all directions,
From his blade of golden colour,
Into heaven's upper spaces,
Into ether's starry pastures.

When a little fire had kindled,
Ukko hid it in the cloud-space,
In a box of gold and silver,
In a case adorned with silver,
Gave it to the ether-maidens,
Called a virgin then to rock it,
That it might become a new-moon,
That a second sun might follow.
On the long-cloud rocked the virgin,
On the blue-edge of the ether,
Rocked the fire of the Creator,
In her copper-coloured cradle,
With her ribbons silver-studded.
Lowly bend the bands of silver,
Loud the golden cradle echoes,
And the clouds of Northland thunder,
Low descends the dome of heaven,
At the rocking of the lightning,
Rocking of the fire of Ukko.
Thus the flame was gently cradled
By the virgin of the ether.
Long the fair and faithful maiden
Stroked the Fire-child with her fingers,
Tended it with care and pleasure,
Till in an unguarded moment
It escaped the ether-virgin,
Slipped the hands of her that nursed it.
Quick the heavens are burst asunder,
Quick the vault of Ukko opens,
Downward drops the wayward Fire-child,
Downward quick the red-ball rushes,
Shoots across the arch of heaven,
Hisses through the startled cloudlets,

Flashes through the troubled welkin,
Through nine starry vaults of ether.

Then the ancient Wainamoinen
Spake and these the words he uttered:
"Blacksmith brother, Ilmarinen,
Let us haste and look together,
What the kind of fire that falleth,
What the form of light that shineth
From the upper vault of heaven,
From the lower earth and ocean.
Has a second moon arisen,
Can it be a ball of sunlight?"

Thereupon the heroes wandered,
Onward journeyed and reflected,
How to gain the spot illumined,
How to find the sacred Fire-child.
Came a river rushing by them,
Broad and stately as an ocean.
Straightway ancient Wainamoinen
There began to build a vessel,
Build a boat to cross the river.
With the aid of Ilmarinen,
From the oak he cut the row-locks,
From the pine the oars he fashioned,
From the aspen shapes the rudder.
When the vessel they had finished,
Quick they rolled it to the current,
Hard they rowed and ever forward,
On the Nawa-stream and waters,
At the head of Nawa-river.

Ilmatar, the ether-daughter,
Foremost daughter of creation,
Came to meet them on their journey,
Thus addressed the coming strangers:
"Who are ye of Northland heroes,
Rowing on the Nawa-waters?"
Wainamoinen gave this answer:
"This the blacksmith, Ilmarinen,
I the ancient Wainamoinen.
Tell us now thy name and station,
Whither going, whence thou comest,
Where thy tribe-folk live and linger?"
Spake the daughter of the ether:
"I the oldest of the women,
Am the first of Ether's daughters,
Am the first of ancient mothers;
Seven times have I been wedded
To the heroes of creation.
Whither do ye strangers journey?"
Answered thus old Wainamoinen:
"Fire has left Wainola's hearth-stones,
Light has disappeared from Northland;
Have been sitting long in darkness,
Cold and darkness our companions;
Now we journey to discover
What the fire that fell from heaven,
Falling from the cloud's red lining,
To the deeps of earth and ocean."
Ilmatar returned this answer:
"Hard the flame is to discover,
Hard indeed to find the Fire-child;
Has committed many mischiefs,
Nothing good has he accomplished;
Quick the fire-ball fell from ether,
From the red rims of the cloudlets,
From the plains of the Creator,
Through the ever-moving heavens,
Through the purple ether-spaces,
Through the blackened flues of Turi,
To Palwoinen's rooms uncovered.
When the fire had reached the chambers
Of Palwoinen, son of evil,
He began his wicked workings,
He engaged in lawless actions,
Raged against the blushing maidens,
Fired the youth to evil conduct,
Singed the beards of men and heroes.

"Where the mother nursed her baby,
In the cold and cheerless cradle,
Thither flew the wicked Fire-child,
There to perpetrate some mischief;
In the cradle burned the infant,
By the infant burned the mother,
That the babe might visit Mana,
In the kingdom of Tuoni;
Said the child was born for dying,
Only destined for destruction,
Through the tortures of the Fire-child.
Greater knowledge had the mother,
Did not journey to Manala,

Knew the word to check the red-flame,
How to banish the intruder
Through the eyelet of a needle,
Through the death-hole of the hatchet."

Then the ancient Wainamoinen
Questioned Ilmatar as follows:
"Whither did the Fire-child wander,
Whither did the red-flame hasten,
From the border-fields of Turi,
To the woods, or to the waters?"
Straightway Ilmatar thus answers:
"When the fire had fled from Turi,
From the castles of Palwoinen,
Through the eyelet of the needle,
Through the death-hole of the hatchet,
First it burned the fields, and forests,
Burned the lowlands, and the heather;
Then it sought the mighty waters,
Sought the Alue-sea and river,
And the waters hissed and sputtered
In their anger at the Fire-child,
Fiery red the boiling Alue!

"Three times in the nights of summer,
Nine times in the nights of autumn,
Boil the waters to the tree-tops,
Roll and tumble to the mountain,
Through the red-ball's force and fury;
Hurls the pike upon the pastures,
To the mountain-cliffs, the salmon,
Where the ocean-dwellers wonder,
Long reflect and well consider
How to still the angry waters.
Wept the salmon for his grotto,
Mourned the whiting for his cavern,
And the lake-trout for his dwelling.
Quick the crook-necked salmon darted,
Tried to catch the fire-intruder,
But the red-ball quick escaped him;
Darted then the daring whiting,
Swallowed quick the wicked Fire-child,
Swallowed quick the flame of evil.
Quiet grow the Alue-waters,
Slowly settle to their shore-lines,
To their long-accustomed places,
In the long and dismal evening.

"Time had gone but little distance,
When the whiting grow affrighted,
Fear befel the fire-devourer;
Burning pain and writhing tortures
Seized the eater of the Fire-child;
Swam the fish in all directions,
Called, and moaned, and swam,
   and circled,
Swam one day, and then a second,
Swam the third from morn till even;
Swam she to the whiting-island,
To the caverns of the salmon,
Where a hundred islands cluster;
And the islands there assembled
Thus addressed the fire-devourer:
'There is none within these waters,
In this narrow Alue-lakelet,
That will eat the fated Fire-fish,
That will swallow thee in trouble,
In thine agonies and torture
From the Fire-child thou hast eaten.'

"Hearing this a trout forth darting,
Swallowed quick as light the whiting,
Quickly ate the fire-devourer.
Time had gone but little distance,
When the trout became affrighted,
Fear befel the whiting-eater;
Burning pain and writhing torment
Seized the eater of the Fire-fish.
Swam the trout in all directions,
Called, and moaned, and swam,
   and circled,
Swam one day, and then a second,
Swam the third from morn till even;
Swam she to the salmon-island,
Swam she to the whiting-grottoes,
Where a thousand islands cluster,
And the islands there assembled
Thus addressed the tortured
   lake-trout:
'There is none within this river,
In these narrow Alue-waters,
That will eat the wicked Fire-fish,
That will swallow thee in trouble,
In thine agonies and tortures,
From the Fire-fish thou hast eaten.'

"Hearing this the gray-pike darted,
Swallowed quick as light the lake-trout,
Quickly ate the tortured Fire-fish.

"Time had gone but little distance,
When the gray-pike grew affrighted,
Fear befel the lake-trout-eater;
Burning pain and writhing torment
Seized the reckless trout-devourer;
Swam the pike in all directions,
Called, and moaned, and swam, and circled,
Swam one day, and then a second,
Swam the third from morn till even,
To the cave of ocean-swallows,
To the sand-hills of the sea-gull,
Where a hundred islands cluster;
And the islands there assembled
Thus addressed the fire-devourer:
'There is none within this lakelet,
In these narrow Alue-waters,
That will eat the fated Fire-fish,
That will swallow thee in trouble,
In thine agonies and tortures,
From the Fire-fish thou hast eaten.'"

Wainamoinen, wise and ancient,
With the aid of Ilmarinen,
Weaves with skill a mighty fish-net
From the juniper and sea-grass;
Dyes the net with alder-water,
Ties it well with thongs of willow.
Straightway ancient Wainamoinen
Called the maidens to the fish-net,
And the sisters came as bidden.
With the netting rowed they onward,
Rowed they to the hundred islands,
To the grottoes of the salmon,
To the caverns of the whiting,
To the reeds of sable colour,
Where the gray-pike rests and watches.
On they hasten to the fishing,
Drag the net in all directions,
Drag it lengthwise, sidewise, crosswise,
And diagonally zigzag;
But they did not catch the Fire-fish.

Then the brothers went a-fishing,
Dragged the net in all directions,
Backwards, forwards, lengthwise, sidewise,
Through the homes of ocean-dwellers,
Through the grottoes of the salmon,
Through the dwellings of the whiting,
Through the reed-beds of the lake-trout,
Where the gray-pike lies in ambush;
But the fated Fire-fish came not,
Came not from the lake's abysses,
Came not from the Alue-waters.

Little fish could not be captured
In the large nets of the masters;
Murmured then the deep-sea-dwellers,
Spake the salmon to the lake-trout,
And the lake-trout to the whiting,
And the whiting to the gray-pike:
"Have the heroes of Wainola
Died, or have they all departed
From these fertile shores and waters?
Where then are the ancient weavers,
Weavers of the nets of flax-thread,
Those that frighten us with fish-poles,
Drag us from our homes unwilling?"

Hearing this wise Wainamoinen
Answered thus the deep-sea-dwellers:
"Neither have Wainola's heroes
Died, nor have they all departed
From these fertile shores and waters,
Two are born where one has perished;
Longer poles and finer fish-nets
Have the sons of Kalevala!"

Rune XLVIII: Capture of the Fire-fish

Wainamoinen, the enchanter,
The eternal wisdom-singer,
Long reflected, well considered,
How to weave the net of flax-yarn,
Weave the fish-net of the fathers.
Spake the minstrel of Wainola:
"Who will plow the field and fallow,
Sow the flax, and spin the flax-threads,

That I may prepare the fish-net,
Wherewith I may catch the
Fire-pike,
May secure the thing of evil?"

Soon they found a fertile island,
Found the fallow soil befitting,
On the border of the heather,
And between two stately oak-trees,
They prepared the soil for sowing.
Searching everywhere for flax-seed,
Found it in Tuoni's kingdom,
In the keeping of an insect.
Then they found a pile of ashes,
Where the fire had burned a vessel;
In the ashes sowed the seedlings
Near the Alue-lake and border,
In the rich and loamy fallow.
There the seed took root and flourished,
Quickly grew to great proportions,
In a single night in summer.
Thus the flax was sowed at evening,
Placed within the earth by moonlight;
Quick it grew, and quickly ripened,
Quick Wainola's heroes pulled it,
Quick they broke it on the hackles,
Hastened with it to the waters,
Dipped it in the lake and washed it;
Quickly brought it home and dried it,
Quickly broke, and combed,
and smoothed it,
Brushed it well at early morning,
Laid it into laps for spinning.
Quick the maidens twirl the spindles,
Spin the flaxen threads for weaving,
In a single night in summer.
Quick the sisters wind and reel it,
Make it ready for the needle.
Brothers weave it into fish-nets,
And the fathers twist the cordage,
While the mothers knit the meshes,
Rapidly the mesh-stick circles;
Soon the fish-net is completed,
In a single night in summer.
As the magic net is finished,
And in length a hundred fathoms,
On the rim three hundred fathoms,
Rounded stones are fastened to it,
Joined thereto are seven float-boards.

Now the young men take the fish-net,
And the old men cheer them onward,
Wish them good-luck at their fishing.
Long they row and drag the flax-seine,
Here and there the net is lowered;
Now they drag it lengthwise, sidewise,
Drag it through the slimy reed-beds;
But they do not catch the Fire-pike,
Only smelts, and luckless red-fish,
Little fish of little value.
Spake the ancient Wainamoinen:
"O thou blacksmith, Ilmarinen,
Let us go ourselves a-fishing,
Let us catch the fish of evil!"

To the fishing went the brothers,
Magic heroes of the Northland,
Pulled the fish-net through the waters,
Toward an island in the deep-sea;
Then they turn and drag the fish-net
Toward a meadow jutting seaward;
Now they drag it toward Wainola,
Draw it lengthwise, sidewise, crosswise,
Catching fish of every species,
Salmon, trout, and pike, and whiting,
Do not catch the evil Fire-fish.

Then the master, Wainamoinen,
Made additions to its borders,
Made it many fathoms wider,
And a hundred fathoms longer,
Then these words the hero uttered:
"Famous blacksmith, Ilmarinen,
Let us go again a-fishing,
Row again the magic fish-net,
Drag it well through all the waters,
That we may obtain the Fire-pike!"

Thereupon the Northland heroes
Go a second time a-fishing,
Drag their nets across the rivers,
Lakelets, seas, and bays, and inlets,
Catching fish of many species,
But the Fire-fish is not taken.

Wainamoinen, ancient singer,
Long reflecting, spake these measures:
"Dear Wellamo, water-hostess,
Ancient mother with the reed-breast,
Come, exchange thy water-raiment,
Change thy coat of reeds
and rushes
For the garments I shall give thee,
Light sea-foam, thine inner vesture,
And thine outer, moss and sea-grass,
Fashioned by the wind's fair daughters,
Woven by the flood's sweet maidens;
I will give thee linen vestments
Spun from flax of softest fibre,,
Woven by the Moon's white virgins,
Fashioned by the Sun's bright daughters,
Fitting raiment for Wellamo!

"Ahto, king of all the waters,
Ruler of a thousand grottoes,
Take a pole of seven fathoms,
Search with this the deepest waters,
Rummage well the lowest bottoms;
Stir up all the reeds and sea-weeds,
Hither drive a school of gray-pike,
Drive them to our magic fish-net,
From the haunts in pike abounding,
From the caverns, and the trout-holes,
From the whirlpools of the deep-sea,
From the bottomless abysses,
Where the sunshine never enters,
Where the moonlight never visits,
And the sands are never troubled."

Rose a pigmy from the waters,
From the floods a little hero,
Riding on a rolling billow,
And the pigmy spake these measures:
"Dost thou wish a worthy helper,
One to use the pole and frighten
Pike and salmon to thy fish-nets?"

Wainamoinen, old and faithful,
Answered thus the lake-born hero:
"Yea, we need a worthy helper,
One to hold the pole, and frighten
Pike and salmon to our fish-nets."

Thereupon the water-pigmy
Cut a linden from the border,
Spake these words to Wainamoinen:
"Shall I scare with all my powers,
With the forces of my being,
As thou needest shall I scare them?"
Spake the minstrel, Wainamoinen:
"If thou scarest as is needed,
Thou wilt scare with all thy forces,
With the strength of thy dominions."

Then began the pigmy-hero,
To affright the deep-sea-dwellers;
Drove the fish in countless numbers
To the net of the magicians.

Wainamoinen, ancient minstrel,
Drew his net along the waters,
Drew it with his ropes of flax-thread,
Spake these words of magic import:
"Come ye fish of Northland waters
To the regions of my fish-net,
As my hundred meshes lower."

Then the net was drawn and fastened,
Many were the gray-pike taken
By the master and magician.
Wainamoinen, happy-hearted,
Hastened to a neighboring island,
To a blue-point in the waters,
Near a red-bridge on the headland;
Landed there his draught of fishes,
Cast the pike upon the seashore,
And the Fire-pike was among them,
Cast the others to the waters.
Spake the ancient Wainamoinen:
"May I touch thee with my fingers,
Using not my gloves of iron,
Using not my blue-stone mittens?"
This the Sun-child hears and answers:
"I should like to carve the Fire-fish,
I should like this pike to handle,
If I had the knife of good-luck."

Quick a knife falls from the heavens,
From the clouds a magic fish-knife,
Silver-edged and golden-headed,

To the girdle of the Sun-child;
Quick he grasps the copper handle,
Quick the hero carves the Fire-pike,
Finds therein the tortured lake-trout;
Carves the lake-trout thus discovered,
Finds therein the fated whiting;
Carves the whiting, finds a blue-ball
In the third cave of his body.
He, the blue-ball quick unwinding,
Finds within a ball of scarlet;
Carefully removes the cover,
Finds the ball of fire within it,
Finds the flame from heaven fallen,
From the heights of the seventh heaven,
Through nine regions of the ether.

Wainamoinen long reflected
How to get the magic fire-ball
To Wainola's fireless hearth-stones,
To his cold and cheerless dwellings.
Quick he snatched the fire of heaven
From the fingers of the Sun-child.
Wainamoinen's beard it singes,
Burns the brow of Ilmarinen,
Burns the fingers of the blacksmith.
Rolling forth it hastens westward,
Hastens to the Alue shore-lines,
Burns the juniper and alder,
Burns the arid heath and meadow,
Rises to the lofty linden,
Burns the firs upon the mountains;
Hastens onward, onward, onward,
Burns the islands of the Northland,
Burns the Sawa fields and forests,
Burns the dry lands of Karyala.

Straightway ancient Wainamoinen
Hastens through the fields and fenlands,
Tracks the ranger to the glen-wood,
Finds the Fire-child in an elm-tree,
Sleeping in a bed of fungus.

Thereupon wise Wainamoinen
Wakes the child and speaks these measures:
"Wicked fire that God created,
Flame of Ukko from the heavens,
Thou hast gone in vain to sea-caves,
To the lakes without a reason;
Better go thou to my village,
To the hearth-stones of my people;
Hide thyself within my chimneys,
In mine ashes sleep and linger.
In the day-time I will use thee
To devour the blocks of birch-wood;
In the evening I will hide thee
Underneath the golden circle."

Then he took the willing Panu,
Took the willing fire of Ukko,
Laid it in a box of tinder,
In the punk-wood of a birch-tree,
In a vessel forged from copper;
Carried it with care and pleasure
To the fog-point in the waters,
To the island forest covered.
Thus returned the fire to Northland,
To the chambers of Wainola,
To the hearths of Kalevala.

Ilmarinen, famous blacksmith,
Hastened to the deep-sea's margin,
Sat upon the rock of torture,
Feeling pain the flame had given,
Laved his wounds with briny water,
Thus to still the Fire-child's fury,
Thus to end his persecutions.

Long reflecting, Ilmarinen
Thus addressed the flame of Ukko:
"Evil Panu from the heavens,
Wicked son of God from ether,
Tell me what has made thee angry,
Made thee burn my weary members,
Burn my beard, and face, and fingers,
Made me suffer deathland tortures?"
Spake again young Ilmarinen:
"How can I wild Panu conquer,
How shall I control his conduct,
Make him end his evil doings?
Come, thou daughter from Pohyola,
Come, white virgin of the hoar-frost,
Come on shoes of ice from Lapland,
Icicles upon thy garments,
In one hand a cup of white-frost,

In the other hand an ice-spoon;
Sprinkle snow upon my members,
Where the Fire-child has been resting,
Let the hoar frost fall and settle.

"Should this prayer be unavailing,
Come, thou son of Sariola,
Come, thou child of Frost from Pohya,
Come, thou Long-man from the ice-plains,
Of the height of stately pine trees,
Slender as the trunks of lindens,
On thy hands the gloves of hoar frost,
Cap of ice upon thy forehead,
On thy waist a white-frost girdle;
Bring the ice-dust from Pohyola,
From the cold and sunless village.
Rain is crystallized in Northland,
Ice in Pohya is abundant,
Lakes of ice and ice-bound rivers,
Frozen smooth, the sea of ether.
Bounds the hare in frosted fur-robe,
Climbs the bear in icy raiment,
Ambles o'er the snowy mountains.
Swans of frost descend the rivers,
Ducks of ice in countless numbers
Swim upon thy freezing waters,
Near the cataract and whirlpool.
Bring me frost upon thy snow-sledge,
Snow and ice in great abundance,
From the summit of the wild-top,
From the borders of the mountains.
With thine ice, and snow, and hoar-frost
Cover well mine injured members
Where wild Panu has been resting,
Where the child of Fire has lingered.

"Should this call be ineffective,
Ukko, God of love and mercy,
First and last of the creators,
From the east send forth a snow-cloud,
From the west despatch a second,
Join their edges well together,
Let there be no vacant places,
Let these clouds bring snow and
hoar-frost,
Lay the healing balm of Ukko
On my burning, tortured tissues,
Where wild Panu has been resting."

Thus the blacksmith, Ilmarinen,
Stills the pains by fire engendered,
Stills the agonies and tortures
Brought him by the child of evil,
Brought him by the wicked Panu.

Rune XLIX: Restoration of the Sun and Moon

Thus has Fire returned to Northland;
But the gold Moon is not shining,
Neither gleams the silver sunlight
In the chambers of Wainola,
On the plains of Kalevala.
On the crops the white-frost settled,
And the cattle died of hunger,
Even birds grew sick and perished.
Men and maidens, faint and famished,
Perished in the cold and darkness,
From the absence of the sunshine,
From the absence of the moonlight.
Knew the pike his holes and hollows,
And the eagle knew his highway,
Knew the winds the times for sailing;
But the wise men of the Northland
Could not know the dawn of morning,
On the fog-point in the ocean,
On the islands forest-covered.

Young and aged talked and wondered,
Well reflected, long debated,
How to live without the moonlight,
Live without the silver sunshine,
In the cold and cheerless Northland,
In the homes of Kalevala.
Long conjectured all the maidens,
Orphans asked the wise for counsel.

Spake a maid to Ilmarinen,
Running to the blacksmith's furnace:
"Rise, O artist, from thy slumbers,
Hasten from thy couch unworthy;
Forge from gold the Moon for Northland,

Forge anew the Sun from silver;
Cannot live without the moonlight,
Nor without the silver sunshine!"

From his couch arose the artist,
From his couch of stone, the blacksmith,
And began his work of forging,
Forging Sun and Moon for Northland.

Came the ancient Wainamoinen,
In the doorway sat and lingered,
Spake these words to Ilmarinen:
"Blacksmith, my beloved brother,
Thou the only metal-worker,
Tell me why thy magic hammer
Falls so heavy on thine anvil?"
Spake the youthful Ilmarinen:
"Moon of gold and Sun of silver,
I am forging for Wainola;
I shall swing them into ether,
Plant them in the starry heavens."
Spake the wise, old Wainamoinen:
"Senseless blacksmith of the ages,
Vainly dost thou swing thy hammer,
Vainly rings thy mighty anvil;
Silver will not gleam as sunshine,
Not of gold is born the moonlight!"

Ilmarinen, little heeding,
Ceases not to ply his hammer,
Sun and Moon the artist forges,
Wings the Moon of Magic upward,
Hurls it to the pine tree branches;
Does not shine without her master.
Then the silver Sun he stations
In an elm-tree on the mountain.
From his forehead drip the sweat-drops,
Perspiration from his fingers,
Through his labours at the anvil
While the Sun and Moon were forging;
But the Sun shone not at morning
From his station in the elm-tree;
And the Moon shone not at evening
From the pine tree's topmost branches.
Spake the ancient Wainamoinen:
"Let the Fates be now consulted,
And the oracles examined;
Only thus may we discover
Where the Sun and Moon lie hidden."

Thereupon old Wainamoinen,
Only wise and true magician,
Cut three chips from trunks of alder,
Laid the chips in magic order,
Touched and turned them with his fingers,
Spake these words of master-magic:
"Of my Maker seek I knowledge,
Ask in hope and faith the answer
From the great magician, Ukko:
Tongue of alder, tell me truly,
Symbol of the great Creator,
Where the Sun and Moon are sleeping;
For the Moon shines not in season,
Nor appears the Sun at midday,
From their stations in the sky-vault.
Speak the truth, O magic alder,
Speak not words of man, nor hero,
Hither bring but truthful measures.
Let us form a sacred compact:
If thou speakest me a falsehood,
I will hurl thee to Manala,
Let the nether fires consume thee,
That thine evil signs may perish."

Thereupon the alder answered,
Spake these words of truthful import:

"Verily the Sun lies hidden
And the golden Moon is sleeping
In the stone-berg of Pohyola,
In the copper-bearing mountain."
These the words of Wainamoinen:
"I shall go at once to Northland,
To the cold and dark Pohyola,
Bring the Sun and Moon to gladden
All Wainola's fields and forests."

Forth he hastens on his journey,
To the dismal Sariola,
To the Northland cold and dreary;
Travels one day, then a second,
So the third from morn till evening,
When appear the gates of Pohya,
With her snow-clad hills and mountains.

Wainamoinen, the magician,
At the river of Pohyola,
Loudly calls the ferry-maiden:
"Bring a boat, O Pohya-daughter,
Bring a strong and trusty vessel,
Row me o'er these chilling waters,
O'er this rough and rapid river!"

But the ferry-maiden heard not,
Did not listen to his calling.
Thereupon old Wainamoinen,
Laid a pile of well-dried brush-wood,
Knots and needles of the fir tree,
Made a fire beside the river,
Sent the black smoke into heaven,
Curling to the home of Ukko.

Louhi, hostess of the Northland,
Hastened to her chamber window,
Looked upon the bay and river,
Spake these words to her attendants:
"Why the fire across the river
Where the current meets the deep-sea,
Smaller than the fires of foemen,
Larger than the flames of hunters?"

Thereupon a Pohyalander
Hastened from the court of Louhi,
That the cause he might discover,
Bring the sought-for information
To the hostess of Pohyola;
Saw upon the river-border
Some great hero from Wainola.

Wainamoinen saw the stranger,
Called again in tones of thunder:
"Bring a skiff, thou son of Northland,
For the minstrel, Wainamoinen!"
Thus the Pohyalander answered:
"Here no skiffs are lying idle,
Row thyself across the waters,
Use thine arms, and feet, and fingers,
To propel thee o'er the river,
O'er the sacred stream of Pohya."

Wainamoinen, long reflecting,
Bravely thus soliloquizes:
"I will change my form and features,
Will assume a second body,
Neither man, nor ancient minstrel,
Master of the Northland waters!"

Then the singer, Wainamoinen,
Leaped, a pike, upon the waters,
Quickly swam the rapid river,
Gained the frigid Pohya-border.
There his native form resuming,
Walked he as a mighty hero,
On the dismal isle of Louhi.
Spake the wicked sons of Northland:
"Come thou to Pohyola's court-room."

To Pohyola's court he hastened.
Spake again the sons of evil:
"Come thou to the halls of Louhi!"

To Pohyola's halls he hastened.
On the latch he laid his fingers,
Set his foot within the fore-hall,
Hastened to the inner chamber,
Underneath the painted rafters,
Where the Northland-heroes gather.
There he found the Pohya-masters
Girded with their swords of battle,
With their spears and battle-axes,
With their fatal bows and arrows,
For the death of Wainamoinen,
Ancient bard, Suwantolainen.
Thus they asked the hero-stranger:
"Magic swimmer of the Northland,
Son of evil, what the message
That thou bringest from thy people,
What thy mission to Pohyola?"

Wainamoinen, old and truthful,
Thus addressed the hosts of Louhi:
"For the Sun I come to Northland,
Come to seek the Moon in Pohya;
Tell me where the Sun lies hidden,
Where the golden Moon is sleeping."
Spake the evil sons of Pohya:
"Both the Sun and Moon are hidden
In the rock of many colours,
In the copper-bearing mountain,

In a cavern iron-banded,
In the stone-berg of Pohyola,
Nevermore to gain their freedom,
Nevermore to shine in Northland!"
Spake the hero, Wainamoinen:
"If the Sun be not uncovered,
If the Moon leave not her dungeon,
I will challenge all Pohyola
To the test of spear or broadsword,
Let us now our weapons measure!"

Quick the hero of Wainola
Drew his mighty sword of magic;
On its border shone the moonlight,
On its hilt the Sun was shining,
On its back, a neighing stallion,
On its face a cat was mewing,
Beautiful his magic weapon.
Quick the hero-swords are tested,
And the blades are rightly measured
Wainamoinen's sword is longest
By a single grain of barley,
By a blade of straw, the widest.

To the court-yard rushed the heroes,
Hastened to the deadly combat,
On the plains of Sariola.
Wainamoinen, the magician,
Strikes one blow, and then a second,
Strikes a third time, cuts and conquers.
As the house-maids slice the turnips,
As they lop the heads of cabbage,
As the stalks of flax are broken,
So the heads of Louhi's heroes
Fall before the magic broadsword
Of the ancient Wainamoinen.

Then the victor from Wainola,
Ancient bard and great magician,
Went to find the Sun in slumber,
And the golden Moon discover,
In the copper-bearing mountains,
In the cavern iron-banded,
In the stone-berg of Pohyola.

He had gone but little distance,
When he found a sea-green island;
On the island stood a birch-tree,
Near the birch-tree stood a pillar
Carved in stone of many colours;
In the pillar, nine large portals
Bolted in a hundred places;
In the rock he found a crevice
Sending forth a gleam of sunlight.
Quick he drew his mighty broadsword,
From the pillar struck three colours,
From the magic of his weapon;
And the pillar fell asunder,
Three the number of the fragments.
Wainamoinen, old and faithful,
Through the crevice looked and wondered.
In the centre of the pillar,
From a scarlet-coloured basin,
Noxious serpents beer were drinking,
And the adders eating spices.
Spake the ancient Wainamoinen:
"Therefore has Pohyola's hostess
Little drink to give to strangers,
Since her beer is drunk by serpents,
And her spices given to adders."

Quick he draws his magic fire-blade,
Cuts the vipers green in pieces,
Lops the heads off all the adders,
Speaks these words of master-magic:
"Thus, hereafter, let the serpent
Drink the famous beer of barley,
Feed upon the Northland-spices!"

Wainamoinen, the magician,
The eternal wizard-singer,
Sought to open wide the portals
With the hands and words of magic;
But his hands had lost their cunning,
And his magic gone to others.

Thereupon the ancient minstrel
Quick returning, heavy-hearted,
To his native halls and hamlets,
Thus addressed his brother-heroes:
"Woman, he without his weapons,
With no implements, a weakling!
Sun and Moon have I discovered,
But I could not force the portals

Leading to their rocky cavern
In the copper bearing mountain."
Spake the reckless Lemminkainen
"O thou ancient Wainamoinen,
Why was I not taken with thee
To become thy war-companion?
Would have been of goodly service,
Would have drawn the bolts or broken,
All the portals to the cavern,
Where the Sun and Moon lie hidden
In the copper-bearing mountain!"
Wainamoinen, ancient minstrel,
Thus replied to Lemminkainen:
"Empty words will break no portals,
Draw no bolts of any moment;
Locks and bolts are never broken
With the words of little wisdom!
Greater means than thou commandest
Must be used to free the sunshine,
Free the moonlight from her dungeon."

Wainamoinen, not discouraged,
Hastened to the forge and smithy,
Spake these words to Ilmarinen:
"O thou famous metal-artist,
Forge for me a magic trident,
Forge from steel a dozen stout-rings,
Master-keys, a goodly number,
Iron bars and heavy hammers,
That the Sun we may uncover
In the copper-bearing mountain,
In the stone-berg of Pohyola."

Then the blacksmith, Ilmarinen,
The eternal metal-worker,
Forged the needs of Wainamoinen,
Forged for him the magic trident,
Forged from steel a dozen stout-rings,
Master-keys, a goodly number,
Iron bars and heavy hammers,
Not the largest, nor the smallest,
Forged them of the right dimensions.

Louhi, hostess of Pohyola,
Northland's old and toothless wizard,
Fastened wings upon her shoulders,
As an eagle, sailed the heavens,
Over field, and fen, and forest,
Over Pohya's many waters,
To the hamlets of Wainola,
To the forge of Ilmarinen.

Quick the famous metal-worker
Went to see if winds were blowing;
Found the winds at peace and silent,
Found an eagle, sable-coloured,
Perched upon his window-casement.
Spake the artist, Ilmarinen:
"Magic bird, whom art thou seeking,
Why art sitting at my window?"
This the answer of the eagle:
"Art thou blacksmith, Ilmarinen,
The eternal iron-forger,
Master of the magic metals,
Northland's wonder-working artist?"
Ilmarinen gave this answer:
"There is nothing here of wonder,
Since I forged the dome of heaven,
Forged the earth a concave cover!"
Spake again the magic eagle:
"Why this ringing of thine anvil,
Why this knocking of thy hammer,
Tell me what thy hands are forging?"
This the answer of the blacksmith:
"'Tis a collar I am forging
For the neck of wicked Louhi,
Toothless witch of Sariola,
Stealer of the silver sunshine,
Stealer of the golden moonlight;
With this collar I shall bind her
To the iron-rock of Ehstland!"

Louhi, hostess of Pohyola,
Saw misfortune fast approaching,
Saw destruction flying over,
Saw the signs of bad-luck lower;
Quickly winged her way through ether
To her native halls and chambers,
To the darksome Sariola,
There unlocked the massive portals
Where the Sun and Moon were hidden,
In the rock of many colours,
In the cavern iron-banded,
In the copper-bearing mountain.

Then again the wicked Louhi
Changed her withered form and features,
And became a dove of good-luck;
Straightway winged the starry heavens,
Over field, and fen, and forest,
To the meadows of Wainola,
To the plains of Kalevala,
To the forge of Ilmarinen.
This the question of the blacksmith:
"Wherefore comest, dove of good-luck,
What the tidings that thou bringest?"
Thus the magic bird made answer:
"Wherefore come I to thy smithy?
Come to bring the joyful tidings
That the Sun has left his cavern,
Left the rock of many colours,
Left the stone-berg of Pohyola;
That the Moon no more is hidden
In the copper-bearing mountains,
In the caverns iron-banded."

Straightway hastened Ilmarinen
To the threshold of his smithy,
Quickly scanned the far horizon,
Saw again the silver sunshine,
Saw once more the golden moonlight,
Bringing peace, and joy, and plenty,
To the homes of Kalevala.

Thereupon the blacksmith hastened
To his brother, Wainamoinen,
Spake these words to the magician:
"O thou ancient bard and minstrel,
The eternal wizard-singer,
See, the Sun again is shining,
And the golden Moon is beaming
From their long-neglected places,
From their stations in the sky-vault!"

Wainamoinen, old and faithful,
Straightway hastened to the court-yard,
Looked upon the far horizon,
Saw once more the silver sunshine,
Saw again the golden moonlight,
Bringing peace, and joy, and plenty,
To the people of the Northland,
And the minstrel spake these measures:
"Greetings to thee, Sun of fortune,
Greetings to thee, Moon of good-luck,
Welcome sunshine, welcome moonlight,
Golden is the dawn of morning!
Free art thou, O Sun of silver,
Free again, O Moon beloved,
As the sacred cuckoo's singing,
As the ring-dove's liquid cooings.

"Rise, thou silver Sun, each morning,
Source of light and life hereafter,
Bring us, daily, joyful greetings,
Fill our homes with peace
and plenty,
That our sowing, fishing, hunting,
May be prospered by thy coming.
Travel on thy daily journey,
Let the Moon be ever with thee;
Glide along thy way rejoicing,
End thy journeyings in slumber;
Rest at evening in the ocean,
When the daily cares have ended,
To the good of all thy people,
To the pleasure of Wainola,
To the joy of Kalevala!"

Rune L: Mariatta – Wainamoinen's Departure

Mariatta, child of beauty,
Grew to maidenhood in Northland,
In the cabin of her father,
In the chambers of her mother,
Golden ringlets, silver girdles,
Worn against the keys paternal,
Glittering upon her bosom;
Wore away the father's threshold
With the long robes of her garments;
Wore away the painted rafters
With her beauteous silken ribbons;
Wore away the gilded pillars
With the touching of her fingers;
Wore away the birchen flooring
With the tramping of her
fur-shoes.

Mariatta, child of beauty,
Magic maid of little stature,
Guarded well her sacred virtue,
Her sincerity and honour,
Fed upon the dainty whiting,
On the inner bark of birch-wood,
On the tender flesh of lambkins.

When she hastened in the evening
To her milking in the hurdles,
Spake in innocence as follows:
"Never will the snow-white virgin
Milk the kine of one unworthy!"

When she journeyed over snow-fields,
On the seat beside her father,
Spake in purity as follows:
"Not behind a steed unworthy
Will I ever ride the snow-sledge!"

Mariatta, child of beauty,
Lived a virgin with her mother,
As a maiden highly honoured,
Lived in innocence and beauty,
Daily drove her flocks to pasture,
Walking with the gentle lambkins.
When the lambkins climbed the mountains,
When they gamboled on the hill-tops,
Stepped the virgin to the meadow,
Skipping through a grove of lindens,
At the calling of the cuckoo,
To the songster's golden measures.

Mariatta, child of beauty,
Looked about, intently listened,
Sat upon the berry-meadow,
Sat awhile, and meditated
On a hillock by the forest,
And soliloquized as follows:
"Call to me, thou golden cuckoo,
Sing, thou sacred bird of Northland,
Sing, thou silver breasted songster,
Speak, thou strawberry of Ehstland,
Tell how long must I unmarried,
As a shepherdess neglected,
Wander o'er these hills and mountains,
Through these flowery fens and fallows.
Tell me, cuckoo of the woodlands,
Sing to me how many summers
I must live without a husband,
As a shepherdess neglected!"

Mariatta, child of beauty,
Lived a shepherd-maid for ages,
As a virgin with her mother.
Wretched are the lives of shepherds,
Lives of maidens still more wretched,
Guarding flocks upon the mountains;
Serpents creep in bog and stubble,
On the greensward dart the lizards;
But it was no serpent singing,
Nor a sacred lizard calling,
It was but the mountain-berry
Calling to the lonely maiden:
"Come, O virgin, come and pluck me,
Come and take me to thy bosom,
Take me, tinsel-breasted virgin,
Take me, maiden, copper-belted,
Ere the slimy snail devours me,
Ere the black-worm feeds upon me.
Hundreds pass my way unmindful,
Thousands come within my hearing,
Berry-maidens swarm about me,
Children come in countless numbers,
None of these has come to gather,
Come to pluck this ruddy berry."

Mariatta, child of beauty,
Listened to its gentle pleading,
Ran to pick the berry, calling,
With her fair and dainty fingers,
Saw it smiling near the meadow,
Like a cranberry in feature,
Like a strawberry in flavor;
But the virgin, Mariatta,
Could not pluck the woodland-stranger,
Thereupon she cut a charm-stick,
Downward pressed upon the berry,
When it rose as if by magic,
Rose above her shoes of ermine,
Then above her copper girdle,
Darted upward to her bosom,
Leaped upon the maiden's shoulder,
On her dimpled chin it rested,

On her lips it perched a moment,
Hastened to her tongue expectant;
To and fro it rocked and lingered,
Thence it hastened on its journey,
Settled in the maiden's bosom.
Mariatta, child of beauty,
Thus became a bride impregnate,
Wedded to the mountain-berry;
Lingered in her room at morning,
Sat at midday in the darkness,
Hastened to her couch at evening.
Thus the watchful mother wonders:
"What has happened to our Mary,
To our virgin, Mariatta,
That she throws aside her girdle,
Shyly slips through hall and chamber,
Lingers in her room at morning,
Hastens to her couch at evening,
Sits at midday in the darkness?"

On the floor a babe was playing,
And the young child thus made answer:
"This has happened to our Mary,
To our virgin, Mariatta,
This misfortune to the maiden:
She has lingered by the meadows,
Played too long among the lambkins,
Tasted of the mountain-berry."

Long the virgin watched and waited,
Anxiously the days she counted,
Waiting for the dawn of trouble.
Finally she asked her mother,
These the words of Mariatta:
"Faithful mother, fond and tender,
Mother whom I love and cherish,
Make for me a place befitting,
Where my troubles may be lessened,
And my heavy burdens lightened."
This the answer of the mother:
"Woe to thee, thou Hisi-maiden,
Since thou art a bride unworthy,
Wedded only to dishonour!"

Mariatta, child of beauty,
Thus replied in truthful measures:
"I am not a maid of Hisi,
I am not a bride unworthy,
Am not wedded to dishonour;
As a shepherdess I wandered
With the lambkins to the glen-wood,
Wandered to the berry-mountain,
Where the strawberry had ripened;
Quick as thought I plucked the berry,
On my tongue I gently laid it,
To and fro it rocked and lingered,
Settled in my heaving bosom.
This the source of all my trouble,
Only cause of my dishonour!"

As the mother was relentless,
Asked the maiden of her father,
This the virgin-mother's pleading:
"O my father, full of pity,
Source of both my good and evil,
Build for me a place befitting,
Where my troubles may be lessened,
And my heavy burdens lightened."

This the answer of the father,
Of the father unforgiving:
"Go, thou evil child of Hisi,
Go, thou child of sin and sorrow,
Wedded only to dishonour,
To the Great Bear's rocky chamber,
To the stone-cave of the growler,
There to lessen all thy troubles,
There to cast thy heavy burdens!"

Mariatta, child of beauty,
Thus made answer to her father:
"I am not a child of Hisi,
I am not a bride unworthy,
Am not wedded to dishonour;
I shall bear a noble hero,
I shall bear a son immortal,
Who will rule among the mighty,
Rule the ancient Wainamoinen."

Thereupon the virgin-mother
Wandered hither, wandered thither,
Seeking for a place befitting,
Seeking for a worthy birth-place
For her unborn son and hero;

Finally these words she uttered
"Piltti, thou my youngest maiden,
Trustiest of all my servants,
Seek a place within the village,
Ask it of the brook of Sara,
For the troubled Mariatta,
Child of sorrow and misfortune."

Thereupon the little maiden,
Piltti, spake these words in answer:
"Whom shall I entreat for succor,
Who will lend me his assistance?"
These the words of Mariatta:
"Go and ask it of Ruotus,
Where the reed-brook pours her waters."

Thereupon the servant, Piltti,
Ever hopeful, ever willing,
Hastened to obey her mistress,
Needing not her exhortation;
Hastened like the rapid river,
Like the flying smoke of battle
To the cabin of Ruotus.
When she walked the hill-tops tottered,
When she ran the mountains trembled;
Shore-reeds danced upon the pasture,
Sandstones skipped about the heather
As the maiden, Piltti, hastened
To the dwelling of Ruotus.

At his table in his cabin
Sat Ruotus, eating, drinking,
In his simple coat of linen.
With his elbows on the table
Spake the wizard in amazement:
"Why hast thou, a maid of evil,
Come to see me in my cavern,
What the message thou art bringing?"

Thereupon the servant, Piltti,
Gave this answer to the wizard:
"Seek I for a spot befitting,
Seek I for a worthy birth-place,
For an unborn child and hero;
Seek it near the Sara-streamlet,
Where the reed-brook pours
her waters."

Came the wife of old Ruotus,
Walking with her arms akimbo,
Thus addressed the maiden, Piltti:
"Who is she that asks assistance,
Who the maiden thus dishonoured,
What her name, and who her kindred?"

"I have come for Mariatta,
For the worthy virgin-mother."

Spake the wife of old Ruotus,
Evil-minded, cruel-hearted:
"Occupied are all our chambers,
All our bath-rooms near the reed-brook;
In the mount of fire are couches,
Is a stable in the forest,
For the flaming horse of Hisi;
In the stable is a manger,
Fitting birth-place for the hero
From the wife of cold misfortune,
Worthy couch for Mariatta!"

Thereupon the servant, Piltti,
Hastened to her anxious mistress,
Spake these measures, much regretting.
"There is not a place befitting,
On the silver brook of Sara.
Spake the wife of old Ruotus:
'Occupied are all the chambers,
All the bath-rooms near the reed-brook;
In the mount of fire are couches,
Is a stable in the forest,
For the flaming horse of Hisi;
In the stable is a manger,
Fitting birth-place for the hero
From the wife of cold misfortune,
Worthy couch for Mariatta.'"

Thereupon the hapless maiden,
Mariatta, virgin-mother,
Fell to bitter tears and murmurs,
Spake these words in depths of sorrow:
"I, alas! must go an outcast,
Wander as a wretched hireling,
Like a servant in dishonour,
Hasten to the burning mountain,
To the stable in the forest,

Make my bed within a manger,
Near the flaming steed of Hisi!"

Quick the hapless virgin-mother,
Outcast from her father's dwelling,
Gathered up her flowing raiment,
Grasped a broom of birchen branches,
Hastened forth in pain and sorrow
To the stable in the woodlands,
On the heights of Tapio's mountains,
Spake these words in supplication:
"Come, I pray thee, my Creator,
Only friend in times of trouble,
Come to me and bring protection
To thy child, the virgin-mother,
To the maiden, Mariatta,
In this hour of sore affliction.
Come to me, benignant Ukko,
Come, thou only hope and refuge,
Lest thy guiltless child should perish,
Die the death of the unworthy!"

When the virgin, Mariatta,
Had arrived within the stable
Of the flaming horse of Hisi,
She addressed the steed as follows:
"Breathe, O sympathizing fire-horse,
Breathe on me, the virgin-mother,
Let thy heated breath give moisture,
Let thy pleasant warmth surround me,
Like the vapor of the morning;
Let this pure and helpless maiden
Find a refuge in thy manger!"

Thereupon the horse, in pity,
Breathed the moisture of his nostrils
On the body of the virgin,
Wrapped her in a cloud of vapor,
Gave her warmth and needed comforts,
Gave his aid to the afflicted,
To the virgin, Mariatta.

There the babe was born and cradled
Cradled in a woodland-manger,
Of the virgin, Mariatta,
Pure as pearly dews of morning,
Holy as the stars in heaven.

There the mother rocks her infant,
In his swaddling clothes she wraps him,
Lays him in her robes of linen;
Carefully the babe she nurtures,
Well she guards her much-beloved,
Guards her golden child of beauty,
Her beloved gem of silver.

But alas! the child has vanished,
Vanished while the mother slumbered.
Mariatta, lone and wretched,
Fell to weeping, broken-hearted,
Hastened off to seek her infant.
Everywhere the mother sought him,
Sought her golden child of beauty,
Her beloved gem of silver;
Sought him underneath the millstone,
In the sledge she sought him vainly,
Underneath the sieve she sought him,
Underneath the willow-basket,
Touched the trees, the grass she parted,
Long she sought her golden infant,
Sought him on the fir tree-mountain,
In the vale, and hill, and heather;
Looks within the clumps of flowers,
Well examines every thicket,
Lifts the juniper and willow,
Lifts the branches of the alder.

Lo! a star has come to meet her,
And the star she thus beseeches:
"O, thou guiding-star of Northland,
Star of hope, by God created,
Dost thou know and wilt thou tell me
Where my darling child has wandered,
Where my holy babe lies hidden?"
Thus the star of Northland answers:
"If I knew, I would not tell thee;
'Tis thy child that me created,
Set me here to watch at evening,
In the cold to shine forever,
Here to twinkle in the darkness."

Comes the golden Moon to meet her,
And the Moon she thus beseeches:
"Golden Moon, by Ukko fashioned,
Hope and joy of Kalevala,

Dost thou know and wilt thou
tell me
Where my darling child has wandered,
Where my holy babe lies hidden?"
Speaks the golden Moon in answer:
"If I knew I would not tell thee;
'Tis thy child that me created,
Here to wander in the darkness,
All alone at eve to wander
On my cold and cheerless journey,
Sleeping only in the daylight,
Shining for the good of others."

Thereupon the virgin-mother
Falls again to bitter weeping,
Hastens on through fen and forest,
Seeking for her babe departed.

Comes the silver Sun to meet her,
And the Sun she thus addresses:
"Silver Sun by Ukko fashioned,
Source of light and life to Northland,
Dost thou know and wilt thou tell me
Where my darling child has wandered,
Where my holy babe lies hidden?"
Wisely does the Sun make answer:
"Well I know thy babe's dominions,
Where thy holy child is sleeping,
Where Wainola's light lies hidden;
'Tis thy child that me created,
Made me king of earth and ether,
Made the Moon and Stars attend me,
Set me here to shine at midday,
Makes me shine in silver raiment,
Lets me sleep and rest at evening;
Yonder is thy golden infant,
There thy holy babe lies sleeping,
Hidden to his belt in water,
Hidden in the reeds and rushes."

Mariatta, child of beauty,
Virgin-mother of the Northland,
Straightway seeks her babe in
Swamp-land,
Finds him in the reeds and rushes;
Takes the young child on her bosom
To the dwelling of her father.

There the infant grew in beauty,
Gathered strength, and light, and wisdom,
All of Suomi saw and wondered.
No one knew what name to give him;
When the mother named him, Flower,
Others named him, Son-of-Sorrow.

When the virgin, Mariatta,
Sought the priesthood to baptize him,
Came an old man, Wirokannas,
With a cup of holy water,
Bringing to the babe his blessing;
And the gray-beard spake as follows:
"I shall not baptize a wizard,
Shall not bless a black-magician
With the drops of holy water;
Let the young child be examined,
Let us know that he is worthy,
Lest he prove the son of witchcraft."

Thereupon old Wirokannas
Called the ancient Wainamoinen,
The eternal wisdom-singer,
To inspect the infant-wonder,
To report him good or evil.

Wainamoinen, old and faithful,
Carefully the child examined,
Gave this answer to his people:
"Since the child is but an outcast,
Born and cradled in a manger,
Since the berry is his father;
Let him lie upon the heather,
Let him sleep among the rushes,
Let him live upon the mountains;
Take the young child to the marshes,
Dash his head against the birch-tree."

Then the child of Mariatta,
Only two weeks old, made answer:
"O, thou ancient Wainamoinen,
Son of Folly and Injustice,
Senseless hero of the Northland,
Falsely hast thou rendered judgement.
In thy years, for greater follies,
Greater sins and misdemeanors,
Thou wert not unjustly punished.

In thy former years of trouble,
When thou gavest thine own brother,
For thy selfish life a ransom,
Thus to save thee from destruction,
Then thou wert not sent to Swamp-land
To be murdered for thy follies.
In thy former years of sorrow,
When the beauteous Aino perished
In the deep and boundless blue-sea,
To escape thy persecutions,
Then thou wert not evil-treated,
Wert not banished by thy people."

Thereupon old Wirokannas,
Of the wilderness the ruler,
Touched the child with holy water,
Gave the wonder-babe his blessing,
Gave him rights of royal heirship,
Free to live and grow a hero,
To become a mighty ruler,
King and Master of Karyala.

As the years passed Wainamoinen
Recognized his waning powers,
Empty-handed, heavy-hearted,
Sang his farewell song to Northland,
To the people of Wainola;
Sang himself a boat of copper,
Beautiful his bark of magic;
At the helm sat the magician,
Sat the ancient wisdom-singer.
Westward, westward, sailed the hero
O'er the blue back of the waters,
Singing as he left Wainola,
This his plaintive song and echo:
"Suns may rise and set in Suomi,
Rise and set for generations,
When the North will learn my teachings,
Will recall my wisdom-sayings,
Hungry for the true religion.
Then will Suomi need my coming,
Watch for me at dawn of morning,
That I may bring back the Sampo,
Bring anew the harp of joyance,
Bring again the golden moonlight,
Bring again the silver sunshine,
Peace and plenty to the Northland."

Thus the ancient Wainamoinen,
In his copper-banded vessel,
Left his tribe in Kalevala,
Sailing o'er the rolling billows,
Sailing through the azure vapors,
Sailing through the dusk of evening,
Sailing to the fiery sunset,
To the higher-landed regions,
To the lower verge of heaven;
Quickly gained the far horizon,
Gained the purple-coloured harbor.
There his bark he firmly anchored,
Rested in his boat of copper;
But he left his harp of magic,
Left his songs and wisdom-sayings,
To the lasting joy of Suomi.

Epilogue

Now I end my measured singing,
Bid my weary tongue keep silence,
Leave my songs to other singers.
Horses have their times of resting
After many hours of labour;
Even sickles will grow weary
When they have been long at reaping;
Waters seek a quiet haven
After running long in rivers;
Fire subsides and sinks in slumber
At the dawning of the morning;
Therefore I should end my singing,
As my song is growing weary,
For the pleasure of the evening,
For the joy of morn arising.

Often I have heard it chanted,
Often heard the words repeated:
"Worthy cataracts and rivers
Never empty all their waters."
Thus the wise and worthy singer
Sings not all his garnered wisdom;
Better leave unsung some sayings
Than to sing them out of season.

Thus beginning, and thus ending,
Do I roll up all my legends,
Roll them in a ball for safety,
In my memory arrange them,
In their narrow place of resting,
Lest the songs escape unheeded,
While the lock is still unopened,
While the teeth remain unparted,
And the weary tongue is silent.
Why should I sing other legends,
Chant them in the glen and forest,
Sing them on the hill and heather?
Cold and still my golden mother
Lies beneath the meadow, sleeping,
Hears my ancient songs no longer,
Cannot listen to my singing;
Only will the forest listen,
Sacred birches, sighing pine trees,
Junipers endowed with kindness,
Alder-trees that love to hear me,
With the aspens and the willows.

When my loving mother left me,
Young was I, and low of stature;
Like the cuckoo of the forest,
Like the thrush upon the heather,
Like the lark I learned to twitter,
Learned to sing my simple measures,
Guided by a second mother,
Stern and cold, without affection;
Drove me helpless from my chamber
To the wind-side of her dwelling,
To the north-side of her cottage,
Where the chilling winds in mercy
Carried off the unprotected.
As a lark I learned to wander,
Wander as a lonely songbird,
Through the forests and the fenlands,
Quietly o'er hill and heather;
Walked in pain about the marshes,
Learned the songs of winds and waters,
Learned the music of the ocean,
And the echoes of the woodlands.

Many men that live to murmur,
Many women live to censure,
Many speak with evil motives;
Many they with wretched voices
Curse me for my wretched singing,
Blame my tongue for speaking wisdom,
Call my ancient songs unworthy,
Blame the songs and curse the singer.
Be not thus, my worthy people,
Blame me not for singing badly,
Unpretending as a minstrel.
I have never had the teaching,
Never lived with ancient heroes,
Never learned the tongues of strangers,
Never claimed to know much wisdom.
Others have had language-masters,
Nature was my only teacher,
Woods and waters my instructors.
Homeless, friendless, lone, and needy,
Save in childhood with my mother,
When beneath her painted rafters,
Where she twirled the flying spindle,
By the work-bench of my brother,
By the window of my sister,
In the cabin of my father,
In my early days of childhood.

Be this as it may, my people,
This may point the way to others,
To the singers better gifted,
For the good of future ages,
For the coming generations,
For the rising folk of Suomi.

THE END.

Witches, Spirits & Mystical Beings

Introduction

THE FIGURE of Suyettar stalks Finnish folklore. A baleful presence in so many stories that she more or less upstages the Devil in her black charisma. Hideous, with snakes for curling locks, Suyettar is the universal anti-mother; monstrous and cruel, she is a glutton for human flesh and a nurturer of all that is ugly, foul and evil. The fly in the world ointment, the grit in the cosmic oyster, she's also the oil in the machine because Finnish folktales could hardly be imagined without her. The need to escape or outwit her drives the narrative of a great many stories, as it does those of 'The True Bride' and 'The Little Sister' here.

Some spirits are more benign, though. The ancestral paganism of the Finns feels as though it echoes in the panentheistic poetic flights of the nineteenth-century storytellers, orthodox as they were for the most part in their Lutheran beliefs. They talk of a "great spirit" lording over Nature as a whole, and of nymph-like beings that flit through Finland's woods and fields; swirling in its streams and lakes and billowing in its Baltic waves. In this respect, the Finnish folktale offered something more than stories to its earlier readers: a whole and powerful vision of Finland and its special place in the universe.

The True Bride

(The Story of Ilona and the King's Son)

THERE WERE ONCE two orphans, a brother and a sister, who lived alone in the old farmhouse where their fathers before them had lived for many generations. The brother's name was Osmo, the sister's Ilona. Osmo was an industrious youth, but the farm was small and barren and he was hard put to it to make a livelihood.

"Sister," he said one day, "I think it might be well if I went out into the world and found work."

"Do as you think best, brother," Ilona said. "I'm sure I can manage on here alone."

So Osmo started off, promising to come back for his sister as soon as he could give her a new home. He wandered far and wide and at last got employment from the king's son as a shepherd.

The king's son was about Osmo's age, and often when he met Osmo tending his flocks he would stop and talk to him.

One day Osmo told the king's son about his sister, Ilona.

"I have wandered far over the face of the earth," he said, "and never have I seen so beautiful a maiden as Ilona."

"What does she look like?" the king's son asked.

Osmo drew a picture of her and she seemed to the King's Son so beautiful that at once he fell in love with her.

"Osmo," he said, "if you will go home and get your sister, I will marry her."

So Osmo hurried home not by the long land route by which he had come but straight over the water in a boat.

"Sister," he cried, as soon as he saw Ilona, "you must come with me at once for the king's son wishes to marry you!"

He thought Ilona would be overjoyed, but she sighed and shook her head.

"What is it, sister? Why do you sigh?"

"Because it grieves me to leave this old house where our fathers have lived for so many generations."

"Nonsense, Ilona! What is this little old house compared to the king's castle where you will live once you marry the king's son!"

But Ilona only shook her head.

"It's no use, brother! I can't bear to leave this old house until the grindstone with which our fathers for generations ground their meal is worn out."

When Osmo found she was firm, he went secretly and broke the old grindstone into small pieces. He then put the pieces together so that the stone looked the same as before. But of course the next time Ilona touched it, it fell apart.

"Now, sister, you'll come, will you not?" Osmo asked.

But again Ilona shook her head.

"It's no use, brother. I can't bear to go until the old stool where our mothers have sat spinning these many generations is worn through."

So again Osmo took things into his own hands and going secretly to the old spinning stool he broke it and when Ilona sat on it again it fell to pieces.

Then Ilona said she couldn't go until the old mortar which had been in use for generations should fall to bits at a blow from the pestle. Osmo cracked the mortar and the next time Ilona struck it with the pestle it broke.

Then Ilona said she couldn't go until the old worn doorsill over which so many of their forefathers had walked should fall to splinters at the brush of her skirts. So Osmo secretly split the old doorsill into thin slivers and, when next Ilona stepped over it, the brush of her skirts sent the splinters flying.

"I see now I must go," Ilona said, "for the house of our forefathers no longer holds me."

So she packed all her ribbons and her bodices and skirts in a bright wooden box and, calling her little dog Pilka, she stepped into the boat and Osmo rowed her off in the direction of the king's castle.

Soon they passed a long narrow spit of land at the end of which stood a woman waving her arms. That is, she looked like a woman. Really she was Suyettar but they, of course, did not know this.

"Take me in your boat!" she cried.

"Shall we?" Osmo asked his sister.

"I don't think we ought to," Ilona said. "We don't know who she is or what she wants and she may be evil."

So Osmo rowed on. But the woman kept shouting:

"Hi, there! Take me in your boat! Take me!"

A second time Osmo paused and asked his sister:

"Don't you think we ought to take her?"

"No," Ilona said.

So Osmo rowed on again. At this the creature raised such a pitiful outcry demanding what they meant denying assistance to a poor woman that Osmo was unable longer to refuse and in spite of Ilona's warning he rowed to land.

Suyettar instantly jumped into the boat and seated herself in the middle with her face towards Osmo and her back towards Ilona.

"What a fine young man!" Suyettar said in whining flattering tones. "See how strong he is at the oars! And what a beautiful girl, too! I daresay the king's son would fall in love with her if ever he saw her!"

Thereupon Osmo very foolishly told Suyettar that the king's son had already promised to marry Ilona. At that an evil look came into Suyettar's face and she sat silent for a time biting her fingers. Then she began mumbling a spell that made Osmo deaf to what Ilona was saying and Ilona deaf to what Osmo was saying.

At last in the distance the towers of the King's castle appeared.

"Stand up, sister!" Osmo said. "Shake out your skirts and arrange your pretty ribbons! We'll soon be landing now!"

Ilona could see her brother's lips moving but of course she could not hear what he was saying.

"What is it, brother?" she asked.

Suyettar answered for him:

"Osmo orders you to jump headlong into the water!"

"No! No!" Ilona cried. "He couldn't order anything so cruel as that!"

Presently Osmo said:

"Sister, what ails you? Don't you hear me? Shake out your skirts and arrange your pretty ribbons for we'll soon be landing now."

"What is it, brother?" Ilona asked.

As before Suyettar answered for him:

"Osmo orders you to jump headlong into the water!"

"Brother, how can you order so cruel a thing!" Ilona cried, bursting into tears. "Is it for this you made me leave the home of my fathers?"

A third time Osmo said:

"Stand up, sister, and shake out your skirts and arrange your ribbons! We'll soon be landing now!"

"I can't hear you, brother! What is it you say?"

Suyettar turned on her fiercely and screamed:

"Osmo orders you to jump headlong into the water!"

"If he says I must, I must!" poor Ilona sobbed, and with that she leapt overboard.

Osmo tried to save her but Suyettar held him back and with her own arms rowed off and Ilona was left to sink.

"What will become of me now!" Osmo cried. "When the King's Son finds I have not brought him my sister he will surely order my death!"

"Not at all!" Suyettar said. "Do as I say and no harm will come to you. Offer me to the king's son and tell him I am your sister. He won't know the difference and anyway I'm sure I'm just as beautiful as Ilona ever was!"

With that Suyettar opened the wooden box that held Ilona's clothes and helped herself to skirt and bodice and gay coloured ribbons. She decked herself out in these and for a little while she really did succeed in looking like a pretty young girl.

So Osmo presented Suyettar to the king's son as Ilona, and the king's son because he had given his word married her. But before one day was past, he called Osmo to him and asked him angrily:

"What did you mean by telling me your sister was beautiful?"

"Isn't she beautiful?" Osmo faltered.

"No! I thought she was at first but she isn't! She is ugly and evil and you shall pay the penalty for having deceived me!"

Thereupon he ordered that Osmo be shut up in a place filled with serpents.

"If you are innocent," the King's Son said, "the serpents will not harm you. If you are guilty they will devour you!"

Meanwhile poor Ilona when she jumped into the water sank down, down, down, until she reached the Sea King's palace. They received her kindly there and comforted her and the Sea King's Son, touched by her grief and beauty, offered to marry her. But Ilona was homesick for the upper world and would not listen to him.

"I want to see my brother again!" she wept.

They told her that the king's son had thrown her brother to the serpents and had married Suyettar in her stead, but Ilona still begged so pitifully to be allowed to return to earth that at last the Sea King said:

"Very well, then! For three successive nights I will allow you to return to the upper world. But after that never again!"

So they decked Ilona in the lovely jewels of the sea with great strands of pearls about her neck and to each of her ankles they attached long silver chains. As she rose in the water the sound of the chains was like the chiming of silver bells and could be heard for five miles.

Ilona came to the surface of the water just where Osmo had landed. The first thing she saw was his boat at the water's edge and curled up asleep in the bottom of the boat her own little dog, Pilka.

"Pilka!" Ilona cried, and the little dog woke with a bark of joy and licked Ilona's hand and yelped and frisked.

Then Ilona sang this magic song to Pilka:

"Peely, peely, Pilka, pide,
Lift the latch and slip inside!
Past the watchdog in the yard,
Past the sleeping men on guard!
Creep in softly as a snake,
Then creep out before they wake!
Peely, peely, Pilka, pide,
Peely, peely, Pilka!"

Pilka barked and frisked and said:

"Yes, mistress, yes! I'll do whatever you bid me!"

Ilona gave the little dog an embroidered square of gold and silver which she herself had worked down in the Sea King's palace.

"Take this," she said to Pilka, "and put it on the pillow where the king's son lies asleep. Perhaps when he sees it he will know that it comes from Osmo's true sister and that the frightful creature he has married is Suyettar. Then perhaps he will release Osmo before the serpents devour him. Go now, my faithful Pilka, and come back to me before the dawn."

So Pilka raced off to the king's palace carrying the square of embroidery in her teeth. Ilona waited and half an hour before sunrise the little dog came panting back.

"What news, Pilka? How fares my brother and how is my poor love, the King's Son?"

"Osmo is still with the serpents," Pilka answered, "but they haven't eaten him yet. I left the embroidered square on the pillow where the king's son's head was lying. Suyettar was asleep on the bed beside him where you should be, dear mistress. Suyettar's awful mouth was open and she was snoring horribly. The king's son moved uneasily for he was troubled even in his sleep."

"And did you go through the castle, Pilka?"

"Yes, dear mistress."

"And did you see the remains of the wedding feast?"

"Yes, dear mistress, the remains of a feast that shamed the king's son, for Suyettar served bones instead of meat, fish heads, turnip tops, and bread burned to a cinder."

"Good Pilka!" Ilona said. "Good little dog! You have done well! Now the dawn is coming and I must go back to the Sea King's palace. But I shall come again tonight and also tomorrow night and do you be here waiting for me."

Pilka promised and Ilona sank down into the sea to a clanking of chains that sounded like silver bells. The king's son heard them in his sleep and for a moment woke and said:

"What's that?"

"What's what?" snarled Suyettar. "You're dreaming! Go back to sleep!"

A few hours later when he woke again, he found the lovely square of embroidery on his pillow.

"Who made this?" he cried.

Suyettar was busy combing her snaky locks. She turned on him quickly.

"Who made what?"

When she saw the embroidery she tried to snatch it from him, but he held it tight.

"I made it, of course!" she declared. "Who but me would sit up all night and work while you lay snoring!"

But the king's son, as he folded the embroidery, muttered to himself:

"It doesn't look to me much like your work!"

After he had breakfasted, the king's son asked for news of Osmo. A slave was sent to the place of the serpents and when he returned he reported that Osmo was sitting amongst them uninjured.

"The old king snake has made friends with him," he added, "and has wound himself around Osmo's arm."

The king's son was amazed at this news and also relieved, for the whole affair troubled him sorely and he was beginning to suspect a mystery.

He knew an old wise woman who lived alone in a little hut on the seashore and he decided he would go and consult her. So he went to her and told her about Osmo and how Osmo had deceived him in regard to his sister. Then he told her how the serpents instead of devouring Osmo had made friends with him and last he showed her the square of lovely embroidery he had found on his pillow that morning.

"There is a mystery somewhere, granny," he said in conclusion, "and I know not how to solve it."

The old woman looked at him thoughtfully.

"My son," she said at last, "that is never Osmo's sister that you have married. Take an old woman's word – it is Suyettar! Yet Osmo's sister must be alive and the embroidery must be a token from her. It probably means that she begs you to release her brother."

"Suyettar!" repeated the king's son, aghast.

At first he couldn't believe such a horrible thing possible and yet that, if it were so, would explain much.

"I wonder if you're right," he said. "I must be on my guard!"

That night on the stroke of midnight to the sound of silver chimes Ilona came floating up through the waves and little Pilka, as she appeared, greeted her with barks of joy.

As before Ilona sang:

"Peely, peely, Pilka, pide,
Lift the latch and slip inside!
Past the watchdog in the yard,
Past the sleeping men on guard!
Creep in softly as a snake,
Then creep out before they wake!
Peely, peely, Pilka, pide,
Peely, peely, Pilka!"

This time Ilona gave Pilka a shirt for the king's son. Beautifully embroidered it was in gold and silver and Ilona herself had worked it in the Sea King's palace.

Pilka carried it safely to the castle and left it on the pillow where the king's son could see it as soon as he woke. Then Pilka visited the place of the serpents and before the first ray of dawn was back at the seashore to reassure Ilona of Osmo's safety.

Then dawn came and Ilona, as she sank in the waves to the chime of silver bells, called out to Pilka:

"Meet me here tonight at the same hour! Fail me not, dear Pilka, for tonight is the last night that the Sea King will allow me to come to the upper world!"

Pilka, howling with grief, made promise:

"I'll be here, dear mistress, that I will!"

The king's son that morning, as he opened his eyes, saw the embroidered shirt lying on the pillow at his head. He thought at first he must be dreaming for it was more beautiful than any shirt that had ever been worked by human fingers.

"Ah!" he sighed at last, "who made this?"

"Who made what?" Suyettar demanded rudely.

When she saw the shirt she tried to snatch it, but the king's son held it from her. Then she pretended to laugh and said:

"Oh, that! I made it, of course! Do you think anyone else in the world would sit up all night and work for you while you lie there snoring! And small thanks I get for it, too!"

"It doesn't look to me like your work!" said the King's Son significantly.

Again the slave reported to him that Osmo was alive and unhurt by the serpents.

'Strange!' thought the king's son.

He took the embroidered shirt and made the old wise woman another visit.

"Ah!" she said, when she saw the shirt, "now I understand! Listen, my Prince: last night at midnight I was awakened by the chime of silver bells and I got up and looked out the door. Just there at the water's edge, close to that little boat, I saw a strange sight. A lovely maiden rose from the waves holding in her hands the very shirt that you now have. A little dog that was lying in the boat greeted her with barks of joy. She sang a magic rime to the dog and gave it the shirt and off it ran. That maid, my Prince, must be Ilona. She must be in the Sea King's power and I think she is begging you to rescue her and to release her brother."

The king's son slowly nodded his head.

"Granny, I'm sure what you say is true! Help me to rescue Ilona and I shall reward you richly."

"Then, my son, you must act at once, for tonight, I heard Ilona say, is the last night that the Sea King will allow her to come to the upper world. Go now to the smith and have him forge you a strong iron chain and a great strong scythe. Then tonight hide you down yonder in the shadow of the boat. At midnight when you hear the silver chimes and the maiden slowly rises from the waves, throw the iron chain about her and quickly draw her to you. Then, with one sweep of your scythe, cut the silver chains that are fastened to her ankles. But remember, my son, that is not all. She is under enchantment and as you try to grasp her the Sea King will change her to many things – a fish, a bird, a fly, and I know not what, and if in any form she escape you, then all is lost."

At once the king's son hurried away to the smithy and had the smith forge him a strong iron chain and a heavy sharp scythe. Then when night fell he hid in the shadow of the boat and waited. Pilka snuggled up beside him. Midnight came and to the sweet chiming as of silver bells Ilona slowly rose from the waves. As she came she began singing:

"Peely, peely, Pilka, pide—"

Instantly the king's son threw the strong iron chain about her and drew her to him. Then with one mighty sweep of the scythe he severed the silver chains that were attached to her ankles and the silver chains fell chiming into the depths. Another instant and the maiden in his arms was no maiden but a slimy fish that squirmed and wriggled and almost slipped through his fingers. He killed the fish and, lo! it was not a fish but a frightened bird that struggled to escape. He killed the bird and, lo! it was not a bird but a writhing lizard. And so on through many transformations, growing finally small and weak until at last there was only a mosquito. He crushed this and in his arms he found again the lovely Ilona.

"Ah, dear one," he said, "you are my true bride and not Suyettar who pretended she was you! Come, we will go at once to the castle and confront her!"

But Ilona cried out at this:

"Not there, my Prince, not there! Suyettar if she saw me would kill me and devour me! Keep me from her!"

"Very well, my dear one," the king's son said. "We'll wait until tomorrow and after tomorrow there will be no Suyettar to fear."

So for that night they took shelter in the old wise woman's hut, Ilona and the king's son and faithful little Pilka.

The next morning early the king's son returned to the castle and had the sauna heated. Just inside the door he had a deep hole dug and filled it with burning tar. Then over the top of the hole he stretched a brown mat and on the brown mat a blue mat. When all was ready he went indoors and roused Suyettar.

"Where have you been all night?" she demanded angrily.

"Forgive me this time," he begged in pretended humility, "and I promise never again to be parted from my own true bride. Come now, my dear, and bathe, for the sauna is ready."

Then Suyettar, who loved to have people see her go to the sauna just as if she were a real human being, put on a long bathrobe and clapped her hands. Four slaves appeared. Two took up the train of her bathrobe and the two others supported her on either side. Slowly she marched out of the castle, across the courtyard, and over to the sauna.

"They all really think I'm a human princess!" she said to herself, and she was so sure she was beautiful and admired that she tossed her head and smirked from side to side and took little mincing steps.

When she reached the sauna she was ready to drop the bathrobe and jump over the doorsill to the steaming shelf, but the king's son whispered:

"Nay! Nay! Remember your dignity as a beautiful princess and walk over the blue mat!"

So with one more toss of her head, one more smirk of her ugly face, Suyettar stepped on the blue mat and sank into the hole of burning tar. Then the king's son quickly locked the door of the sauna and left her there to burn in the tar, for burning, you know, is the only way to destroy Suyettar. As she burned the last hateful thing Suyettar did was to tear out handfuls of her hair and scatter them broadcast in the air.

"Let these," she cried, yelling and cursing, "turn into mosquitos and worms and moths and trouble mankind forever!"

Then her yells grew fainter and at last ceased altogether and the king's son knew that it was now safe to bring Ilona home. First, however, he had Osmo released from the place of the serpents and asked his forgiveness for the unjust punishment.

Then he and Osmo together went to the hut of the old wise woman and there with tears of happiness the brother and sister were reunited. The king's son to show his gratitude to the old wise woman begged her to accompany them to the castle and presently they all set forth with Pilka frisking ahead and barking for joy.

That day there was a new wedding feast spread at the castle and this time it was not bones and fish heads and burnt crusts but such food as the king's son had not tasted for many a day.

To celebrate his happy marriage the king's son made Osmo his chamberlain and gave Pilka a beautiful new collar.

"Now at last," Ilona said, "I am glad I left the house of my forefathers."

The Three Chests

(The Story of the Wicked Old Man of the Sea)

THERE WAS ONCE an honest old farmer who had three daughters. His farm ran down to the shores of a deep lake. One day as he leaned over the water to take a drink, wicked old Wetehinen reached up from the bottom of the lake and clutched him by the beard.

"Ouch! Ouch!" the farmer cried. "Let me go!"

Wetehinen only held on more tightly.

"Yes, I'll let you go," he said, "but only on this condition: that you give me one of your daughters for wife!"

"Give you one of my daughters? Never!"

"Very well, then I'll never let go!" wicked old Wetehinen declared and with that he began jerking at the beard as if it were a bellrope.

"Wait! Wait!" the farmer spluttered.

Now he didn't want to give one of his daughters to wicked old Wetehinen – of course not! But at the same time he was in Wetehinen's power and he realized that if he didn't do what the old reprobate demanded he might lose his life and so leave all three of his daughters orphans. Perhaps for the good of all he had better sacrifice one of them.

"All right," he said, "let me go and I'll send you my oldest daughter. I promise."

So Wetehinen let go his beard and the farmer scrambled to his feet and hurried home.

"My dear," he said to his oldest daughter, "I left a bit of the harness down at the lake. Like a good girl will you run down and get it for me."

The eldest daughter went at once and when she reached the water's edge, old Wetehinen reached up and caught her about the waist and carried her down to the bottom of the lake where he lived in a big house.

At first he was kind to her. He made her mistress of the house and gave her the keys to all the rooms and closets. He went very carefully over the keys and pointing to one he said:

"That key you must never use for it opens the door to a room which I forbid you to enter."

The eldest daughter began keeping house for old Wetehinen and spent her time cooking and cleaning and spinning much as she used to at home with her father. The days went by and she grew familiar with the house and began to know what was in every room and every closet.

At first she felt no temptation to open the forbidden door. If old Wetehinen wanted to have a secret room, well and good. But why in the world had he given her the key if he really didn't want her to open the door? The more she thought about it the more she wondered. Every time she passed the room she stopped a moment and stared at the door. It looked just exactly like the doors that led into all the other rooms.

"I wonder why he doesn't want me to open just that door?" she kept asking herself.

Finally one day when old Wetehinen was away she thought:

"I don't believe it would matter if I opened that door just a little crack and peeped in once! No one would know the difference!"

For a few moments she hesitated, then mustered up courage enough to turn the key in the forbidden lock and throw open the door.

The room was a storeroom with boxes and chests and old jars piled up around the wall. That was unexciting enough, but in the middle of the floor was something that made her start when she saw what it was. It was blood – that's what it was, a pool of dark red blood! She was about to slam the door shut when she saw something else that made her pause. This was a lovely shining ring that lay in the midst of the pool.

"Oh!" she thought to herself, "what a beautiful ring! If I had it I'd wear it on my finger!"

The longer she looked at it, the more she wanted it.

"If I'm very careful," she said, "I know I could reach over and pick it up without touching the blood."

She tiptoed cautiously into the room, wrapped her skirts tightly about her legs, knelt down on the floor, and stretched her arm over the pool. She picked up the ring very carefully but even so she got a few drops of blood on her fingers.

"No matter!" she thought, "I can wash that off! And see the lovely ring!"

But later, after she had the door again locked, when she tried to wash the blood off, she found she couldn't. She tried soap, she tried sand, she tried everything she could think of, but without success.

"I don't care!" she thought to herself. "If Wetehinen sees the blood, I'll just tell him I cut my finger by accident."

So when Wetehinen came home, she hid the ring and pretended nothing was the matter.

After supper Wetehinen put his head in her lap and said:

"Now, my dear, scratch my head and make me drowsy for bed."

She began scratching his head as she had many nights before but, at the first touch of her fingers, he cried out:

"Stop! You're burning my ear! There must be some blood on your fingers! Let me see!"

He reached up and caught her hand and, when he saw the blood stains, he flew into a towering rage.

"I thought so! You've been in the forbidden room!"

He jumped up and without allowing her time to say a word he just cut off her head then and there with no more concern than if she had been a mosquito! After that he took the body and the severed head and threw them into the forbidden room and locked the door.

"Now then," he growled, "*she* won't disobey me again!"

This was all very well but now he had no one to keep house for him and cook and scratch his head in the evening and soon he decided he'd have to get another wife. He remembered that the farmer had two more daughters, so he thought to himself that now he'd marry the second sister.

He waited his chance and one day when the farmer was out in his boat fishing, old Wetehinen came up from the bottom of the lake and clutched the boat. When the poor old farmer tried to row back to shore he couldn't make the boat move an inch. He worked and worked at the oars and wicked old Wetehinen let him struggle until he was exhausted. Then he put his head up out of the water and over the side of the boat and as though nothing were the matter he said:

"Hullo!"

"Oh!" the farmer cried, wishing he were safe on shore, "it's you, is it? I wondered what was holding my boat."

"Yes," wicked old Wetehinen said, "it's me and I'm going to hold your boat right here on this spot until you promise to give me another of your daughters."

What could the farmer do? He pleaded with Wetehinen but Wetehinen was firm and the upshot was that before the farmer again walked dry land he had promised Wetehinen his second daughter.

Well, when he got home, he pretended he had forgotten his ax in the boat and sent his second daughter down to the lake to get it. Wicked old Wetehinen caught her as he had caught her sister and carried her home with him to his house at the bottom of the lake.

Wetehinen treated the second sister just exactly as he had the first, making her mistress of the house and telling her she might use every key but one. Like her sister she, too, after a time gave way to the temptation of looking into the forbidden room and when she saw the shining ring lying in the pool of blood of course she wanted it and of course when she reached to get it she dabbled her fingers in the blood. So that was the end of her, too, for wicked old Wetehinen when he saw the blood stains just cut her head right off and threw her body and the severed head into the forbidden room beside the body and head of her sister and locked the door.

Time went by and the farmer was living happily with his youngest daughter when one day while he was out chopping wood he found a pair of fine birch bark brogues. He put them on and instantly found himself walking away from the woods and down to the lake. He tried to stop but he couldn't. He tried to walk in another direction but the brogues carried him straight down to the water's edge and out into the lake until he was in waist deep.

Then he heard a gruff voice saying:

"Hullo, there! What are you doing with my brogues?"

Of course it was wicked old Wetehinen who had played that trick to get the farmer into his power again.

"What do you want this time?" the poor farmer cried.

"I want your youngest daughter," Wetehinen said.

"What! My youngest daughter!"

"Yes."

"I won't give her up!" the farmer declared. "I don't care what you do to me. I won't give her up!"

"Oh, very well!" Wetehinen said, and immediately the brogues which had been standing still while they talked started walking again. They carried the farmer out into the lake farther and farther until the water was up to his chin.

"Wait – wait a minute!" he cried.

The brogues stopped walking and Wetehinen said:

"Well, do you promise to give her to me?"

"No!" the farmer began. "She's my last daughter and—"

Before he could say more, the brogues walked on and the water rose to his nose. In desperation he threw up his hands and shouted:

"I promise! I promise!"

So when he got home that day he said to his youngest daughter whose name was Lisa:

"Lisa, my dear, I forgot my brogues at the lake. Like a good girl won't you run and get them for me?"

So Lisa went to the lake and Wetehinen of course caught her and carried her down to his house as he had her two sisters.

Then the same old story was repeated. Wetehinen made Lisa mistress of the house and gave her keys to all the doors and closets with the same prohibition against opening the door of the forbidden room.

"If I am mistress of the house," Lisa said to herself, "why should I not unlock every door?"

She waited until one day when Wetehinen was away from home, then went boldly to the forbidden room, fitted the key in the lock, and flung open the door.

There lay her two poor sisters with their heads cut off. There in the pool of blood sparkled the lovely ring, but Lisa paid no heed to it.

"Wicked old Wetehinen!" Lisa cried. "I suppose he thinks that ring will tempt me but nothing will tempt me to touch that awful blood!"

Then she rummaged about, opening boxes and chests, and turning things over. In a dark corner she found two pitchers, one marked *Water of Life*, the other *Water of Death*.

"Ha! This is what I want!" she cried, taking the pitcher of the *Water of Life*.

She set the severed heads of her sisters in place and then with the magic water brought them back to life. She used up all the *Water of Life*, so she filled the pitcher marked *Water of Life* with the water from the other pitcher, the *Water of Death*. She hid her sisters each in a big wooden chest, she shut and locked the door of the forbidden room, and Wetehinen when he came home found her working at her spinning wheel as though nothing unusual had happened.

After supper Wetehinen said:

"Now scratch my head and make me drowsy for bed."

So Lisa scratched his wicked old head and she did it so well that he grunted with satisfaction.

"Uh! Uh!" he said. "That's good! Now just behind my right ear! That's it! That's it! You're a good girl, you are! You're not like some of them who do what they're told not to do! Now behind the other ear! Oh, that's fine! Yes, you're a good girl and if there's anything you want me to do just tell me what it is."

"I want to send a chest of things to my poor old father," Lisa said. "Just a lot of little nothings – odds and ends that I've picked up about the house. I'd be ashamed to have you open the chest and see them. I do wish you'd carry the chest ashore tomorrow and leave it where my father will find it."

"All right, I will," Wetehinen promised.

He was true to his word. The next morning he hoisted one of the chests on his shoulder, the one that had in it the eldest sister, he trudged off with it, and tossed it up on shore at a place where he was sure the farmer would find it.

Lisa then wheedled him into carrying up the second chest that had in it the second sister. This time Wetehinen wasn't so good-natured.

"I don't know what she can always be sending her father!" he grumbled. "If she sends another chest I'll have to look inside and see."

Now Lisa, when the second sister was safely delivered, began to plan her own escape. She pulled out another empty chest and then one evening after she had succeeded in making old Wetehinen comfortable and drowsy she begged him to carry this also to her father. He grumbled and protested but finally promised.

"And you won't look inside, will you? Promise me you won't!" Lisa begged.

Wetehinen said he wouldn't, but he intended to just the same.

Well, the next morning as soon as Wetehinen went out, Lisa took the churn and dressed it up in some of her own clothes. She carried it to the top of the house and perched it on the ridge of the roof before a spinning wheel. Then she herself crept inside the third chest and waited.

When Wetehinen came home he looked up and saw what he thought was Lisa spinning on the roof.

"Hullo!" he shouted. "What are you doing up there?"

Lisa, in the chest, answered in a voice that sounded as if it came from the roof:

"I'm spinning. And you, Wetehinen, my dear, don't forget the chest that you promised to carry to my poor old father. It's standing in the kitchen."

Wetehinen grumbled but because of his promise he hoisted the chest on his shoulder and started off. When he had gone a little way he thought to put it down and take a peep inside. Instantly Lisa's voice, sounding as if it came from the roof, cried out:

"No! No! You promised not to look inside!"

"I'm not looking inside!" Wetehinen called back. "I'm only resting a minute!"

Then he thought to himself:

"I suppose she's sitting up there so she can watch me!"

When he had gone some distance farther, he thought again to set down the chest and open the lid but instantly Lisa's voice, as from a long way off, called out:

"No! No! You promised not to look inside!"

"Who's looking inside?" he called back, pretending again he was only resting.

Every time he thought it would be safe to put down the chest and open the lid, Lisa's voice cried out:

"No! No! You promised not to!"

"Mercy on us!" old Wetehinen fumed to himself, "who would have thought she could see so far!"

On the shore of the lake when he threw down the chest in disgust he tried one last time to raise the lid. Instantly Lisa's voice cried out:

"No! No! You promised not to!"

"I'm not looking inside!" Wetehinen roared, and in a fury he left the chest and started back into the water.

All the way home he grumbled and growled:

"A nice way to treat a man, always making him carry chests! I won't carry another one no matter how much she begs me!"

When he came near home he saw the spinning wheel still on the roof and the figure still seated before it.

"Why haven't you got my dinner ready?" he called out angrily.

The figure at the spinning wheel made no answer.

"What's the matter with you?" Wetehinen cried. "Why are you sitting there like a wooden image instead of cooking my dinner?"

Still the figure made no answer and in a rage Wetehinen began climbing up to the roof. He reached out blindly and clutched at Lisa's skirt and jerked it so hard that the churn came clattering down on his head. It knocked him off the roof and he fell all the way to the ground and cracked his wicked old head wide open.

"Ouch! Ouch!" he roared in pain. "Just wait till I get hold of that Lisa!"

He crawled to the forbidden room and poured over himself the water that was in the pitcher marked *Water of Life*. But it wasn't the *Water of Life* at all, it was the *Water of Death*, and so it didn't help his wicked old cracked head at all. In fact it just made it worse and worse and worse.

Lisa and her sisters were never again troubled by him nor was anyone else that lived on the shores of that lake.

"Wonder what's become of wicked old Wetehinen?" people began saying.

Lisa thought she knew, but she didn't tell.

The Little Sister

(The Story of Suyettar and the Nine Brothers)

THERE WAS ONCE a woman who had nine sons. They were good boys and loved her dearly but there was one thing about which they were always complaining.

"Why haven't we a little sister?" they kept asking. "Do give us a little sister!"

When the time came that another child was to be born, they said to their mother:

"If the baby is a boy we are going away and you will never see us again, but if it is a little girl then we shall stay home and take care of it."

The mother agreed that if the child were a girl she would have her husband put a spindle outside on the gatepost and, if it were a boy, an ax.

"Just wait," she said, "and see what your father puts on the gatepost and then you will know whether it is another brother God has sent you or a little sister."

The baby turned out to be a girl and the mother was overjoyed.

"Hurry, husband!" she cried, "and put a spindle on the gatepost so that our nine sons may know the good news!"

The man did so and then quickly returned to the mother and baby. The moment he was gone Suyettar slipped up and changed the tokens. She took away the spindle and put in its place an ax. Then with an evil grin she hurried off mumbling to herself:

"Now we'll see what we'll see!"

She hoped to bring trouble and grief and she succeeded. As soon as the nine sons saw the ax on the gatepost they thought their mother had given birth to another son and at once they left home vowing never to return.

The poor mother waited for them and waited.

"What is keeping my sons?" she cried at last. "Go out to the gate, husband, and see if they are coming."

The man went out and soon returned bringing back word that someone had changed the tokens.

"The spindle that I put on the gatepost is gone," he said, "and in its place is an ax."

"Alas!" cried the poor mother, "some evil creature has done this to spite us! Oh, if we could only get word to our sons of the little sister they were so eager to have!"

But there was no way to reach them for no one knew the way they had gone.

In a short time the husband died and the poor woman, abandoned by her nine sons, had only her little daughter left. She named the child Kerttu. Kerttu was a dear little girl and her face was as beautiful as her heart was good. Whenever she found her mother weeping alone she tried to comfort her and, as she grew older, she wanted to know the cause of her mother's grief. At last the mother told her about her nine brothers and how they had gone away never to return owing to the trick of some evil creature.

"My poor mother!" she cried, "how sorry I am that I am the innocent cause of your loss! Let me go out into the world and find my brothers! When once they hear the truth they will gladly come home to you to care for you in your old age!"

At first the mother would not consent to this.

"You are all I have," she said, "and I should indeed be miserable and lonely if anything happened you!"

But Kerttu continued to weep every time she thought of her poor brothers driven unnecessarily from home and at last the mother, realizing that she would nevermore be happy unless she were allowed to go in search of them, gave up opposing her.

"Very well, my daughter, you may go and may God go with you and bring you safely back to me. But before you go I must prepare you a bag of food for the journey and bake you a magic cake that will show you the way."

So she baked a batch of bread and at the same time mixed a little round cake with Kerttu's own tears and baked it, too. Then she said:

"Here now, my child, are provisions for the journey and here is a magic cake that will lead you to your brothers. All you have to do is throw it down in front of you and say:

"Roll, roll, my little cake!
Show me the way that I must take
To find at last the brothers nine
Whose own true mother is also mine!"

"Then the little cake will start rolling and do you follow wherever it rolls. But, Kerttu, my child, you must not start out alone. You must have some friend or companion to go with you."

Now it happened that Kerttu had a little dog, Musti, that she loved dearly.

"I'll take Musti with me!" she said. "Musti will protect me!"

So she called Musti and Musti wagged his tail and barked with joy at the prospect of going out into the world with his mistress.

Then Kerttu threw down the magic cake in front of her and sang:

"Roll, roll, my little cake!
Show me the way that I must take
To find at last the brothers nine
Whose own true mother is also mine!"

At once the cake rolled off like a little wheel and Kerttu and Musti followed it. They walked until they were tired. Then Kerttu picked up the little cake and they rested by the wayside. When they were ready again to start the cake a-rolling, all Kerttu had to do was throw it down in front of her and say the magic rime.

Their first day was without adventure. When night came they ate their supper and went to sleep in a field under a tree.

The second day they overtook an ugly old woman whom Kerttu disliked on sight. But she said to herself:

"Shame on you, Kerttu, not liking this woman just because she's old and ugly!" and she made herself answer the old woman's greetings politely and she made Musti stop snarling and growling.

The old hag asked Kerttu who she was and where she was going and Kerttu told her.

"Ah!" said the old woman, "how fortunate that we have met each other for our ways lie together!"

She smiled and petted Kerttu's arm and Kerttu felt like shuddering. But she restrained herself and told herself severely:

"You're a wicked girl not to feel more friendly to the poor old thing!"

Musti felt much as Kerttu did. He no longer growled for Kerttu had told him not to, but he drooped his tail between his legs and, pressing up close to Kerttu, he trembled with fright. And well he might, too, for the old hag was none other than Suyettar who had been waiting all these years just for this very chance to do further injury to Kerttu and her brothers.

Kerttu, poor child, was, alas! too good and innocent to suspect evil in others. She said to Suyettar:

"Very well, if our ways lie together then we can be companions."

So Suyettar joined Kerttu and Musti and the three of them walked on following the little cake. As the day advanced the sun grew hotter and hotter and at last when they reached a lake Suyettar said:

"My dear, let us sit down here for a few moments and rest."

They all sat down and presently Suyettar said:

"Let us go bathing in the lake. That will refresh us."

Kerttu would have agreed if Musti had not tugged at her skirts and warned her not to.

"Don't do it, dear mistress!" Musti growled softly. "Don't go in bathing with her! She'll bewitch you!"

So Kerttu said:

"No, I don't want to go in bathing."

Suyettar waited until they were again journeying on and then when Kerttu wasn't looking she turned around and kicked Musti and broke one of the poor little dog's legs. Thereafter Musti had to hop along on three legs.

The next afternoon when they passed another lake, Suyettar tried again to tempt Kerttu into the water.

"The sun is very hot," she said, "and it would refresh us both to bathe. Come, Kerttu, my dear, don't refuse me this time!"

But again Musti tugged at Kerttu's skirts and, licking her hand, whispered the warning:

"Don't do it, dear mistress! Don't go in bathing with her or she will bewitch you!"

So again Kerttu said politely:

"No, I don't feel like going in bathing. You go in alone and I'll wait for you here."

But this was not what Suyettar wanted and she said, no, she didn't care to go in alone. She was furious, too, with Musti and later when Kerttu wasn't looking she gave the poor little dog a kick that broke another leg. Thereafter Musti had to hop along on two legs.

They slept the third night by the wayside and the next day they went on again always following the magic cake. In mid-afternoon they passed a lake and Suyettar said:

"Surely, my dear, you must be tired and hot. Let us both bathe in this cool lake."

But Musti, hopping painfully along on two legs, yelped weakly and said to Kerttu:

"Don't do it, dear mistress! Don't go in bathing with her or she'll bewitch you!"

So for a third time Kerttu refused and later, when she wasn't looking, Suyettar kicked Musti and broke the third of the poor little dog's legs. Thereafter Musti hopped on as best he could on only one leg.

Well, they went on and on. When night came they slept by the roadside and then next morning they started on again. The sun grew hot and by mid-afternoon Kerttu was tired and ready to rest. When they reached a lake Suyettar again begged that they both go in bathing. Kerttu was tempted to agree when poor Musti threw himself panting at her feet and whimpered:

"Don't do it, dear mistress! Don't go in bathing with her or she will bewitch you!"

So Kerttu again refused.

"That's right, dear mistress!" Musti panted, "don't do it! I shall soon be dead, I know, for she hates me, but before I die I want to warn you one last time never to go in bathing with her or she will bewitch you!"

"What's that dog saying?" Suyettar demanded angrily, and without waiting for an answer she picked up a heavy piece of wood and struck poor Musti such a blow on the head that it killed him.

"What have you done to my poor little dog?" Kerttu cried.

"Don't mind him, my dear," Suyettar said. "He was sick and lame and it was better to put him out of his misery."

Suyettar tried to soothe Kerttu and make her forget Musti but all afternoon Kerttu wept to think that she would never again see her faithful little friend.

The next afternoon when Suyettar begged her to go in bathing there was no Musti to warn her against it and at last Kerttu allowed herself to be persuaded. She was tired from her many days' wandering and it was true that the first touch of the cool water refreshed her.

"Now splash water in my face!" Suyettar cried.

But Kerttu didn't want to splash water into Suyettar's face for she supposed Suyettar was an old woman and she thought it would be disrespectful to splash water into the face of an old woman.

"Do you hear me!" screamed Suyettar.

When Kerttu still hesitated, Suyettar looked at her with such a terrible, threatening expression that Kerttu did as she was bidden. She splashed water into Suyettar's face and, as the water touched Suyettar's eyes, Suyettar cried out:

"Your bonny looks give up to me.
And you take mine for all to see!"

Instantly the two changed appearance: Suyettar looked young and beautiful like Kerttu, and Kerttu was changed to a hideous old hag. Then too late she realized that the awful old woman to whom she had been so polite was Suyettar.

"Oh, why," Kerttu cried, "why didn't I heed poor Musti's warning!"

Suyettar dragged her roughly out of the water.

"Come along!" she said. "Dress yourself in those rags of mine and start that cake a-rolling! We ought to reach your brothers' house by tonight."

So poor Kerttu had to dress herself in Suyettar's filthy old garments while Suyettar, looking like a fresh young girl, decked herself out in Kerttu's pretty bodice and skirt.

Unwillingly now and with a heavy heart Kerttu threw down the cake and said:

"Roll, roll, my little cake!
Show me the way that I must take
To find at last the brothers nine
Whose own true mother is also mine!"

Off rolled the little cake and they two followed it, Kerttu weeping bitterly and Suyettar taunting her with ugly laughs. Then suddenly Kerttu forgot to weep for Suyettar took from her her memory and her tongue.

The little cake led them at last to a farmhouse before which it stopped. This was where the nine brothers were living. Eight of them were out working in the fields but the youngest was at home. He opened the door and when Suyettar told him that she was Kerttu, his sister, he kissed her tenderly and made her welcome. Then he invited her inside and they sat side by side on the bench and talked and Suyettar told him all she had heard from Kerttu about his mother and about the tokens which had been changed at Kerttu's birth. The youngest brother listened eagerly and Suyettar told her story so glibly that of course he supposed that she was his own true sister.

"And who is the awful looking old hag that has come with you?" he asked pointing at Kerttu.

"That? Oh, that's an old serving woman whom our mother sent with me to bear me company. She's dumb and foolish but she's a good herd and we can let her drive the cow out to pasture every day."

The older brothers when they came home were greatly pleased to find what they thought was their sister. They began to love her at once and to pet her and they said that now she must stay with them and keep house for them. She told them that was what she wanted to do and she said that now she was here the youngest brother need no longer stay at home but could go out every morning with the rest of them to work in the fields.

So now began a new life for poor Kerttu. In the morning after the brothers were gone Suyettar would scold and abuse her. She would bake a cake for her dinner to be eaten in the fields and she would fill the cake with stones and sticks and filth. Then she would take Kerttu as far as the gate where she would give her back her tongue and her memory and order her roughly to drive the cow to pasture and look after it all day long. In the late afternoon when Kerttu drove home the cow, Suyettar would meet her at the gate and take from her her tongue and her memory and then in the evening the brothers would see her as a foolish old woman who couldn't talk. Every morning and every evening Kerttu begged Suyettar to show her a little mercy, but far from showing her any mercy Suyettar grew more cruel from day to day.

Suyettar was very proud to think that nine handsome young men took her for a beautiful girl and she felt sure they would never find out their mistake for only Kerttu knew who she really was and Kerttu was entirely in her power.

At night seated in the shadow in a far corner of the kitchen with her nine brothers laughing and talking Kerttu felt no sorrow for at such times of course she had no memory. But during the day it was different. Then when she was alone in the meadow she had her memory and her tongue and she thought about her poor mother at home anxiously awaiting her return and she thought of her nine sturdy brothers all of whom might now through her mistake fall victims to Suyettar. These thoughts made her weep with grief and as the days went by she put this grief into a song which she sang constantly:

"I've found at last the brothers nine
Whose own true mother is also mine,
But they know me not from stick or stone!
They leave me here to weep alone,
While Suyettar sits in my place
With stolen looks and stolen face!
She snared me first with evil guile
And now she mocks me all the while:
By night she takes my tongue away,
She feeds me sticks and stones by day!...
Oh, little they guess, the brothers nine,
That their own true mother is also mine!"

The brothers as they worked in nearby fields used to hear the song and they wondered about it.

"Strange!" they said to one another. "Can that be the old woman singing? In the evening at home she never opens her mouth and our dear sister always says that she's dumb and foolish."

One afternoon when Kerttu's song sounded particularly sad, the youngest brother crept close to the meadow where Kerttu was sitting in order to hear the words. He listened carefully and then hurried back to the others and with frightened face told them what he had heard.

"Nonsense!" the older brothers said. "It can't be so!"

However, they, too, wanted to hear for themselves the words of the strange song, so they all crept near to listen.

It looked like an old hag who was singing but the voice that came out of the withered mouth was the voice of a young girl. As they listened they, too, grew pale:

"I've found at last the brothers nine
Whose own true mother is also mine,
But they know me not from stick or stone!
They leave me here to weep alone,
While Suyettar sits in my place
With stolen looks and stolen face!
She snared me first with evil guile
And now she mocks me all the while:
By night she takes my tongue away,
She feeds me sticks and stones by day!...
Oh, little they guess, the brothers nine,
That their own true mother is also mine!"

"Can it be true?" they said, whispering together.

They sent the youngest brother to question Kerttu and he, when he had heard her story, believed it true. Then the other brothers went to her one by one and questioned her and finally they were all convinced of the truth of her story.

"It is well for us," they said, "if we do not all fall into the power of that awful creature! How, O how can we rescue our poor little sister!"

"I can never get back my own looks," Kerttu said, "unless Suyettar splashes water into my eyes and unless I cry out a magic rime as she does it."

The brothers discussed one plan after another and at last agreed on one that they thought might deceive Suyettar.

They had Kerttu inflame her eyes with dust and come groping home one midday. The brothers, too, were at home and as Kerttu came stumbling into the kitchen they said to Suyettar:

"Oh, sister, sister, see the poor old woman! Something ails her! Her eyes – they're all red and swollen! Get some water and bathe them!"

"Nonsense!" Suyettar said. "The old hag's well enough! Let her be! She doesn't need any attention!"

"Oh, sister!" the youngest brother said, reproachfully, "is that any way for a human, kind-hearted girl like you to talk? If you won't bathe the old creature's eyes, I will myself!"

Then Suyettar who of course wanted them to think that she was a human, kind-hearted girl said, no, she would bathe them. So she took a basin of water over to Kerttu and told her to lean down her head. As she splashed the first drop of water into Kerttu's eyes, Kerttu cried out:

"My own true looks give back to me
And take your own for all to see!"

Instantly Suyettar was again a hideous old hag though still dressed in Kerttu's pretty bodice and skirt, and Kerttu was herself again, young and fresh and sweet, though still incased in Suyettar's rags. But the brothers pretended that they saw no difference and kept on talking to Suyettar as though they still thought her Kerttu. And Suyettar because her eyes were blinded with the dust supposed that they were still deceived.

Then one of the brothers said to Suyettar:

"Sister dear, the *sauna* is all heated and ready. Don't you want to bathe?"

Suyettar thought that this would be a fine chance to wash the dust from her eyes, so she let them lead her to the sauna. Once they got her inside they locked the door and set the *sauna* a-fire. Oh, the noise she made then when she found she had been trapped! She kicked and screamed and cursed and threatened! But Kerttu and the brothers paid no heed to her. They left her burning in the sauna while they hurried homewards.

They found their poor old mother seated at the window weeping, for she thought that now Kerttu as well as her sons was lost forever. As Kerttu and the nine handsome young men came in the gate she didn't recognize them until Kerttu sang out:

"I bring at last the brothers nine
Whose own true mother is also mine!"

Then she knew who they were and with thanks to God she welcomed them home.

The Water Lily

WERE YOU EVER last summer at that pretty little island, where the graceful birches dally with the breeze, and where the water is so crystal clear that you can see the little fishes swimming over the white sandy bottom? If you have been there, you will be sure to remember the big boulder-stone on the strand, and the little water lily bathing at its feet, and perhaps observed how every evening, when she grew sleepy, she folded her petals together and hid her chalice under her broad green leaves. Gossips said she was in love with the sun, for she was seen early every morning to open her floral eyes and gaze with a pure innocent look at the dazzling orb of the heavens. But the snowy water lily was not so presumptuous as to dream of becoming wedded to such a mighty and illustrious lord, placed so high, and, besides, who was so much older than she, that she did not even venture to call him her godfather. Oh dear no; the water lily had no such wishes. She had become intimately acquainted with a young birch which grew on the strand, and mirrored his long flowing locks in the water, where the water lily swam without ever abandoning her parent root.

The water lily was not only beautiful, but also meek and good, which was far better; and in consequence she was everybody's favourite, and her suitors were innumerable. There was a whole company of sedges (bulrushes) quite near, and one of the sedge-fronds was continually bowing to her whenever there came the slightest breath of wind across the water. "Your most humble servant," said the sedge, as it made a reverence so deep that it almost dipped its tip on the crystal floor. But the water lily did not like a humility which only consisted in bowing, for she observed the sedges could look as stiff and haughty as anybody when the frolicsome little perches gambolled on the surface of the water.

There was also another suitor, still more stiff and erect than anyone else; it was a pole near the strand, to which an old fisherman used to tie his nets, that the waves might not carry them away. That pole was jealous of his position, and went out of the road for no man; no, not for fishes either, and had many a "set to" with those who came too near him.

The water lily did not approve of that, for she was kind and forgiving, and never quarrelled with anybody, not even with the flat old boat, which at an abrupt turn sometimes would dip her in the water, when it had a chance.

The third suitor was the great big boulder-stone himself, who was called the landmark, for he constituted the boundary in the fishery that was divided between two hamlets. The boulder-stone grew quite warm at heart on sunshiny days, when he stood staring at the water lily, but he was so awfully old, some said sixty thousand years, and crisp moss grew in all his fissures, and made him look so hoary and wrinkled. The water lily was perfectly awed by the reverence of the landmark, but to wed him would have been to carry admiration a great deal too far.

In one word, the water lily loved a green young birch very much that was always nodding to her so friendly when he mirrored himself in the glassy waters, and that he may have been said to have done a little too often; but it was only to behold his own image side by side with the lovely water lily, his little sweetheart.

I had nearly forgotten to tell you the water lily's pedigree. She was the youngest and most beloved child of the water-sprite, and he had cradled her in his arms when she was a wee thing, and now he frequently lifted her on his broad shoulders when she rose at dawn day from her soft and transparent bed. And when night came, and the sun sank in the west, and the water lily rested her white head beneath her leafy coverlet, then the weird old water-sprite would sing mystic songs to her, and she was gently cradled by the wave until her petals closed, and in the balmy summer night she dreamt bright dreams of all the beauty which the seas embrace.

"Don't come too near me, old Nixie!" said the pole to the water-sprite. But the sedge, which was always ready to cringe to those in power, twisted himself into every conceivable attitude, and kept on whispering: "Your humble servant, sir; your most obedient humble servant, sir!"

"Never mind those fools," said the boulder-stone to the water-sprite, for they were old acquaintances. "You had better give your child to me, and she will enjoy a life of luxury and ease," he continued.

"What things one must hear, to be sure," said the water-sprite, and laughed till the spray was thrown in showers from his beard. "What would everybody say if I were to remove my darling floral daughter into your crib?"

"Well, what does it matter," replied the boulder-stone, "if I am some thousands of years old? I am a steady old fellow, and not carried away by the whirlwinds of life and passion, like the young dandies."

"Well, I think we had better leave the subject, 'tis only one of your whims; and let us remain firm friends as of old." But the boulder-stone, the pole, and the sedge-frond were each determined to obtain the water lily for his wife.

The landmark one night roused the young dashing southwest wind, who had gone to sleep at the foot of the rock, and said to him: "Seeing that you have chosen my place for your lodging this night, you might do me a service in return."

"What is it?" asked the southwest wind.

"At sunrise tomorrow morning you must blow with all your might till you succeed in breaking off the young birch which grows on the strand, because it is for him, forsooth, that the water lily won't become my wife."

"Very well," answered the reckless wind, "I have broken cedars and palm trees as if they had been sticks; why shouldn't I break off a puny little birch stripling?"

The sedge again addressed himself to the billow, who slowly and sleepily, with the surf, surged in through the firth: "Your most humble servant, mighty swell of the ocean!" he greeted the wave. "Pray be so kind as to do me a little service as you pass by."

"What might that be?" the huge wave yawned.

"If you please, to surge on to the young birch on the strand and pull him down. He is the cause, forsooth, of the water lily refusing to become my bride."

"Very well," answered the billow, "I have flooded forests and cities; it is a mere bagatelle for me to sweep away such a stripling of a birch. But I am falling asleep just now; we will wait till tomorrow morning."

"Your most humble servant," said the sedge-frond.

The pole was also annoyed with the birch, and managed to vex the fisherman when he was the same evening tying his nets to the pole. "You rascally pole!" the fisherman said. "You are tearing the net to pieces!"

"Well, it isn't my fault that I am so knotty," the pole replied. "On the strand grows a birch that would suit you far better; cut him down tomorrow and stick him into the bottom of the creek."

"Very well advised," said the fisherman; "I will think of it tomorrow."

The evening passed, and night came on, and the water lily folded again the white petals of her chalice, and the birch looked quite joyous with delight as he beheld her in the soft twilight of the summer night. There were no forebodings of evil, and the water lily enjoyed the sweet sleep of a child. A large yellow moth, whose nature it was to flit about at night, hovered anxiously about the birch, but the birch observed it not. He was busy washing himself in the dew, which fell in little tiny trickling pearls in an almost invisible shower over him, and his thoughts were only how he should become quite spruce and elegant till his little water lily again should look at him with her beaming floral eyes.

And it was not very long before a crimson streak was seen in the northeast, tinging the whole land, spreading and increasing every moment in intensity, until the vast expanse of the sky, east and north, was one terrific conflagration, where the clouds seemed like monster dragons vomiting fire.

The fisherman chanced to be awake, and looking out through the window of his hut, he said, rather surprised: "It betokens that we are going to have a regular gale today. I had better hasten out and take in the nets."

But as yet it was calm, and so perfectly still that not even the verdant ringlets of the young birch moved in the cool morning breeze. The water lily began to open her chalice, and with a sleepy look, said, "Good morning" to her friend the birch. Never had the birch appeared so spruce before, she thought, and she had never appeared so charming before to him. They felt so happy and loving; and at this moment the sun rose in his full glory behind the crimson clouds and looked benignly down upon them in their youthful happiness in the early morning.

Then the boulder-stone impatiently shook his lodger the southwest wind, who moved in the soft grass. "Get up and work," said the landmark.

"Let me alone," answered the wind, and spread his great cloudy wings abreast, which he had used as a blanket. But the rock allowed him no peace. "Since you insist upon it, I will rage so that it shall whiz about your ears," the aerial depredator said, vexed; and barely awake, he tore roaring into the air, so that the tree-tops bowed dismayed.

He was quite wild that morning, the young madcap southwest wind. The sky soon became darkened with his gigantic wings, and his wrath crested the billows of the sea. But the birch and the water lily lived leeward of the isle, so they were not aware of the storm. They had charged a gilded little butterfly with messages of love from one another, and amused themselves in despatching and receiving these, and watching his aerial passage across the water that lay between them.

The storm increased, the trees creaked with the labour of trying to withstand it, the billows dashed the spray aloft, and it whizzed and roared around the cliffs and rocks as if a hundred thousand kittens were in battle with as many yelping whelps. The billows came rushing madly through the estuary, so that the little sedge-frond felt ill at ease, and writhed and twisted himself in an inconceivable manner to enable himself to hold his ground. "How stupid I was to ask the mighty billow to aid me," he thought; but it was too late now to repent. He already saw in the distance quite a watery mountain, showing the froth of his wrath. "There he is, the wave I bespoke!" he said, terrified; and on the instant the weird water-monster surged over him and tore him from his root, and the last the sedge-frond said on being hurried into the deep was, "Your most obedient humble servant, sir!"

It fared no better with the intriguing pole. He set to and jostled with the waves, and cried, "For shame!" to his assailants.

But when the huge billow came, it was all up with him. He was snapped like a reed, and flung far away amongst the angry waves.

The boulder-stone, who had witnessed so many storms in his days, remained quite callous during all this uproar, and his stony heart laughed at the havoc and devastation around.

The lovers were not aware that the southwest wind with his wild behaviour had awoke the majestic thunder, slumbering in the clouds. "Reetch!" there whizzed a long, terrific zig-zag flash of lightning, lighting up all the heavens for a moment, and then flinging its wrathful dart to the doomed boulder-stone, splitting its stony heart, though thousands of ages old; and that was the end of the wicked suitor.

The weird old water-sprite had enough to do to keep his coral palace in repair that day, for the warring billows pursued each other in such wild chase that they nearly set afloat the tiles of his silvery roof. But when evening came, and the boisterous southwest wind had hied away on his dark wings, and a genial friendly breeze from the south had replaced him, the water-sprite papa went out of his castle to look at his little darling, the water lily, and he found her with her slender stem broken and her white chalice crushed, at the foot of the birch; but it was still visible on her snowy cheek, and her petals (even beautiful in their decay), that she had been deprived of her life at a moment when her happiness had reached its height, and when her young floral heart was replete with joy and innocent love.

Then the weird old water-sprite shed tears as large as the eggs of little sparrows, and they trickled down his long flowing beard.

This beloved child (the water lily) he buried in the earth, beneath the roots of the birch. And the poor birch wept till the tears fell like rain from his foliage, and the gilded little butterfly cried till she lost her eyes and became stone-blind, and the dew wept till the whole meadow was quite wet, and the golden setting sun wept in the cloud until a beautiful rainbow grew out of his tears and arched the whole heavens over the verdant wood.

But the boulder-stone could not shed any tears, if he had wanted, for his heart was broken in twain, and the sedge-frond lay withered at his feet. The old fisherman looked for his pole in vain; he first thought he would cut down the birch, and make himself a new one, but then it seemed to him it was a pity to cut down such a beautiful young tree, so he allowed it to remain, and that was very properly done by the old fisherman. What do you say?

Next spring, perhaps, a new water lily will grow at the foot of the birch, near the strand. That will be the child of the beautiful water lily. I wonder if it will be as meek and humble as its mother.

The White Violet

DOWN IN THE VALLEY grew a white violet; she was neither prettier nor plainer than other white violets, and, considering that all such little spring flowers are pretty, of course this one was as beautiful and white as any of the others. "Was she not a little prettier than the others?" "Well, I am sure I don't know." Where flowers grow there butterflies always flirt about. Where else should they flirt? It is the same old story over and over again, and yet there is always something new in them!

The most splendid-looking of the butterflies was called "Apollo"; he had white wings with golden stars, by way of orders of distinction. Butterflies generally may be presumed to be a little vain, and love tinsel and display; of course they cannot help being gaudy, they are born aristocratic flirts.

One day Apollo came on a visit to the white violet, and said: "Love me, and I will love you!"

"I cannot help but love you," answered the little flower, for she was quite taken with his splendid appearance, and was too artless to make believe to the contrary.

"Well, but is it quite sure?" asked the butterfly.

"Of course," answered the dainty flower, "I cannot live without you!"

"That's right," said the the honey from her chalice. Butterflies like honey, but they are rather improvident, and don't store it up as the bees do. He had his feast and then flew away.

"He is sure to return," thought the floweret; but she was mistaken, Apollo stayed away, he hadn't time to think of her.

One day, however, he was fluttering around near another little flower close by. "Now I have an opportunity of speaking to him," thought the little white violet. Then she nerved her enfeebled petals a little, and called out, as loud as a little white violet possibly can: "Love me, and I will love you."

"I don't love you a litttle bit," answered the heartless flirt, quite unconcerned, for he did not care one whit.

"But I love you," remonstrated the discarded little love.

"Very likely, so much the worse for you," responded the aristocrat, and away he flew again. But now he stayed away yet longer. The little white violet was left quite lonely on the sward, the hours slowly dragged on, and she began to wither.

At last Apollo came again, quite by accident, looking even more splendid than before, and the artless little flower asked once more: "Don't you love me?"

"Not a bit," answered he.

"But I love you," repeated the rejected little thing.

"Well, what is that to me?" answered the cruel flirt. "That is the same old story which cruel flirt. I have heard a hundred times before," and in a moment he was off again.

"Just listen to me, Miss Violet," said a knotty juniper-bush, which grew near at hand; "it is not proper to lay bare one's feelings in the way you do. We must appear a little saucy if a weak little flower like you can be taught to show off such pertness. If anybody cuts you, why, cut them again; and if anybody makes you feel that he despises you, you must show off who you are. Just look at me; only just let the sparrows dare to slight me! No, Miss Violet, we must have some self-respect. It is quite old-fashioned, I can tell you, to return love for contempt."

"But, really, I can't help it," said the despised little thing. "I love him with my whole fragrance, and will continue to do so until I wither and die."

"You are a spooney little mushroom!" answered the juniper-bush, and that was the very worst he could say, for these fungi were said not to be very choice in the selection of their acquaintance, and the spruce prided himself upon his great knowledge of the sylvan world.

The sun was scorching hot, and the white violet grew paler, and every hour became more withered. Then some boys came running into the wood, and one of them flaunted about a butterfly-net, and then he caught sight of Apollo. "Look, what a splendid butterfly!" he cried; "that will be a fine specimen to stick with a pin in my collection of insects." And he began chasing his gaudy prey over the sward.

Apollo was now in dire distress. How he flew! how he fluttered! Hey! the net touched him on the wing and down he tumbled, head over heels, defenceless, upon the green grass, close to where his discarded violet still lingered. "He fell down somewhere hereabout," called out the boy, and bent down to search for the captive, but when he did not find him, he ran away to chase other butterflies.

And it was no easy thing to find Apollo, for the white violet had hidden him under her leaves, which formed quite an arbour above him. But her slender stalk had been trampled upon, and she was quite torn off and lay crushed amongst the grass.

"It was well I escaped," said Apollo, and he crept out from his hiding-place, which was the nether garments of the little white violet herself.

"Do you love me now?" said the little withering floweret, cut off from her parent root.

"Oh, it is you!" said the incorrigible coxcomb. "Look, my stars and ribbons have been most horribly defiled! Really I shall not be able to show myself in society again." "Have you no love for me at all?" asked the dying violet.

"Nay; but look how dirty my beautiful costume has become!" continued Apollo.

"Have you a dew-drop in your chalice, my dear? if so, do give it to me, that I may wash myself, for I am as black as a mole."

"Then have you no love for me at all?" asked the flower for the last time.

"My dear friend, I have no time just now for such trivial questions," answered the dandy. "Ah! just what I feared, my frill is quite rumpled! What will they say at the Court of the Roses?"

"But I love you still," sighed the violet, and breathed her last scarcely perceptible fragrance, and all her withered petals fell off from her chalice, and there was the end of her.

"Oh, dear me! look at the poor thing now," said the butterfly, lamenting, for his heart was not altogether bad; he was only very flighty, and took things so easy, like the rest of them, that was all. "And the worst of it is, I shan't be able to get any water to titivate myself with now, before the night-dew falls. Really I am a most cruelly used butterfly; my dress-coat is quite destroyed, my frill rumpled dreadfully, and my stars and medals look like copper coin – how very annoying! It will create an awful sensation in the world, and everybody will pity me – that is some consolation – I shall be considered highly interesting: how they will talk about me at the Court of Roses!" And, with these words, the gay Apollo again took wing, but he had not gone very far when a sparrow, who had lain in wait for him in a tree, pounced down upon him. "Smack!" and the beautiful flutterer became a mere mouthful for his ravenous foe, though he thought himself highly interesting to the last moment.

The prickly juniper-bush had witnessed all this, but he kept his thoughts to himself. The fault was (he tried to reason), that the little white violet was far too amiable. "No; it is far better to be a little more self-confident, and sting again if anybody is too impertinent. Why don't they take example of me?"

But everybody did not think alike. When the evening zephyr sighed in the long grass, it took up and carried away a gentle whisper amongst the remaining white violets, which meant, "Love me, and I will love you"; and then they added, "And when you do not love me any longer, I will still love you."

It certainly was an old and common-enough story, but the white violets loved to repeat it very often.

Knut Fairyflute

KNUT WAS A POOR BOY who had no father nor mother, so he lived with his grandmother in a little cottage by the side of a lake called Perlebanks. He had a shirt, a coat, a pair of trousers, and a cap; he did not require anything more in summer. For winter he had woollen stockings and birch-bark shoes; that wasn't so very bad. He was always contented and happy, but always hungry. It is not easy to be at the same time both happy and hungry.

The misfortune was that his kind grandmother seldom had enough food to really satisfy the boy. She spun wool, and then sent Knut to sell the yarn at Herr Peterman's large farm, called Asa, about a mile distant. When Knut returned with the money which he had got for the wool, the old woman bought meal with it to bake cakes. She had also a fishing-net, so that she could sometimes have fish, when the son of Fisherman Jonas was able to help Knut to set the net. If the wool sold well they were able to have sour milk, and also potatoes, grown on a little croft near the cottage, which was not larger than the floor of a room; but things were not always so prosperous, and Knut's appetite often demanded satisfaction, yet still he was always cheerful.

He sat one morning by the shore of Perlebanks, and gathered yellow pebbles, which looked like soft, hot, cooked potatoes. Poor Knut! they were not good to eat, so he laughed and threw them away, and as he did so he saw something lying amongst the stones. Knut lifted it, and found it was a little reed pipe, such as children often make when playing by the water's edge. There was nothing at all remarkable about it, but Knut tried it to see if it made any noise, and truly it did; one could sound three notes on it – pu, py, pt. When Knut found that he stuffed the pipe into his jacket pocket. That was a real fast day: Knut had had no breakfast. "If only I were in Herr Peterman's kitchen at Asa!" said he to himself, and tried to imagine that he smelt fried herring.

He had nothing else to do, so he sat down on a stone and tried to fish, but not a fish would even nibble. There had been a storm the day before, and the water was now as calm as a mirror, the sun shone, and the billows heaved like crystal mountains against the shore and kissed the sea's foot-prints in the sand.

'I wonder what Granny has for dinner today,' thought Knut to himself. One wave approached so near that it wet Knut's bare feet, and there was heard a babbling in the water: Knut, have you found the Princess's reed pipe? It can sound three notes – *pu*, to sleep; *py*, to weep and *pi* to laugh."

"What!" said Knut. "Is it a fairy pipe? Go away, Wave; I have found the pipe, and I mean to keep it."

The wave mumbled something, no one ever knew what, rolled away, and never came back.

Knut took the pipe out of his pocket, and examined it. "Oh ho; so you are a fairy pipe, and can work magic? Now, come, do charm me a fish on to the hook," and with that he blew *pu, pu*.

He had not long piped when a trout, then a dace, and finally a pike floated to the surface of the water, lying on their sides as if asleep.

'Fish are straying about here!' thought Knut, continuing to pipe. Soon all the water near the shore was covered with floating fish – sticklebacks, perch, roach, dace, salmon, and all the smart-tailed fry which live in the water. 'Here is a fine haul of fish!' thought Knut, and ran up to the cottage to fetch a landin gnet.

When he returned he saw the shore covered with water-fowl. The gulls were the greediest and screamed, "Ta-i-an! ta-i-an!" so loud that they might have been heard half a mile away. There were many others to keep them company: goosanders, gannets, wild geese, and even swans. All these rapacious visitors were hard at work devouring the floating fish, and in the midst of the swarm there swooped down a great sea-eagle, and seized in his claws a half-pound trout.

"Stop, thieves!" cried Knut, as he took up some stones, and began throwing them at the birds. Some were hit on the wings, and some on the legs, but none were inclined to leave their prey. Then a shot was heard, and then another, and another, the sound being quite near.

Some of the birds turned on their sides and floated on the water beside the fish. The firing continued, till at last, of the whole flock of birds, some were shot down, and the rest scattered screaming in every direction. A boat, in which were three sportsmen, landed on the shore to collect the game. It was Herr Peterman, who had rowed out with three of his friends to shoot game. They stepped on shore in great spirits.

"Look at Knut!" said Herr Peterman. "How in all the world have you managed to collect so many birds to Perlebanks?"

"I played to attract fish, and the birds wanted to keep them company," answered Knut craftily.

"Well, you must be an extra fine player," said Herr Peterman. "From this time you should be called Knut Fairyflute."

"All right," said Knut. He never had possessed a surname, so might just as well be called Fairyflute, as Andersson, Séderlund, or Matsson.

"But how is it, Knut Fairyflute, that you look so poorly today? You are as thin as a hop-pole," said Herr Peterman.

"How can I help looking poorly, when I have seen so much food, and yet have eaten none since yesterday's dinner?" answered Knut, with his usual cheerfulness.

"You don't mean to say so. Come today and dine at Asa, since you have procured us such a good bag! But do not come before four o'clock, as the birds could not be plucked and roasted earlier."

"Thank you humbly," answered Knut, while thinking at the same time, "That is late enough for one who has eaten nothing since dinner-time yesterday."

Herr Peterman rowed away home, and Knut went back to his grandmother.

"Well, Knut, have you seen any fish today?"

"I have seen plenty, but the birds ate up the fish, and Herr Peterman shot the birds."

"How unfortunate, Knut! We have only two herrings, four potatoes, and half a roll of bread for dinner today."

"Never mind, Granny! You shall eat it. I am asked to dine at Asa, and shall bring you home a bit of cheese in my pocket."

"Don't go the short cut through Kükkale Wood, Knut; fairies live there, as well as three fairy kings – a mountain king, snow king, and woodland king. Go along the shore road; it is safer, but beware of the mermaid!"

"The shore road is so long, Granny, and I have had nothing to eat since yesterday's dinner."

"Well, well, go whichever way you please, but don't think about food; it leads into temptation."

"No, Granny; I shall think about the next Sunday-school lesson."

Knut started, and thought about the lesson, but when he came to the shortcut, he thought:

'I would certainly be a fool, if, when I am so hungry, I were to walk two miles instead of one.'

Thus, he turned down the shortcut through Kükkale Wood and resolved to hear himself say the Catechism while he went through the wood. He had not gone far when he saw a little thin man dragging behind him a cart laden with twelve bars of iron.

"Well, good-day to you, Knut Fairyflute," said the old man. "Why do you look so poorly?"

"How can I help looking poorly when I have swallowed nothing but the Catechism since yesterday's dinner? But how do you know my name?"

"I know all names," said the old man.

"Can I help you? Such a load makes you breathless."

"Shove if you like, Fairyflute."

Knut shoved, and soon they came to a high hill in the wood.

"I live here," said the old man. "Step in; as you have helped me with my load, I shall give you something good."

The old man went inside the hill. Knut's stomach said, "Follow," and Knut followed.

Soon they found themselves in a great underground palace, which was all shining with gold, silver, and precious stones.

"Do you live here?" asked Knut.

"Of course I do," said the old man. "I am the King of the Mountain, and tomorrow my daughter will celebrate her wedding. All my attendants are in such a bustle that I have had to fetch my food home myself from the forge."

"Was that iron which you were dragging in the cart?" asked Knut.

"Pig-iron, my boy, pig-iron of the best quality. It is somewhat better than ordinary iron ore. Pig-iron is my favourite food, especially when glowing at a white heat. Have you ever eaten pig-iron?"

"No," said Knut, "not that I can remember."

"Then you are going to taste something extra good. Now look while I put two pieces in my flaming furnace. In three minutes, they will glow at a white heat; creep into the furnace and bite a bit of the red-hot roast."

"Many thanks; but I would rather you gave me a bit of bread and butter, and a good junket."

"But you don't know what is good. Be off with you into the furnace; the iron is red-hot already."

"I well believe it; it is far too hot in there."

"What nonsense you talk! It is only the moderate heat of a room," growled the old man, and tried with all his might to stuff Knut into the burning furnace. But then the one who took to his heels was Knut! He ran for dear life, luckily found the door, and was soon once more on the forest path.

'Granny was right,' thought Knut. 'I will hear myself say the Catechism.'

While Knut was thinking of the answer to the difficult question: *What is that*? he began to feel cold. The reason was soon manifested, for although it was summer, there suddenly appeared a snow mountain. 'That is extraordinary,' thought Knut. 'Wherever shall one be able to get a little hot food?'

With that, he climbed up on the snow and thought of food, when all of a sudden, he fell plump through a deep hole and found himself in a beautiful palace of shimmering ice. It was bright with stars and lit by the moon. All the halls were adorned with mirrors of crystal ice, and all the floors bestrewn with hoarfrost that glittered like diamonds. Clumsy snowmen crawled on their bodies across the floor. One only was standing upright; he was a tall, stalwart giant, with icicles in his hair, icicles in his beard, a robe of thin ice, and shoes made of the frozen juice of berries.

"Well, good-day, Knut Fairyflute," said the giant. "Why do you look so poorly?"

"How could I look anything else but poorly, I who have had nothing but a hot bar of iron since yesterday's dinner?" answered Knut, all his teeth chattering.

"You are too hot, young man, you are too hot," said the giant. "I am the Snow King; I bring up all my subjects to be lumps of ice, and I will turn you into one. High Chamberlain, dip the boy seven times in ice water, hang him up on a peg, and let him freeze!"

"No, stop a minute," rejoined Knut. "Please give me a mug of beer posset instead – I am a lump of ice already."

"High Chamberlain, give him a bit of frozen quicksilver and a draught of ague before you dip him!" ordered the giant.

Knut tried to run away, but it was now too late. The High Chamberlain seized him by the collar, and it would have been all up with poor Knut if it had not occurred to him to have recourse to the reed pipe. He did not know what to do except to blow it, and this time it turned out *pi*! *pi*!

Immediately the features of the tall snow king were relaxed to a grin, which might have been mistaken for mirth, but which was nothing else than rage at the inclination to laugh which completely overpowered him. He laughed – yes, he laughed, so that the icicles fell from his hair and chin; his knees gave way, his head fell off, and broke in pieces. All the snowmen laughed themselves to bits; the High Chamberlain fell to pieces as he sat, and became slush; the ice mirrors cracked into atoms, and all the snow mountain changed into a snowstorm. With the greatest difficulty could Knut keep his lips together to blow, he himself laughed so much. In the midst of the snowstorm, he observed he was again on the forest path; the snow ran to swell the brook, and once more it was summer.

'Now I shall take care,' thought Knut.

He scrambled steadily forward and began to con over his recollections of '*What is that?*', but he had not gone far when he found himself beside the most beautiful green forest slope among the mountains, where the grass gleamed with wild strawberries.

'It cannot be dangerous to gather some wild strawberries, especially when one is not going to get food until four o'clock in the afternoon', thought Knut, as he climbed up the bank.

Scarcely was he there when he perceived that what he had taken to be wild strawberries were nothing else than thousands of little fairies dressed, like them, in red. They were not taller than strawberry stalks, and danced merrily around a green tuft, upon which sat their queen, who was three inches high.

"Well, good day to you, Knut Fairyflute," said the elf queen. "Why do you look so poorly?"

"And how could I look anything else but poorly when I have had nothing to eat since yesterday's dinner except hot iron and frozen quicksilver? I thought that you were a strawberry."

"Poor boy, he is hungry," said the elf queen to her lady-in-waiting. "Give him a dewdrop and an ant leg, that for once he may have a satisfying meal."

"Thank you heartily," said Knut. "Could I not have, instead, a tub of strawberries and a pailful of milk?"

"He is a gross feeder!" said the elf queen, greatly offended at such an outrageous appetite. "You know very well, human child, that you have come into my kingdom without leave, and trampled to death a thirtieth part of my faithful subjects, as more than one red streak can tell. Wood spiders, do your duty!"

Scarcely were the words uttered when a legion of long-legged spiders dropped down from the trees and began to weave innumerable fine spider webs around Knut. He did not like this sort of fun, so he tried to rub away the spiders' webs and get once more to the forest path. He could not move. His feet were entangled in the strong net, his arms were glued to his side, his eyes pasted together, and soon he fell down on the grass. He could see nothing, but he heard all the forest laughing. The elves formed a circle around him, and danced on the top of him, nipped his cheek like midges, and were beside themselves with merriment at such a comical prank.

"Lie there and starve, until you can learn to be satisfied with a drop of dew and the leg of an ant!" said they.

Knut implored their pity.

"Listen to me, little elves," said he. "A little piece of reed which I am carrying in my jacket pocket will satisfy me. Will anyone be good enough to put it in my mouth?"

The elves were indescribably amused at the idea of such a greedy human child being satisfied with a bit of reed. Four of them climbed into his jacket pocket, and by means of their combined strength dragged out the magic pipe, which, with much difficulty, they succeeded in putting into his mouth. Whereupon they danced still more merrily round about and over the top of him, so that the forest echoed with their laughter, which sounded just like millions of mosquitoes. Knut hardly felt the pipe between his lips when he began to blow, and this time it was *py*! *py*! First, the merry laughter in the forest ceased, and soon was heard on all sides a sobbing – not unlike the sound one hears in summer when a torrent of rain is lashing the brook. Knut could not see, but he understood that the fairies were weeping, and he thought that, after all, it was a shame to make such merry things sob so piteously.

"Let me go, and then you may laugh again," said Knut to the fairies.

The greatest joy of the fairies is to laugh, and they laugh away their short lives all through the summer evenings. Soon, hundreds of them were prepared to sweep away the cobwebs, to release him from his prison, to free his arms and legs, and to open his sealed eyes. Knut could now see his little tormentors, and was malicious enough to blow another *py*, *py*.

Oh! What faces the poor little beings made! They wanted so much to laugh, and yet they had to cry, because of that horrid *py*.

Knut could not in his heart plague them longer. Therefore, for a change, he blew *pi*, *pi*, and then all the fairies became mad with delight. They jumped so high that they nearly jumped up to the larks in the sky, and some of them fell right down on Knut, and then he had to shake them off. He never noticed that one of the fairies had fallen into his jacket pocket and could not find her way out again.

"Goodbye, little fairies," said Knut, as he resumed his wandering on the forest path. 'I must beware of the Woodland King', he thought. Where was I in my lesson – '*What is that?*'

In a short time, Knut came to a bed of cloudberries by the side of the road.

'There can be no harm in gathering some cloudberries in passing, when I shall not get food until four o'clock in the afternoon,' thought he.

A large fir tree lay there, and in order to reach the cloudberries, he had to climb over the tree. Scarcely did he find himself amid the thick and leafy foliage, when the fir tree, to Knut's great alarm, raised itself up and said in a gruff voice:

"Well, how are you, Knut Fairyflute? Why do you look so poorly today?"

Knut was hanging high up on the top of the tree, but summoned sufficient courage to answer: "How can I look anything else but poorly when I have had nothing to eat since yesterday's dinner except hot pig-iron, frozen quicksilver, a drop of dew, and one ant leg?"

"Well, why do you disturb my after-dinner nap?" asked the fir tree. "Don't you know that I am the king of the forest and rule over all woods and marshes for seven miles round? This is my castle. Is it not a fine abode?"

Knut saw nothing but a wild waste, but he asked if he might not be allowed to descend to gather a few cloudberries.

"What do I hear? Cloudberries!" roared the forest king. "Take the fir tree for a spade and dig yourself up seven cart-loads of peat. That is what I call a substantial meal. It is my favourite food."

"Perhaps I might have a cart-load of apple marmalade, and just a moderate-sized pot filled with honey?" asked Knut.

"Apple marmalade! I shall make you into apple marmalade for disturbing my mid-day slumber. Golden Eagle, I give the little rascal to you; you can chop him into mince-collops for your youngsters!"

Now Knut perceived an enormous eagle sitting on the top of the fir tree, looking at him with ravenous eyes. He could not jump down – his arms and legs were held fast by the branches, and he would soon be chopped up into mince-meat. Knut had never tasted mince-collops; but much as he liked food, it seemed dreadful to him to become food for an eagle.

At this critical point, he felt something as delicate as a flower clamber up his arm, the collar of his jacket, his chin, and from there to his mouth. It was the little fairy, which had lain forgotten in his pocket, and now with great difficulty was dragging the fairy pipe – which was six times as long as herself.

"Blow!" said the fairy.

Knut felt the pipe in his mouth and began to blow. It was *pi* again.

The fir tree commenced to gape, stretched out its branches, and mumbled something about its mid-day sleep having been disturbed whereupon it threw itself full length down on the turf, and in its fall crushed the enormous eagle beneath it.

Knut crept from between the branches. He heard the forest snore like a hundred bears growling for a wager, and set off on foot as hard as he was able.

'Now I shall take good care,' thought he. 'It is dangerous in the forest. I will rather go by the shore road, along by the sea.'

Soon, he had made his way over the fallen, slumbering trees to a fence round a farm. He climbed over it and found himself on the shore road. The great wide sea lay before him, much larger than it was at Perlebank. The west wind was blowing – not a wild, rushing wind such as one often has on the water, but a slight fresh breeze such as sailors love, when the boat dances on the waves. And those little waves – how graceful and fascinating they were, with their rounded crests and their joyous plunge as they chased each other! They would have been like little, frolicsome children splashing in their bath, if only they had not been clad in sea-green coats and skirts edged with fine white frillings. Knut felt tired, so he sat down by the roadside and looked at the waves. He loved them as far back as he could remember, for had he not grown up on the shore beside them? Next to swimming among them, Knut knew nothing nicer than to watch their merry gambols. If only he had not been so very, very hungry! 'Had I all the flat stones I have skipped along the surface of the water, and were they all real bread and butter – how I would eat!' thought Knut.

A wave rolled so far up on the shore that it wet Knut's bare feet. Out of the foam there rose a white shoulder, and immediately afterward the fairest little maid sat down by Knut's side. She was about as tall as himself, with light-green clothing, a silver bracelet on her arm, and in her long fair hair she wore a golden comb and a wreath of the whitest water lily.

"Well, good day, Knut Fairyflute!" said she, in a voice like the purling of a brook among the pebbles in spring. "Why do you look so poorly?"

Knut gazed at her in amazement.

"How could I look anything else but poorly? I, who have had nothing to eat since yesterday's dinner but hot pig-iron, frozen quicksilver, a drop of dew, one ant leg, and seven cartloads of peat from the bog!"

"Poor boy," said the pretty little maid, as she stroked back the hair from his forehead. "Come to me, and I will feed you with sea foam and real pearls."

"Many thanks," said Knut. "I would rather have a plate of grilled flounders and fifteen pieces of bread and butter spread with jam."

The little maid laughed.

"Have you never eaten fresh-fallen snow with lots of sugar? I'll tell you something. I am Unda Marina's favourite waiting-maid, and Unda Marina is the sea king's favourite child – she who lives in the lovely coral palace far away down in the sea, and imprints her dainty footsteps in the sand when she plays in the waves. Yesterday we played at fox and geese on the shore at Perlebank, and there Unda Marina lost her reed pipe. The Billow told me that you had found it. Will you follow me and give it back to Unda Marina, and as a reward, you shall have a whole mountain of the sea's most precious pearls?"

"No, thank you," said Knut. "I have been invited to dine at Asa, and I have had nothing to eat since yesterday."

"Don't you think that I am rather pretty?" said the sea maiden, taking both his hands and looking him through and through with her blue twinkling eyes. "Won't you kiss my rosy lips?"

"You are certainly not ugly," said Knut, "but I would rather kiss a good roast fowl."

"Just listen to that!" said the sea maiden with her ringing laugh. "I will tell you something more, Knut Fairyflute! If you follow me and give back the pipe, you shall be my very dearest sweetheart. I shall be your loving bride; we shall dress in silk and pearls, and live happily for a thousand years."

"That is all very fine," answered Knut. "But I have eaten nothing fit for food since yesterday, and am invited to dine at Asa. Goodbye to you, dripping damsel; I am now going on."

"You are pretending," said the sea maiden slyly. "You have not got the pipe."

"Have I not?" exclaimed Knut, pulling the pipe out of his pocket.

With that, he felt a big wave come swish over his head and landed him full-length on the hillside. He remembered nothing more until he wakened, and found himself lying on the grass. The Sun was seen in the western sky, which showed that it must now be afternoon. There stood Kükkale Wood, with all its fairy kings, where he had survived so many adventures, and where he had been invited to partake of such curious meals. There was the wide sea which still lapped the shore with its rippling waves, and splashed up its foam as it lay. But where was Unda Marina's waiting maid? She was not to be seen; she had floated away on the dancing waves. And where was the fairy pipe? Where was the tiny fairy who had so cleverly saved him from the eagle's claws? On the hill beside him lay an old broken bit of reed, but it gave forth no sound. In his jacket pocket he felt a little wet spot, but whether it were some sea spray, or the remains of the little fairy, which he had crushed against the hillside, no one could ever tell.

Knut began to think that he had fallen asleep in the sun and dreamt nonsense. "Yes, but I am asked to dine at Asa," he exclaimed.

In a trice he started to his feet, and meant to run the shortest way he knew through the forest. That was not easily done. The juniper bushes picked a quarrel with his trousers, the spruce branches hung fast by his coat, the blaeberry bushes and heather pricked his bare legs. But through them Knut was determined to go, and through them he went without further mishaps, tired, hungry, and hot, just as the clock struck four in the afternoon.

"Welcome, Knut," said Herr Peterman, "you look really happy today."

"Why should I not look happy, when have been invited to partake of hot pig-iron, frozen quicksilver, a drop of dew, an ant leg, seven cart-loads of peat, a dish of sea-foam, and a mountain of pearls?" rejoined Knut.

"That was a large number of dishes for one day," said Herr Peterman. "One ought never to think much about food, for if constantly thinking about it, one falls a prey to the fairies who scoff at mankind. Perhaps you are hungry, my boy?"

Knut looked confused, squeezed his cap in his hands, and answered, "That he was not exactly starving."

"Well, I am glad of that," said Herr Peterman, "I have been out since breakfast, and my servants have not had time to pluck the birds. You can wait till eight o'clock, and then you will have supper."

'This is even worse than hot pig-iron and seven cart-loads of peat,' thought Knut to himself, but he bit his nails, and answered that he could well enough wait. 'I can think of the Catechism,' thought he.

It was too bad of Herr Peterman. He himself had once been a poor boy, and knew well what it meant to wait hungry for four hours.

"Knut," said he, "I see that you can do something else besides think of food. You know that it is a heroism to conquer oneself, and to deny ourselves those necessities upon which our mind is set. I like you, my boy, and shall care for you, so that you may go to school, and learn to be a clever fellow. But – what is that? I thought I smelt roast fowl! Step in, my boy; you shall sit with me, and for once eat real food."

"*What is that*?" It sounded just like the Catechism. The door into the dining room opened; a large dinner table stood ready prepared awaiting the hungry guests. Herr Peterman led in Knut, and he sat there like a real grown-up gentleman, and there he would have sat to this day – he was *so* hungry – had he not long ago carried home a bit of cheese to his grandmother, and been sent to school.

Sikku

IN THE TIME OF CHARLES XII, there lived in the north of Finland a poor cowboy whose name was Sikku. It ought to have been Sixtus, but the Finnish tongue can only wag in a certain way, so that it usually reconstructs names after its own manner, according to how it can best pronounce them.

Sikku was very poor. He had neither cap, shirt, nor shoes, but that did not in the least trouble him, for he was always happy and contented, and when he herded the cows at the foot of Sipuri Mountain, he sang songs from morn to night, blew his bark horn, and his greatest pleasure was hearing the mountain echoes mimic him. Sikku had an old clasp-knife; that was his wealth, and in addition he had a comrade by the name Kettu, which means in Finnish "fox," although he really was a dog; a long-nosed, long-tailed, yellow cur, faithful and ferocious. The two friends, kept together in joy and sorrow; Kettu drove in the cows, Kettu watched while Sikku took his midday nap, and Sikku shared with Kettu the hard bread which was their usual breakfast and dinner. Besides the bread, they feasted every day on an excellent soup of clear spring-water, and almost every day they had a nice dessert: strawberries, cloudberries, blaeberries, whortleberries, hagberries, or rowan-berries, according to the time of summer. But those dainties Kettu despised. Sikku thought himself a prince in the forest, but when the evenings became rainy and cold, he began to long for the porridge-pot. Oh, how comforting was the hot pan, which he used to scrape to get off any scraps that he could find on the edge of it, but Kettu only licked the ladle and stole Pussycat's milk out of the broken dish, which stood on the floor by the watertub. This seldom happened without a battle. The farmer in Anttila farm was miserly, and his wife mean, but what did that matter to Sikku? He had liberty.

He alone was responsible for the fifteen cows coming safely back to the farm to be milked every evening.

For a time all went well, and no other care in the world had Sikku.

One day he climbed to the top of the highest hill, while Kettu looked after the cows in the valley. There was a splendid view over forests, bogs, and small lakes, but not a single house was to be seen.

Never in his life had Sikku thought the – world was so big. His heart glowed as he saw the sun glittering in the lakes, amid the dark green woods, and as the clouds floated across the sky, one after another sparkled and vanished into shade, and gleamed anew on some other part. Sikku sang and blew his bark horn between times, which sounded so musical among the mountains that it seemed to change into a song:

"Sipuri Mountain, too-too!
Falidoo!
In the whole world no boy is found
Who herds his cows upon such a ground!
Too-too! Too-too!
Falidoo!"

While he sang, there suddenly stood before him on the mountain a little hunchbacked old woman, who said to him: "All that you see shall be yours, if you will be my boy and obey me."

"Oh, ho!" said Sikku, as he looked at the old woman, whom he recognized – she was the witch from the neighbouring village of Allis.

"Give me the white cow Kimmo!" said the old woman. "And say when you go home that the wolves devoured her."

Sikku opened his eyes wide, and answered:

"No! I'm not so foolish as that."

"Then you will have yourself to blame," said the old woman. And with that she hopped like a crow down the mountain-side.

Kettu was heard barking in the valley. Sikku ran down, and found that Kimmo had sunk in the bog, so that only her horns were to be seen above the quagmire. Sikku tried to drag her out, but his strength was not sufficient, and when he had pulled and pulled till he was tired, he had to go home with the fourteen cows. The bell-cow, Mansikka, lowed, Kettu howled, Sikku related the misfortune, got a beating, and was sent next day to the valley without any food.

This time he did not sing, but sat, miserable and hungry, at the foot of the mountain.

Then there came to him the bearded wizard from Allis, and said:

"Give me the black cow, Musikka – say that wolves devoured her – and I will give you all the land you see from Sipuri Mountain."

"No! I am not so foolish," answered Sikku angrily.

"Then you will have yourself to blame," said the wizard, and with that he turned a somersault down the mountain.

Kettu began to bark, Sikku rushed forward, and found Musikka dead on the forest slope. She had eaten some poisonous plant, and would never walk again. Sikku wept. He brought some water from the spring in a bit of bark, and dashed it over Musikka's head, but that did no good. He had to go home with the thirteen cows and tell of the accident.

This time he was shut up three days in the cellar without food.

On the fourth day he was sent again to the valley with the thirteen cows, and got a bag of provisions. Being hungry, he opened his bag when he reached the entrance to the field, but found only a grey stone in it.

Sikku drove the cows to the mountain, ate some wild berries which he found in the forest, and sat down dejectedly on a stump beside the animals, for fear any further misfortune should happen.

Then there appeared the pretty little fairy maid from Allis, who always had a squint, who held out to him a crumbly wheaten loaf, patted his thin cheeks, and said:

"Give me the red cow Mansikka, and say when you go home that the bears devoured her, then you shall have the wheaten loaf and all the land you can see from Sipuri Mountain."

Sikku was so hungry that he could have devoured a loaf of moss. He looked at the wheaten loaf, he looked at the pretty little fairy maid, and had to bite his tongue for fear he should immediately answer Yes.

But the fairy maid laughed, and this made Sikku angry.

"No!" said he; "I am not so foolish."

"Well then, you have yourself to blame," said the fairy maid, and with that she flapped like a magpie into the forest.

Sikku feared a fresh disaster, and ran to Mansikka, who had just been browsing near him, and Mansikka lay full length on the grass, a viper hung fast by her nose, and in a short time she too was dead.

What did it avail that Sikku instantly killed the viper? He had to go home with only twelve cows, and tell of the misfortune.

"What punishment do you think you deserve?" said the enraged farmer. "Whether would you choose to be put into the boiler or to be thrown down the deep well?"

"I cannot help it," answered Sikku crying; "Three times have I been promised all the land seen from Sipuri Mountain if I will lie and steal, but that I won't do."

"Well," said the farmer, "that is all my land which you see from Sipuri Mountain, and I promise to give it to you if, before the next full moon, you drive into the field nine good cows in the place of Kimmo, Musikka, and Mansikka, which lie dead upon the mountain. But what shall I do to you now? You must have some punishment."

"Bind him hand and foot, and leave him at the topmost point of Sipuri Mountain, and let him satisfy his hunger by gazing at the view!" said the farmer's wife, who could not forgive Sikku, for she missed her cows.

This suggestion pleased the farmer. Sikku was bound hand and foot, and left on the topmost peak of the mountain, and everyone was forbidden to give him either food or drink. The remaining twelve cows were driven by another cowboy to graze on the open ground of the farm far away from the mountain. Sikku lay bound and half dead with hunger. The woods smelt sweet, the lakes glittered in the sunshine between the fir branches. Evening drew on, night came, the dew fell, the thrush sang, the stars twinkled, the moon looked down on the poor boy, and no one in the world was the least concerned about him. But high above the woods, the lakes, the dew, the thrush, and the stars, is one who looks down on all the desolate ones of earth. He saw even poor Sikku. God sent a kind friend to him, and who could it be but Kettu? Kettu might have had porridge at home, Kettu might have stolen his milk, as he was accustomed to do, out of Pussycat's broken dish by the water tub, but instead of that Kettu ran, hungry as he was, to the mountain, laid himself down by Sikku's bound feet, and – licked his hands. This so comforted Sikku that he was once more happy and contented, and so they both fell asleep in the moonlight.

Now in the time of Charles XII, there was a great war in the southern part of the country. The northern part did not know much about it, and all beyond the immense forests remained in peace, when suddenly there appeared an enemy fleet on the sea coast, and landed an army of soldiers, who spread themselves over the country, ravaging and plundering everywhere. One of these troops reached Sikku's part of the country, attacked, burned, and plundered Anttila Farm, carried off all the cattle, and took the farmer himself prisoner.

When this was done the enemy dispersed, that they might proceed to do the same with other villages. Some Cossacks were left behind to guard the prisoners and stolen cattle, until they should be taken on board ship.

Early in the morning Sikku was awakened by Kettu biting a man in the leg. Two savage-looking, bearded men had climbed to the top of the mountain to have a good view, and see where they might now betake themselves. They found the boy bound, and enemies though they were, they had pity on him, loosed his fetters, gave him bread out of their wallets, and carried him off. At the foot of the mountain they had left their horses tied to trees. One of the men lifted the boy up beside him on to the back of a horse, and chased Kettu away. They set off at a gallop, and soon drew near to the shore of a vast ocean.

Here there was much booty and many prisoners taken by the enemy, but as the Cossacks were eager to get further plunder, they had left six men to guard the prisoners and the spoils, while the rest were away.

Night approached, and the six were afraid of being overpowered by the peasants during the darkness; therefore they entered a boat, took Sikku with them, and rowed out to an island, so that they might pass the night in safety; the cattle were left to graze on the shore, and the prisoners, as well as the six horses, were fast tied to trees.

Sikku lay beside the Cossacks on the desert island. The night was dark, the big waves rolled against the white pebbles on the beach, and the wind blew towards land. Sikku lay awake and listened to the slow regular breathing of the tired soldiers as they slept by his side. Five of them were there, but the sixth was in the boat as watch Sikku sat up softly and listened. One of the Cossacks spoke in his sleep, and flung his arms about. Sikku lay down again but could not rest. In a short time he sat up again, and when all was quiet he stepped over the slumbering soldiers down to the boat. Here even the watch was asleep, and slept so heavily that he was never aware that Sikku shot out the boat to sea, and let the wind drift them back to *terra firma*.

The Cossack in the boat slept soundly. He had ridden many miles; no wonder that he slept like a log!

When Sikku felt the boat bump on the shore, he climbed noiselessly out, took his clasp-knife out of his pocket and cut the prisoners' bonds. The Cossack still slept. The prisoners could hardly realize their deliverance. They followed Sikku and bound their enemy in the boat with the same rope from which they had just been released. And now the Cossack awoke, but too late – he himself was now the captive of his prisoners.

"Kill him at once! Let us row to the island and kill them all while they sleep!" called out one of those who had just been set free.

"No," answered Sikku, who recognized his master's voice, "rather let us remove their plunder and betake ourselves to a place of safety!"

"They have burned my farm and carried off all that I possess!" sighed the farmer.

"They have loosed my fetters and given me food," said Sikku, who seemed suddenly to have become a man.

Most of the people agreed with Sikku. Some rode off on the Cossacks' horses, others drove the cattle to a hiding-place in the forest, one and all took what they could of the enemy's plunder, and Sikku took his share. Some days after the enemy set sail.

The peasants returned from the woods and clefts of the mountains, where they had sought refuge in the hour of danger.

Many came from their burned farms and assembled at the church to consult with each other what should now be done. And what were they to do with the six Cossack prisoners, for the five on the island had also been captured?

"Kill them at once," several again called out.

"No; give them to Sikku!" said some of the others; "he has caught them."

Sikku got the six prisoners, extracted a promise from them that they would no longer take part in the war against his country, and let them go free to seek their comrades.

The farmer and his wife at Anttila had taken shelter in a barn, which the enemy in their haste had not burned. "Ah," said he, "if we only had our fine cows!"

At the same time they saw a little bareheaded, barefooted, shirtless boy driving, with the help of a yellow dog, nine beautiful cows down the hillside to the barn.

"Is not that Sikku and Kettu?" exclaimed the farmer.

"Are those not our cows?" shrieked the farmer's wife.

Yes, it was Sikku and Kettu, and the veritable cows from Anttila Farm, which had been carried off by the enemy. The Cossacks had killed three, nine were left, and those Sikku had taken as his share of the spoil.

"Look, I am bringing you nine cows!" Sikku called out, and he would like to have waved his cap for joy, but he had not got one.

"Bless me, is it really you?" shrieked the farmer and his wife, in their delight embracing Sikku and patting the cows. Kettu had already vanished in the barn, to see if by any chance Pussy-cat's broken dish stood there by the water-tub. Pussycat fuffed, and again there was war in the camp.

"Are you hungry?" said the farmer's wife to Sikku. She had a guilty conscience.

"No; many thanks," said Sikku. "It is not yet full moon," he remarked after a pause.

The farmer brought his hand slowly down behind his long ears. He thought differently of Sikku, and remembered his hasty vow.

"Listen now, Sikku," said he; "let us make an agreement. What will you do with so much land while you are so young? Serve me faithfully for seven years, and then I will fulfil my promise, and you shall have all the land which you can see from Sipuri Mountain."

"Agreed," said Sikku. So Sikku served faithfully for seven years on Anttila Farm, became big and strong, bought a cap, shirt, and shoes, married the farmer's daughter, the winsome Greta, and with her got not alone all the land to be seen from Sipuri, but also the newly built farm of Anttila.

"Kettu and Pussycat were both buried at the foot of the mountain; but of the wizard nothing is known, except that there is now a crow's nest at Allis, and folk say the crows are not to be depended on.

Animal Stories

Introduction

ANIMALS ABOUND IN Finnish folktale – perhaps no surprise, in the mythology of a country only ever sparsely settled by humans, overwhelmingly outnumbered in an open, empty land of lakes and forests. Finns would see animals all around, leading parallel existences to theirs; only occasionally impinging on them; seeing them, they would get a sense of other possibilities, alternative ways of living. Like people the world over, though, they came to see quasi-human quirks in them and to sense personalities: the quiet dignity of a deer; the cheekiness of a sparrow; the sinister solemnity of a crow. A fox who can talk, like the one who becomes companion and counsellor to 'Mighty Mikko' in the Finnish folktale of that name, is already an extraordinary animal. Why would he not then be capable of gratitude? Why would he not additionally be able to secure his friend a treasure, to win him a wife – no ordinary one but a princess, daughter of his country's king? Still more miraculous, it might be felt, is the power of folktale to transmute the low cunning of the stereotypically sly old fox into a wonderfully benign resourcefulness underpinned by deep affection and unshakeable loyalty.

Mighty Mikko

(The Story of a Poor Woodsman and a Grateful Fox)

THERE WAS ONCE an old woodsman and his wife who had an only son named Mikko. As the mother lay dying the young man wept bitterly.

"When you are gone, my dear mother," he said, "there will be no one left to think of me."

The poor woman comforted him as best she could and said to him:

"You will still have your father."

Shortly after the woman's death, the old man, too, was taken ill.

"Now, indeed, I shall be left desolate and alone," Mikko thought, as he sat beside his father's bedside and saw him grow weaker and weaker.

"My boy," the old man said just before he died, "I have nothing to leave you but the three snares with which these many years I have caught wild animals. Those snares now belong to you. When I am dead, go into the woods and if you find a wild creature caught in any of them, free it gently and bring it home alive."

After his father's death, Mikko remembered the snares and went out to the woods to see them. The first was empty and also the second, but in the third he found a little red Fox. He carefully lifted the spring that had shut down on one of the Fox's feet and then carried the little creature home in his arms. He shared his supper with it and when he lay down to sleep the Fox curled up at his feet. They lived together some time until they became close friends.

"Mikko," said the Fox one day, "why are you so sad?"

"Because I'm lonely."

"Pooh!" said the Fox. "That's no way for a young man to talk! You ought to get married! Then you wouldn't feel lonely!"

"Married!" Mikko repeated. "How can I get married? I can't marry a poor girl because I'm too poor myself and a rich girl wouldn't marry me."

"Nonsense!" said the Fox. "You're a fine ,well set up, young man and you're kind and gentle. What more could a princess ask?"

Mikko laughed to think of a princess wanting him for a husband.

"I mean what I say!" the Fox insisted. "Take our own Princess now. What would you think of marrying her?"

Mikko laughed louder than before.

"I have heard," he said, "that she is the most beautiful princess in the world! Any man would be happy to marry her!"

"Very well," the Fox said, "if you feel that way about her then I'll arrange the wedding for you."

With that the little Fox actually did trot off to the royal castle and gain audience with the King.

"My master sends you greetings," the Fox said, "and he begs you to loan him your bushel measure."

"My bushel measure!" the King repeated in surprise. "Who is your master and why does he want my bushel measure?"

"Ssh!" the Fox whispered as though he didn't want the courtiers to hear what he was saying. Then slipping up quite close to the King he murmured in his ear:

"Surely you have heard of Mikko, haven't you? Mighty Mikko as he's called."

The King had never heard of any Mikko who was known as Mighty Mikko but, thinking that perhaps he should have heard of him, he shook his head and murmured:

"H'm! Mikko! Mighty Mikko! Oh, to be sure! Yes, yes, of course!"

"My master is about to start off on a journey and he needs a bushel measure for a very particular reason."

"I understand! I understand!" the King said, although he didn't understand at all, and he gave orders that the bushel measure which they used in the storeroom of the castle be brought in and given to the Fox.

The Fox carried off the measure and hid it in the woods. Then he scurried about to all sorts of little out of the way nooks and crannies where people had hidden their savings and he dug up a gold piece here and a silver piece there until he had a handful. Then he went back to the woods and stuck the various coins in the cracks of the measure. The next day he returned to the King.

"My master, Mighty Mikko," he said, "sends you thanks, O King, for the use of your bushel measure."

The King held out his hand and when the Fox gave him the measure he peeped inside to see if by chance it contained any trace of what had recently been measured. His eye of course at once caught the glint of the gold and silver coins lodged in the cracks.

"Ah!" he said, thinking Mikko must be a very mighty lord indeed to be so careless of his wealth; "I should like to meet your master. Won't you and he come and visit me?"

This was what the Fox wanted the King to say but he pretended to hesitate.

"I thank Your Majesty for the kind invitation," he said, "but I fear my master can't accept it just now. He wants to get married soon and we are about to start off on a long journey to inspect a number of foreign princesses."

This made the King all the more anxious to have Mikko visit him at once for he thought that if Mikko should see his daughter before he saw those foreign princesses he might fall in love with her and marry her. So he said to the Fox:

"My dear fellow, you must prevail on your master to make me a visit before he starts out on his travels! You will, won't you?"

The Fox looked this way and that as if he were too embarrassed to speak.

"Your Majesty," he said at last, "I pray you pardon my frankness. The truth is you are not rich enough to entertain my master and your castle isn't big enough to house the immense retinue that always attends him."

The King, who by this time was frantic to see Mikko, lost his head completely.

"My dear Fox," he said, "I'll give you anything in the world if you prevail upon your master to visit me at once! Couldn't you suggest to him to travel with a modest retinue this time?"

The Fox shook his head.

"No. His rule is either to travel with a great retinue or to go on foot disguised as a poor woodsman attended only by me."

"Couldn't you prevail on him to come to me disguised as a poor woodsman?" the King begged. "Once he was here, I could place gorgeous clothes at his disposal."

But still the Fox shook his head.

"I fear Your Majesty's wardrobe doesn't contain the kind of clothes my master is accustomed to."

"I assure you I've got some very good clothes," the King said. "Come along this minute and we'll go through them and I'm sure you'll find some that your master would wear."

So they went to a room which was like a big wardrobe with hundreds and hundreds of hooks upon which were hung hundreds of coats and breeches and embroidered shirts. The King ordered his attendants to bring the costumes down one by one and place them before the Fox.

They began with the plainer clothes.

"Good enough for most people," the Fox said, "but not for my master."

Then they took down garments of a finer grade.

"I'm afraid you're going to all this trouble for nothing," the Fox said. "Frankly now, don't you realize that my master couldn't possibly put on any of these things!"

The King, who had hoped to keep for his own use his most gorgeous clothes of all, now ordered these to be shown.

The Fox looked at them sideways, sniffed them critically, and at last said:

"Well, perhaps my master would consent to wear these for a few days. They are not what he is accustomed to wear but I will say this for him: he is not proud."

The King was overjoyed.

"Very well, my dear Fox, I'll have the guest chambers put in readiness for your master's visit and I'll have all these, my finest clothes, laid out for him. You won't disappoint me, will you?"

"I'll do my best," the Fox promised.

With that he bade the King a civil good day and ran home to Mikko.

The next day as the Princess was peeping out of an upper window of the castle, she saw a young woodsman approaching accompanied by a Fox. He was a fine stalwart youth and the Princess, who knew from the presence of the Fox that he must be Mikko, gave a long sigh and confided to her serving maid:

"I think I could fall in love with that young man if he really were only a woodsman!"

Later when she saw him arrayed in her father's finest clothes – which looked so well on Mikko that no one even recognized them as the King's – she lost her heart completely and when Mikko was presented to her she blushed and trembled just as any ordinary girl might before a handsome young man.

All the Court was equally delighted with Mikko. The ladies went into ecstasies over his modest manners, his fine figure, and the gorgeousness of his clothes, and the old greybeard Councillors, nodding their heads in approval, said to each other:

"Nothing of the coxcomb about this young fellow! In spite of his great wealth see how politely he listens to us when we talk!"

The next day the Fox went privately to the King, and said:

"My master is a man of few words and quick judgement. He bids me tell you that your daughter, the Princess, pleases him mightily and that, with your approval, he will make his addresses to her at once."

The King was greatly agitated and began:

"My dear Fox—"

But the Fox interrupted him to say:

"Think the matter over carefully and give me your decision tomorrow."

So the King consulted with the Princess and with his Councillors and in a short time the marriage was arranged and the wedding ceremony actually performed!

"Didn't I tell you?" the Fox said, when he and Mikko were alone after the wedding.

"Yes," Mikko acknowledged, "you did promise that I should marry the Princess. But, tell me, now that I am married what am I to do? I can't live on here forever with my wife."

"Put your mind at rest," the Fox said. "I've thought of everything. Just do as I tell you and you'll have nothing to regret. Tonight say to the King: 'It is now only fitting that you should visit me and see for yourself the sort of castle over which your daughter is hereafter to be mistress!'"

When Mikko said this to the King, the King was overjoyed for now that the marriage had actually taken place he was wondering whether he hadn't perhaps been a little hasty. Mikko's words reassured him and he eagerly accepted the invitation.

On the morrow the Fox said to Mikko:

"Now I'll run on ahead and get things ready for you."

"But where are you going?" Mikko said, frightened at the thought of being deserted by his little friend.

The Fox drew Mikko aside and whispered softly:

"A few days' march from here there is a very gorgeous castle belonging to a wicked old dragon who is known as the Worm. I think the Worm's castle would just about suit you."

"I'm sure it would," Mikko agreed. "But how are we to get it away from the Worm?"

"Trust me," the Fox said. "All you need do is this: lead the King and his courtiers along the main highway until by noon tomorrow you reach a crossroads. Turn there to the left and go straight on until you see the tower of the Worm's castle. If you meet any men by the wayside, shepherds or the like, ask them whose men they are and show no surprise at their answer. So now, dear master, farewell until we meet again at your beautiful castle."

The little Fox trotted off at a smart pace and Mikko and the Princess and the King attended by the whole Court followed in more leisurely fashion.

The little Fox, when he had left the main highway at the crossroads, soon met ten woodsmen with axes over their shoulders. They were all dressed in blue smocks of the same cut.

"Good day," the Fox said politely. "Whose men are you?"

"Our master is known as the Worm," the woodsmen told him.

"My poor, poor lads!" the Fox said, shaking his head sadly.

"What's the matter?" the woodsmen asked.

For a few moments the Fox pretended to be too overcome with emotion to speak. Then he said:

"My poor lads, don't you know that the King is coming with a great force to destroy the Worm and all his people?"

The woodsmen were simple fellows and this news threw them into great consternation.

"Is there no way for us to escape?" they asked.

The Fox put his paw to his head and thought.

"Well," he said at last, "there is one way you might escape and that is by telling everyone who asks you that you are the Mighty Mikko's men. But if you value your lives never again say that your master is the Worm."

"We are Mighty Mikko's men!" the woodsmen at once began repeating over and over. "We are Mighty Mikko's men!"

A little farther on the road the Fox met twenty grooms, dressed in the same blue smocks, who were tending a hundred beautiful horses. The Fox talked to the twenty grooms as he had talked to the woodsmen and before he left them they, too, were shouting:

"We are Mighty Mikko's men!"

Next the Fox came to a huge flock of a thousand sheep tended by thirty shepherds all dressed in the Worm's blue smocks. He stopped and talked to them until he had them roaring out:

"We are Mighty Mikko's men!"

Then the Fox trotted on until he reached the castle of the Worm. He found the Worm himself inside lolling lazily about. He was a huge dragon and had been a great warrior in his day. In fact his castle and his lands and his servants and his possessions had all been won in battle. But now for many years no one had cared to fight him and he had grown fat and lazy.

"Good day," the Fox said, pretending to be very breathless and frightened. "You're the Worm, aren't you?"

"Yes," the dragon said, boastfully, "I am the great Worm!"

The Fox pretended to grow more agitated.

"My poor fellow, I am sorry for you! But of course none of us can expect to live forever. Well, I must hurry along. I thought I would just stop and say goodbye."

Made uneasy by the Fox's words, the Worm cried out:

"Wait just a minute! What's the matter?"

The Fox was already at the door but at the Worm's entreaty he paused and said over his shoulder:

"Why, my poor fellow, you surely know, don't you? that the King with a great force is coming to destroy you and all your people!"

"What!" the Worm gasped, turning a sickly green with fright. He knew he was fat and helpless and could never again fight as in the years gone by.

"Don't go just yet!" he begged the Fox. "When is the King coming?"

"He's on the highway now! That's why I must be going! Goodbye!"

"My dear Fox, stay just a moment and I'll reward you richly! Help me to hide so that the King won't find me! What about the shed where the linen is stored? I could crawl under the linen and then if you locked the door from the outside the King could never find me."

"Very well," the Fox agreed, "but we must hurry!"

So they ran outside to the shed where the linen was kept and the Worm hid himself under the linen. The Fox locked the door, then set fire to the shed, and soon there was nothing left of that wicked old dragon, the Worm, but a handful of ashes.

The Fox now called together the dragon's household and talked them over to Mikko as he had the woodsmen and the grooms and the shepherds.

Meanwhile the King and his party were slowly covering the ground over which the Fox had sped so quickly. When they came to the ten woodsmen in blue smocks, the King said:

"I wonder whose woodsmen those are."

One of his attendants asked the woodsmen and the ten of them shouted out at the top of their voices:

"We are Mighty Mikko's men!"

Mikko said nothing and the King and all the Court were impressed anew with his modesty.

A little farther on they met the twenty grooms with their hundred prancing horses. When the grooms were questioned, they answered with a shout:

"We are Mighty Mikko's men!"

"The Fox certainly spoke the truth," the King thought to himself, "when he told me of Mikko's riches!"

A little later the thirty shepherds when they were questioned made answer in a chorus that was deafening to hear:

"We are Mighty Mikko's men!"

The sight of the thousand sheep that belonged to his son-in-law made the King feel poor and humble in comparison and the courtiers whispered among themselves:

"For all his simple manner, Mighty Mikko must be a richer, more powerful lord than the King himself! In fact it is only a very great lord indeed who could be so simple!"

At last they reached the castle which from the blue smocked soldiers that guarded the gateway they knew to be Mikko's. The Fox came out to welcome the King's party and behind him in two rows all the household servants. These, at a signal from the Fox, cried out in one voice:

"We are Mighty Mikko's men!"

Then Mikko in the same simple manner that he would have used in his father's mean little hut in the woods bade the King and his followers welcome and they all entered the castle where they found a great feast already prepared and waiting.

The King stayed on for several days and the more he saw of Mikko the better pleased he was that he had him for a son-in-law.

When he was leaving he said to Mikko:

"Your castle is so much grander than mine that I hesitate ever asking you back for a visit."

But Mikko reassured the King by saying earnestly:

"My dear father-in-law, when first I entered your castle I thought it was the most beautiful castle in the world!"

The King was flattered and the courtiers whispered among themselves:

"How affable of him to say that when he knows very well how much grander his own castle is!"

When the King and his followers were safely gone, the little red Fox came to Mikko and said:

"Now, my master, you have no reason to feel sad and lonely. You are lord of the most beautiful castle in the world and you have for wife a sweet and lovely princess. You have no longer any need of me, so I am going to bid you farewell."

Mikko thanked the little Fox for all he had done and the little Fox trotted off to the woods.

So you see that Mikko's poor old father, although he had no wealth to leave his son, was really the cause of all Mikko's good fortune, for it was he who told Mikko in the first place to carry home alive anything he might find caught in the snares.

The Forest Bride

(The Story of a Little Mouse Who Was a Princess)

THERE WAS ONCE a farmer who had three sons. One day when the boys were grown to manhood he said to them:

"My sons, it is high time that you were all married. Tomorrow I wish you to go out in search of brides."

"But where shall we go?" the oldest son asked.

"I have thought of that, too," the father said. "Do each of you chop down a tree and then take the direction in which the fallen tree points. I'm sure that each of you if you go far enough in that direction will find a suitable bride."

So the next day the three sons chopped down trees. The oldest son's tree fell pointing north.

"That suits me!" he said, for he knew that to the north lay a farm where a very pretty girl lived.

The tree of the second son when it fell pointed south.

"That suits me!" the second son declared thinking of a girl that he had often danced with who lived on a farm to the south.

The youngest son's tree – the youngest son's name was Veikko – when it fell pointed straight to the forest.

"Ha! Ha!" the older brothers laughed. "Veikko will have to go courting one of the Wolf girls or one of the Foxes!"

They meant by this that only animals lived in the forest and they thought they were making a good joke at Veikko's expense. But Veikko said he was perfectly willing to take his chances and go where his tree pointed.

The older brothers went gaily off and presented their suits to the two farmers whose daughters they admired. Veikko, too, started off with brave front but after he had gone some distance in the forest his courage began to ebb.

"How can I find a bride," he asked himself, "in a place where there are no human creatures at all!"

Just then he came to a little hut. He pushed open the door and went in. It was empty. To be sure there was a little mouse sitting on the table, daintily combing her whiskers, but a mouse of course doesn't count.

"There's nobody here!" Veikko said aloud.

The little mouse paused in her toilet and turning towards him said reproachfully:

"Why, Veikko, I'm here!"

"But you don't count. You're only a mouse!"

"Of course I count!" the little mouse declared. "But tell me, what were you hoping to find?"

"I was hoping to find a sweetheart."

The little mouse questioned him further and Veikko told her the whole story of his brothers and the trees.

"The two older ones are finding sweethearts easily enough," Veikko said, "it will shame me to have to go home and confess that I alone have failed."

"See here, Veikko," the little mouse said, "why don't you take me for your sweetheart?"

Veikko laughed heartily.

"But you're only a mouse! Whoever heard of a man having a mouse for a sweetheart!"

The mouse shook her little head solemnly.

"Take my word for it, Veikko, you could do much worse than have me for a sweetheart! Even if I am only a mouse I can love you and be true to you."

She was a dear dainty little mouse and as she sat looking up at Veikko with her little paws under her chin and her bright little eyes sparkling Veikko liked her more and more.

Then she sang Veikko a pretty little song and the song cheered him so much that he forgot his disappointment at not finding a human sweetheart and as he left her to go home he said:

"Very well, little mouse, I'll take you for my sweetheart!"

At that the mouse made little squeaks of delight and she told him that she'd be true to him and wait for him no matter how long he was in returning.

Well, the older brothers when they got home boasted loudly about their sweethearts.

"Mine," said the oldest, "has the rosiest reddest cheeks you ever saw!"

"And mine," the second announced, "has long yellow hair!"

Veikko said nothing.

"What's the matter, Veikko?" the older brothers asked him, laughing. "Has your sweetheart pretty pointed ears or sharp white teeth?"

You see they were still having their little joke about foxes and wolves.

"You needn't laugh," Veikko said. "I've found a sweetheart. She's a gentle dainty little thing gowned in velvet."

"Gowned in velvet!" echoed the oldest brother with a frown.

"Just like a princess!" the second brother sneered.

"Yes," Veikko repeated, "gowned in velvet like a princess. And when she sits up and sings to me I'm perfectly happy."

"Huh!" grunted the older brothers not at all pleased that Veikko should have so grand a sweetheart.

"Well," said the old farmer after a few days, "now I should like to know what those sweethearts of yours are able to do. Have them each bake me a loaf of bread so that I can see whether they're good housewives."

"Mine will be able to bake bread – I'm sure of that!" the oldest brother declared boastfully.

"So will mine!" chorused the second brother.

Veikko was silent.

"What about the Princess?" they said with a laugh. "Do you think the Princess can bake bread?"

"I don't know," Veikko answered truthfully. "I'll have to ask her."

Of course he had no reason for supposing that the little mouse could bake bread and by the time he reached the hut in the forest he was feeling sad and discouraged.

When he pushed open the door he found the little mouse as before seated on the table daintily combing her whiskers. At sight of Veikko she danced about with delight.

"I'm so glad to see you!" she squeaked. "I knew you would come back!"

Then when she noticed that he was silent she asked him what was the matter. Veikko told her:

"My father wants each of our sweethearts to bake him a loaf of bread. If I come home without a loaf my brothers will laugh at me."

"You won't have to go home without a loaf!" the little mouse said. "I can bake bread."

Veikko was much surprised at this.

"I never heard of a mouse that could bake bread!"

"Well, I can!" the little mouse insisted.

With that she began ringing a small silver bell, tinkle, tinkle, tinkle. Instantly there was the sound of hurrying footsteps, tiny scratchy footsteps, and hundreds of mice came running into the hut.

The little Princess mouse sitting up very straight and dignified said to them:

"Each of you go fetch me a grain of the finest wheat."

All the mice scampered quickly away and soon returned one by one, each carrying a grain of the finest wheat. After that it was no trick at all for the Princess mouse to bake a beautiful loaf of wheaten bread.

The next day the three brothers presented their father the loaves of their sweethearts' baking. The oldest one had a loaf of rye bread.

"Very good," the farmer said. "For hardworking people like us rye bread is good."

The loaf the second son had was made of barley.

"Barley bread is also good," the farmer said.

But when Veikko presented his loaf of beautiful wheaten bread, his father cried out:

"What! White bread! Ah, Veikko now must have a sweetheart of wealth!"

"Of course!" the older brothers sneered. "Didn't he tell us she was a Princess? Say, Veikko, when a Princess wants fine white flour, how does she get it?"

Veikko answered simply:

"She rings a little silver bell and when her servants come in she tells them to bring her grains of the finest wheat."

At this the older brothers nearly exploded with envy until their father had to reprove them.

"There! There!" he said. "Don't grudge the boy his good luck! Each girl has baked the loaf she knows how to make and each in her own way will probably make a good wife. But before you bring them home to me I want one further test of their skill in housewifery. Let them each send me a sample of their weaving."

The older brothers were delighted at this for they knew that their sweethearts were skilful weavers.

"We'll see how her ladyship fares this time!" they said, sure in their hearts that Veikko's sweetheart, whoever she was, would not put them to shame with her weaving.

Veikko, too, had serious doubts of the little mouse's ability at the loom.

"Whoever heard of a mouse that could weave?" he said to himself as he pushed open the door of the forest hut.

"Oh, there you are at last!" the little mouse squeaked joyfully.

She reached out her little paws in welcome and then in her excitement she began dancing about on the table.

"Are you really glad to see me, little mouse?" Veikko asked.

"Indeed I am!" the mouse declared. "Am I not your sweetheart? I've been waiting for you and waiting, just wishing that you would return! Does your father want something more this time, Veikko?"

"Yes, and it's something I'm afraid you can't give me, little mouse."

"Perhaps I can. Tell me what it is."

"It's a sample of your weaving. I don't believe you can weave. I never heard of a mouse that could weave."

"Tut! Tut!" said the mouse. "Of course I can weave! It would be a strange thing if Veikko's sweetheart couldn't weave!"

She rang the little silver bell, tinkle, tinkle, tinkle, and instantly there was the faint scratch-scratch of a hundred little feet as mice came running in from all directions and sat up on their haunches awaiting their Princess's orders.

"Go each of you," she said, "and get me a fibre of flax, the finest there is."

The mice went scurrying off and soon they began returning one by one each bringing a fiber of flax. When they had spun the flax and carded it, the little mouse wove a beautiful piece of fine linen. It was so sheer that she was able when she folded it to put it into an empty nutshell.

"Here, Veikko," she said, "here in this little box is a sample of my weaving. I hope your father will like it."

Veikko when he got home felt almost embarrassed for he was sure that his sweetheart's weaving would shame his brothers. So at first he kept the nutshell hidden in his pocket.

The sweetheart of the oldest brother had sent as a sample of her weaving a square of coarse cotton.

"Not very fine," the farmer said, "but good enough."

The second brother's sample was a square of cotton and linen mixed.

"A little better," the farmer said, nodding his head.

Then he turned to Veikko.

"And you, Veikko, has your sweetheart not given you a sample of her weaving?"

Veikko handed his father a nutshell at sight of which his brothers burst out laughing.

"Ha! Ha! Ha!" they laughed. "Veikko's sweetheart gives him a nut when he asks for a sample of her weaving."

But their laughter died as the farmer opened the nutshell and began shaking out a great web of the finest linen.

"Why, Veikko, my boy!" he cried, "however did your sweetheart get threads for so fine a web?"

Veikko answered modestly:

"She rang a little silver bell and ordered her servants to bring her in fibers of finest flax. They did so and after they had spun the flax and carded it, my sweetheart wove the web you see."

"Wonderful!" gasped the farmer. "I have never known such a weaver! The other girls will be all right for farmers' wives but Veikko's sweetheart might be a princess! Well," concluded the farmer, "it's time that you all brought your sweethearts home. I want to see them with my own eyes. Suppose you bring them tomorrow."

"She's a good little mouse and I'm very fond of her," Veikko thought to himself as he went out to the forest, "but my brothers will certainly laugh when they find she is only a mouse! Well, I don't care if they do laugh! She's been a good little sweetheart to me and I'm not going to be ashamed of her!"

So when he got to the hut he told the little mouse at once that his father wanted to see her.

The little mouse was greatly excited.

"I must go in proper style!" she said.

She rang the little silver bell and ordered her coach and five. The coach when it came turned out to be an empty nutshell and the five prancing steeds that were drawing it were five black mice. The little mouse seated herself in the coach with a coachman mouse on the box in front of her and a footman mouse on the box behind her.

"Oh, how my brothers will laugh!" thought Veikko.

But he didn't laugh. He walked beside the coach and told the little mouse not to be frightened, that he would take good care of her. His father, he told her, was a gentle old man and would be kind to her.

When they left the forest they came to a river which was spanned by a footbridge. Just as Veikko and the nutshell coach had reached the middle of the bridge, a man met them coming from the opposite direction.

"Mercy me!" the man exclaimed as he caught sight of the strange little coach that was rolling along beside Veikko. "What's that?"

He stooped down and looked and then with a loud laugh he put out his foot and pushed the coach, the little mouse, her servants, and her five prancing steeds – all off the bridge and into the water below.

"What have you done! What have you done!" Veikko cried. "You've drowned my poor little sweetheart!"

The man thinking Veikko was crazy hurried away.

Veikko with tears in his eyes looked down into the water.

"You poor little mouse!" he said. "How sorry I am that you are drowned! You were a faithful loving sweetheart and now that you are gone I know how much I loved you!"

As he spoke he saw a beautiful coach of gold drawn by five glossy horses go up the far bank of the river. A coachman in gold lace held the reins and a footman in pointed cap sat up stiffly behind. The most beautiful girl in the world was seated in the coach. Her skin was as red as a berry and as white as snow, her long golden hair gleamed with jewels, and she was dressed in pearly velvet. She beckoned to Veikko and when he came close she said:

"Won't you come sit beside me?"

"Me? Me?" Veikko stammered, too dazed to think.

The beautiful creature smiled.

"You were not ashamed to have me for a sweetheart when I was a mouse," she said, "and surely now that I am a princess again you won't desert me!"

"A mouse!" Veikko gasped. "Were you the little mouse?"

The Princess nodded.

"Yes, I was the little mouse under an evil enchantment which could never have been broken if you had not taken me for a sweetheart and if another human being had not drowned me. Now the enchantment is broken forever. So come, we will go to your father and after he has given us his blessing we will get married and go home to my kingdom."

And that's exactly what they did. They drove at once to the farmer's house and when Veikko's father and his brothers and his brothers' sweethearts saw the Princess's coach stopping at their gate they all came out bowing and scraping to see what such grand folk could want of them.

"Father!" Veikko cried, "don't you know me?"

The farmer stopped bowing long enough to look up.

"Why, bless my soul!" he cried, "it's our Veikko!"

"Yes, father, I'm Veikko and this is the Princess that I'm going to marry!"

"A princess, did you say, Veikko? Mercy me, where did my boy find a princess?"

"Out in the forest where my tree pointed."

"Well, well, well," the farmer said, "where your tree pointed! I've always heard that was a good way to find a bride."

The older brothers shook their heads gloomily and muttered:

"Just our luck! If only our trees had pointed to the forest we, too, should have found princesses instead of plain country wenches!"

But they were wrong: it wasn't because his tree pointed to the forest that Veikko got the Princess, it was because he was so simple and good that he was kind even to a little mouse.

Well, after they had got the farmer's blessing they rode home to the Princess's kingdom and were married. And they were happy as they should have been for they were good and true to each other and they loved each other dearly.

The Enchanted Grouse

(The Story of Helli and the Little Locked Box)

THERE WAS ONCE an old couple who lived with their married son and his wife. The son's name was Helli. He was a dutiful son but his wife was a scold. She was always finding fault with the old people and with her husband and for that matter with everybody else as well.

One morning when she saw her husband taking out his bow and arrows she said:

"Where are you going now?"

"I'm going hunting," he told her.

"Isn't that just like you!" she cried. "You're going off to have a good time hunting and you don't give a thought to me who have to stay home alone with two stupid old people!"

"If I didn't go hunting," Helli said, "and shoot something, we'd have nothing to put in the pot for dinner and then you would have reason to scold."

At that the woman burst into tears.

"Of course, as usual blame me! Whatever happens it's my fault!"

Poor Helli hurried off, hoping that by the time he returned his wife would be in a calmer state of mind. He had small success with his hunting. He shot arrow after arrow but always missed his mark. Then when he had only one arrow left he saw a Grouse standing in some brushwood so near that there was little likelihood of his missing it.

He took good aim but before he could fire the Grouse said:

"Don't shoot me, brother! Take me home alive."

Helli paused, then he shook his head.

"I've got to shoot you for we've nothing to put in the pot for dinner."

Again he aimed his arrow and again the Grouse said:

"Don't shoot me, brother! Take me home alive."

For the second time Helli paused.

"I'd like to spare you," he said, "but what would my wife say if I came home empty-handed?"

He took aim again and a third time the Grouse said:

"Don't shoot me, brother! Take me home alive."

At that Helli dropped his arrow.

"I don't care what she says! I can't shoot a creature that begs so pitifully for its life! Very well, Mr. Grouse, I'll do as you say: I'll take you home alive. But don't blame me if my wife wrings your neck."

He took the Grouse up in his arms and started homewards.

"Feed me for a year," the Grouse said, "and I'll reward you."

When they reached home and Helli's wife saw the Grouse, she cried out petulantly:

"Is that all you've got and out hunting all morning! That won't be dinner enough for four!"

"This Grouse isn't to be killed," Helli announced. "I'm going to keep it for a year and feed it."

"It won't take much to feed a Grouse," the old man remarked.

But the wife flew into a passion.

"What! Feed a useless bird when there isn't enough to feed your own flesh and blood!"

But Helli was firm and despite her threats his wife did not dare to maltreat the Grouse.

At the end of a year the Grouse grew a copper feather in its tail which it dropped in the dooryard. Then it disappeared.

"Ha!" laughed Helli's wife. "A copper feather! That's your reward for feeding that thankless bird a whole year! And now it's escaped!"

But the next day the Grouse returned.

"Feed me for another year," it said to Helli, "and I'll reward you."

His wife raised an awful to-do over this, but Helli was firm and for another year he fed and petted the Grouse.

At the end of the second year the Grouse grew a silver feather in its tail which it dropped in the dooryard. Then it disappeared.

"One silver feather!" Helli's wife cried. "So that's all you get for feeding that thankless bird a whole year! And now it's escaped!"

But it hadn't. It returned the very next day.

"Feed me for another year," it said to Helli, "and I'll reward you."

At the end of the third year the Grouse grew a golden feather in its tail and when it dropped that in the dooryard the scolding wife hadn't so much to say, for a golden feather was after all pretty good pay for a few handfuls of grain.

For a day the Grouse disappeared and then when it returned it said to Helli:

"Get on my back and I'll reward you."

Helli did so and the Grouse, rising high in the air, flew far away. On, on it flew until it reached the broad ocean. Over the ocean it flew until Helli could see nothing but water in whatever direction he looked.

"Ha!" he said to himself with a shudder, "I hope I can hold on!"

As he spoke, the Grouse slipped from beneath him and he fell down, down, down. However, before he touched water the Grouse swooped under him and caught him up again high into the air. He had this same terrible experience a second time and a third time and each time he thought his last moment had arrived.

"Now," the Grouse told him, "you know what my feelings were when you threatened three times to shoot me with your arrow."

"You have taught me a lesson," Helli said.

After that the Grouse flew on and on. At last it said:

"Look straight ahead, master, and tell me what you see."

Helli shaded his eyes and looked.

"Far, far ahead I see what looks like a copper column."

"Good!" the Grouse said. "That is the home of my oldest sister. She will be overjoyed to see us and when she hears how you have spared my life she will want to make you a present and will offer you various things. Take my advice and tell her that the only thing you want is her little locked box the key to which is lost. If she won't give you that, accept nothing."

The Grouse's oldest sister received them most hospitably and when she had heard their story at once offered Helli anything he might like from among her treasures.

"Then give me your little locked box the key to which is lost," Helli said.

The oldest sister shook her head.

"My little locked box! Who told you about that? I'm sorry, but I cannot give you that! Take anything else!"

"No," Helli said, "that or nothing!"

When the oldest sister could not be prevailed upon to give away her little locked box, the Grouse had Helli mount his back once more and off they flew.

"We'll visit my second sister now," he said. "If she offers you a present, ask her for her little locked box without a key and accept nothing else."

On, on they flew until the oldest sister's castle was far behind.

"Look, master," the Grouse said, "look straight ahead and tell me what you see."

Helli shaded his eyes and looked.

"Far ahead I see something that is like a silver cloud."

"That," said the Grouse, "is the silver castle of my second sister."

At the silver castle the second sister received them with joy and when she heard who Helli was at once declared that she wanted to show him her gratitude by making him a gift.

"Ask from me what you will," she said, "and you shall have it."

But when he asked for her little locked box without a key, she cried out:

"No! No! Not that! Anything else!"

"But I don't want anything else!" Helli said.

When the Grouse saw that his second sister was not to be parted from her little locked box, he bade Helli mount his back and off they flew again.

"We'll go to my youngest sister this time," he said. "If she offers you a present, ask for the same thing."

On, on they flew until the silver castle was lost to view.

"Now, master, look ahead and tell me what you see."

Helli shaded his eyes and looked.

"I seem to see a golden haze like the sun behind a cloud."

"That is the golden castle of my youngest sister."

They arrived and the youngest sister threw her arms about the Grouse for she loved him dearly and had not seen him for a long time.

"Welcome, brother!" she said. "And welcome also to you, Helli!"

Then she offered Helli a present and when he asked for her little locked box without a key she gave it to him at once.

"It is my most precious possession," she said, "but you may have it for you spared my dear brother's life when you might have taken it."

After they had rested and feasted they bade the youngest sister farewell and Helli with his precious box held tightly in one hand mounted the Grouse's back and off they flew towards home.

"Be carcful of thc box," the Grouse said, "and don't let it out of your hands until we reach some beautiful spot where you'd like always to live."

They passed high mountains and wooded lakes and fertile valleys.

"Shall we stop here?" the Grouse asked. "Or here? Or here?"

But always Helli said:

"No, not here."

At last they reached home and the Grouse told Helli that now they must part forever.

"By sparing my life three times," the Grouse said, "and then feeding me for three years you have broken the enchantment that bound me and now I shall not have to go about any longer as a grouse but shall be able to resume my natural shape. Farewell, Helli, and when you find the spot where you think you would like always to live, drop the box and you will find you have a treasure that will more than reward you for your kindness to me."

The Grouse disappeared and Helli said to himself:

"Where do I want to live always but right here at home with my dear old father and mother and my wife who is my wife even if she does scold me sometimes!"

So there at home after they all had supper together, he dropped the box on the floor. It broke and out of it arose a beautiful castle with servants and riches and everything that Helli had always wanted and never had. And Helli and his old father and mother and his wife lived in it and were happy. And gradually his wife got over her habit of scolding for when you're happy you haven't anything to scold about.

The Six Hungry Beasts

ONCE UPON A TIME THERE LIVED A MAN who dwelt with his wife in a little hut, far away from any neighbours. But they did not mind being alone, and would have been quite happy, if it had not been for a marten, who came every night to their poultry yard, and carried off one of their fowl. The man laid all sorts of traps to catch the thief, but instead of capturing the foe, it happened that one day he got caught himself, and falling down, struck his head against a stone, and was killed.

Not long after the marten came by on the look out for his supper. Seeing the dead man lying there, he said to himself: "That is a prize, this time I have done well," and dragging the body with great difficulty to the sledge which was waiting for him, drove off with his booty. He had not driven far when he met a squirrel, who bowed and said: "Good morning, godfather! what have you got behind you?"

The marten laughed and answered: "Did you ever hear anything so strange ? The old man that you see here set traps about his hen-house, thinking to catch me; but he fell into his own trap, and broke his own neck. He is very heavy; I wish you would help me to draw the sledge." The squirrel did as he was asked, and the sledge moved slowly along.

By-and-by a hare came running across a field, but stopped to see what wonderful thing was coming. "What have you got there?" she asked, and the marten told his story and begged the hare to help them pull.

The hare pulled her hardest, and after a while they were joined by a fox, and then by a wolf, and at length a bear was added to the company, and he was of more use than all the other five beasts put together. Besides, when the whole six had supped off the man he was not so heavy to draw.

The worst of it was that they soon began to get hungry again, and the wolf, who was the hungriest of all, said to the rest:

"What shall we eat now, my friends, as there is no more man?"

"I suppose we shall have to eat the smallest of us," replied the bear, and the marten turned round to seize the squirrel who was much smaller than any of the rest. But the squirrel ran up a tree like lightning, and the marten remembering, just in time, that he was the next in size, slipped quick as thought into a hole in the rocks.

"What shall we eat now?" asked the wolf again, when he had recovered from his surprise.

"We must eat the smallest of us," repeated the bear, stretching out a paw towards the hare; but the hare was not a hare for nothing, and before the paw had touched her, she had darted deep into the wood.

Now that the squirrel, the marten, and the hare had all gone, the fox was the smallest of the three who were left, and the wolf and the bear explained that they were very sorry, but they would have to eat Liini. Michael, the fox, did not run away as the others had done, but smiled in a friendly manner, and remarked: "Things taste so stale in a valley; one's appetite is so much better up on a mountain." The wolf and the bear agreed, and they turned out of the hollow where they had been walking, and chose a path that led up the mountain side. The fox trotted cheerfully by his two big companions, but on the way he managed to whisper to the wolf: "Tell me, Peter, when I am eaten, what will you have for your next dinner?"

This simple question seemed to put out the wolf very much. What would they have for their next dinner, and, what was more important still, who would there be to eat it? They had made a rule always to dine off the smallest of the party, and when the fox was gone, why of course, he was smaller than the bear.

These thoughts flashed quickly through his head, and he said hastily: "Dear brothers, would it not be better for us to live together as comrades, and everyone to hunt for the common dinner? Is not my plan a good one?"

"It is the best thing I have ever heard," answered the fox and as they were two to one the bear had to be content, though in his heart he would much have preferred a good dinner at once to any friendship.

For a few days all went well; there was plenty of game in the forest, and even the wolf had as much to eat as he could wish. One morning the fox as usual was going his rounds when he noticed a tall, slender tree, with a magpie's nest in one of the top branches. Now the fox was particularly fond of young magpies, and he set about making a plan by which he could have one for dinner. At last he hit upon something which he thought would do, and accordingly he sat down near the tree and began to stare hard at it.

"What are you looking at, Michael?" asked the magpie, who was watching him from a bough.

"I'm looking at this tree. It has just struck me what a good tree it would be to cut my new snow-shoes out of." But at this answer the magpie screeched loudly, and exclaimed: "Oh, not this tree, dear brother, I implore you! I have built my nest on it, and my young ones are not yet old enough to fly."

"It will not be easy to find another tree that would make such good snow-shoes," answered the fox, cocking his head on one side, and gazing at the tree thoughtfully; "but I do not like to be ill-natured, so if you will give me one of your young ones I will seek my snow-shoes elsewhere."

Not knowing what to do the poor magpie had to agree, and flying back, with a heavy heart, he threw one of his young ones out of the nest. The fox seized it in his mouth and ran off in triumph, while the magpie, though deeply grieved for the loss of his little one, found some comfort in the thought that only a bird of extraordinary wisdom would have dreamed of saving the rest by the sacrifice of the one. But what do you think happened ? Why, a few days later, Michael the fox might have been seen sitting under the very same tree, and a dreadful pang shot through the heart of the magpie as he peeped at him from a hole in the nest.

"What are you looking at ?" he asked in a trembling voice.

"At this tree. I was just thinking what good snow-shoes it would make," answered the fox in an absent voice, as if he was not thinking of what he was saying.

"Oh, my brother, my dear little brother, don't do that," cried the magpie, hopping about in his anguish. "You know you promised only a few days ago that you would get your snow-shoes elsewhere."

"So I did; but though I have searched through the whole forest, there is not a single tree that is as good as this. I am very sorry to put you out, but really it is not my fault. The only thing I can do for you is to offer to give up my snow-shoes altogether if you will throw me down one of your young ones in exchange.'

And the poor magpie, in spite of his wisdom, was obliged to throw another of his little ones out of the nest and this time he was not able to console himself with the thought that he had been much cleverer than other people.

He sat on the edge of his nest, his head drooping and his feathers all ruffled, looking the picture of misery. Indeed he was so different from the gay, jaunty magpie whom every creature in the forest knew, that a crow who was flying past stopped to inquire what was the matter. "Where are the two young ones who are not in the nest?" asked he.

"I had to give them to the fox," replied the magpie in a quivering voice; "he has been here twice in the last week, and wanted to cut down my tree for the purpose of making snow-shoes out of it, and the only way I could buy him off was by giving him two of my young ones."

"Oh, you fool," cried the crow, "the fox was only trying to frighten you. He could not have cut down the tree, for he has neither axe nor knife. Dear me, to think that you have sacrificed your young ones for nothing! Dear, dear! how could you be so very foolish!" And the crow flew away, leaving the magpie overcome with shame and sorrow.

The next morning the fox came to his usual place in front of the tree, for he was hungry, and a nice young magpie would have suited him very well for dinner. But this time there was no cowering, timid magpie to do his bidding, but a bird with his head erect and a determined voice.

"My good fox,' said the magpie – putting his head on one side and looking very wise – "my good fox, if you take my advice, you will go home as fast as you can. There is no use your talking about making snow-shoes out of this tree, when you have neither knife nor axe to cut it down with!"

"Who has been teaching you wisdom?" asked the fox, forgetting his manners in his surprise at this new turn of affairs.

"The crow, who paid me a visit yesterday," answered the magpie.

"The crow was it?" said the fox, "well, the crow had better not meet me for the future, or it may be the worse for him."

As Michael, the cunning beast, had no desire to continue the conversation, he left the forest; but when he came to the high road he laid himself at full length on the ground, stretching himself out, just as if he was dead. Very soon he noticed, out of the corner of his eye, that the crow was flying towards him, and he kept stiller and stiffer than ever, with his tongue hanging out of his mouth. The crow, who wanted her supper very badly, hopped quickly towards him, and was stooping forward to peck at his tongue until the fox gave a snap, and caught him by the wing. The crow knew that it was of no use strugghng, so he said:

"Ah, brother, if you are really going to eat me, do it, I beg of you, in good style. Throw me first over this precipice, so that my feathers may be strewn here and there, and that all will see them may know that your cunning is greater than mine." This idea pleased the fox, for he had not yet forgiven the crow for depriving him of the young magpies, so he carried the crow to the edge of the precipice and threw him over, intending to go round by a path he knew and pick him up at the bottom. But no sooner had the fox let the crow go than he soared up into the air, and hovering just out of reach of his enemy's jaws, he cried with a laugh,"Ah, fox! you know well how to catch, but you cannot keep."

With his tail between his legs, the fox slunk into the forest. He did not know where to look for a dinner, as he guessed that the crow would have flown back before him, and put everyone on their guard. The notion of going to bed supperless was very unpleasant to him, and he was wondering what in the world he should do, when he chanced to meet with his old friend the bear.

This poor animal had just lost his wife, and was going to get someone to mourn over her, for he felt her loss greatly. He had hardly left his comfortable cave when he had come across tlue wolf, who inquired where he was going. "I am going to find a mourner," answered the bear, and told his story.

"Oh, let me mourn for you," cried the wolf.

"Do you understand how to howl?" said the bear.

"Oh, certainly, godfather, certainly," replied the wolf; but the bear said he should like to have a specimen of his howling, to make sure that he knew his business. So the wolf broke forth in his song of lament: "Hu, hu, hu, hum, hoh," he shouted, and he made such a noise that the bear put up his paws to his ears, and begged him to stop.

"You have no idea how it is done. Be off with you," said he angrily.

A little further down the road the hare was resting in a ditch, but when she saw the bear, she came out and spoke to him, and inquired why he looked so sad. The bear told her of the loss of his wife, and of his search after a mourner that could lament over her in the proper style. The hare instantly offered her services, but the bear took care to ask her to give him a proof of her talents, before he accepted them. "Pu, pu, pu, pum, poh," piped the hare; but this time her voice was so small that the bear could hardly hear her. "That is not what I want," he said, "I will bid you good morning."

It was after this that the fox came up, and he also was struck with the bear's altered looks, and stopped. "What is the matter with you, godfather?" asked he, "and where are you going?"

"I am going to find a mourner for my wife," answered the bear.

"Oh, do choose me," cried the fox, and the bear looked at him thoughtfully.

"Can you howl well?" he said.

"Yes, beautifully, just listen," and the fox lifted up his voice and sang – weeping: "Lou, lou, lou! the famous spinner, the baker of good cakes, the prudent housekeeper is torn from her husband! Lou, lou, lou! she is gone! she is gone!"

"Now at last I have found someone who knows the art of lamentation," exclaimed the bear, quite delighted; and he led the fox back to his cave, and bade him begin his lament over the dead wife who was lying stretched out on her bed of grey moss. But this did not suit the fox at all.

"One cannot wail properly in this cave," he said, "it is much too damp. You had better take the body to the storehouse. It will sound much finer there." So the bear carried his wife's body to the storehouse, while he himself went back to the cave to cook some pap for the mourner. From time to time he paused and listened for the sound of wailing, but he heard nothing. At last he went to the door of the storehouse, and called to the fox:

"Why don't you howl, godfather? What are you about?"

And the fox, who, instead of weeping over the dead bear, had been quietly eating her, answered:

"There only remain now her legs and the soles of her feet. Give me five minutes more and they will be gone also!"

When the bear heard that he ran back for the kitchen ladle, to give the traitor the beating he deserved. But as he opened the door of the storehouse, Michael was ready for him, and slipping between his legs, dashed straight off into the forest. The bear, seeing that the traitor had escaped, flung the ladle after him, and it just caught the tip of his tail, and that is how there comes to be a spot of white on the tails of all foxes.

Mikko the Fox

(Adventure II: The Partners)

THE BEAR AND THE WOLF AND THE FOX made houses quite close together and the Wolf and the Fox decided to go into partnership.

"The first thing we ought to do," said Pekka, the Wolf, "is make a clearing in the forest and plant some crops."

The Fox agreed and the very next day they started out to work. Each had a crock with three pats of butter for his dinner. They left their crocks in the cool water of a little spring in the forest not far from the place where they had decided to make a clearing.

It was hard work felling trees and the Fox, soon tiring of it, made some sort of excuse to run off. When he came back he said to the Wolf:

"Pekka, the folks at the Farm are having a christening and have sent me an invitation to attend."

"It's too bad we're so busy today," the Wolf said. "Another day you might have gone."

"But I must go," the Fox insisted. "They've been good neighbors to us and they'd be insulted if I refused."

"Very well," the Wolf said, "if you feel that way about it you better go. But hurry back for we have a lot to do."

So the Fox trotted off but he got no farther than the spring where the butter crocks were cooling. He took the Wolf's crock and licked off the top layer of butter. Then after a while he went back to the clearing.

"Well, Mikko," the Wolf said, "is the christening over?"

"Yes, it's over."

"What did they name the child?"

"They named it Top."

"Top? That's a strange name!"

In a few moments the Fox again ran off and returned with the announcement that there was to be another christening at the Farm and again they wanted him to attend.

"Another christening!" the Wolf exclaimed. "How can that be?"

"This time the daughter has a baby."

"You're not going, are you, Mikko? You can't always be going to christenings."

"That's true, Pekka, that's true," said the Fox, "but I think I must go this time."

The Wolf sighed.

"You will hurry back, won't you? This work is too much for me alone."

"Yes, Pekka dear," the Fox promised, "I'll hurry back as quickly as I can."

So he trotted off again to the spring and the Wolf's butter crock. This time he ate the middle pat of the Wolf's butter, then slowly sauntered back to the clearing.

"Well," said the Wolf, pausing a moment in his work, "what did they name the baby this time?"

"This one they named Middle."

"Middle? That's a strange name to give a baby!"

For a few moments the Fox pretended to work hard. Then he ran off again. When he came back, he said:

"Pekka, do you know they're having another christening at the Farm and they say that I just must come."

"Another christening! Now, Mikko, that's too much! How can they be having another christening?"

"Well, this time it's the daughter-in-law that has a baby."

"I don't care who it is," the Wolf said, "you just can't go. You've got some work to do, you have!"

The Fox agreed:

"You're right, Pekka, you're right! I'm entirely too busy to be running off all the time to christenings! I'd say, 'No!' in a minute if it wasn't that we are new settlers and they are our nearest neighbors. As it is I'm afraid they'd think it wasn't neighborly if I didn't come. But I'll hurry back, I promise you!"

So for the third time the Fox trotted off to the little spring and this time he licked the Wolf's butter crock clean to the bottom. Then he went slowly back to the clearing and told the Wolf about the christening and the baby.

"They've named this one Bottom," he said.

"Bottom!" the Wolf echoed. "What funny names they give children nowadays!"

The Fox pretended to work hard for a few minutes, then threw himself down exhausted.

"Heigh ho!" he said, with a yawn, "I'm so tired and hungry it must be dinner time!"

The Wolf looked at the sun and said:

"Yes, I think we had better rest now and eat."

So they went to the spring and got their butter crocks. The Wolf found that his had already been licked clean.

"Mikko!" he cried, "have you been at my butter?"

"Me?" the Fox said in a tone of great innocence. "How could I have been at your butter when you know perfectly well that I've been working right beside you all morning except when I was away at the christenings? You must have eaten up your butter yourself!"

"Of course I haven't eaten it up myself!" the Wolf declared. "I just bet anything you took it!"

The Fox pretended to be much aggrieved.

"Pekka, I won't have you saying such a thing! We must get at the bottom of this! I tell you what we'll do: we'll both lie down in the sun and the heat of the sun will melt the butter and make it run. Now then, if butter runs out of my nose then I'm the one that has eaten your butter; if it runs out of your nose, then you've eaten it yourself. Do you agree to this test?"

The Wolf said, yes, he agreed, and at once lay down in the sun. He had been working so hard that he was very tired and in a few moments he was sound asleep. Thereupon the Fox slipped over and daubed a little lump of butter on the end of his nose. The sun melted the butter and then, of course, it looked as if it were running out of the Wolf's nose.

The Wolf awoke and felt his nose with his tongue.

"Why, Mikko," he said in surprise, "so there is! Well, I suppose I must have eaten that butter myself but I give you my word for it I don't remember doing it!"

"Well," said the Fox, pretending still to feel hurt, "you shouldn't always suspect me."

When they went back to the clearing, the Wolf began pulling the brush together to burn it up and the Fox slipped away and lay down behind some bushes.

"Mikko! Mikko!" the Wolf called. "Aren't you going to help me burn the brush?"

"You set it a-fire," the Fox called back, "and I'll stay here to guard against any flying sparks. We don't want to burn down the whole forest!"

So the Wolf burned up all the brush while the Fox took a pleasant nap.

Then when he was ready to plant the seed in the rich wood ashes, the Wolf again called out to the Fox to come help him.

"You do the planting, Pekka," the Fox called back, "and I'll stay here and frighten off the birds. If I don't they'll come and pick up every seed you plant."

So Mikko, the rascal, took another nap while the poor Wolf planted the field he had already cleared and burned.

Mikko the Fox

(Adventure III: The Fox and the Crow)

IN A SHORT TIME THE FIELD THAT PEKKA, the Wolf, had planted began to sprout. Pekka was delighted.

"See, Mikko," he said to the Fox, "our grain is growing and we shall soon be harvesting it!"

The Fox turned up his nose indifferently.

"If we don't get something to eat before that grain ripens," he said, "we'll starve, both of us! While we wait for the harvest I think we better go out hunting. I'm going this minute for I tell you I'm hungry!"

The Fox went sniffing into the forest and finally came to the tree where Harakka, the Magpie, had her nest. The Fox, cocking his head, paced slowly round and round the tree, looking at it from every angle. Harakka, the Magpie, sitting on her nest among her fledglings, began to feel nervous.

"Say, Mikko," she called down, "what are you looking at?"

At first the Fox made no answer. Deep in thought, apparently, he nodded his head and murmured:

"Yes, the very tree!"

Harakka, the Magpie, again called down:

"What are you looking at, Mikko?"

The Fox started as though he had heard the question for the first time.

"Ah, Harakka, is that you? Good day to you! I hope you are well! I hope the children are all well! I was so busy looking for the right tree that I didn't recognize you at first. You see I have to cut down a tree to get wood for a new pair of skis. This tree is just the one I want."

"Oh, mercy me!" the Magpie cried. "You can't cut down this tree! Do you want to kill all my children? This is our home!"

Mikko, the rascal, pretended to be very sympathetic.

"I'm awfully sorry to have to disturb you, truly I am, but I'm afraid I do have to cut down this tree. I can't find another that suits me as well."

The Magpie flapped her wings in despair.

"You hard-hearted wretch! What will you take not to cut down this tree?"

The Fox put his paw to his head and pretended to think hard. After a moment he said:

"Well, Harakka, I'll make you this offer: I'll leave this tree standing provided you throw me down one of your fledglings."

"What!" the poor Magpie shrieked. "Give you one of my babies! I'll never do that! Never! Never! *Never*!"

"Oh, very well! Just as you like! If I cut the tree down I can get them all. But I thought for the sake of old times I'd ask for only one. However, do as you think best."

What could the poor Magpie say? If the tree were felled and her fledglings thrown out of the nest they would certainly all perish. Perhaps it would be wise to sacrifice one to save the rest.

"You promise to let the tree stand," she said, "if I give you one of my children?"

"Yes," the rascal promised, "just drop me one of your fledglings, a nice plump one, and I won't cut down the tree."

With shaking claw Harakka pushed one of her children over the edge of the nest. It fluttered to the ground and Mikko carried it off.

Well, the next day what did that Fox do but come back and begin pacing around the tree again.

"Yes," he said, pretending to talk to himself, "this is the best tree I can find. I might as well cut it down at once."

"But, Mikko!" cried the Magpie, "you forget! You said you wouldn't cut down this tree if I gave you one of my children and I did give you one!"

The Fox flipped his tail indifferently.

"I know," he said, "I did promise but I thought then I could find another tree that would suit me as well as this one, but I can't. I've looked everywhere and I can't. I'm sorry but I'm afraid that I'll just have to take this tree."

"O dear, O dear, O dear!" the poor distracted Magpie wept. "Will nothing make you leave this tree stand?"

The Fox smacked his lips.

"Well, Harakka, drop me down another of your fledglings and I won't disturb the tree. I promise."

"What! Another of my babies! Oh, you wretch!"

"Well, suit yourself," Mikko said. "One of your fledglings and you can keep the others safe in the nest, or I'll cut the tree down."

What could the poor Magpie do? Wouldn't it be better to sacrifice another fledgling on the chance of saving the rest? Yes, it would! So she pushed another out of the nest. It fluttered to the ground and Mikko, the rascal, carried it off.

That afternoon Varis, the Crow, came to call on the Magpie.

"Why, my dear," she said, looking over the fledglings, "two of your children are missing! Whatever has become of them?"

"It's that rascally Mikko!" the Magpie cried, and thereupon she told her friend the whole story.

Varis, the Crow, listened carefully and then said:

"My dear, that miserable Fox has been fooling you! Why, he can't cut down this tree or any other tree for that matter! He hasn't even got an ax! Don't let him impose on you a third time!"

So the very next day when the Fox came and again tried the same little trick, Harakka, the Magpie, tossed her head scornfully and said:

"Go along, you rascal! You can't fool me again! How can you cut down this tree or any other for that matter when you haven't even got an ax!"

The Fox was furious at being cheated of his dinner.

"You didn't think that out yourself, Harakka!" he said. "Someone's been talking to you! Who was it?"

"It was my dear friend, Varis," the Magpie said. "She's on to your tricks!"

"I'll teach that Crow to interfere with my affairs!" the Fox muttered to himself as he trotted off.

He went to an open field and lay down with his mouth open, pretending to be dead.

"I'm sure Varis will soon spy me!" he said to himself.

He was right. Presently the Crow began circling above him. She flew nearer and nearer and at last alighted on his head. His tongue was lolling out and Varis decided to have her first bite there. She gave it a sharp peck at which the Fox jumped up and caught her in his paws.

"Ha! Ha!" he cried. "So you're the one who spoiled my little game with Harakka, are you? Well, I'll teach you not to interfere with me! As I haven't got one of Harakka's fledglings for my dinner, I'm going to take you!"

"You don't mean you're going to eat me!" cried the Crow in terror.

"That's exactly what I mean!"

"No, no, Mikko! Don't do that!"

"Yes, that's exactly what I'm going to do! I'm going to teach you birds that I'm not an animal to be played jokes on!"

"I suppose," the Crow said, sighing, "if it must be, it must be! But, Mikko, if you really want to use me as a warning to the other birds, you oughtn't to eat me right down. It would be much better if you dragged me along the ground first. Then they'd see a wing here, a leg there, and a long trail of feathers. That really would terrify them."

"I believe you're right," the Fox said.

He put the Crow down on the ground and lifted his paw for a moment to change his hold. The Crow instantly jerked away and escaped.

"Ha! Ha!" she cawed as she flew off. "You were clever enough to catch me, Mikko, but you weren't clever enough to eat me when you had me!"

So this was one time when Mikko, the Fox, was worsted.

Mikko the Fox

(Adventure IV: The Chief Mourner)

"MERCY ME!" THOUGHT MIKKO TO HIMSELF as he watched Varis, the Crow, fly away, "this is certainly my unlucky day! There I had my dinner right in my hand and then lost it!"

Sighing and shaking his head he sauntered slowly back to the forest.

Now it happened that Osmo, the Bear, had just lost his wife and was out looking for someone to bewail her death. The first person he met was Pekka, the Wolf.

"Pekka," he said, "my wife's dead and I'm out looking for a good strong mourner. Can you mourn?"

"Me? Indeed I can! Just listen!"

Pekka, the Wolf, pointed his nose to the sky and let out a long shivery howl.

"There!" he said. "I don't believe you'll find anyone that can do any better than that!"

But Osmo, the Bear, shook his head.

"No, Pekka, you won't do. I don't like your mourning at all!"

The Bear ambled on and presently he met the Hare.

"Good day, Jussi," he said. "Are you any good at mourning? Show me what you can do."

The Hare gave some frightened squeaks as his idea of mourning the dead.

"No, no," Osmo said, "I don't like your mourning either."

So he walked on farther until by chance he met the Fox.

"Mikko," he said, "my wife's dead and I'm out looking for a good strong mourner. Can you mourn?"

"Can I? Indeed I can!" the Fox declared. "I'm a marvel at mourning! I can wail high and low and soft and loud and just any way you want! Listen!" And Mikko, beginning with a little whimpering sound, slowly rose to a high heart-rending cry. This is what he wailed:

"*Med*! *Med*! *Med*!
The Bear's Wife is dead!
Lax! *Lax*! *Lax*!
No more she'll spin the flax!
Eyes! *Eyes*! *Eyes*!
No more she'll bake the pies!
Air! *Air*! *Air*!
No more she'll drive the mare!
Shakes! *Shakes*! *Shakes*!
There'll be no more little cakes!

Darth! Darth! Darth!
Throw the pots on the hearth!
For the Bear's Wife is dead!
Med! Med! Med!"

Osmo, the Bear, was deeply moved.

"Beautiful! Beautiful!" he grunted hoarsely. "How well you knew her! Come along home with me, Mikko, and start right in! Oh, how beautifully you wail!"

So Mikko went home with the Bear. The old Bear Wife was laid out on a bench in the kitchen.

"Now then," the Bear said, "you begin the wailing while I cook the porridge."

"No, no, Osmo," the Fox said, "I couldn't possibly wail in here! The place is full of smoke and my voice would get husky in two minutes! Can't you lay her out in the storehouse?"

The Bear demurred but the Fox insisted and at last had his way. So together they dragged the body of the old Bear Wife out to the storehouse. The Fox stood beside the body ready to begin his wailing and the Bear went back to the kitchen.

The moment the Bear was out of sight Mikko, the rascal, instead of bewailing the old Bear Wife began gobbling her up! He just gobbled and gobbled and gobbled as fast as he could.

"What's the matter?" the Bear called out after a few minutes. "Why don't you begin?"

The Fox made no reply but kept on gobbling as hard as he could.

"Mikko! Mikko!" the Bear called out again. "What's the matter? Why aren't you howling?"

By this time the Fox had made a good dinner, so he called back:

"Don't bother me! I'm busy eating! Yum! Yum! Yum! Bear meat is awful good! Just give me a few more minutes and I'll be finished!"

At that the Bear rushed out of the kitchen in a terrible rage but the Fox was already running off and the Bear was unable to catch him. He did hit the end of his tail with the long spoon with which he had been measuring the meal, but that was all.

Mikko, the rascal, got safely away. However, to this day his tail shows the white mark of the meal.

Mikko the Fox

(Adventure V: Mirri, the Cat)

ONE DAY WHILE THE FOX was out walking in the forest he met a stranger.

"Good day," he said. "Who are you?"

"I am Mirri," the stranger said, "a poor unfortunate Cat out of employment. I had service in a decent family but I've had to leave them."

"Did they treat you badly?" the Fox asked.

"No, it wasn't that. They were considerate enough but they kept getting poorer and poorer until finally they hadn't food enough to feed us animals. Then I overheard the master say that soon they'd be forced to eat us and that they'd begin with me. At that I decided it was time for me to run away and here I am."

"My poor Cat," Mikko said, "you've had a cruel experience! Why don't you take service with me?"

"Will I be safe with you?" the Cat asked. "Will you protect me?"

"Will I?" the Fox repeated boastfully. "My dear Mirri, once it becomes known that you are Mikko's servant all the animals will show you a wholesome respect."

"Well then, I'll enter your service," the Cat said.

So the bargain was struck and the Fox at once began to train his new servant.

"Now, Mirri, tell me: what would you do if you suddenly met a Bear?"

"There's just one thing I could do, master: I'd run up a tree."

The Fox laughed.

"You must have more ways than one to meet such a situation! Take me now: there are any of a hundred things that I could do if I met a Bear!"

Just then Osmo, the Bear, ambled softly up behind the Fox. The Cat saw him and instantly flew up a tree. Before the Fox could move Osmo clutched him firmly on the shoulder with his teeth.

"Oh, master, master!" the Cat called down from the tree. "What's this? I with my one way have escaped and you with your hundred are caught!"

But the Fox paid no heed to the Cat. He twisted his head around and looked reproachfully at the Bear.

"Why, Osmo, my dear old friend!" he said, "what in the world do you mean taking hold of me so roughly! Ouch! You're nipping my shoulder, really you are! I don't understand why you're acting this way! Here I've always been such a good friend to you, so faithful, so true, so—"

"What!" rumbled the Bear. "Faithful! True! Oh, you—"

Osmo's feelings overcame him to such an extent that he opened his jaws to roar out freely his denial of the Fox's hypocrisy.

That gave the Fox just the chance he wanted. He jerked quickly away and fled and the Bear was left standing with his mouth wide open.

Later when the Bear had ambled off the Fox returned and called the Cat down from the tree.

"You see, Mirri," he remarked casually, "it wasn't anything at all for me to get the best of the Bear!"

He could see that he had vastly impressed the Cat, so he let the subject drop.

"Come along, Mirri," he said, "it's time for us to go home."

TRICKERY, ENCHANTMENT & MAGIC

Introduction

WONDER, ARGUABLY, IS IN THE END what fairy stories are all about. We go to them to be transported to an enchanted realm, at an infinite imaginative distance from our own. A secondary function of such stories, though, is to give us a new perspective on our everyday existence; to reveal the exoticism latent in our lives, however humdrum they may seem. Magic may be a curse, a punishment, but in these tales it is as often a force for good. A mighty leveller, it's the power that can place a woodcutter's son on the level of his king, or allows a peasant's cottage to become a castle. Trickery depends on down-to-earth thinking: it is unshiftably rooted in the real world and so in certain respects is the opposite of enchantment. Yet it is analogous to magic in its ability to transform situations; to find a winning way out of what appears a hopeless spot; to reimagine realities in a more advantageous way. In 'The Devil's Bride', quick-wittedness is what gives Erkki an edge over the very personification of evil, enabling him to prevail over the Prince of Darkness himself.

The Mysterious Servant

(The Story of a Young Man Who Respected the Dead)

THERE WAS ONCE A RICH MERCHANT who had an only son. As he lay dying, he said:

"Matti, my boy, my end is approaching and there are two things I want to say to you: The first is that I am leaving you all my wealth. If you are careful you will have enough to suffice you for life. The second thing I have to say is to beg you never to leave this, your native village. At your birth there was a prophecy which declared that if ever you left this village you would have to marry a woman with horns. Now that I have warned you in time it will be your own fault if ever you have to meet this fate."

The merchant died and Matti was left alone. He had never before wanted to travel but now that he knew of the fate which would overtake him if he did, he couldn't bear the thought of remaining forever a prisoner in his native village.

"What is the use of riches," he asked himself, "if one can't travel over the broad world and see wonderful sights? Besides, if it's my fate to marry a horned woman, I don't see why sitting quietly at home is going to save me. No! I'm going to take my chances like a man and come and go as I like!"

So he gathered his riches together, closed the old house where he had been born, and started out into the bright world. He travelled many days, meeting strange people and seeing strange sights. At last he settled down in a large city and became a merchant like his father.

One afternoon as he was out walking, he saw a crowd of men dragging the body of a dead man in the gutter. They were kicking and abusing the dead body and calling it evil names.

Matti stopped them.

"What is this you are doing?" he demanded. "Don't you know that disrespect to the dead is disrespect to God? Give over abusing this poor dead body and bury it decently or God will punish you!"

"Let us alone!" the men cried. "He deserves the abuse we are giving him! When he was alive he borrowed money from us all and then he died without repaying us. Are we to have no satisfaction at all?"

With that they resumed their abuse of the dead body.

"Wait!" Matti cried. "Tell me what the dead man owed you and I will pay it!"

"He owed me ten ducats!" said one.

"And me a hundred!" shouted another.

"And me five hundred!"

"And me a thousand!"

"Come all of you to my house," Matti said, "and I will pay you, but only on condition that first you hand over the body to me and help me give it a decent burial."

The men agreed. They helped Matti bury the dead man and then went home with him.

Each told Matti the amount the dead man owed him and, true to his promise, Matti paid them all.

When he had paid the last man he found that he had nothing left for himself but nine silver kopeks. The dead man's debts had exhausted all the wealth his father had left him.

"No matter!" Matti thought to himself. "My riches would have done me no good if I had stood by and allowed a poor dead man to be abused. What if I have nothing left? I'm young and strong and I can go out into the world and make my livelihood somehow. I'll go home and have one last look at my native village and then begin life anew."

So, dressed in shabby old clothes with nothing in his pockets but the nine silver kopeks, Matti left the city where people were beginning to know him as a merchant and started back to his native village. He was soon met by a man who addressed him respectfully and asked to be engaged as his servant.

"My servant!" Matti repeated with a laugh. "My dear fellow, I'm too poor to have a servant! All I have in the world are nine silver kopeks!"

"No matter, master," the man said. "Take me anyhow. I will serve you well and I promise you will not regret our bargain."

So Matti agreed and they walked on together. The sun was hot and by mid-afternoon Matti was feeling faint with hunger and fatigue.

"Master," the servant said, "I will run ahead to the next village and order the landlord at the inn to prepare you a fine dinner. Do you come along slowly and by the time you arrive the dinner will be ready."

"But remember," Matti warned him, "I have no money to pay for a fine dinner!"

"Trust me!" the servant said and off he hurried.

At the next village he hunted out the best inn and ordered the landlord to prepare his finest dinner without delay. He was so particular that everything should be the best that the landlord supposed his master must be some great lord.

When Matti arrived on foot, tired and travel-stained and shabby, the landlord was amazed.

"It's fine lords we have nowadays!" he muttered scornfully, and he wished he had not been in such haste to cook the best food in the house. But it was cooked and ready to serve and so, with an ill grace, he served it.

Matti and his man ate their fill of good cabbage soup and fish and fowl tender and juicy.

It quite enraged the landlord to see poor men with such good appetites.

"They eat as if their pockets were lined with gold!" he muttered angrily. "Well, let them eat while they can for they'll lose their appetites once they see the reckoning!"

When they finished eating, they rested and then called for the reckoning. It was much more than it should have been but neither Matti nor the servant objected.

"Like a good fellow," the servant said, "will you please to lend me your half peck measure?"

"Like a good fellow, indeed!" the landlord muttered to himself. "Who are you to call me a good fellow I'd like to know!"

Nevertheless he went out and got the measure.

"Now, master," the servant said, "give me three of your nine silver kopeks."

The servant threw the three silver kopeks into the measure, shook the measure three times and lo! it was filled to the brim with silver kopeks! The servant counted out the amount of the reckoning and handed the rest of the money to his master. Then he and Matti went on their way leaving the landlord gaping after them with open mouth.

Day after day the servant paid the reckoning in the same way at the various inns where they stopped until they reached at last Matti's native village and the old house that still belonged to him.

They settled themselves there and one day the servant said to Matti:

"Now, master, you know your fate: for having left your native village you know you are destined to marry a horned woman. You might as well do it at once for you'll have to do it sooner or later."

"That is true," Matti said, "and if I knew the whereabouts of the horned woman who is my fate I should marry her at once."

"In that case we'll lose no more time," the servant said. "The king has three daughters all of whom are horned. This isn't generally known but it is true. Let us go to the palace and present your suit. The king will give friendly ear for there are not many suitors for daughters with horns. He will try to make you take the oldest who has big horns and a hoarse voice. When she sees you, she'll whisper: 'Take me! Take me!' But do you shake your head and answer: 'No! Not this one!' Then the king will send for his second daughter. Her horns are not so big nor is her voice so hoarse. She, too, will whisper you: 'Take me! Take me!' But do you again shake your head and answer: 'No! Not this one!' Be firm and the king will finally have to send for his youngest daughter. Her horns are just soft little baby horns and her voice is just a little husky. Take her and soon all will be well."

So Matti and the servant went to the palace and got audience with the King.

"My master, Matti," the Servant said, addressing the King, "is desirous of marrying a wife with horns."

The King was interested at once.

"As it happens I have a daughter with horns," he said. "I'll have her come in."

He sent for his oldest daughter and presently she appeared. Her horns were long and thick.

"Take me! Take me!" she whispered hoarsely as she passed Matti.

"See what a fine girl she is!" the king said, "and what well-grown horns she has!"

But Matti shook his head.

"No, Your Majesty, I don't think I want to marry this one."

"Of course you must follow the dictates of your heart," the king said drily. "However, come to think of it, my second daughter also has horns. Maybe you'd like to consider her."

So the second daughter was called in. Her horns were not so large as her sister's nor was her voice so hoarse. But Matti, remembering the servant's warning, refused her, too. The King seemed surprised and even annoyed that Matti should refuse his daughters so glibly, but when he found that Matti was firm he said:

"I have got another daughter, my youngest, but, if it's horns you're looking for, I don't believe you'll be interested in her at all since her horns are so small and soft that they are hardly noticeable at all. However, as you're here, you might as well see her."

So the youngest princess was sent for and at once Matti knew that she was the one he wanted to marry. She wasn't as beautiful as a princess should be but she was gentle and modest and when she passed Matti her cheeks flushed and she wasn't able to whisper anything. But Matti felt very sure that if she had whispered her voice would have been scarcely husky.

"This, O King," he said, "is my choice! Let me marry your youngest daughter and I promise to be a faithful husband to her."

The king would have preferred to marry off the older princesses first for their horns were getting to be very troublesome, but as they all had horns he was afraid to refuse Matti's offer.

So after a little talk he gave Matti the youngest and in a short time they were married.

After the wedding feast the king led the young couple to the bridal chamber and closed the door.

Matti's servant meantime had gone out to the woods and cut some stout switches of birch. When the palace was quiet and all were asleep, he crept softly into the bridal chamber and, dragging the bride out of bed, he beat her unmercifully.

"Oh! Oh!" she cried in pain.

Her screams woke Matti and in fright he jumped out of bed and tried to stop the servant.

"Wait!" the servant said. "She is under an evil enchantment and I am delivering her!"

So he kept on beating her until he had drawn blood. Then instantly the horns fell from her head and there she stood a beautiful young girl released from the evil enchantment that had disfigured her.

The servant handed her over to her husband who fell in love with her on sight and has loved her ever since.

"Now farewell, Matti," the servant said. "My work is done and you will need me no longer. You have married a beautiful princess and the king will soon make you his heir."

With these words the servant disappeared and Matti was left alone with his lovely bride.

And that was Matti's reward for having respected the dead. God Himself in the form of the servant had come down and taken care of him.

The Gifts of the Magician

ONCE UPON A TIME THERE WAS AN OLD MAN who lived in a little hut in the middle of a forest. His wife was dead, and he had only one son, whom he loved dearly. Near their hut was a group of birch trees, in which some blackgame had made their nests, and the youth had often begged his father's permission to shoot the birds, but the old man always strictly forbade him to do anything of the kind.

One day, however, when the father had gone to a little distance to collect some sticks for the fire, the boy fetched his bow, and shot at a bird that was just flying towards its nest. But he had not taken proper aim, and the bird was only wounded, and fluttered along the ground. The boy ran to catch it, but though he ran very fast, and the bird seemed to flutter along very slowly, he never could quite catch up with it; it was always just a little ahead. But so absorbed was he in the chase that he did not notice for some time that he was now deep in the forest, in a place where he had never been before. Then he felt it would be foolish to go any further, and he turned to find his way home.

He thought it would be easy enough to follow the path along which he had come, but somehow it was always branching off in unexpected directions. He looked about for a house where he might stop and ask his way, but there was not a sign of one anywhere, and he was afraid to stand still, for it was cold, and there were many stories of wolves being seen in that part of the forest. Night fell, and he was beginning to start at every sound, when suddenly a magician came running towards him, with a pack of wolves snapping at his heels. Then all the boy's courage returned to him. He took his bow, and aiming an arrow at the largest wolf, shot him through the heart, and a few more arrows soon put the rest to flight. The magician was full of gratitude to his deliverer, and promised him a reward for his help if the youth would go back with him to his house.

"Indeed there is nothing that would be more welcome to me than a night's lodging," answered the boy; "I have been wandering all day in the forest, and do not know how to get home again."

"Come with me, you must be hungry as well as tired," said the magician, and led the way to his house, where the guest flung himself on a bed, and fell fast asleep. But his host returned to the forest to get some food, for the larder was empty.

While he was absent the housekeeper went to the boy's room and tried to wake him. She stamped on the floor, and shook him and called to him, telling him that he was in great danger, and must take flight at once. But nothing would rouse him, and if he did ever open his eyes he shut them again directly.

Soon after, the magician came back from the forest, and told the housekeeper to bring them something to eat. The meal was quickly ready, and the magician called to the boy to come down and eat it, but he could not be wakened, and they had to sit down to supper without him. By-and-by the magician went out into the wood again for some more hunting, and on his return he tried afresh to waken the youth. But finding it quite impossible, he went back for the third time to the forest.

While he was absent the boy woke up and dressed himself. Then he came downstairs and began to talk to the housekeeper. The girl had heard how he had saved her master's life, so she said nothing more about his running away, but instead told him that if the magician offered him the choice of a reward, he was to ask for the horse which stood in the third stall of the stable.

By-and-by the old man came back and they all sat down to dinner. When they had finished the magician said: "Now, my son, tell me what you will have as the reward of your courage?"

"Give me the horse that stands in the third stall of your stable," answered the youth. "For I have a long way to go before I get home, and my feet will not carry me so far."

"Ah! my son," replied the magician, "it is the best horse in my stable that you want! Will not anything else please you instead?"

But the youth declared that it was the horse, and the horse only, that he desired, and in the end the old man gave way. And besides the horse, the magician gave him a zither, a fiddle, and a flute, saying: "If you are in danger, touch the zither; and if no one comes to your aid, then play on the fiddle; but if that brings no help, blow on the flute."

The youth thanked the magician, and fastening his treasures about him mounted the horse and rode off. He had already gone some miles when, to his great surprise, the horse spoke, and said: "It is no use your returning home just now, your father will only beat you. Let us visit a few towns first, and something lucky will be sure to happen to us."

This advice pleased the boy, for he felt himself almost a man by this time, and thought it was high time he saw the world. When they entered the capital of the country everyone stopped to admire the beauty of the horse. Even the king heard of it, and came to see the splendid creature with his own eyes. Indeed, he wanted directly to buy it, and told the youth he would give any price he liked. The young man hesitated for a moment, but before he could speak, the horse contrived to whisper to him: "Do not sell me, but ask the king to take me to his stable, and feed me there; then his other horses will become just as beautiful as I."

The king was delighted when he was told what the horse had said, and took the animal at once to the stables, and placed it in his own particular stall. Sure enough, the horse had scarcely eaten a mouthful of corn out of the manger, when the rest of the horses seemed to have undergone a transformation. Some of them were old favourites which the king had ridden in many wars, and they bore the signs of age and of service. But now they arched their heads, and pawed the ground with their slender legs as they had been wont to do in days long gone by. The king's heart beat with delight, but the old groom who had had the care of them stood crossly by, and eyed the owner of this wonderful creature with hate and envy. Not a day passed without his bringing some story against the youth to his master, but the king understood all about the matter and paid no attention. At last the groom declared that the young man had boasted that he could find the king's war horse which had strayed into the forest several years ago, and had not been heard of since. Now the king had never ceased to mourn for his horse, so this time he listened to the tale which the groom had invented, and sent for the youth. "Find me my horse in three days," said he, "or it will be the worse for you."

The youth was thunderstruck at this command, but he only bowed, and went off at once to the stable.

"Do not worry yourself," answered his own horse. "Ask the king to give you a hundred oxen, and to let them be killed and cut into small pieces. Then we will start on our journey, and ride till we reach a certain river. There a horse will come up to you, but take no notice of him. Soon another will appear, and this also you must leave alone, but when the third horse shows itself, throw my bridle over it."

Everything happened just as the horse had said, and the third horse was safely bridled. Then the other horse spoke again: "The magician's raven will try to eat us as we ride away, but throw it some of the oxen's flesh, and then I will gallop like the wind, and carry you safe out of the raven's clutches."

So the young man did as he was told, and brought the horse back to the king.

The old stableman was very jealous, when he heard of it, and wondered what he could do to injure the youth in the eyes of his royal master. At last he hit upon a plan, and told the king that the young man had boasted that he could bring home the king's wife, who had vanished many months before, without leaving a trace behind her. Then the king bade the young man come into his presence, and desired him to fetch the queen home again, as he had boasted he could do. And if he failed, his head would pay the penalty.

The poor youth's heart stood still as he listened. Find the queen? But how was he to do that, when nobody in the palace had been able to do so! Slowly he walked to the stable, and laying his head on his horse's shoulder, he said: "The king has ordered me to bring his wife home again, and how can I do that when she disappeared so long ago, and no one can tell me anything about her?"

"Cheer up!" answered the horse, "we will manage to find her. You have only got to ride me back to the same river that we went to yesterday, and I will plunge into it and take my proper shape again. For I am the king's wife, who was turned into a horse by the magician from whom you saved me."

Joyfully the young man sprang into the saddle and rode away to the banks of the river. Then he threw himself off, and waited while the horse plunged in. The moment it dipped its head into the water its black skin vanished, and the most beautiful woman in the world was floating on the water. She came smilng towards the youth, and held out her hand, and he took it and led her back to the palace. Great was the king's surprise and happiness when he beheld his lost wife stand before him, and in gratitude to her rescuer he loaded him with gifts.

You would have thought that after this the poor youth would have been left in peace; but no, his enemy the stableman hated him as much as ever, and laid a new plot for his undoing. This time he presented himself before the king and told him that the youth was so puffed up with what he had done that he had declared he would seize the king's throne for himself.

At this news the king waxed so furious that he ordered a gallows to be erected at once, and the young man to be hanged without a trial. He was not even allowed to speak in his own defence, but on the very steps of the gallows he sent a message to the king and begged, as a last favour, that he might play a tune on his zither. Leave was given him, and taking the instrument from under his cloak he touched the strings. Scarcely had the first notes sounded than the hangman and his helper began to dance, and the louder grew the music the higher they capered, till at last they cried for mercy. But the youth paid no heed, and the tunes rang out more merrily than before, and by the time the sun set they both sank to the ground exhausted, and declared that the hanging must be put off till tomorrow.

The story of the zither soon spread through the town, and to the following morning the king and his whole court and a large crowd of people were gathered at the foot of the gallows to see the youth hanged. Once more he asked a favour – permission to play on his fiddle, and this the king was graciously pleased to grant. But with the first notes, the leg of every man in the crowd was lifted high, and they danced to the sound of the music the whole day till darkness fell, and there was no light to hang the musician by.

The third day came, and the youth asked leave to play on his flute. "No, no," said the king, "you made me dance all day yesterday, and if I do it again it will certainly be my death. You shall play no more tunes. Quick! the rope round his neck."

At these words the young man looked so sorrowful that the courtiers said to the king: "He is very young to die. Let him play a tune if it will make him happy." So, very unwillingly, the king gave him leave; but first he had himself bound to a big fir tree, for fear that he should be made to dance.

When he was made fast, the young man began to blow softly on his flute, and bound though he was, the king's body moved to the sound, up and down the fir tree till his clothes were in tatters, and the skin nearly rubbed off his back. But the youth had no pity, and went on blowing, till suddenly the old magician appeared and asked: "What danger are you in, my son, that you have sent for me?"

"They want to hang me," answered the young man; "the gallows are all ready and the hangman is only waiting for me to stop playing."

"Oh, I will put that right," said the magician; and taking the gallows, he tore it up and flung it into the air, and no one knows where it came down. "Who has ordered you to be hanged?" asked he.

The young man pointed to the king, who was still bound to the fir; and without wasting words the magician took hold of the tree also, and with a mighty heave both fir and man went spinning through the air, and vanished in the clouds after the gallows.

Then the youth was declared to be free, and the people elected him for their king; and the stable helper drowned himself from envy, for, after all, if it had not been for him the young man would have remained poor all the days of his life.

The Raspberry Worm

"THEW!" cried Lisa.

"Ugh!" cried Aina.

"What now?" cried the big sister.

"A worm!" cried Lisa.

"On the raspberry!" cried Aina.

"Kill it!" cried Otto.

"What a fuss over a poor little worm!" said the big sister scornfully.

"Yes, when we had cleaned the raspberries so carefully," said Lisa.

"It crept out from that very large one," put in Aina.

"And supposing someone had eaten the raspberry," said Lisa.

"Then they would have eaten the worm, too," said Aina.

"Well, what harm?" said Otto.

"Eat a worm!" cried Lisa.

"And kill him with one bite!" murmured Aina.

"Just think of it!" said Otto laughing.

"Now it is crawling on the table," cried Aina again.

"Blow it away!" said the big sister.

"Tramp on it!" laughed Otto.

But Lisa took a raspberry leaf, swept the worm carefully on to the leaf and carried it out into the yard. Then Aina noticed that a sparrow sitting on the fence was just getting ready to pounce on the poor little worm, so she took up the leaf, carried it out into the wood and hid it under a raspberry bush where the greedy sparrow could not find it. Yes, and what more is there to tell about a raspberry worm ? Who would give three straws for such a miserable little thing? Yes, but who would not like to live in such a pretty home as it lives in; in such a fresh fragrant dark-red cottage, far away in the quiet wood among flowers and green leaves!

Now it was just dinner time, so they all had a dinner of raspberries and cream. "Be careful with the sugar, Otto," said the big sister; but Otto's plate was like a snowdrift in winter, with just a little red under the snow.

Soon after dinner the big sister said: "Now we have eaten up the raspberries and we have none left to make preserve for the winter; it would be fine if we could get two baskets full of berries, then we could clean them this evening, and tomorrow we could cook them in the big preserving pan, and then we should have raspberry jam to eat on our bread!"

"Come, let us go to the wood and pick," said Lisa.

"Yes, let us," said Aina. "You take the yellow basket and I will take the green one."

"Don't get lost, and come back safely in the evening," said the big sister.

"Greetings to the raspberry worm," said Otto, mockingly. "Next time I meet him I shall do him the honour of eating him up."

So Aina and Lisa went off to the wood. Ah! how delightful it was there, how beautiful! It was certainly tiresome sometimes climbing over the fallen trees, and getting caught in the branches, and waging war with the juniper bushes and the midges, but what did that matter? The girls climbed well in their short dresses, and soon they were deep in the wood.

There were plenty of bilberries and elder berries, but no raspberries. They wandered on and on, and at last they came ... No, it could not be true! ... they came to a large raspberry wood. The wood had been on fire once, and now raspberry bushes had grown up, and there were raspberry bushes and raspberry bushes as far as the eye could see. Every bush was weighed to the ground with the largest, dark red, ripe raspberries, such a wealth of berries as two little berry pickers had never found before!

Lisa picked, Aina picked. Lisa ate, Aina ate, and in a little while their baskets were full.

"Now, we shall go home," said Aina. "No, let us gather a few more," said Lisa. So they put the baskets down on the ground and began to fill their pinafores, and it was not long before their pinafores were full, too.

"Now we shall go home," said Lisa. "Yes, now we shall go home," said Aina. Both girls took a basket in one hand and held up her apron in the other and then turned to go home. But that was easier said than done. They had never been so far in the great wood before, they could not find any road nor path, and soon the girls noticed that they had lost their way.

The worst of it was that the shadows of the trees were becoming so long in the evening sunlight, the birds were beginning to fly home, and the day was closing in. At last the sun went down behind the pine tops, and it was cool and dusky in the great wood.

The girls became anxious but went steadily on, expecting that the wood would soon end, and that they would see the smoke from the chimneys of their home.

After they had wandered on for a long time it began to grow dark. At last they reached a great plain overgrown with bushes, and when they looked around them, they saw, as much as they could in the darkness, that they were among the same beautiful raspberry bushes from which they had picked their baskets and their aprons full. Then they were so tired that they sat down on a stone and began to cry.

"I am so hungry," said Lisa.

"Yes," said Aina, "if we had only two good meat sandwiches now."

As she said that, she felt something in her hand, and when she looked down, she saw a large sandwich of bread and chicken, and at the same time Lisa said: "How very queer! I have a sandwich in my hand."

"And I, too," said Aina. "Will you dare to eat it?"

"Of course I will," said Lisa. "Ah, if we only had a good glass of milk now!"

Just as she said that she felt a large glass of milk between her fingers, and at the same time Aina cried out, "Lisa! Lisa! I have a glass of milk in my hand! Isn't it queer?"

The girls, however, were very hungry, so they ate and drank with a good appetite. When they had finished Aina yawned, stretched out her arms and said: "Oh, if only we had a nice soft bed to sleep on now!"

Scarcely had she spoken before she felt a nice soft bed by her side, and there beside Lisa was one, too. This seemed to the girls more and more wonderful, but tired and sleepy as they were, they thought no more about it, but crept into the little beds, drew the coverlets over their heads and were soon asleep.

When they awoke the sun was high in the heavens, the wood was beautiful in the summer morning, and the birds were flying about in the branches and the tree tops.

At first the girls were filled with wonder when they saw that they had slept in the wood among the raspberry bushes. They looked at each other, they looked at their beds, which were of the finest flax covered over with leaves and moss. At last Lisa said: "Are you awake, Aina?"

"Yes," said Aina.

"But I am still dreaming," said Lisa.

"No," said Aina, "but there is certainly some good fairy living among these raspberry bushes. Ah, if we had only a hot cup of coffee now, and a nice piece of white bread to dip into it!"

Scarcely had she finished speaking when she saw beside her a little silver tray with a gilt coffee-pot, two cups of rare porcelain, a sugar basin of fine crystal, silver sugar tongs, and some good fresh white bread. The girls poured out the beautiful coffee, put in the cream and sugar, and tasted it; never in their lives had they drunk such beautiful coffee.

"Now I should like to know very much who has given us all this," said Lisa gratefully.

"I have, my little girls," said a voice just then from the bushes.

The children looked round wonderingly, and saw a ittle kind-looking old man, in a white coat and a red cap, limping out from among the bushes, for he was lame in his left foot; neither Lisa nor Aina could utter a word, they were so filled with surprise.

"Don't be afraid, little girls," he said smiling kindly at them; he could not laugh properly because his mouth was crooked. "Welcome to my kingdom! Have you slept well and eaten well and drunk well?" he asked.

"Yes, indeed we have," said both the girls, "but tell us . . ." and they wanted to ask who the old man was, but were afraid to.

"I will tell you who I am," said the old man; "I am the raspberry king, who reigns over all this kingdom of raspberry bushes, and I have lived here for more than a thousand years. But the great spirit who rules over the woods, and the sea, and the sky, did not want me to become proud of my royal power and my long life. Therefore he decreed that one day in every hundred years I should change into a little raspberry worm, and live in that weak and helpless form from sunrise till sunset. During that time my life is dependent on the little worm's life, so that a bird can eat me, a child can pick me with the berries and trample under foot my thousand years of life. Now yesterday was just my transformation day, and I was taken with the raspberry and would have been trampled to death if you had not saved my life. Until sunset I lay helpless in the grass, and when I was swept away from your table I twisted one of my feet, and my mouth became crooked with terror; but when evening came and I could take my own form again, I looked for you to thank you and reward you. Then I found you both here in my kingdom, and tried to meet you both as well as I could without frightening you. Now I will send a bird from my wood to show you the way home. Goodbye, little children, thank you for your kind hearts; the raspberry king can show that he is not ungrateful." The children shook hands with the old man and thanked him, feeling very glad that they had saved the little raspberry worm. They were just going when the old man turned round, smiled mischievously with his crooked mouth, and said: "Greetings to Otto from me, and tell him when I meet him again I shall do him the honour of eating him up."

"Oh, please don't do that," cried both the girls, very frightened.

"Well, for your sake I will forgive him," said the old man, "I am not revengeful. Greetings to Otto and tell him that he may expect a gift from me, too. Goodbye."

The two girls, light of heart, now took their berries and ran off through the wood after the bird; and soon it began to get lighter in the wood and they wondered how they could have lost their way yesterday, it seemed so easy and plain now.

One can imagine what joy there was when the two reached home. Everyone had been looking for them, and the big sister had not been able to sleep, for she thought the wolves had eaten them up.

Otto met them; he had a basket in his hand and said: "Look, here is something that an old man has just left for you."

When the girls looked into the basket they saw a pair of most beautiful bracelets of precious stones, dark red, and made in the shape of a ripe raspberry and with an inscription: 'To Lisa and Aina'; beside them there was a diamond breast pin in the shape of a raspberry worm: on it was inscribed 'Otto, never destroy the helpless!'

Otto felt rather ashamed: he quite understood what it meant, but he thought that the old man's revenge was a noble one.

The raspberry king had also remembered the big sister, for when she went in to set the table for dinner, she found eleven big baskets of most beautiful raspberries, and no one knew how they had come there, but everyone guessed.

And so there was such a jam-making as had never been seen before, and if you like to go and help in it, you might perhaps get a little, for they must surely be making jam still to this very day.

The Sea King's Gift

THERE WAS ONCE A FISHERMAN who was called Salmon, and his Christian name was Matte. He lived by the shore of the big sea; where else could he live? He had a wife called Maie; could you find a better name for her? In winter they dwelt in a little cottage by the shore, but in spring they flitted to a red rock out in the sea and stayed there the whole summer until it was autumn. The cottage on the rock was even smaller than the other; it had a wooden bolt instead of an iron lock to the door, a stone hearth, a flagstaff, and a weathercock on the roof.

The rock was called Ahtola, and was not larger than the market-place of a town. Between the crevices there grew a little rowan tree and four alder bushes. Heaven only knows how they ever came there; perhaps they were brought by the winter storms. Besides that, there flourished some tufts of velvety grass, some scattered reeds, two plants of the yellow herb called tansy, four of a red flower, and a pretty white one; but the treasures of the rock consisted of three roots of garlic, which Maie had put in a cleft. Rock walls sheltered them on the north side, and the sun shone on them on the south. This does not seem much, but it sufficed Maie for a herb plot.

All good things go in threes, so Matte and his wife fished for salmon in spring, for herring in summer, and for cod in winter. When on Saturdays the weather was fine and the wind favourable, they sailed to the nearest town, sold their fish, and went to church on Sunday. But it often happened that for weeks at a time they were quite alone on the rock Ahtola, and had nothing to look at except their little yellow-brown dog, which bore the grand name of Prince, their grass tufts, their bushes and blooms, the sea bays and fish, a stormy sky and the blue, white-crested waves. For the rock lay far away from the land, and there were no green islets or human habitations for miles round, only here and there appeared a rock of the same red stone as Ahtola, besprinkled day and night with the ocean spray.

Matte and Maie were industrious, hard-working folk, happy and contented in their poor hut, and they thought themselves rich when they were able to salt as many casks of fish as they required for winter and yet have some left over with which to buy tobacco for the old man, and a pound or two of coffee for his wife, with plenty of burned corn and chicory in it to give it a flavour. Besides that, they had bread, butter, fish, a beer cask, and a buttermilk jar; what more did they require? All would have gone well had not Maie been possessed with a secret longing which never let her rest; and this was, how she could manage to become the owner of a cow.

"What would you do with a cow?" asked Matte. "She could not swim so far, and our boat is not large enough to bring her over here; and even if we had her, we have nothing to feed her on."

"We have four alder bushes and sixteen tufts of grass," rejoined Maie.

"Yes, of course," laughed Matte, "and we have also three plants of garlic. Garlic would be fine feeding for her."

"Every cow likes salt herring," rejoined his wife. "Even Prince is fond of fish."

"That may be," said her husband. "Methinks she would soon be a dear cow if we had to feed her on salt herring. All very well for Prince, who fights with the gulls over the last morsel. Put the cow out of your head, mother, we are very well off as we are."

Maie sighed. She knew well that her husband was right, but she could not give up the idea of a cow. The buttermilk no longer tasted as good as usual in the coffee; she thought of sweet cream and fresh butter, and of how there was nothing in the world to be compared with them.

One day as Matte and his wife were cleaning herring on the shore they heard Prince barking, and soon there appeared a gaily painted boat with three young men in it, steering towards the rock. They were students, on a boating excursion, and wanted to get something to eat.

"Bring us a junket, good mother," cried they to Maie.

"Ah! if only I had such a thing!" sighed Maie.

"A can of fresh milk, then," said the students; "but it must not be skim."

"Yes, if only I had it!" sighed the old woman, still more deeply.

"What! haven't you got a cow?"

Maie was silent. This question so struck her to the heart that she could not reply.

"We have no cow," Matte answered; "but we have good smoked herring, and can cook them in a couple of hours."

"All right, then, that will do," said the students, as they flung themselves down on the rock, while fifty silvery-white herring were turning on the spit in front of the fire.

"What's the name of this little stone in the middle of the ocean?" asked one of them.

"Ahtola," answered the old man.

"Well, you should want for nothing when you live in the Sea King's dominion."

Matte did not understand. He had never read Kalevala and knew nothing of the sea gods of old, but the students proceeded to explain to him.*

"Ahti," said they, "is a mighty king who lives in his dominion of Ahtola, and has a rock at the bottom of the sea, and possesses besides a treasury of good things. He rules over all fish and animals of the deep; he has the finest cows and the swiftest horses that ever chewed grass at the bottom of the ocean. He who stands well with Ahti is soon a rich man, but one must beware in dealing with him, for he is very changeful and touchy. Even a little stone thrown into the water might offend him, and then as he takes back his gift, he stirs up the sea into a storm and drags the sailors down into the depths. Ahti owns also the fairest maidens, who bear the train of his queen Wellamos, and at the sound of music they comb their long, flowing locks, which glisten in the water."

"Oh!" cried Matte, "have your worships really seen all that?"

"We have as good as seen it," said the students. "It is all printed in a book, and everything printed is true."

"I'm not so sure of that," said Matte, as he shook his head.

But the herring were now ready, and the students ate enough for six, and gave Prince some cold meat which they happened to have in the boat. Prince sat on his hind legs with delight and mewed like a pussy cat. When all was finished, the students handed Matte a shining silver coin, and allowed him to fill his pipe with a special kind of tobacco. They then thanked him for his kind hospitality and went on their journey, much regretted by Prince, who sat with a woeful expression and whined on the shore as long as he could see a flip of the boat's white sail in the distance.

Maie had never uttered a word, but thought the more. She had good ears, and had laid to heart the story about Ahti. 'How delightful,' thought she to herself, 'to possess a fairy cow! How delicious every morning and evening to draw milk from it, and yet have no trouble about the feeding, and to keep a shelf near the window for dishes of milk and junket! But this will never be my luck.'

"What are you thinking of?" asked Matte.

"Nothing," said his wife; but all the time she was pondering over some magic rhymes she had heard in her childhood from an old lame man, which were supposed to bring luck in fishing.

'What if I were to try?' thought she.

Now this was Saturday, and on Saturday evenings Matte never set the herring-net, for he did not fish on Sundays. Towards evening, however, his wife said:

"Let us set the herring-net just this once."

"No," said her husband, "it is a Saturday night."

"Last night was so stormy, and we caught so little," urged his wife; "tonight the sea is like a mirror, and with the wind in this direction the herring are drawing towards land."

"But there are streaks in the north-western sky, and Prince was eating grass this evening," said the old man.

"Surely he has not eaten my garlic," exclaimed the old woman.

"No; but there will be rough weather by tomorrow at sunset," rejoined Matte.

"Listen to me," said his wife, "we will set only one net close to the shore, and then we shall be able to finish up our half-filled cask, which will spoil if it stands open so long."

The old man allowed himself to be talked over, and so they rowed out with the net. When they reached the deepest part of the water, she began to hum the words of the magic rhyme, altering the words to suit the longings of her heart:

Oh, Ahti, with the long, long beard,
Who dwellest in the deep blue sea,
Finest treasures have I heard,
And glittering fish belong to thee.
The richest pearls beyond compare
Are stored up in thy realm below,
And Ocean's cows so sleek and fair
Feed on the grass in thy green meadow.

King of the waters, far and near,
I ask not of thy golden store,
I wish not jewels of pearl to wear,
Nor silver either, ask I for,
But one is odd and even is two,
So give me a cow, sea king so bold,
And in return I'll give to you
A slice of the moon, and the sun's gold.

"What's that you're humming?" asked the old man.

"Oh, only the words of an old rhyme that keeps running in my head," answered the old woman; and she raised her voice and went on:

Oh, Ahti, with the long, long beard,
Who dwellest in the deep blue sea,
A thousand cows are in thy herd,
I pray thee give one unto me.

"That's a stupid sort of song," said Matte. "What else should one beg of the sea king but fish? But such songs are not for Sunday."

His wife pretended not to hear him, and sang and sang the same tune all the time they were on the water. Matte heard nothing more as he sat and rowed the heavy boat, while thinking of his cracked pipe and the fine tobacco. Then they returned to the island, and soon after went to bed.

But neither Matte nor Maie could sleep a wink; the one thought of how he had profaned Sunday, and the other of Ahti's cow.

About midnight the fisherman sat up, and said to his wife:

"Dost thou hear anything?"

"No," said she.

"I think the twirling of the weathercock on the roof bodes ill," said he; "we shall have a storm."

"Oh, it is nothing but your fancy," said his wife.

Matte lay down, but soon rose again.

"The weathercock is squeaking now," said he.

"Just fancy! Go to sleep," said his wife; and the old man tried to.

For the third time he jumped out of bed.

"Ho! how the weathercock is roaring at the pitch of its voice, as if it had a fire inside it! We are going to have a tempest, and must bring in the net."

Both rose. The summer night was as dark as if it had been October, the weathercock creaked, and the storm was raging in every direction. As they went out the sea lay around them as white as snow, and the spray was dashing right over the fisher-hut. In all his life Matte had never remembered such a night. To launch the boat and put to sea to rescue the net was a thing not to be thought of. The fisherman and his wife stood aghast on the doorstep, holding on fast by the doorpost, while the foam splashed over their faces.

"Did I not tell thee that there is no luck in Sunday fishing?" said Matte sulkily; and his wife was so frightened that she never even once thought of Ahti's cows.

As there was nothing to be done, they went in. Their eyes were heavy for lack of slumber, and they slept as soundly as if there had not been such a thing as an angry sea roaring furiously around their lonely dwelling. When they awoke, the sun was high in the heavens, the tempest had ceased, and only the swell of the sea rose in silvery heavings against the red rock.

"What can that be?" said the old woman, as she peeped out of the door.

"It looks like a big seal," said Matte.

"As sure as I live, it's a cow!" exclaimed Maie. And certainly it was a cow, a fine red cow, fat and flourishing, and looking as if it had been fed all its days on spinach. It wandered peacefully up and down the shore, and never so much as even looked at the poor little tufts of grass, as if it despised such fare.

Matte could not believe his eyes. But a cow she seemed, and a cow she was found to be; and when the old woman began to milk her, every pitcher and pan, even to the baler, was soon filled with the most delicious milk.

The old man troubled his head in vain as to how she came there, and sallied forth to seek for his lost net. He had not proceeded far when he found it cast up on the shore, and so full of fish that no mesh was visible.

"It is all very fine to possess a cow," said Matte, as he cleaned the fish; "but what are we going to feed her on?"

"We shall find some means," said his wife; and the cow found the means herself. She went out and cropped the seaweed which grew in great abundance near the shore, and always kept in good condition. Everyone, Prince alone excepted, thought she was a clever beast; but Prince barked at her, for he had now got a rival.

From that day the red rock overflowed with milk and junket, and every net was filled with fish. Matte and Maie grew fat on this fine living, and daily became richer. She churned quantities of butter, and he hired two men to help him in his fishing. The sea lay before him like a big fish tank, out of which he hauled as many as he required; and the cow continued to fend for herself. In autumn, when Matte and Maie went ashore, the cow went to sea, and in spring, when they returned to the rock, there she stood awaiting them.

"We shall require a better house," said Maie the following summer; "the old one is too small for ourselves and the men."

"Yes," said Matte. So he built a large cottage, with a real lock to the door, and a store-house for fish as well; and he and his men caught such quantities of fish that they sent tons of salmon, herring, and cod to Russia and Sweden.

"I am quite overworked with so many folk," said Maie; "a girl to help me would not go amiss."

"Get one, then," said her husband; and so they hired a girl.

Then Maie said: "We have too little milk for all these folk. Now that I have a servant, with the same amount of trouble she could look after three cows." "All right, then," said her husband, somewhat provoked, "you can sing a song to the fairies."

This annoyed Maie, but nevertheless she rowed out to sea on Sunday night and sang as before:

Oh, Ahti, with the long, long beard,
Who dwellest in the deep blue sea,
A thousand cows are in thy herd,
I pray thee give three unto me.

The following morning, instead of one, three cows stood on the island, and they all ate seaweed and fended for themselves like the first one.

"Art thou satisfied now?" said Matte to his wife.

"I should be quite satisfied," said his wife, "if only I had two servants to help, and if I had some finer clothes. Don't you know that I am addressed as Madam?"

"Well, well," said her husband. So Maie got several servants, and clothes fit for a great lady.

"Everything would now be perfect if only we had a little better dwelling for summer. You might build us a two-storey house, and fetch soil to make a garden. Then you might make a little arbour up there to let us have a sea-view; and we might have a fiddler to fiddle to us of an evening, and a little steamer to take us to church in stormy weather."

"Anything more?" asked Matte; but he did everything that his wife wished. The rock Ahtola became so grand and Maie so great that all the sea-urchins and herring were lost in wonderment. Even Prince was fed on beefsteaks and cream scones till at last he was as round as a butter jar.

"Are you satisfied now?" asked Matte.

"I should be quite satisfied," said Maie, "if only I had thirty cows. At least that number is required for such a household."

"Go to the fairies," said Matte.

His wife set out in the new steamer and sang to the sea king. Next morning thirty cows stood on the shore, all finding food for themselves.

"Know'st thou, good man, that we are far too cramped on this wretched rock, and where am I to find room for so many cows?"

"There is nothing to be done but to pump out the sea."

"Rubbish!" said his wife. "Who can pump out the sea?"

"Try with thy new steamer, there is a pump in it."

Maie knew well that her husband was only making fun of her, but still her mind was set upon the same subject. 'I never could pump the sea out,' thought she, 'but perhaps I might fill it up, if I were to make a big dam. I might heap up sand and stones, and make our island as big again.'

Maie loaded her boat with stones and went out to sea. The fiddler was with her, and fiddled so finely that Ahti and Wellamos and all the sea's daughters rose to the surface of the water to listen to the music.

"What is that shining so brightly in the waves?" asked Maie.

"That is sea foam glinting in the sunshine," answered the fiddler.

"Throw out the stones," said Maie.

The people in the boat began to throw out the stones, splash, splash, right and left, into the foam. One stone hit the nose of Wellamos's chief lady-in-waiting, another scratched the sea queen herself on the cheek, a third plumped close to Ahti's head and tore off half of the sea king's beard; then there was a commotion in the sea, the waves bubbled and bubbled like boiling water in a pot.

"Whence comes this gust of wind?" said Maie; and as she spoke the sea opened and swallowed up the steamer. Maie sank to the bottom like a stone, but, stretching out her arms and legs, she rose to the surface, where she found the fiddler's fiddle, and used it as a float. At the same moment she saw close beside her the terrible head of Ahti, and he had only half a beard!

"Why did you throw stones at me?" roared the sea king.

"Oh, your majesty, it was a mistake! Put some bear's grease on your beard and that will soon make it grow again."

"Dame, did I not give you all you asked for – nay, even more?"

"Truly, truly, Your Majesty. Many thanks for the cows."

"Well, where is the gold from the sun and the silver from the moon that you promised me?"

"Ah, Your Majesty, they have been scattered day and night upon the sea, except when the sky was overcast," slyly answered Maie.

"'Til teach you!" roared the sea king; and with that he gave the fiddle such a 'puff' that it sent the old woman up like a sky-rocket on to her island. There Prince lay, as famished as ever, gnawing the carcase of a crow. There sat Matte in his ragged grey jacket, quite alone, on the steps of the old hut, mending a net.

"Heavens, mother," said he, "where are you coming from at such a whirlwind pace, and what makes you in such a dripping condition?"

Maie looked around her amazed, and said, "Where is our two-storey house?"

"What house?" asked her husband.

"Our big house, and the flower garden, and the men and the maids, and the thirty beautiful cows, and the steamer, and everything else?"

"You are talking nonsense, mother," said he. "The students have quite turned your head, for you sang silly songs last evening while we were rowing, and then you could not sleep till early morning. We had stormy weather during the night, and when it was past I did not wish to wake you, so rowed out alone to rescue the net."

"But I've seen Ahti," rejoined Maie.

"You've been lying in bed, dreaming foolish fancies, mother, and then in your sleep you walked into the water."

"But there is the fiddle," said Maie.

"A fine fiddle! It is only an old stick. No, no, old woman, another time we will be more careful. Good luck never attends fishing on a Sunday."

Sampo Lappelill

(A Story from Lappland)

ONCE UPON A TIME THERE WAS A LAPPLANDER and his wife. Do you know what that means? The Lapps are a people who live in the extreme north, far beyond Norway, Sweden, and Finland. In Lappland there are no fields, nor fine forests, nor houses such as we are accustomed to see, but only desolate stretches of country and high mountains and little huts into which one must creep through a hole, and that is the country where the Lapps live. Theirs is a strange land. Part of the year it is always light, for the sun never goes down in summer, and the rest of the year there is almost perpetual darkness, for in winter the stars are shining all day. Winter lasts for ten months of the year – there is sledging all that time – and one may see the squat little Lapps driving over the snow in things like boats, which are called "pulkas" there is no horse harnessed to the "pulka," only a reindeer. Have you ever seen a reindeer? It is about the size of a pony, with great branching horns, a short neck, and pretty little head with large bright eyes; when he runs he flies like a whirlwind over mountain and brook, so that his hoofs strike against each other, and sound crack – crack! This the Lapp thinks great fun, as he sits in his "pulka" and he would like to have such fine sledging all the year round.

There was once, as before mentioned, a Lapp and his wife. They lived far away in Lappland, at a place called Aimio, which is situated between the Rivers Tenejoki and Tana. You may see it in the top part of a map of Finland, where the boundary line of Lappland comes down like a big white nightcap on Finland's high head. That place is desolate and wild, but the old Lapp and his wife thought that in no place in all the world was there to be found such white snow and such bright stars, and such lovely northern lights as just there in Aimio. They built themselves a hut there, after exactly the same pattern as all the other Lapp huts. Trees do not grow there, only small spindly birches, which were more like bushes than trees, so where could they find wood to build a cottage? To make the hut, they took long straight sticks, and stuck them in the snow, and tied them together at the top. Then they hung reindeer skins over the poles, which made it look just like a grey sugar-loaf, and then their hut was finished. At the top of the sugarloaf they left a little hole, through which the smoke might escape when a fire was lit in the hut, and another little hole in the south side by which one could creep in and out. That is what the Lapp hut was like, and the Lapps themselves thought it delightful and warm, and quite grand inside, although they had no bed and no floor, nothing but the white snow.

The peasant and his wife had a little boy called Sampo, which is considered a lucky name in Lappland. But Sampo was rich, for he had two names – one was not enough.

Once there had come strangers – gentlemen in big fur coats, and they had stayed in the hut. They brought with them a hard white bit of snow of a kind which the Lapps had never seen before, and which was called sugar. They gave some bits of the sweet snow to Sampo, patted him on the cheek, and said, "Lappelill, Lappelill!" which means "little Lapp" They could not say more, for none of them spoke the Lapp language. And then they travelled away still farther north to the White Sea, and to the most northern point of Europe, which is called the North Cape. But the Lapp woman often thought of the strangers and their sweet snow, and so she began to call her boy "Lappelill."

"I think Sampo is a much better name," said the man, somewhat angered. "Sampo means wealth, and I tell you, mother, don't you spoil the name! Our Sampo will yet be a king among the Lapps and reign over a thousand reindeer and fifty huts. You shall see mother, you shall see!"

"Yes, but Lappelill sounds so uncommon," said the woman, and she called her boy Lappelill, and the father called him Sampo.

Now you must know that the boy had not yet been baptized, for at that time there was no priest to be found for twenty miles round. "Next year we shall drive to the priests and have the boy baptized," the father used to say. But next year they were prevented, and the journey was put off, and the boy remained unchristened.

Sampo Lappelill was now a little chubby boy of seven or eight years old, with black hair, brown eyes, a snub nose, and wide mouth, just like his own papa's, but in Lappland that is looked upon as a mark of beauty.

Sampo was no weakling for his years; he had his own little skates on which he shot down the steep sides of the Tana and his own little reindeer which he used to harness, and his own little "pulka." Swish! you should have seen how the snow whirled around him as he was carried across the ice and through the drifts which were so deep that nothing was seen of the youngster but a tuft of his black pow!

"I shall never feel happy until the boy has been baptized," said the Lapp woman. "The wolves might make off with him some fine day on the fjeld, or he might encounter Hüsi's reindeer with the golden. horns, and the Lord pity him then if he were not baptized!"

Sampo heard these words, and began to wonder what kind of a reindeer it could be that had golden horns.

"It must be a beautiful deer," said he. "Wouldn't I like to drive him some day and go to Rastekais!"

Rastekais is a high and lonely mountain about five or six miles distant from Amio.

"How can you dare to chatter so foolishly, you thoughtless rascal?" scolded the mother. "Rastekais is the place where the Trolls have their home, and their too lives Hüsi."

"Hüsi; who's that?" asked Sampo.

The mother was taken aback.

"So the youngster has ears," thought she to herself. "Perhaps I should not speak of such things in this hearing, but it might be as well to put an end to his fancy for an excursion to Rastekais." So she said:

"Lappelill, dear, don't go to Rastekais, for that is where Hüsi, the great King of the Fjeld lives – he who eats a reindeer at one mouthful, and swallows little boys like midges!"

At these words Sampo looked very thoughtful, but he remained silent, while at the same time saying to himself:

"It would be at least interesting for once to see such a monster as the Fjeld King – but only at a distance!"

Although it was now three or four weeks since Christmas, still it was quite dark in Lappland. There was no morning, nor noon, nor evening, it was always night, and the moon shone, and the Northern Lights crackled, and the stars twinkled all the day long.

Sampo began to weary. It was so long since he had seen the sun that he had almost forgotten what it looked like, and when anybody spoke of summer, Sampo remembered nothing about it except that it was the season when midges were so nasty and tried to eat him up. So Sampo thought it would not matter if summer went away altogether, if only it would get light enough for him to see to skate.

One day at twelve o'clock (but it was quite dark) the Lappman said:

"Come here, and you will see something!"

Sampo crept out of the hut and looked intently towards the south to where his father pointed. There he saw a little red streak on the horizon.

"Do you know what that is?" asked the Lapp.

"That is the Southern Aurora," said the boy.

He had a good idea of the directions of the wind, and knew very well that one never saw the Northern Lights in the south.

"No," said the father. "That is the forerunner of the sun. Tomorrow or next day we shall see the sun itself. See how wonderfully the red light glows on the top of Rastekais!"

Sampo turned westwards, and saw how the snow in the far distance was tinged with red on the dark, gloomy top of Rastekais, a place which he had not seen for so long. Immediately again the thought flashed through his brain, "How delightfully exciting it would be to see the Fjeld King at a distance."

Sampo pondered over the subject all day and half the night. He ought to have slept, but could not.

'No,' thought he, 'it would be interesting just for once to see the Fjeld King,' and as he thought and thought, at last he crept quietly from under the reindeer skin coverlet where he lay, and out through the door hole. It was so cold that the stars glistened and the snow crackled under foot, but Sampo Lappelill was not a coddled youth, so he did not mind this in the least. Besides, he had on a fur jacket, fur trousers, fur shoes, fur cap, and fur gloves. Thus equipped, he looked at the stars, and wondered what he should do next. Just then he heard his little reindeer, not far off, scraping in the snow. 'Perhaps I might drive a bit?' thought Sampo. No sooner said than done, Sampo harnessed the reindeer to the "pulka," which he was well accustomed to do, and drove out with all speed on to the vast dreary snow plain. 'Twill drive a little way towards Rastekais, but only quite a little way,' thought he to himself; and then he was carried over the frozen river, and up the other side of the Tana, and then he was at the frontier of the kingdom of Norway, because the Tana forms the boundary, but this Sampo did not know. He sat and sang to himself—

"Short is the day,
And long is the way,
Rest we dare not, here,
For the wolves are near,"

and as he sang he saw the wolves, like grey dogs, running in the darkness all around the sledge and snapping at the reindeer. Sampo was not the least afraid, for he well knew that no wolf was so nimble of foot as his clever reindeer. Oh! how it carried him over hills and stones, till the latter rattled about his ears! Sampo Lappelill just let him go. Crack went the reindeer's hoofs, and the moon in heaven ran a race with him, and the high fjelds seemed to be running backwards, but still Sampo Lappelill let him go. It was such fun driving, and that was all he thought of. It happened, in taking a sharp turn down hill, that the "pulka" upset, and Sampo fell out on the snow. The reindeer did not notice this, but thought that Sampo was still sitting quietly in the "pulka," so he ran on, and Sampo, having his mouth filled with snow could not call out – "*Ptrroh, ptrroh*!" (stop, stop!) – only that is what one says to horses, but not to reindeer! There he lay, like a footless field-mouse, out in the dark night, and in the middle of the vast plain, where no one lived within many miles.

Sampo, as is not to be wondered at, was somewhat astounded at first. He crawled up out of the snow, and was not in the least hurt; but that did not comfort him. All around him, as far as he could see by the pale moonlight, there were nothing but drifts and fields of snow, and high mountains. One mountain was much higher than all the others, and Sampo now knew that he was quite near

Rastekais. Suddenly it occurred to him that here lived the savage King of the Fjeld, who ate up a reindeer at a mouthful, and swallowed little boys like midges. Then Sampo Lappelill began to be afraid. Ah, how gladly would he now have been safe at home in the warm hut beside his father and mother, but how was he ever to get there? And perhaps the Fjeld King would find him in the drift and swallow him up, trousers, and gloves, and all, just like any other poor little midge.

Yes, there sat Sampo Lappelill alone in the snow and darkness, on Lappland's dreary plains; it was all so weird and awesome as he looked towards the high dark form of the mountain Rastekais where the Fjeld King lived. What use was it to sit there and cry? for all his tears turned at once into ice, and rolled like peas down his hairy skin coat.

Sampo saw it was useless, so he got up out of the snowdrift and ran about to warm himself.

"If I stay here, I shall be frozen to death," said he to himself; "well, it would be better to face the Fjeld King than that.

If he eat me up, I'm eaten, but I shall tell him he had better eat up the wolves on the fjeld. They would make a fatter roast than I, and he would have less trouble with the skin," whereupon Sampo started to climb the high mountain. He had not been climbing long when he heard something rustle in the snow, and a great shaggy wolf sprang up close by him. Then Sampo's little Lappish heart went pit-a-pat, but he resolved to appear as if he were not the least afraid.

"Don't stand in my way," he called out to the Wolf. "I have an errand to the Fjeld King, and look out for your skin if you come too near me!"

"Gently, gently, not so fast," said the Wolf (for on Rastekais all the animals can talk). "What little dwarf are you trudging along in the snow?"

"My name is Sampo Lappelill," answered the boy; "and who are you?"

"I am Grand Marshal to the Fjeld King," answered the wild animal, "and I have been running round the mountain to summon his people to the great Sun Festival. As you are going the same way as I am, you may sit on my back, and get a ride to the mountain."

Sampo did not long consider, but climbed up on the Wolf's shaggy coat, and was carried at a gallop over cliffs and precipices.

"What does that mean, 'the Sun Festival'?" asked Sampo.

"Don't you know?" said the Wolf. "After the winter's darkness in Lappland, and the sun is seen for the first time in the heavens, then we have the Sun Festival. All the wild animals and all the Trolls in the north assemble at Rastekais, and for that day they are quite harmless. It is lucky for you, Sampo Lappelill, otherwise I would have eaten you up long ago."

"Does the Fjeld King obey the same law?" asked Sampo.

"Of course," said the Wolf. "For one hour before the sun rises, and for one hour after it sets, the Fjeld King himself would not venture to touch a hair of your head. But beware when the time is up, for should you still be tarrying on the field, a hundred thousand wolves and a thousand bears would rush upon you, and then there would be a speedy ending of Sampo Lappelill."

"Perhaps you will be so kind as to help me back again when it is time to start?" timidly asked Sampo.

The Wolf began to laugh (for on Rastekais the wolves could laugh). "Don't imagine that, Sampo dear," said he. "On the contrary, I shall be the first to dig my teeth into you. You are a plump and dainty morsel; I see that you have been fattened on reindeer milk and cheese. You will be a delicious breakfast for me early in the morning."

Sampo wondered if it would not be as well to jump down at once from the Wolf's back, but it was now too late. They had already reached the top of the mountain, and there they saw an extraordinary sight. The Fjeld King sat on his throne, which was made of rocks that nearly reached the sky, and he gazed out into the darkness over mountain and valley. On his head he wore a cap of white snow clouds; his eyes were like the full moon, as it rises over the forest; his nose was as the top of a mountain, and his mouth like the cleft of one; his beard was like a bunch of long icicles; his arms were as thick as the thickest fir tree; his hands were like fir-cones; his legs and feet were like a toboggan hill in winter, and his wide fur coat was like a snow mountain. But, if you ask, how could the Fjeld King and his people be seen in the darkness, you must know that the snow shone all around them, and far across the arch of heaven there glistened the most brilliant Aurora, which lit up the whole expanse.

Around the Fjeld King were seated millions of trolls and fairies, so small, that when they tripped upon the snow their footprints were no larger than those of a squirrel. They had gathered together from the remotest parts of the world, from Nova Zembla, Spitzbergen, Greenland, and Iceland, even from the North Pole itself, in order to worship the sun – not that they really liked it, for the Trolls would have been very well pleased to see the sun sink, and never rise again. It was from fear, just as savages worship evil spirits. And, farther away, stood all the big and little animals which live in Lappland. They stood in long, close rows, thousands and thousands of them, from bears, wolves, and gluttons, down to the harmless reindeer, the little field-mouse, and the active reindeer-flea; the mosquitoes were prevented from coming, as they had been frozen to death.

Sampo Lappelill saw all this with much amazement. He climbed stealthily down from the Wolf's back, and hid himself behind a large stone, to see what would happen next. The Fjeld King raised his massive head, which made the snow whirl about him, and then the Aurora seemed to shine like a glory round him. It shot out in long, starry, pale red streaks, across the blue night heavens; it crackled and it whizzed, just as when a forest is on fire the flames twist and twine up the trees; it expanded and contracted, it grew denser and paler by turns, so that one gleam of light after another flashed across the snowy fjeld. This amused the Fjeld King. He clapped his icy hands, which echoed like thunder through the mountains, the Trolls shrieked with delight, and the animals squealed from fear. But this only amused the Fjeld King the more, so he called out loud over the mountain:

"That's it! that's it! Eternal winter and night! That is what I like!"

"That is right! that is right!" shrieked the Trolls at the top of their voices, for they all liked winter and darkness better than summer and sunshine. There was much grumbling heard amongst the animals, for all the beasts of prey, including field-mice thought. the same as the Trolls, but the reindeer and the others had no fault to find with summer, if only they had not remembered Lappland's mosquitoes. The Flea was the only one who wished to have summer without any alterations, so she piped as loud as she could:

"My Lord King, I thought we were assembled here to greet the returning sun!"

"Silence! you miserable insect!" roared the White Bear beside her. "We only assemble here because of an old custom. It is at least pleasurable this year, the sun seems to have gone away altogether. The sun is extinguished! the sun is dead!"

"The sun is extinguished! the sun is dead!" murmured all the animals, and all Nature shuddered. The Trolls from the North Pole laughed so much that their caps fell off. The great Fjeld King upraised his thunder voice and called out anew over the desert plains:

"That is right! that is right! The sun is dead! All the world shall fall down and hail me 'King of Eternal Winter and Darkness!'"

This enraged Sampo Lappelill as he sat behind the stone. He rose up, his little saucy nose in the air, and cried out:

"You are telling lies, Fjeld King, as big as yourself. Yesterday I saw the first streak of sunlight in the sky, and the sun is not dead. Your beard shall suffer when midsummer comes."

At these words the Fjeld King's forehead darkened like a thunder-cloud; he forgot the rule of that day, and lifted his terrifying arm to try to crush Sampo Lappelill. With that the Northern Lights paled, a red streak appeared in the heavens and lit up the frosty face of the Fjeld King, so that it quite blinded him, and he had to let his arm drop. Then the gilded edge of the sun rose slowly and majestically above the horizon and lit up the fjeld, the drifts, the cliffs, the Trolls, the animals, and the little manly Sampo Lappelill. All at once there shone a beam of light on the snow, and it looked as if millions of roses had been showered down on it, and the sun shone into every one's eyes, and right down into every heart. Even those who had rejoiced most that the sun was dead were now secretly glad to see it again. It was comical to see the amazement of the Trolls. They blinked at the sun with their little grey eyes from under their red night-caps, and although it was against their wish to see it, they were so charmed that they stood on their heads in the snow with delight. The Fjeld King's beard began to melt, and to drop down his enormous mantle in a trickling stream.

After all had gazed for some time with more or less joy at the sun, and the first hour had nearly passed, Sampo Lappelill heard one of the Reindeer say to her young one: "Come, come, dear child, or else we shall be devoured by the wolves!"

And then Sampo remembered what would happen to him if he tarried longer, so when he caught sight of a fine Reindeer near him, with branching golden horns, he hesitated no longer, but jumped on the animal's back, and was carried off at a sweeping pace down the mountain-side.

"What is that strange rustling which hear behind us?" asked Sampo after a while, for he had to take breath after his rapid run.

"Those are the thousand bears scampering after us to devour us," answered the Reindeer. "But don't be afraid. I am the Fjeld King's enchanted Reindeer, and no bear has ever nagged my heels."

So they rode a little farther. Then Sampo asked:

"What is that strange blowing which I hear behind us?"

The Reindeer answered: "Those are the hundred thousand wolves which havestarted at full gallop after us to tear you and me to pieces. But don't be afraid; no wolf has ever beaten me in a race across the fjeld."

So they rode a little farther, and Sampo Lappelill asked: "Do you think it is thundering behind us on the fjeld?"

"No," said the Reindeer, beginning to tremble in every limb; "it is the Fjeld King himself, who strides after us with giant steps, and now it will be all over for us both, for no one can escape him."

"Is there nothing to be done?" asked Sampo.

"No," said the Reindeer, "we can do nothing, except to try to reach the Parson's house at Enare, if we possibly can. Should we reach it, we are saved, for the Fjeld King has no power to touch those who have been christened."

"All right," said Sampo; "fly, my nimble Reindeer, over mountains and rocks, and I shall feed you with golden oats out of a silver trough!"

And the Reindeer ran and ran for dear life, and they had just got inside the Parson's house when the Fjeld King arrived and thundered so loudly on the door that everybody thought the house would fall down.

"Who is there?" asked the Priest.

"It is I," answered the thunder voice out in the garden. "Open to His Majesty the King of the Fjeld! There is an unchristened child here, and all heathens belong to me."

"Wait a little, till I get on my gown and bands, in order to receive so distinguished a personage in a becoming manner!" answered the Priest from within.

"All right," roared the Fjeld King; "best make haste, or else I will kick the walls of your house down."

"Coming, coming, your gracious Majesty!" answered the Priest, and with that he took a bowl of water and baptized Sampo Lappelill in the name of the Father, Son, and Holy Ghost.

"Well, are you ready yet?" roared the Fjeld King, who had just raised his terrible foot to knock the house down.

The Priest then opened the door and said: "Begone, you king of winter and darkness, for with this child you have nothing more to do! God's mercy now shines upon Sampo Lappelill, and he no more belongs to yours, but to God's kingdom."

This so enraged the Fjeld King that he at once blew up into a snowstorm, and the snow fell so very, very thick upon the house, and covered it up all over the roof, that all expected to find their graves in the drift. The Priest alone was calm, read his prayers out of his book of devotion and waited for morning. When morning dawned, the sun shone upon the snow, and the snow melted, and the Parsonage was saved, but the Fjeld King had disappeared, and no one is quite sure, but everybody imagines that he still lives and reigns in Rastekais.

Sampo Lappelill thanked the kind priest, and begged of him to lend him a "pulka." Then Sampo harnessed the Reindeer with the golden horns to the sledge, and thus he drove home to his parents at Aimio. But how Sampo afterwards became a great man, and fed his Reindeer with golden oats out of a silver trough, is another story, which would be too long to relate now.

It is said that the Lapps no longer delay, as they once used to do, bringing their children to be baptized, for who would willingly see his child eaten up by the Fjeld King? Sampo Lappelill knows what that means. He knows what is going on when the thunder rolls through the mountains.

Castles in the Air

SOMETIMES AT SUNSET IN THE SPRING TIME, the sky appears more than usually transparent: rosy and violet veils are spread before the sun to make his glow endurable. It happens then, that small golden clouds rise at the furthermost view of the horizon, and flit playfully about amongst each other. They constantly change colour, form, and places: they glimmer gloriously, but the tracings are so airy and ephemeral, that they seem to be the embodiment of mutability, they do not at all resemble the other clouds, that night and day are busy weaving their mystic veils in the heavens.

Why are they so beautiful and changeable? Why do they only float in those far distant regions? I will tell you. They are not rain-clouds but abodes of light, the castles in which the angels dwell in the azure sky, the beauteous supernal spirits who exist in those radiant realms of the universe. How can you fancy they could endure palaces of brick and marble, with sombre walls and zinc roofs, which would hide from their view the sun and stars? Radiant, transparent, airy and ever-changing forms like themselves are these abodes. They construct them of rays and sparkling gems, with walls of silvery moonbeams, and roof them in with the golden sunset. There they enjoy their gladsome existence in the freedom of the air, far above the mists of the earth, and thither not even the song of the lark nor the tumult of the strife below can penetrate; there brightness, serenity, beauty, and tranquillity adore God's presence. His love, His magnificence, His sanctity, and His greatness, are spread like an eternal broad daylight throughout the lustrous worlds.

Who of you dare to assert that the transparent air cannot support the fairy homes of the angels? Have you forgotten all the tales of your childhood? In the bowels of the earth dwell gnomes and dwarfs. In the fire triumphantly breathes the salamander. In the sea reigns Neptune, and the beautiful, bewitching sea-nymphs with their green flowing tresses of sea-weed. On the earth men, and all around them, in the woodlands and on the mountains, is heard the echo; and every hill and every vale, every spring and brook, every leaf and frond, abounds with myriads of living beings, some of which are seen, but far more are invisible. Yea, far away beyond the sun and moon, and far away where the stars glimmer from immeasurable distances, glorious beings are said to exist, very different from us, or anything we can conceive of, who gaze with strange and wondering vision upon our planet.

And do you imagine that the air alone is void because the birds do not nestle therein? The air which floods the earth like an unfathomable ocean, invisible to all, but felt and inhaled by every creature? Do you observe how the wind swells the sails of the vessels, and turns the wings of the mill, how it supports the fleet wings of the birds, and the flaunting kite with its long wavy tail? There is no such thing throughout the universe as void. Everywhere life and light; everywhere is spirit and beauty, and adoration. Every atom hath its inhabitants, every star hath beings; and you think that in the sky dwells nothing! Have you heard the story of Radigundis, the princess of the swans, floating in the air, a star amongst dark clouds, and scattering her white feathers over the meadows in the spring?

Are you acquainted with Cheristane, the elfin queen of eternal youth, and who is subject to no changes, though all the world around her withers and decays in old age?

Have you seen Oberon, the monarch of the air, who with his pipe makes everybody dance? or Titania, his wife, whose beauty and jealousy form the subject for so many tales?

Have you heard the Finnish tale of the girl who sits upon the evening clouds, and weaves a golden shade with silver shuttle ?

Would you like to see them and many more of the beauteous creatures of the fairy tales? If so, listen to what I tell you. Go down to the seashore one evening at sunset, press your right hand against the left side of your breast, and feel if your heart beats warmly and freely, eager for what is beautiful and pure in the world. Look then around you with the eye of a child, and you shall behold wonderful things in the rosy clouds of the sunset.

But if you glance at them with an indifferent eye and a cold heart, you will perceive nothing but fleeting clouds and the evening mist, foreboding rain on the morrow. All that is beautiful in the world must be beheld with innocent eyes, or it dissolves into vapour, perishes, and becomes naught. This is the canon law of beauty, once for all, I cannot help it.

Often when I was a wee lad I used to sit on the craggy shore, and admire the dancing waves glittering in the sunset. Round and round they went in circles and long shimmering rows far out on the blue deep, and in the distance they could no longer be distinguished one from another, till they all at last reached the uttermost limit of the main where the sea ceased and heaven began. That was the place where at midsummer time the sun dived into the sparkling waves for a short time. It was the shore of Wonderland, enchanting and delightful, the loved spot where the phantoms of fancy and the airy inhabitants of the sunset clouds gambolled with each other in the faint, blushing billows. They darted in the shape of rosy flickering flames to and fro over the mirroring waters, they danced, they chased each other, they had a "set to," and tumbled about and fought playfully, and then kissed each other in earnest. A merry race they were. They gathered long veils of haze that lay over the woodlands, rolled them together, and tied them over each other's eyes, and had a game at blind man's buff. Then it sometimes happened that one of them darted into the deep, and immediately a whole flock of the others followed in a shower of rosy sparkles; but the next moment the brilliant playmates rose anew, and with a gigantic leap were again seated astride on a golden cloud which slowly floated through the blue ether.

Some of the radiant beings were larger and stronger than others. They would pluck a starry gem from the heavens, and send it whizzing through the air. Many thousands of the little ones then stretched out their hands to catch the shooting star; but it followed the curve of the vaulted heavens, and fell into the sea like a display of fireworks, and burst into millions of sparkling atoms, besprinkling the waves like a spray of silver, a rain of diamonds, and this pleased the airy creatures beyond comprehension. They joined hands and danced all round the welkin, and the clouds hurriedly made way for them, and soon nothing was to be seen but the waving locks of their golden hair, which streamed behind, flashing like the Northern Lights, or electric waves and flames fanned by the evening wind. Such things we can see only when we are children. When we grow up there comes a film over our eyes, so that we no longer can perceive the iridescent bloom on the wings of the butterfly, or the soft and roseate colour on the petals of the flower, or the playful gambols of the ariels in the sunset of a summer evening.

There lived a little boy, named Elias, at the homestead of his father, which lay halfway between the great gloomy forest in the east, and the glorious ocean main stretching westward. He was a quiet and meek lad, with a great love for pretty fairytales.

"I am sure I don't know what will become of the lad when he grows up," was frequently uttered by the father, who was a sturdy farmer, and could draw a straighter furrow than any man in the county. "The lad has far too soft a heart and the complexion of a girl, and that is not the stuff to make a bluff hearty farmer of. Aye, but his brother Eric is made of stronger stuff, with arms of iron and sturdy legs as if they were brazen mould; and Elias gazes into the air as if he would take a census of the gnats, while Eric carts the manure into the fields, and don't care for anybody. Believe me, sir, Eric will become a rich man, while Elias will dwell in the clouds with sunbeams for breakfast and moonshine for supper."

"Well, but that depends upon what he will be taught," said the schoolmaster, who had read many books, and knew a thing or two. "'Tis all very well to have a strong arm, and the country may even yet need such; but clever heads are also needed, to guide the arms and comprehend superior things in the world. Send Elias to school, and we will soon find out what he is meant for."

"Well, I think I will take your advice," answered the father, and Elias forthwith became a private pupil of the schoolmaster.

One evening in the autumn, when twilight had set in, the legitimate time for telling fairytales and adventures, all the children were seated around the fire, which threw out a ruddy glare on all things, eagerly listening to deaf old Kajsa, who knew more stories than anybody else, and could not be interrupted in her narratives by troublesome questions. By her they were at once introduced into Wonderland, where princesses dwelt in enchanted castles surrounded by orange groves, where sang the gorgeous birds of paradise, and the children wondered if old Kajsa had really been there herself, since she seemed so thoroughly at home in describing its details. She recited to her wondering audience legends of silver palaces, where the good fairies live, where everything sparkles with precious gems, and of the mystic home of the water-sprite, who dwells at the bottom of the lake, and sits on a throne of mother-of-pearl; and she spoke of the hazy mountains in Ginnistan, where the golden pheasants build their nests, but which constantly recede before the wanderer's foot, even if he proceeds in the same direction for twenty years.

"Oh, don't I wish I could only once see a castle of silver and rubies," said little Peter, the son of the village carpenter.

Elias lifted up his head at these wistful words, and his big soft eyes beamed with love, and he nodded with a friendly smile and said: "That you also easily may do; I see that almost every day."

"You!" cried all the children. "You!" reiterated Eric, and laughed derisively; "well, what next! I don't think you will find many castles of silver about here, amongst the firs and junipers."

"Well, then, all of you come with me tomorrow evening a little before sunset," Elias remarked quietly.

"Agreed," all cried, and the following evening all the children accompanied Elias to a cliff on the seashore, where there was a fine view of the sea.

"It is not such a glorious sight now as at midsummer," Elias said. "The ariels grieve that the summer has fled; they don't dance now so merrily as before, but we need not wait long, they will soon appear." And the children gazed with wonder and great expectation over the main to the horizon which was being painted in purple and gold by way of prelude, and the performers were waiting to enter upon the scene.

The golden disc had barely touched the margin of the sea before a flood of rosy light suffused the waves and illumed the clouds, and towering castles with silver turrets and colonnades of gold burst upon their vision, and airy phantoms were seen to emerge and join in the festive dance amongst the floating clouds.

It was a glorious and enchanting sight. Elias clapped his hands in ecstasy, and called out: "Look! look! here they come!" And all the children looked to where he pointed; but some of them discerned nothing but clouds, others beheld the castles but not the phantoms; only one little ragged girl, like Elias, clapped her hands and cried quite beyond herself with joy, "I see them, I see them, here they come!"

"Who are come?" asked Eric, who was also one of the party. "I see nothing but a few ragged clouds moved by the wind. The clouds are only humid vapours, Father has told me, and I happen to know something more about those things than you."

"Well, do tell us what you know!" said the children.

"I know a proverb that says:

'Evening red and morning grey,
Are two sure signs of one fine day.'"

"No, that's not it," said one of the other boys, "this is it:

'Evening grey and morning red
Brings rain upon the shepherd's head.'"

"Why, you lout, that is the end of the same proverb!"

"No, it isn't," cried the other.

"Yes, it is, and I'll prove it to you," and with that Eric gave his adversary a box on the ear, and then the two boys began fighting furiously in the glowing sunset.

"Nay, but look how beautiful it is!" exclaimed Elias, and the little beggar-girl and several of the children repeated with delight, "Nay, but look how beautiful it is!" Just then broad streaks spread in the azure vault, the airy phantoms formed a circle around their golden castle, and moved in a graceful undulating dance, and some scattered themselves along the blue main of the sky, and with renewed impetus began travelling in fantastic gyrations, as if they had been swift skaters, inscribing their hieroglyphic names on crystal ice.

"Just you wait a bit," cried the boy who had been beaten by Eric; "I'll go home and tell Father."

"Oh, but why don't you look?" Elias cried out. "Now a tower rises high in the air on the principal castle in the sky, tipped with a silver spire, carrying aloft a golden cross, and red flames flicker all around."

"I don't care for any such foolery," said Eric, annoyed.

"Oh, but stay yet awhile," entreated little Peter, who, like Elias and the girl, had eyes for the gorgeous display of the heavens. "Oh, what beautiful clear colours! Look at the opposite shores, lit up with bright green and gold! Look how the mountain-ridges shimmer against the sky, and how the swans swim in the creek, and the lazy swell of the rose-coloured wave against the cliff yonder, dissolving into a spray of silver."

"And listen to the lullaby of the billows, and how the trees and sedges are humming the same tune," observed the beggar-girl.

"And look there," resumed Elias; presses a multitude of warrior phantoms, with flashing swords and glittering helmets, to storm the castle, and there comes the king with a crown on his head, leading by the hand a princess clad in dazzling white robes. Nay, but look how beautiful she is! And down there in that dark chasm waits a hideous dragon with fiery jaws, and all the flaming spirits, the king's champion-subjects, rush back from the sea; they now gather into dense masses near the battlements of the castle; they throw a shower of golden darts upon the enemy, and now the belligerent forces meet in battle array! Look how the bright helmets and coronets are cloven asunder by the flashing swords. A whirlwind comes from the sea in the east, and shakes the very foundations of the castle, it trembles! totters! ah, it falls into crumbling ruins! It is on fire! but through the ambient flames are still descried the glaives of the phantom warriors, the wide-flowing robes of the princess, woven from the first faint rays of the rising moon."

"Well, it is all moonshine with you," muttered Eric contemptuously. "Did ever anybody hear such stuff? Now I am off home to have my supper of stirabout."

"Yes, let us all go home and have our porridge!" cried most of the children in chorus.

Only Elias and the little beggar-girl, with litte Peter, remained on the strand until the last flush of the golden sunset had faded away, and the airy play of the celestial band had flitted into the starry regions of the night.

Since that evening twelve years have sped, bringing many changes in the lives of the children. Eric had become a sturdy, well-to-do farmer, who managed his father's lands with skill and foresight, turning the soil, draining the marshes, and clearing new spaces in the wilderness. Elias had for several years been travelling in foreign lands, and when he returned he had written many beautiful books on the prodigious wonders of nature.

One evening two young men stood on the cliff by the sea, and gazed with thoughtful yet childlike eyes upon the gambols of the aerials in the sky. The immortal spirits never grow old, but the two friends had travelled with time. It was Elias, and his companion was little Peter, who had been most struck with the transparency of the colours in the landscape, and had observed the swans. The little fellow had now grown up and had become a painter. He was an artist famed for the glorious blending of colours in his works. Elias was a poet – one of the few who transcribe direct from nature.

They looked at the sunset, then glanced at each other and smiled; brotherly love lighting up their faces when they read each other's thoughts.

"Well, yes, everything is as it used to be," they said, "only our eyes are not so keen as when we were children; a filmy veil is already thrown over some of the aerial's display and the brightness of creation, but let us humbly thank God, who has endowed our eyes with capacity to penetrate the mystic veil and behold the glorious forms."

"Do you remember that evening," asked Peter gaily, "when we stood here enchanted by the gorgeous display in the clouds at sunset, and Eric, in the midst of our joy and ecstasy, urged us to go home and eat stirabout?"

"Yes," answered Elias, "I remember it perfectly well; and the porridge has given Eric strong sinewy arms, while our love for the beautiful in nature has endowed us with the wings of poetry and art. But there was with us that evening a third, who saw and heard more than the others. It was a poor beggar-girl. She was the only one who heard the music quavering over the billows. It was the third gift which lay dormant amongst us children, the entrancing power of music, by the influence of which men's hearts melt like wax. Where is this our sister now? Sister in the chosen family of the few. What may have become of poverty's step-child?"

"Oh, she was destitute, besides like ourselves being untaught, and may not, like us, have been fortunate enough to get her great gift developed by proper training, to make her conscious of the heavenly spark within. Alas! many great and glorious endowments are thus lost to the world."

While Elias was still speaking, they heard from the forest a clear resonant voice singing a ballad, pure and simple as if the verdant wood itself had composed it in a peaceful sylvan glade. From amongst the trees appeared a shepherd-girl driving her cattle home for the evening, and approaching the place where the two young friends were standing, and they recognized in her the little beggar-girl of bygone times. She also knew them again, and greeted them joyfully in her simple manner, and she sang to them beautiful ballads, quaint pretty ditties, such as are only to be learnt from conversing with the flowers of the meadows and the whisperings in the wood. And the poet and the painter both listened attentively, while their hearts beat responsive to those simple lays, sung in the clear stillness of the evening.

"Ah!" said Elias with emotion; "God's beautiful gifts are never bestowed in vain. They have a mission of joy to spread amongst the poor and unlearned, as well as amongst he rich and refined; and I thank Thee, great Heaven, that Thou dost allow what is beautiful upon earth constantly and eternally to make its way through trial and privation, contempt and neglect, and we know now that if many gifts are lost because they are not properly nurtured, new flowers of equally exquisite fragrance are constantly growing up in the fertile soil of nature. We also shall perish, but that eternal beauty, which we humbly strive to attain in our efforts, shall not die, but live evermore in new successions of glorious flowers. And thus we sing and paint with joyous hearts, for we sing and picture that which is eternal."

The disc of the sun again touched the margin of the sea, and the whole heavens flushed with joy; and then again appeared the beautifully shimmering castles in the air, with crystal colonnades and towers, and spires of glittering silver; and the spirits again floated through its portals, and dived into the sea, so that the silvery billows laughed with sparkling glee, and then again they formed a ring-dance around their mystic azure world. Hills and vales basked in the glory, snowy swans swam towards the shore, and over the water floated a crystal tone, and the rays of the setting sun spread gloriously over the three chosen ones on the cliff – the poet, the painter and the songstress from the verdant wood.

The Silver Chalice

A WATER LILY WHISPERED TO ME THE FOLLOWING STORY:

They possessed a small flat-bottomed boat, and four nets, with which they went out fishing during the summer months; and when the strawberries began to ripen on the hillsides, the old man sat alone in the boat with his fishing-rod, while his granddaughter went up the hills to gather the fruit. One day when the sun was scorching hot, they went out in the boat and rowed towards the furthermost isle on the coast, when the old man became thirsty, and said:

"Lizzie, my child, take the jar and fetch me a little water from some spring on the hill-side, for you know I can't drink the salt sea water."

"Yes, Grandfather," she answered readily, and at once took the earthenware jar and leaped ashore. It was a wild and uncultivated tract of mountain and dark forest-land. Little Lizzie ran along over hill and vale, until she was quite red in the face from exertion and the heat, but she found no spring, for it was such a hot summer that they had all dried up. At last she became very tired and went but slowly, and as she passed under the sombre fir trees strange thoughts arose within her, the like of which she had never before experienced. She fancied that the tall trees looked strangely at her, and she felt so lonely in the great wide world.

Then something rustled in the woods, and a shrill piping voice cried out: "Why are you so lonely, Lizzie dear; where is your sweetheart?"

She looked up startled, but saw nothing except a ptarmigan perched on the waving branches of an old birch. She felt frightened and began to run, but stumbled over an old tree-trunk that lay in her way, and, smash! there lay the earthen jar broken into many pieces.

"There! goodbye to you," she said ruefully. She was now in a fix. Grandfather was waiting all the time in the boat, and poor Lizzie had nothing to fetch water in to quench the old man's thirst.

She seated herself on the luckless tree stump and began to cry, and then she heard another faintly purring sound distinctly asking: "Why are you so lonely, Lizzie, dear; where is your sweetheart?"

She looked around, but could see nothing but a squirrel that peered at her slyly from among the branches of a luxuriant fir tree. This vexed her. What business was it of the squirrel's if she chose to go alone in the woods? She turned her back upon him ungraciously and went away. But she had not proceeded far before she heard the same question repeated for the third time; "Why are you so lonely, Lizzie dear; where is your sweetheart?" This time it came from a beautiful and strange bird, with gold shimmering on his wings, soaring in the sky.

What stupid talk is this?" she said. "Grandfather is still waiting in the boat for me to take him some water, and here I have broken our only jar."

"Maybe; but where is your sweetheart?" asked the golden bird from on high.

"Well, how stupid you are, to be sure!" rejoined Lizzie. "Don't you know that I love my grandfather better than anybody else in the whole world? How, then, can I have a sweetheart?" And the little girl thought these questions were quite irreverent and uncalled for, and she turned her steps towards the seashore to find her grandfather again; but she did not escape her tormentors for all that, oh dear no. All the trees and the brushwood and stones around her seemed endowed with life, and began chattering, scattered old tree-stumps began to mutter, the blueberry shrubs whispered at her feet, and the mossy grey mountains on which she trod sighed softly: "Lizzie dear, Lizzie dear, where is your sweetheart?" This the girl thought was going a little too far, and no wonder; so she took to her heels and ran as fast as she could, crying out right and left: "Stupid old wood! crazy old mountains! who cares for you? Yah!"

At last she came to her grandfather in the boat. "Oh dear, oh dear!" she cried, " I have broken the jar, and have got nothing else to fetch water in, Grandfather."

"Ah! that is always the way," muttered the old man, "when a child is sent on an errand. But, Lizzie, why have you been so long away?"

She told him where she had been, and what she had heard in the wood. "Never mind that, child," said he; "'tis only tittle-tattle in the trees, when the branches rustle against each other, and it only means that we shall have rain tomorrow. A sweetheart, what nonsense that is!"

"Well, but I've got one, you know," said Lizzie.

"Yes, the kitten."

"Then I've two, Grandfather. Why, you are the other."

"You are a good little girl. Take the empty little butterbox, and try once more to find some water for me, for I am nearly parched with thirst."

She took the small vessel and resumed her search for water in the forest, which was now perfectly quiet; in fact, so quiet that it was almost too quiet. "If, at least, I could hear a linnet twitter," she thought to herself, but all the little birds kept silent. She saw a wild briar which had burst into bloom that day, and which spread an uncommonly strong and delightful scent for such a flower.

Lizzie culled some of the pretty little blossoms to give to her grandfather, but there was something traced on the petals; and when she looked at it and began spelling to see what it meant, she found the same vexing question: "Why are you so lonely, Lizzie dear; where is your sweetheart?"

"Are you also worrying yourself about me?" she asked, and at once flung the flowers away. "Has the wood grown daft? I can't make it out. Has it got nothing else to think of?"

She continued her search for water, but found no spring; she found instead what she did not expect, viz. that on all the stones and bushes was scribbled the same tiresome question: "Why are you so lonely, Lizzie dear; where is your sweetheart?"

"Well, I am sure the wood is quite crazy; I must keep my eyes shut," thought Lizzie, and she pressed her eyes as hard together as she could, but was compelled to peep just a little at times, so as not to stumble on the stones and trunks of trees. At last she came to the shore, but without having found any water to fill Grandfather's butter-box with. She already bethought herself to return to the boat a second time, when she descried a deep cleft in the mountain side, which sloped towards the shore, and in the chasm was still some fresh water, for it lay shaded from the sun. Lizzie was very glad at this discovery, and descended the steep cliff as carefully as possible to reach the water, but when she put out the little vessel to fill it she slipped, and was nearly falling down, at which she let go the butter-box to clutch the branch of a tree, and the little thing rolled down the mountain into the sea; a gust of wind caught the little box and carried it far from the shore. "There it goes. Goodbye little butterbox!"

"Dear me," said Lizzie; "now it is as bad as ever again. What shall I use now to take Grandfather some water in?" And she seated herself on a stone and cried so bitterly that the tears rolled like tiny pearls down her cheeks.

After a while she thought to herself: "Well, I do no good here crying, while poor old Grandfather is dying almost from thirst. I had better make a box of birch-bark and take some water in that."

No sooner said than done. She quickly made a little box of bark, which answered the purpose excellently, and she began again to descend the slope. She chanced to look down into the sea, and saw something glitter at the bottom, and she waded in the water and stretched out her hands to reach the bright object. It lay in shallow water, and presently she held in her hands a beautiful chalice of purest silver.

* * *

Neptune was seated in his emerald hall, and all his court waited upon him in silence; the king's brow was sad, for he missed his youngest daughter, Unda Marina, whom he had sent on a mission to gather corals on the coast of Australia. The pet, as was her custom, had dallied on a distant shore, to imprint her footsteps on the white sandy beach. The young prince of the forest, who was her betrothed, had thrown roses and narcissi to her among the cresting billows, and Unda Marina had gracefully caught them as they descended, and the time had rapidly passed away, and she had thrown, in mirth and play, the shell in which she was to fetch the corals, to the prince, and he had kept it; then she remembered her father's command, and sank into the sea to fetch a new shell from the paternal repository.

An envious sea monster, a tattling busybody, had hastened to inform the king that his daughter had spent her time with the forest prince, who was her sweetheart, and that she had given him the shell for a keepsake. This roused the wrath of mighty Neptune, for there existed implacable and eternal war between him and the king of the forest; but he calmed himself, and commanded his informer to fetch him the silver chalice. The monster obeyed and brought the precious cup, which possessed the strange virtue that everyone who drank from it forgot that which was most dear to him in life.

Unda Marina quietly floated into the emerald palace in the shape of a silver-crested wave, and curtsied gracefully to her father.

"Where have you been all this time?" asked the king.

"Playing on the beach at catching flowers with Prince Florian; but he has kept my shell, and I have come back to fetch another."

"Disobedient child!" answered the king, angrily; "I will forgive you this time, but see you do not the like again. Take this silver chalice instead of the shell, and fetch me some cool and sweet water from a spring in the north, for I am getting tired of always drinking salt-water." But he thought to himself, "My daughter will herself drink out of the silver chalice, and forget the forest prince for ever."

Unda Marina took the chalice and swam across the mirroring waters, until she found the spring in the cleft on the shore. She filled the chalice brimful of the cool water, and at once raised it to her own coral lips, for she felt thirsty in the summer heat. In an instant she forgot him who lay nearest her heart, the young Prince Florian of the forest; he had so engrossed her thoughts that she had forgotten about everything else in the world, and now floated thoughtlessly away in company with all the other senseless billows, which constantly chase each other across the blue main.

She had also forgotten the silver chalice in the shallow water near the shore; and there little Lizzie found it that day when she went in search of water for her grandfather.

She turned the cup round examining it on every side, and thought how beautiful it was, and how it glittered. "It will be a grand thing to take water in such a beautiful cup to Grandfather," she thought to herself, and immediately she filled the chalice with water from the cleft. How limpid the water appeared, like living silver. She could not resist the temptation, she drank, and—

In an instant she felt her blood curdle in her veins, and turn cold as ice; a strange dull numbness seized her every limb, and her heart grew almost still within her. Her childish and irregular thoughts, which but a moment since had flown in all directions in unbounded flight, came all at once to the ground with flagging wings, as if they had been brought down by grape-shot; and there she sat, poor little girl, like one in a dream, without remembering the tittle-tattle in the woods, or her grandfather in the boat, who after all was what she most loved in the world.

How long she remained thus entranced nobody knows, but it must have been for a considerable time, for she grew in the meanwhile to a tall girl; the birds in the forest twittered as before, and the trees indulged in much tittle-tattle as interludes between their more sage whisperings, but Lizzie did not listen to either. Who cares for senseless foolish talk, or prudent either in this world, when one has nobody to love?

Then came many visitors to the spring, and drank out of Unda Marina's silver chalice; for of some use Lizzie liked to be, or else why should she be sitting there. Once there came an old widow after a fisherman; she had wept for twenty years the loss of the loved one, whom the sea had robbed her of; and she took a deep draught out of the charmed chalice, and grieved no more. Another time there came a vain girl, who thought of nothing but combing her long golden tresses, and when she had drunk from the chalice, she dropped her comb into the sea. And yet another time a gentleman was seated with his fishing-rod in hand on the rock; he loved nothing in the world so well as himself, and when he had drunk, he suddenly remembered that while he was living and feasting upon the very best of the land every day, his poor old mother and his sister had to endure cold and hunger. How many people would require to drain Unda Marina's silver chalice to the very bottom, so that they should forget their own selves?

The most to be pitied was the poor, blind, old grandfather. Perhaps he is still seated in the boat, waiting for the water that is so long in coming, to slake his thirst. There are so many slips between the cup and his lips.

One day came a young sailor to the seashore where the spring was. He had come to cut some timber from which to make oars. He saw Lizzie sitting on the cleft, and he felt inclined to jest, so he said: "Why do you sit so lonely, Lizzie dear; where is your sweetheart?" She looked up and knew him at once, for they had often played together as children. She gazed at him and he looked at her. Then the birds in the forest began to sing and twitter all around, and on every tree and branch, every shrub and leaf, every hill and stone, was once more scribbled that most incomprehensible question which before had so thoroughly vexed and puzzled little Lizzie when she had gone in search of the spring.

"I recollect Grandfather is waiting for me seated in the boat," she said, and at once sprang from the cliff, and ran away over stones and stumps at such a rate, that half of the water was spilled out of Unda Marina's chalice.

"What a fleet little thing!" said the sailor, and by mistake made a cut in a stone, so that he blunted the edge of his axe.

Lizzie ran as fast as she could, and found her grandfather seated in the boat, waiting patiently for her.

"Where can you have been all this time?" he asked.

She told him what had befallen her, and how she had found the silver cup, but she did not mention anything about the young sailor, for she had quite forgotten that there ever existed any sailors at all, and the moment she forgot him she recollected her grandfather.

"Now you must drink at last, Grandfather," she said cheerfully and lovingly, and she held the cup to his lips.

The old man drank eagerly, and, like the others who had quaffed from the enchanted cup, he quite forgot what he most loved in the world, which was the use of his eyes. He thought that to be blind was quite natural, and he remembered not that he had ever beheld the sun, the moon and stars, the blue deep, and the verdant woods and meadows. Meanwhile, Neptune sat in his kingly palace, waiting in vain for his daughter's return. He then despatched the sea-monster to find her, but he quickly returned with the intelligence that Unda Marina had forgotten everything, and now floated a listless billow over the ocean main.

The submarine monarch became infuriated, and flung the sea-monster, transformed to a slimy rock, into the Gulf of Finland, on which many a tall ship founders when a gale is raging in the dark autumnal nights.

But that did not bring his truant daughter back. She never returned, and the king's long beard has grown silvery white with grief for his lost darling.

Lizzie rowed her grandfather to their island home, and there they found everything just as they had left it, and the old man again mended nets, and the girl made switches and set the nets to catch the fish.

Unda Marina's silver chalice they sold to a silversmith, and who knows where now it is to be found? Perhaps somebody has bought it for a cream-jug, and maybe the gossips round the tea-table wonder how it is that so many of them that use it now so soon forget what before they had loved most in the world.

It sometimes happens that the young sailor rows to the beach, close by where Lizzie's hut is, and he looks sorrowfully up at the little window. But she knows him not. She works at her switches, and listens to the trees that whisper outside her home: "Why are you so lonely, Lizzie dear; where is your sweetheart?"

"I wish I knew!" she answers, and would fain laugh at the thought, but she cannot find it in her heart to do that either, for somehow there is something strange and melancholy in the sigh, which she cannot quite understand.

You little bird with golden shimmer on your wings, and who sings so sweetly up in the blue ether, repeat once more the words for dear little Lizzie, and sing them also to the billow of Unda Marina on the shoreless sea. Perhaps they may listen to you, and their memories may return to them. Sing to the giddy billow, "Unda Marina, Unda Marina, have you forgotten your friend in the forest?" Then again repeat your song to the poor girl in the hut: "Lizzie dear, Lizzie dear, why are you so lonely; where is your sweetheart?"

The Devil's Bride

(The Story of the Boy Who Wouldn't Lose His Temper)

THERE WAS ONCE a Finnish boy who got the best of the Devil. His name was Erkki. Erkki had two brothers who were, of course, older than he. They both tried their luck with the Devil and got the worst of it. Then Erkki tried his luck. They were sure Erkki, too, would be bested, but he wasn't. Here is the whole story:

One day the oldest brother said: "It's time for me to go out into the world and earn my living. Do you two younger ones wait here at home until you hear how I get on."

The younger boys agreed to this and the oldest brother started out. He was unable to get employment until by chance he met the Devil. The Devil at once offered him a place but on very strange terms.

"Come work for me," the Devil said, "and I promise that you'll be comfortably housed and well fed. We'll make this bargain: the first of us who loses his temper will forfeit to the other enough of his own hide to sole a pair of boots. If I lose my temper first, you may exact from me a big patch of my hide. If you lose your temper first, I'll exact the same from you."

The oldest brother agreed to this and the Devil at once took him home and set him to work.

"Take this ax," he said, "and go out behind the house and chop me some firewood."

The oldest brother took the ax and went out to the woodpile.

'Chopping wood is easy enough,' he thought to himself.

But at the first blow he found that the ax had no edge. Try as he would he couldn't cut a single log.

"I'd be a fool to stay here and waste my time with such an ax!" he cried.

So he threw down the ax and ran away thinking to escape the Devil and get work somewhere else. But the Devil had no intention of letting him escape. He ran after him, overtook him, and asked him what he meant leaving thus without notice.

"I don't want to work for you!" the oldest brother cried, petulantly.

"Very well," the Devil said, "but don't lose your temper about it."

"I will so lose my temper!" the oldest brother declared. "The idea – expecting me to cut wood with such an ax!"

"Well," the Devil remarked, "since you insist on losing your temper, you'll have to forfeit me enough of your hide to sole a pair of boots! That was our bargain."

The oldest brother howled and protested but to no purpose. The Devil was firm. He took out a long knife and sliced off enough of the oldest brother's hide to sole a pair of big boots.

"Now then, my boy," he said, "now you may go."

The oldest brother went limping home complaining bitterly at the hard fate that had befallen him. "I'm tired and sick," he told his brothers, "and I'm going to stay home and rest. One of you will have to go out and get work."

The second brother at once said that he'd be delighted to try his luck in the world. So he started out and he had exactly the same experience. At first he could get no work, then he met the Devil and the Devil made exactly the same bargain with him that he had made with the oldest brother. He took the second brother home with him, gave him the same dull ax, and sent him out to the woodpile. After the first stroke the second brother threw down the ax in disgust and tried to run off and the Devil, of course, wouldn't let him go until he, too, had submitted to the loss of a great patch of hide. So it was no time at all before the second brother came limping home complaining bitterly at fate.

"What ails you two?" Erkki said.

"You go out into the cruel world and hunt work," they told him, "and you'll find out soon enough what ails us! And when you do find out you needn't come limping home expecting sympathy from us for you won't get it!"

So the very next day Erkki started out, leaving his brothers at home nursing their sore backs and their injured feelings.

Well, Erkki had exactly the same experience. At first he could get work nowhere, then later he met the Devil and went into his employ on exactly the same terms as his brothers.

The Devil handed him the same dull ax and sent him out to the woodpile. At the first blow Erkki knew that the ax had lost its edge and would never cut a single log. But instead of being discouraged and losing his temper, he only laughed.

"I suppose the Devil thinks I'll lose my hide over a trifle like this!" he said. "Well, I just won't!"

He dropped the ax and, going over to the woodpile, began pulling it down. Under all the logs he found the Devil's cat. It was an evil-looking creature with a gray head.

"Ha!" thought Erkki, "I bet anything you've got something to do with this!"

He raised the dull ax and with one blow cut off the evil creature's head. Sure enough the ax instantly recovered its edge and after that Erkki had no trouble at all in chopping as much firewood as the Devil wanted.

That night at supper the Devil said: "Well, Erkki, did you finish the work I gave you?"

"Yes, master, I've chopped all that wood."

The Devil was surprised. "Really?"

"Yes, master. You can go out and see for yourself."

"Then you found something in the woodpile, didn't you?"

"Nothing but an awful-looking old cat."

The Devil started. "Did you do anything to that cat?"

"I only chopped its head off and threw it away."

"What!" the Devil cried angrily. "Didn't you know that was my cat!"

"There now, master," Erkki said soothingly, "you're not going to lose your temper over a little thing like a dead cat, are you? Don't forget our bargain!"

The Devil swallowed his anger and murmured: "No, I'm not going to lose my temper but I must say that was no way to treat my cat."

The next day the Devil ordered Erkki to go out to the forest and bring home some logs on the ox sledge. "My black dog will go with you," he said, "and as you come home you're to take exactly the same course the dog takes."

Well, Erkki went out to the forest and loaded the ox sledge with logs and then drove the oxen home following the Devil's black dog. As they reached the Devil's house the black dog jumped through a hole in the gate.

"I must follow master's orders," Erkki said to himself.

So he cut up the oxen into small pieces and put them through the same hole in the gate; he chopped up the logs and pitched them through the hole; and he broke up the sledge into pieces small enough to follow the oxen and the logs. Then he crept through the hole himself.

That night at supper the Devil said:

"Well, Erkki, did you come home the way I told you?"

"Yes, master, I followed the black dog."

"What!" the Devil cried. "Do you mean to say you brought the oxen and the sledge and the logs through the hole in the gate?"

"Yes, master, that's what I did."

"But you couldn't!" the Devil declared.

"Well, master," Erkki said, "just go out and see."

The Devil went outside and when he saw the method by which Erkki had carried out his orders he was furious. But Erkki quieted him by saying:

"There now, master, you're not going to lose your temper over a trifling matter like this, are you? Remember our bargain!"

"N-n-no," the Devil said, again swallowing his anger, "I'm not going to lose my temper, but I want you to understand, Erkki, that I think you've acted very badly in this!"

All that evening the Devil fumed and fussed about Erkki. "We've got to get rid of that boy! That's all there is about it!" he said to his wife.

Of course whenever Erkki was in sight the Devil tried to smile and look pleasant, but as soon as Erkki was gone he went back at once to his grievance. He declared emphatically:

"There's no living in peace and comfort with such a boy around!"

"Well," his wife said, "if you feel that way about it, why don't you kill him tonight when he's asleep? We could throw his body into the lake and no one would be the wiser."

"That's a fine idea!" the Devil said. "Wake me up some time after midnight and I'll do it!"

Now Erkki overheard this little plan, so that night he kept awake. When he knew from their snoring that the Devil and his wife were sound asleep, he slipped over to their bed, quietly lifted the Devil's wife in his arms, and without awakening her placed her gently in his own bed. Then he put on some of her clothes and laid himself down beside the Devil in the wife's place.

Presently he nudged the Devil awake.

"What do you want?" the Devil mumbled.

"Sst!" Erkki whispered. "Isn't it time we got up and killed Erkki?"

"Yes," the Devil answered, "it is. Come along."

They got up quietly and the Devil reached down a great sword from the wall. Then they crept over to Erkki's bed and the Devil with one blow cut off the head of the person who was lying there asleep.

"Now," he said, "we'll just carry out the bed and all and dump it in the lake."

So Erkki took one end of the bed and the Devil the other and, stumbling and slipping in the darkness, they carried it down to the lake and pitched it in.

"That's a good job done!" the Devil said with a laugh. Then they went back to bed together and the Devil fell instantly asleep.

The next morning when he got up for breakfast, there was Erkki stirring the porridge.

"How did you get here?" the Devil asked. "I mean – I mean where is my wife?"

"Your wife? Don't you remember," Erkki said, "you cut off her head last night and then we threw her into the lake, bed and all! But no one will be the wiser!"

"W-wh-what!" the Devil cried, and he was about to fly into an awful rage when Erkki restrained him by saying:

"There now, master, you're not going to lose your temper over a little thing like a wife, are you? Remember our bargain!"

So the Devil was forced again to swallow his anger. "No, I'm not going to lose my temper," he said, "but I tell you frankly, Erkki, I don't think that was a nice trick for you to play on me!"

Well, the Devil felt lonely not having a wife about the house, so in a few days he decided to go off wooing for a new one.

"And, Erkki," he said, "I expect you to keep busy while I'm gone. Here's a keg of red paint. Now get to work and have the house all blazing red by the time I get back."

"All blazing red," Erkki repeated. "Very well, master, trust me to have it all blazing red by the time you get back!"

As soon as the Devil was gone, Erkki set the house a-fire and in a short time the whole sky was lit up with the red glow of the flames. In great fright the Devil hurried back and got there in time to see the house one mass of fire.

"You see, master," Erkki said, "I've done as you told me. It looks very pretty, doesn't it? All blazing red!"

The Devil almost choked with rage. "You – you—" he began, but Erkki restrained him by saying:

"There now, master, you're not going to lose your temper over a little thing like a house a-fire, are you? Remember our bargain!"

The Devil swallowed hard and said: "N – no, I'm not going to lose my temper, but I must say, Erkki, that I'm very much annoyed with you!"

The next day the Devil wanted to go a-wooing again and before he started he said to Erkki:

"Now, no nonsense this time! While I'm gone you're to build three bridges over the lake, but they're not to be built of wood or stone or iron or earth. Do you understand?"

Erkki pretended to be frightened.

"That's a pretty hard task you've given me, master!"

"Hard or easy, see that you get it done!" the Devil said.

Erkki waited until the Devil was gone, then he went out to the field and slaughtered all the Devil's cattle. From the bones of the cattle he laid three bridges across the lake, using the skulls for one bridge, the ribs for another, and the legs and the hoofs for the third. Then when the Devil got back, Erkki met him and pointing to the bridges said: "See, master, there they are, three bridges put together without stick, stone, iron, or bit of earth!"

When the Devil found out that all his cattle had been slaughtered to give bones for the bridges, he was ready to kill Erkki, but Erkki quieted him by saying: "There now, master, you're not going to lose your temper over a little thing like the slaughter of a few cattle, are you? Remember our bargain!"

So again the Devil had to swallow his anger. "No," he said, "I'm not going to lose my temper exactly but I just want to tell you, Erkki, that I don't think you're behaving well!"

The Devil's wooing was successful and pretty soon he brought home a new wife. The new wife didn't like having Erkki about, so the Devil promised her he'd kill the boy.

"I'll do it tonight," he said, "when he's asleep."

Erkki overheard this and that night he put the churn in his bed under the covers, and where his head ordinarily would be he put a big round stone. Then he himself curled up on the stove and went comfortably to sleep.

During the night the Devil took his great sword from the wall and went over to Erkki's bed. His first blow hit the round stone and nicked the sword. His second blow struck sparks.

"Mercy me!" the Devil thought, "he's got a mighty hard head! I better strike lower!"

With the third stroke he hit the churn a mighty blow. The hoops flew apart and the churn collapsed.

The Devil went chuckling back to bed. "Ha!" he said boastfully to his wife, "I got him that time!"

But the next morning when he woke up he didn't feel like laughing for there was Erkki as lively as ever and pretending that nothing had happened.

"What!" cried the Devil in amazement, "didn't you feel anything strike you last night while you were asleep?"

"Oh, I did feel a few mosquitoes brushing my cheek," Erkki said. "Nothing else."

"Steel doesn't touch him!" the Devil said to his wife. "I think I'll try fire on him."

So that night the Devil told Erkki to sleep in the threshing barn. Erkki carried his cot down to the threshing floor and then when it was dark he shifted it into the hay barn where he slept comfortably all night.

During the night the Devil set fire to the threshing barn. In the early dawn Erkki carried his cot back to the place of the threshing barn and in the morning when the Devil came out the first thing he saw was Erkki unharmed and peacefully sleeping among the smoking ruins.

"Mercy me, Erkki!" he shouted, shaking him awake, "have you been asleep all night?"

Erkki sat up and yawned. "Yes, I've had a fine night's sleep. But I did feel a little chilly."

"Chilly!" the Devil gasped.

After that the Devil's one thought was to get rid of Erkki. "That boy's getting on my nerves!" he told his wife. "I just can't stand him much longer! What are we going to do about him?"

They discussed one plan after another and at last decided that the only way they'd ever get rid of him would be to move away and leave him behind.

"I'll send him out to the forest to chop wood all day," the Devil said, "and while he's gone we'll row ourselves and all our belongings out to an island and when he comes back he won't know where we've gone."

Erkki overheard this plan and the next day when they were sure he was safely at work in the forest he slipped back and hid himself in the bedclothes. Well, when they got to the island and began unpacking their things there was Erkki in the bedclothes!

The Devil's new wife complained bitterly. "If you really loved me," she said, "you'd cut off that boy's head!"

"But I've tried to cut it off!" the Devil declared, "and I never can do it! Plague take such a boy! I've always known the Finns were an obstinate lot but I must say I've never met one as bad as Erkki! He's too much for me!"

But the Devil's wife kept on complaining until at last the Devil promised that he would try once again to cut off Erkki's head.

"Very well," his wife said, "tonight when he's asleep I'll wake you."

Well, what with the moving and everything the wife herself was tired and as soon as she went to bed she fell asleep. That gave Erkki just the very chance he needed to try on the new wife the trick he had played on the old one. Without waking her he carried her to his bed and then laid himself down in her place beside the Devil. Then he woke up the Devil and reminded him that he had promised to cut off Erkki's head.

The poor old Devil got up and went over to Erkki's bed and of course cut off the head of his new wife.

The next morning when he had found out what he had done, he was perfectly furious.

"You get right out of here, Erkki!" he roared. "I never want to see you again!"

"There now, master," Erkki said, "you're not going to lose your temper over a little thing like a dead wife, are you?"

"I am so going to lose my temper!" the Devil shouted. "And what's more it isn't a little thing! I liked this wife, I did, and I don't know where I'll get another one I like as well! So you just clear out of here and be quick about it, too!"

"Very well, master," Erkki said, "I'll go but not until you pay me what you owe me."

"What I owe you!" bellowed the Devil. "What about all you owe me for my house and my cattle and my old wife and my dear new wife and everything!"

"You've lost your temper," Erkki said, "and now you've got to pay me a patch of your hide big enough to sole a pair of boots. That was our bargain!"

The Devil roared and blustered but Erkki was firm. He wouldn't budge a step until the Devil had allowed him to slice a great patch of hide off his back.

That piece of the Devil's hide made the finest soles that a pair of boots ever had. It wore for years and years and years. In fact Erkki is still tramping around on those same soles. The fame of them has spread over all the land and it has got so that now people stop Erkki on the highway to look at his wonderful boots soled with the Devil's hide. Travelers from foreign countries are deeply interested when they hear about the boots and when they meet Erkki they question him closely.

"Tell us," they beg him, "how did you get the Devil's hide in the first place?"

Erkki always laughs and makes the same answer: "I got it by not losing my temper!"

As for the Devil, he's never again made a bargain like that with a Finn!

The Natural World

Introduction

IT SEEMS FAIR TO SAY THAT THE NATURAL WORLD, which lies so emphatically at the centre of the *Kalevala*, looms large in the Finnish consciousness more generally, it seems fair to say. The Land of a Thousand Lakes has a fair few other natural features too, ranging from woods and rivers to moors and mountains. Even now, only a small proportion of the country has been brought into agricultural production – and that has had to be hacked clear and painstakingly ploughed in sweat and blood. Finns accordingly have a vivid sense of the presence of the wilderness all around them; while they feel deep love for it, they experience a touch of fear as well. Theirs is an untamed country in which they know they have no more than a modest foothold, as they know. This is the context in which they encounter Finland's folktales: it is an atmospheric and at times unsettling one. However successful storytellers of the Christian era have been in reimagining their country's wooded glades as a second Eden, we continue to hear overtones from a more distant – and now more disturbing – pagan past. Wonderful as nature's beauties are in revealing to us the glories of God's creation, they hint at darker mysteries as well.

The Two Brooks

"NOW THERE IS REALLY SOMETHING very queer about this brook," said Richard, "it seems to me as if he wanted to speak to me sometimes; whenever I make a dam with a few stones, to allow my ships to get into deep smooth water, he throws his spray up into my face, and gurgles and murmurs as if he would say, 'Listen to me!' but it is impossible to understand him when he speaks a language which nobody knows."

"Well, do you know," answered Rose, "that is exactly how it is with my brook; whenever I splash in the water, or wash my doll's clothes, I fancy I can see somebody looking at me, and nodding, as much as to say, 'I know something you don't know!"

"It is only your own self you see in the water," said Richard, "just as in a mirror."

"As if I didn't know that," quickly responded Rose slightly annoyed; "but I tell you that the girl in the brook is a different creature, and we are more like two sisters; when I open my lips she opens her mouth, but though I speak she never says anything."

"She is, perhaps, the daughter of the spirit of the brook; you just take care, or she will do like her father, pull you by the feet and drag you in."

To this Rose didn't answer, for she was slightly offended again.

"Now don't get out of temper, Rose," said Richard; "our brooks are so close to each other that they very likely come from the same source. They must be brother and sister; but see, my brook is broader and deeper than yours, and sometimes he is quite turbulent in temper, so I will call him the 'Madcap' brook."

"My brook is smaller and flows more gently, he murmurs words of love at quiet eventide, so I will call him the 'Gentle' stream," Rose answered.

"Yes," said Richard approvingly, "and the Madcap brook is my brother, while the Gentle one is your sister; we shall like them all the more since we have given them names."

"It is for all the world like as if the two brooks were two little children," said Rose; "I wonder what becomes of them when they run away from here?"

"They go out in the wide world, of course," said Richard. "Come, now, let each of us follow each other's brook in his course to see how they fare, and when we have come to where they end we will turn back home again."

"Yes, so we will; but only stay a little, while I run home to fetch some bread and butter," said provident little Rose.

"Very well, make haste, and bring me some as well," said Richard.

After a short time Rose returned with sandwiches, and they each set out on their different journeys. "Goodbye, goodbye!" said Rose.

"Ta-ta," answered her brother gaily, he following the course of the Madcap brook, while she took that of the Gentle stream.

And now my story naturally divides itself into two different parts, so we will concern ourselves with the little girl first. Rose walked along the bank of her stream, saying, "You darling little child of a brook, you are only just learning to creep now, I wonder what will become of you when you grow big? Flow gently and peacefully, and show me your fate when you have got abroad in the world."

Rose continued her wandering, the brook meandering quietly at her side, watering the flowers on the bank, nourishing himself with the moisture from the meadows, and soon he grew gradually stronger and bigger. As he expanded, the water became more transparent and his course more subdued, and he fell into a gentle murmur of meditation, while his banks became more verdant and fertile. At last he was welcomed and embraced by a deep sylvan lake that was longing for this union. Birch and mountain-ash, the latter in full bloom, had formed a living ring round the shores, and the sun from the sky reflected his heaven-born splendour in the calm waters of the lake, while swans floated peacefully upon its bosom, and the lingering rays of the setting sun tinged their lovely down with rosy colours.

Little Rose unconsciously folded her hands together, and softly whispered to the brook, "How happy you are, beloved stream; during your whole course of existence you have been the means of spreading many untold blessings to herbs and trees, and fertilizing your banks, and when your life has come to an end God allows you to sink into the embrace of the lake, radiant and sparkling with heavenly joy. God grant that I also may live and die like my darling brook."

Rose now turned back, grateful and joyous, and ere nightfall had arrived home, but Richard had not returned yet. "He will come soon," thought the little girl.

But Richard came not, either during the night or the following day; he was not heard of for many years. "My poor brother," thought Rose, "and he had only a sandwich for his journey!"

At last everybody was sure Richard was lost for ever, and the sorrow was general and sincere; only the Madcap brook and the Gentle stream blustered and murmured respectively, quite plainly in the summer evenings, "Only wait, only wait, he will come back," but nobody believed them.

Time passed on and Rose grew up, and forgot to wash any more of her doll's clothes in the Gentle stream, and also to nod to the little girl in it who had formerly been her dear playmate, and last of all she almost forgot to grieve any more about Richard; new thoughts were constantly born which dispelled the memories of the past. But the two brooks murmured incessantly, "Only wait, only wait, he will come back."

One day arrived a traveller, a stranger with a long black beard, and asked of a young lady in the garden if she knew anything of a child called Rose, and the girl accosted was no other than Rose herself, but she did not answer, for she was so surprised, and could not understand what business the stranger had there.

He then appeared to be very grieved and added, "Nobody remembers me in this place, and Rose, my darling sister, is away; I will go to our two brooks, the Madcap and the Gentle stream, and ask them for my little sister."

By this Rose perceived at once that the stranger was her long lost brother, and she very nearly flung herself into his arms to cry, "Don't grieve, Richard; here I am, your own sister, and we will never more part," but she subdued her emotions, and instead added, "Come, let us go to the two brooks."

They went on to the narrow slip of land which lay between the two rivulets, and which was covered with the greenest of grass. "I recognize my Madcap brook," said the traveller. "Though a stranger, would you like to hear the story of this, my own brook?"

"Yes, do tell it," answered Rose with quickly beating heart.

Richard began: "I was only a wee lad when I left my sister and my home to follow this brook and see what became of him when he grew big. The Madcap brook, as we called him, leapt boisterously on from his very commencement like a frolicsome boy, and could bear no obstacles in his way. When he encountered a stone he grew quite white with rage, and hurled it aside as he proceeded on his way. When he came to a firm projecting cliff he fought for a while a fierce battle for supremacy, but had sense enough to yield and take his onward course. The further the Madcap went, the more increased his strength; rills and rivulets became his vassal tributaries, and he soon grew into a broad stream. I followed his course faithfully; when I became hungry, people that dwelt in cottages on his bank gave me food; of water to slake my thirst he himself gave me an abundant supply; and when I was tired I slept upon the soft grass on his banks; but the stream still increased in power and showed his real madcap nature. He yielded to no more cliffs, but with accumulated power sprang over them and descended as a swift rapid, after which he would take a rest before beginning new strifes. The mills built upon his banks he worked briskly, turning the wheels which ground corn for many hamlets. Saw-mills were constructed to take advantage of his power, and he cut planks and beams, working diligently night and day. He carried big rafts of timber on his broad shoulders, and floated them safely down his foaming rapids. He increased every way, and by this time he had grown into a mighty river; yes, one of the greatest in the world. I followed his course for months and years, and saw rivers and streams, themselves great, become his tributaries, and now the Madcap brook had acquired giant strength; I saw him carry whole fleets of proud vessels on his broad back, and course through mighty cities, whose very existence he had called into life; and the inhabitants said, 'Have you ever seen such a mighty river before?' 'No, I answered,' but I knew him when he was a wee thing, a child like myself, and I have stanked him often at his sylvan source with a few small stones, and the very first vessel he ever floated was a little boat I made of a pea-pod.'"

"The greater became the stream the more useful was he, but also the more dangerous; they constructed large mounds to guard against his indomitable spirit, which at times would leap over all boundaries. One spring day, when the sun had melted the snow upon the mountains, countless new-born streams and rills rushed down the slopes, to swell his size; this infused new life into the Madcap stream and made him feel as of yore; he grew wild, overbearing, and threw himself with a fierce clamour over the mounds that bound him in, and flooded a fertile and thickly populated district. But now a mountain stood in his way to oppose his course, he paused for a short time to gather all his forces into a large lake with which he besieged the mountain, but the giant fortress stood firm. However, he increased the lake until he reached the mountain ridge, when mad with victory he threw himself headlong down the steep cliff on the other side; this formed one of the grandest and most beautiful cataracts, and with tumultuous uproar he revelled in his own valour, sending the spray on high, so that it glittered in all the colours of the rainbow, like a halo of glory, and then again he made for his great goal, the ocean, in the distance. But he had yet a long way to travel ere he could reach his destination, and at last he grew tired of his own greatness and divided himself into several arms, which shallow and sluggishly made their way through a marshy land. Now the Madcap stream had grown old, and having led an adventurous life, he grew feeble in his old age. Men mastered him once more, and led his main course into new channels, and dammed him up whenever they chose; and when the time had come that he must merge into the ocean main, then the former Madcap stream stole through many little unknown rillets into the unfathomable mystic deep before him, when he ceased to exist as a stream, but became an unit of the pristine element.

"But I repeated to myself, 'I thank Thee, O God, that Thou hast allowed me to see, in the course of this stream, the picture of man's life in its grandeur, its usefulness, its arrogance, and its ultimate feebleness; and now know I that neither power nor greatness are eternal, but that the great ocean, Death, awaits us all alike; therefore let us try and seek our greatness, our power, and our ultimate goal in Thee alone, everlasting God, and let us learn to subdue our proud passions, and become useful toilers for Thy kingdom of heaven upon earth.'"

"And here," added Richard, "ends my story about the Madcap brook; I have returned a wiser man, but as I cannot find my sister I feel very lonely, in spite of all my rich treasures of memory."

"No, not alone any longer," answered Rose, "for now your own sister twines her arms around your neck, and her lips kiss yours, and her joyous tears mingle with yours. Let us build a cottage here on the meadow, between the Madcap brook and the Gentle stream, so that we may always see them, and constantly remember their different fates. Tell me, Richard dear, if you agree to that."

"Yes, I do," he answered, and lovingly kissed her brow and hands; and they then made their home between the two brooks, and always remembered that God has a deep-fraught meaning in every image He shows his children in the multitudinous variety of creation.

Rose and Richard in time grew old, but the two brooks remained young, the one the same placid mirror out of which peeped a little head to every child that looked into it, and the other, ever eager to float the tiny pea-shell boats which little boys consigned to his care; the Gentle stream murmured lovingly at eventide as of yore; and the Madcap brook danced away as frolicsome as ever, over stones and pebbles. Neither of them knew or cared what would be their future lot, but Rose and Richard knew it well, for it had taught them a wholesome lesson which they remembered as long as they lived.

The Most Beautiful Thing in the Wood

WELL, IT WAS A SWEET, BEAUTIFUL MORNING, I can tell you, and early too, I really don't think it was more than 5 o'clock ; the sun had barely risen, and the shadows of the birches fell long and attenuated over the green sward. Father and Mother did not like us to sleep long of a morning, and there lived near us an old fisherman, who was in the habit of calling out under our bedroom window every morning as the clock struck 4: "Reef topsails and haul in your sheets, boys," which sailors shout to each other when a storm arises in the night. Like a shot we darted out of bed as this greeting reached us; before we got accustomed to it we thought it very hard, but soon we saw the truth of the old saying, "The morning light hath golden mouth," but then you know a little fellow must get into his hammock by 9 o'clock of an evening.

I have often thought we ought not to sleep away those glorious summer nights in Finland, almost radiant with brightness and only slightly obscured with a thin veil of twilight, the dew glittering on the grass, and the birds singing the whole livelong night but the mandates of nature must be obeyed, so sleep one must.

Frederick the Great, of Prussia, was a monarch highly appreciating the value of time, and it vexed him that he was compelled to sleep away one-third or one-fourth of his life. He, therefore, once resolved upon accustoming himself to do away altogether with such a wasteful habit. The first night he worked all the time, and that so far succeeded very well; the next night he also wrote the whole time, without so much as nodding once, and now he fancied he had achieved a great thing. But what was the consequence, think you? The following day, when he was seated in his Council Chamber, surrounded by his ministers, and they began to speak to him on important matters of State, they suddenly noticed that His Majesty began to nod and nod, and that he fell asleep where he sat nodding, in all the dignity of royalty.

I am, therefore, most loyally of the opinion that we must do as nature bids. Sleep is a blessing to the weary and the suffering, and to the troubled mind a great relief; but that is no reason why one should encourage oneself to be lazy on a glorious morning like this; no, far better to imagine that the old fisherman stands outside the window bawling, "Haul in the sheets and reef topsails, boys."

But I must tell you how the forest appeared on the morning in question. There was a delightful fresh verdure and a cool genial air, upon which floated occasional breaths of lime-blossom and the balm of fir trees. There were numerous trees of various kinds, from the towering pine, meditating upon the time when he would become a tall mast and sail round the world, down to the little juniper bush, who consoled himself with the thought that he could become a tree if somebody would take the trouble to lop his branches and tie him to a pole. "But I don't care for that, I prefer my liberty," he said, "and if I grew tall, then the little children would not be able to reach my branches, when the time comes to chop off some of my twigs to strew on the floor of the kitchen on a Sunday morning."

"And that is the only thing you are good for," observed a tall fir, who actually thought himself of a higher rank in creation; "such things as you, are only made to be trampled upon," he sneered.

"Well, what then?" answered the juniper. "I am quite content that I can gladden the hearts of men with my fragrance, fresh from the forest, besides which, I am useful for many other things as well; for instance, I chase away the gnats with my smoke, when anyone lights a few of my twigs, and I am first-rate to make bows of, which any schoolboy knows, and they can also brew small beer with my berries, and also use them for medicine, and they can—"

"Stop short there, Friend," interposed the mountain-ash, "for it is very conceited to enumerate one's own merits that way. I should really like to know which of us all might justly be considered to be the most beautiful and useful in the wood. What do you say to that?" And the mountain-ash waved gracefully his white airy branches, for he happened to be covered all over with blossoms, it being midsummer time.

"What a question!" called out a lime tree, also redolent with blossoms. "Let us carefully consider who might gain the palm," he said, and artfully perfumed the air with his luscious sweet breath to gain their favour.

The lady birch also approved of the proposed contest, for she had had her long flowing ringlets curled by the morning breeze, and now waved them conquettishly to all her admirers. "I rather fancy that I am the most charming," thought the lady of the wood to herself.

A willow, who stood close by the lake, and was always mirroring himself in the water, thought that he surely was the most luxuriant, graceful, and charming, and he, therefore, nodded to the others, saying, "Well, it is really a question to be deeply considered."

An aspen tree stood close to them, and trembled for fear lest he should not gain the admiration of all; he was always trembling, the poor aspen, for though he was big and tall he had a faint heart and fragile branches.

A wild briar grew near also, but kept her secret hopes to herself within her thorny bosom; her pink blossoms smiled at the mere thought that anyone could fancy himself more lovely than they were.

"Let us refer to the flowers," said the beech, and spread his exuberant foliage patronisingly over tufts of violets and cranberry blossoms to protect them from the sun.

"There is no occasion for that," objected a giant pine haughtily, "to be supreme one must be big and strong. Look at me, am I not handsome? When I 'shiver my timbers' thousands of my prickles fall to the ground, which whole regiments of emmets gather and use as spears when they wage war against each other. That I am a warlike champion I presume no one can deny," and the pine looked fierce, trying to frighten the others.

The oak listened calmly to the strife. "It is ridiculous to judge of ourselves," he said, "I am pretty sure that each of you thinks himself the best; let us, therefore, refer to the bullfinch, seated in the birch-tree top. He favours no one in particular, and he will impartially judge who is the most charming in the wood."

This proposal was agreed to, and they asked the opinion of the little songster, but he was reserved and rather shy of telling them the unvarnished truth.

Then there came two little children, a boy and a girl, who lived in a little cottage close by, and when they came into the sylvan glade betimes, this glorious morning, they folded their hands in admiration, saying: "O kind God, how beautiful is Thy wood! how grand Thy whole world! Kind, loving, God, grant us poor children that we may grow up in Thy knowledge, and that our whole lives may be devoted to serve and praise Thee gratefully, O Lord!"

When the forest trees heard the children's prayer they felt astonished and reproved, and their murmurs died away into inaudible whispers, and the twitter of the bullfinch in the birch was distinctly heard:

"Beautiful and glorious is our verdant wood, and all God's nature! but I tell you trees, who are vying with each other as to which is the most beautiful, that of all the pretty and delightful things that God has allowed to grow in this forest, there is nothing more lovely, more innocently pretty, than these two little children, who praise God from the fulness of their hearts, this glorious summer morning. For beauty and wisdom and power and grandeur are naught where there is not a meek and humble heart that gives God the praise for everything. The trees hold forth their arms in adoration, the flowers offer up their incense, and the birds sing many a joyous 'Te Deum.' The same eternal spirit moves and speaks within us all; we all grow in the sunshine of heavenly grace; but the children's prayer is ever more acceptable to God than the songs of the birds, the adoration of the trees, or the fragrance of the flowers. God bless you, little children, and protect you, tender little plants, in the great forest of life, and may you ever increase in knowledge and grace!"

Nature's Secret

A LITTLE BOY WHOM I ONCE KNEW was called David, and he had a little sister named Hester. Their father was a settler in the deep forests of Finland, where he had made a clearing, and tilled some land, and called himself Wood, because of his sylvan home. His wife was a kind body, who tended their two cows, two calves, the two goats, two pigs, and the two children, besides a horse, a dog, and a cat, and well, really that is all I know about *her*. There were many weird old legends told about the forest in which they lived, but this did not frighten the family; on the contrary, they thought it quite in the order of things, and properly belonging to an old forest.

The children assisted their parents during the whole winter, indeed, there was no spare time for growing lazy. The boy was kept busy all the day with axe and other tools, helping his father to make implements for their husbandry, besides which he had to chop wood, carry in the fuel, and give the horse water. Little Hester also had her duties, she had to sweep the dust away, clean the pots, comb the wool, and feed the cows and pigs. Spring-time had arrived, and the cattle were for the first time to be let out to graze in the woodlands, and now everything would be delightful for everybody concerned. The cow who carried the bell was called "The Star," and she kicked up her heels and scampered off in her clumsy way, so that a merry peal rang out from her bell. The calves, with tails erect, danced about for very joy, and the goats skipped with agile legs from stone to stone, shaking their beards in evident enjoyment, and David and Hester laughed so merrily and long that at last they were compelled to support themselves against the gate.

"Here is an oatmeal cake, a bit of cheese, and four dried herrings," said the mother; "now be off with the cattle and behave yourselves, and bring them home at nightfall; the goats will be sure to follow the cow-bell." The children needed not to be told this twice, and they hurriedly snatched up the provision wallet, and were off like two little sprites, capering and dancing with the two calves, while the mother remained for a short time listening, with a smile, to their merry ringing laughter, until it died away in the distance.

The snow had melted away from field and meadow, but still lay in fleecy flocks in shaded places of the hills sloping northwards; birds were singing and chirruping in almost every tree; the green grass and the early violets were peeping forth from amongst the withered leaves of all shades and colours which lay strewn over the ground of the birch coppice. David and Hester felt supremely happy, they thought that everything smiled around them for very joy of existence. The trees nodded to them, the birds greeted them with song, the fresh green grass invited them to sit down, and the boulder-stones, that were abundantly scattered about, seemed to stare at them with grey eyes from under mossy eyebrows. The wind whispered in confidence to them, the clouds followed their progress from on high, the brook asked them to listen to his recital, the gnats and flies danced in the sunlight to please them, and the gay squirrels leaped from branch to branch among the tall trees to show them what clever trapezists they were. There seemed particularly bright sunshine especially spread on their road, and through the azure sky glowed the orb of day in all its splendour, as if God himself had looked down upon them and meant to say, "How dearly I love you, little children!"

In the wood was a large mountain, with many clefts and caves, and in one of these fissures a hermit had built himself a small hut, partly supporting its walls against the mountain, and in which he lived. This hermit was a remarkable man, who for more than half a century had there lived a life of seclusion from the world, devoted to thought and study; he was quite a sage, this venerable old greybeard, deeply read in learned lore, and some hinted even in the black art and witchcraft; he was for ever meditating why the world was created just this way and not the reverse. "Old Greybeard," as he was generally called, could hear the grass grow, and knew the nature of every herb, plant, and tree, he also knew the names of all animals, and of all races of man; but he thought he only just required to know a little more and he would then have mastered all knowledge; as yet he had not been able to count the stars, nor compute the number of the ocean sands, nor had he measured how broad and deep and long eternity might be. Upon these mighty problems were the old man's meditations fixed when the children arrived at his study in the cleft.

"Good morning, Gaffer Greybeard," cried the children, for they were not a bit afraid of him, and they had many times before chatted to the old man.

"Good morning, children," answered he, without looking up from the withered leaf he held in his hand and which he was dissecting.

"Why are you looking so closely into that withered old leaf, Gaffer?" asked David, while he was busy making a pipe from a willow twig. He first cut the bark through all round, then he knocked upon it, until the young bark became loosened from the wood, and then he cut a hole and made a gash, after which the pipe was complete and ready for use.

"I am seeking to find out nature's secret, and am accustoming myself to count the veins in the leaf; then I shall be able to compute the sands of the sea, and calculate the vastness of eternity. But these are things you don't understand, little children."

"Indeed," rejoined David; and really he did not understand anything more of it than that it was a strange occupation. "What do you mean by nature's secret?"

"I wish to discover why everything is created the way it is, and the use of it, and whether it has come of itself," answered the hermit. "You see, my little lad, in that consists the secret of nature."

But David did not comprehend this. He took a bit of bread and cheese from his wallet, and seating himself on a big stone, commenced eating: that was one of nature's secrets he did understand. Hester was seated a little further off, making a fine switch for vapourbathing purposes, from sapling birch twigs, and "The Star" went clanking the bell amongst the herd grazing. This, again, was for them a secret of nature they had discovered.

After a short time David, who had been sitting and thinking for himself, said to the hermit: "Don't you know, Gaffer, that God has created everything, and that what He has made is good?"

"Well, that may be," answered the hermit; "but I will tell you, lad, that I have sought God ever since I began to reason, and so has many a learned man before me, but we have never found Him. I have tried to discover Him in the withered leaves, in the dead maggots, and in the mystic arts. I have analysed the flowers of the field, but I found Him not. I have pounded stones and ores to atoms, and sought him in the crystals, but I found Him neither there. I have dissected the lark to find out what made her sing, but her instrument was silent to me. Once I found a man lying dead in the wood; I opened his heart and his brains, but all in vain still no God. Look you, child; this is the only marvel I cannot comprehend. You smile. Can you, then, tell me where God dwells?"

"Yes," quickly responded the boy; "anybody might tell you that. God is everywhere."

"But I cannot see Him; I want to feel Him with my hands," said the hermit, and looked so wretched and unhappy. At this moment a dark cloud hid the sun, which made David feel sad and dejected, almost as if God had withdrawn His presence from the world, and left it a cold, dark, and desolate waste.

But this gloom lasted but for a short time; the cloud passed on, the sun glowed anew as if with increased power, the birds sang, the gnats danced, the cow-bell tinkled, the squirrels sprang gaily about among the branches of the trees, the birches looked quite gladsome, swaying their soft yielding foliage in the sunshine, and Hester, seated on a mossy stone, sang a song of which the echo took up the burden:

"Come listen to a noble song,
Which I have heard the thrushes 'mong;
God's bounteous kindness I will praise
Throughout the length of all my days.

"The flashing brook doth sing His love,
The shifting clouds speak from above,
The gorgeous blossoms of the flower –
All own, and wide proclaim His power.

"The stars shine forth at His command,
The sun reveals His mighty hand;
The whole wide world He fills with light,
And all unite to prove His might,
And show that God dwells everywhere,
Even within myself."

"Yes, that is just what I meant to say," cried David, quite elated, for the little girl had, unawares, happened to sing what he thought but could not find words to express. And then he began making a large horn of the bark of trees, such as graziers use to sound when they wish to call their scattered herd together.

"Well, now, this is astounding. I never thought of that before," said the hermit, and fell into deep thought. "If that is the truth that one can actually see God in everything, without dissecting it, and that He is really to be found within ourselves too."

"There is no doubt of it," said David, and the sun shone straight in his face, so that he was obliged to shade his eyes with his hands.

"I must have discovered nature's secret, then, at last," muttered Old Greybeard with consternation and surprise.

"That you may depend upon, Gaffer," quickly rejoined David, though he did not understand one whit of the old man's troubles, and then he began trying his new horn, to hear if it echoed from the hills.

"Well, now, truly, this is extraordinary," said the hermit, who seemed quite lost with astonishment. "Here have I in my time spent half a century in reading nature, and have found nothing but withered leaves and foul corruption; and then comes along a stripling like this, who is barely more than a babe, and brings me face to face with that which I have sought after so long. Is it possible that a little child can behold God, and solve the enigma of creation? when I myself, who have spent a lifetime in trying to unravel deep mysteries, and am thought to be one of the most learned men in the world, have taken so much labour in vain. But it is really the truth for all that, and it annoys me. Ah, after all, this little rascal is wiser than any of my school."

At these words Old Greybeard grew very small from sheer vexation, and seemed quite ashamed to look the children in the face; and then he retired into the dark recesses of the mountain cleft.

Hester had, by this time, finished making the switches, and David had been sounding his new horn, after which they began to search for the cattle and goats.

Never before had the wood appeared to them so delightful. Everything that had life sang and bloomed in the bright sunshine; every animal could speak, every tree look about itself, and the very stones appeared grey with wisdom. It seemed to them that God had written two great, beautiful, and holy Bibles, for man to read. In the one He had caused His revealed word to be written, His holy commandments, and the sacred evangels which speak of Christ and eternal life. In the other great holy and glorious Bible, the book of creation, which everywhere lies open for us to read, He has written on every leaf and living thing His omnipotence, His wisdom, and His eternal love, if only we can decipher His scroll. But in this the old sage failed, and therefore he lived in the darkness of earth.

And it must not be wondered at that he felt vexed to think how he had wasted half a century (as well as others before him from time immemorial) to discover nature's secret, and how a mere babe, as it were, hits upon the right solution, and with no more concern than if he had found a berry in the wood.

But this is a striking fact in the world, that little children easiest find God, and though they cannot comprehend the deep mysteries of nature's secret, yet they feel within themselves that it is nothing less than that God himself dwells everywhere, and in everything, and in everyone.

The Pine and Fir Trees

IN THE WILDERNESS OF A FINLAND FOREST, near each other, grew two gigantic trees, a pine and a fir. They were so very old that no one could guess the time when they had been saplings, and they could be seen far and wide, for their dark tops towered high over all other trees of the forest. When spring-time came the bullfinch sang delightful melodies, perched on their branches, and the pink and pale blossoms of the heather looked meekly and admiringly up at the grand old giants, as if to say, "Great heavens! is it possible that anything can grow so tall, and become so great and so old in this world?" But when the wintry storms came, and enveloped the whole tract in snow, and the heather had fallen asleep under the white sheet, the raging winds shook the snow from their ever verdant branches, and swelling to a hurricane swept, like an invisible flood, the houses from the surface of the earth, and laid low myriads of trees in the forest, like soldiers fallen in battle.

But the two mighty trees laughed at the storm-god, as he hurled obstacles from his path in his fury; there they stood, invincible and strong, nor ever once quaked, as everything else broke down around them; they might well feel proud, these champions of the wilderness!

Not far from them may be seen a small hill, on the top of which stands a humble hut, covered with turf and small stones to keep the sods in their places. The little dwelling has only two tiny windows and a low door. A potato-plot and a small patch of tillage ground adjoined the hut, in which lived a poor man and his wife. During winter the poor cutter earned his living by felling trees in the forest, and transporting them to a large saw-mill some miles distant, and was thereby enabled to make just enough to keep them in bread and butter, milk and potatoes; and that he thought was very fine, as many others had to live only upon bread, half the ingredients of which were made up of the bark of trees ground to flour, and had no butter at all to make it go down a little easier.

The poor people had two little children, a boy and a girl, whom they had named Sylvester and Sylvia; these were rather strange names, but yet appropriate on account of their sylvan home. One wintry day, it was New Year's Eve, the two children went into the woods to look at the snares and gin traps, for hares and snipe were plentiful, and they had good luck, for there was a beautiful white hare caught in Sylvester's gin trap, and a pretty little snipe in Sylvia's snare, but both the hare and the bird were alive and struggling to be free, for each had been caught by the leg, and they cried so piteously that the children's little hearts were quite touched. "Let me go, and I will give you something nice," said the hare; "Let me free and I will reward you," twittered the poor little bird.

They took pity upon the captives and let them loose; the hare scampered off quick as thought into the brushwood, and the little bird darted off swift as lightning upon her wings, and both cried out as they were leaving, "Ask Skyhigh and Mossbeard, ask Sky-high and Mossbeard!"

"Did you ever!" said the boy, vexed; "such ungrateful little brutes, they did not even say 'thank you'!"

"They told us instead to ask Skyhigh and Mossbeard; who may they be, having such queer names?" said the girl.

"I never heard of them before," rejoined Sylvester.

At this moment a keen northeasterly wind stole through the foliage of the tall trees quite near, creating strange sounds, and the children listened eagerly and could plainly hear the trees whispering to each other:

"Do you stand firm yet, brother Sky-high?" said the fir.

"To be sure I do," rejoined the pine, "but how fares it with you, brother Mossbeard?"

"I am getting old, I feel it," replied the fir, "for the storm tore a limb from my body."

"Oh! you are only a child compared with me," said Sky-high the pine; "only 350 years, and I have completed my 388th year, quite a child yet you are."

"Now the storm returns," said Mossbeard, "we had better sing a little, to give my branches something to do."

And they began singing together, accompanied by the storm:

"List to our words!
High in the north,
Far back in time, and deep in the earth
Are we rooted,
Securely footed;
Therefore, we can weather all storms:
Old winter's shrouds,
Soft summer's rain,
Swift fleeting clouds,
All fall in vain
Upon our brows
Centuries old.
The sons of men
They come and go,
But we remain.
Little children,
Spring-time saplings,
Grow like we
Strong and great,
Firmly rooted
In mountain ground.
Grow in the storm,
Far up in air,
Grow in the light
Heavenwards!
Lift high your brows as we our tops,
Seeking to grow nearer to God."

"Let us talk to these children," quoth Skyhigh.

"I wonder what they are going to say to us?" said the boy.

"Let us go home," whispered his sister; "I feel afraid of the tall trees, and their strange singing."

"Stay a little, here is Father coming, with an axe on his shoulder," and in a short time the cotter came up to them.

"Ah! here are just two such trees as I am in want of!" and he raised his axe to fell Skyhigh.

The children began crying. "Father dear, don't cut down Skyhigh," said Sylvester. "Dear kind Father, pray don't cut down Mossbeard," begged Sylvia; "they are so very old, and have treated us to a song."

"What fool's tales are you telling now, children?" said the cotter; "old trees can't sing. But it is all the same. Since you beg for their lives I'll spare them, and try and find two others to suit me."

And he went further into the woods, but the children remained, for they were curious to hear what Skyhigh and Mossbeard would say to them now.

The wind (which had been away busily engaged in turning the wings of the mill, so swiftly that the mill-stones had nearly struck fire in the dust and floss flying about), ere long returned, and began moaning in the trees; then the children could again plainly discern what their forest friends said.

"You have saved our lives, and we will reward you," they said; "you may now, each of you, ask for something in return, and whatever your wishes may be, we will see them fulfilled."

This made the children very happy, but at the same time also very perplexed what to choose. They had no particular desire for anything in this world; at length, Sylvester said, "I should like to have more sunshine, that we may better see the footprints of the hares upon the snow."

"Yes," exclaimed Sylvia, "and I should like for spring-time to come, so that the snow might melt away, for then the birds would again sing in the wood."

"What little fools you are," said the trees, "you might have wished for all beautiful things in the world, and instead you have only wished for things that will occur whether you wish them or not. But you have saved our lives, and therefore we will fulfil your wishes in the best possible manner. Upon you, Sylvester, we bestow the gift, that wherever you go and wherever you look a laughing sunshine shall spread about; and upon you, Sylvia, we bestow the gift, that wherever you go and whenever you open your pretty little mouth, spring-time will bud, and the snow will melt. Do you like that?" asked the trees.

"Oh yes! yes!" cried the children, highly delighted, "It is much more than we asked for. Many, many thanks, dear old trees, for your kind gifts."

"Now goodbye," said the trees, " and we wish you much joy."

"Goodbye, goodbye," the children called out, and wended their way homeward. As they proceeded along the forest path, the boy often looked round to spy for snipes, as he was wont to do; and, lo! how strange! wherever he looked, it seemed as though a sunbeam illumed the way; it shone clear and bright, and gilded the branches and foliage of the trees. Sylvia saw with amazement that the snow melted away on each side of their forest-path. "Look! look!" she cried out to her little brother, and she had barely opened her mouth before green grass was growing at her feet, and the trees began to display their swelling buds, and the first skylark of the year trilled his joyous strains high up in the air.

"Well, this is nice," the children cried with delight, and they ran home to their mother, the one exclaiming, "I can see sunshine everywhere," and the other, "I can melt snow."

"Well, anybody might do that," said the mother, laughing; but soon she got her eyes opened, for although the shades of evening fell all around the hut, within all was sunshine, which only faded away when Sylvester grew sleepy and gradually closed his eyes; and although it was early in the winter, such a balmy air of spring-time was felt in the cottage that the broom which was standing in a corner of the room began shooting tiny leaves, and the cock which was shut up in a small pen crowed with ecstasy to awaken his hens, and tell them of the unexpected season; and all this continued until Sylvia had fallen asleep.

When the father came home the mother said: "I am afraid, good man, that the children have met with something uncanny in the wood, for everything seems bewitched around them."

"You only fancy that, Wife," said the cotter. "But what think you? I have great news! guess what it is. Well, then, the King and Queen are journeying through the land, and are expected to halt at our parish church tomorrow! What say you? Shall we go and take the children with us, and have a look at royalty?"

"That I think we ought to do. I should like it above all things," answered the wife, "for I have never seen a king and queen before."

Early the following morning the cotter and his family set out for the church, and they were all in such great expectations about what they were going to see, that no one thought of the strange things that had occurred the preceding evening.

When they arrived at the church they found a great concourse of people assembled there, but everybody looked downcast and dismayed. The King, they said, had expressed great dissatisfaction at finding the country so wild and uncultivated, and, being a rather hard master, he laid the blame on the people, and they expected he would punish them severely. Of the Queen they knew that she felt the cold in the land very much, and had been dejected and annoyed during the whole of their journey.

This rumour had been made known beforehand, so everybody trembled, and felt anxious when they saw the royal sledges coming at a great speed along the road. As they came near, the people saw that the King looked stern, and the Queen was weeping; but yet they stopped near the church, while fresh horses were being harnessed to the sledges, and the royal travellers looked around.

"How beautifully the sun shines out, all of a sudden," said the King, and smiled graciously, just like any other human being. "I can't make it out, but I feel quite in a good humour."

"That is because Your Majesty has partaken of a good breakfast," rejoined the Queen. "I, also, feel quite happy."

"The reason is, Your Majesty passed such a good night," answered the King. "But look around! How beautiful appears this desolate land; how the sun gilds those two tall trees, a pine and a fir. What if we should have a royal villa built here?"

"Yes, by all means let it be done, my liege," added the Queen. "For see, it is surprisingly mild here, although it is still winter-time."

At this moment they observed Sylvester and Sylvia, who had climbed up on a rustic wooden paling that ran along the road, the better to observe the royal party; and little Sylvia was chattering away in high glee, and at such a rate that the uncouth branches, of which the enclosure was made, suddenly shot forth green leaves.

"Look, Your Majesty, there are two darling little children," exclaimed the Queen; "let them be brought to the sledge."

The children were immediately brought forward at the royal command, both sucking their thumbs, as seems to be the approved fashion among little folks when they are presented to someone of whom they are a little shy.

"My little ones," said the King, "I like you, and I feel quite happy and warm at heart when I see you. Get up into the sledge, and I will take you to my royal court, and dress you up in cloth of gold, and you shall have the opportunity of making everybody happy around you.'

"No, thank you, please Mr. King," answered both Sylvester and Sylvia. "We like better to make Father and Mother happy at home; at your court we should only fret after Sky-high and Mossbeard."

"Could you not bring them with you?" asked the Queen, who now felt quite warm at heart.

"No thank you, Mrs. Queen," said the children, laughing; "that we can't do, for they grow in the wood."

"What queer ideas get into children's heads, to be sure," said the King and Queen; and they both laughed so heartily that the royal sledge fairly shook from the effect. And the King commanded that a royal villa should be erected on this very spot; every poor person received a golden ducat from the King, and Sylvester and Sylvia besides had a present of a huge festive royal-cake, which the purveyor had purposely baked for the journey, and which was so big that it had to be drawn by four horses. And the children in their turn gave freely of this to everybody in the hamlet; and yet there was so much left that the cotter's horse had a tough job to draw the rest home.

During the journey home to the cottage, the wife said to the husband, "Do you know why the King and Queen were so merry?"

"No," answered he.

"Why, it was because our children looked at them. Don't you remember what I told you yesterday?"

"Yes," said the husband; "but don't tell the children of it. It is better that they don't know of their marvellous gifts which nobody can explain."

But the boy and his little sister were so happy at the remnants of the big cake that they quite forgot all about their gifts of spreading sunshine and melting snow; they were not aware themselves how happy and cheerful everybody became that went near them, and since they were good and loving little children, everybody naturally concluded that was the cause. Certain it is they made their parents very happy, and the wild country around the hut gradually became transformed into fertile corn-fields and rich pasture; where the birds of early spring-time twittered the whole year round; and Sylvester after a few years was made gamekeeper over the demesne belonging to the royal villa; and Sylvia was appointed to tend the flowers in the garden, and, strange to say, wherever these children moved, everything seemed to thrive, that it made one's heart laugh with delight to behold it.

One day Sylvester and Sylvia paid a visit to their old friends, Sky-high and Moss-beard; a mighty snow-storm arose on the occasion, and the wind as of yore sighed and moaned heavily as it swept through the dark foliage of the giant trees, for they were again chanting one of their old lays:

"List, oh! list,
We are growing old, we are growing grey,
Yet to defy thee, O storm, we dare and may;
During verdant spring,
During summer's heat,
During moon's harvest ring,
During winter's snow and sleet,
During misty night,
At dawn so bright.
List, oh! list,
To our song as of old,
We are grey but—"

"Bold," shouted the storm with a hoarse laugh, and crash! – there lay both the mighty champions in the snow. Sky-high had reached the age of 399 years, and Mossbeard 361 years. They had not themselves noticed how their own limbs, with which they were rooted in the earth, at last had withered and lost their hold, so that the mighty storms of winter could vanquish these champions of the forest, no longer invincible.

But the brother and sister patted in a friendly way the mossy stems of the slain old giants, and spoke to them words of loving gratitude, that the snow melted all around them and the pale and pink blossoms of the heather burst out in all their beauty, and intertwined among the branches of the fallen heroes, which thus became buried in a grave of living flowers.

It is now a very long time since I heard anything more about Sylvester and Sylvia, and I suppose that long before this they have themselves grown old and grey, since it is now many, many years when last any king and queen journeyed through Finland. But whenever I see two good and merry little children who everybody loves, then I fancy that they must be Sylvester and Sylvia, and that they have obtained their sparkling merry little eyes by way of reward from some Sky-high and Moss-beard. Not long ago, I saw two such darling children, and it was really remarkable that wherever they looked there seemed to spread sunshine from the merry glances of their eyes; a sunshine which dispelled the clouds from men's furrowed brows and brightened up the faces of those who but a moment before had gazed listlessly around them. The children themselves were not aware of their magical influence, but it was impossible to look at them without feeling a living joy beat responsive in your own breast, which we do feel when we see innocence and kindliness dwell in the same heart. Then thaws the frost which obscured the view on our window-panes; then melts the snow around us, and then men's ice-bound hearts throb with joy, and a new spring-time of life takes birth within, though in the winter of our lives; and, so to say, the very broom, as the meanest thing, begins to bud anew, and the dry branches of the rustic enclosure are once more covered with imaginary blossoms, and the winged and joyous harbinger of spring, the lark, trills his sweet melodies of love and light in the azure sky. And for all this we are beholden to some Sky-high and Mossbeard – or rather say to that God of eternal love who allows love and mirth to spring up like a new spring in the hearts of men.

The Ambitious Birch

IN THE WOOD, NOT FAR FROM THE HIGH ROAD, grew a beautiful birch tree. He was only a sapling yet, and it being early spring-time, he had begun to throw out numerous tiny buds and leaflets, of a soft delicate green, the dainty costume in which Mother Nature attires these, her curled darlings, in their childhood.

"Now, really I am very pretty," thought the young birch tree to himself. " I am sure I am a good deal handsomer than any of those crooked old mountain-ashes yonder. I should think so, indeed," and he tried to straighten himself out more than ever. "Now I wonder what I shall become in the world; perhaps the titmouse could guess." With that he asked the little bird.

But his adviser was a little rascal, who wished to keep friends with the birch, to be allowed to peck with his beak at his fresh swelling buds, so the titmouse answered, "Well, really now, master birch, you are certainly good-looking, and, I should say, destined to become something superior in this world. I would almost wager anything that they will make a basket of your twigs for the princess, to be placed on the marble slab of her table and filled with golden apples."

"Oh, indeed! how delightful!" exclaimed the conceited birch.

"That you may depend upon," said the little storyteller of a titmouse, and flew away to a big spruce fir which grew a little way off, and made him believe that out of his trunk would be made a rocking-chair for no less a personage than the king himself. He knew not that the sly bird wished to shelter himself under his thick branches when it rained, that he might feed in peace and comfort upon his tasty spruce-cones.

How artfully they are taken in, who listen to the flatterer's voice!

Near to the main road was a hut, from which one day a number of children came into the wood, and being provided with knives, began to cut off twigs from the young birch. 'Ah, here they have come already,' thought the sapling, 'to make a basket for the princess,' and he was so pleased with himself that he quite trembled with delight, and his little buds quivered in ecstasy.

"The leaves are not big enough yet to do for bathing switches," the children said, "rather let us make regular brooms of the long twigs."

"What," sighed the birch, dismayed, "dare anyone turn me into a broom?"

"What a fine broom it will make, to be sure," said the children, and then they made such a useful domestic implement of him, that is to say, not of the whole of him, but from his twigs, but that meant all the same, for every twig thought himself as good as the entire tree, and the ambitious little things consoled themselves with the thought that they at least should have the honour of sweeping the princess's parlour, even if they were not permitted to become a casket for golden apples on a marble-slab.

When the children returned home, their mother, on beholding the new broom, said, "Well done, children, that is a good strong one, I will keep that for myself to sweep the kitchen floor with"; and she applied him to the task. The conceited twigs could have dropped all the buds from very fear and shame if they had not already been deprived of them during the making of the broom. After this trial he was thrust into a corner near the fireplace, and where at leisure he began chatting with the pail by his side.

"I belong to a fine family, though they have made a menial of me," he said, "but my lineage can easily be traced; isn't there something light, airy, and elegant about me still?"

"I can't see it," answered the pail, "but I myself belong to a very ancient race, who for ages have been the bulwark of the land. I was intended for a rocking-chair for the king, and a most important position that is, I can tell you, but I was spoiled in the making, and was fashioned into a pail instead. A little titmouse had predicted that great destiny for me; he staked his life, he said, but then, you know, a little bird stakes his life too frequently."

"Oh, fie upon that little rascal," interrupted the broom, "he has cheated me in the very same way, and he has told you fibs. Tell me, neighbour, what do you intend to become by and by?"

"Oh, I shall remain a pail all my life," answered the spruce-fir's descendant. "If only I get my fill of bones, and peelings, and dishwater I am quite content. And then the pigs are really very fond of me; directly I go to fling them their victuals, they hear me coming, and crowd round quite eagerly to see me. I say, friend, as our lot in life has been thrown together, what do you say to our marrying?"

"Well, I'm sure, I never heard of such presumption!" exclaimed the broom. "Do you imagine that I intend to remain all my life in this position? A broom, forsooth! Oh dear no! You will witness my rise in the world yet."

"Well, those who live shall see," answered the pail.

The housewife at this moment came to the fireplace, and looking at the broom, said, "I see it is already a good deal used up, I had better make a switch to chastise the children with; it is really needed at times, when they are disobedient." And she at once set about making it, not of the whole of the broom, only from a few of the softest twigs, but of course each twig thought himself as good as the broom entire.

With the switch the mother beat her children, and since he was so frequently in use, he must have been sadly needed. Whenever they quarrelled, pulled each other by the hair, or tore their clothes, the switch had to perform his duties, and it was really wonderful how well he did his business; the children must have quite enjoyed it, for they marvellously improved.

The switch at first rather disliked his new profession, but he gradually became so accustomed to it, that he was always ready for work, and whenever the children quarrelled he used to say to himself, where he sat stuck up between the door-post and the wall, "Now then, I shall soon be amongst you!"

"A mighty fine position you are raised to, and no mistake," sneered the pail.

"You be quiet, or I will treat you as I do the children," muttered the chastiser. "Nobody knows yet what may become of me if fortune comes in my way."

"Well, we shall see," answered the incredulous pail.

"Heaven be thanked, the children have now been taught to behave themselves," said the mother. "Dear me, the switch is quite worn out; I will just put it together with the remnants of the broom as a bed for the little pigs, they are in want of something soft to lie upon."

The stumps of sprigs were now thrown into the sty; not a very nice place. "Enough, enough," grunted the inhabitants, and turned them over with their miry snouts.

"Good gracious me, how you look!" exclaimed the pail, when she was brought with the pigs' food into the sty.

"Keep your pity to yourself," answered the twigs, "you don't know what may become of me yet." But really now he was in a most deplorable plight; if a switch could shed tears instead of drawing them from others, he had cause to weep enough to fill the whole pail.

Now you may think the story has come to an end, but it is nothing of the kind. The birch had not been allowed to supply a basket for the princess, and as a broom had not been appointed to sweep her royal floors, or as a switch called upon to beat the golden-stitched jackets of the princelings, not even been used as a bed for the royal sucking-pigs. Instead of his ambitious plans in the spring-time (when he was budding with youth and hope) having been realized, he had been subjected to many humiliating tasks.

The titmouse one day perched on the railings of the pig sty. The twigs recognized him at once. "Well met, Titmouse; how do you do?" they shouted.

But the little rascal was off like a shot. He did not care to renew an acquaintance with those who had so sadly come down in the world that even some trampled upon them; besides, he felt no longer any interest in them whatsoever, now they could not treat him to any more dainty buds in exchange for his flattery. After some time the abject remnants of twigs were thrown out on the land, and there they lay embedded in mud and snow, summer and winter. The corn grew up and hid their miseries. The pail, as well as the housewife and the titmouse, had long ago forgotten their very existence. However, during all these misfortunes they had managed to preserve just one tiny little mite of a bud, which carried a germinating seed within it. From this small seed grew in the middle of the ditch a wee birchen plant, softly tinged with green. The king and queen were out travelling in the land this season, together with their young children.

One sultry summer day they passed near to the little homestead and the little corn-field, which lay close to the high road, and as the landscape was charmingly inviting, they halted for a while to enjoy the cool shade which the luxuriant foliage of a clump of trees afforded. Their little daughter, the princess, expressed her joy at quitting the close carriage, and danced away with delight along the side of the green-covered dyke, to where the little birch plant grew.

"Oh, look what a pretty little thing grows here!" she cried. "Oh, I should like to plant that in my garden."

"It is only a little sapling-birch," said the king. "What do you want with it? Oaks, and poplars, and chestnuts, or fruit-trees are far better worth planting, my child; of them you may have as many as you like."

"I have plenty of them already," answered the little princess, "but I have not a single birch; do let me take it home to the castle with me," said she, beseechingly.

"Allow her to do that, my dear Lord," said the indulgent queen. "There can be no harm in so doing."

"Most willingly, you foolish little child," answered the king; "only, don't take all the pretty trees you see with you, or there will be no room for ourselves in the carriage."

The young princess carefully loosened the small plant from its birth-place, placed it in a basket filled with moistened moss, and thus brought it to her castle home. Once there, she transplanted the birch with her own hands into a fine garden, and placed soft mould around its roots, and watered and tended the birch every day, as if it had been her foster child. The birch thrived and grew tall, and gradually became a fine large tree, alone of its kind among a number of exotic luxuriant trees the simple child of the woodlands, born and nurtured in the freedom of nature. And he grew really magnificent and grand, and was the acknowledged favourite of the princess. Of all places she preferred to sit under his graceful leafy canopy, and all thought that this was the foremost tree on the royal demesne.

The ambitious birch-tree of the forest was vain; consequently had to endure a fall. His longings were influenced by false ambition; he was therefore condemned to suffer humiliation, disgrace and death. But he had cherished an everlasting hope of a better future, which no humiliation could crush, and for this he was now rewarded in the glory of his offspring planted in the king's garden. The yearnings of hope and faith are always sooner or later realized, though inscrutable are the ways that lead thereto, through trials severe and frequent.

The pail had also in her youth nourished ambitious dreams of future fame and fortunc; but she was of coarser grain, and had grown habituated to her drudgery, and at last thought of nothing but her daily food. Every sapling in the forest of life indulges in hopeful daydreams of future greatness. But some only become plodders and drudges like the pail, others nothing at all, while still others become the source of happiness to their kin.

This yearning never ceases in the budding spring-time, and the youthful period of our forest life is full of these ambitious dreams. Dream, young sapling, of your future, hope for greatness, but beware of false ambition. Ever retain a pure and humble heart, hope humbly, purge yourself of pride, and then you will not have to be buried in the cold earth before the princess of the future chances to seek and transplant you into her garden, where you may find your right mission of giving shelter and joy to the weary wanderers of life.

Human Stories, Heroes & Morality

Introduction

ALWAYS AN OUTLIER, ALWAYS STRANDED far away on the unfashionable edge of Europe, Finland learned to take a down-to-earth view of valour and to see the heroism in more everyday courage. Consider the bravery exemplified with which 'The Terrible Olli' resists the wicked Troll. Meanwhile, four centuries of Lutheranism encouraged Finns to find a romance in doing the right thing and a satisfaction in stoic suffering, which more than made up for what was lost in glory and derring-do. By and large, it is fair to say that heroism here is understated, while morality is depicted modestly and without drama. Ultimately, however, these virtues are no less impressive, no less moving.

Log

(The Story of the Hero Who Released the Sun)

THERE WAS ONCE A POOR COUPLE who had no children. Their neighbours all had boys and girls in plenty but for some reason God didn't send them even one.

"If I can't have a flesh and blood baby," the woman said one day, "I'm going to have a wooden baby." She went to the woods and cut a log of alder just the size of a nice fat baby. She dressed the log in baby clothes and put it in a cradle. Then for three whole years she and her husband rocked the cradle and sang lullabies to the log baby.

At the end of three years one afternoon, when the man was out chopping wood and the woman was driving the cows home from pasture, the log baby turned into a real baby! It was so strong and hearty that by the time its parents got home it had crawled out of the cradle and was sitting on the floor yelling lustily for food. It ate and ate and ate and the more it ate the faster it grew. It wasn't any time at all in passing from babyhood to childhood, from childhood to youth, and from youth to manhood. From its beginnings it was known in the village as Log and never received any other name.

Log's parents knew from the first that Log was destined to be a great hero. That was why he was so strong and so good. There was no one in the village as strong as he nor anyone as kind and gentle.

Now just at this time a great calamity overtook the world. The sun and the moon and the dawn disappeared from the sky and as a result the earth was left in darkness.

"Who have taken from us the sun and the moon and the dawn?" the people cried in terror.

"Whoever they are," the king said, "they shall have to restore them! Where, O where are the heroes who will undertake to find the sun and the moon and the dawn and return them to their places in the sky?"

There were many men willing to offer themselves for the great adventure but the king realized that something more was needed than willingness.

"It is only heroes of exceptional strength and endurance," he said, "who should risk the dangers of so perilous an undertaking."

So he called together all the valiant youths of the kingdom and tested them one by one. He had some waters of great strength and it was his hope to find three heroes the first of whom could drink three bottles of the strong waters, the second six bottles, and the third nine bottles.

Hundreds of youths presented themselves and out of them all the king found at last two, one of whom was able to take three bottles of the strong waters, the other six bottles.

"But we need three heroes!" the king cried. "Is there no one in all this kingdom strong enough to drink nine bottles?"

"Try Log!" someone shouted.

All the youths present instantly took up the cry:

"Log! Log! Send for Log!"

So the king sent for Log and sure enough when Log came he was able to drink down nine bottles of the strong waters without any trouble at all.

"Here now," the king proclaimed, "are the three heroes who are to release the sun and the moon and the dawn from whoever are holding them in captivity and restore them to their places in the sky!"

He equipped the three heroes for a long journey furnishing them money and food and drink of the strong waters, each according to his strength. He mounted them each on a mighty horse with sword and arrow and dog.

So the three heroes rode off in the dark and the women of the kingdom wept to see them go and the men cheered and wished that they, too, were going.

They rode on and on for many days that seemed like nights until they had crossed the confines of their own country and entered the boundaries of an unknown kingdom beyond. Here the darkness was less dense. There was no actual daylight but a faint greyness as of approaching dawn.

They rode on until they saw looming up before them the towers of a mighty castle. They dismounted near the castle at the door of a little hut where they found an old woman.

"Good day to you, Granny!" Log called out.

"Good day, indeed!" the old woman said. "It's little enough we see of the day since the evil one cursed the sun and handed it over to Suyettar's wicked offspring, the nine-headed serpent!"

"The evil one!" Log exclaimed. "Tell me, Granny, why did the evil one curse the sun?"

"Because he's evil, my son, that's why! He said the sun's rays blistered him, so he cursed the sun and gave him over to the nine-headed serpent. And he cursed the moon, too, because at night when the moon shone he could not steal. Yes, my son, he cursed the moon and handed her over to Suyettar's second offspring, the six-headed serpent. Then he cursed the dawn because he said he couldn't sleep in the morning because of the dawn. So he cursed the dawn and gave her over to Suyettar's third offspring, the three-headed serpent."

"Tell me, Granny," Log said, "where do the three serpents keep prisoner the sun and the moon and the dawn?"

"Listen, my son, and I will tell you: When they go far out in the ocean they carry with them the sun and the moon and the dawn. The three-headed serpent stays out there one day and then returns at night. The six-headed serpent stays two days and then returns, and the mighty nine-headed monster does not return until the third night. As each returns a faint glow spreads over the land. That is why we are not in utter darkness."

Log thanked the old woman and then he and his companions pushed on towards the castle. As they neared it they saw a strange sight which they could not understand. One half of the great castle was laughing and rocking as if in merriment and the other half was weeping as if in grief.

"What can this mean?" Log cried out. "We had better ask the old woman before we go on."

So they went back to the hut and the old woman told them all she knew.

"It is on account of the dreadful fate that is hanging over the king's three daughters," she said. "Those three evil monsters are demanding them one by one. Tonight when the three-headed serpent comes back from the ocean he expects to devour the eldest. If the king refuses to give her up, then Suyettar's evil son will devour half the kingdom, half of the castle itself, and half the shining stones. O that some hero would kill the monster and save the princess and at the same time release the Dawn that it might again steal over the world!"

Log and his fellows conferred together and the one they called three bottles, because his strength was equal to three bottles of the strong waters, declared that it was his task to fight and conquer the three-headed serpent.

In the castle meanwhile preparations for the sacrifice of the oldest princess were going forward. As the king sewed the poor girl into a great leather sack, his tears fell so fast that he could scarcely see what he was doing.

"My dear child," he said, "it should comfort you greatly to think that the monster is going to eat you instead of half the kingdom! Not many princesses are considered as important as half the kingdom!"

The princess knew that what her father said must be true and she did her best to look cheerful as they slipped the sack over her head. Once inside, however, she allowed herself to cry for she knew that no one could see her. The sack with the princess inside was carried down to the beach and put on a high rock near the place where Suyettar's sons were wont to come up out of the water.

"Don't be frightened, my daughter!" the king called out as he and all the court started back to the castle. "You won't have long to wait, for it will soon be evening."

Log and his companions watched the king's party disappear and then Three Bottles solemnly drank down the three bottles of strong waters with which his own king had equipped him. As he was ready to mount his horse, he handed Log the leash to which his dog was attached.

"If I need help," he said, "I'll throw back my shoe and do you then release my dog."

With that he rode boldly down to the beach, dismounted, and climbed up the rock where the unfortunate princess lay in a sack. With one slash of the sword he ripped open the sack and dragged the princess out. She supposed of course that he was the three-headed serpent and at first was so frightened that she kept her eyes tightly shut not daring to look at him. She expected every minute to have him take a first bite and, when minutes and more minutes and more minutes still went by and he didn't, she opened her eyes a little crack to see what was the matter.

"Oh!" the princess said.

She was so surprised that for a long time she didn't dare to take another peep.

"You thought I was the three-headed serpent, didn't you?" a pleasant voice asked. "But I'm not. I'm only a young man who has come to rescue you."

The princess murmured, "Oh!" again, but this time the "Oh!" expressed happy relief.

"Yes," repeated the young man, "I am the hero who has come to rescue you. My comrades call me Three Bottles and you, too, may call me that. And while we are waiting for the serpent to come in from the ocean I wish you would scratch my head."

The princess wasn't in the least surprised at this request. Heroes and monsters and fathers alike seemed always to want their heads scratched.

So Three Bottles stretched himself at the princess's feet and put his head in her lap. He settled himself comfortably and she scratched his head while he gazed out over the dark ocean waiting for the serpent to appear. At first there was nothing to break the glassy surface of the water. They waited and at last far out they saw three swirling masses rolling landward.

"Quick, my princess!" Three Bottles cried. "There comes the monster now! Get you down behind the rock and hide there while I go meet the creature and chop off his ugly heads!"

The princess, quivering with fright, crouched down behind the rock and Three Bottles, mounting his horse, rode boldly down to the water's edge awaiting the serpent's coming.

It came nearer and nearer in long easy swirls, slowly lifting its three scaly heads one after another.

As it approached shore it sniffed the air hungrily.

"Fee, fi, fo, fum!" it muttered in a deep voice, repeating the magic rime it had learned from its evil mother, Suyettar:

"Fee, fi, fo, fum!
I smell a Finn! Yum! Yum!
I'll fall upon him with a thud!
I'll pick his bones and drink his blood!
Fee, fi, fo, fum!
Yum! Yum!"

"Stop boasting, son of Suyettar!" Three Bottles cried. "You'll have time enough to boast after you fight!"

"Fight?" repeated the serpent as if in surprise. "Shall we fight, pretty boy, you and I? Very well! Blow then with your sweet breath, blow out a long level platform of red copper whereon we can meet and try our strength each with the other!"

"Nay," answered Three Bottles. "Do you blow with your evil breath and instead of red copper we shall have a platform of black iron."

So the serpent blew and on the iron platform that came of his breath Three Bottles met him in combat. Back and forth they raged, Three Bottles striking right and left with his mighty sword, the serpent hitting at Three Bottles with all his scaly heads and belching forth fire and smoke from all his mouths. Three Bottles hacked off one scaly head and at last a second one, but he was unable to touch the third.

"I shall have to have help," he acknowledged to himself finally, and reaching down he took one of his shoes and threw it over his shoulder back to his comrades who were awaiting the outcome of the struggle. Instantly they loosed the dog which bounded forward to its master's assistance and soon with the dog's help Three Bottles was able to dispatch the last head.

He was faint now with weariness and his comrades had to help him back to the old woman's hut where he soon fell asleep.

Night passed and Dawn appeared. A great cry of relief and thanksgiving went up from all the earth.

"The dawn! The dawn!" people cried. "God bless the man who has released the dawn!"

Only at the castle was there sorrow still.

"My poor oldest daughter!" the king cried with tears in his eyes. "It was my sacrifice of her that has released the dawn!"

Then he called his slaves and gave them orders to gather up his daughter's bones and to bring back the leather sack.

"We shall need it again tonight," he said. He wiped his eyes and for a moment could say no more. "Yes, tonight we shall have to sew up my second daughter and offer her to the six-headed serpent, him that holds captive the moon. Otherwise the monster will devour half my kingdom, half the castle, and half the shining stones. Ai! Ai! Ai!"

But the slaves when they went to the high rock on the seashore found, not the princess's bones, but the princess herself, sitting there with her chin in her hand, gazing down on the beach which was strewn with the fragments of the three-headed serpent.

They led her back to her father and reported the marvel they had seen.

"There, O King, lies the monster on the sand with all his heads severed! So huge are the heads that it would need three men with derricks to move one of them!"

"Some unknown hero has rescued my oldest daughter!" the king cried. "Would that another might come tonight to rescue my second child likewise! But, alas! what hero is strong enough to destroy the six-headed monster!"

So when evening came they sewed the second princess in the sack and carried her out to the rock.

Log and his companions saw the procession move down from the castle and they saw that the castle was again disturbed, one half of it laughing and one half weeping.

"It's the second princess tonight," the old woman told them. "Unless her father, the king, gives her to the six-headed serpent, the monster will come and devour half the kingdom, half the castle, and half the shining stones. He it is that holds the moon captive and the hero that slays him will release the moon."

Then he whom his comrades called Six Bottles cried out:

"Here is work for me!"

He drank bottle after bottle of the strong waters until he had emptied six.

"Now I am ready!" he shouted.

He mounted his mighty horse and as he rode off he called to his comrades:

"If I need help I'll throw back a shoe and do you then unleash my dog!"

He rode to the rock on the shore and dismounted. Then he climbed the rock and released the second princess. He told her who he was and as they awaited the arrival of the six-headed serpent he lay at the princess's feet and she scratched his head.

This time the serpent came in six mighty swirls with six awful heads that reared up one after another. In terror the second princess hid behind the rock while Six Bottles, mounting his horse, rode boldly down to the water's edge.

Like his brother serpent this one, too, came sniffing the air hungrily, muttering the magic rime he had learned from his mother, wicked Suyettar:

"Fee, fi, fo, fum!
I smell a Finn! Yum! Yum!
I'll fall upon him with a thud!
I'll pick his bones and drink his blood!
Fee, fi, fo, fum! Yum! Yum!"

"Stop boasting, son of an evil mother!" Six Bottles cried. "You will have time enough to boast after you fight!"

"Fight?" repeated the serpent scornfully. "Shall we fight, little one, you and I? Very well! Blow then with your sweet breath, blow out a long level platform of white silver whereon we can meet and try our strength one with the other."

"Nay!" answered Six Bottles. "Do you blow, blow with your evil breath, and instead of white silver we shall have a platform of red copper."

So the serpent blew and on the copper platform that came of his breath Six Bottles met him in combat. Back and forth they raged, Six Bottles striking left and right with his mighty sword, the serpent hitting at Six Bottles with every one of his six scaly heads and belching forth fire and smoke from all his mouths. Six Bottles hacked off one head, then another, then another. At last he had disposed of five heads. He tried hard to strike the last, but by this time the serpent had grown wary and Six Bottles' own strength was waning. So he reached down and took one of his shoes and threw it over his shoulder back to his comrades who were awaiting the outcome of the struggle. Instantly they loosed the dog which bounded forward to its master's assistance and soon with the dog's help Six Bottles was able to dispatch the last head.

Then his comrades led him, weary from the fight, to the old woman's hut and soon he fell asleep.

While he slept the Moon appeared in the sky and a great cry of relief and thanksgiving went up from all the world:

"The moon! The moon! God bless the man who has released the moon!"

The king who was awakened by the sound looked out the castle window and when he saw the Moon, returned to its place in the sky, his eyes overflowed with grief.

"My poor second daughter!" he cried. "It was my sacrifice of her that has released the moon! Tomorrow morning I will send the slaves to gather up her bones and to bring back the leather sack into which, alas! I must then sew my youngest daughter for evil Suyettar's third son, the nine-headed serpent. Ai! Ai! Ai! How sad it is to be a father!"

But on the morrow when the slaves went to the rock they found the second princess sitting there alone gazing down upon the scattered fragments of the six-headed serpent.

"Here she is, safe and sound!" they reported to the king as they led the second princess into his presence, "and, marvel of marvels! on the beach below the rock lies the body of the six-headed serpent torn to pieces! Its heads, O King, are so monstrous that six men with derricks could scarcely move one of them!"

"God be praised!" the king cried. "Another unknown hero has come and saved the life of my second child! Would that a third might come tonight and rescue the life of my youngest child! Alas, she is dearer to me than both the others, but I fear me that even if there be heroes who could dispatch the first two serpents, there is never one who can touch him of the nine heads that holds the mighty sun a captive!"

And the poor king wept, so sure was he that nothing could save the life of his youngest child.

When Log and his companions heard of the king's grief, Log at once stood forth and said: "This last and mightiest battle is for me!"

He opened the strong waters and drank bottle after bottle until he had emptied nine.

"Now let night come as soon as it will!" he cried. "I am ready for the monster!"

He started forth telling his comrades he would throw back a shoe if he needed help from his dog.

So it was Log himself who slashed open the sack for the third time and released the youngest princess who was much more beautiful than her sisters. She fell in love with the mighty hero on sight and was so thrilled with his godlike beauty that when he put his head in her lap she hardly knew what to do although her father always declared that she scratched his head much better than either of her sisters.

They had not long to wait for soon all the ocean was a-glitter with the swirls of the ninefold monster who was coming to shore with the captive sun in his keeping.

"Await me behind the rock!" Log cried to the princess as he leapt upon his horse and started forward.

"Oh, Log, my hero, be careful!" the princess cried after him.

Nearer and nearer came the swirls of the nine-coiled monster. One after another of his nine heads rose and fell as he approached, and every head sniffed more hungrily as it came nearer, and each head rumbled as it sniffed:

"Fee, fi, fo, fum!
I smell a Finn! Yum! Yum!
I'll fall upon him with a thud!
I'll pick his bones and drink his blood!
Fee, fi, fo, fum!
Yum! Yum!"

"Stop boasting, evil son of an evil mother!" Log cried. "You will have time enough to boast after you fight!"

"Fight?" roared the awful monster. "Shall we fight, poor infant, you and I? Very well! Blow then with your sweet breath, blow out a long level platform of shining gold whereon we can meet and try our strength each with the other!"

"Nay!" Log answered boldly. "Do you blow, blow with your evil breath and instead of shining gold we shall have a platform of white silver."

So the monster blew and on the silver platform that came of his breath Log met him in combat. Back and forth they raged, Log striking right and left with his mighty sword, the serpent hitting at

Log with all his nine scaly heads and belching forth fire and smoke from all his nine mouths. Log hacked off head after head until six lay gaping on the sand. But the last three he could not get.

Suddenly he pointed behind the serpent and cried:

"Quick! Quick! The sun! It is escaping!"

The serpent looked around and Log hacked off a head. Now only two remained, but try as he would Log could get neither of them.

Again he tried subterfuge.

"Your wife, O Son of Suyettar! See, yonder, they're abusing her!"

The monster looked and Log whacked off another head. But one now remained and as usual it was the hardest of them all to get. Log felt his strength waning while the Monster seemed more nimble than ever.

'I shall have to have help,' Log thought.

He threw back his shoe to his comrades and they at once loosed his dog. With the dog's help Log was soon able to dispatch the last head. Then Three Bottles and Six Bottles helped him off his horse and supported him to the old woman's hut where he soon fell into a deep sleep.

The next morning the blessed Sun rose at his proper time and people all over the world, falling on their knees with thanksgiving and weeping with joy, cried out:

"The sun! The sun! God bless the man who has released the sun!"

At the castle they woke the king with the good news but the king only shook his head and murmured in grief:

"Yes, the sun is released but what care I since my favourite child, my youngest daughter, has been sacrificed!"

He dispatched the slaves to gather up her bones and presently these returned bringing the princess herself and telling a marvellous tale of the beach littered with nine severed heads so huge that it would need nine men with derricks to move one of them.

"What manner of heroes are these who have rescued my daughters!" cried the king. "Let them come forth and I will give them my daughters for wives and half my riches for dowry! But they will have to prove themselves the actual heroes by bringing to the castle the heavy heads of the monsters they have slain."

When Log and his fellows heard this they laughed with happiness and, strengthening themselves with deep draughts of the strong waters, they gathered together the many heads of the mighty serpents, bore them to the castle, and piled them up at the king's feet.

Then Log stepped forward and said:

"Here we are, O King, come to claim our reward!"

The king, true to his promise, gave them his daughters in marriage, the oldest to Three Bottles, the second to Six Bottles, and the lovely youngest to Log. Then he apportioned them the half of his riches and, after much feasting and merrymaking, the heroes took their brides and their riches and bidding the king farewell started homewards.

As they rode through a great forest they sighted a tiny hut and Log, motioning his comrades to wait for him quietly, crept forward to see who was in the hut. It was well he was cautious for inside the hut was Suyettar herself talking to two other old hags.

"Ay," she was saying, "they have slain my three beautiful sons, my mighty offspring that held captive the sun and the moon and the dawn! But I tell you, sisters, they will pay the penalty..."

To hear better Log changed himself into a piece of firewood and slipping inside the hut hid himself in the woodpile near the stove.

"Ay, they will pay the penalty!" Suyettar repeated. "I shall have my revenge on them! A fine supper Suyettar shall soon have, yum, yum!

I'll fall upon them with a thud!
I'll pick their bones and drink their blood!

Fools, fools, to think they can escape Suyettar's anger!"

"But sister, sister," the two old hags asked, "how will you get them?"

Suyettar looked this way and that to make sure that no one was listening. Then she whispered:

"This is how I shall get them: As they come through this forest, the three men with their brides, I shall send upon them a terrible hunger. Then they shall come suddenly upon a table spread with tempting food. One bite of that food and they are in my power, he-he! Ay, sisters, tonight Suyettar will have a fine supper! Nothing can save them unless, before they touch the food, someone make the sign of the cross three times over the table. Then table and food would disappear and also the ravening hunger. But even if that happens Suyettar shall still get them!"

"How, sister, how?" the other two asked.

"Presently I should send upon them consuming thirst, and then put in their pathway a spring of cold sparkling water. One drop of that water and they are in my power, he-he! Nothing can save them from me unless, before their lips touch the water, someone make the sign of the cross three times over the spring. At that the spring would disappear and also their thirst. But even if they escape the spring, I shall still get them. I shall send great heaviness on them and a longing for sleep, then let them come upon a row of soft inviting feather beds. If they cast themselves upon the beds, they are mine, he-he! to feast upon as I will! Nothing can save but that someone make the sign of the cross three times over the beds before they touch them. Oh, sisters, I shall get them one way or another for there is no one to warn them. If there was any one to warn them, he wouldn't dare tell them what he knows for he would also know that if he told them he would himself be turned into a blue cross and have to stand forever in the cemetery."

As Log knew now all the dangers that threatened, he slipped away from the woodpile and, when he was outside, took his own shape and hurried back to his comrades.

"Away!" he cried. "We are in great danger!"

They all spurred their horses and rode swiftly on until Three Bottles suddenly cried:

"Hold, comrades, hold! I am faint with hunger!"

"Me, too!" cried Six Bottles.

At that instant a great table, laden with delicious food, appeared before them.

"Look!" cried the one of them.

"Food!" cried the other.

They flung themselves from their horses and ran towards the table. But quick as they were, Log was quicker. He reached the table first and, raising his hand, made the sign of the cross three times. The table disappeared as suddenly as it had come and with it the strange hunger that had but now consumed them.

"Strange!" Three Bottles exclaimed. "I thought I was hungry, but I'm not!"

"I thought I saw food just now," Six Bottles said. "I must have been dreaming."

So they mounted again and pushed on.

"Danger threatens us," said Log. "We must hurry and not dismount no matter what the temptation."

They agreed but presently one of them cried out and then the other:

"Water! Water! We shall soon perish unless we have water!"

Instantly by the wayside appeared a spring of cool sparkling water and it was all Log could do to reach it before his fellows. He did get there first and make the sign of the cross three times whereat the spring disappeared and with it the thirst which had but now consumed them all.

"I thought I was thirsty," Three Bottles said, "but I'm not!"

"Why did we dismount?" Six Bottles asked. "There's no water here."

So again they mounted and went forward and Log, warning them again that danger threatened, begged them not to dismount a third time no matter what the temptation.

They promised they would not but presently, complaining of fatigue, they wanted to. Their brides, too, swayed in the saddle, overcome with weariness and sleep.

"Dear Log," they said, "let us rest for an hour. See, our brides are drooping with fatigue! One hour's sleep and we shall all be refreshed!"

Instantly beside them on the forest floor they saw three soft white feather beds. Log leaped to the ground but before he was able to make the sign of the cross over more than one of the beds, his comrades and their brides had fallen headlong on the other two.

And that was the end of poor Three Bottles and Six Bottles and their two lovely brides. There was no way now of saving them from Suyettar. She had them in her power and nothing would induce her to give them up.

As Log and his bride sadly mounted their horse and rode on they heard an evil voice chanting out in triumph:

"I'll fall upon them with a thud, he-he!
I'll pick their bones and drink their blood, he-he!"

"Poor fellows! Poor fellows!" Log said, and the princess wept to think of the awful fate that had overtaken her two sisters.

Well, Log and his bride reached home without further adventure and were received by the king with great honours.

"I knew my heroes were succeeding," the king said, "when first the dawn appeared again, and then the moon, and last the mighty sun. All hail to you, Log, and to your two comrades! But, by the way, where are Three Bottles and Six Bottles?"

"Your Majesty," Log said, "Three Bottles and Six Bottles were brave men both. By their prowess they released the one the dawn, the other the moon. Then in an evil adventure on the way home they perished. I can tell you no more."

"You can tell me no more?" the king said. "Why can you tell me no more? What was the evil adventure in which they perished?"

"If I told you, O King, then I, too, should perish, for I should be turned into a blue cross and stood forever in the cemetery!"

"What nonsense!" the king exclaimed. "Who would turn you into a blue cross and stand you forever in the cemetery?"

"That is what I cannot tell you," Log said.

The king laughed and pressed Log no further, but the people of the kingdom, scenting a mystery, insisted on knowing in detail what had happened the other two heroes. Presently the rumour began to spread that Log himself had done away with them in order that he might gather to himself all the glory of the undertaking.

The king was forced at last to send for him again and to demand a full account of everything.

Log realized that his end was near. He met it bravely. Commending to the king's protection his lovely bride, the youngest princess, Log related how the three mighty serpents whom they had killed were sons of Suyettar, and how in revenge Suyettar had succeeded in destroying Three Bottles and Six Bottles together with their brides. Then he told the fate about to overtake himself.

He finished speaking and as the king and the court looked at him, to their amazement he disappeared.

"To the cemetery!" someone cried.

They all went to the cemetery where at once they found a fresh blue cross that had come there nobody knew how. There it stands to this day, a reminder of the life and deeds of the mighty hero, Log.

The king was overcome with sorrow at losing such a hero. He took Log's bride under his protection and he found her so beautiful and so gentle that soon he fell in love with her and married her.

The Terrible Olli

(The Story of an Honest Finn and a Wicked Troll)

THERE WAS ONCE A WICKED RICH OLD TROLL who lived on a Mountain that sloped down to a Bay. A decent Finn, a farmer, lived on the opposite side of the Bay. The farmer had three sons. When the boys had reached manhood he said to them one day:

"I should think it would shame you three strong youths that that wicked old Troll over there should live on year after year and no one trouble him. We work hard like honest Finns and are as poor at the end of the year as at the beginning. That old Troll with all his wickedness grows richer and richer. I tell you, if you boys had any real spirit you'd take his riches from him and drive him away!"

His youngest son, whose name was Olli, at once cried out:

"Very well, father, I will!"

But the two older sons, offended at Olli's promptness, declared:

"You'll do no such thing! Don't forget your place in the family! You're the youngest and we're not going to let you push us aside. Now, father, we two will go across the Bay and rout out that old Troll. Olli may come with us if he likes and watch us while we do it."

Olli laughed and said: "All right!" for he was used to his brothers treating him like a baby.

So in a few days the three brothers walked around the Bay and up the Mountain and presented themselves at the Troll's house. The Troll and his old wife were both at home. They received the brothers with great civility.

"You're the sons of the Finn who lives across the Bay, aren't you?" the Troll said. "I've watched you boys grow up. I am certainly glad to see you for I have three daughters who need husbands. Marry my daughters and you'll inherit my riches."

The old Troll made this offer in order to get the young men into his power.

"Be careful!" Olli whispered.

But the brothers were too delighted at the prospect of inheriting the Troll's riches so easily to pay any heed to Olli's warning. Instead they accepted the Troll's offer at once.

Well, the old Troll's wife made them a fine supper and after supper the Troll sent them to bed with his three daughters. But first he put red caps on the three youths and white caps on the three Troll girls. He made a joke about the caps.

"A red cap and a white cap in each bed!" he said.

The older brothers suspected nothing and soon fell asleep. Olli, too, pretended to fall asleep and when he was sure that none of the Troll girls were still awake he got up and quietly changed the caps. He put the white caps on himself and his brothers and the red caps on the Troll girls. Then he crept back to bed and waited.

Presently the old Troll came over to the beds with a long knife in his hand. There was so little light in the room that he couldn't see the faces of the sleepers, but it was easy enough to distinguish the white caps from the red caps. With three swift blows he cut off the heads under the red caps, thinking of course they were the heads of the three Finnish youths. Then he went back to bed with the old Troll wife and Olli could hear them both chuckling and laughing. After a time they went soundly to sleep as Olli could tell from their deep regular breathing and their loud snores.

Olli now roused his brothers and told them what had [160]happened and the three of them slipped quietly out of the Troll house and hurried home to their father on the other side of the Bay.

After that the older brothers no longer talked of despoiling the Troll. They didn't care to try another encounter with him.

"He might have cut our heads off!" they said, shuddering to think of the awful risk they had run.

Olli laughed at them.

"Come on!" he kept saying to them day after day. "Let's go across the Bay to the Troll's!"

"We'll do no such thing!" they told him. "And you wouldn't suggest it either if you weren't so young and foolish!"

"Well," Olli announced at last, "if you won't come with me I'm going alone. I've heard that the Troll has a horse with hairs of gold and silver. I've decided I want that horse."

"Olli," his father said, "I don't believe you ought to go. You know what your brothers say. That old Troll is an awfully sly one!"

But Olli only laughed.

"Goodbye!" he called back as he waved his hand. "When you see me again I'll be riding the Troll's horse!"

The Troll wasn't at home but the old Troll wife was there. When she saw Olli she thought to herself:

"Mercy me, here's that Finnish boy again, the one that changed the caps! What shall I do? I must keep him here on some pretext or other until the Troll comes home!"

So she pretended to be very glad to see him.

"Why, Olli," she said, "is that you? Come right in!"

She talked to him as long as she could and when she could think of nothing more to say she asked him would he take the horse and water it at the Lake.

"That will keep him busy," she thought to herself, "and long before he gets back from the Lake the Troll will be here."

But Olli, instead of leading the horse down to the Lake, jumped on its back and galloped away. By the time the Troll reached home, he was safely on the other side of the Bay.

When the Troll heard from the old Troll wife what had happened, he went down to the shore and hallooed across the Bay:

"Olli! Oh, Olli, are you there?"

Olli made a trumpet of his hands and called back:

"Yes, I'm here! What do you want?"

"Olli, have you got my horse?"

"Yes, I've got your horse but it's my horse now!"

"Olli! Olli!" his father cried. "You mustn't talk that way to the Troll! You'll make him angry!"

And his brothers looking with envy at the horse with gold and silver hairs warned him sourly:

"You better be careful, young man, or the Troll will get you yet!"

A few days later Olli announced:

"I think I'll go over and get the Troll's money-bag."

His father tried to dissuade him.

"Don't be foolhardy, Olli! Your brothers say you had better not go to the Troll's house again."

But Olli only laughed and started gaily off as though he hadn't a fear in the world.

Again he found the old Troll wife alone.

"Mercy me!" she thought to herself as she saw him coming, "here is that terrible Olli again! Whatever shall I do? I mustn't let him off this time before the Troll gets back! I must keep him right here with me in the house."

So when he came in she pretended that she was tired and that her back ached and she asked him would he watch the bread in the oven while she rested a few moments on the bed.

"Certainly I will," Olli said.

So the old Troll wife lay down on the bed and Olli sat quietly in front of the oven. The Troll wife really was tired and before she knew it she fell asleep.

"Ha!" thought Olli, "here's my chance!"

Without disturbing the Troll wife he reached under the bed, pulled out the big money-bag full of silver pieces, threw it over his shoulder, and hurried home.

He was measuring the money when he heard the Troll hallooing across to him:

"Olli! Oh, Olli, are you there?"

"Yes," Olli shouted back, "I'm here! What do you want?"

"Olli, have you got my money-bag?"

"Yes, I've got your money-bag but it's my money-bag now!"

A few days later Olli said:

"Do you know, the Troll has a beautiful coverlet woven of silk and gold. I think I'll go over and get it."

His father as usual protested but Olli laughed at him merrily and went. He took with him an auger and a can of water. He hid until it was dark, then climbed the roof of the Troll's house and bored a hole right over the bed. When the Troll and his wife went to sleep he sprinkled some water on the coverlet and on their faces.

The Troll woke with a start.

"I'm wet!" he said, "and the bed's wet, too!"

The old Troll wife got up to change the covers.

"The roof must be leaking," she said. "It never leaked before. I suppose it was that last wind."

She threw the wet coverlet up over the rafters to dry and put other covers on the bed.

When she and the Troll were again asleep, Olli made the hole a little bigger, reached in his hand, and got the coverlet from the rafters.

The next morning the Troll hallooed across the Bay:

"Olli! Oh, Olli, are you there?"

"Yes," Olli shouted back, "I'm here! What do you want?"

"Have you got my coverlet woven of silk and gold?"

"Yes," Olli told him, "I've got your coverlet but it's my coverlet now!"

A few days later Olli said:

"There's still one thing in the Troll's house that I think I ought to get. It's a golden bell. If I get that golden bell then there will be nothing left that had better belong to an honest Finn."

So he went again to the Troll's house taking with him a saw and an auger. He hid until night and, when the Troll and his wife were asleep, he cut a hole through the side of the house through which he reached in his hand to get the bell. At the touch of his hand the bell tinkled and woke the Troll. The Troll jumped out of bed and grabbed Olli's hand.

"Ha! Ha!" he cried. "I've got you now and this time you won't get away!"

Olli didn't try to get away. He made no resistance while the Troll dragged him into the house.

"We'll eat him – that's what we'll do!" the Troll said to his wife. "Heat the oven at once and we'll roast him!"

So the Troll wife built a roaring fire in the oven.

"He'll make a fine roast!" the Troll said, pinching Olli's arms and legs. "I think we ought to invite the other Troll folk to come and help us eat him up. Suppose I just go over the Mountain and gather them in. You can manage here without me. As soon as the oven is well heated just take Olli and slip him in and close the door and by the time we come he'll be done."

"Very well," the Troll wife said, "but don't be too long! He's young and tender and will roast quickly!"

So the Troll went out to invite to the feast the Troll folk who lived on the other side of the Mountain and Olli was left alone with the Troll wife.

When the oven was well heated she raked out the coals and said to Olli:

"Now then, my boy, sit down in front of the oven with your back to the opening and I'll push you in nicely."

Olli pretended he didn't quite understand. He sat down first one way and then another, spreading himself out so large that he was too big for the oven door.

"Not that way!" the Troll wife kept saying. "Hunch up little, straight in front of the door!"

"You show me how," Olli begged.

So the old Troll wife sat down before the oven directly in front of the opening, and she hunched herself up very compactly with her chin on her knees and her arms around her legs.

"Oh, that way!" Olli said, "so that you can just take hold of me and push me in and shut the door!"

And as he spoke he took hold of her and pushed her in and slammed the door! And that was the end of the old Troll wife!

Olli let her roast in the oven until she was done to a turn. Then he took her out and put her on the table all ready for the feast.

Then he filled a sack with straw and dressed the sack up in some of the old Troll wife's clothes. He threw the dressed up sack on the bed and, just to glance at it, you'd suppose it was the Troll wife asleep.

Then Olli took the golden bell and went home.

Well, presently the Troll and all the Troll folk from over the Mountain came trooping in.

"Yum! Yum! It certainly smells good!" they said as they got the first whiff from the big roast on the table.

"See!" the Troll said, pointing to the bed. "The old woman's asleep! Well, let her sleep! She's tired! We'll just sit down without her!"

So they set to and feasted and feasted.

"Ha! Ha!" said the Troll. "This is the way to serve a troublesome young Finn!"

Just then his knife struck something hard and he looked down to see what it was.

"Mercy me!" he cried, "if here isn't one of the old woman's beads! What can that mean? You don't suppose the roast is not Olli after all but the old woman! No! No! It can't be!"

He got up and went over to the bed. Then he came back shaking his head sadly.

"My friends," he said, "we've been eating the old woman! However, we've eaten so much of her that I suppose we might as well finish her!"

So the Troll folk sat all night feasting and drinking.

At dawn the Troll went down to the water and hallooed across:

"Olli! Oh, Olli, are you there?"

Olli who was safely home shouted back:

"Yes, I'm here! What do you want?"

"Have you got my golden bell?"

"Yes, I've got your golden bell but it's my golden bell now!"

"One thing more, Olli: did you roast my old woman?"

"Your old woman?" Olli echoed. "Look! Is that she?"

Olli pointed at the rising sun which was coming up behind the Troll.

The Troll turned and looked. He looked straight at the sun and then, of course, he burst!

So that was the end of him!

Well, after that no other Troll ever dared settle on that side of the Mountain. They were all too afraid of the Terrible Olli!

Little Lasse

THERE WAS ONCE A LITTLE BOY whose name was Lars, and because he was so little he was called Little Lasse; he was a brave little man, for he sailed round the world in a pea-shell boat.

It was summer time, when the pea shells grew long and green in the garden. Little Lasse crept into the pea bed where the pea stalks rose high above his cap, and he picked seventeen large shells, the longest and straightest he could find.

Little Lasse thought, perhaps, that no one saw him; but that was foolish, for God sees everywhere.

Then the gardener came with his gun over his shoulder, and he heard something rustling in the pea bed.

"I think that must be a sparrow," he said. "Ras! Ras!" But no sparrows flew out, for Little Lasse had no wings, only two small legs. "Wait! I will load my gun and shoot the sparrows," said the gardener.

Then Little Lasse was frightened, and crept out on to the path.

"Forgive me, dear gardener!" he said. "I wanted to get some fine boats."

"Well, I will this time," said the gardener. "But another time Little Lasse must ask leave to go and look for boats in the pea bed."

"I will," answered Lasse; and he went off to the shore. Then he opened the shells with a pin, split them carefully in two, and broke small little bits of sticks for the rowers' seats. Then he took the peas which were in the shells and put them in the boats for cargo. Some of the shells got broken, some remained whole, and when all were ready Lasse had twelve boats. But they should not be boats, they should be large warships. He had three liners, three frigates, three brigs and three schooners. The largest liner was called Hercules, and the smallest schooner The Flea. Little Lasse put all the twelve into the water, and they floated as splendidly and as proudly as any great ship over the waves of the ocean.

And now the ships must sail round the world. The great island over there was Asia; that large stone Africa; the little island America; the small stones were Polynesia; and the shore from which the ships sailed out was Europe. The whole fleet set off and sailed far away to other parts of the world. The ships of the line steered a straight course to Asia, the frigates sailed to Africa, the brigs to America, and the schooners to Polynesia. But Little Lasse remained in Europe, and threw small stones out into the great sea.

Now, there was on the shore of Europe a real boat, father's own, a beautiful white-painted boat, and Little Lasse got into it. Father and Mother had forbidden this, but Little Lasse forgot. He thought he should very much like to travel to some other part of the world.

'I shall row out a little way – only a very little way,' he thought. The pea-shell boats had travelled so far that they only looked like little specks on the ocean. "I shall seize Hercules on the coast of Asia," said Lasse, "and then row home again to Europe."

He shook the rope that held the boat, and, strange to say, the rope became loose. Ditsch, ratsch, a man is a man, and so Little Lasse manned the boat.

Now he would row – and he could row, for he had rowed so often on the steps at home, when the steps pretended to be a boat and Father's big stick an oar. But when Little Lasse wanted to row there were no oars to be found in the boat. The oars were locked up in the boat-house, and Little Lasse had not noticed that the boat was empty. It is not so easy as one thinks to row to Asia without oars.

What could Little Lasse do now? The boat was already some distance out on the sea, and the wind, which blew from land, was driving it still further out. Lasse was frightened and began to cry. But there was no one on the shore to hear him. Only a big crow perched alone in the birch tree; and the gardener's black cat sat under the birch tree, waiting to catch the crow. Neither of them troubled themselves in the least about Little Lasse, who was drifting out to sea.

Ah! how sorry Little Lasse was now that he had been disobedient and got into the boat, when Father and Mother had so often forbidden him to do so! Now it was too late, he could not get back to land. Perhaps he would be lost out on the great sea. What should he do?

When he had shouted until he was tired and no one heard him, he put his two little hands together and said, "Good God, do not be angry with Little Lasse." And then he went to sleep. For although it was daylight, old Nukku Matti was sitting on the shores of the 'Land of Nod,' and was fishing for little children with his long fishing rod. He heard the low words which Little Lasse said to God, and he immediately drew the boat to himself and laid Little Lasse to sleep on a bed of rose leaves.

Then Nukku Matti said to one of the Dreams, "Play with Little Lasse, so that he does not feel lonesome."

It was a little dream-boy, so little, so little, that he was less than Lasse himself; he had blue eyes and fair hair, a red cap with a silver band, and white coat with pearls on the collar. He came to Little Lasse and said, "Would you like to sail round the world?"

"Yes," said Lasse in his sleep, "I should like to."

"Come, then," said the dream-boy, "and let us sail in your pea-shell boats. You shall sail in Hercules and I shall sail in The Flea."

So they sailed away from the 'Land of Nod,' and in a little while Hercules and The Flea were on the shores of Asia away at the other end of the world, where the ice sea flows through the

Bering Strait into the Pacific Ocean. A long way off in the winter mist they could see the explorer Nordenskiold with his ship Vega trying to find an opening between the ice. It was so cold, so cold; the great icebergs glittered strangely, and the huge whales now lived under the ice, for they could not make a hole through with their awkward heads. All around on the dreary shore there was snow and snow as far as the eye could see; little grey men in shaggy skins moved about, and drove in small sledges through the snow drifts, but the sledges were drawn by dogs.

"Shall we land here?" asked the dream-boy.

"No," said Little Lasse. "I am so afraid that the whales would swallow us up, and the big dogs bite us. Let us sail instead to another part of the world."

"Very well," said the dream-boy with the red cap and the silver band; "it is not far to America—" and at the same moment they were there—

The sun was shining and it was very warm. Tall palm trees grew in long rows on the shore and bore coconuts in their top branches. Men red as copper galloped over the immense green prairies and threw their arrows at the buffaloes, who turned against them with their sharp horns. An enormous cobra which had crept up the stem of a tall palm tree threw itself on to a little llama that was grazing at the foot. Knaps! it was all over with the little llama.

"Shall we land here?" asked the dream-boy.

"No," said Little Lasse. "I am so afraid that the buffaloes will butt us, and the great serpent eat us up. Let us travel to another part of the world."

"Very well," said the dream-boy with the white coat, "it is only a little way to Polynesia—" and then they were there.

It was very warm there, as warm as in a hot bath in Finland. Costly spices grew on the shores: the pepper plant, the cinnamon tree, ginger, saffron; the coffee plant and the tea plant. Brown people with long ears and thick lips, and hideously painted faces, hunted a yellow-spotted tiger among the high bamboos on the shore, and the tiger turned on them and stuck its claws into one of the brown men. Then all the others took to flight.

"Shall we land here?" asked the dream-boy.

"No," said Little Lasse. "Don't you see the tiger away there by the pepper plant? Let us travel to another part of the world."

"We can do so," said the dream-boy with the blue eyes. "We are not far from Africa—" and as he said that they were there.

They anchored at the mouth of a great river where the shores were as green as the greenest velvet. A little distance from the river an immense desert stretched away. The air was yellow; the sun shone so hot, so hot as if it would burn the earth to ashes, and the people were as black as the blackest jet. They rode across the desert on tall camels; the lions roared with thirst, and the great crocodiles with their grey lizard heads and sharp white teeth gaped up out of the river.

"Shall we land here?" asked the dream-boy.

"No," said Little Lasse. "The sun would burn us, and the lions and the crocodiles would eat us up. Let us travel to another part of the world."

"We can travel back to Europe," said the dream-boy with the fair hair. And with that they were there.

They came to a shore where it was all so cool and familiar and friendly. There stood the tall birch tree with its drooping leaves; at the top sat the old crow, and at its foot crept the gardener's black cat. Not far away was a house which Little Lasse had seen before; near the house there was a garden, and in the garden a pea bed with long pea shells. An old gardener with a green coat walked about and wondered if the cucumbers were ripe. Fylax was barking on the steps, and when he saw Little Lasse he wagged his tail. Old Stina was milking the cows in the farmyard, and there was a very familiar lady in a check woollen shawl on her way to the bleaching green to see if the clothes were bleached. There was, too, a well-known gentleman in a yellow summer coat, with a long pipe in his mouth; he was going to see if the reapers had cut the rye. A boy and a girl were running on the shore and calling out, "Little Lasse! Come home for bread and butter!"

"Shall we land here?" asked the dream-boy, and he blinked his blue eyes roguishly.

"Come with me, and I shall ask Mother to give you some bread and butter and a glass of milk," said Little Lasse.

"Wait a little," said the dream-boy. And now Little Lasse saw that the kitchen door was open, and from within there was heard a low, pleasant sizzling, like that which is heard when one whisks yellow batter with a wooden ladle into a hot frying-pan.

"Perhaps we should sail back to Polynesia now?" said the dream-boy.

"No; they are frying pancakes in Europe just now," said Little Lasse; and he wanted to jump ashore, but he could not. The dream-boy had tied him with a chain of flowers, so that he could not move. And now all the little dreams came about him, thousands and thousands of little children, and they made a ring around him and sang a little song:

The world is very, very wide,
Little Lasse, Lasse,
And though you've sailed beyond the tide,
You can never tell how wide
It is on the other side,
Lasse, Little Lasse.
You have found it cold and hot,
Little Lasse, Lasse;
But in no land is God not,
Lasse, Little Lasse.
Many men live there as here,
But they all to God are dear,
Little Lasse, Lasse.
When His angel is your guide,
Little Lasse, Lasse,
Then no harm can e'er betide,
Even on the other side
Where the wild beasts wander.
But tell us now,
Whene'er you roam,
Do you not find the best is home
Of all the lands you've looked upon,
Lasse, Little Lasse?

When the dreams had sung their song they skipped away, and Nukku Matti carried Lasse back to the boat. He lay there for a long time quite still, and he still heard the frying-pan sizzling at home on the fire, the sizzling was very plain, Little Lasse heard it quite near him; and so he woke up and rubbed his eyes.

There he lay in the boat, where he had fallen asleep. The wind had turned, and the boat had drifted out with one wind and drifted in with another while Little Lasse slept, and what Lasse thought was frizzling in a frying-pan was the low murmur of the waves as they washed against the stones on the shore. But he was not altogether wrong, for the clear blue sea is like a great pan in which God's sun all day makes cakes for good children.

Little Lasse rubbed the sleep out of his eyes and looked around him. Everything was the same as before; the crow in the birch tree, the cat on the grass, and the pea-shell fleet on the shore. Some of the ships had foundered, and some had drifted back to land. Hercules had come back with its cargo from Asia, The Flea had arrived from Polynesia, and the other parts of the world were just where they were before.

Little Lasse did not know what to think. He had so often been in that grotto in the 'Land of Nod' and did not know what tricks dreams can play. But Little Lasse did not trouble his head with such things; he gathered together his boats and walked up the shore back to the house.

His brother and sister ran to meet him, and called out from the distance, "Where have you been so long, Lasse? Come home and get some bread and butter." The kitchen door stood open, and inside was heard a strange sizzling.

The gardener was near the gate, watering the dill and parsley, the carrots and parsnips.

"Well," he said, "where has Little Lasse been so long?"

Little Lasse straightened himself up stiff, and answered: "I have sailed round the world in a pea-shell boat."

"Oh!" said the gardener.

He had forgotten Dreamland. But you have not forgotten it; you know that it exists. You know the beautiful grotto and the bright silver walls whose lustre never fades, the sparkling diamonds which never grow dim, the music which never ceases its low, soft murmur through the sweet evening twilight. The airy fairy fancies of happy Dreamland never grow old; they, like the glorious stars above us, are always young. Perhaps you have caught a glimpse of their ethereal wings as they flew around your pillow. Perhaps you have met the same dream-boy with the blue eyes and the fair hair, the one who wore the red cap with the silver band and the white coat with pearls on the collar. Perhaps he has taken you to see all the countries of the world and the peoples, the cold wastelands and the burning deserts, the many coloured men and the wild creatures in the sea and in the woods, so that you may learn many things, but come gladly home again. Yes, who knows? Perhaps you also have sailed round the wide world once in a pea-shell boat.

Adalmina's Pearl

ONCE UPON A TIME there was a king and a queen who had a little girl, and since she was the daughter of a king she was styled a princess.

She was called Adalmina, and was their only child. The consequence was that they loved her very dearly, almost too much, for God does not like us to idolize anyone or anything, for that is ignoring the precepts of the Bible, which says, "that we must love God with all our heart."

When the little princess was christened there were two good fairies invited to act as sponsors, such was the custom with the kings; one was attired in red and the other in blue, and the two beneficent fairies did not forget to bestow upon the little princess their customary gifts. The red fairy gave a real pearl of priceless value, which was of such peerless beauty that its equal was nowhere to be found, and with it followed three endowments. "As long as Adalmina wears the pearl," said the fairy, "she will every day increase in beauty, wealth, and wisdom; but if she loses it, no one can prevent that at the same time she will lose the three precious gifts, and they will never return unless she recover the pearl." That was the decision of the first fairy.

But the blue fairy said: "On Adalmina has been bestowed three such splendid gifts, that few wish for anything better in this world. Still there is one gift remaining which exceeds them all, and that I will bestow upon her, on one condition as long as the princess holds possession of the pearl, and the three endowments appertaining, my gift will be of no avail; but should she lose her pearl, her beauty, wealth, and wisdom, then she will get in exchange from me the fourth gift, which is a humble heart: such is my decision." And with that the two fairies nodded farewell and disappeared like fleeting clouds in the summer sky.

The king and queen were highly delighted. They thought to themselves: "If Adalmina becomes beautiful, rich, and wise, it will not much matter about her heart. We will take great care of the pearl, and then we can very well do without the mean gift bestowed by the blue fairy. Aye, but the red fairy knew better what becomes a princess; her gifts were right royal endowments. But the blue fairy was very niggardly, that must be owned; she threw the dear child alms as we throw a penny to a beggar-girl on the high road."

The king caused a golden crown to be made which fitted the head of the little princess exactly; but it was so contrived that as Adalmina grew bigger the crown increased in proportion, and fitted always as well as at first; but for everybody else the remarkable crown was either too large or too small. Topmost in the crown was the precious pearl, encompassed so firmly and securely that it was quite impossible to lose it.

The crown was placed on the Princess Adalmina's head, and she wore it constantly, both when she slept in her gilded cradle, and also when she ran about playing in the castle.

But since the king and queen were very anxious less she should lose the pearl, they had sternly commanded that the attendants were not to allow the princess to go beyond the gate which separated the royal gardens from the park. She was constantly escorted by four valets and four ladies-in-waiting whenever she went out. They were all strictly enjoined to guard well the princess and her wonderful pearl. Indeed, if they were to prove negligent they were in immediate danger of making a fatal acquaintance with the grim headsman, attired all in scarlet, wearing an awful big beard, and carrying the dreadful axe, which was anything but a plaything.

Thus the princess grew up, and everything came to pass exactly as the red fairy had promised. She developed into the most perfect princess the world had ever seen. Yes, of such exceeding rare beauty that her eyes sparkled like two silvery stars of an evening in spring; and wherever she went golden sunshine spread around her, and all the gorgeous flowers in the garden made a low obeisance to her, at the same time saying, "You are far prettier than we!"

And she grew so immensely rich that inexhaustible treasures seemed to be showered upon her by the fairy of fortune. The floor in her room was made of silver and mother-of-pearl; the walls consisted of huge mirrors, reflecting in a dazzling maze the brilliant rubies inlaid in the golden ceiling, and which told with marvellous effect when the perfumed lamps were lit at night. The Princess Adalmina took her food from golden vessels, she slept in a golden bed, and dressed in robes of golden tissue; yea, if it had been possible she would have eaten gold, but it was too hard to bite; and she was so shrewd that she at once could solve the most difficult riddles; and as for her lessons, she had only just to glance at them and she would remember them perfectly. All the sages of the realm came to the court to put puzzling questions to the princess, and they all agreed that so wise and shrewd a princess as Adalmina had never existed in the world before, and never would again.

This was all very well, and it is no sin to be beautiful, rich, and wise when one knows rightly how to use these heaven-bestowed gifts, but that is very difficult.

The king and queen thought in the excess of their joy that their daughter was the best and most perfect being in the whole world, and as ill-luck would have it, Adalmina began to think so too. When everybody constantly repeated that she was a thousand times more beautiful, wealthy, and wise than anybody else, she readily believed it, but this engendered pride in her heart, which made her look with scorn upon everybody else, her own parents included.

Deplorable child! it was a dark spot on the brightness of her beauty, it was poverty in all her wealth, it was the greatest folly in all her wisdom; and she was very nearly lost to herself through that, for her pride increased with her years, and thus her vainglory was accompanied by many sins, so that she gradually became bad at heart, cruel, avaricious, and envious. When she saw a pretty flower in the garden she eagerly put her foot upon it, crushing it to death, for she allowed no one to be admired but herself. When she saw some princess riding in a gilded carriage she felt very much annoyed, for she did not like anyone to be rich but herself; and if anybody spoke of any young girl who was amiable, good, and prudent, she cried from sheer vexation, for she could not bear to hear anybody being praised but herself. Adalmina chided all who did not flatter her, and followed out the bent of her inclinations, and yet she despised the most abject slaves of her will. She was a perfect tyrant, whom all dreaded and no one loved. The king and queen were the only persons in the whole realm who did not feel scandalized at her intolerable pride.

One day when she was about fifteen years of age she went for a walk in the royal garden. When she came to the gate that opened into the park it was locked, and no one dared to open it contrary to the king's command. The four ladies-in-waiting and the four valets attending her, all refused for the first time to obey the princess's command to open it. Then she became so awfully angry that it appeared as if a dark veil had obscured her radiant beauty. She struck her faithful servants in the face, ran away from them, and escaped over the gate, and when the amazed attendants began to pursue her she increased her speed until she was quite lost in the intricacies of the wild woodlands.

She at last felt tired and thirsty for the first time in her life, and seated herself at a sylvan spring to rest; she even condescended to fetch water with her own royal and dainty hands, and drink in the primitive manner which poor people do, who have no servant curtseying to them with a glass on a tray. She observed her own image reflected in the clear water. "Ah, how beautiful I am!" she said to herself, and with that she leaned her head over the false mirror the better to behold herself, when, splash! in tumbled the golden crown with the pearl from off her head, and disappeared in an instant in the rippling water of the deep spring. She scarcely noticed it, for she was so taken with her own beauty. But an extraordinary change now took place, for the troubled spring had barely regained its wonted smooth surface before she saw reflected quite another being. She saw no longer a young princess of fabulous beauty in gold embroidered garb, with jewels in her tresses, and earrings of sparkling diamonds; instead she beheld only a poor, ugly beggar girl, bareheaded, barefooted, clothed in rags, and with matted hair. And on the instant all her vaunted wisdom vanished, she became as foolish and stupid as if she had never been taught anything in her life; but the strangest of all, she at the same moment lost all her memory, so that she no longer knew who she was, whence she came, or where she was going. She was only half conscious of some wonderful change having taken place within her, and this frightened her, so that she ran away from the spring further into the forest, without aim or intention.

The night deepened the darkness of the forest, and the wolves began to howl around her. She trembled with fear, and ran frantically along at random, until at last she descried a faint light glimmering among the trees. When she arrived at the place she found a small hut where lived a poor old woman. "Poor child," said she, "where do you come from so late at night?"

But the girl could give her no answer, she could neither tell her name, nor where her parents lived. This the old woman thought strange, and took pity upon her, saying: "Since you are so poor and lonely in the world, you may remain with me; I am just now in need of someone to tend my goats in the wood, and you shall have the place, poor child, if you are kind and good, and content to live on bread and water with a cup of goat's milk sometimes for a treat." For this the child felt very grateful, and kissed the hands of the poor old woman. Although Adalmina was not aware of it, yet the blue fairy had kept her word. She now possessed that which was better than beauty, wisdom, and wealth, a pure and meek heart; she felt far happier now she tended the goats and lived upon her meagre fare, and slept upon a bed of straw and moss; and she was also far better off than before, for a humble heart brought many precious blessings with it, such as a good conscience, a contented mind, peace, quiet, charity, and love, though lowly now her lot in life; and wherever she went there seemed to flow a genial sunshine around her, not caused by any external beauty, but that produced by peace and love, which, like an aureole, surrounds the kind-hearted and pious in this world, whose very souls beam with love, like the radiant and beautiful faces of the angels when they on soft white wings float gently into the habitations of men.

In the king's palace was a terrible to-do when the princess disappeared. It was to no avail that the poor ladies-in-waiting and the valets had almost grown mad with fear and despair, for having allowed their charge to escape over the gate. They were all thrown into a deep dungeon, where they could see neither the sun nor the moon, and to complete their terrors the scarlet-clad headsman was posted at the door with his axe.

The king and queen were quite inconsolable in their grief. All their subjects were compelled to put on deep mourning, and all public places were draped in sables, and upon all church doors notices were placed informing everybody "that whoever could discover the Princess Adalmina should have her for wife, if nothing else would satisfy him, besides half the kingdom for a dowry, as a reward." Those were the customary terms offered in those times on the like occasions, as everybody well knows.

It was a splendid reward, certainly, for anyone who might chance to find the lost princess. Many were the princes and knights who essayed to earn it. For three years they traversed the world in all directions, both winter and summer, and eagerly continued their search without even finding so much as the gilt heel of Adalmina's shoe.

At last it happened that the young and clever Prince Sigismund, of Gaul, during his endeavours to find the princess, chanced to go to the hut of the old woman, where she sat attired in deep mourning, though of coarsest stuff. But black it was at any rate, and even the goats on the hill-side were black and white, as if in obedience to the king's behests.

"Who are you mourning for, old dame?" asked the prince.

"Know you not that the king has commanded everybody to put on mourning for the lost princess?" answered the old woman. "Though I really don't think there was much harm done in losing her, though, forsooth, she was both comely and rich, and shrewd withal; but people say she was shamefully proud and cruel at heart, so that nobody could love her."

At this moment Adalmina returned with the goats from the wood. The prince looked at her and thought it strange that a girl who was so poor and ugly could attract him so; in fact, so much, that he felt a warm regard spring up in his heart for her at once, though he had scarcely seen the tip of her nose. He asked her if she had seen the princess. "No," answered Adalmina.

"It is very strange," continued the prince. "For three long years I have scarcely thought of anything else but my little princess. But now I will seek her no longer, but have a castle built for me in this forest, and dwell here for the rest of my days."

And he had a castle built quite near the spring where Adalmina had undergone the transformation. Then it happened to him on a sultry day that he felt himself thirsty, and leaned over the spring to drink.

"What might that be that glitters so beautifully in the water?" he said to himself. "I will find out what it is."

The prince bent further over the spring, and thrust his arm into the water, and brought up a most beautiful crown, tipped with a real pearl! Then the thought struck him: "What if it be Adalmina's pearl!" He went at once to the royal castle, and no sooner had the king and queen seen the precious gem than they both simultaneously exclaimed:

"Lo! Adalmina's crown and the fairy's gift. Oh, where can she herself be, our beautiful, darling little princess?"

Then the king bethought himself that if his daughter were still alive, she would by this time be eighteen years of age. He remembered the conditions the red fairy had laid down when she bestowed her gift, and he began to surmise the course of events which had really taken place. He therefore again announced from the church portals, "that all girls who were eighteen years of age should come to the royal castleyard, to try on the crown, and she on whose head it fitted exactly should be accepted as the real and long-lost princess, and Prince Sigismund of Gaul would espouse her for his wife." It need scarcely be said that all the girls in the kingdom eagerly hastened to the courtyard of the palace, and those who were more or less than eighteen pretended not to be aware of the fact.

It was a glorious summer day, and at least a thousand girls were arranged in rows to try their fortune. From early dawn until late in the evening the crown was passed from head to head, after having in vain been tried upon everyone; but nobody did it fit. At last the assembled girls began to murmur, and complain that the king was only making fools of them, and they said:

"Let us cast lots, and whoever wins shall have both the crown and the prince."

The Prince Sigismund took this very ill, and asked them to wait until the evening. To this the girls assented. Shortly before sunset a watchman was posted near the high road to see if any more aspirants for the crown might come that way. The prince called out:

"Time wanes, Guard; do you see anyone coming along?"

The watchman answered: "I see the flowers already nodding their heads in sleep, for night is fast approaching, but I can descry no one on the high road."

Again the prince said: "Eventide has come, Guard; do you see no one on the high road?"

The watchman answered: "A cloud is passing before the setting sun, and the birds in the wood are hiding their sleepy heads under their weary wings. Night stands on the threshold, but no one is to be seen on the high road."

The prince asked yet once more: "Evening has waned, Guard; do you see no one coming along the high road?"

The watchman again answered: "I see a small cloud of dust rising near the margin of the big forest. It is fast approaching. Now I see a poor shepherd-girl driving her goats in front of her along the high road."

"Let us try the crown on the shepherd-girl," said the prince.

But the girls, who all considered themselves far superior, cried, "No, no." But the king had the shepherd-girl brought forward, and lo! when they tried the crown on her head, it fitted exactly!

By this time the sun had quite set, and darkness fell upon the land, so that no one could see what the shepherd-girl was like. But Prince Sigismund thought in his heart, "Heaven itself wishes me to take the poor girl for my wife, and I gladly obey, for I have seen her before in the hut of the poor old woman in the forest, and I know that she brings sunshine with her wherever she goes."

And the populace shouted, "Long live Prince Sigismund and the Princess Adalmina!" But many people thought to themselves, "It is after all only a poor shepherd-girl." Then she was brought, with the crown on her head, into the royal hall, brilliantly illuminated with a thousand wax candles. But brighter far than all this sea of light beamed forth the wondrous beauty of Adalmina, when she suddenly appeared before the throng in robes of golden tissue, for with the pearl also returned all the other endowments of the red fairy. But best of all, she was also allowed to retain the gift of the blue fairy, a pure and humble heart; and since her good memory also returned, she remembered perfectly that pride had formerly dwelt in her heart, and how she had become transformed; and she knew now how that the poor and ugly are far happier with a good conscience than the rich and beautiful in all their haughty pride. She humbly knelt before her parents, imploring them and all others to forgive her her former sinful pride, and as a proof of how much her heart was changed for the better, she led forward the poor old woman that had come from her forest hut, and embraced her, saying:

"The charitable are rich in their poverty, but the stony heart of the wealthy is impoverished even in the midst of his treasures."

And all present who witnessed this could scarcely believe their senses. But Prince Sigismund said: "I knew all along that this would happen. Adalmina's pearl is exceedingly rare and beautiful, but infinitely more precious is a humble and contrite heart."

The nuptials of the prince and princess were then celebrated with great pomp and joy in the castle of the king; and the four ladies-in-waiting, with the four valets, were liberated from the dungeon; and the scarlet-clad headsman with the big, frightful beard placed his axe in a corner. And all the people in the realm shouted joyfully:

"Rare and beautiful is Adalmina's pearl, but far more precious is a humble heart."

Pikku Matti

ON YONDER HILL STANDS A LOG-HUT, with only one little window, and that so small, that when the dumpling-faced, flaxen-haired little boy who dwells within peeps out, his rosy features seem to fill the whole frame. Formerly the cot possessed a chimney, was painted red, and a neat wooden paling enclosed the place including a potato-plot. But now it is wretchedly dilapidated, the smoke finding its way out through a hole in the roof, and the wooden railing has long ago tumbled down. The reason of this sad change is because now it is inhabited by only a blind old soldier and his aged wife; they are extremely poor and cannot repair the place themselves, and they would certainly die from sheer starvation if the old man did not at times earn a trifle by mending fishing-nets, and the old woman make brooms for sale, and the parish doled out to them three sacks of flour a year.

Times were better some four or five years ago, for then there lived with them their son and his wife, a thrifty young couple, who both worked hard to keep everything nice. And then they were all so happy together, until one day misfortune came. One Sunday morning the big boat which brought all the people of the hamlet across the lake to their parish church, was more than usually crowded, and was upset by a heavy squall when far from the shores, and both the son and his wife perished with many others in the treacherous deep. But the old folks had that morning remained at home, the old man because of his blindness, and the old woman to take care of the little child. When the church bells that morning rang out their chimes calling together the flock, it was a funeral dirge for those who so unexpectedly had been called through the portals of death, to gather into the tabernacle of eternal rest and adoration.

The poor old people were thus left to themselves in their lonely hut, alone with their grief, their poverty, and their little grandchild. The only thing they inherited from the dear departed ones was this little lad, called Matti and because he was an uncommonly wee thing they gave him the name of Pikku Matti. Anyone who does not understand the Finnish language must just guess at the meaning of that. His face was round and rosy as a ripe winter-apple; he had large blue, honest eyes, and quite golden hair, in fact that was the only gold he possessed in this world. It was his chubby face that was wont to fill the little window of the cot whenever anything remarkable happened on the turnpike road. If you are travelling that way you are sure to see him. Perhaps it is a dark, dismal evening in the autumn; then you will see, by the fitful glare of the logs that crackle in the big fire-place of the lonely hut, how the blind old soldier is mending his nets, while his old wife is reading aloud from the Bible, about the poor blind who dwell in darkness, and that to them has been given a great light which will guide them on their road to heaven, the name of Jesus Christ. And the ruddy light falls upon Pikku Matti, where he sits close by with the kitten on his knees; he listens attentively, as if he understands what his grandmother reads, but at last sleep steals into his dreamy blue eyes, and he leans his soft rosy cheek against the knee of the old dame, and if you are snugly ensconced in your elegant travelling-carriage on the dark road, your eye will glance with mingled joy and envy into the abode of poverty, for there dwell innocence and true devotion, and that peace which prayer produceth to the grieved and afflicted, and that trust in God which is never relied upon in vain. That house contains greater treasures probably than your own home of luxury and splendour.

But if you journey this way on a fine summer day, you will observe near the hut a five-barred gate, and then you must stop until it is opened. But in a minute Pikku Matti comes running to his post; he appears already in the doorway of the hut, how nimbly his little feet trot over stones and tree-trunks that lie in his way, and his yellow hair streaming in the wind. Now he has come to the gate, throw a coin to him not to disappoint him, give one that shines bright and new, for that is his delight; though so poor, he knows not yet the value of money, and a bright penny creates in him as much happiness as a golden ducat. But be sure you do not throw the coin down before your carriage has quite passed through the gate, for the little boy does not think an inch before his nose, and if he sees the bright object roll in the centre of the road, he will heedlessly throw himself upon his reward, and letting go his hold of the gate it will bang right on your horse's nose, or catch in the carriage, and cause an accident; but don't scold him, for when you were a little boy you were not a bit wiser.

The poor lad lives upon black bread and dumpling, with small-beer, but sometimes he gets a few potatoes and sour milk, which is considered a great feast.

But he thrived on his homely fare and grew plumper every year. Read he could not, but he could say his prayers, and knew the Ten Commandments; and he could stand on his head, and turn somersaults where the grass was soft; and he could make ducks and drakes on the limpid surface of the lake, when he accompanied his grandmother to the strand to see her wash his shirts; he could also drive a horse and cart along an even road, ride a neighbour's horse to the brook to water it, particularly if anybody went with him; he could detect the difference between the traces of a snipe and a magpie on the newfallen snow; he could tell the footprints of the wolf on his track; he could make a sledge from small twigs, and create horses and cattle from fir tree cones with little sticks for legs.

These were his accomplishments, and he was considered very clever for such a wee fellow, but it was barely enough to cover a great deficiency which poor Pikku Matti suffered from, and, in fact, I don't know if I dare tell you what it was, he had no breeches! But the cause of it was, first, his grandparents were so extremely poor, and then it was the highest fashion among all the little lads in the hamlet to do without such habiliments, so poor Pikku Matti had to go without; but that was only the custom on weekdays: when Sunday came they were all attired like other people. But our little friend had neither for Sunday nor for weekdays that which he ought to have possessed, and at times it became a source of great unhappiness to him.

It was a long happy time before he understood that he really was in want of anything, and he was as brave and merry in his little shirt as if there never had existed any unnecessary trammels of other garments. One Sunday morning, however, when the villagers crowded on the shore to embark in their boats for church, Pikku Matti declared that he would go as well.

"That you can't, my dear," said his grandmother.

"Why?" asked Pikku Matti.

"You have no clothes."

This answer set the little boy thinking and wondering.

"I have an old petticoat you might put on," she said, "but then everybody would take you to be a girl."

"I don't want to be a girl, I mean to be a man," declared the boy.

"Well, did you ever? They are all alike," laughed his grandmother. "A man must be a man, if he ain't bigger than an elf. You stay at home this time, my boy."

And poor Pikku had to submit.

Some short time after this there was an assize to be held in the neighbouring village. Of course a great concourse of people gathered together. Amongst others came Wipplusti with his peep-show. Of course you know Wipplusti. Everybody wanted to have a peep at his show, for there was to be seen the Emperor Boney with his golden crown on his head, and a Turkish sabre trailing at his feet, and there was the great Mogul with his hoops around his waist, and with his horrible big beard, and the giant Bumburrifex, and the hobgoblin of the ancient castle of Åbo, the old capital of Finland. Some people gave Wipplusti a few pence, others a small loaf of bread, while others gave him nothing at all. Indeed, there were some that only bantered him; but everybody enjoyed themselves thoroughly.

These wonderful things were told to Pikku Matti by other youngsters, and he immediately determined to have a peep at the show.

"It really can't be done, my child," declared his grandmother.

"Why not, Granny?" he asked.

"Because there will be such a great number of the gentry, my lad. The judge and his secretary, and the writer, and the bailiff, and the constable himself, and the road-surveyor, and I don't know who; you can't go among them without breeches."

Pikku Matti had a severe struggle with himself, but Wipplusti's peep-show was a very great temptation, and so at last he said:

"What if you should lend me your petticoat, Granny?"

"There he is at last," said his grandmother, and laughed heartily when he had got the petticoat on, and was cutting rather a sorry figure in the centre of the kitchen floor. "Now you do look like a little girl."

"If I do look like a girl I won't go to the village," said Matti, nearly crying; "I don't want to be a girl, but to be a man."

"Certainly you look like a lass," said the old woman, "but you can always tell anybody you meet that you are not a girl, but a boy."

"Well, so I can," thought Pikku, and off he started.

Not far from home he was overtaken by a gentleman, who stopped him and asked :

"Can you tell me, my little girl, if it is far to where the assizes are held?"

"I am not a girl, I am a boy!" quickly answered Matti.

"That you don't look, anyhow," said the traveller.

Pikku Matti had nothing to say for himself, but when he came to the place where the court was held, he cried out aloud so that everybody could hear him:

"I am not a girl, though I look like one; I am a young man!"

All the old men and women laughed heartily, and the lads and lasses gathered around him, and clapped their hands, and cried: "Well, Maggie, my dear girl, who gave you that fine gown?"

"It is my grandmother's petticoat, you boobies, and not mine," answered Pikku. "I am no Maggie, my name is Matti, that you might see."

Then one of the biggest and most teasing of the boys lifted up Pikku Matti on to his shoulders, and galloped with him to where the peep-show was being exhibited, and called out loudly:

"Look and behold! a penny a peep to see a young man cut a dash in his granny's petticoat!"

Pikku grew white with anger, and tugged his tormentor's woolly hair with all his might.

"It is not my petticoat, it is my grandmother's," he bawled, and began crying with vexation; but the cruel jester continued:

"Look at a lad in an old woman's petticoat!" and off they again started, jumping and struggling all round the courtyard.

Never was boy in such perplexity before. He wept, and yelled, and kicked, and fought to get free, and when at last he became too troublesome for his foe and got loose, he took to his heels as fast as he could run away, was tripped up by his long skirts, then got on his feet again, nearly choked with anger, stumbled anew, rose again, gathered up the petticoat around him, and cut along the road as quickly as his nimble little feet would allow him, till from sheer fatigue, on reaching home, he tumbled head over heels once more on the threshold, and out of breath he panted :

"Take off the petticoat, I will have no more of this, I am a boy."

"Don't cry, Pikku dear," said his grandmother kindly. "When you become a man, you will show them what stuff you are made of."

"Yes, that you will, my lad," said his grandfather, " and then I will lend you my old regimental trousers!"

They loved poor Pikku Matti, these simple old folks, for, next to God, he was the only joy and consolation in their hard life. They would gladly have bestowed gold-stitched velveteens upon him if it had been in their power. He got a piece of bread and butter, and that was so great a solace to him in his grief, that he soon forgot all about his annoying adventure. He seated himself in a corner of the hut, enjoying his extra treat, and soon thought no more of the shame and insults heaped upon him when dressed in an old woman's petticoat.

Some time after this frequent clouds of dust rose in the high road, so many messengers were sent past there on foot and on horseback, for a great man who was travelling through the country was expected this way. Rumour said, "he was such a great dignitary that the King could not be grander." People congregated from all parts to have a look at him, and wonderful things were told of him. It was said, indeed, that "he rode in a golden carriage, drawn by a team of twelve horses, and that from head to foot he was dressed in silver and brass-foil," which latter was the grandest thing they could think of. The little children imagined that the great man would carry a knapsack on his back, filled with silver coins and sticks of liquorice, which he would liberally scatter among them while passing along the road.

These rumours reached the ears of Pikku Matti, and he immediately declared, as usual, that he would go to meet the great mysterious traveller. He had a will of his own, poor little Matti, as often is the case with grandchildren pets.

"Little boys must obey their elders," observed his grandmother.

"And you know that you have no clothes," added the grandfather mildly, " or maybe you wish to borrow Granny's petticoat again?"

"I don't want any more petticoat," cried poor Matti, and turned as red as a raspberry at the bare recollection of all the insults he had been exposed to on account of that hated garment. "No, never more in this world will I put on a petticoat – I want Grandfather's regimentals."

"Do you hear that, Wife?" said the old man. "Well, lead me up to the garret, and we will try if the things can be made to fit you." Agile as a kitten, he darted up the ladder that his aged grandfather had such difficulty in mounting. They went to the big green box that stood in a corner, and which had always inspired Pikku Matti with a lively curiosity whenever he had been in the loft to set traps for mice.

The first thing that caught his eager eyes was a large sabre with a bright scabbard.

"I want that sword," cried he, impatiently.

"You pigmy!" said his grandfather. "Here hold the sabre while I get the regimentals out of the box."

Pikku Matti received the sabre from his hands, but it was so heavy that he could scarcely hold it.

The old soldier patted him on the cheek and said: "Aha!". "What, all of them? That depends upon whom you fight against."

"Yes," rejoined the little belligerent, and wondered for a moment whom the grandfather meant. "I shall cut off the heads of the wolves, and hawks, and all stinging-nettles, and everybody who may do any ill to my grannies. Yes, that I will, and cut off the heads of anybody who dares to call me a girl, besides."

"Well, well, laddie, bridle your courage a bit, and give a little quarter to some of them. Here are the trousers – I suppose I must give you the coat as well."

"Yes, Gran, and the sword and the cap too."

"Well, you are a fire-eater, and no mistake!" rejoined the old man. "You shall have them all on one condition, that you go no further than the five-barred gate when the great man comes."

"Yes, Grandfather."

The two had scarcely descended the ladder again, before the bailiff came tearing like a whirlwind along the road, and bawling right and left to the people to keep out of the way of the great dignitary who would pass by in a few minutes. Everybody seemed in a flurry, and how they bustled about in the hut! Grandfather's trousers were hastily pulled on Matti's tiny legs. They were grey, with narrow light blue stripes, but they were so big and roomy that Pikku could perfectly well have crept into one leg. What a sight it was! but on they must go. They were turned up at the bottom half-way, and tied under his arms with a kerchief. As much trouble gave the coat, which was made of the same kind of grey stuff with blue facings, and seemed rather intended for a giant than a pigmy. When he had it on the sleeves reached the ground, and the skirts swept the floor.

"That will never do," said the grandmother, and at once began to pin up the sleeves and lappets.

Pikku Matti thought all this was unnecessary bother. To crown the work the big shako was put on his head, and would most assuredly have extinguished him quite had it not been well lined with hay. At last the heavy sabre was hung trailing from his side, and now the pigmy warrior was declared fully equipped.

No hero ever returned from a victory prouder than Pikku Matti was, as he marched forth in his first uniform. His rotund little figure disappeared amongst the clothes like a mouse in a sack. Nothing was to be seen but his blue honest little eyes, his chubby cheeks, and his little upturned nose, peeping out from the narrow space between the standing collar and the shako.

When thus martially accoutred, with great gravity he emerged from the door, then the sabre rattled against the loose stones in the yard, the pins fell out, and the sleeves and lappets had it all their own way; the shako became top-heavy, and took bearings right and left, while the brave warrior seemed almost overpowered by the weight of his glory. The poor old couple had not laughed so heartily for many a day. The old man, who could hear everything distinctly, though he saw nothing, turned the wee lad round several times and kissed by mistake his little tilted nose, that protruded beyond the coat collar, and said, "Bless you, Pikku Matti, my boy; may never a worse man than you will be ever wear the uniform of the Old Guards."

"Right wheel, march! Halt, attention!" called out the old man now; "when the great man comes you must salute him this way," and then he taught the young recruit to stand straight as a gun-rod, to look fierce, to keep his left arm stiff by his side, and with the right hand to salute.

"Yes, Grandfather," said Matti, who was an apt recruit.

Pikku Matti had barely arrived at his post by the five-barred gate before a dense cloud of dust was descried on the road, and the great man soon came along, travelling at a fearful speed, which made the carriage wheels strike fire against the stones; now he was nearing hey! how he goes, then the coachman suddenly called out, "Whoa! Hi, there, open the gate quick!" The road-surveyor had placed himself at the five-barred gate, to see that everything would pass off with military precision in the twinkle of an eye, which would convey to the great man a very favourable opinion of the order and efficiency of the roads. But when the carriage came dashing along, the road-surveyor, waiting to bow very humbly to his superior, forgot that he was standing on the edge of the dyke which skirted the road, lost his balance, and tumbled over into the muddy water, and his man, who was placed ready at the gate, was so astonished by the sudden disappearance of his master, from whom he was to receive the word of command, that he never thought to open the gate, and thus it remained closed in the very face of the grand traveller.

The carriage was, therefore, stopped, the dignitary looked astonished, and the coachman continued to bawl, "Open the gate!" Then Pikku Matti bethought himself and advanced, though dreadfully encumbered, opened the gate and saluted exactly as his grandfather had taught him, though looking somewhat like a dog who had been trained to sit upright.

The coachman cracked his whip, the horses started forward, but the gentleman in the carriage cried out at the same moment, "Stop, stop!" and the equipage came once more to a standstill.

"What funny little fellow is that in the uniform of the Old Guards?" asked the traveller, and laughed so heartily that the carriage almost shook.

Pikku Matti was not in the least degree disconcerted by this, he only thought how his grandfather had taught him to make the salutation, and he repeated it, but this time with the left hand, looking all the time as grave as possible.

This amused the inquirer very much, and he asked of the bystanders, "Who are the parents of the lad?"

The surveyor had by this time crept out of the ditch, and hastened to inform him that he was a poor orphan, who lived at the hut of his grandfather, close by, a blind old soldier kept by the parish and named Havok.

The officious narrator imparted this information in a contemptible tone, which seems to be the orthodox way when a man in power condescends to speak of a pauper; but he was very much astonished when he found that his superior, on hearing this, alighted from his carriage and went straight to the hut.

I wish you had been there! The old woman nearly fell off her chair when such a visitor entered her humble abode; but the old man, who could not see anything, had more courage, and with due respect, indicated where he knew the settle stood. "The blessings of the day upon you, my friends," said the stranger, and heartily shook their hands. "Somehow, I fancy that I know you, old comrade," he continued, scrutinizing the wrinkled features of the aged soldier; "are you not Havok, No. 39, from my regiment?"

"Yes, Captain," answered he promptly, recognizing with amazement the voice of his former commanding officer.

"How glad I am that at last I have found you!" said the former captain, now governor of a province. "Have you forgotten how, at the Battle of Jutas, during the thick of the fight, when I was sore wounded and exhausted, you carried me on your back across the ford, and saved me from falling into the hands of the enemy? If you have forgotten it, do you think I can ever do so? After peace was proclaimed I quite lost sight of you; I sought long but in vain, and at last I gave you up for dead; but now I have found you I will provide for yourself, your wife, and the little lad – a fine boy!" And the hero of many battles caught up Pikku Matti in his arms, and gave him such a smacking kiss that the shako tumbled off his head, the sabre rattled, and all the pins came out and let down his coat and trousers.

"Let me alone," vociferated Matti to his new-found friend; now you have knocked off my hat, and Grandfather will scold me!"

"Gracious, sir!" said the old woman, who felt quite put out on account of Pikku Matti; "please take no notice of what the lad says. Alackaday! he is not used to speak to great folks."

"We will get a new hat for old Grandfather," said the governor, consoling him; "and you, kind old dame, have no concern for the lad's straightforward talk, I like a good-spirited boy. Listen to me, Pikku Matti. You look to me as if you mean to be a fine fellow when you grow up; would you like to become a brave soldier, like your grandfather has been?"

"Grandfather says that depends upon whom I fight against," answered Matti.

"You are a smart little fellow," said the governor, laughing; "you have no lack of courage, at any rate."

"Yes, gracious sir, but the reason is, this is the first day he ever wore trousers, and you know courage comes with a lad's first breeches."

"Say, rather, that he adheres to the uniform of the Old Guards," answered the governor. "Much glory still clings with the smell of powder to these threadbare garments, and such rich treasures of memories, are transmitted as heirlooms from one generation to another; but new times have come, and the boy may yet be needed for the defence of his country. Are you strong, my little man?"

Pikku Matti did not answer, he only held out the middle finger of his right hand, challenging the governor to a trial of strength that way.

"I see by the look of you that you will become a very bear in strength when you have grown up to be a man. Will you come with me, and you will then have white bread to eat, and as much milk as you can drink, and it is not unlikely that sometimes you may get a stick of liquorice and a bun, when you have been uncommonly good."

"Shall I have a horse to ride on?" asked Matti.

"Yes, that you shall," answered the governor.

Pikku thought for a while of these things, his small blue eyes wandered from the governor to his grandfather, and from him to his grandmother, and again from her back to the traveller, but at last he crept behind his blind old grandfather saying, "I will stay with my grandfather and grandmother."

"But," said the old soldier, his voice trembling with emotion, "dear lad, if you remain with us, you will only get black bread and water, and salt dumpling. Did you not hear what the gentleman offers you? White bread and milk, and a horse to ride on."

"I will stay with you, Grandfather, I will not leave you," Pikku answered, nearly choking with tears.

"You are a fine lad, such as a boy ought to be," said the governor, his eyes filling with tears, and he patted the little fellow on his chubby cheeks. "You remain with your grandfather, my boy, and I will take care that neither he, your grandmother, nor yourself ever want for anything; and when you are a man come then to me, and I will give you land to till and a forest to cut wood for yourself; and if you become a peasant or a soldier it matters not, so long as you remain an honest and faithful son to your country. Am I in the right, Pikku?"

"Yes, sir," answered the boy, stiff.

"God bless you, child," said the grandparents simultaneously, deeply touched at heart.

"God bless our dear country, and give to it many faithful sons like you, Pikku," said the governor, "for many a one deserts the dear old land on account of its poverty, and seeks to gain the leaven loaves abroad. But what do they gain thereby? God and their conscience only know, but the land of their birth gains nothing by them. Honour thy father and thy mother in their poverty, that thy days may be long in the land which the Lord thy God giveth thee."

"That stands in my spelling book," observed Pikku Matti.

"But it does not stand in everyone's heart," rejoined the governor.

Biographies & Sources

Tiina Porthan

Foreword

Tiina Porthan, Master of Arts, is a Finnish author who writes about mythology with the focus on the creepy, magical side of folk poems and tales. She collaborates with artist Tero Porthan to make this tradition known worldwide. Her books include *The Finnish Book of Spells: The Finnish Spell System from Curses to Exorcisms* (2024), *Women of Might and Magic: Witch Queens, Deities of Death and Nature Goddesses in Finnish Mythology* (2023), *The Finnish Book of the Dead: Gods, Spirits and Creatures of the Underworld in Finnish Mythology and Folklore* (2022).

Albert Alberg

The Water lily, Tracings on the Beach, Adalmina's Pearl, The Two Brooks, The Most Beautiful Thing in the Woods, Nature's Secret, The Pine and Fir Trees, The White Violet, The Ambitious Birch, Castles in the Air, The Silver Chalice

Albert Alberg (1838–1924) was a writer, translator and actor from Sweden. As a published author, he translated (from the Swedish of Zacharias Topelius) and wrote *Whisperings in the Wood: Finland Idyls for Children* (1881). Other famous works by Albert Alberg is *Fabled Stories From the Zoo* (1885).

Ella R. Christie

The Wood Anemone, Sampo Lappelill, Sikku, Knut Fairyflute

Ella Robertson Christie (1861–1949) was a Scottish explorer and traveller. She also loved gardening. Ella was a pioneer for travelling, especially as a woman – she went all over the world from Borneo to Cuba. She journalled her travels in diaries. She translated (from the Swedish of Zacharias Topelius) and wrote *Fairy Tales From Finland* (1896).

John Martin Crawford

Kalevala: The Epic Poem of Finland (translated into English)

John Martin Crawford (1845–1916) was an American physician and scholar. While Crawford was in attendance at Lafayette College, he was inspired by Professor Thomas Conrad Porter to translate the *Kalevala*. He translated the Finnish epic the *Kalevala* into English and it was published in 1888.

Parker Fillmore

The True Bride, Mighty Mikki, The Three Chests, Log, The Little Sister, The Forest Bride, The Enhanted Grouse, The Terrible Olli, The Devil's Bride, The Mysterious Servant, Mikko the Fox Adventures II–V

Parker Fillmore (1878–1944) was an American author born in Cincinnati, Ohio. Upon taking a job as a teacher in the Philippines, Fillmore was given no textbooks to teach his students English, and so he crafted his own stories for this purpose, launching his career in writing. Returning to the US and moving to a primarily Czech neighbourhood in New York City, he gained a great passion for the Czechoslovakian folklore that his neighbours shared with him. This led to his publication of several collections of these stories including *Czechoslovak Fairy Tales* (1919) and *The Shoemaker's Apron* (1920).

Andrew Lang

The Gifts of the Magician, The Six Hungry Beasts, Little Lasse, The Raspberry Worm, Sea King's Gift

Poet, novelist and anthropologist Andrew Lang (1844–1912) was born in Selkirk, Scotland. He is now best known for his collections of fairy stories and publications on folklore, mythology and religion.. Inspired by the traditional folklore tales of his home on the English-Scottish border, Lang complied twelve coloured fairy books (such as *Red, Blue, Crimson* and *Yellow*) which collected 798 stories from French, Danish, Russian and Romanian sources, amongst others. This hugely successful series further encouraged the increasing popularity of fairy tales in children's literature.

Elias Lönnrot

Kalevala: The Epic Poem of Finland

Elias Lönnrot (1802–1884) was a Finnish physician and philosopher. He was a collector of traditional Finnish oral poetry. It was Elias who first compiled and synthesized the short ballads and poems to curate the Finnish Epic poem, the *Kalevala* in 1835.

Zacharias Topelius

The Water lily, Tracings on the Beach, Adalmina's Pearl, The Two Brooks, The Most Beautiful Thing in the Wood, Nature's Secret, The Pine and Fir Trees, The White Violet, The Ambitious Birch, Castles in the Air, The Silver Chalice, The Wood Anemone, Sampo Lappelill, Sikku, Knut Fairyflute

Zacharias Topelius (1818–1898) was a Finnish author and historian and a key figure in Finnish literature. He was professor of Finnish history at University of Helsinki. In his later years he wrote stories based on Finnish folktales. Many translators and authors went on to translate his stories.